THE CHRON
BOOK FIVE

THE
BATTLE
OF
TORRY
NORTH

BENJAMIN SANFORD

STENOX PUBLISHING
Clarksburg, MD

Cover Art by Karl Moline

ISBN 979-8-9890221-0-6 (paperback)
ISBN 979-8-9890221-1-3 (digital)

Printed in the United States of America

CHAPTER 1

Valera stood before the long mirror, adorned in a golden gown, with silver stitching along its high neckline and hem, its beauty unable to conceal her belly swollen with child. The servants washed her hair, styling it into an upturned do, with jeweled pins holding it in place, each probably worth more then all her possessions. They could be worth a thousand-fold, and she would still see them for what they were… chains. She cared nothing for the trappings of court, having sacrificed that very life to be with her beloved Jonas. She doubted Tyro knew that she could have been the Torry Queen. If he did, he would know she couldn't be appeased with beautiful dresses and rich jewelry. Yet, here she stood with a dozen maid servants doting on her, fussing over the most trivial of things. She wanted nothing more than to rest after arriving midday, but was ushered to the throne room, and then bathed and escorted here, to a richly furnished room, designated as her private chamber.

"That should more than suffice, you needn't trouble yourself," Valera said to the maids attending her hands peeking beyond her billowy sleeves, coloring her nails in hues of gold and silver. She was taken aback by the strange custom that was a common practice in the southern parts of Arax, and apparently had taken root here as well. It was just another annoyance to test her patience.

"The emperor insists that you are properly attended, Mistress," the maid called Aina said, kneeling beside her, attending her right hand, stroking it carefully with a narrow brush.

"You needn't call me by that appellation, Aina. My name is Valera," she gifted the young girl a smile. She had lived these past two decades as a wife and mother, tending her own household, without the pampering of servants. Though born of a great noble house, she did not regret giving up the pleasures of that life. It was a small sacrifice to be with Jonas. She had grown quite comfortable through the years doing things for herself, and certainly didn't need to be waited on now.

"That would be improper, Mistress. The emperor has given us to you to tend to your needs and comfort," Aina said.

"Given to me?" Valera's eyes narrowed severely, her withering look frightening the comely girl.

"Yes, Mistress," Aina answered with a trembling lip, immediately prostrating herself before her, the other maids acting in kind.

"Stand, all of you," Valera ordered, pulling her hands free of their grasp, her voluminous skirts swirling about her ankles.

The nervous maids gathered themselves, slowly coming to their feet, each clutching their skirts. They certainly didn't look like slaves by their rich attire, each adorned in shimmering calnesian gowns of black or gray, with silver slippered feet. They were all quite lovely, obviously handpicked for their position in the palace.

"Am I to understand that you are each a slave, and given to me?" Valera asked sternly.

"Yes, Mistress," the one called Mayla answered. She appeared to be the eldest, with long auburn tresses, and soulful brown eyes, looking no older than twenty years.

"I am no one's Mistress. I do not abide slavery. If you are mine, then I release you," Valera said.

"Oh, please no, Mistress. Should you reject us we will fall to another, one who is certain to be cruel and harsh," Aina pleaded, giving Valera pause.

"Where are you from, Aina?" She asked, her heart breaking for these poor girls.

"I was born in Mordicay, Mistress," Aina said.

"And how did you come to be here?"

"I… My grandfather was a Menotrist merchant. His estate was attainted long ago, and all his kin, including my mother, were so ascribed and sold at auction. I was born in her master's house in Mordicay, and sold to the emperor when I was ten years, Mistress," Aina said ashamedly, lowering her eyes.

Such needless suffering, Valera thought miserably. She could only imagine the shame Jonas felt for his father's cruelty. Did Tyro even consider how his actions would hurt his wife and child?

"And you?" Valera called upon another girl to answer to her origin. And so it went, each girl revealing how they came to be a slave in the imperial court. Most were Menotrist, with two from other northern tribes, one from Corpi, one purchased from the Troan markets and another from Yatin. Valera rightly suspected at least one to be Benotrist, placed among them to spy on her, as if that even mattered at this juncture, though Tyro was desperate for anything she might reveal.

Valera resolved to do what she could to shield these slave girls from any further abuse, with what little power she had, or Tyro might lend her. It might not matter in the grand affairs of state or effect the war, but it was something she could do, some small virtuous act to which she could occupy herself, taking her mind from her dilemma. It would be a silent quest, as she could hardly voice aloud her intentions, lest Tyro use it against her, leveraging the welfare of her maids to coerce her to his will.

"I am Valera, as I assume most of you are aware. I am the daughter of a noble Torry house, and am wed to the emperor's son. I have lived many years from court, longer than any of you have lived, my husband and I working our own small farm by ourselves with our son. As I have spent much of the last two decades away from court, you may find me ignorant of many of the protocols you are each familiar with. If you see me about to misstep, I consider it your duty to put voice to it. Am I understood?"

"Yes, Mistress," they chorused, each bobbing a deep curtsy, where she finally noticed their slave collars peaking above the neck of their gowns, each silver, and polished to a bright sheen.

Win this war, my beloved Jonas and Terin, and I shall see those hateful things struck from their necks, she silently vowed.

The maids returned to their work, preparing her for her private audience with the emperor. No sooner had they finished then her escort arrived at the door of her chamber, Larus Braxus, Castellan of Fera. She noted his rich purple robes and unyielding gray eyes that matched her own. His once dark mane was silvered with age, and his nondescript face belied his cunning intellect. He was accompanied by four members of the imperial Elite, clad in red tunics and polished gold breastplates, with their sigil emblazoned upon their chests, a sword and whip dividing a sun and moon.

"My lady Valera, we are to escort you," Larus Braxus declared evenly, his eyes silently appraising her, revealing nothing of his assessment.

"Very well, Castellan Braxus," she followed him without.

* * *

Tyro couldn't have selected a less interesting minion to escort her through the halls of the palace. Valera wondered if Larus ever smiled? He was as humorless as a plant, not speaking a word until she found herself before a stone archway with two porian doors opened to receive her.

"My lady," Larus waved an open hand toward the chamber, where torchlight filtered through the large entryway, bathing the outer corridor in light.

She regarded him respectfully before stepping within, the imperial Elite following after, each posting to a separate corner of a surprisingly modest dining chamber. Impressive frescos decorated each wall, depicting scenes from the Benotrists' storied past, including the capture of Fera during Tyro's revolution. Her gaze swept the richly adorned chamber, with its wooden framework contrasting nicely with its black and gray stone walls. There were two adjoining corridors, one in each opposite corner of the chamber, each leading to another set of chambers as far as she could tell. Her eyes finished at the small table centered in the chamber, where sat the Benotrist

Emperor, standing from his place at the table's opposite end, dressed in flowing golden robes over a long silver tunic.

"Your seat, Daughter," Tyro directed her to a place opposite him, which she quietly took, while he retook his seat. A snap of his fingers brought several servants from an adjoining passageway that led to an attached kitchen, each impeccably attired in black gowns with large decorative aprons.

"Mistress," A serving girl greeted, offering to fill her goblet with wine, which she refused, asking for water instead.

"Keeping your wits about you lest your tongue freely offer what your mind has closely guarded," Tyro nodded approvingly, appreciating Valera's strength and intellect.

"Wine dulls a child's wit if the mother partakes, so our Torry matrons tell it," she said, the mention of anything Torry souring his mood.

"Then water shall suffice, in the event they are right," Tyro said, taking a generous sip from his goblet while the servants brought forth platters of food.

"You spoke earlier of questions and answers?" Valera decided to cut to the meat of it, despising theatrics.

"In time, daughter. Let us partake. I am sure you are famished from your lengthy journey, and food on the road is barely edible, as my years of warfare can attest," he forked a serving of meat into his mouth, watching as she relented, taking a generous portion as well.

"Is the food to your liking?" He asked.

"It is delightful," she smiled politely, playing his game. Her father instructed her on the many forms of extracting information in formal settings. *The banquet hall is as much a battlefield as any other, and requires a keen mind to know the players from the obtuse,* he often repeated.

"And do you find the meat to your favor?"

"It is especially good," she answered as simply as he asked, with a slight nod of her head.

"Hotis spoke of your home, a very quaint cottage and farm that you and Joriah worked yourselves," he ventured.

"We did. I fear what shall become of it in our absence," she regarded him, studying his response to that, reminding him of the harm he had done.

"Farming is an honorable vocation, the very lifeblood of every realm of Arax, though an odd choice for the daughter of a great house, such as you were," he took another sip of wine, gauging her reaction to that. He wondered how much she knew that he knew of her, just as she wondered the same in reverse. Would she freely admit to her rich lineage? There was much that he pieced together, and much he was ignorant of.

"I am not too proud to raise a blister. When the food you eat is of your own sweat and effort, you savor its taste more greatly," she spooned another helping to her mouth, doing her best to conceal just how famished she was.

"I see it now," a rare smile touched his lips, staring at her intently.

She knew her expected response was to answer naively, asking what it was that he saw, only to be caught off guard with a revelation that would make her uncomfortable. So be it.

"See what?" she asked as innocently as she dare feign.

"You share many attributes with Cordela, especially her strength and practical thinking, unlike most of those of the feminine persuasion."

"A most flattering comparison, equating myself to Jonas' mother, and your first wife," she smiled evenly, noticing the twitch in his eye at her using the name of Jonas over Joriah.

"I assume Joriah spoke with you of his heritage?"

How should she answer? How much should she divulge?

"He did," she decided that he already knew this and answered honestly.

"And what did he speak of? His mother's kin, or his father's?"

"Both," she continued with honesty, sensing the tortured look in his eyes, and needing to placate him in some measure.

He restrained himself from shouting the questions he truly wanted answered, biding his time, carefully weighing each question and answer. She sensed what he wanted to ask, deciding to put him off balance by answering.

"He spoke of his mother's special heritage, and the unique power of her blood and the ancient King she was descended from," she didn't name Kal aloud with the ears of his servants so near. "He also spoke of his father, the man he loved, and still loves, despite the worlds that separate them," those last words taking him aback.

As hard as he tried, he couldn't fully shield his emotion with that revelation. He was the Emperor of the Benotrist Gargoyle Empire, conqueror of northern Arax, and the most feared ruler the world had ever known, yet the mention of his son still loving him was almost too much to bear. Valera could see the conflict in his golden eyes, with the specks of purple visible in the soft light.

"Does it surprise you that you still hold his affection?" She asked, pressing her advantage, pleased to see some emotion emerge from his icy veneer.

"A son should hold his father in such regard, but words are as cheap as watered wine. Actions speak to one's true nature. My son and wife disappeared long ago, without a trail or even a word to assuage my grief. Had Terin done so to you, would you not desire an answer?" He asked, steeling his heart. He needed, no… he demanded an answer to this question.

"You left them little choice," she said, looking at him over the rim of her goblet while taking another sip.

"Little choice?" He asked in a deathly whisper.

Valera was no fool, knowing her very life, and that of her un-born child, rested on Tyro remaining Emperor here, and speaking loosely of how the Kalinian bloodline could not abide gargoyles, would hardly do either of them any good. She regarded the servants and guards warily, before looking back to him, silently expressing her concern.

"Guards, leave us. Take the servants with you!" Tyro ordered, the guards bowing before herding everyone from the chamber, leaving the two of them alone.

"Are you not afraid of spies in the walls?" She asked, not trusting anything about this foul place.

"You are not very trusting," he said, admiring that about her.

"Neither are you," she repaid the compliment, neither seeing a trusting nature as an attribute to be admired.

"There are no spies in these walls. My many years living here has seen to that. Now, my dear, you were speaking of choices."

"You once made a choice, convincing your son to find a Sword of Light, and giving it to you, using it to slay your evil brother."

"At least you were correctly informed of Aleric's nature," he said, naming his brother.

"And you are curious as to what transpired after your assault upon Aleric's holdfast," she surmised, recalling what Jonas had spoken of regarding that perilous time. Tyro's eyes narrowed severely, recalling his attack on his brother, where he saved Regula from execution, and slew many of Aleric's men, but failed to kill Aleric himself, a failure that would forever haunt him.

"Aleric escaped my blade, losing three fingers in the exchange. Seeking revenge, he led his men to the Kalinian Vale, slaying all who dwelt there, so few they were at that time. I came upon the ghastly scene, but failed to find Cordela or Joriah's bodies among the slain. I did not know if they were taken or escaped," Tyro stated truthfully what he knew, waiting upon her to complete the holes in his knowledge.

"They hid in the upper vale, having dwelt there after you had departed, Cordela unable to face her kin after your betrayal…"

"I did not betray them," Tyro said, remaining as calm as his temper would allow.

"In your view, you obtained the sword to slay your brother to protect Cordela and her kin from his cruel intentions, but you did so against her father's wishes."

"The fool wouldn't listen. I warned him of my brother's nature, and that he would slay them all unless we killed him first. I did what any man of reason would do, I took the sword to spare my wife and child."

"But you didn't spare them. He still attacked, and slew everyone who dwelt there, save for Cordela and Jonas. They were only spared by the fickle wind of fate, having dwelt in the upper vale affording them time to hide while everyone else was slaughtered. They emerged two days after, gathering what they could of value, though Aleric left them little to scavenge. They journeyed south a fair distance, avoiding murderous brigands, slavers and gargoyles, until learning of your alliance with gargoyles. It was then they had no choice but to flee farther, far beyond your reach, for no Kalinian could abide a gargoyle's presence. You left them no choice but to abandon you," she said, her words striking his heart like a cruel dagger.

"It did not matter who I chose to ally with. They were my family and belonged with me. She would have been my empress, and Joriah an imperial prince. They would have wanted for nothing. I would have placed them above my own life," he growled, his demeanor losing its practiced calm.

"They cannot abide the gargoyles. You know this. Cordela told you this," she wondered why she even tried to reason with him, the look in his eyes proving it pointless.

"The gargoyles fear them. Who better to be my heir than one with such blood?"

"Because the power would reverse, and exchange the gargoyles fear for hatred and bloodlust. They would devour any Kalinian that aligned with them," she regretted saying thus, but he had to know the madness of his plans.

"Lies! Lies to rob me of my son and heir. Speak not of it again."

"As you wish," she mentally retreated, allowing her words time to take root.

After a long moment he broke the uncomfortable silence.

"They fled to Torry North. Was that the first land they sought out, or did they go elsewhere?"

"They went straight there, choosing there as their new home."

"They chose my enemy over me," he shook his head disgustedly.

"The Torry Realms were not your enemy then. You were still mired in your revolution. Our realms are only at war now because you made it so," she dared state the truth.

"They were always my enemy. Where were the Torries when the Menotrists oppressed my people? They did nothing to help us, and anyone ignoring such crimes share in the guilt. Gargoyles never hurt or enslaved our people. They fought beside us, casting down the evil Menotrists, and you would have me call them my enemy? You might despise me, child, but I am loyal to my blood and my friends," he said.

"Jonas is your kin, where is your loyalty to him?"

"Joriah. I have warned you not to speak that bastardized twisting of his true name."

"Very well. Joriah is your kin. Where is your loyalty to…"

"My loyalty is in sparing his life and seeing that he remains safe, both him and his brood. I take care of my own, daughter, even if they must wear chains for me to do so," he warned.

"Safe? How is my unborn child safe surrounded by gargoyles?"

"Your child is MY blood. I protect my own."

"Jonas… Joriah will not see it thus. He will hold you to account."

"He will do nothing but present himself to his rightful Emperor, and swear obedience to my throne. And if you think he shall raise his sword against me, then you are ignorant to another facet of his Kalinian blood. He can do no harm to those he loves. He is helpless against me," Tyro said, his bold claim taking her aback.

She didn't believe him until the certainty in his eyes broke that confidence.

"He didn't tell you of that? Interesting. Ironic, is it not, that for all the power wielded by Joriah, he is helpless against the emperor of the very realm he is sworn to destroy," Tyro mused aloud.

"Love can die. What then shall become of you?" She asked.

"Perhaps, but I doubt so. Joriah seems a man of great passion. I would know how he came to wed you, the daughter of a great house, the daughter of the great Torg Vantel?" He asked, taking her aback with that knowledge.

"I see you are well apprised of my kinship."

"I am, but there is more I would know."

"There is more I would know as well, particularly of Terin. I would know every detail that you are privy of, everything that transpired from the first moment he entered this castle to his liberation from slavery," she said.

"A fair bargain," he nodded.

And so, they each relayed their tales, with her detailing Jonas' arrival in Torry North, including Cordela's tragic death, which struck his heart, though he tried not to show her such weakness. He was surprised and angered by his son's groveling when he confessed his love of Valera to King Lore, offering up his life and his sword for the offense of his own heart. He was further taken aback by Lore's mercy and the promise of their then unborn child to the service of the throne, that child now destroying all of Tyro's plans wherever he went. He was equally proud and angered by Terin's fell deeds, so great as they are. Tyro then told her of Terin's brief time at Fera, and the events that followed as far as he understood them. He learned of his deeds at Telfer and Corell, and later at Mosar and Carapis. The tale of him being plucked from the beach by slavers tore her heart. He left unsaid that if he knew of his sorry state, he would have left him in Darna's keeping in exchange for his male heirs. What better place to keep him safely off the battlefield, and still give him the heirs he required? The very idea of his grandson suffering in slavery was an affront to his honor, but considering the alternatives, he could think of no better option to deal with the troublesome boy. Of course, all those wonderful plans were waylaid by his troublesome son by marriage, the insufferable Raven. Must all his kin confound him so? Once they finished their tales, they sat there for a time, both overwhelmed with so many tidings.

"And to think he was here in my very presence, unbeknownst to him or myself," he mused. Not a day went by without him pondering that failed opportunity. Had he taken Terin then, the disaster at Corell would have certainly been avoided, and this war all but over. He would have Terin, and through him, Joriah as well. Not to mention Tosha's sons. Letha would have little choice but to submit to his demands. Perhaps she could again take her rightful place as his Empress. He could have further bound his house to Darna, allowing her to rule the Sisterhood just as she planned, her sons and daughter bound to his many heirs.

Valera groaned, reading his thoughts so clearly.

"None of your plans would bring you joy. What do you truly gain by gathering such power? Once you die it would all fall apart. Your heirs want nothing to do with it. They oppose you at every turn. You could come back into fellowship with them if you would only make peace," she pleaded, losing all sense of control, vainly hoping to sway him to reason. Could he not see all that life could offer him if he only forsook this madness?

"Peace," he shook his head. "We are too far beyond that now, child. My gargoyles and Benotrists will sweep away the last vestiges of Tarelian rule, and their allies, bringing all of Arax under one rule. Only then shall we know peace."

"Is war worth the lives of your son and grandson? They will sacrifice their very lives to stop you. Would you do that for victory?"

"We shall see," he said, dismissing her.

He watched as the guards escorted her out, his mind a maelstrom of conflicting emotions, anger, hate, love, longing, and so many more, each tearing him in a thousand directions. He sat there for a long while, considering his options. He slowly gained his feet, following the corridor opposite the one leading to the kitchen, following the long passageway that ended outside his private chamber, the guards bowing as he passed within. He stepped toward his open window, the starlit sky offering him a breathtaking view, its mysterious beauty beckoning. He pondered all the decisions he made through the years that led him to this place and time. What would he have done different? Hindsight was meaningless unless you considered the alternative to your actions. The only true regret he had was not killing his brother in their first engagement, which would have stopped him from attacking Cordela's kin. Of course, that action led him to possess other wondrous gifts, his gaze drifting to the corner of the floor off his right.

He stepped nigh, drawing away the fitted stone that only lifted easily if one knew where to look. There before him rested three swords, each clothed in simple, nondescript scabbards. Lifting one in his hand sent a pulse of unfettered power coursing his flesh, filling him with euphoria as if he were still a young man. He stood, drawing the sword, a bright golden hue emitting along its blade.

"I may yet have need of you, old friend," he whispered, feeling the hypnotic power the *Sword of the Stars* invoked, filtering throughout.

CHAPTER 2

Tro Harbor.

All was in ruin.

Smoke, black and gray as a tortured sky twisted toward the heavens above. Tro's wounds were ablaze in the morning light, lamentations echoing mournfully through the wharves and streets. Fires burned unchecked throughout the harbor. Along the north shore of the inlet bay, another ape galley listed, foundering beneath the waves. Several warships drifted with the current in the middle of the harbor, their crews abandoning them with flames scorching their upper decks. The Troan Bioars *Fairer Maiden* and *Falling Star* were entangled, their blackened hulls pressed against one another, refusing to succumb, the former listing at the bow, and the later listing to port, leaning on the other. The bioar *Blazing Torch* was aptly named, fires ravaging its portside bow, and upper deck, but her savvy crew managed to save her, the Troan vessel requiring extensive repairs to make her sea worthy. The once proud Troan fleet was reduced to a mere seventeen vessels, many of those damaged, or suffering extensive casualties. The once powerful 1st Ape Fleet suffered far worse, only twelve of its sixty vessels surviving the battle, with the *Angry Fist* the latest to succumb, going down at her bow, before dipping fully beneath the waves.

Most offensive to the nose and virgin eye were the corpses strewn across the bay, their lifeless forms drifting and bobbing in a morbid dance. Ape, man and gargoyle forms littered the shore and bay, their stench threatening to overwhelm the survivors in the coming days, with disease following in its wake. Schools of carka fish swarmed the bay, their dorsal fins riding the surface as they fed on the fallen.

Terin stood atop the *Stenox*, observing the devastation with a heavy heart. Cronus stood at his side, resting a hand on the low wall circling three sides of the deck, the two friends barely able to share words since Cronus' arrival, attaining Tro just before the deadly attack. With the Ape Fleet smashed and the *Stenox* still Crippled, Tro seemed without hope.

"Such waste," Terin sighed, taken aback by the horror of it all. It was the same wherever his fool of a grandfather sent his minions, Tuft's, Corell, Yatin and here, all suffering in kind.

"Morac will soon return to Corell with fresh legions, and once Tro falls, they will be easily resupplied," Cronus stated coldly, the grim facts steeling his heart.

Terin thought on Cronus' words, knowing full well the dire straits that Corell was in. Morac was held at bay by King El Anthar's battlegroups, but with Nayboria stirring in the south, he could spare no more to Corell's defense. Prince Lorn was occupied with the Macon Campaign, and the Yatin armies were decimated by Yonig's invasion. That left only General Fonis' 2nd Torry Army at Central City. If he moved to defend Corell, then Tyro would send a legion against Rego, Central City and the Torry heartland.

"We have spent so much blood keeping the enemy at bay to this point, I don't know where we will draw the strength to continue," Terin lowered his head, hating the defeat in his voice.

"I know of what you speak. We have bled Tyro at every turn, and he still brings overwhelming numbers to bear. He knows as well as we that the fate of the war will be decided before the walls of Corell, and he shall empty his realm of strength to see it through," Cronus said.

"He is without mercy and will never relent," Terin left unsaid what was truly gnawing at his heart, though Cronus could well surmise.

"His sins are not yours, Terin. He may share your blood, but not your soul," he placed a comforting hand to his friend's shoulder, Terin turning his head sharply to him with that revelation.

"You know?" Terin couldn't mask the shame in his voice.

"Yes. Your father had Elos reveal it to me during our journey here."

"Cronus, I am so very sorry for all that he did to you," Terin couldn't help but think of the torment Cronus suffered in his grandfather's dungeon.

"Sorry? You did not place me there, or torture me there. It was you that rescued me from that foul place, you, Lorken and Raven. I will never forget that."

"I once thought I could never know what you suffered there, but I have a fairly good idea. The others don't understand," Terin lowered his head sadly, painfully recalling his captivity.

"Your Princess could," he reminded him of her capture by Monsoon.

"Yes, but she was held for ransom, with some hope of rescue. I never thought I would ever see any of you again, especially near the end. Every time I close my eyes, I find myself bound to that pole, suffering the lash. Even worse was the boredom of it all, day after day of mindless drudgery, time passing so painfully slow. Just when I couldn't fathom it being worse, I rebelled against Yah, and he forsook me, or at least I felt as if he had. I also thought Corry had died, stripping me of every dream I hoped for. You cannot suffer such things without it forever changing you in some way, and not for the good," Terin looked up, gazing across the water, the horrific scenery reflecting his morose spirit.

"Hopelessness," Cronus sighed, knowing well that torturous emotion. "I barely speak of what I endured in that foul dungeon, the torture, mutilation and death of my men, watching as they were dragged away one by one, to slavery or death. Just as your torment culminated in the stripping of your divine gift, mine ended with Kriton revealing that I had betrayed to him Leanna's name in my nightmares. He promised to see that she suffer by his hands, threatening to present to me her corpse while I endured in the dungeon for all eternity," Cronus kept his voice as dead as he could manage, lest he break with emotion.

"Thank you for sharing that, Cronus," he looked at his friend, their kindred spirits further joined by their suffering.

"I was blessed with a wonderful brother, a brother I lost. The fates have been kind enough to bless me with another," Cronus regarded him fondly, the early spring breeze lifting his dark mane.

"I have no brother or sister, and if I did, none would compare to the brother Yah has given me," Terin smiled.

* * *

"Try it again, Zem!" Brokov shouted down the hallway of the 1st deck, where Zem was working in the weapon's room, while he laid on his stomach, reaching through the open floor panel in the diving room, tools in hand.

Zem initiated the energy storage system, the ship's readouts indicating success. They spent the better part of the previous night sealing the energy leaks throughout the ship, which limited their energy restoration to five percent. Now Zem saw a healthy 5.002 percent on the readout, indicating success.

"System success! I will monitor its progress!" Zem's booming metallic voice echoed back from the end of the hall.

"Whew," Brokov sighed, rolling over on his back, staring at the ceiling, completely exhausted.

"You should rest. You have certainly earned it," he heard Kendra say, finding her standing in the doorway, her arms crossed.

"I certainly have," he smiled, not even bothering to stand up, enjoying her attractive form filling his vision.

"Are you well?" She gave him a mischievous look, knowing the affect she was having on him, dressed in her shorter leather tunic, her legs displayed to great effect.

"Just tired, what about you?" He asked, thankful they were able to heal her before she succumbed to the vicious wound to her neck.

"Better, thanks to you," she ambled toward him as he rose to a sitting position, leaning back with his hands on the floor, supporting him.

18

"I couldn't let you die and leave me all alone with all these idiots," he grinned as she knelt beside him.

"No, you couldn't. That would be a most insufferable fate," she smiled, brushing her lips across his.

"Aw hell," he relented, crushing his lips to hers. The one thing Raven did right was bringing her along with him from Axenville. He would be sure to thank him someday… maybe.

* * *

Their magantor swept through the heavens, the midday sun bearing overhead with the landscape passing swiftly below. They followed the coastline north at first light, before circling back, completing their brief reconnaissance, Elos steering the great avian, with Lorken sitting behind him. Following the coastline back south, they spied the outline of the Troan Bay along the horizon. From afar the harbor displayed a tranquil charm, before their descent brought the tortured city into view. Lorken shook his head, disgusted by the wreckage of the ape and Troan fleets, and the fire ravaged landscape circling the bay.

"What a pitiful sight," Lorken said, observing the *Stenox* dead in water, moored along the central harbor district on the south shore.

"Your ship still floats. Take comfort in that," Elos said, maneuvering the great avian through the mouth of the bay, before crossing the face of the great sentinel, the giant statue's sapphire eyes staring past them to the open sea.

"It won't stay afloat for long if they haven't fixed the power leaks," Lorken snorted as they circled the *Stenox*, setting down alongside it upon the stone wharf.

"We shall know that answer soon," Elos said.

"Yes, and then we can share the bad news," Lorken said, seeing Raven exit the bridge, watching them dismount while he stood upon the second deck.

"What did you find out?" Raven asked as they climbed aboard.

"Nothing good. I'll tell you on our way to the forum. Gather up whoever is going," Lorken said.

"Most of them are already there," Raven said, as Cronus, Lucas and Terin escorted Corry there prior to their arrival, while Ular and Argos were there much of the morn with their respective delegations.

* * *

It was late in the day when they finally gathered in the city forum, with the many emissaries and ruling patriarchs seated along the lower tiers of stone benches circling the central circled platform, where stood Klen Adine, the Magistrate of Tro. Beside him stood Admiral Purvis and Commander Balkar, the ranking Troan commanders. The ruling families were represented by their five patriarchs, each suffering great loss from the attack, nearly all of their manses damaged or destroyed. The representatives of Bedo and Gotto attended on behalf their cities, each realizing the precarious position their people were in. Pors Vitara and Porlin Galba sat stone faced, determined to return to their native Casia and lobby for a declaration of war. Pors still nursed his aching leg and burnt hands and face, each a gift from Tyro, gifts he looked to repay. Among the apes were chiefs Hukor and Gargos, along with Admiral Zorgon and Argos. Ular stood beside chief Ilen of Enoructa, the later eager to return to Linkortis to rally his people for war. Cronus, Lucas and Terin sat behind Corry, who led the Torry delegation, her role changing from neutral arbiter to ally among peers. Last in attendance were Raven and Lorken, each standing off to the side of the chamber alongside Elos, the former leaning against the wall. Lorken felt the icy stares of Marcus Talana and Ortus Maiyan, both men forced to tolerate his presence, though hating him profusely.

"We find ourselves gathered to discuss our position, and the options that lay before us," Klen began, eying each of them briefly before continuing.

"Just before dawn, I dispatched several of our available magantors to scout the northern approaches of Gotto, while Lorken and Elos searched along our northern coast. Our scouts discovered large columns of gargoyles marching south toward Gotto. They place their strength between fifteen and thirty telnics," Klen said, though the estimate was irrelevant compared to its greater meaning. It was either a part of a legion, or a detachment from a legion, meaning Tyro was moving against them in strength.

"Lorken, what did you discover?" Klen asked, causing Lorken and Elos to stand forth.

"We spotted a large Benotrist fleet moving south, approximately seventy-five leagues to our direct north," Lorken said.

"How large of a fleet?" Admiral Zorgon asked gruffly.

"More than a hundred ships if I were to guess," Lorken said, causing a collective groan from many of those gathered.

"The nearest major Benotrist port is Pagan, and that's a fair distance. They must have sailed long ago to pull this off," Raven said.

"Aye, and they probably are moving other forces against the northeastern city states to secure their lines of communication. They wouldn't be venturing this far south if that was in doubt," Admiral Purvis said, his words greatly effecting the representative from Bedo.

"One hundred warships and at least a legion of gargoyles? What hope have we of repelling a force of that size?" Varin, Patriarch of House Corbin lamented.

"Let us remove emotion from our thinking, Patriarch Varin. Lorken and Elos have spotted a sizable fleet, though its exact strength is unknown. Our scouts report a partial legion of gargoyles advancing upon Gotto. Whether this land force is merely a part of a full legion moving against us or marches alone, we can only surmise. Morac's greater strength rests at Notsu, suffering tremendously from his failed siege of Corell. Should he move at us with greater strength, he would doom his planned renewed attack upon Corell. His plan to destroy this port, the ape fleet, and the Earthers in one fell strike, has met with failure," Klen stated.

"Failure! Have you a care to look across the harbor? Tro is in ruin, the ape fleet smashed, and your Earth friends' vessel sits dead in the water!" Marcus Talana growled.

"We ain't dead yet, Marcus," Raven grunted, refuting that notion.

"Nor are you alive, Earther! What of the great power you boasted just yester morn? You sit helpless as the rest of us, and I doubt that…" Marcus countered, before Raven cut him off.

"Tyro just made the biggest mistake of his sorry life. He's a dead man, whether he knows it or not. Hell, even if he managed to sink the *Stenox*, we'd still kick his ass from one side of Arax to the other!" Raven growled.

"Your arrogance is boundless!" Ortus Maiyan glared daggers at him.

"Oh, I'm just getting started!" Raven said, coming off the wall, stepping onto the stone circle, giving everyone around him a hard look. "Once we restore full power, we'll sink every ship Tyro has from one coast to the other. And while we're at it, we'll flatten every port city from Tinsay to Pagan. By the time we're done not even a Benotrist paddling a canoe will be spared. Then we'll blast every dwelling within miles of the coast. If we see as much as a pup tent with a pitiful Benotrist huddling inside it, we'll blow it apart in so many pieces even the bugs won't find it! And then we'll start hunting down Benotrist and gargoyle generals and ministers, cutting them up for fish bait. Then we'll move down the food chain, taking out every unit commander and above. And don't get me started about Tyro's Elite. We'll start with Morac. I'll personally take that magic sword of his and shove it up his…"

"I think you made your point, Raven," Klen stopped him from going any further, everyone, save the apes and Lorken, looking on with their mouths agape.

"Before we can properly plan for all contingencies, we need a full listing of available forces. Admiral Purvis," Klen stepped aside for the Troan Admiral.

"The Troan fleet suffered thirty-three vessels sunk, and four severely damaged, leaving thirteen fit for sea. The damaged vessels are presently moored, undergoing repairs. Casualties exceed fourteen hundred killed, missing or wounded," Purvis related the grim assessment, before yielding to Commander Balkar.

"Municipal forces suffered twenty-eight hundred dead or missing, and another eight hundred wounded. Our archer barracks suffered 327 dead, 61 wounded, leaving Tro with 112 trained bowmen. Civilian casualties are heavy, and as yet uncounted. I have ordered all tributary dominions to marshal all reserves to Tro's defense. They have eight days to call their levies, which shall bring our garrison to six full telnics," Commander Balkar stated grimly.

"What of enemy casualties, Commander?" Lubion Tobian, the ranking Patriarch of Tro, asked.

"At least twenty gargoyle telnics, along with countless Benotrist merchant sailors, and thousands of pirates. I can only guess their total losses, but it was exceedingly high," Balkar gave the Earthers a wary look, knowing that many of those deaths were attributed to their terrible power.

"Admiral Zorgon!" Klen offered the ape admiral the floor, Purvis and Balkar each backing a step, giving the large ape a wide berth.

"Forty-eight ships sunk, three severely damaged, leaving nine fit for sea. Of my crews, nearly half of the lost ships' crews were killed, missing or wounded. If the survivors are being organized into infantry, we can field five telnics to support your garrison," Zorgon reported grimly, the losses suffered by the 1st Ape Fleet staggering to behold. With only forty galleys in the 2nd Ape Fleet at Torn, the apes had little means of projecting strength, especially if Tyro's fleet bypassed Tro to engage the remains of the ape navy.

"Eleven telnics against a gargoyle legion," Farbo Fixus, Patriarch of House Fixus, bemoaned.

To that, Ortus Maiyan protested vehemently, coming to his feet, the death of his son Orvis still painfully burned into his heart. "That is if Tyro sends a full legion against us, which he might not spare. Anything less will not subdue us. If Darkhon wants our city, he will pay a heavy toll. We will fight him street to street, house to house, bleeding him for every step. My house has endured here since the foundations of Tro were first laid. I'll not give one stone, one coin, one once of blood to this Benotrist upstart!" Ortus declared emphatically. Whatever strength age had robbed of him, his hunger for vengeance returned to him five fold.

Klen regarded the aged head of House Maiyan carefully. His sources informed him of his son Orvis' subterfuge, conspiring with agents of Tyro to undermine Tro's defenses prior to the attack, though he would not present that evidence. It would serve little use considering that Orvis was himself betrayed, murdered by agents of

Tyro sometime during the attack. He was likely lured to betray them with false promises of making him regent of Tro and its surrounding fiefdoms. Once Tro was compromised, and the attack commenced, Tyro had little need to prop up an ignorant fool to rule the city. Ortus Maiyan's current bold defiance seemed genuine, giving Klen reason to believe that the patriarch of House Maiyan was unaware of the plot. Since the elder Maiyan was pushing to resist Tyro, Klen saw no benefit in revealing the truth. He would use Ortus' thirst for vengeance to forward his own war agenda.

It was at this moment that Lubion Tobian addressed the assemblage, the ranking patriarch Klen's strongest supporter, his voice holding sway over the entire council.

"As we've elected to resist Darkhon, you stated yester eve that you would present a plan to do so. Have you done so?" Lubion asked of Klen.

"I have, Patriarch Tobian," Klen bowed his head to the elder statesman, a man who held his deepest trust. He then raised his chin, projecting the strength for which his post demanded at such times. "Half measures and empty words will only fail us in this endeavor. The crisis at hand requires adherence to the recommendations I shall put forth, though extreme they might appear to any or even all of you. I fear if they are not adhered to, we shall fall."

"Speak them, Adine!" Marcus Talana ordered sternly; his eyes fixed upon the fingertips of his right hand as he rubbed them together.

"One! Designate Admiral Zorgon supreme commander of all municipal forces," he said, holding up one finger to emphasis this point. "Two! Full manumission of all male slaves exceeding twenty five years of age in return for conscription. Three! Removal of all non-essential citizens to the Ape Republic. Four! Declaration of absolute law, authorizing the post of harbor magistrate to arrest, detain and execute any citizen or non-citizen for treason or suspicion of treason. Five! Authorize the post of harbor magistrate power to negotiate freely with mercenaries, pirates and privateers, including those outlawed by Tro. Six! Provide the harbor magistrate the authority to seize any dwelling or property deemed necessary for Tro's defense," Klen finished, preparing for the blowback of his audacious plan.

"Outrageous!" Farbo Fixus protested.

"Manumission of slavery?" Marcus Talan spat.

"Are you to be our king?" Farbo sneered.

"All provisions are temporary, and emergency powers granted the office of magistrate shall be rescinded once the danger has passed, or when the ruling families decide," Klen added, assuaging their concerns.

"If we support such measures, we shall have little wealth worth saving," Farbo argued.

To this, Lubion Tobian stood to address the assemblage, his steely gaze giving his fellow patriarchs pause. "The wealth of Tro is not in our legions of slaves, our treasury or the riches we have stored. Our reputation and our geography are the true sources of our power. If we survive this incursion, our trade routes shall be restored, and we shall again prosper. Should our city fall, then we shall lose all. Darkhon's reputation in treating conquered lands is well known, and none of you should contemplate submitting yourselves to his mercy, for he has none. If Magistrate Adine recommends that we take these actions he has listed, then we would be wise to do so. I speak for House Tobian in support of his measures. Our city is worth fighting for… no matter the cost!"

"I stand with Lubion, and support these measures," Varin Corbin, Patriarch of House Corbin declared.

"Before I cast my vote, I would hear from our ape friends their intentions. Will the forces they have here stay and defend our city?" Marcus Talana asked, looking directly to Admiral Zorgon.

"Aye! We'll stand with you. Not one of my sailors shall retreat. We hold this city until relieved!" Zorgon affirmed, giving steel to their collective spines.

"Very well, and what of the Earthers? Will you stay and fight beside us?" Marcus asked of Lorken and Raven. Though he despised them intensely, he respected their power and their word.

"We aren't going anywhere, but we have conditions that aren't negotiable," Raven said.

"And they are?" Klen asked, preparing for the bad news whenever Raven opened his mouth.

"Don't give me that look, Klen, it ain't that bad," Raven disarmed his protest before he could give it voice.

"There are only two," Lorken added.

"The first is you just forget all about our previous differences, especially the little matter surrounding the sinking of the *Lady Talana*, and Lorken's wedding Jenna," Raven said, drawing reluctant nods from the patriarchs of Houses Talana and Maiyan.

"The second is far more important. We want a restricted fly zone for the center of the harbor, where the *Stenox* will take up position until our ship is fully operational. That means no magantors flying over the water. If we see one anywhere near our ship, we blast it out of the sky. Limit your magantors to specific landing zones at the city's edge," Lorken explained, which the patriarchs relented to.

"It appears those terms are agreeable," Klen said, receiving nods of approval from the ruling patriarchs. There was still a grave matter to discuss upon their overall strategic position, one that involved Corell, their fates interlinked at this time. He spent much of the morning discussing this at length with the Torry Princess, finding her knowledge on strategic matters most impressive, as well as her understanding of the geographical challenges of the terrain resting between Corell and Tro, as well as all of eastern Arax. With that, he invited her to stand forth to address the assemblage.

Corry stepped into the stone circle, sensing the doubts of the ruling patriarchs, as well as the Casian and Gotto delegates, none fully accepting the words of a woman. She cared not, knowing her true worth. Where were these men when Morac assailed the walls of Corell? Unlike them, her sword was stained with the blood of many enemies, both gargoyles and the men and women she slew at Bansoch.

"Tyro has made a strategic blunder in his poorly planned assault upon your harbor. It is no secret that Morac intends to renew his assault upon Corell with spring upon us, with fresh levies from the north. Throughout our history, few invasions from the north availed passing east of the Plate Mountains, the unforgiving landscape of the Kregmarin Plain hindering supply routes to feed a host as large as Morac's. Adding to this, our Jenaii allies have waylaid many caravans from the north at many points along that perilous route, as well as fomenting rebellion throughout the eastern half of the Benotrist Empire," Corry began, receiving a confirming look from Elos before continuing.

"Supplying his vast host to assail Corell is Tyro's greatest weakness. The overland route is arduous under the best of situations, and nigh impossible under the current environment thanks to the efforts of our Jenaii allies. Tyro would prefer the full use of your harbor, moving food and provisions by the safer and more efficient sea route," she explained, most of those assembled understanding the lengthy supply chains the Benotrists required. Their nearest farmlands supporting the invasion were along the headwaters of the Tur River, and the large estates south of Nisin. Any provisions from these lands required transport across the Kregmarin Plain. The use of Tro, however, required provisioning from lands tributary to Terse, which meant those lands along the northeastern coast would have to fall under Benotrist influence, or be allowed neutrality as long as they fed the Benotrist war effort. For all the council knew, those lands might have already fallen, a fact weighing heavily upon the Bedoan emissary. The delegate from Terse perished in the attack, proving he was likely unaware of any subterfuge between his city and Tyro.

"It is apparent that Tyro meant to destroy the ape fleet and the *Stenox* in one fell strike, and take the harbor intact. His clumsy attack may have slain many of your people, sunk much of the ape fleet, and temporarily damaged the *Stenox*, but none of these blows are permanent. You have more than enough strength among you to resist a gargoyle legion. If Tyro wants to seize Tro, he will need far more than one legion, and any commitment of forces that size will greatly hinder his assault upon Corell. Even if he were successful, the cost in blood and time would mean Tro would not be able to supply his legions at Notsu until midsummer, dooming any attack upon Corell for another year. One year is all our armies in the south require to finish the Macon Campaign and neutralize Nayboria, bringing all our might north to face whatever Tyro can send at us the following spring," Corry's keen strategic assessment now had their collective attention.

"It is my opinion that Tyro has little choice but to commit all his strength to Morac's renewed attack upon Corell, leaving very little to assail you here. This will force him to commit nearly all his magantor and cavalry to reinforce his supply caravans along the Kregmarin. All you would need to do is stand firm, hold this city at all cost, and wait for President Matuzak to rally the Ape Republic to come to your aid. And know this, every day the *Stenox* grows stronger, standing as an unmovable block in the center of the Troan Bay, denying Tyro access by sea and air. Should we defeat Morac a second time at Corell, Tro and all lands to its south shall be secure from Tyro," she said, her words winning them to her cause.

"Aye, you're a fiery lass, Princess. You remind me of my aunt Becta, as fierce an ape lass who ever wielded an ax. We'll hold this city, Tyro and his filthy gargoyles be damned!" Admiral Zorgon bellowed, his voice giving spine to the council.

"Tro will not fall before all our blood is spilt!" Marcus Talana Growled, standing from his stone bench.

"Aye!" Ortus Maiyan seconded, coming to his feet.

"Aye!" The others agreed, one after another coming to his feet, adding his voice to the affirmation.

Corry regarded the men in the chamber, taken aback by their willingness to stand together, united in purpose despite their many differences. She then knew that this was their great hope, all the peoples of Arax united in cause and purpose, to bring down the tyrant threatening to destroy them all. She looked to one after another, before stopping at Terin, who stared at her with unbridled love, proud of her strength and courage. She couldn't help but smile back at him, overcome with emotion every time she looked into those soulful sea blue eyes. They could have looked upon one another for eternity if not distracted by Raven's loud voice.

"Now that's settled, let's get to work!" The big Earther grunted, heading for the exit.

* * *

"I would advise against it," Brokov warned.

The late evening found them gathered in the dinning cabin of the *Stenox*, the crew and their Torry friends, along with Elos, who stood at the doorway between Zem and Argos. The ship restored enough power to light the cabin, though the food processor was still inoperable, a fact causing much grief among Argos, Orlom, Lorken and Raven, their appetites exceeding the others. They compensated by setting up a makeshift grill on the stone wharf where they were presently moored, cooking up fish from the ship's storage, nearly causing Klen an apoplexy. Only the Earthers would deign to erect such an eyesore near the harbor magistrate, but Brokov assured him they would soon fix their food preparation unit and take up position in the middle of the harbor. Brokov wisely fed power to the food storage unit, and water purification and plumbing sections, prioritizing those essential functions first.

"Your council is wise, but I dare not delay my return to Corell," Corry said, urgent to attain Corell long before Morac's invasion commenced.

"I would caution a much more southern route, far from any patrols Morac might have lurking about," Brokov warned, preferring they return to the ape republic, retrieve their other magantor riders, thus taking a much safer approach to Corell.

"Elos and Cronus took a similar path from Corell," Corry said.

"And were fortunate. You can be assured that Morac will look to sever any contact between Tro and Corell in the coming days, especially along key geographical features like the Falls of Flen," Brokov pointed out, naming the juncture where Corry planned to cut west from. The Falls of Flen rested far upriver, halfway between Tro and the Ape Hills.

"I trust our speed and stealth to safeguard our journey, as well as the Jenaii and Torry champions, each wielding a Sword of the Moon, along with two of the Torry Elites' greatest warriors," she added, regarding Cronus and Lucas proudly.

"And three Troan magantors as escort," Lucas added, Corry having negotiated their aid during her morning meeting with Klen Adine, convincing him the necessity of her quest. Tro and Corell's fates were now linked. Should Corell fall, Tro was doomed, convincing

Klen the urgency of returning the Torry Princess and champion to the White Castle before Morac's invasion.

A long silence followed, each of them weighing the difficult options before them. The way to Corell was fraught with peril, but Terin and Corry needed to reach the palace, and soon.

"This seems familiar," Lorken quipped, recalling the last time they had a similar debate, after Cronus and Raven reached Tro upon their escape from Fera. Kato was the one voice among the Earthers to insist upon their full intervention on the Torries behalf, venturing forth on his own to aid their desperate cause.

"No, the last time we were debating whether to help at all. This time we're in it. The only question is, what do we do," Kendra said, sitting beside Corry at the table, most of the others pressed about, a few sitting, the rest standing, crowding the small cabin. The others debated the pros and cons with each choice, coming to no conclusion. Some debated waiting for the Torry magantors to come to Tro, and proceed in force to Corell. Others thought they should travel to Gregok, and join with the Torry magantors there, before heading for Corell. A few thought it best to hold position, and strike Morac's legions from the east, once the Ape Armies arrived, using both swords and the power of the earthers to overwhelm the enemy where they were weakest. Nearly everyone had an opinion, save for Raven, who simply stood off to the side, unusually quiet, which Lorken noticed.

"Rav?" Lorken called out to his friend, causing the room to quiet, all eyes looking to Raven, who seemed unaffected by the direction of the conversation, as if his mind were already made up.

"This war will be decided at Corell. Ben will be there, and I'll be there to kill him," Raven said bluntly, the others taken aback by this declaration.

"Are you coming with us?" Cronus asked, wondering if his ears deceived him. How he longed for this moment, when his dearest friend fought beside him defending the Torry realm.

"Yep. You're going to need an Earther to face an Earther, but I'll be staying out of sight until Ben shows himself. Once I kill him, then I'll help you kill the rest of the sorry bastards. I trust the rest of you to get the ship in order. Once Corell is secure, I'll come back, and then we can take the fight to Tyro, starting with his navy," Raven's words sent ripples across Terin's flesh, believing for the first time that they had a true chance for victory.

"I am coming with you," Ular said with his distinct watery voice, regarding Lucas knowingly, the Torry smiling happily, welcoming his friend on their journey.

"We would be pleased with your company, Ular," Corry said, holding the Enoructan Champion in the highest regard.

"Can I come, Boss?" Orlom looked to Raven from across the cabin, his usual playful banter replaced with serious determination, so much so, that Raven didn't have the heart to say no.

"Alright, but no shooting until I get Thorton. Can you do that?" Raven asked, the others doubting his ability to do so.

"Aye, I can do that," Orlom said, his sad look nearly breaking Corry's heart. Even though he and Grigg were constant troublemakers, it was never done so purposely, their antics quite comical if you could see them from afar. His friend's death tore away much of his wide-eyed innocence, giving him a determined resolve to kill every gargoyle he could lay his hands on, or blast to pieces.

"You should take one of our tissue regenerators. I have two almost fully charged," Brokov said, the third he had lent to the harbor matrons, who were treating the many wounded with it after a brief instruction on its use.

"Not a bad idea. There will be no shortage of wounded needing it. Hopefully Your brother still has the one Kato left him," Raven said, looking to Corry.

"We shall see," was all she could say, looking at Raven with mixed emotions. He was the most impossible, frustrating man she had ever known, but she was eternally thankful he was coming to help them.

"And don't expect any of that kneeling nonsense from me or Orlom. You best tell your royal court about that when we arrive. No need for the first person I kill at Corell to be one of your people," Raven reminded her, stepping for the door, pausing before passing fully through. "Tell Klen we should leave just before sunrise. Fewer people seeing me leave the better. Get some sleep, we have a long journey ahead of us."

* * *

It was before dawn the following morn when they gathered upon the wharf beside the *Stenox,* the three Troan magantors joining *Wind Racer* and Elos' warbird, requiring each mount to bear two riders, and one of them three. *Wind Racer* being the largest would carry Terin, Corry and Ular, the rest flying in pairs. With Raven being the heaviest he would pair with Elos, who could jump off if the Magantor ever struggled with their weight. They each took advantage of the *Stenox's* shower one last time before disembarking, knowing the journey ahead would lack any such amenities. There were few if any settlements along their planned route of travel. As the others bid their farewells upon the wharf, Raven joined Brokov, Lorken and Zem upon the bridge, the four Earthers sharing one last moment before Raven departed.

"Take good care of the ship," Raven said, looking at each of them as they stood upon the bridge in a small circle.

"It will still be floating when you get back," Lorken said.

"Especially with our biggest Klutz and Orlom on their way to Corell," Brokov smiled.

"I was being serious," Raven gave him a not so gentle shove.

"So was I," Brokov couldn't help himself.

"Where did you put the healing thingy?" Raven asked, looking around as if it to find it somewhere on the floor.

"You mean the tissue regenerator? I gave it to Ular. He has been well schooled with its operation," Brokov said.

"You sure that was a good idea? These things are very complicated and require…" Raven began to argue, but Brokov was having none of it.

"It's not that complicated. Even a child could use it with proper instruction. That goes for just about anyone, except you. You'd just find some way to break it, Captain Klutz," Lorken grinned, receiving a shove as well.

"My friends, my wonderful friends," Raven shook his head, looking at the three of them, wondering what he did to deserve being stranded on Arax with these idiots?

"In all seriousness, Rav, just watch your back out there, and if you get a chance to kill Ben, don't hesitate," Brokov said, patting him on the shoulder.

"Same goes for you if he somehow shows up here," Raven said, considering that a possibility.

"Take good care of Cronus and the kid," Lorken said, using the moniker they often ascribed to Terin.

"And Corry, Ular and Lucas," Zem added.

"And Orlom. Make sure he doesn't do anything too stupid, like taking a dump in the throne room," Lorken shook his head, just imagining the look on the Torries faces when he showed up at the palace. He only wished they had a live feed so they could enjoy the show from a safe distance.

"Or mistake the good guys for the bad guys," Brokov voiced that concern in all seriousness, considering only he and Raven were carrying Laser weapons, both he and Raven with a pistol and a rifle strapped over their shoulders. Cronus and Ular left their pistols with the *Stenox,* as many of the crew's weapons were as yet not fully operational, the safety of the ship taking precedence over lesser considerations.

"I'll keep an eye on him," Raven said, knowing Grigg's death went far in Orlom's maturity. With that, he bid them one last farewell, stepping toward the door.

"Rav," Zem called out, catching them by surprise with his use of that abbreviated name for Raven.

"Yeah?" Raven said, looking back at him.

"Remember all the mean and hurtful things we all have said and done to each other these past years?" Zem recalled with his deep metallic voice, his tone one of profound sincerity.

"Yeah," Raven said, making a face, wondering where he was going with this.

"I look forward to your return so we can do them all over again."

"Thanks, Zem," Raven shook his head before stepping out.

CHAPTER 3

Sawyer.

Squid Antillius made his way through the festive streets, the good citizens spilling out of their homes, celebrating their joyous liberation. The midday sun shone brightly overhead, heralding the end of winter with a wondrous gift of peace. The sound of flutes and horns echoed through the air, matching the celebratory atmosphere. Young men and women joined hands, dancing through the streets. Members of the ruling forum stood upon the lip of the great fountain in the center of the city, speaking to the gathered crowds, heralding the virtues of their brave defenders and Torry allies. Young lovers embraced everywhere he looked, the stress of the siege lifting, overwhelming their restraint. Squid smiled, catching sight of a soldier embracing his lady, taking her in his arms, their lips pressed one to the other. In another direction he saw a young father twirling his infant daughter in the air, both laughing.

Squid paused briefly, looking skyward, the largest smile breaking upon his aged face, taking a moment to praise his god.

"Thank you, Yah," he said aloud, doubting anyone heard him over the raucous noise. It didn't matter who heard or not. He merely expressed his gratitude to the most high, to him whom he placed his trust. Yah rewarded his trust with a victory unlooked for. He could think of no flowery words to match the unfettered joy emanating from his heart, no poetic prose worthy to praise him. All he could muster was a simple *Thank You,* the unassuming utterance perfectly reflecting his childlike faith.

"Antillius!" He turned as an overzealous Minister Sounor rushed to greet him.

"Sounor," he greeted in kind, embracing his friend, the Sawyeran Minister's guards struggling to keep pace with their charge in the gathering crowd.

"What are you doing alone in the streets in your condition? And without your guards," Sounor shook his head.

"My wounds are more than healed, old friend. And I hardly require protection, especially now," Squid smiled.

Word reached the city early that morn, emissaries from Fleace arriving to lift the siege by order of King Mortus. General Bram Vecious called for a parlay with the forum of Sawyer under the blue flag of truce, relaying the news of Prince Lorn and King Mortus agreeing to accords. The arrival of General Dar Valen leading a joint contingent of Torry and Macon warbirds confirmed the good tidings, with word quickly spreading throughout the city. The news found Squid in his chambers, where he immediately rushed outside, making his way to the city forum while caught up in the crowds spilling out into the streets.

"Very well. Come, the others are gathering in the forum," Sounor urged, tugging on his sleeve.

"Not all of them it seems," Squid pointed out the several forum members atop the fountain, giving speeches.

"Bah, they are junior members looking to bolster their placement," Sounor dismissed the crowd pleasers, drawing Squid away from the gathering throng. They didn't make it more than a few paces before the Torry Minister was recognized, drawing the crowds attention.

"Bless you Ambassador Antillius! Bless your realm and bless your Prince!" A woman with a belly swollen with child, shouted tearfully, rushing forth to kneel at his feet, showering his hands with kisses. Before he could respond, helping her to her feet, others pressed forth, shouting praises, trying to touch him, with Sounor trying to give him space, but to no avail. Eventually the Sawyeran Minister laughed, shrugging his shoulders in defeat as poor Antillius was hugged, kissed and touched by a thousand pairs of hands. Squid eventually managed to calm the passionate mob enough to say a few words.

"My good people, I am humbled by your adulation, but I am merely a servant of the Torry Prince and his mighty God. Reserve your praise for them, and for your brave soldiers, who have held the enemy at bay for these many fortnights, ensuring your banners still fly above your ramparts," he pointed to the city forum behind them, where the sigil of Sawyer lifted in the late morning breeze, a silver ship upon a field of black.

"Hail Prince Lorn! Hail Antillius! Hail Sawyer!" The chants began to echo, building into a deafening crescendo, causing Sounor and Squid to shake their heads and again embrace before lifting their hands into the air, their gesture invigorating the crowd.

* * *

When Squid finally reached the forum, he was greeted by a sea of smiling faces in the members of the ruling council, and their many retainers. Standing in the center circle stood General Dar Valen, commander of the Torry Magantor forces, and Bram Vecious, General of the 2nd Macon Army, the former enemy and new ally to the city.

"Minister Antillius, Prince Lorn sends his regards, and is most eager to receive you at Fleace," General Valen greeted him as he stepped forth, taking Squid aback by the sudden change sweeping the city and the Macons who as recently as this morn opposed them. It was the strangest thing to stand in the presence of General Vecious as allies, this manifestation brought about by a simple message, peace replacing war, causing enemies to become friends, though forgiveness would come grudgingly in some corners.

"I would be honored, General Valen. Am I expected immediately or am I to wait upon my replacement?" Squid asked.

"He asks that you return with me this day," General Valen said, taking him aback with the urgency.

General Valen was apprised of the state of the city, and the Macon forces surrounding it. He requested a representative of the Sawyeran

Council accompany them on their return to Fleace, to attend the joint council of war hosted by the Macon King. He further advised the Sawyeran council to prepare the city for the campaign ahead once the current celebration ended, and to coordinate with General Vecious the movement of forces across the lake once provisions were secure for their advance. This last request took the entirety of the council aback, dampening their mood. It was a stern reminder that the war in the southwest might be over, but the greater war continued, their eventual fate to be decided far from home. General Valen ordered the city to gather all of their wounded to be brought to the city square, and to be categorized by severity of their injuries. When asked why, he simply said *compliments of the lady Ilesa*.

* * *

The Macon encampment north of the city.

Squid wondered General Valen's insistence that he immediately follow him to their former enemy's encampment upon leaving the forum, only to be greeted by the sight of hundreds of wounded Macon soldiers lined up upon the open ground, numbering well over four hundred, suffering everything from broken limbs to severe burns. Those recently injured with mortal wounds were prioritized, but were thankfully few. He was further surprised to find a Torry Matron tending them with what appeared to be Kato's healing device, which he remembered him using after the siege of Corell. Dar drew Squid aside before introducing him to the comely Matron, telling him of Kato's death, and his wedding the Lady Ilesa, which he had not learned of. He also told of Terin's fall at Carapis, but said that the prince had good reason to believe that he was alive. The last bit of ill tidings struck Squid like a blow to the head, knowing what Terin's death might do to his old friend Jonas, let alone the cost to the realm. Losing Kato was bad enough, but Terin also? He hoped Lorn was correct to believe otherwise, giving him hope that the boy lived. With that weighing upon his heart, he followed Dar to the young Matron, who was surprisingly guarded by several members of the

37

Torry and Macon Elite, each accompanying Dar here to safeguard the Lady Ilesa at the insistence of Prince Lorn and King Mortus. Both monarchs knew the importance of her work, and the value of Kato's wondrous gift.

"My Lady Ilesa, Minister Antillius," Dar introduced them.

"My Lady, I am honored to meet the wife of one of the bravest and most honorable men I have ever known. I can see why he chose you, as you are lovely and as kind as I remember him to be," Squid gave her an empathetic smile, imagining her suffering.

"You are kind to say so, Minister Antillius," Ilesa smiled wanly, wiping her bloody hands on the apron tied about her skirt, its material already soiled from her day's labors, though she had recently arrived. The device was currently recharging, with the next man waiting for its use laying upon the ground, his broken back rendering him crippled below the waist.

Squid grasped her hand, lifting it to his lips despite her protest that it was filthy. "The hand of Kato's wife could never soil my lips, no matter what they have touched, my fair Ilesa," Squid assuaged her protest, kissing her left hand, followed by her right.

"The lady Ilesa came here at her own insistence, Minister Antillius, after treating many of the wounded at Fleace. She was moved by the tidings of the many wounded here that the Macons were unable to remove from the siege, as well as the many wounded men among Sawyer," Dar said proudly, impressed by Ilesa's undertaking this journey considering her own condition, which he advised Squid of with his next utterance, Causing Ilesa to look away, uncomfortable with his undo praise.

"To travel so far upon a magantor and with child." Squid shook his head. "You are a most zealous and kind soul, My Lady," Squid sighed, touched by her bravery.

"I do this to honor him, and would not have it any other way," she couldn't bring herself to say Kato's name, or the token of his affection that was a part of him, and now her. She touched a hand to her heart, reassuring herself that it rested where she placed it upon her bosom, beneath the folds of her dress, her most treasured possession.

Squid noticed the odd gesture, but had the decency not to inquire what was so important that it rested next to her heart.

"Lady Ilesa shall remain here treating the wounded, under the joint protection of the Torry and Macon Elite sent to safeguard her," Dar Valen added.

"When shall she rejoin us?" Squid asked as she stepped away with the device showing itself fully restored, ready to heal the Macon soldier with the broken back.

"That is the wrong question, Minister," Dar said, bidding Ilesa farewell, while drawing Squid away.

"And what is the right question?" Squid inquired.

"When shall we rejoin Lady Ilesa?" Dar gave him a knowing look.

* * *

Fleace. The Macon capital.

"Something amuses you, husband?" Deliea asked, amused by the stupid grin gracing Lorn's face. He lay atop of her, his hands pressing into the bed on either side of her head, looking down into her alluring green eyes.

"Just admiring the plunder I have taken from the Macon royal treasury," he smiled, his gaze drifting to her breasts before returning to her eyes.

"Is that so?" Deliea lifted a brow, trying so hard to scowl, and failing miserably.

"That is so," he gently caressed her cheek with his right hand, tracing his thumb around her eye and along her nose, the sensual touch sending tendrils of arousal across her flesh.

"Did you go to war with my father just to gain me as your wife?" She asked, her steely countenance breaking with amusement, her question not even phasing him in the least.

"I can't think of a better reason, can you?"

His silly answer made her laugh. There were many reasons to go to war, and the desire to bed a Princess was not among them, but it was a pleasant endeavor, and the only means to truly unify the warring realms. She loved looking into his eyes, losing herself in their comforting embrace. She found him strikingly handsome, especially with the morning sun alighting the side of his face as it broke through the window. 'Twas another evening and morning of romantic bliss, the continuous joining of their flesh time and again since their wedding night, a night she had both longed for and feared all her life. As a maiden, Deliea longed for the physical joining to a desirable man, but feared the sundering of her maidenhood, and the pain that might entail. With Lorn it was all pleasure, and none of the pain. He was gentle, yet invigorating, playful and yet serious, and most important of all, he desired her, just as she desired him.

"You went to war with my father to gain me as your wife. That will be our answer should our children one day ask," she smiled, liking that answer.

"And how many children shall that be?" He smiled back.

"Two, perhaps three," she ventured, gauging his response.

"So few?" He gave her a look.

"Do you desire more?"

"Yes. I was looking forward to eleven or twelve," he said in all seriousness.

"Twelve!" She gasped, hoping it was a jest. In truth she wanted more than three, but didn't wish to scare him, but twelve?

"Is that too few? We could try for twenty, but I think that a bit much."

"Twenty it is then," she decided to play along. She would have to see to the expansion of the royal nursery.

"Whether it is three, twelve or twenty, we have to start with the first," he reminded her.

"These past few days have not lacked for effort," she pointed out.

"True, and I hope to maintain this rigorous pace, if my Princess is equally enthused."

"She is enthused, and so much more, my Prince," she reached up to kiss him, their lips melding one to the other.

Lorn returned her fervor, pressing his lips to hers, losing himself in her caress. He lost track of time, joined to her in their intimate embrace before finally relenting, drawing briefly away to again look upon his beloved.

"Why do you stop?" She asked, tilting her head to the side, searching his beautiful eyes for the answer.

"I love looking at you," he couldn't stop smiling, pleased with his choice of wife, admiring her perfect face, with her large expressive eyes that were alive with desire and intelligence. Her voice was soft and sultry, her every utterance causing his heart to race.

"And I, you, but there is more at work in that mind of yours," she said, running her hands along his handsome jaw and cheeks.

"I… I have seen enough death and war to last a thousand lifetimes. The battles in Yatin and with your people rend my heart. I have prepared for this war for many years, guided by Yah's providence, sacrificing all else to see it through, giving my people hope for victory, though small it is. In all that time I hadn't the time for the pleasures of life, or to think beyond eventual victory, my every thought consumed with the war against Tyro. But now…" he paused, seeking the words his heart wanted to say.

"But now, you are distracted, distracted by me," her smile eased, seeing the conflict in his stormy eyes.

"No, not distracted. You are a gift, a blessing from Yah, a safe harbor in the storm that surrounds me. I never realized how much I needed this, this peaceful respite from my labors. Deliea, I don't know what shall befall me, befall us, in the battles ahead. I have seen so many lives cut short, and lovers losing one or the other in the battles we fought. It is heartbreaking. We have no guarantees other than the day we are in. But being here with you these past days has given me something to live for beyond duty and the welfare of my people. For the first time in a long time, I have something to look forward to… you," he pressed a gentle kiss to her forehead, pulling briefly away to look again into her eyes.

"I can see the burden you carry in your eyes, like a heavy stone weighing upon you. I wish I had the strength to lift it from your back, but alas, I cannot. If all I can do is to grant you respite from your worries, then that is what I shall do."

"Thank you," he said, pressing his forehead to hers.

"I must ask though," she said, causing him to again draw briefly away so as to look in her eyes.

"Ask me whatever you wish."

"I must confess that I have long harbored feelings for you, since I first saw you all those years ago. Strange, is it not, that you chose me to be your wife, fulfilling my deepest desire?" She bravely confessed the leanings of her heart, something only the bonds of their matrimony granted her courage to do so.

"It is not strange at all. It was the will of Yah. It was he that told me what I must do to bring peace between our peoples, and the face and name of the woman who was to be my wife and Queen. I knew little about you, Deliea, other than your beguiling beauty. I simply trusted his plan, and again I have been rewarded. It is as simple as that," he shrugged, revealing all, hiding nothing from her. He went on to explain the vision he had as a child, the terrible future that would come to pass unless he followed the will of Yah. He told her of all the visions since, from the ones urging him to prepare the realm for war to the one that led him to meet Terin in the wilderness after his flight from Telfer, and his visions leading him to out maneuver her father's armies, leading him to the gates of Fleace.

"…so you see, my love, I am simply doing as I am told," he said, concluding his tale.

"I urged my father not to assail Sawyer, pleading with him to not threaten the Torry southern flank whilst you were occupied holding back Tyro's hordes in the north and west, but he wouldn't listen," she sighed sadly.

"He was simply doing what he thought best for your people, Deliea. Do not begrudge him for that."

"You are defending him? I am surprised," she could hardly believe her ears.

"It is simple geography," he shrugged.

"Explain?" She asked, his blunt response piquing her interest.

"If you look at a map, you can understand his motivation. The Macon Empire has natural borders to its south where it meets the sea, and the foothills separating it from Torry South to the west…"

"Which you circumvented," she pointed out.

"A simple trick, which will not be repeated," he said, recalling the horns of Borin.

"Continue," she said, not meaning to interrupt him.

"To the east, the Clev river separates Macon from the Jenaii, and the Monata River guards much of your northern flank. Sawyer, however, is inconveniently positioned to the northeast, a dagger to the heart of the realm, and controlling the upper Monata and the western half of the lake. Though Sawyer never raised its swords to Maconia, the threat always remained," he said.

"And how will you rectify that to appease my father?"

"Our children will rectify that. The unification of our realms and people will remove any threat Sawyer could impose upon your father's realm. The true threat Sawyer held was not its own strength, but the strength of another using its position against Maconia. Torry North was the likeliest threat, but should we fall, then whoever controlled our realm after, could similarly threaten Macon. If we win this war, then greater Maconia joined with the Torry Realms, will secure these lands indefinitely," Lorn further explained.

"Torry South, Torry North and Macon forming a new Kingdom, an Empire really. Such a power has not been seen since the days of Kal," she mused.

"Tyro would disagree," he shrugged, considering the size of his empire.

"I meant a power aligned with Kal's value, a power to permanently stand against the gargoyles," she added.

"Yes, but a kingdom, not an empire."

"A kingdom?" She questioned, the melding of so many regions and people could be nothing but an empire.

"We will become one people, one realm, one purpose to unite us. Soldiers from Macon shall serve in Torry North and South, while those in the Torry Realms serve in Macon and the other in turn. They will take wives from one of the other two lands, further unifying our bloodlines. Merchants shall only be permitted to trade with the other regions as long as their heirs are wed to those outside their region. Eventually Teso and Zulon shall join, unifying all the realms along the Nila and Monata Rivers, save for Sawyer. As a colony of old Tarelia, they shall be named friend of our new kingdom, and in a show of faith, we shall commission the reestablishment of Tarelia," he revealed just a few of his grandiose plans that he hadn't shared with any other.

Deliea looked upon him with deep admiration, proud of her husband's dreams and ambition.

"A new kingdom shall require a new capital city," she said.

"Yes, it does, and I know who I shall put forward to oversee such a task," he smiled knowingly.

"Who?" She asked, wondering which of the Macon or Torry Ministers or regents he intended to put forth, one that her father would approve.

"I have already discussed it with your father, and he agrees."

"Who is it?"

"You shall find out during our war council," he smiled.

"Shall I be in attendance?"

"You are my wife and future queen of the Torry Realms. Of course, you shall be in attendance, not only this council, but all councils concerning matters of state."

She smiled, taken aback by his trust in her, thankful that she was more than a decoration of his triumph, but a true partner in every sense.

"Shall we?" He asked, stealing a glance to the door.

"Must we? I am so enjoying my husband's company."

"Perhaps a slight delay," he conceded, crushing his lips to hers.

* * *

"You needn't shadow me like I'm an invalid," Jentra snorted, annoyed with Criose, who followed so closely on his heels that he struggled from bumping into him whenever Jentra stopped.

"Forgive my clumsiness, Elite Prime, but his Highness insisted I guard you wherever you go," Criose insisted, holding tight to his vows.

"I know what he said, but I am the one who guards, not the one who is guarded. Whoever heard tell of a guard for a guard?" Jentra shook his head, waiting for the next moment to speak with his prince and straighten this mess out, but the lad was mostly unavailable the past few days, occupied in his bedchambers with his Macon Princess.

"My apologies, Elite Prime, but I am charged by Prince Lorn to protect you," Criose said, holding firm.

"I know what he blasted told you, Criose, and stop apologizing. I am charged with protecting our future king, and since you are charged with protecting me, that means your first duty is to protect him also. Fair enough?"

"Aye, that seems fair," Criose grinned, finding the cantankerous Jentra a man after his own heart.

"Good," Jentra snorted, glad that that was settled as they made their way through the encampment just outside the city walls, beyond the north bank of the Monata River. Several commanders of rank accompanied them as they went from unit to unit of the Cagan garrison troops in his command, sorting out volunteers for the newly formed Macon-Torry Army to be commanded by General Ciyon.

"Commander Jelen, what unit is next?" Jentra called the commander of 2nd Telnic closer to identify the next group of men waiting just ahead, most standing to attention in ordered ranks, the others quickly falling into place.

"4th Unit, Elite Prime," Commander Jelen quickly answered as they made there way between rows of pitched tents and pavilions placed along the matted grass that ran some distance north of the river.

"Have you sorted the married men from the others?" Jentra asked, weary of having to go through that tedious task with the last unit he inspected.

"Aye, the ones to the left are unwed," Jelen pointed out the nearly even split among the men, half aligned to their left and the others to their right, the groups facing each other as they passed between them.

"And the unwed understand what's expected of them?" Jentra asked, looking upon them as if they were condemned men awaiting the headman's block.

"Yes, their summoning is this afternoon, along with the designated men from the 5ᵗʰ and 6ᵗʰ Units," Jelen said. The unwed men were led into the amphitheater of Fleace in smaller groups where the unwed maidens of the city were gathered. It was a surreal, and strange event, the forced marital union of men and women from each realm. The unwed Macon soldiers were similarly sorted out, half being sent to Cagan to wed maidens from Torry South. Others would be wed to maidens from Torry North, once their armies eventually made their way north.

"What of you, Jelen, are you wed?" Jentra asked as they moved briskly along.

"Yes, twenty-one years wed to my lovely Kalista," Jelen said, thankful to be spared the hastened nuptials.

"And you, Criose?" Jentra spared the poor soldier a brief glance, not breaking stride.

"Ah… well… no," Criose shrugged nervously, recalling the unwanted advances of Guardian Darna's vice steward, Veya Cluse, who took him to bed on every occasion she was able. He still shuddered at the memory of the hard faced woman with her shaved head and foul temper. He never thought a woman could be the source of so many nightmares, but she certainly tormented his sleep. He just hoped Jentra wasn't suggesting what he thought he was suggesting?

"Well, you'll have to pick one that strikes your fancy. Of course, she'll have to be in agreement as well. Our Prince may be forcing this, but he wants everyone to find favor in this duty," Jentra would have smiled if he was able, but smiling never suited him. It just wasn't his nature.

And so, it went, with Jentra going from unit to unit in all the telnics he commanded, sorting out the men that wanted to volunteer for the newly formed joint army, finding more than half eager to do so.

* * *

Dadeus Ciyon stood in his pavilion overlooking the scrolled parchments strewn across his table, trying to make sense of it all.

Prince Lorn wanted him to piece together a new army using the castoff parts of the garrisons of Cagan, Fleace and Cesa, and detachments from the Torry 1st and 4th Armies, along with many of the men of his own battered 3rd Macon Army, most of whom were taken captive at Borin. General Lewins of the Torry 1st Army, was kind enough to gift him one of his ablest telnic commanders, Gorin Houn. Dadeus was pleased that Gorin was good humored and liked to cuss, two promising traits sure to make the times ahead less tedious. If there was one thing Dadeus Ciyon hated, it was boredom. He was also pleased to learn that Gorin came with his entire telnic, each capable warriors trained to his exacting standards. The rest of his new army was another matter. He was overjoyed to have two of his former telnic commanders, Kellis Havel and Jex Fortev, rejoin him as well, each busying themselves reordering the ranks. Every telnic and unit was to be half Torry and half Macon, Prince Lorn encouraging the blending of the two peoples. Such a thing was never done, and would require much coordination and training to bring all soldiers to a uniform standard. Lorn left it to Dadeus to assign his commanders accordingly, and select a uniform. He chose tan tunics with either gray or dark mail, which nearly all soldiers from either side possessed. The problems arose in swords, with the Torries favoring a shorter sword, meant for jabbing between shields, while the Macons favored a longer version, to give them greater reach. Horn signals needed sorting as well, with the Torry signal for retreat sounding too similar to the Macon signal to flank left.

"This appears to be a missive from Commander Clyvo," Guilen said, opening the sealed parchment just delivered to them. Upon arriving after his flight from the federation, Guilen thought to begin his life anew as a merchant, using his mother's gold, but decided to aid Prince Lorn in the interim, the prince assigning him to be Dadeus' aide de camp. His reading improved every day, showing steady improvement. He owed that to Terin, who somehow managed to instruct him as well as any master sage, and doing so in secret without Darna learning of it.

"And what does our illustrious Commander have to say?" Dadeus snorted, while reviewing another parchment.

"Fifteen units of his garrison have agreed to transfer to our army," Guilen shrugged, impressed it was so many.

"Well, half wits are better than no wits at all," Dadeus quoted one of his uncle Dorven's favorite sayings, Guilen appreciating his dry humor.

"That brings us to nearly twelve telnics, once all the men of 3rd Army are returned to you," Guilen said.

"No, nearly half of them are unwed, and will continue their march to Cagan, joining the Torry 4th Army while Torry maidens find them," Dadeus said in good humor, almost breaking a smile at his tasteless pun.

"You sound as if they await the gallows. There are far worse fates than wedding and bedding an attractive maid," Guilen said.

"Such as?"

"Wedding and bedding an unattractive and vicious maid, whose entire passion is making your life miserable."

"You speak from experience, I surmise."

"Unfortunately. I wedded one odious creature and nearly a second, had I not escaped. Neither was as lovely as any of the maidens I have seen paraded before our soldiers, I assure you that."

"Such is the price one must pay to live a pampered life. You were a noble son of the Sisterhood, with no labors to tax you beside pleasing your wife. I could think of many worse fates than that. I can think of many a Macon maid that I would gladly bend my knee to, letting them lay about while I fed grapes to their lovely lips, and kiss them farewell whilst they busied themselves with the affairs of the realm," Dadeus smiled with a faraway look.

"The maidens you would wed in the Sisterhood do not match what you are picturing in your brain, I assure you," Guilen frowned.

"They were that hideous?" Dadeus made a face.

"More than hideous, and mean."

"I shall take you at your word, my brave fellow. Drink?" Dadeus pulled out two goblets from under the table, and a jug of wine, pouring his new friend a cup.

"With pleasure," Guilen smiled, wishing his mother could see him now, sharing a drink with a Macon General, preparing an army for war. She would be aghast, and he would revel in her disgust.

After downing their drinks Dadeus resigned themselves to the task ahead.

"We best step lively. Our dear Prince Lorn requires our attendance," he sighed, straightening his tunic and mail, reaching for his helm.

"You sound as if it is you who is to be wed," Guilen smirked, following Dadeus to the door.

"Mine shall be worse, unless our illustrious prince is kind to his servants."

"You are not to choose from a multitude of Torry maidens? I would think many a fair maid would desire a match to the dashing and handsome General Ciyon?" Guilen smirked.

"That might be so, but our dear Prince Lorn asks that I first consider a certain maid that he has in mind, a fair flower from his northern realm."

"Did he give you name for said flower?"

"No. When I asked, he simply said the greatest gifts are often a mystery."

"If Prince Lorn says so, I lean toward believing it, unlike my mother. If she spoke of gifting me a fair flower, it would be certain to be a pile of ocran dung," Guilen said in all seriousness, causing Dadeus to chuckle.

"Guardian Darna seems an entertaining treasure. Perhaps I shall call upon her if she ever deigns to visit our realm. Come, my friend, let us revel in others misery," Dadeus wrapped an arm around his shoulder, taking him in tow.

* * *

"Shall we, my love?" Lorn offered Deliea his arm as he escorted her from the palace courtyard, through the main gates to the city beyond, with a unit of royal guards clearing their way to the amphitheater. Young Dougar trailed them, attired in a rich burgundy tunic and black cape, acting as Lorn's squire and personal aide. Deliea looked back from time to time, giving the former orphan boy a reassuring smile. The boy couldn't stop smiling, despite the cross looks some of the nobles of the city sent his way seeing one of his station so highly placed. Dougar cared not, overjoyed with Lorn's kindness and trust. If the Torry Prince asked him to follow him into a tempest or raging fire, he would gladly do so.

Throngs of people greeted them along the way, throwing voli petals into the air, hailing their Crown Princess and her groom. Lorn couldn't help but smile seeing peace replacing war, and friends replacing enemies. When Cronus arrived at Maeii informing him of Macon assailing Sawyer, he was beset with worries. Kato was dead and Terin believed lost, with their army far to the north. He wondered how he could overcome the obstacles before them in the south while the threat to the north hung ominously nigh. But Yah again answered, forcing him to focus only on the step before him, bringing him to this glorious moment, joined hand in hand with the woman Yah picked to be his wife, sparing so many a needless death in battle.

"Hail Princess Deliea!" The throngs shouted, tossing their blue petaled flowers into the air, carpeting their path.

They waved to the crowds before passing through the entrance to the amphitheater, the great edifice towering over the surrounding plazas. They traversed the wide corridor of the structure which emptied out into a vast open aired arena, with long stone benches circling a large open area below. The royal box rested opposite the entrance, but they had no need for that, for this night was like the previous four, with scores of Macon maidens and Torry soldiers gathered upon the open ground below, greeting one another. Upon Lorn and Deliea's entrance the crowd immediately took a respectful knee, greeting their monarchs.

"Arise my good people and brave warriors. This is a time of merriment and romance, and perhaps love if the fates are kind!" Deliea called them to their feet, urging them to continue.

Lorn smiled at his beloved's gracious words, knowing what a great queen she would be. He couldn't miss Jentra and Criose approaching from their left, and Dadeus and Guilen from their right. For some reason, Criose's disposition seemed ashen, as if he swallowed sour milk. Dadeus looked little better. He rightly guessed Dadeus was wondering with whom he would be paired, Lorn saving that surprise for their return to Torry North.

"Gentlemen, how fare you this fine day?" Lorn greeted them.

"Come to see the condemned on their final walk," Jentra snorted, though Lorn saw the amusement in his eyes.

"Taking delight in others' happiness is virtuous indeed, old friend," Lorn goaded.

"Virtuous, that is me, here to send off my new guard to wedded bliss," Jentra pushed Criose forward, directing him to the open area below to join the other bachelors.

Criose gave him a sour look before relenting, going to seek out a bride.

"Young love is quite romantic," Jentra snorted happily, watching the former sailor mingle with the ladies.

"You are a generous soul, my good sir," Deliea smiled.

"I do make an effort, Princess," Jentra bowed, enjoying Criose's misery a bit much.

"And your efforts have been well noted. I was speaking at length with my cousin about your brave exploits at Mosar and Carapis, guarding my Prince and your Torry Champion. She is most eager to make your acquaintance," Deliea said, her true intentions not revealed until said cousin made her way from the opposite direction, causing Jentra's grin to falter.

"And here she is now, Jentra. May I introduce the Lady Neiya," Lorn introduced them as Neiya drew nigh, a comely, auburn haired mature beauty, with discerning green eyes that took Jentra aback. She was of a noble house, the king's niece through his wife's elder sister.

Jentra gave Lorn a dark look, realizing he was to make an honest effort to court the fair maid.

"My Lady," Jentra bowed stiffly, taking her hand, pressing a kiss to the back of her fingers.

"Elite Prime, I am honored to make your acquaintance," she said in kind, before drawing him away, giving him a tour of the amphitheater.

"That was quite devious, My Prince," Dadeus remarked as poor Jentra passed beyond earshot, hopelessly drawn into Neiya's web.

"We all must do our duty to forge lasting peace, Dadeus, even you shall not escape the marital bonds, I assure you," Lorn remarked, enjoying Dadeus' olive skin turning bright red. For a man notorious for wooing the ladies, Dadeus seemed most shy in actually courting them.

"Fair enough, My Prince, but might I ask, what of our dear Guilen here? Should he be the only bachelor to escape such a fate?" Dadeus gave his new aide de camp a most mischievous look, Guilen not sharing in his mirth.

"Guilen is not Torry or Macon, thus evading our edict… for now," Lorn said, Guilen exhaling a relieved sigh. After finally escaping his mother's noose, he was in no hurry to bind himself to another, though he hoped to eventually find a wife to his liking, and live far away from the Sisterhood.

And so, as the day grew late, most of the soldiers found a desirable match, and were brought before Lorn and Deliea, who oversaw their marital union, the maidens' families gathering to receive them upon their joining. It was another successful evening of matchmaking, nearly two thirds of the men brought forth finding agreeable matches. Those that remained would come again tomorrow where the process was repeated, with additional men from other units. Eventually Lorn would work his way through the entire 1st Torry Army and their Cagan garrison. Though time was of the essence, this process couldn't be further rushed. He needed the Macon and Torry realms united in blood and purpose, and Dadeus' new army trained enough to work in concert.

As the evening grew late, Jentra found Lorn after escorting the Lady Neiya to her home, before returning to have words with his Prince.

"How fares the Lady Neiya?" Lorn asked, drawing Jentra aside, while Deliea spoke with several of her ladies and courtesans.

"She is well," Jentra snorted, wishing to freely speak his mind.

"Just well? Did you not favor her company?"

"Yes, she is lovely and intelligent, not an empty headed fool like most pampered women of wealth," he hated finding her so damn likable, giving Lorn smug satisfaction with his little game.

"I am not forcing you to wed her, Jentra, but if she is to your liking, and you to hers, then why not consider it? We all have a duty to forge this alliance with unshakable bonds, and nothing is stronger than bonds of blood and matrimony."

"I'll consider it, but on my terms, not yours, or your Princess. I shall court her as a lady of her station deserves," Jentra lifted his chin, holding his ground.

"So, you do like her," Lorn smiled, causing Jentra to shake his head, wondering how Lorn managed to put him in these situations.

"It is one thing to drag my poor carcass all over creation trying to keep you from getting your fool self killed, but another to lead me into marriage with a lady I hadn't met before tonight. Sometimes you are insufferable," Jentra growled.

"So, you do like her," Lorn smiled, reading his friend like an open parchment.

"Aye, she is acceptable."

* * *

Two days hence.

They spotted the great city from afar, its curtain walls straddling the banks of the Monata, and its towering citadels rising above the golden palace, presiding over the Macon capital like mountain peaks above a lowly plain. Squid Antillius held tight to General Valen, memories of his last flight upon a magantor still vivid in his memory. A half dozen Torry warbirds trailed off their left, and an equal number of Macon upon their right, soaring through the heavens, a symbol of their new alliance. They followed General Valen as he circled Fleace, before setting down upon the raised magantor platforms of the inner palace, their long approach giving time to alert the garrison of their arrival. Squid was pleasantly surprised to find Prince Lorn waiting for him atop the battlements, where the magantor platforms met the inner palace, with Princess Deliea beside him, joined hand in hand.

Within moments he dismounted, handlers hurrying forth to attend to their mounts, the other magantors setting down upon the adjoining platforms. Lorn thanked General Valen profusely for returning Squid in good health and prompt order. Dar Valen pressed a fist to his heart, saluting his future king before stepping away to attend his men, and see to the Sawyeran Minister and Commanding General, Gaive Dolom, who came on behalf of the Sawyeran Council.

Squid and Lorn paused before embracing each other, each man recalling fondly their last parting at Squid's country home outside of Central City. It seemed so long ago, with so many events transpiring since then.

"Your father would be proud," Squid said, his admiration for Lorn evident in his sparkling gray eyes.

"And of you. You have been busy on behalf the realm, old friend," Lorn smiled, placing his hands upon the minister's shoulders before fully embracing him.

Deliea looked on as the two of them hugged for an eternal moment, taken aback by their warm affections. She found it endearing, the Prince of the Torry Realms unafraid to share his brotherly love so openly. Or was it fatherly, considering the difference in their ages. Lorn spoke glowingly of his friend and mentor, the man who shared his faith in Yah, guiding Lorn through the years when others would have scoffed at their beliefs and preparations.

"My dearest princess, you make a fitting future Queen," Squid greeted upon breaking his embrace of Lorn, kissing her hand.

"Your words are most kind, Squid Antillius. Much has changed since our last parting. I again offer my deepest gratitude for your intervention at Molten Isle. It was you that recruited the Earthers to oversee our rescue. Had you not done so, I would certainly have perished," she said.

"Fortune smiled upon us during that time, and even now, so it appears," he said, looking to each of them.

"More Yah than good fortune," Lorn humbly confessed.

"Yes, Yah indeed. I beseeched his help for Sawyer, and he answers in the most unexpected way. Never in my imaginings could I foresee what you have accomplished. Defeating Yonig and then turning back south, turning a foe to a friend. Your father would be so very proud of you, my boy, so very proud indeed," Squid said, his eyes moistening at the mention of the fallen king.

"He would, but our work is not finished. This alliance merely grants us a fighting chance. The war will be decided before the walls of Corell," Lorn said.

"I agree. Let us put such plans into motion, shall we," Squid said.

"Yes, and there is little time to waste," Lorn said leading him to King Mortus' council chambers where the others were gathering.

CHAPTER 4

The Council of Fleace.

Squid Antillius entered the large council chamber recognizing most the faces gathered therein, including ministers and commanders from Macon, Torry and Sawyer along with King Mortus and the Macon Queen Mother Demaya, who stood at her son's side, a strong and shrewd woman who often sat the throne when her son was otherwise occupied. The chamber was brightly lit, with stone arched windows set high upon its white stone walls, bathing the chamber with sunlight. Statues, twice the height of a man, circled the chamber, each crafted in the likeness of Macon monarchs that ruled the realm since its founding, the tallest of which was of Mortun, the first Macon King. A large cupola ceiling presided above the open floor where a massive table was positioned at its center, around which the congregants were gathered.

Of the Torry commanders present, he noted General Lewins of 1st Army standing prominently among the Torry delegation on the opposite side of the council table, his eyes fixed studiously to the map of Arax unfurled across its surface. Flanking Lewins was General Dar Valen and his kin Denton Valen, commanding the Torry magantor forces. General Avliam commanded the Torry cavalry, whose numbers were growing with more mounts arriving daily from Cagan, after redeploying from the Yatin Campaign. Jentra stood as acting commander of the Cagan garrison telnics present, with the others still positioned at Cesa.

The other Torry Minister present was Gregor Vors, the steward of Soren Palace and chief Minister to Vintor Ornovis, regent of Cagan. He came on behalf the Cagan regent, and was attended by his Scribe Valen Croftus, the buttercup haired youth who matched Gregor's slight build and condescending airs. Squid recalled their rudeness to Terin and himself upon their return from Molten Isle, questioning Terin's suitability as Princess Corry's escort. If Terin's exploits made them ashamed of their behavior toward him, they certainly didn't show it. Squid had to temper his anger, treating both men with curtesy, for pride never served an acolyte of Yah.

From Sawyer came his old friend Minister Sounor, who held his deepest confidence, along with the Sawyeran General Gaive Dolom, commander of all Sawyeran forces. His performance throughout the siege proved his astute generalship, managing to persevere until the siege was lifted.

From the kingdom of Zulon was King Sargov, uncle of Prince Lorn, and his able General Zubarro. Representing Zulon's sister kingdom of Teso was General Velen, whose surname was strikingly similar to General Dar Valen, likely a distant kin, if one traced the familial lineages.

The Macons were the largest delegation, led by their monarch, King Mortus, who presided over the assemblage at the head of the table, his stern countenance reflecting the grim task before them, as they transitioned from celebrating their alliance to the greater conflict against Tyro. Beside him stood the Queen Mother, and his Chief Minister Orton Lorvius, who just recently returned from the Sawyer campaign where he constantly urged General Vecious to assail the city, often leading to disastrous results. Beside him was his fellow Macon high Minister Hulan, a less assuming and more astute diplomat, in Squid's honest opinion. Beside the Macon ministers stood their commanders of rank, including General Noivi, commander of the Macon 1st Army, and Novin, the commander of the garrison of Fleace, and Clyvo, commander of the garrison of Cesa.

Lorn took up position to King Mortus' right, with his bride

at his side, the lovely Deliea. Squid found the match exceptional, her intellect and charm perfectly complimenting Lorn's strength and even temperament.

The most interesting character at the table was General Ciyon, commanding the newly formed army of Macon and Torry soldiers, flamboyantly attired in golden mail, greaves and tunic, with his long black mane framing his handsome face. If his confidence seemed lacking from his recent defeat at the Horns of Borin, he showed it not, organizing his new command with determined efficiency. Beside him stood his aid de camp, Guilen Estaran, who recently escaped from the Sisterhood with the help of Terin, if what Lorn said was true. Of course, Lorn and Squid had little time to discuss many details in the brief time they shared before the commencement of this council. Squid would be certain to share a long conversation with Guilen, and learn all he knew of Terin's captivity.

"Let us commence this gathering with a disposition of land forces," King Mortus declared, looking to his ranking Commander, General Noivi of the 1st Macon Army.

"I have reconstituted most of the ten telnics of 1st Army just east of the city. We have suffered a few hundred casualties throughout the siege of Sawyer and our redeployment to Fleace. Reprovisioning should be complete within a few days," General Noivi stated firmly.

"And the 2nd and 4th?" King Mortus asked of his General.

"General Farin remains at Null with the fully mustered eight telnics of the 4th Army. General Vecious remains at Sawyer with the 2nd Army, with thirteen of his original fifteen telnics fit for duty," General Noivi added.

"And his orders to remain there have been communicated?" King Mortus asked.

"It has, Sire. He is currently coordinating with the garrison of Sawyer, preparing to receive our armies should we choose Sawyer as a staging area before advancing to Torry North," Noivi said, looking to the Sawyer delegation to confirm these details.

"General Vecious and I have coordinated the redisposition of forces, both my own and those of the Macon 2nd Army, as well as treatment of the wounded, which has been most greatly enhanced by the arrival of Mistress Ilesa and her powerful device," General Dolom, Commander of the Sawyer garrison stated, acknowledging both Lorn and Noivi gratefully.

"I can attest to its magical properties," Squid added, working his shoulder, demonstrating his full recovery, Ilesa having treated him before his departing Sawyer.

"As can so many of our wounded soldiers," General Lewins said, recalling the many men healed after the battle at Borin that would have otherwise died, both Macon and Torry.

"The Earthers' magic is quite impressive," Squid said, recalling the many wonders he had seen them do during his brief time in their company. He didn't miss the conflicted reaction of the Macon King. Squid would later learn of the source of his misgivings, as Lorn revealed to Mortus the nature of the powerful *sea beast* they used in the battle of Cesa. They would keep that information between themselves, using it as leverage should certain allies think to betray them, in particularly the unstable Emperor Yangu.

"And your status, Commanders?" Mortus asked his garrison commanders.

"The Cesa Garrison is fully redeployed here at the capital, Sire," Commander Clyvo said of his five telnics.

"The Fleace garrison is fully mustered at five telnics, Sire," Commander Noivi stated.

"Very good," Mortus nodded, though he already knew the status of his city's defenses, being apprised of them daily. He briefly regarded General Ciyon, but would hear from him last, as they would further discuss which forces would be reassigned to his new army.

King Sargov next addressed the council, speaking on behalf his small kingdom of Zulon and its sister realm of Teso.

"I have come with more than half my kingdom's strength, the three telnics of the 2nd Zulon Army, leaving the 1st with its two telnics to guard our home. General Velen has brought two telnics of the 2nd Teso Army, leaving the four telnics of the 1st Teso Army to guard their homes. We are both at your service for the campaign to come," King Sargov regarded both Mortus and Lorn, standing firmly in agreement with whatever plan they came to.

"Minister Sounor?" Mortus acknowledged the Sawyer delegation, an uncomfortable exchange considering their recent hostilities.

"Our city stands ready to receive you should it be required to stage a movement upon Torry North. Should another route be proposed, we are in position to lend half our garrison to the cause. General Dolom," Sounor signaled his colleague to state the readiness of the city garrison.

"We have forty-three hundred men fit for duty. Two telnics shall be ascribed to the expedition force you are gathering," Gaive Dolom stated.

Squid knew that two telnics was not much in the grand scheme of things, but a little strength gathered form many corners would make a great difference when brought together.

Lorn next addressed the council to give a full accounting of Torry forces both in the North and South, and the likeliest invasion route Tyro would employ. He called upon General Lewins to begin.

"The 1st Torry Army is currently positioned to the south of the city, nearly ninteen full telnics, and another telnic reassigned to General Ciyon's command," Lewins began. "The 4th Torry Army is currently being redeployed to Cagan, now commanded by General Farro. Once fully reconstituted, it should number twelve telnics. The Cagan garrison is currently split with two telnics at Cesa and three here. The five units of the Tuk garrison have been sent back to fortify that vital holdfast. Moving to Torry North, General Fonis and the 2nd Torry Army are currently at Central city. With reserves replacing his casualties at Tuft's Mountain, his command again numbers twenty full telnics. The Garrison at Central City is fully mustered, standing at five telnics. The garrison at Cropus stands at five telnics. The garrison of Corell stands at three telnics plus whatever troops that have been conscripted since the siege was broken. General Bode and the 3rd Torry Army are currently positioned near Corell with anywhere from twelve to thirteen telnics. Also complimenting Corell's defense is the Jenaii 1st battlegroup numbering between twelve to fourteen telnics. The 2nd battlegroup has repositioned to the Naybin border, with the likelihood of war starting there very soon," Lewins finished, looking to General Valen who nodded in agreement with his assessment of their northern forces.

"General Ciyon?" Lorn looked to the Macon General to conclude the assessment of their land forces, his new command the source of much of their vital planning in this council.

"Sires," he began, acknowledging both Lorn and Mortus. "My new command currently includes the eight telnics from the 3rd Macon Army, most of which were captured at Borin and are currently enroute to Fleace. Those that are unwed are being sent to Cagan as per the orders of King Mortus and Prince Lorn. Another telnic from the Torry 1st Army has been graciously added by General Lewins. Another seven units from the Cagan garrison have volunteered to join, and more may do so as we continue to review their ranks. Once fully reconstituted, my new army will require extensive drill and training to bring them to acceptable combat standards," Ciyon reported.

"How many of your men from the previous 3rd Macon Army are unwed?" King Mortus inquired.

"Nearly half, Sire," Ciyon said, much reducing his ranks until the men could be wed to Torry maidens and return to Fleace.

"The unwed men shall remain in Cagan after their nuptials and join their strength to General Farro's battered army. I have sent orders to General Farro to reassign half of his strength to you," Lorn said, which would increase his army by two telnics if his assessment was correct, the six telnics of Farro's 4th Army exchanging places with the four telnics of Ciyon's army.

"How soon will they be dispatched, Highness?" Ciyon asked, for time was essential.

"I will send word to them today. Many of Farro's telnics are still enroute from Faust."

"With Farro's six telnics, four of my original, one from General Lewins, and the units from the Cagan garrison, my army will stand between eleven and twelve telnics," Ciyon said.

"Commanders Clyvo and Novin will dispatch two telnics apiece form their garrisons, adding them to your army," King Mortus commanded, both commanders bowing their heads, acknowledging his edict.

"And the Cagan garrison will add three telnics of their five," Lorn added, bringing Ciyon's total above nineteen telnics, a near even split among Torries and Macons.

"A full accounting of our naval forces should be addressed before we commence with our strategic aims," King Mortus exclaimed, looking again to General Noivi to detail the Macon position.

"The 1st and 3rd Macon Fleets are presently east of Cesa, while the 2nd holds at Null. Each have twenty warships in their full complement," General Noivi stated, the omission of the 4th Fleet leaving a sour taste in the Macons' collective mouths, with its total destruction by the Torries mysterious *Sea Beast*.

Lorn regarded General Lewins to give the state of the Torry Navy.

"The Torry 2nd and 5th Fleets are currently at Cesa, with a combined 67 warships. The 1st, 3rd and 4th Fleets are in transit between Faust and Cagan with a combined strength of seventy four warships," Lewins stated.

With that, they all firmly understood their disposition of forces, leaving them the difficult choices of where to move them, and when.

"Now, we must fully ascertain Tyro's next offensive. By your collective judgement, you believe he shall again assail Corell. If you would, state why you believe this to be so?" King Mortus asked of Lorn.

"There are three primary avenues of invading southern Arax from the far north. The first is through Yatin. Yonig's invasion proved the feasibility of this approach, but he was strangely not supported with any reinforcements, and weakly provisioned. Another legion committed to the invasion probably would have toppled the Yatin Empire before our forces could've intervened. We would now be looking at Tyro's legions on the doorstep of Torry South," Lorn began.

"Will he return?" Mortus asked.

"I don't believe so," Lorn sighed, extending a pointing stick to the western side of the map, making a triangle from Tinsay, Telfer and Tenin by tapping each point on the map. "With Yonig dead, and most of his legions destroyed, Tyro would have to commit several legions to conquer Yatin. They would have to be gargoyle legions that could feed off the land, most of which was ravaged during the first invasion. Benotrist Legions would require massive logistical support, which due to the narrow coastal route along the Benotrist Yatin border, requiring provisions to be moved by ship, and parallel the legions advance. This would be perilous considering our combined naval strength between both of our navies, and the Yatin 3rd Fleet. That means the invasion would have to be all gargoyle legions, and Tyro doesn't have enough of them left to do so, with so many still at Notsu," Lorn stated.

"And to make certain that he cannot invade with Benotrist legions, we should concentrate our navies at Cagan," Mortus said, drawing nods of agreement form both the Macon and Torry commanders gathered around the table, as Lorn continued.

"The second pathway to invade is the broad gap between the Mote and Plate Mountains," Lorn began.

"Where Tyro launched his attack upon Tuft's Mountain," Mortus said, his eyes fixed keenly to that region on the map.

"Yes, a swift and bold strike he hoped would overwhelm our armies and seize Rego. Only a gargoyle army could move across that area with enough speed to gain surprise. The terrain is uneven in many places, and its thick forests difficult to navigate for a human army. It could be done, but would require patience and time, time Tyro will not give us," Lorn explained.

"But there are plenty of resources for an army to forage, and fresh water from the headwaters of the Cot River along its course, which any army would make good use of," General Noivi pointed out.

"Yes, but it would take time, time Tyro shall not give us," Lorn repeated that vital point.

"Time for him, not for us. Wouldn't it be Tyro that needs the time to move his army, Prince Lorn?" Noivi asked.

"You misunderstand, General. Tyro will not send an army that we have time to prepare for, and would threaten Rego and Central City, which is far easier for our armies here to respond to, than the farther distance to Corell. He could again use gargoyle legions to hasten the crossing, but without Benotrist support, we could destroy them in detail. What sets Tyro apart from previous threats is his using gargoyle and human armies in concert. The only pathway that allows him to bring his full might to bear is across the Kregmarin to Notsu, where Morac's legions have staged since the breaking of the siege. Commander Valen," Lorn ordered his magantor General to address the assemblage, being most familiar with the recent happenings in the north.

"Since the breaking of the siege, Morac returned to Notsu, reconstituting his battered legions. By our best estimates, he suffered nearly fifty percent casualties, nearly all dead or captured, though mostly dead. His tenuous supply lines across the Kregmarin have been ripe targets for Jenaii ambushes, which have spread as far north as the approaches of Nisin. Despite these setbacks, he has persisted at Notsu, strengthening his hold on the region. We have spied reinforcements moving south to reinforce him, each telnic size and above, though we haven't gotten close enough to identify them," General Dar Valen said.

"Gargoyle or human reinforcements, General?" Jentra asked.

"Human, either Benotrist or local conscripts from annexed regions of the eastern empire," Dar said.

"Would you surmise their total reinforcements greater than a legion?" General Noivi asked.

"A conservative estimate would be twenty to thirty telnics, but if I were to guess, I would say at least a legion. Considering we believed they were moving a single legion before the battle of Kregmarin, and they brought six... well, you can see why I don't place much faith in guesses," Dar sighed, recalling that bitter failure that cost King Lore and the 5th Army their lives.

"There is a difference between guesses and informed assumptions, General," Lorn said, his eyes trained on the northeast regions of the map. "The only uncommitted gargoyle legions left to Tyro are the 12th and 14th, and the 12th is still near the northeastern border by last account. The 14th was last believed to be at Laycrom, but that report is over a year old," Lorn tapped his pointer to the northwest corner of the map, where Laycrom sat.

"Then Morac means to renew his assault with mostly Benotrist legions. That would mean a lengthy siege," General Ciyon said.

"It would be, if the gate was still intact," Jentra snorted, that information causing a stir throughout the chamber.

"What ails the gate?" General Noivi asked in alarm.

"General Valen, you are best informed on this matter," Lorn called upon Dar to again share information he was most privy to.

"During the siege, Morac and Dethine tore apart the main gate, and all the gates leading to the inner courtyard. Princess Corry has since recruited the finest smiths in all the realm to affect its repairs, but the task may not be completed before Morac's return."

"They tore it apart, how?" King Sargov asked.

"With their damnable swords!" Jentra growled, the Swords of Light causing nearly as much harm than good at this juncture.

"What shall prevent them from tearing them apart again should the repairs be made?" General Noivi rightly asked.

"We have swords to counter them," Lorn said.

"You are speaking of your Champion, but last we heard he was lost at sea," King Mortus asked, though Lorn informed him before the council began that he had a great amount of information to share, and this was likely part of it.

"We have reason to believe Terin lives," Lorn said, looking across the table to Guilen, who stood beside General Ciyon. This was the reason Guilen was allowed to attend this war council, to share what he knew. Lorn had asked him and Criose to not speak of Terin until he gave them leave to do so. Only a few knew what he was about to reveal. Lorn debated whether to allow this information to be revealed, but felt Yah's will guiding him, needing to give these men gathered here hope for victory.

"Terin lives. He survived the battle at Carapis and was washed ashore before being taken by slavers and sold at Bansoch," Guilen said, his revelation taking many of them aback. The very idea that the hero of Corell and Yatin could have been taken slave was almost unthinkable.

"Sold to whom?" Minister Lorvius asked.

"My mother," Guilen said, before going on to explain all that transpired up to his escape.

"If he lives, then we must retrieve him before Corell is assailed,"

Mortus said. If anyone had told him he would be keen to see the Torry Champion returned to battle a fortnight ago, he would've thought them mad, but the winds of war often shift, with allies becoming enemies, and enemies becoming friends.

"It is being addressed. In the meantime, we must do our part to counter Tyro's plans," Lorn said.

"Then we base that upon our informed assumptions," Mortus regarded Lorn briefly, repeating his words. "That means we must reinforce Corell, and looking at the map, we can all agree that Corell is a long way off."

"We have to decide which forces to send, how to provision them, and which route of advance they shall take," General Ciyon said.

"With spring upon us, provisioning will be difficult. We have used most of our winter stores through the recent campaigns," General Noivi stated, and was quickly chorused by General Lewins, summarizing the similar plight of both the Torries and Macons.

"General Vecious had enough provisions for a year long siege when I departed Sawyer," Minister Lorvius said.

"Provisions for his army perhaps, but not enough for all the forces we are planning to move," General Noivi refuted.

"Last year's harvest was exceedingly good. Nearly all of our granaries in the interior are more than half full. I shall order all excess stores removed to the capital immediately," King Mortus declared, taking the council aback with this revelation. Only the Minister of agriculture was privy to this detail, as Mortus kept each minister ignorant of their fellow ministers' information. It was a means of control Mortus employed to keep each part of his command structure dependent upon him for all information beyond their purview.

"I will order the same for all granaries in Torry South," Lorn said, knowing their stores were much depleted, but still above adequate levels going into planting season.

"What of Teso and Zulon? Was not your recent harvest exceedingly strong?" Minister Vors, steward of Cagan, inquired, looking expectantly to King Sargov of Zulon.

"Our harvest was strong, but much of our surplus has been sold," King Sargov revealed.

"Sold! To whom?" Mortus asked.

"Princess Corry purchased much of our yield after the siege of Corell was lifted," King Sargov said.

"Very wise," King Mortus raised an approving brow, impressed with Corry's forward thinking as a spring siege would likely happen after winter thinned Corell's stores.

"Her Highness has proven herself worthy of the House of Lore, bravely leading the defense of the palace throughout the siege and demonstrating astute planning after. I have had the great honor of serving both the son and the daughter of King Lore, each worthy of great praise," Dar Valen said proudly, regarding his future King with deepest respect.

"She has done well, far better than I would have done in her place. She relied upon our northern armies and Jenaii allies to break the first siege of Corell. Should there be a second, I intend to be there," Lorn's words swept the chamber with firm authority.

"And I would be with you!" Mortus affirmed. The Macon King felt renewed by his alliance with the Torry prince. All his life he was tormented by his confounding visions, believing he had to overcome the Torry realms or be overcome by them, the visions plaguing his waking thoughts. At times the visions were almost unbearable and all consuming, driving him to the brink of madness. When he learned of Prince Lorn's victory at the Horns of Borin, the madness nearly took him, his visons coming to fruition, wondering if he would destroy Lorn, or Lorn destroy him. He would never forget that moment before the gates of the city when he faced the son of Lore below the clouded sky. It was there when Lorn revealed the truth of his visions before the parting of the clouds and the glorious sunlight breaking upon them, as if that moment was forever ordained. It was at that pivotal moment he received Yah's mercy and blessing, knowing the truth of the ancient deity. From that moment forth he belonged to Yah, just as Lorn and Deliea belonged to each other. He looked back upon the apparent failures of his life, realizing they were in fact blessings. He oft lamented not having a son, a true heir, foolishly overlooking his four beautiful and intelligent daughters. Had he son, the alliance with Lorn would have disinherited him, or sowed the seeds of a future civil war. He looked upon his beloved Deliea with fierce pride. She was wiser than he, and complimented the Torry Prince in every way. She would make a fine Queen, and with their union, she would reign over a far greater realm than the one he could have given her. Of course, their union must bear fruit to solidify their alliance, but he felt the hand of Yah comforting his heart in this regard. Deliea would give Lorn a son, and many more children. With that revelation, Mortus would give all that he had, even his very life, to protect the realms of men from the gargoyle threat.

"And I!" Ciyon added, his spirit invigorated by their new cause. Leading an army against gargoyles was the thing of legend and renown. Should they carry the day, his name would be long remembered. He had to caution himself, lest pride and glory cloud his judgement, as it had at Borin.

"We are all with you. The question we now must ask, is where shall we move our armies?" King Sargov asked.

A long silence followed, each of them studying the map intently, weighing the positives and detriments of each course of action. Jentra tried to use good sense and logic in formulating a plan, but for once decided to trust in Lorn and his God.

"I know fool well I will regret this, but we have leaned on your strange connection to your God up to this point, Prince Lorn. What is he telling you now?" Jentra asked, the others strangely agreeing with him, all looking to Lorn for an answer.

"I believe Tyro will strike at Corell with all his might, but there remain the other possibilities. Moving all our southern armies along a single route of travel shall be difficult to provision with our alternate sources of resupply. Contrary to what you believe, Jentra, Yah doesn't often give me specific instructions. He often merely points me in the direction he wishes me to go, and leaves the specifics to we mortals. In this we must trust our own good sense. I believe we should concentrate our efforts in countering an attack upon Corell, while allocating forces to counter possible incursions through Yatin and the eastern gap of the Mote Mountains. King Mortus' suggestion to concentrate our naval strength at Cagan is the wisest choice in countering another invasion through Yatin. I shall order all our fleets to return to Cagan immediately, along with the Macon 1st and 2nd Fleets, if your Grace is in agreement?" Lorn asked of Mortus.

"Aye. I shall order it done," Mortus declared.

"In addition, they shall return the remnant of the Cagan garrison to its proper position. The Torry 4th Army shall remain at Cagan, and shall be available to reinforce our Yatin allies if the need arises. As that army shall be half its original size, and split among Macon and Torry soldiers, general Farro can use this vital time to meld them into a suitable fighting force," Lorn said, drawing nods of approval from the commanders gathered around.

"That leaves Torry North," King Sargov said.

"Yes, and with two likely pathways for Tyro to assail it. In this, I believe we should divide our forces," Lorn said, drawing the expected disapproving looks from the congregants. The thought of dividing their forces against a foe potentially many times stronger, went against all military doctrine. Lorn continued before they voiced their objections.

"I believe we should send one force up the Nila, toward Central City, where it can join with General Fonis' 2nd Torry Army. By the time it arrives, we will know if Tyro is sending a force through the gap of Mote. If the threat is not present, that force can continue on toward Corell. The second, and larger force should proceed to Sawyer, taking the swifter and more direct route to Corell, taking ship across Lake Monata, disembarking beyond the Arian Hills, likely at Tarelis," Lorn suggested, naming the largest Torry port along the northeast shore of Lake Monata.

"Should Tyro move in force at Yatin or the Mote gap, it would be difficult to return this force in time to give battle," Minister Vors stated, fearing for the safety of Cagan and all points south.

"True, but that is a calculated risk we must decide. To be in position to relieve Corell or even Central City, we must depart far in advance," General Noivi stated.

"As a fair portion of my army is still at Cagan, I should take the Nila route. I could join the forces currently here with those in Cagan at a point somewhere in between, perhaps Tuk. From there we can proceed up river," General Ciyon said, his gaze keenly focused upon the confluence of the Nila and Monata Rivers, where the fortress city of Tuk lay.

"That would be wise, and the armies of Zulon and Teso could join you enroute," King Sargov said, the plan allowing his army to return briefly home before continuing its march north, perhaps bringing more forces to bear. He would send word ahead, ordering his son and heir to muster what other forces he could spare for the battles in the north.

"Then we can send the rest of our armies to Sawyer, taking ship across the lake. Of course, that shall require a great many vessels," King Mortus said.

"We can summon all the merchant ships of Lake Monata to Sawyer. Most are Torry, Sawyer or Jenaii flagged, and have kept away throughout the siege," Minister Sounor stated, estimating that such a merchant fleet could ferry the armies and provisions across the lake.

"We can provide an additional fifty merchant vessels to the cause," King Mortus added.

"That leaves us with the decision of which armies to send," Lorn said.

"Should we not bring all of them?" General Noivi asked.

"I think it wise to leave one army here at Fleace to respond in any direction if needed, while committing the rest to Corell. It would be wise to send the largest of our armies, the Torry 1st, and the Macon 2nd, to Corell, leaving you, General Noivi, to remain here with the Macon 1st Army," Lorn said, looking to both Noivi and King Mortus for consensus.

Noivi thought to protest, not wishing to be held back while the great battle for their time was decided, but his King interjected, further complicating his position.

"The plan is sound, but I would render one change. Exchange the unwed men of the Torry 1st Army with the unwed soldiers of General Noivi's army. This will give them time to find Macon brides, and the Macon soldiers can find suitable matches in the north, once we are victorious," Mortus said, contemplating nothing but victory, his confidence putting steel in the hearts of those gathered about the

THE CHRONICLES OF ARAX

table. The danger in this would be the blending of two armies while preparing to march.

"I agree," Lorn said, balancing the need to unify the two realms with the speed needed to reach Corell in time. He had to trust in Yah in this, for he guided him here to begin with for the very purpose of unifying the south, bringing their combined force to bear in the north.

"Generals, see that the exchange is done, and begin training the blended armies over the next days before we begin our march!" Mortus ordered Noivi and Lewins, who nodded in kind.

"General Avliam, you shall go ahead to Central City and co-ordinate with General Meborn. I want our disembarkation sites rein-forced all along the northeastern Monata shoreline," Lorn ordered, pointing out the likeliest areas the merchant fleets would land their troops after leaving Sawyer, running his pointer along the Monata shore on the map where it met Torry North, with the port of Tarelis the likeliest target.

"Shall I go with what I have, or wait for my full complement, Highness?" General Avliam asked, with most of his riders still arriving from Torry South, and many more still in Yatin.

"With what you have. Those that are yet to arrive shall remain with General Farro. Speed is now of the essence."

"It will take some time to sort out the reconstituted armies and for the new commands to adequately blend their ranks. This needs to be complete before we march," General Lewins advised.

"You have five days, General. Generals Avliam and Valen have to move out come the morrow. Corell will have need of all our mag-antors, and Avliam's cavalry will help secure our landing areas and will be long engaged with the enemy before we arrive," Lorn said.

Another long silence followed, each of them looking for fault in the plan, weighing the positives and negatives with the uncertainties any war engendered.

"It is agreed then?" King Mortus asked, looking to each of them, a chorus of silent nods affirming their consent.

"Very well. That concludes the strategic planning of this council. Let us debate the political matters that weigh upon us," Lorn redirected them to the next task at hand.

"We represent many realms and a city state," Mortus added, regarding Minister Sounor with surprising respect.

"Perhaps many realms, but Macon and the Torry Realms constitute the vast share of the power here. My small Kingdom pales beside your combined might," King Sargov stated honestly.

"True, uncle, but we shall forever regard you with the deepest respect. We are family, you and I, and Teso as well. Sawyer is a colony of old Tarelia, and shall endure as a free and independent city state as long as she desires. As for Greater Maconia and the Torry Realms, we shall remain separate until Princess Deliea and I have a child that shall share our crowns. Until then, we shall work to our utmost to gift that child a truly united kingdom, the blood of our monarchs and the blood of our people forever joined," Lorn said.

"My Kingdom shall also be joined to yours, as well as Teso, with the marriage of my daughter Zevana to your heir, King Sargov, and my daughter Bedela to the heir of Teso. Beyond this, each of us shall lead armies into battle, shedding blood side by side against the gargoyle curse. Once we are victorious, we shall make our world anew. With the Torry and Macon Realms united, your kingdoms will fall within our protection, and yet remain independent, allied by location, by blood, and by cause," King Mortus declared.

"Which leaves us with a question that requires answering, though that answer may not be forthcoming," Lorn smiled wanly.

"And what question should that be, Highness?" Jentra asked, knowing when Lorn was going to say something surprising.

"The very important question of where our new capital shall be. King Mortus and I have decided to commission a person to oversee this important decision, trusting them to balance practicality and location."

"And you have already decided upon a person, Highness?" Minister Vors asked, unable to mask his own suitability for such a task.

"We have. We have chosen someone with a keen intellect and discerning eye. We have chosen the Princess Deliea, my wife and future Queen," Lorn turned to her, his declaration taking her by surprise.

"My love, I…" she thought to protest, but words failed her.

"You are very wise, Deliea, and are well suited to this task. Yah led me to your arms, arms that I trust with my life and our child's future. You are the Crown Princess of the Macon Empire, and I the Crown Prince of the Torry Realms. We shall rule our lands together, yet separate until we pass on our crowns to our first born. Your father and I shall be consumed with the war before us, and leave it to you to oversee all else, including the place for a new capital, one suited for both of our realms," Lorn smiled, touching a hand to her cheek.

"Very well," she smiled in kind, never loving him more, her partner, her friend, her future King.

CHAPTER 5

They soared through the air, coursing the heavens, the lands passing quietly below like ghostly shadows, open farmland giving way to lush forest, with the Flen River cutting its path from one to the other. They shadowed the Flen since coming upon it, following its course southward, searching for the fabled Falls that rested mid distance between Gotto and the Ape Hills. They departed Tro, angling south-west, avoiding Gotto altogether, lest anyone spy their movements, before again finding the Flen, its riverbanks swelling with the early spring rains fueling its strength.

Corry held tight to Terin, wrapping her slender arms around his waist, as Ular held tight to her. Her head pressed to Terin's back, feeling the thick material of the jacket he wore against her cheek. Her left leg pressed to his thigh, feeling the sheath of the Sword of the Moon squeezed between them. It was the only Araxan vestment he retained; the rest of his garb borrowed from the Earthers. She felt the wind in her face, lifting her golden mane in the spring air, much of it slapping poor Ular in the head, though he would not voice a complaint. Wind Racer responded to Terin's commands, maneuvering through the air as if their minds were one. It was similar to his mastery of his blade, the two moving in unison. Corry marveled at his mysterious power, able to do things he had no right to. It was equally breathtaking and frightening to be in his presence, and yet, she never felt more alive. He was life itself, her life, and she couldn't imagine her world without him, causing her to hold ever tighter, lest he slip her grasp. She vowed to never be parted from him again, lest the winds of fate and war carry him away.

"Packaww!"

The sound of another magantor echoed off her right, with Elos and Raven seated upon it, Elos pointing ahead toward something in the distance, the others trailing them. Corry lifted her head, looking over Terin's shoulder. There ahead, the river widened, its rocky banks pushing back the forest to either side as if the arms of a giant swatted away the trees to scoop water in its hands. Just farther ahead, Corry could make out an impressive fall, stretching the width of the river, dropping nearly thirty feet, water spraying heavily along its base. They continued on, finding the next fall just beyond the first, the river forming a significant curve around the fall, water funneling to its center. Their magantors circled overhead, sweeping across the face of the inspiring sight, water cascading nearly eighty feet to a maelstrom of swirling currents below, kicking up a great fountain of water, spraying high into the air at its base.

Corry looked farther afield, the next fall resting half a league to the south, a broad shallow drop, half the height of the first fall. She stared in wonder, beholding the impressive sight in all its splendor. The fabled Falls of Flen were a series of five drops along the Flen River as it cut through the Vale of Flen, each a marvel of creation, the most majestic of nature's wonders. They circled the second falls one last time before continuing to the third, circling it once before angling to the fourth.

The fourth rested around a sharp bend, dropping over one hundred feet in a vertical plunge, with narrowing cliffs to either side, the narrow chasm creating a dangerous swirling current at its base, masked by the tumultuous spray of water. Corry gasped at its terrible beauty, a sight few Araxans had ever seen, but nearly all had heard tell. If the first four falls caused her to gaze in wonder, the fifth nearly made her weep. A fair distance beyond the fourth, the great wonder rose imperiously above the forested vale, water cascading across its broad face, dropping two hundred and thirty feet into a hazy pool, mist rising high into the firmament. The midday sun shone brightly across the vale, streams of blinding light reflecting off the face of the rushing waters.

"It is beautiful," she said, her loud voice but a whisper in Terin's ear, deafened by the thunderous roar of the falls, and the wind pressing their faces.

"Yes, but I have seen greater beauty," he shouted, looking back to her with a knowing smile.

She kissed his cheek, hearing enough of his garbled words to know his meaning. If they died this very moment, she would could think of no better way to meet her end, soaring above such wondrous beauty, her arms wrapped around the man she loved.

They followed Elos' lead as he swept over the falls, before circling back, finding a small clearing some distance downstream upon the eastern bank, a sizable patch of green grass between the river's edge and the forest. Elos' magantor set down first, its strong legs imprinting in the soil, Raven easing off the saddle, happy to be again on the ground. Elos followed, before running his hand along the bird's beak, the subtle command keeping it in place as Raven stretched his legs, already complaining about his sore back.

"You know, Elots, the last time I flew on one of these I had the saddle all to myself, now I'm riding the bitch seat," Raven grumbled, mangling Elos' name, the poor Jenaii warrior trying to figure out what a *Bitch Seat* was.

"Packaww!" Wind Racer sounded overhead before setting down beside them, Ular bounding off its back in a swift leap, landing perfectly, with Corry and Terin following.

"You make that look too easy, Ular. Nobody likes a show off," Raven smiled, slapping his green scaled friend on the back.

"I like him," Corry refuted, stepping beside them as the other magantors set down around them, Orlom, Lucas and Cronus soon joining them with their three Troan escorts.

"We shall set camp here for the night," Elos said, familiar with this area, having journeyed here long ago. Many Jenaii warriors made the arduous trek to the fabled Falls of Flen as a rite of passage before reaching adulthood. He never thought to return and see the wondrous sight again, pleased for a second chance to behold its majesty.

* * *

They spent the afternoon gathering kindling and wood for their cookfire, while Raven sent a few hurried blasts into the river, stunning a bounty of fish, which Orlom and Ular quickly rounded up. Lucas and Cronus set up a spit after Ular cleaned their catches, rapidly gutting them with practiced ease. They gathered around the blazing fire as the sun set, its wanning rays filtering through the upper boughs of the far bank. The sound of the falls echoed strongly even here, a constant torrent of unending thunder. Lucas and Ular volunteered for first watch, taking up position within the forest behind them, keeping a watchful eye up and downstream.

"This fish s preeetty gggood. Whaz it?" Raven asked with his mouth full, already on his third helping, struggling with the many bones the fish had, which kept getting stuck in his teeth.

"It is called a gako, a rather common and tasty species, native to the Flen and Veneba River basins," one of their Troan escorts answered.

"Iiyy littkeee it too," Orlom mumbled, tearing off another piece in his mouth.

"You are quite the fisherman, Rav," Cronus smiled wryly, recalling when Tosha discovered his ability to simply stun fish with his pistol after watching her trying to catch them by hand.

"Didn't he just use his pistol?" Corry asked, standing between Terin and Cronus on the opposite side of the fire, thinking it looked quite easy.

"Yes," Cronus said, his smile indicating there was more to this than he was saying.

"Not this again. That's all Tosha bitched about for days," Raven said, after swallowing the portion in his mouth, recalling the days leading up to Axenville, where she escaped them and recruited a mob to attack him.

"There is that word again... *bitch*. What does that mean?" Elos asked curiously, lifting a serious brow over his silver eye. He stood beside Raven, his stoic demeanor in stark contrast to the big Earther's natural irreverence. Seeing them stand beside each other, Corry

77

couldn't think of any two individuals more different than Elos and Raven. Of course, the Earthers looked and acted different from every Araxan, but with the Jenaii, it was far more pronounced.

"Well, it has a lot of meanings, Elost. For one, when I said Tosha did a lot of bitching on our journey, it means she complained, complained a lot. When I said riding bitch…" Raven went on to explain that reference, as well as a dozen other uses for the word, none of which Elos felt comfortable with. If there was one thing the Jenaii never did, it was curse. They rarely even got angry, as far as Raven could tell, which was a good thing since he managed to mangle Elos' name every time he spoke it.

"Boss's lady was just testing him, making sure he was the strongest male to breed her. Our ape lasses always do that," Orlom added, reaching for another fish.

"Breed her?" Corry said under her breath, wondering how they could civilize Orlom before attaining Corell. Terin placed his hand in hers, gently squeezing it, calming her ire. She looked over to him, his small laugh reminding her the silliness of it all. Orlom was Orlom, and nothing they said would change his behavior. At least with Orlom he didn't mean to offend. With Raven, it was intentional. He was the most insufferable man she had ever known, bombastic, rude and arrogant to extremes, but Terin loved him, and for that she could overlook all those faults. Whenever anything threatened to sour her mood, all she had to do was look into his beautiful sea blue eyes and all was right with her heart. The constant dull thunder of the falls reminded her of where she stood, camped beside the most beautiful natural wonder, hand in hand with the man she loved. A part of her, a very large part, regretted returning to court, the pomp and ceremony seeming so tedious now. She wanted nothing more than for the war to be over and begin to share her life with Terin, someplace far from court. Just as her mind entertained that joyous thought, Raven's loud voice interrupted her dream.

"What's the story with this place, anyway? Where did the name Flen come from?" Raven asked no one in particular. It was one of their escorts, the Troan named Samor, that answered.

"The legends say Flen was a wise man or king of great renown, or perhaps a wealthy merchant. Some claim he was the father of the Troan city state. No matter his wealth or power, all the legends agree that his greatest love was his beloved wife and four daughters. They were his greatest achievement and passion. Alas, they were killed, whether lost at sea, or in a great conflagration, no one truly knows. Such was his lament, it caused a great ground quake, splitting these lands into five parts, with a massive river of his tears flowing over them, creating the river and falls that share his name," Samor said with a faraway look.

Corry had heard this tale, but with subtle differences, like his origin being of the Lone Hills, and his children being two sons and two daughters, but the quake and river of tears being the same. It was a woeful tale filled with such sorrow to rend her heart. Heartbreak was a powerful thing, shattering the most stalwart of men or women, crushing them under burdensome pain and loneliness. She thought of the dreadful day when Lucas brought her tidings of Terin's fall, leading her to the palace battlements where she considered throwing herself from the wall, ending her pain. What held her back? Only duty and hatred for her enemies gave her strength to endure, until Jonas spoke those wonderful and terrible words, giving her hope of finding Terin, but fear of losing him to another. But what if he had truly died? Would her breaking heart be powerful enough to shake the land, or her tears enough to fuel a river?

"Well that story sucks. How about coming up with a happier tale than that?" Raven said, his blunt speech ruining her thoughts.

"Most tales are sad," Samor shrugged.

Corry thought to say something, but the look in Raven's eyes reminded her that there was more in his words than the tale of Flen. Heartbreak destroyed his friend Thorton, killing the man he knew in every meaningful way. Part her of her could sympathize with Thorton, a very small part, but a part all the same.

"Sorrow is the fuel of poets and bards," Elos bluntly stated. The greatest works of man were oft penned by calamity, inspiring the creative bent of the artist, singer and story teller.

"Or a hideous face, like that rotten minstrel we picked up in

Axenville. One look in a mirror probably inspired everything he sang," Raven growled, hoping to never run into that fool Galen again.

"Minstrel? Are you speaking of Galen?" Corry asked, taken aback by his vitriol.

"He's the only minstrel I know, and if the rest are anything like him, I'd just as soon not meet any more," Raven said, taking another fish off the spit.

"I expect you to treat him kindly once we reach Corell, Raven," she said, not wishing any conflict at court.

"When we reach Corell? He's there?" Raven growled with the fish halfway to his mouth, thoughts of Galen nearly ruining his appetite… nearly.

"He journeyed with me to Sawyer, Maeii, to Cagan and finally back to Corell," Cronus spoke in Galen's defense.

"You put up with him for that long? Did you hit your head on something, Cronus?" Raven would've tossed Galen off the palace rooftop if he was Cronus.

"Galen has served the crown admirably during the siege and the journeys he has taken since. He is a valued friend," Corry said.

"He's a moron," Raven snarled.

"He has redeemed himself many times since that unfortunate incident at Axenville, Rav. He deserves a second chance," Cronus regarded his friend kindly, empathizing with his point of view.

"Redeemed himself? Hell, I wouldn't trust that weasel anymore than I'd trust Argos guarding our supper," Raven snorted.

"Yeah, Fatty eats everything," Orlom added for good measure, causing Cronus to smile, shaking his head.

"I am not asking you to like Galen, Raven, just to make peace with him while you are our guest," Corry said.

"I won't kill him, if that's what you're worried about. Just keep him out of my hair," Raven grunted.

"You don't have much hair, Boss," Orlom said, looking at his short haircut.

"I think he means to keep Galen away from him, Orlom," Cronus explained. All that time crossing the northern wilderness with Raven helped him pick up many of his odd sayings.

"Do you regret coming with us, Rav?" Terin asked warily.

"No. I came to kill Thorton, and then Morac's army. Once Corell is secure I'll go back to the *Stenox* and finish what's left of Tyro's empire."

"It won't be so easy, Raven. Tyro has many legions. Even with your great power, it will take more than…" Corry tried to explain, but he was having none of it.

"Listen, Tyro just made the dumbest mistake in his miserable life. He declared war on us and the Ape Republic. Once we get the *Stenox* up and running at full power, that's the end of his navy, and every dwelling within fifty miles of the coast. And have you ever seen a pissed off ape before? Well, it ain't a pretty sight, and he just pissed off their whole nation. What do you think will happen when they come barreling over the ape hills, swarming over eastern Arax like a tsunami during high tide? I almost pity the poor bastards," Raven said, slapping Orlom on the back, the young gorilla grinning in agreement.

"That's right, Boss. We gonna slaughter 'em," Orlom swung his fists, as if shadow punching an invisible foe.

Cronus smiled, shaking his head with his friend's over confidence. Leave it Raven to make light of the direst of situations. Perhaps a little confidence is what they needed instead of sad faces and pessimism. How could anyone stay in the fight if they held no hope for victory? This was especially true if you had something to live for, something very special. He wanted nothing more than for this war to be ended, and to spend the rest of his days with Leanna and their child.

"Come on, Cronus, I think our shift is about to start," Raven said, drawing him from his thoughts. It was well past sundown, and it was their turn to stand guard.

"Yes, Lucas and Ular are probably hungry," Cronus said, reminding the others to leave some food for their friends.

* * *

Terin and Corry walked south along the river bank as the others began to bed down for the night, while Cronus and Raven took up position within the tree line, standing watch. The sound of the falls grew ever louder the farther south they went, from a low thunder to a deafening roar if they ventured any farther. She slipped her hand in his, enjoying that small affection that would be denied them once they reached Corell. A Princess of the realm could not be so forward in her subjects' eyes, even with the man she intended to wed. But here in the wilderness, such restrictions were overlooked, at least with their present company. These men were Terin's friends and brothers, and her friends as well if she was being forthright.

"What a beautiful night," Terin said, gazing skyward, the stars shining in their full glory in the clear night sky, with the sound of the falls echoing in the air.

"A beauty one overlooks when not in the arms of the one they love," she wistfully recalled all those nights before his rescue when she would look at the night sky with profound loneliness, fearing his fate.

"How true," he sighed, his eyes drifting to hers, his thoughts very much the same as they stopped along the river bank.

"These same stars brought me no comfort when I thought you had perished, and little when I knew you were held captive. Only now can I appreciate their wonder," she caressed his cheek with her free hand, holding tight to his grasp with the other. He closed his eyes, kissing her palm, while leaning into her touch.

"I thought of you constantly since departing Corell, though every step led me farther from your arms. My longing only grew with every battle, pushing me to finish the enemy, hastening my return to you, and then…" his voice trailed, the bitter memory of his enslavement rearing its head.

"I know, you needn't say it, or even think of it. Look at me, Terin," she said, drawing his eyes to hers. "Whatever happened there doesn't matter, not to me. You are mine, Terin Caleph. Mine and no others. I would fight a thousand battles to return you to my arms. I would slay Darna a thousand times if need be, to bring you home. These past fortnights we have spent since Bansoch have been the happiest in my life. I didn't seek out Raven to help me rescue the Torry Champion. I sought him out to help me rescue you, the man

I love," she pressed her forehead to his underneath the starlit sky in the shadow of the Falls.

* * *

"Well, this brings back memories," Raven said, standing beside Cronus within the foliage of the forest, with their campsite between them and the river, and his rifle slung over his shoulder. They just watched as Terin and Corry returned from their walk, bedding down for the night.

"That was a long journey," Cronus reflected on their arduous trek to Tro across the Benotrist Empire.

"It would've been a whole lot shorter if those critters didn't eat our magantors. I sure as hell ain't letting that happen this time," Raven growled, leaning his shoulder against the thick trunk of a paccel tree, his right hand resting on his holstered pistol.

"You needn't worry, Rav. Graggloggs are not native to these regions as far as I know."

"Why not? Is there something worse that eats them?"

"No, at least I hope not," Cronus smiled.

"Guess I'll have to take your word for it," Raven shook his head, half expecting something to take a bite out of him as soon as he bedded down.

"I have missed your blunt speech. It has been unusually boring since we last parted," Cronus said.

"Boring? You're in the middle of a war."

"War can be boring, Raven. Terrifying for brief moments followed by endless stretches of tedium. You always seemed to make those in between periods entertaining."

"Somebody has to be the life of the party," Raven said in all seriousness. Cronus didn't know the reference, but understood what he was saying, causing him to laugh.

"Believe this as you will, but I even miss all your arguments with Tosha."

"She's a handful. You should've seen the reception she gave me when I showed up after the babies were born. Thought she was going to plant an ax in my head."

"I thought you were on good terms with her?"

"We are, but that was after I explained why I was late. Saving her mother's throne helped a whole lot too. Her mother's not so bad. I can't believe the two of them are related," Raven shrugged.

Cronus started to laugh.

"What's so funny?" Raven made a face.

"Just imagining you at Bansoch. I wish I was there to see it," Cronus kept laughing, shaking his head.

"What's so funny about me in Bansoch? Just so you know, me and Tosha's mom got along just fine. I think she likes me, and who can blame her."

"Tosha's mom? You mean Queen Letha," Cronus couldn't stop laughing, rightly guessing that Raven used that familiar moniker when addressing the queen. "How did you not lose your head?"

"Lose my head? Things may have been a little awkward at first, but the Queen and her people started to really warm up to us before we left."

"I'll take your word for it," Cronus said, using one of Raven's phrases. After spending so much time together on their journey to Tro, he couldn't help but learn them all.

"I wish you were there. I know you would have liked to help rescue the kid," Raven looked to where Terin was now sleeping beside their dying fire, resting an arms length from Corry.

"I wish I was too. I owe him one after Fera. I owe all of you for that," Cronus sighed, rarely talking about Fera, still tormented from the memories.

"I still owe you, if we're keeping score," Raven said, referencing Cordi's death, and Cronus saving his life when first they met.

"Cordi wasn't your fault, Rav, and even if it was, you more than made up for it at Cesa."

"I still can't believe you were there. Just another strange coincidence. How did you figure it was us?"

"I was there, riding Terin's warbird. I just arrived over the Macon fleet as you began sinking their ships. It wasn't hard to figure out, especially when I recognized the familiar shape swerving below the waves, cutting open the hulls of the Macon vessels."

"That was Lorken, Brokov and me. Can't believe you were there. If we had known, we'd have stopped and said hello," Raven shook his head.

"I would've come with you to rescue Terin. Prince Lorn will be most pleased when he learns that Terin lives. Your sinking of that Macon fleet proved most helpful to our cause. Prince Lorn extends his gratitude for that as well. If I haven't said it enough, just know I am thankful for your friendship, Raven," Cronus placed a hand to his friend's shoulder.

"I'm thankful for yours, Cronus. You stuck your neck out for me when we were just strangers. I won't forget that. I might be an ornery cuss, but I'm not ungrateful."

"You're not ornery, Raven, you just like to sound like you are. Just as you won't forget our first encounter, I shall never forget when I looked up at your wonderful face from the floor of Fera's dungeon. I never thought to escape that foul place, and without you, I wouldn't have. We may die tomorrow or at Corell, for only the fates know our destiny, but I won't meet my end chained helplessly in Tyro's dungeon. I have you to thank for that."

"I was just paying back an old debt. And we aren't dying tomorrow or at Corell. It's like I said, Tyro just made the biggest mistake in his sorry life. Once I kill Thorton, I'll help your people destroy whatever army Morac brings to Corell. That should take a grand total of five minutes. I'd almost feel sorry for the miserable bastards if they weren't such… miserable bastards," he couldn't think of a better word.

"It will be good to have you at our side, Rav," Cronus smiled at that.

"Morac won't know what hit him. Between you, me, and the gang over there, we should be alright," Raven jerked a thumb toward their friends resting around the fire.

"Ular seems an impressive warrior, as is Elos, I assure you. Your crewmate Orlom looks dangerous as well," Cronus said.

"Throw in a couple of magical swords, and I like our chances.

If we stick together, we can avoid repeating past mistakes," Raven thought of Arsenc and Kato, Cronus rightly guessing his reference.

"So many good men have fallen in this war. I grow weary of it."

"Like in any war. I am sorry to hear of Arsenc. He was a good friend," Raven said.

"He was like a brother, same as you and Terin, and all your crew. Raven, I am sorry about Kato. He… well, he was a great friend to my people. I know what he meant to you," Cronus closed his eyes, pained by that brutal loss.

"I know," Raven sighed.

"His wife is stricken with grief. I wish you could meet her. She is a fierce and caring woman. She rides with Prince Lorn though she is with child, insisting to treat the wounded with Kato's healing device."

"She's pregnant?" Raven made a face.

"Yes. Kato never knew."

"Damn you, Ben," Raven growled.

"For what it is worth, Prince Lorn believes Thorton didn't mean to kill him. Kato stepped aside when they drew upon each other. During every engagement between them at Mosar, neither tried to kill the other, each targeting anything but a mortal blow."

"It was the same for me and Ben at Fera. We didn't go for kill shots, but that doesn't matter now. I have to kill him, and next time I won't hesitate," Raven resigned himself to that awful fact. After Kato and the attack on the *Stenox*, all bets were off.

"I grieve for your loss, Raven. I know he was your greatest friend, greater than any of us. To have to kill him…" Cronus shook his head sadly, at a loss for words.

Raven felt sick with the whole rotten mess, wondering how it all came to this, when he noticed Cronus suddenly shift, a strange look passing his face.

"You alright?"

"I spent enough time around gargoyles to sense when I am being watched," Cronus shifted slowly, so not to alert any foes to his sudden movement, sparing a glance across the river, searching the far bank.

That was enough for Raven to unsling his rifle, using the night vision on the lens to scan afield, sweeping the forest across the river, south to north, with all lifeforms outlined in bright red on its green field. He scanned upriver, shifting north, finding nothing but small critters and nesting birds before stopping just downriver of their position.

"Crap," he growled, seeing the distinct outline atop a high branch of a paccel, a gargoyle with its wings silhouetted behind its hunched form.

"Rav?" Cronus could tell by his tone that something was amiss.

"We got company. Better wake the others," Raven said, scanning deeper into the forest, finding a dozen more waiting behind the first, some perched high in the trees, others waiting afoot.

"How many?" Cronus asked before stepping away.

"A dozen so far," Raven said, sweeping further downstream, before finding more popping into view. "Make that two dozen. Now three," he added, the news just getting worse by the moment.

Cronus' felt that unsettling feeling coursing his back, creeping along his neck, of danger pressing perilously close. He drew his blade, spinning about, finding a set of glowing red eyes starring back several paces behind them on their side of the river.

ZIP!

Raven sent a hurried blast to where he was looking, blue laser striking the creature through the chest, chaos suddenly erupting all around them.

ZIP! ZIP! ZIP!

More blasts followed, striking targets emerging behind the first amidst the thick tree trunks of towering paccels.

"Kai-Shorum!"

Gargoyle battle cries screamed in the night air, above, behind and all around them. They could hear their bodies moving through the trees, leaping between branches high above the forest floor, or flying overtop altogether. Others moved afoot, shifting from tree to tree, their eyes fixed to their prey, closing on Raven and Cronus from all points along the east bank of the Flen.

"Wake them up! I'll hold them here!" Raven growled, lifting his aim skyward.

ZIP! ZIP!

Laser streamed through the upper boughs of the tree above, drilling a passing gargoyle through its center, its entrails spewing in its wake. The second blast found purchase through the left wing of the next creature, its right working to keep it aloft, veering sharply left through its rapid descent, before crashing through the branches below. Raven fired rapidly, dropping two more before shifting back to the ground, where a dozen more were running afoot from truck to truck, brandishing their scimitars.

Cronus raced toward their campsite, shouting aloud as he ran, Elos and Terin already standing with swords drawn, with Ular coming to his feet. Breaking in the open he could see his comrades silhouetted before their cookfire, with dozens of winged forms breaking through the trees along the far side of the river. The sound of the falls dulled much of the battle, war cries and shouts greatly muted. Laser flashed from the left side of the fire, streaming toward the west bank of the river. It was obviously Orlom taking aim. Whether he hit his target, Cronus couldn't discern in the dark.

THUD!

Cronus ducked, a gargoyle corpse dropping beside him, taken down by Raven's aim, with another dropping off his right. Cronus kept his feet, angling to the right side of the campsite where Lucas and Ular stood back to back, while their Troan escorts had their swords drawn, staring expectantly across the river, where the gargoyles drew nigh, their wings spread in flight above the rushing water. Cronus slipped to the right of Ular, a gargoyle scimitar glancing off his raised blade, twisting to avoid its foot from kicking his chest, his follow swing taking it across the back of its right leg. Cronus let it continue on, bringing his blade overhead to receive the next creature swooping down from above.

* * *

SPLIT! THRUST!

Terin scored his first kill, a creature that set down between Elos and himself. Corry stayed close to his side, struggling to spot the creatures moving swiftly in the moonlight, her blade at the ready. She turned sharply right, where a gargoyle arm dropped at her feet, Terin's follow strike taking the creature across its chest, its legs and lower torso falling away. She lost sight of Terin as he moved around her, cutting down gargoyles to her left and back, the creatures oblivious to his presence, their eyes fixed solely upon her and Elos. With the fire to their back and the river to their front, they were the first to observe the gargoyles springing from the far bank.

Moonlight illuminated Elos' blade, bathing his stoic countenance in its emerald light. His feet moved deftly in concert with his blade, his slashes quick and short, cutting down gargoyles in quick order. Terin was deadlier, cutting down most before their feet touched the ground, with those that did faring just as poor. Corry shifted her blade, blocking a gargoyle head flying off Terin's blade, watching as he and Elos stepped closer to the river's edge, closing on the gargoyles setting down along the riverbank.

* * *

Lucas sliced the wing from a creature pressing his front, its crimson eyes raging with hate, blood issuing from the severed appendage, his shield blocking its maddened counter strike. Ular stood behind him, ducking under a clumsy swing, trapping the creature's sword arm with one hand, gutting the gargoyle with the other. He spun away, his blade meeting another's hasty blow, letting the first creature drop to the ground.

Orlom kept behind the others, spewing laser fire across the river, dropping several gargoyles, their bodies splashing short of the bank, the current taking them swiftly downstream and over the next fall. The Troan escort fended poorly, unaccustomed to fighting gargoyles. One of them was upon the ground, his stomach slashed open, writhing in pain.

* * *

ZIP! ZIP! ZIP!

Raven couldn't help but hit targets this close, gargoyles coming at him from his left, right and front, moving tree to tree before bursting straight for him. They eventually stopped, their numbers sufficiently thinned, Raven blasting the last one though the nose, the creature's blazing eyes dulling as it dropped to his feet.

"Ugly little suckers," Raven snorted, scanning one last time before rejoining the others.

Stepping from the trees he was greeted with chaos, gargoyles swooping overhead, his friends fending them off, some faring better than others. Keeping his rifle tucked to his shoulder, he used the lens to scan afield. Terin, Elos and Corry stood closest to the river bank, gargoyle corpses piled at their feet. He spotted several floating downstream, before slipping over the next falls, cut down by Terin and Elos, or shot by Orlom, who stood to the side of their cookfire showering laser blasts across the river. Lucas and Ular accounted well of themselves, cutting down every creature that came near them, without receiving the slightest of a scratch. Cronus stood among the Troans, helping them guard their magantors, one of the avian nursing a damaged wing.

"Not this time," Raven swore not to repeat the incident with the graggloggs, when their magantors were slain, forcing them to ride ocran all the way to Tro harbor.

"PACKAWW!"

Wind Racer sounded, sweeping overhead, gargoyles clutched in both talons, depositing them into the river. Raven didn't notice him missing from the others, having sprung into the air at the outset, the only magantor not tethered, granting him free reign.

"Looks like the whole gang is getting in on the action," Raven mumbled to himself, struggling to find targets, the enemy dying everywhere he looked.

ZIP!

His next blast found a creature creeping closer to Cronus, moving low along the river bank, laser taking it through the head, spilling brains where it dropped. A quick scan found several gargoyles retreating afoot upstream, heading for the base of the first falls.

ZIP! ZIP! ZIP!

Three blasts dropped them in quick succession, their bodies dropping on the rock strewn embankment. And… that was about it, no other gargoyles in sight. Scanning up and downstream showed nothing, not even a retreating form. Raven lowered his rifle, approaching the others as Ular rushed to treat the wounded Troan, with the Tissue regenerator in hand.

"Nasty critters!" Raven said, kicking a gargoyle carcass laying between Cronus and Lucas who were looking afield, trying to pick out movement in the moonlight. "It's all clear, at least as far as I can see with this," he added, lifting his rifle.

"We need a full count. This was a large group, and far more organized than a mere raiding party," Lucas said.

"Maybe not. They could just as easily have been deserters or bandits. Gargoyles have been using these tactics for thousands of years," Cronus said, lowering his sword while scrubbing his chin with his free hand.

"One way to find out. See if any are alive and get them to talk. Just be sure they're crippled before sticking your nose near them," Raven advised, stepping away to check on Orlom.

Lucas thought that was sound advice, hacking off the right hand of the nearest corpse, moving on as it failed to respond.

Cronus went to check on the others as Lucas went about his search, finding Elos and Terin with swords still drawn, staring out across the river to the trees lining the far embankment, with Corry standing behind them, guarding their backs.

"Are any of you wounded?" Cronus asked, Terin and Elos turning around to face him, blood staining their clothes. He noticed Terin's blade dark as a turbid sky, whilst Elos' emitted its usual luster.

"We are unscathed," Elos bluntly stated, moonlight reflecting off his piercing silver eyes. Cronus thought the Jenaii warrior looked ethereal beneath the starlit sky.

"I doubt any of us shall rest tonight," Terin sighed, sparing a glance to the corpses piled along the riverbank.

"We'll split guard duty, half and half. A little sleep is better than none. We'll leave at first light. I thought this would be far enough south to avoid gargoyle patrols or raiders, but apparently not," Cronus said as Wind Racer swept overhead, setting down beside the other magantors, where Ular finished healing the wounded Troan, moving on to help the avian with the damaged wing.

"We should continue upstream before breaking west, reducing our chances of encountering any more," Corry said, wiping the blood off her sword on the tunic of the dead gargoyle at her feet.

"I agree, Highness. It might delay our reaching Corell, but is a safer and wiser path. I suggest we go as far as the headwaters of the Flen before turning west. Hopefully none escaped. If any did, they might inform Morac that an Earther was here," Cronus said, knowing Raven's desire to keep his presence at Corell hidden until Thorton revealed himself. Of course, any Earther spotted here could be headed to the Ape Republic instead of Corell or points west, but the possibility would still be in Morac's line of thought.

* * *

"Good work, little buddy," Raven ruffled Orlom's head, the young gorilla holstering his pistol with a large grin on his face.

"I hit a lot of them, Boss, did you see?" He exclaimed with his toothy smile.

"I saw you in the end. I was a little busy myself. Most importantly, you kept your weapon on the enemy, not our own friends. First two rules of shooting, don't shoot yourself, and don't shoot your friends," Raven said.

"What's rule three?" Orlom asked, bouncing on his feet in excitement.

"Shoot the bad guys."

* * *

The sunrise fully revealed the carnage of the battle, scores of gargoyle corpses strewn along the near river bank, with several caught in tree branches along the west bank, victims of Orlom's deadly fire. One corpse rested in the water, caught on the remains of a fallen tree rotting in the river. With the light of day, they expanded their search up and downstream, making sure of their kills. Lucas' search for a prisoner to question the night before proved futile, their collective martial skills proving too effective by the condition of the bodies they discovered.

It was Elos that led them to a grim discovery upstream, where a large enclave was cut along a cliff face near the base of the falls, where the sound of the water echoed like thunder claps though the cavern. It was wide and shallow, but deep enough for scores of men to take shelter, though the misty air would soak your clothing if your lingered there for very long. The river passed before the face of the enclave, though obscured by the water thrown up by the falls just south of it. Cronus, Terin, Corry and Raven followed Elos into the broad opening, the sound of the falls forcing them to nearly shout to be heard.

All across the wet rocky floor were scattered bones, enough for dozens if not scores of victims. Cronus knelt near the back wall, picking up a set of rusty shackles, with bones slipping between their manacles as he lifted it.

"Human bones," Elos' voice thundered above the sound of the falls, handing what appeared to be a femur to Raven, who recognized the teeth marks up and down the bone.

"Looks like a feeding ground," Raven handed the grizzly item to Terin, who examined it while Corry stepped toward a smaller pile, lifting a tiny, fractured skull, likely that of a child, before setting it gently back down and closing her eyes with the horror of it all.

"Do you believe our attackers last night were responsible for this?" Cronus asked Elos.

"I found one of their corpses just downstream from here, as if crawling in this direction with its last breath," Elos did not add that the creature's entrails were dragged along behind it, smearing along the riverbank.

Whether the gargoyles were posted here to waylay travelers, or were deserters making this their home, they could only speculate.

It did lesson the odds of any survivors reporting back to Morac any time soon.

"It's time for gargoyles to go extinct," Raven said, before exiting the cave.

They quickly packed their gear, and took to the sky, heading upstream for the headwaters of the Flen before turning west to the Lone Hills.

CHAPTER 6

Notsu.

Notsu stood in ruin, her once proud towers now casting meek shadows. The outer plain about the city was ravaged, its vegetation gnawed away at the root. The gargoyles winter hunger left nothing in their wake, the legions feasting on the land, devouring all and leaving naught for the coming season. From atop the highest citadel, one could look in any direction and see only mud caked fields crisscrossed with hollows and ruts. The listless streets rang hallow with doors bared, fearing bands of Benotrist soldiers looting any household if the opportunity presented itself, despite Morac's harsh disciplinary measures to curb such behavior. The old and infirm citizens of Notsu were handed over to the gargoyle legions for food, serving no purpose to Morac's strategic aims. They were merely idle mouths to feed, and needed to be culled. The people of Notsu were now vassals of the Benotrist Empire, and unlike the Menotrist slaves and Venotrist serfs who performed menial agrarian tasks, the city's populace provided servants with a wide variety of skills. Artisans were rounded up and dispersed throughout the empire to construct majestic monuments and sculptures glorifying the Emperor and the Empire he rules. Merchants still coordinated some trade routes northeast and south, providing Notsu its vital, yet greatly weakened commercial lifeline. Comely wenches were gathered up, and given as brides or concubines to citizens of Notsu that found favor with Morac. Fairer maidens of wealthy families were taken by Morac himself, joining his growing collection, after losing several of his favorites in the aftermath of the siege.

Morac stood on the terrace of his headquarters, the former estate of Tevlan Nosuc, the wealthiest citizen of Notsu. He was lord of all he surveyed. The home he now claimed was richly decorated with gold, marble and black stones. Crafted archways and pillars supported each entryway. Each wall was painted in scenic detail, with frescos depicting the great events in the city's storied past, along with newer commissioned works, such as Morac's victory at Kregmarin. He looked upon it fondly, the artist emphasizing his attributes, portraying his bravery in fine detail, from his handsome face to his outstretched arms holding aloft the severed head of King Lore. The work covered each wall of the central atrium, giving a panoramic view of the battlefield, from the gargoyle and Benotrist legions storming the hillsides, to the Torries pitiful ranks yielding under the impressive attack. The great chamber would host his council of war this afternoon, once the newest arrivals were settled in.

He observed three flax of cavalry parading in the street below. He spent the winter outfitting as many ocran as he could from the eastern half of the empire, recalling the painful lesson of his prior campaign when the Torry cavalry wreaked havoc on his flanks and lines of communication.

"Our reinforcements," Daylas, the acting governor said, standing at his side, pointing north of the city where long lines of infantry drew nigh, soon approaching the north gate.

"The 10th Legion," Morac affirmed, one of several additions to his spring campaign.

"I shall greet their commander, and escort him hither," Daylas bowed and withdrew.

"Soon," Morac whispered as Daylas stepped away. Soon his legions would march west, sweeping the last vestiges of Torry power form the face of central Arax.

* * *

The city gates were drawn open, receiving a vast host of Benotrist soldiers clad in gray mail over black tunics, bearing the sigil of the 10th Benotrist Legion, a black cloven shield upon a field of red. They marched from the port city of Pagan in the far north, traveling hundreds of leagues, one of several legions sent to bolster Morac's army for his renewed campaign upon the Torry realm. The beleaguered citizens of Notsu looked on with knowing dread at the endless procession of Benotrist warriors adding their numbers to the vast host already sheltered within their walls, swelling Morac's numbers to immeasurable strength. The city was already on the brink of starvation, most of their food stores plundered, and Morac's legions given precedence over what remained.

"Greetings, General Gavis," Emperor's Elite Daylas, the acting governor of Notsu, hailed the Commander of the 10th Benotrist Legion just beyond the city gates, watching as the soldiers paraded past.

"Emperor's Elite," the grizzled General greeted in kind. A veteran of the Benotrist revolution, Gavis was Tyro's most experienced and capable Legion Commander. His once handsome countenance was marred by his misshapen nose and a vicious scar running from his left ear to his chin. He regarded Daylas with mismatched gray and black eyes that unsettled the acting governor.

"Notsu welcomes you, General. Lord Morac awaits you at his headquarters. I am to escort you there," Daylas said.

"Aye, but my men require attending," General Gavis retorted.

"Emperor's Elite Tovus shall see to their accommodations. He is my second," Daylas assured him.

"Very well. Lead on."

* * *

Morac's headquarters and former estate of Tevlan Nosuc.

Morac oversaw his war council, his cruel brown eyes fixed upon the map of eastern Arax unfurled across the table centered in the great atrium of the spacious manse, with ranking members of the Imperial Elite and Commanders of Legion gathered about. The scenic fresco depicting his victory at Kregmarin circled the large chamber, impressing upon his commanders his glorious triumph over the Torry King. He tested his left leg, stretching it to its utmost, comforting himself of its restoration. It became habit, a constant reassurance that he was fully healed. The Torries would feel his full measure when the siege was renewed. Their only salvation the last time was their pathetic champion, whose sword turned back every assault upon the castle. He would negate that advantage when next they met, allowing his vast host to decide the battle, and decide they shall, with overwhelming strength. Said strength was represented by the Generals circling the table.

General Concaka, commander of the 5th Gargoyle Legion, stood to his left, his crimson eyes dulled with studious calm as he surveyed the approaches of Corell displayed upon the map. The 5th Legion was an amalgamation of the shattered 4th, 5th and 7th Legions, their combined strength numbering forty-four telnics after suffering terrible losses throughout the Corell campaign. With the 6th Legion completely destroyed at Corell, and the 4th and 7th added to the 5th, those three Legion markers were removed from the map, a grim reminder of the devastation wrought upon their ranks. The 5th Legion was represented upon the map by its sigil, a black mailed fist upon a field of white.

General Felinaius stood to Concaka's left, commander of the Benotrist 11th Legion. Much of his strength was preserved with nearly half his telnics assigned to garrison Notsu and secure their lines of supply throughout the campaign. The 11th Legion consisted of thirty-nine telnics, and were represented on the map by their sigil, two silver crossed daggers upon a field of black.

Next stood General Vlesnivolk, commander of the 8th Benotrist Legion. His legion was much reduced to twenty-two telnics, but was recently bolstered by ten telnics from the Nisin Garrison, and five from the Pagan Garrison, bringing his strength to thirty-seven telnics. The 8th Legion's marker upon the map was represented by a gray hammer upon a field of red.

The 5th, 8th and 11th Legions represented all that remained of Morac's army from the previous campaign. Knowing the importance of victory in Torry North, Tyro reinforced him with three additional Legions, two of which were currently present, with the third underway.

The first of the new arrivals stood across the table from Morac, General Trimopolak, commander of the 14th Gargoyle Legion, previously garrisoned at the Benotrist capital city of Laycrom, near the western coast. Tyro redeployed them upon first hearing of the defeat at Corell. They marched with all haste to reach Notsu for the spring campaign, numbering a full complement of fifty telnics. They were represented on the map by their sigil, a red headless corpse upon a field of black.

Beside the gargoyle general, stood the commander of the Benotrist 10th Legion, the newly arrived General Gavis, his mismatched eyes studying the map intently. He was keenly aware of Morac's shortcomings in the previous campaign, and would be certain to avoid them this time. His legion numbered a full fifty telnics, and were represented by their sigil, a black cloven shield upon a field of red.

The last legion was currently enroute along the Kregmarin, still many days march to their north. It was the fabled 9th Benotrist Legion, the very legion Tyro led into battle at Glauston, the pinnacle battle of the revolution, where they decimated the last and greatest of the Menotrist armies, securing total victory over their age old foes. The 9th Legion was commanded by General Marcinia, and was represented by its sigil, a gray sword upon a field of white.

Besides these six legions, Morac also commanded the Gargoyle 12th Legion, which currently stood north of Gotto, much of its strength reduced from the raid on Tro. It was commanded by General Krakeni, and was represented by its sigil, clashing red fists upon a field of green.

Joining the Generals of Legion were several ranking members of the Imperial Elite, including Kriton, who stood to Morac's right, along with Borgon, Daylas and Hossen Grell, who just returned from Tro. Also in attendance was Dethine, the Nayborian Champion, recently returned form his native realm, where he apprised his King of the happenings in the north. With most of his contingent destroyed at the siege of Corell, he now commanded a mere two hundred Naybin warriors.

"Victory shall soon be ours if we plan accordingly," Morac began, his fierce brown eyes sweeping around the table, taking the measure of the men he commanded. "The enemy waits upon us at Corell, greatly reduced by our previous campaign. General Bode's 3rd Torry Army has reinforced them, but suffered much in the breaking of the siege, and they can no longer count his army among their potential relief forces. The Torry 2nd Army is repositioned at Central City, if our reports are to be believed. The garrisons of Cropus and Central City can field a combined ten telnics. That is the total forces available to the enemy in Torry North."

"What of the Jenaii battlegroups?" General Gavis asked, knowing they positioned many telnics at Corell since the breaking of the siege.

"Some forces remain, but most have been withdrawn to counter the Naybin army demonstrating along the Elaris," Dethine said, running a pointer along the Elaris River that divided the Jenaii Kingdom from Nayboria.

"And what of the Torry cavalry and magantor forces that devastated our forces during the previous siege? They are still a threat to our lines of supply as we currently stand, let alone when we again advance into Torry North," Gavis pointed out.

"We have made contingencies to deal with them, General. And I would caution casting aspersions on the conduct of current and past campaigns," Daylas interjected, regarding the Benotrist General with a calm veneer. Daylas was an able administrator, who was not prone to emotional outbursts, unlike many of his fellow elite. He also took upon his dutiful role as Morac's advocate in the presence of their commanders.

"General Naruv has allotted more than half of all our magantor forces for this campaign, led by his second, General Polis," Borgon, who stood 8th among Tyro's Elite, said. He was a noted ruffian, with a loud and boisterous demeanor, who survived the assault upon the gate of Corell where so many of his fellow Elite fell.

"And where is General Polis?" Gavis asked, leery of advancing into enemy territory without proper protection from enemy warbirds.

"He is currently overseeing the security of our supply lines. Be assured that his forces shall be in control of the air once we cross into Torry North," Borgon said, staring intently at General Gavis with his even set gray eyes.

"What of cavalry?" Gavis asked.

"We have gathered over three thousand mounts from across the eastern half of the empire to secure our supply trains and oppose the enemy cavalry. Kriton shall lead five hundred mounts himself, preceding the vanguard of our invasion," Daylas said.

"Three thousand?" Gavis asked. To gather that many so quickly brought into question their competence. Since the revolution, the Benotrists relied on their swift moving gargoyle allies to serve the function of most contemporary cavalries, but the Torries dispelled that notion, devastating their lines of communication in the lead up to the breaking of the siege. Gargoyles might move swiftly afoot, but could not outpace ocran. Gargoyles could fly, but only for short distances.

"I believe General Gavis is concerned with the ability of our new cavalry," General Felinaius, commander of 11th Legion said. "It takes years of riding to match the skill of our Torry counterparts. Casual rides through the countryside or running messages for your local proctor is poor substitute for riding in combat or in coordination with others," Felinaius ventured. It was not lost on him the danger of questioning Lord Morac's planning considering the fate of the late General Maglakk, who Morac struck down amid a council of war at Corell.

"Our rawest recruits shall be used securing our supply trains along the Kregmarin, freeing our better riders for contesting the Torry cavalry," Daylas affirmed.

"You shall find our cavalry and magantor forces more than adequate, General Gavis. With the soon arrival of General Marcinia's 9th Benotrist Legion, we shall have more than enough forces to decisively finish Torry North. With the only remaining enemy forces far away in the south, none shall reach the battle before it is decided," Morac said.

"What of Prince Lorn and their southern armies? The latest

reports show he was victorious in Yatin. What prevents him from shifting all his armies north?" Gavis asked.

"That would be a concern had he not redirected his meager southern forces to Maconia. Should he carry the day, his armies would no doubt be severely reduced, and pose little threat to the army we are bringing to bear. His victory in Yatin did little more than ensure the Yatin Empire would not crumble. What remains of Emperor Yangu's armies are no threat beyond their shrunken border," Morac explained.

"The greater news from the Yatin campaign is the death of the Earther Kato. He did much to spoil our plans during the first siege of Corell. He is not there to aid them this time," Kriton's eyes blazed with cold fury.

"Perhaps not, but the other Earthers are ever a concern. You have information on this matter, Emperor's Elite Grell?" Daylas called upon Hossen Grell, who just returned from the Troan raid, which he took the greatest part in planning.

"The Earthers are in no position to interfere with our plans for the foreseeable future, if ever," Hossen stroked his beard, the unusual trait proving he was native to the Lone Hills.

"Do continue," Daylas ordered, weary of Hossen's smug demeanor.

"Their vessel was severely damaged during the raid on Tro. It is doubtful many of their crew survived. Their vessel may soon sink as well, never to trouble us again," Hossen proudly boasted.

"You are certain of this?" Borgon asked, fear and elation painting his face with equal aplomb.

"Indeed. I witnessed the devastation. It was most exhilarating," Hossen smiled knowingly.

"And how was this done? Thorton was very explicit that the attack was to be delayed if the Earthers were present?" Daylas asked, concern visible on his usually stoic face.

"Thorton's advice was considered, but the opportunity presented itself, and I adjusted our plan accordingly. The weapon he gifted us was used much more effectively against their ship than the city forum. We have neutralized the *Stenox* and decimated the Ape Navy, rendering their Republic helpless to respond."

"You are certain that the Earthers are impaired if not destroyed?" Gavis asked warily.

"Most assuredly, General," Hossen assured him.

"Then the harbor should soon fall, and greatly strengthen our supply routes?" Gavis asked, since that was the point of attacking Tro to begin with.

"The 12th gargoyle Legion did suffer a great many casualties in the raid, and many of our agents were slain along with most of our contracted mercenaries and Benotrist merchants that were recruited for that delicate task," Hossen tempered expectations of seizing Tro quickly.

"Then when can we off load supplies there? That was the point in that whole exercise, was it not?" Gavis asked, wondering why he was the only one raising these questions.

"Guard yourself, General. Hossen is a member of the Imperial Elite, and deserving your full respect," Daylas warned.

"The status of the Troan Campaign, Hossen?" Morac asked with a deathly quiet voice.

"General Krakeni is moving upon Gotto as we speak, his 12th Legion strong enough to seize it before advancing upon Tro. Our 3rd and 6th fleets are advancing upon Tro from the north, and shall cut their lifeline to the sea. Tro shall soon be surrounded by land and sea, forcing their capitulation. Our 4th fleet is currently at Terse, ensuring their ruling council agrees to our generous terms of cooperation in these troubling times," Hossen explained. Terse was critical to their plans for Tro, supplying much of the needed grain to feed the legions.

It wasn't lost on Gavis the dangerous ground upon which they tred. The Troan campaign committed all their naval resources from the eastern half of the Empire. The Campaign in Torry North would exhaust nearly all the Empire's strength. Should things turn poorly, the very fate their Empire would hang perilously on the precipice.

"Inform General Krakeni that Tro must be seized immediately. We cannot depend solely upon our current resupply routes that run through the Kregmarin," Morac ordered. The state of the Kregmarin was a weak point in their tenuous hold upon Notsu. Their engineers spent the winter season digging new wells along the arduous trek, as well as cleansing many of the wells the Torries poisoned in the wake of their defeat.

"Should we reinforce Krakeni, perhaps with one of the legions presently here?" Gavis asked, knowing the diminished 12th Legion might lack the strength to complete the task.

"Nay. We march upon Corell with our full might. I'll not waste time with the dregs of Tro whilst Corell is reinforced. We strike now!" Morac proclaimed, his eyes fixed upon the white castle displayed upon the center of the map, the source of his tortured dreams since his defeat there.

"General Felinaius, you shall again split your command. You shall garrison fifteen telnics here at Notsu, securing the city," Daylas said. With much of the populace removed, there were few left to stir rebellion. The youngest and healthiest males were either conscripted as auxiliaries or taken north as slave labor. Fifteen telnics would suffice to protect the city from threats without.

"Aye, I shall see it done, Governor Daylas," General Felinaius affirmed.

"Very good. We shall now review the order of march, and targeted objectives for each legion," Daylas continued as Dethine followed Morac to his private sanctum.

* * *

Dethine followed Morac through the wide lit corridors of the expansive estate, passing large pottery bowls and figurines twice the height of a man, serving artistic flare over practicality, with decorative sandstone walls lining the passageways. Several slaves bowed as they passed, dropping to their knees with their heads pressed to the floor. Dethine noticed nearly four in five slaves were female, and those that were male were no older than twelve years. After occupying the city for so long, most of Notsu's able bodied men were culled, conscripted or enslaved. It was a wise action, lessening the need for a stronger garrison. Morac led him through two large chambers before stopping before an impressive archway, with guards posted to either side, bowing as their lord passed within.

Dethine was greeted by an impressive chamber, ornately decorated with gold flooring and silken drapes adorning its spacious windows, granting a scenic view of the city below. The walls were painted with erotic frescos, naked bodies intimately joined covering every portion of their surface, their view only obscured by several gold pillars circling the room, supporting its domed roof. Even the ceiling was covered in lewd images of females in the throes of passion. Below this impressive visage were several beds, with several smaller mattresses circling a larger bed in the center of the floor. Various tables and chests circled the room, with pitchers of wine and water and trays of delicious smelling food adorning them.

They were greeted by sixteen kneeling slave girls, adorned in flowing calnesian gowns, that fell high above their knees, their small bodices squeezing their ample breasts. Upon entering the chamber, the girls pressed their heads to the floor, bowing to their master in complete obeisance.

"Lift your heads!" Morac clapped his hands, stopping in front of them, with Dethine standing to his right, admiring his comrade's *collection*.

Dethine recognized a few of them from Morac's pavilion at Corell, though several were missing, replaced with newcomers. He noted several golden collars among the recent additions, including a beautiful wench with midnight black hair draping a delicate neck, and large expressive brown eyes staring sadly at the floor before her.

"You like her?" Morac grinned, seeing his comrade's response.

"Fetching. A worthy addition," Dethine returned the grin.

"She is yours. Belicia, attend your new master!" Morac ordered, the girl hurrying from her place in line to kneel at Dethine's feet, pressing her lips to his sandaled boot.

"A most generous offering, Lord Morac," Dethine nodded agreeably.

"A worthy gift for a friend of my people. Your King's generosity in lending his most able asset to our cause, has not gone unnoticed by myself, or my Emperor. Nayboria shall profit greatly by your loyal friendship," Morac said, acknowledging the Naybins loan of Dethine to this campaign whilst their own border was threatened by the Jenaii. King Lichu correctly understood that the fate of his realm rested upon a Benotrist victory at Corell. Should the Torries win the day, nothing they did in the south would protect their realm from falling.

"The Torries and Jenaii shall rue the day they failed to slay us during the last siege. When next we take the field, we shall smite them between our fell blades," Dethine smiled, drawing forth his bronze hued blade, its golden light bathing the chamber in ethereal brilliance.

Morac did the same, drawing forth the *Sword of the Sun*, its crimson light exploding in the chamber, outshining its sister blade, bathing his countenance in otherworldly light. The power of the swords illuminated every crevice in the chamber, alighting Morac's macabre trophy resting in the far corner. It was the severed head of the Troan Minister Denin Regs, dipped in tar to preserve it long enough for it to be delivered to the beleaguered city.

"Yes, a fitting tribute to their avarice. Never more shall they profit off the desperation of their betters," Morac answered Dethine's unspoken question as they shared a look before sheathing their blades.

"Justice finds the unrighteous," Dethine nodded in agreement, voicing his disdain for greedy merchants and oligarchs. Man was rightfully ruled by a monarch, not the effeminate petty money lenders and merchants who were too weak to raise a sword themselves. As the son of the Naybin King's bastard brother Dethar, Dethine was ever loyal to his kingly uncle, entrusted to wield the sacred weapon of his people. As King Lichu had no legitimate son to trust the *Sword of the Stars* to, he named his baseborn nephew his Champion to lead his armies into battle.

"Yes, justice," Morac nodded agreeably. "This night we celebrate the destruction of the Ape Fleet, the *Stenox*, and with them, the Troan-Ape alliance," Morac said, snatching a golden-haired girl from the line of kneeling slaves, her golden collar marking her a maiden, and recently acquired. She was a true prize, one he took unusual interest in, and the only one of his *collection* from a common household. Her father was a tanner in Notsu, but she possessed three attributes that caught his attention. She was a maiden, beautiful and her given name was… Corry.

CHAPTER 7

"Why are we here?" Caben Dotin, commander of telnic of the Nisin garrison, asked, starring blankly in the dark night air, wondering what the Earther was looking at.

"Keep quiet," Thorton growled lowly, staring through the lens of his rifle, scanning the valley floor below. They stood at the edge of a copse of trees, the open near slope of the high ridge affording them a clear view of the valley below. They settled within the trees earlier in the day, their magantors hidden far behind them, guarded by a dozen ocran riders accompanying them.

Revolution was sweeping across the eastern Benotrist Empire, from the northern slopes of the Plate Mountains, across the Nisin Plain to the coast, and from the head waters of the Tur in the east to the Reguh River Valley in the west. Menotrist and Venotrist serfs, slaves and the displaced, joined in ever greater numbers. Random acts of sabotage and dissent soon festered to outright revolt. The gargoyles and Benotrists put out the rebellion with fierce savagery, but it only fanned the flames engulfing the countryside. The sack of Nivek and the slaying of its governor, sent a chilling effect across the empire, causing the castellans and governors to fortify in place, fearing to weaken their garrisons lest they be overwhelmed. Thorton knew such a response was wrong headed, and played into the enemy's hands.

Thorton knew most revolutions coalesced around charismatic leaders that inspired followers to take up arms and persevere despite pitiful odds and brutal oppression. The name Alen was quickly spreading across the land, passing the lips of the oppressed, giving them hope. His name came to embody that hope, his legend over-shadowing the man himself. The *legend* was the slave that defied Tyro, battled for his freedom in the arena of Fera, and then escaped the Black Castle. The *man* was fortunate to fight beside others more capable, and escaped while Tyro's forces were otherwise occupied. The *Legend* defended Corell from Morac's legions, repelling each assault. The *Man* merely acted as a message runner throughout the siege, and engaged the enemy sparingly. The *Legend* set out from Corell and organized open revolt in the Benotrist Empire, with cunning and tactical brilliance. The *Man* merely followed the plan set by Elos, methodically building a growing rebellion. With Elos now gone, Alen slowly transitioned into the leader his legend portrayed him to be, each decision and order he gave building his confidence and skill.

It fell to Thorton to root him out, and quash this legend before it spread. Even more pressing was the rebel attacks upon Morac's tenu-ous supply trains, which the rebels were attacking at their source, the very farmlands from which they started. With winter behind them, the upcoming planting season was crucially important to replenish their quickly thinning ottein stores. While the Benotrists concen-trated their forces in their strongholds, the rebels attacked their supply chains, concentrating their larger attacks upon larger estates, killing or freeing the slaves, serfs and beasts that worked the land, crippling the next harvest in its infancy. To harry the current supply chains, they targeted wherever the Benotrists were weak, poisoning wells where the caravans passed, especially those between larger sources of water. Trees were cut down wherever the road narrowed, blocking their path, costing them precious time to clear the way. Thorton had to admire the rebel's creativity in causing mayhem. He thought it prudent to drag a commander of rank into the field to show him what the rebels were up to, over his heated protest.

After a painfully long wait, Thorton's patience paid off, the clear images coming into view through his lens. They were alit a bright crimson on the green backfield, taking shape as eight figures emerged from the far side of the vale through the tree line gracing its summit.

Breaking into the open, they rushed toward a watering point below, a large well resting beside the roadway that passed through the valley floor.

"Zelo, lend the commander your pistol so he can have a look," Ben said, scanning the rebels running down the opposite ridge, several carrying some sort of bags over their shoulders.

Commander Dotin scowled looking through the alien device, until his eyes drew wide with what he was seeing.

"What are they doing?" He gasped.

"Poisoning the well, if I were to guess," Ben shrugged.

"Then stop them!" Commander Dotin screeched.

"Relax," Thorton dismissed his alarm, directing him to return Zelo's pistol. "Aim for their legs, Zelo. I want a few alive for questioning."

ZIP! ZIP! ZIP!

The flash of blue laser alit the night sky, striking the small line of men descending the opposite ridge, several tumbling face first, laser piercing their legs and hips. Two dropped with laser passing through their abdomens, laser aiming higher than intended. Zelo's initial shots were scattered, showering around his intended targets, before he settled down, finding purchase in the trailing man in the group, his blast taking the fellow in the shoulder, his next cutting him down through the middle. Thorton started with the first man in the group, working his way up the ridge while Zelo worked his way down until all eight men lay dead, wounded or dying upon the far ridge.

"They're all yours Dotin, go get 'em," Ben said, scanning afield for any other targets that might emerge along the far ridgeline.

No sooner had he spoken, then the Benotrist cavalry burst from the trees all around them, hurrying down the near slope. Thorton thought they should ride a little slower considering the lack of visibility, but assumed they knew what they were doing. There was enough moonlight to partially illuminate the valley floor, and Thorton fired off several more blasts around the enemy fallen to direct the Benotrist cavalry to their location.

They found three of the men dead, and two dying, leaving three alive struggling with wounds to their legs. One of the survivors ripped open his inner thigh with a knife rather than be taken captive just before the Benotrists were upon them. The two survivors were bound and dragged to the valley floor where Commander Dotin, Thorton and Zelo joined them. The men were babbling incoherently, their disordered state a result of trauma and blood loss. Thorton ordered their leg wounds bound up before they bled out. A search of their things revealed satchels of poison they intended to dump into the wells. Under threat of torture, the men revealed they were previously part of a larger group before breaking off into smaller elements attacking different targets throughout the region. These men were equipped with poison, thus targeting wells. Others burned estates, others were given axes to cut down trees, blocking roadways. Some set traps that targeted the legs of ocran pulling carts, a cruel and effective tactic in hampering supply caravans. Commander Dotin was mortified with the grim tales, knowing the effect it had on their war effort.

"Now you understand, commander. You can't afford to fortify in place while these rebels gut your infrastructure and sever your supply trains," Thorton said, looking down at the two prisoners moaning on the ground, their legs painfully impaired, before drawing his pistol and braining them where they lay.

"Why? They deserved a torturous end, not your mercy!" Dotin shrieked.

"You didn't listen, Dotin. We don't have time for torture and useless fear tactics. Kill them and be done with it. You got the information you asked for. Take this fight to the rebels wherever they are or where you think they shall be. Success will not come in one glorious battle, but in a thousand small engagements. My advice, remove most of your servants from each holdfast, keeping only the barest essential personnel, and preferably female servants over male. Outside of your fortresses, take your essential laborers' womenfolk hostage until we have victory in Torry North. Keep them safe, but as leverage for their husbands and fathers' loyalty. As for what else you can do, use your imagination. That's what these rebels are doing quite well," Ben kicked one of the corpses.

"What of you, Thorton? Are you staying to help in this?" Dotin asked.

"I'll lend a hand where I can, Commander, but my first task is to find Alen and kill him, where ever he has run off to."

* * *

Gostovar. One hundred twenty leagues southeast of Pagan along the Tur River.

Gostovar was a key trading hub straddling the banks of the Tur River. Caravans of Calnesia, spices, slaves and ottein passed the town heading east, west and points south. It was a key stopover between Nisin, Pagan and the free ports of the northeast including Bedo and Terse. It was most noted for its local ocran breeders, who supplied the empire with the finest mounts for its cavalry and supply caravans. Rolling grasslands surrounded the region, providing vital feedstock for their ocran breeders, fueling the growth of the larger estates that doted the landscape.

A sturdy five meter wall circled the city, with five gates liberally spaced along its circumference, with a single stone bridge straddling the river. No one entered Gostovar without passing inspection. This day a large caravan approached from the east, laden with spice, cloth and a thousand slaves locked in coffle, their hands confined in wooden stocks that circled their necks and jutted prominently to their sides, stretching their arms to their utmost. They were driven by Filoan slavers dressed in black tunics, brandishing leather whips and riding ocran. The slavers were liberal with the lash, the whips biting the miserable wretches without mercy, driving their charges through the south gate. The slaves were caked in filth, their woolen tunics stinking of urine, feces, sweat and vomit, permeating the air around them, causing the inspectors to quickly approve their entrance to the city, advising the slavers to clean their products before selling them. Other Filoans drove wagons filled with goods, while keeping a distance from the foul smelling chattel that were led to the center of the city. Amidst the procession, was a posh litter born by a dozen slaves, carrying the master of the caravan, a surprisingly young man of slight build, wearing a long robe over a calnesian tunic and Bedoan sandals, a merchant of great wealth, no less.

The guards posted at the south gate halted the litter bearers, after waving the slave coffles within.

"Hold!" They commanded as a Filoan rider rode nigh, an apparent lieutenant of the wealthy merchant, who looked on from his litter with visible disinterest.

"Greetings!" The Filoan rider hailed the guards.

"Your business and your name?" One guard asked, eying the merchant sitting comfortably upon the litter before them.

"I am Garris Terez, Guardian of Poncour Roulle, Merchant of Filo. My benefactor has journeyed long to sell his wares in your fair municipality after learning of the high prices recently offered, if the rumors we have heard are true," the rider explained.

"Prices are always high in war, stranger, but Filo is a long way off for this time of year," the guard said, his gaze drifting between Garris and Poncour Roulle, the pampered merchant looking far too comfortable upon his litter.

"Far off perhaps, but not too far. We hurried here with all haste, as you can smell by the state of our chattel," Garris japed, referring to the unkempt condition of the slaves in coffle, which was often expected when moving captives over long distances.

"Aye, and I suggest you clean them before sale. Our local purchasers like to see what they're buying," the guard advised. Gostovar was accustom to receiving and selling slave stock, with large holding pens in the center of the city.

"That would benefit their view and our noses," Garris japed, his jovial mood having little effect on the guard.

"Our pens might not be large enough to hold all your chattel," the guard added, watching the last of the slaves in coffle shuffle forth.

"We can always keep the least quality stock outside the pens. They have grown used to long periods in their bonds. By now most should look forward to their sale," Garris smirked.

"Very well. Proceed to the designated areas for arriving merchandise. The exchange agents shall meet with you there," the guard waved them on.

* * *

The caravan of Poncour Roulle advanced to the center of the city, where only half of his slaves could be housed in the pens provided for arriving chattel. The prisoners held without were kept in their stocks, painfully knelt upon the unforgiving stone of the wide avenue that adjoined the holding pens. To the surprise of many, the slaves within the pen were also kept in their stocks, as Poncour Roulle chose to keep them fully restrained until the next morn, where they would be cleaned in small groups and displayed for sale to local merchants and estates. The slave pens rested along the south bank of the Tur River, near the lone bridge that connected the two sides of the city, the area forming a prominent junction that broke off into five directions, each leading to one of the gates of the city.

The caravan's other goods were already being displayed for sale, drawing a small crowd of local shoppers, causing many to overlook the sorry condition of the slaves housed nearby. The slavers' harshness with their charges merely eased the people's minds, knowing the slaves' vast numbers were well secured as the waning daylight gave way to dusk. To honor his generous hosts, Poncour Roulle broke open casks of Bedoan ale, inviting the good people of Gostovar to freely partake, his charity seen as way for him to ingratiate himself before putting his slaves up for sale on the morrow. Great cheers went out throughout the evening, celebrating the great city of Filo, and Gostovar's new favorite merchant, Poncour Roulle.

As the night drew on, the congregants slowly dispersed in a drunken stupor, including ranking members of Gostovar's garrison. Few noticed as the slavers, all of whom appeared drunk throughout the night, suddenly moved with a lively step among their captives with keys in hand.

Free of their chains, the slaves stretched their arms, easing their burdensome stocks carefully to the ground. Hidden within the lengths of each stock were swords, which they quickly retrieved. The citizens still assembled in the city center screamed in alarm as Poncour's men descended upon them, cutting them down where they stood, while others broke off toward the south and southeastern gates.

114

Alen discarded the robes of Poncour Roulle, throwing the disguise into the street while drawing his blade, leading a cohort of his men toward the city barracks. His men drove two of the wagons that were among their caravan to the front and rear entrances of the two level wooden structure, setting the oil laden wagons ablaze, trapping many within.

Across Gostovar, the southern gates of the city fell in detail, allowing thousands of rebels to pour into the city proper. Those first to enter the city proceeded to Alen's siege of the barracks, surrounding the structure with archers and pike men. Those trapped within escaped a few at a time, squeezing through windows or breaks in the wall, before they were cut down by rebel spears and arrows. Others were engulfed in flames, running freely, lighting the night air as they screamed. The freed slaves chased down people in the streets, cutting them down where they fled.

Alen's men swept the city, freeing any slaves they found, while killing every Benotrist where they found them, slaying many in their beds, whether man, woman or child, sparing none. They burned every wooden structure, slaying ocran that were herded in corrals. The governor of the city was dragged from his bed, bound to a stake and set ablaze, his screams echoing over the ruin of his city.

By dawn the task was complete. Alen sent his men to the local ocran breeding estates throughout the region, where they slew every beast they could find, denying them to the empire. Alen dispersed his small army, ordering them to break up into smaller groups to further spread their revolt, while he led a small cohort with his Jenaii guides back west, circumventing Nisin to spread revolt along the Reguh, never remaining in place long enough to be found.

CHAPTER 8

Fera.

Valera took a sip from her goblet, regarding the emperor evenly, sitting across from him at his table. Another evening found her in his company, as it had every evening since her arrival. Again, the servants and guards were dismissed after their dinner was served, affording them privacy to speak freely, which she could never truly exercise considering whom she was speaking with. She felt the baby move within her, taking comfort in its forceful kick, reassuring her of its good health. The child was the one thing she took comfort in, the one thing that made sense in the madness that surrounded her. How could Tyro not see that? He looked at her with those yellow eyes of his, with specks of purple tainting their iris', wondering what he was thinking? The man was a complete mystery, a paradox of emotions and motives that she couldn't fully ascertain. Tyro loved her husband, as far as she could understand, but it felt a more possessive love than genuine affection, more cold than heartfelt, cold and unbending, and all consuming. Was it obsession or madness that fueled him? Or was it simple pride?

"Joriah carved for you?" Tyro asked, forking a morsal into his mouth, using that as a starting point for the night's conversation.

"He did," she took another sip of water.

"That is not very specific, daughter. What works of art did he produce for you?"

"He carved many figurines from both stone and wood, each equal to your impressive skill," she complimented, having seen his many works decorating the halls of the palace.

"What images did he carve? What was the source of his inspiration?" Tyro asked, curiosity evident in his golden eyes.

"He mostly carved…" she was embarrassed to say, not one to boast, her humility very much equal to Jonas'.

"You," Tyro rightly guessed, her soft nod affirming his answer.

"Joriah was mostly inspired by my appearance, my beauty as he generously called it," she smiled at the memory.

"The boy is not blind. I was similarly inspired by his mother. Though I took a second wife, it was many years after I thought she was dead, but no other could replace her in my heart," he confessed with a faraway look.

She could almost pity the man for his suffering if he was someone other than himself. She could never bring herself to pity the monster Taleron had become, and could only imagine the conflict that stormed within her poor husband's mind concerning his father. Since the first night she arrived, their conversations remained on trivial things, with Valera not wishing to rouse his ire, and Tyro happily gleaning the most mundane of details involving his son and his kin. And so, she detailed Jonas' many sculptures that he made of her, displaying them about their home.

"You lived simply for someone born of such privilege, Joriah as well. Tell me of this home you shared with Joriah?" He asked, wondering why neither had riches to draw upon considering her high birth and Joriah's skill with the sword.

Valera struggled to quickly answer, considering the nature of their exile from court, which served more as a proving ground for Terin than a punishment for her and Jonas.

"Jonas desired to live simply, to raise our son away from the corrupting influence of court, to foster in him the values we both cherish. One could hardly instill humility and kindness in a child when they are waited upon by doting servants and applauded for the simplest of achievements," she began.

"Joriah is an imperial prince, my rightful heir. What need has he of humility? Or his son?" Tyro refuted that notion.

"Joriah is no prince. He is a simple Torry farmer and warrior, who has committed his life to raising our family in quite obscurity. We have no need of fancy titles and lordly estates and castles. Is there any greater joy for a father than teaching his son to hunt, fish, dress game or to use a sword? Could he have done all of that with Terin if he was distracted by the games of court? I am proud of the man Joriah has become, and the simple life we have built together," she gifted Tyro a genuine smile, hoping for him to see Jonas' choices as selfless acts for his family rather than rejection of his father.

"He taught him well," Tyro conceded, taking a generous sip of his wine. "I remember well the lessons I shared with Joriah when he was a boy. He was so quick to learn, and handled a sword better than most grown men even then. His Kalinian blood played a part, no doubt, but I like to think I taught him much of what he knew."

"My father spoke well of his skill, claiming Jonas was the finest swordman he had ever known. Father is never one to pay false praise, or throw about compliments. My Jonas, your Joriah, is the finest warrior of the Torry Realm, but do you care to know what he said of you?" She smiled, her inviting voice disarming him with ease.

"Speak of it," he said, eager to hear it.

"He said that his father was the greatest warrior he had ever known. He spoke fondly of sitting beside you along the stream that meandered the vale, fishing for much of the day, with you telling him stories, or teaching him how to skin game or throw knives. He spoke of your training him with the sword and bow, recalling each moment he had with you as the greatest in his young life. He wanted to give Terin that same experience, to raise him by ourselves, savoring every moment with him, just as he did with you, all those years ago, before war and vengeance drew you away," she regretted that last part, unable to curb her true thoughts.

"Those were simpler times," was all he could say, his eyes going out of focus, lost in a memory.

It pained her to see what had become of this man, wondering what could bring about such a change in a person. From what Jonas told her, he was once a good man, and a doting father, a man that he loved so very much. How could the man he so lovingly described become this monster? The very fact she shared a table each of these past nights with the greatest tyrant Arax had ever known, still hadn't settled in her brain. What did he want of her? Oh, he spoke at length of claiming what was his, or what he thought he had a right to, including her, but there had to be more to this obsession. He never asked of her anything too critical to the war effort, or the Torry Realm, only details of Jonas, Cordela and Terin, along with herself of course. Was her place here simply to assuage the loneliness of this man? She knew her true purpose was to lure Jonas here, and silently prayed that he would not be so foolish. The Torry Realm needed the blood of Kal upon the battlefield. What purpose would coming here serve, other than to remove Jonas from the war? He must know that she was safe from his father, the man being as protective of her as Jonas was. No matter how alone she felt, she didn't want her beloved Jonas to join her in this strange captivity.

Please stay away, my beloved, her thoughts whispered desperately.

"Tell me of Terin? What was he like as a child? What did you teach him?" Tyro was eager to learn what he knew so little of.

"He is a wonderful boy, dutiful, loving and loyal," she almost cried, but kept her emotions in check, struggling to not show weakness to him. "Jon… Joriah enjoyed hunting with him, teaching him to track game and use a bow. He was masterful at starting fires, and cooking what they caught, impressing Joriah with his eagerness to learn. He was a hard worker as well. They would work the fields well into the night, neither complaining about their labors. Most farmers had several sons and daughters to help them, but we had only Terin until now," she said running a hand over her bulging womb.

Tyro never considered the possibility that his son lived or that he was a simple farmer, laboring in self imposed exile. Tyro spent all his life as a warrior, first as the second son of his noble father, then as a revolutionary, then as a conqueror and Emperor. His son was greater than him with blade and bow, this he did not doubt, but how much greater would Joriah be if he fully dedicated himself to his martial craft? A farmer? What a waste of his skill, but to hear Valera speak of it, it was a gloriously simple and pure life, as if the life he offered was beneath them. This angered him, though he showed it not. It was a conversation he would have with his son when he presented himself, and he WOULD present himself. He knew Joriah loved Valera just as strongly as he loved Cordela, and if she were held by his own father, nothing would stop him from coming for her.

The one thing he was uncertain of, was what Joriah would do when they met? He hadn't seen him since he was a child. Valera said that he still loved him, but that could merely be a lie to appease him. He honestly didn't know what the boy would do. If Cordela was still alive she would scold him for what he did, but he needed to take Valera to force Joriah from his lair. He needed to see his son. He needed to know the truth of where he has been and why. And most importantly, he needed to know the truth of what Valera said of his Kalinian blood, if Joriah would be set upon by his gargoyles if he accepted his rightful place at his side.

He was drawn from his musings by Valera's sudden discomfort, her eyes drawn wide with alarm. Tyro sprang from his chair with the vigor of his youth, coming quickly to her side.

"What ails you?" He placed a firm hand to her shoulder, keeping her steady.

"The child quickens," she said breathily, a wave of erotic euphoria sweeping over her, signaling the beginning of her labor.

Tyro knew well that look, recalling his beloved Cordela before birthing Jonas, and Letha before birthing Tosha. It was a wondrous and possibly dangerous time if things went poorly. He immediately called for his guards, ordering her moved to the birthing chamber he arranged for her, summoning the small army of matrons he kept on hand to attend her.

* * *

Chief Matron Lesela ordered her charges about the birthing chamber with the skill of a seasoned general, preparing the bed, cleansing the instruments and seeing to the comfort of their patient. Lesela served as the chief matron of the Empire, holding her post since the revolution, named to her high post by Tyro himself for her valiant service to their cause. Born the bastard daughter of a Menotrist noble and Benotrist slave girl, she was apprenticed to the Matron's Guild upon her fifth year, eventually forsaking the Menotrists to help her long suffering Benotrist kin, quickly finding favor with Tyro while tending the many wounded in nearly all the major battles he fought. Well into her sixth decade, silver tainted her once vibrant black mane, and her brown eyes bespoke her years of service. She was ever loyal to the emperor, their similar mixed Benotrist and Menotrist heritage giving them common cause.

"Rest easy, My Lady," Lesela smoothed Valera's hair behind her ear, while another Matron ran a wet cloth over her forehead, the Chief Matron's usual harsh tone softening whenever addressing Valera. She was one of a very few close confidants of the emperor that knew Valera's connection to him.

"You mustn't fuss over me, Chief Matron. I have born a child before. This doting is unnece…" Valera tried to say, but Lesela was having none of it.

"You are a Princess of the realm, and bearing the emperor's grandchild. I'll hear none of this nonsense. Now rest, My Lady," Lesela softly scolded her, stepping into the outer corridor where the emperor awaited her.

Lesela smoothed the folds of her long white matron's gown, before stepping without. The Chief Matron in the empire wore a white gown, whilst her sisters wore the traditional red of their guild, though during the actual birthing, she would don a deep burgundy shift. She spared one last glance to her surroundings, making certain all was properly attended. The spacious circular chamber had a high domed ceiling and light blue stained walls, with torches liberally spaced along its circumference. The Lady Valera was placed upon a large bed in the room's center, with a table of instruments at its foot, many of which would hopefully not be needed. Satisfied with their preparations, she stepped without.

She found Tyro waiting in the outer corridor, his imperial elite standing vigilant watch behind him, their hands always resting upon their sword hilts, prepared to draw steel at the slightest threat. She began to kneel when Tyro waved off such formality.

"Remain standing, Chief Matron. How is she?" Tyro asked, torch-light enhancing the intensity of his vibrant golden eyes.

"She is well, My Emperor. She is still quite early, and these sorts of things often take days to complete fruition. Others take but a brief time, but we shall be ever vigilant in our watch."

"What of complications?" He asked, ever wary of the dangers of the birthing bed.

Though Araxan women felt wondrous erotic stimulation through-out the birthing process, certain dangers still persisted. Tyro bitterly recalled the fate of his own dear mother, who died giving birth to his still dead sister, victim of her wicked matron who was the devoted creature of his father's first wife, the Menotrist crone hating his mother for his father's amorous affections. Tyro never doubted that his mother bled out upon the birthing bed purposely at the hand of that matron. He voiced his suspicion to his father, who turned a stone ear to his complaint. He recalled the sneering look upon his step mother's face when his father rebuked him. Whenever he thought to show Menotrists mercy, he simply reminded himself of the cruel nature of his father's first wife, and her evil get, his brother Aleric. To sooth his rage at the memory, he recalled the satisfaction he had when he impaled his wretched stepmother and her matron when he attacked their holdfast, where his brother escaped their fate, though losing three fingers in their exchange. He remembered the woman's screams as she hung on that pole, her pierced innards matching beautifully her dying screech.

"There are few complications, My Emperor, but I shall be ever watchful for them. The greatest concern is the position of the child, particularly the position of the head. From what I have felt, it seems it has dropped perfectly into position. another concern for the child is with the cord, whether it is knotted or wound around its neck. This cannot be determined until it emerges from the womb. As for the mother, the greatest concern is bleeding. Some, but very few, women suffer intense bleeding after the birth. Any bleeding near the entrance we can sew, but should it happen further within…. well, there is naught we can do but hope for the best. I fear this is not what you wish to hear, but any assurances beyond what I stated would be false assurances, which I would never offer you. We have endured too much together for me to disrespect you in such a way, My Emperor," she bowed her head with deep reverence.

"I honor your honest counsel, Lesela. What I ask of you remains between us and no other," Tyro said.

"As always, My Emperor," she bowed her head dutifully.

"You must do all in your power to make certain the Lady Valera survives the birthing bed, but should you be forced to choose between the child and the mother, the child must live," he regarded her knowingly.

"The child is ever my utmost priority, My Emperor, and the mother thereafter."

"Very good. Keep me apprised," he said, before stepping away.

* * *

The Benotrist Border. West of the Mote Mountains.

Jonas' gaze swept the horizon, looking for any sign of civilization beyond the rolling, barren hills that stretched from the Cress Mountains in the west to the Mote Mountains to their direct east. It was an inhospitable, difficult barrier that separated the Benotrist Empire from the wilderness that divided the Yatin Empire from Torry North, preventing each of the three realms from settling this desolate and isolated region.

Jonas shared the saddle with Davin Pesera, a seasoned magantor rider that joined him on his quest once he attained Central City. He needed to reach the Benotrist Empire with all haste, to make certain his dear Valera was truly safe, but would not gift them a Torry magantor should he be detained. Davin would return the valued mount once Jonas presented himself to the border garrison commander, wherever he could find one, and by the way thinks were looking, it would be no time soon. They followed the Nila north, and then the Tuss River, which led to the foothills of the Mote Mountains, which they skirted west before breaking fully north, keeping the towering peaks of the Mote Range to their east.

Jonas' mind was a torrent of emotions, fear, grief and angst taking their toll on him. It was with a heavy heart he returned to these lands, lands that took so much from him. It was also a place of many a fond memory, he reminded himself. Logic would caution him from coming here, knowing his death was likely, despite his father's intentions. What would they say when they meet? His last memory of his father was the fateful night in the Kalinian Vale when he placed the Sword of the Sun in his hands, gifting him the power to destroy the world. Had he only known, he thought he might have acted differently, but what child could refuse their father such a thing? His parents were his world, and he loved them both so fiercely.

Yah, forgive me my weakness, he lamented his choices, both the one as a child, and the one now, forsaking his adoptive home to save the woman he loved. Part of him hoped he could reason with his sire, convince him of the folly of this war, but deep inside his heart, he knew it a fool's quest. Another part of him felt he had more than done his duty to the Torry Realm, raising up Terin to fulfill the role appointed him, and gifting him the Sword of the Moon to contest the Sword of the Sun he gifted his sire. Terin's Kalinian blood enhanced the lesser sword, making him more than a match for Morac's fell blade.

Yah revealed much of his plan to Jonas, revealing the roles both Terin and Lorn were appointed to. With his own role complete, he often struggled with what Yah expected of him. Fighting at Corell seemed the logical choice, and he did so gladly, helping break the siege, and staying long enough to convey his visions to Corry on Terin's whereabouts. He was even willing to heed Torg's advice and bring Valera to Corell when that damnable missive arrived, shattering his world. What choice had he but to answer his father's summons? It was a meeting he always knew would have to happen, especially with the war now upon them, and he and Terin aligned opposite his father.

"Jonas, look yonder!" Davin, his guide and companion, shouted over the wind, his finger reaching out around him, from his position behind, pointing to the horizon where a small holdfast rested beyond the hills upon a flattening plain.

Jonas drew a deep breath, steeling his nerve for the task ahead, hoping the parchment he carried would serve its intended purpose. If not, he would learn just how deadly his sword arm still was.

They pressed on, the early spring air contorting their faces as they sped through the firmament, the Benotrist holdfast growing larger in their view. The small fortress consisted of a curtain wall surrounding a small garrison, with a stone keep gracing its center. A minaret rose above the stone keep, where lookouts perched upon its highest floor were first to spot their approach, alerting the garrison to their presence. At the base of the minaret, a large flat platform graced the roof of the fortress, with a small magantor stable along its north face. Even from afar, Jonas could see two great avian strutting forth across the keep's flat roof, their dark wings standing out against the light gray stone of the keep's roof. Both birds took flight as they drew nigh, circling the holdfast before closing the distance between them, easing their ascent before drawing level.

"Raise the signal, Davin!" Jonas shouted over the wind, his comrade hoisting a blue flag above their heads, the gesture indicating their peaceful intent.

Jonas spotted a narrow stream skirting the east side of the holdfast, with a dozen small thatched huts resting along its length farther downstream, likely peasant homes tributary to the holdfast. Their magantor continued at an easy pace toward the roof of the keep as the Benotrist warbirds drew up alongside them upon seeing the flag of truce, following them through their descent. A flax of soldiers met them upon the roof of the keep, armed with long spears, and clad in gray mail and matching helms over black tunics. A commander of rank stood behind them, his cold eyes observing their approach guardedly as they set down, their magantor's talons scrapping to a stop upon the gray stone. Jonas and Davin eased slowly off their mount, so as not to alarm the Benotrists with any sudden movements. Jonas' sea blue tunic and silver mail and helm alerted the Benotrists that he was a member of the Torry Elite, his physical presence giving off a powerful aura they found unsettling.

"We come peacefully at the request of your emperor! I would speak with your commander!" Jonas declared with authority, refusing to show any weakness that might give these men idea to take them captive, at which point he would draw steel and slay them to a man. One look into his piercing purple eyes gave these men little doubt that he could do just that. His stoically bold statement caused the commander of the garrison to stand forth.

"I am the Commander of garrison, Gul Balik. I would have your name," the Benotrist commander stated, stepping forward, adorned in the matching armor of his men, with a row of red feathers running the middle of his gray helm, with a matching red cape draping his shoulders.

"I am known to your Emperor as Joriah Taleron. I was given this parchment written by the hand of Emperor's Elite Hutis Vlenok," Jonas drew the missive given him at Corell, handing it to the Benotrist commander, who readily accepted it. Jonas sensed that he was expected, by the commander's response when he uttered his name.

The commander quickly read the parchment, nodding his head expectantly as the other magantors set down behind their own.

"You were expecting us?" Jonas asked.

"We were told it was a possibility. Now that you are here, I would ask for your sword," Commander Balik said.

"You'll not have it. I am not a prisoner. I am here under the flag of truce to parlay with your emperor. If he asks for my sword, I shall give it to him, but no other. You are to provide escort for me to Fera, and my comrade here shall be given liberty to return to my people, informing them of my safe arrival," Jonas stated firmly, brokering no room for compromise. He would not surrender himself into captivity without first seeing that his father was actually Tyro, though he had no reason to base such doubts. Even then, he doubted he would surrender his blade, the very one gifted to him by Princess Corry after the breaking of the siege of Corell.

The commander's face quickly morphed into complete acquiescence, strangely conceding to Jonas' demands.

"So be it. My magantor scouts shall deliver you to Fera," Gul Balik agreed.

CHAPTER 9

They soared over the land like leaves on the wind, the trees, homes and farms of the Torry countryside dotting the landscape below with their familiar charm. They approached Corell from the south, passing over lands untouched by Morac's invasion. Corell was the rock upon which the invasion broke, protecting the lands west and south of it from the gargoyles scourge. Scenic green valleys and lush farm lands gave way to a scorched and tortured terrain, still bearing the scars of Morac's sins. The fetid smell of decay and rotting flesh had long since dissipated, but much of the landscape yet lingered in that moment of time where it suffered the gargoyles darkest inclinations. The blanched bones of men and gargoyles littered much of the countryside, glistening brightly in the late day sun. The devastation bled into the horizon with downed trees, burnt out dwellings and devoured fields. The gargoyles' path was as the locust, consuming all in its terrible wake.

Corry eyed the ruin with a heavy heart, knowing the suffering inflicted upon her people. She could only pray that Corell endure, lest the whole realm share in this fate. Her gaze shifted to the northeast, imagining that fell place far beyond the horizon upon the Kregmarin Plain where her father met his end. What would he think if he saw her now? Would he be proud of her managing the realm in his and Lorn's absence, or be ashamed for her abandoning her post to rescue Terin? Oh, how she missed him, longing for him to hold her in his protective arms, kissing her forehead, driving off all her worries. She almost cried every time she thought of him, the pain too much to bear. She hugged Terin tighter, leaning on his warmth and love to fill the cavernous hole her father's death hollowed within her. She pressed her head tight to his back as they sped through the sky, taking comfort in his closeness, savoring his touch. She could sense his presence even with her eyes closed, his aura feeling more familiar with every passing day.

"I love you, Terin Caleph!" She shouted into his ear, not caring if Ular overheard her utterance from his place behind her.

Terin looked back over his shoulder, gifting her the most beautiful smile, sending her heart aflutter. She marveled at how easily he melted her heart and scrambled her brain. At times she felt like a helpless fool, driven to madness in his presence. He claimed she had the same effect upon him, though she didn't fully believe it. No one could possibly feel as foolish as she felt all the times in his company. How ever could she manage the realm when they reached Corell? Everyone would be able to see that she was now a blubbering idiot, Terin causing her to smile constantly with his impossible charm. Oh, how she loved this boy, and if the realm thought her a silly girl for going after him, so be it. She would rather suffer the ridicule of the realm than live without Terin.

Terin couldn't help smiling either, Corry's love mending his heart the very moment she appeared in Darna's dungeon, sweeping away his pain like a cleansing wind. Even with his power stripped away, and transformed into whatever it was now, he could only thank Yah for giving him his heart's greatest desire… HER. She was what he wanted above all else. She was what he was now fighting for. He would rather die than live in a world without her. Was this what his father felt with his mother? He remembered that Jonas was willing to forfeit his life when he confessed his love for Valera to King Lore, willing to offer up his sword and life than live in a world where he couldn't have her. He darkly thought of Tyro and his obsession with Cordela, willing to destroy the world in order to protect her, but unwittingly driving her away with his actions. The love his father and grandfather had for their wives was all consuming, but ended differently, with Jonas' pure heart holding on to the woman he loved, while Taleron caused his beloved Cordela to slip away.

Which am I? Terin pondered, determined to follow Yah's guidance to insure he didn't repeat his grandfather's folly.

Amidst his musings the horizon came alive with winged forms filling the heavens, too distant to determine if they were friend or foe. Their numbers were too grand and too high to be gargoyles, and their wings too small to be magantors, though at this distance, he could be mistaken. Within moments their allegiance was clear, the silver and gray wings of the Jenaii with their distinct blue armor setting his heart at ease. His heart grew elated with their vast numbers, unable to count them, but guessing their strength over a hundred. Elos drew up alongside Terin's left, giving him a knowing look before advancing ahead, with Raven seated in front of him, giving Terin a modified Earth salute with just the two fingers of his right hand. He could almost hear Raven mangling Elos' name as they flew on ahead, with the Jenaii Champion pointing north over Raven's thick shoulder, explaining the V shaped formation of his countrymen. The Jenaii used larger sized patrols to scout in force for protection as well as striking targets of opportunity. Able to fly many times farther than gargoyles, and gain greater lift, the Jenaii were masters of the sky, countered only by the gargoyles' greater numbers.

Terin marveled as Elos and Raven drew farther ahead, before the Jenaii Champion sprang from the back of their magantor, spreading his wings, soaring gracefully toward his brethren as they drew nigh, meeting them in mid flight. Their formation opened up, allowing him to pass freely between them, as they broke off, half veering left and the others veering right, circling the magantors before drawing alongside them, escorting them north to Corell. Terin's heart sang at the beautiful scene, sunlight playing off the Jenaii warriors' silver wings. Cronus and Elos assured him that ten thousand Jenaii warriors guarded Corell, along with General Bode's 3rd Army. With he and Elos, as well as Raven and the others fighting beside them, he favored their chances. His power to drive off the gargoyles might be gone, but the garrison was much stronger than last time. The burden wouldn't fall solely upon his shoulders to defend Corell. His brothers would fight beside him, brothers born from friendship rather than blood, but brothers all the same.

Raven managed flying the magantor well enough to keep it in a straight line, as long as he didn't need to make any sharp turns or perform some crazy stunt as some of his comrades were prone to do.

How did Lorken manage to maneuver these birds so well? He wondered. Compared to Lorken he flew like a nervous grandmother with the shakes, which was ironic considering Raven was a much better Space Fleet pilot. He recalled all the times he and the others poked fun at the shuttle pilots ferrying crews and supplies from ship to ship, commenting on their pitiful skills flying those painfully slow barges. This is what being stranded on Arax brought him to, flying on a giant bird like one of those shuttle idiots. Orlom's magantor drew up alongside of his, the young gorilla pointing excitedly toward the horizon where a slender sliver of white jutted into the sky. The slender silhouette was quickly joined by several others, all white, save for a golden one. They were obviously the towers of Corell, with the whole palace swiftly coming into view, its towering walls rising above the land in all their glory. He had to admit, the scene was quite impressive, wondering how the Torries constructed the blasted thing? The same went for Fera, its walls even higher than Corell's. No wonder it supposedly took these people a hundred years to construct each of these monstrous castles. Corell looked more like a giant block of stone than a walled fortress, with its towering outer walls overshadowed by the inner walls set higher still, let alone the large inner keep with its towers rising high into the heavens.

Orlom looked on so happily, he began to bounce up and down in the saddle. Raven winced, hoping his young friend wouldn't foolishly jump to his death in all the excitement, a sentiment shared by Orlom's saddle mate, the Troan magantor rider that suffered the gorilla's presence throughout their entire journey.

Terin's heart soared as the familiar walls arose upon the horizon. How he longed to see Corell, recalling all his fevered dreams where the palace walls always lingered briefly in his sight before he was dragged away, returned to his captivity in Darna's foul keep. But now, the walls were real, their overwhelming presence a balm to his tortured soul. He felt Corry's comforting arms around him, a reminder of all the gifts Yah had restored to him.

"Welcome home," Corry shouted through the crisp air, before kissing his cheek.

* * *

The lookouts atop the tower of Celenia descried their arrival, heralding the news of approaching magantors to those below, who relayed it throughout the command. Arriving magantors were a common occurrence of late, with curriers arriving regularly from Central City, and General Valen's recent return from the Macon Campaign. The fact that these magantors approached from the south with an entire Jenaii patrol joining to escort them, indicated their importance.

When word reached Leanna that magantors were approaching from the south, she hurried to the roof of the inner keep, her labored breath hindering her efforts with her growing womb. She made her way up the wide stairwell that emptied upon the central roof, with the palace towers rising up all around her from that high, flat surface. Her frantic gaze swept the heavens, looking in each direction, struggling to spot the approaching avian, and determine which of the platforms above they would set down upon. There was no assurance that any of the war birds carried Cronus, but she found herself excited with every arrival in recent days, hoping he would be among them.

Her eyes found the approaching Jenaii escort in the southern sky between the Golden Tower and the Tower of Zar, their winged forms filling the heavens. Her heart pounded finding the lead magantor, with a strangely clad rider sitting its saddle, strangely attired but familiar all the same.

Raven? She thought her eyes betrayed her, closing them briefly before looking again. By then he was gone, his mount passing behind the Tower of Zar, obscured from view. Her eyes then fell upon the next magantor with another Earther she could not determine, before recognizing the familiar feminine form of Princess Corry sitting behind the Earther, and an Enoructan sitting behind her. The beast they rode upon was wondrously beautiful, until she recognized it as *Wind Racer,* the very warbird Cronus departed upon, which gave her hope and worry. Hope that he should be among these arrivals, and worry that he was not riding upon the great avian. The next magantor bore two riders, a man she did not know, and a gorilla, though one much smaller than Argos. The next riders quickly doused her fears, lifting her heart in joyous rapture. There upon a mighty warbird, sat Cronus behind another man she did not know. She quickly looked to her left, where Raven's magantor angled toward the southeast platform.

* * *

Luckily for Raven, Elos returned to his mount just before they set down upon the stone lip of the magantor platform, helping him ease the bird's descent, its outstretched talons scrapping the stone surface. He eased himself off the saddle, happy to feel something solid beneath his feet. A cursory glance gave doubt to this solid ground he felt. A few steps in any direction would end in a quick drop and death. The grandiose view overlooked the outer and inner walls of the palace, towering above the castle and the surrounding lands like sitting upon a mountain peak.

The scars of the siege were still visible in each direction, though winter frost and rain dulled much of the horror that was visited upon Corell. He could see the filled in siege trenches circling the palace at a distance, where the scorched remains of so many corpses were piled and burnt, before covered with soil. Even now, he could see bones bleached by the sun peaking above the makeshift graveyards. Stable attendants hurried forth to attend his mount, guiding it into a stall farther within the stable, just as Wind Racer set down.

By now, a flax of royal guards spilled out onto the platform, attired in their distinct silver armor and gold tunics with wings affixed to their matching helms. Their spears lowered upon recognizing Elos. Their sudden relief upon seeing Elos transformed to dismay when Corry dismounted from Wind Racer, causing the men to take a respectful knee, welcome smiles gracing their collective faces with the return of their Princess.

"Arise, my brave warriors," Corry smiled, overcome with joy upon seeing her home and people once more.

No sooner had they gained their feet, their eyes went straight to Ular and Raven. Few if any of the royal court had ever seen an Earther, save for Kato, and fewer still had seen an Enoructan. Their curious stares shifted from one to the other until one of them recognized Terin standing beside the Princess, attired in Earth garb.

"Champion!" One soldier cried out, his infectious joy quickly spreading to his comrades, relieved to see their mightiest hero returned to them. Terin stepped forth, embracing the royal guards, taking them aback by his familiar gesture. He didn't care if he looked the fool, he loved his comrades, even those he didn't know. They had all shed blood during the siege, forging unbreakable bonds of brotherhood. He went from one to the other, taking each in his embrace, just as Orlom's magantor set down, followed soon by the others. Seeing an ape took the guards further aback, overwhelmed by the strange diversity of the new arrivals.

Corry shook her head, unable to hide her smile, watching Terin embrace the royal guards like long lost brothers. It was this wholesome innocence that he so easily exhibited that she found so endearing. The Terin of old often held back from such affections, ever guarded by the protocols of court and what was expected of him. He didn't care about those things anymore. His enslavement in Darna's keep made him realize that life was precious and brief, and he would no longer be bound by expectations. He was the Champion of the realm, and was responsible for no one but serving the crown and realm. He could be friends with everyone if he chose, and that was what he would do.

"Terin!" Leanna's voice drew their attention as she stepped onto the platform, rushing into his arms, planting kisses across his blushing face.

"You are as beautiful as I remember," Terin smiled.

"You found him," Leanna said, taking Corry into her embrace.

"Yes, with a little help from some old friends," Corry smiled, pointing out Raven and the others.

"Raven, I have missed you so," she started to cry, stepping into his arms.

"Your husband is one lucky man, Leanna," he lifted her off the floor, twirling her around just as Cronus' magantor set down. Raven lowered her to her feet, pointing her in Cronus' direction.

She could barely constrain herself, waiting for him to dismount and step clear of the shifting bird before rushing into his arms. Time lost all relevance as they kissed, sharing an eternal embrace while the others tried to look away, each pretending not to notice, with only Orlom hooting excitedly, cheering them on.

"She's a fine lass, Cronus. Give her a twirl like Boss did!" Orlom grinned, ignoring Corry's reproachful look, though Cronus couldn't disagree, gently lifting her off the floor, giving her a slow twirl before setting her back down, giving the young gorilla a knowing wink.

Leanna opened her eyes with their lips parting, her slender hands lingering upon his shoulders, drinking in the sight of him. His dark mane lifted in the spring breeze as her blue eyes met his forest green, her mind naked before his piercing gaze. He read her soul as if it were written in stone. A tingling sensation rippled through her body, lingering at her fingertips as she moved her hands to his chest.

"Soon," she whispered as his eyes lowered to her swollen belly. As he took in all that his eyes beheld, he realized all that he endured was worth the gifts of this life. He would endure all that he suffered ten fold for the love of this woman and the child she carried. Here in his arms was all that he desired.

They were soon drawn from their loving embrace by the words of the palace guard.

"Master Vantel awaits you in the throne room, Highness," the guard said to Corry, who was rather enjoying her friends' embrace.

"Very well. Everyone, if you would follow me. I'd rather Master Torg see each of you for himself than leaving it to me to describe you to him," Corry said, giving Raven a knowing look, reminding him to behave, which he would certainly ignore.

* * *

Torg Vantel miserably sat the throne, presiding over court as if it were the worst task he ever performed, slightly below carrying buckets of waste or shoveling ocran dung. He spent the better part of the morn hearing one case after another, some as mundane as two farmers squabbling over the rights of a newborn moglo that was sired by one farmer's bull and the other's sow. He immediately scolded them for bringing such a trivial claim before the throne, wondering how their case made the docket before ordering the sow's owner to gift the bull's owner ten loaves of bread as compensation, which made neither of them happy. And, so it went for much of the session until he was informed of the arriving magantors. He ordered all arriving riders brought immediately to him, a standard practice he employed ever since Corry departed to rescue Terin. He wasn't yet aware of who just arrived, but heard that it was a large group, with multiple riders to each magantor, and demanded the entire company be brought to the throne room. It was the palace steward who rushed ahead of the arriving party, entering the throne room with a determined gait, his robes swirling in his wake.

"Keep your feet and speak to your purpose!" Torg growled before the man could kneel.

"Master Vantel, the recent arrivals shall be here in moments," the steward said.

"And?" Torg knew by the man's tone there was more he wasn't saying.

"Her Highness, Princess Corry has returned, and with many others."

Corry? Torg's old heart began to race.

"Guards, clear the room!" Torg bellowed, coming swiftly to his feet, descending the dais to stand in the center of the chamber.

Chief Minister Eli Monsh and commander Nevias entered the chamber soon after, upon hearing of the Princess' arrival. The Chief Minister had recently returned from Central City, traveling through-out Torry North since the breaking of the siege, managing the state of the realm. They were soon followed by General Bode, commander of 3rd Torry Army, and General El Tuvo, commander of the 1st Jenaii Battle Group. They each took up position beside Torg, awaiting the Torry Princess.

Torg steeled his heart, awaiting her entrance with guarded optimism. He feared for her since her departure, wishing he had the power to command her to stay, though nothing could stay her hand in her quest to rescue his grandson. His thoughts drifted to Terin, wondering if her quest was successful, and if it was, wondering if he was with her. If that was true, he knew he would have to speak with the boy on his father's whereabouts, a conversation he truly dreaded. He also wondered if Cronus and Elos where with them? They were determined in their belief that Terin was waiting for them at Tro. There was also the dozen magantors Corry took with her, and he rightly wondered if they returned as well, for they would be needed for the battles to come. Before the next thought came to mind, the court crier heralded Corry's arrival.

"Her Highness, Princess Corry, acting regent of Torry North!" The crier proclaimed, announcing her entrance.

Torg couldn't hide the smile on his craggy face as she passed through the doors of the throne room, her head held high as she approached. He was immediately taken aback by her strange entourage, which included an ape, an Enoructan warrior and two Earthers which he determined by their similar garb as Kato. One was particularly large, towering above the rest, while the second was far smaller, but looked familiar, again taking him aback as he recognized his face.... Terin. Torg's heart soared, his eyes fixed on his grandson walking beside Corry so intently he failed to quickly notice Cronus, Elos and Lucas standing farther back.

"Master Vantel, I have returned something precious of yours," Corry smiled, waving an open hand to his grandson, who shrugged sheepishly, an easy smile gracing his lips.

"Welcome home, boy. You gave this old man a terrible fright, taking years that I can ill afford. And as for you, Highness, the throne is yours," Torg almost scolded her, before stepping forth, planting a kiss to her forehead. "No more running off and torturing me with that foul chair," he added, jerking a thumb over his shoulder in the direction of the throne.

"As long as your grandson doesn't get his fool self captured, I shall have no need to abandon you to such torture," she smiled.

"Aye, between the two of us we shall keep him in place," Torg snorted, ruffling Terin's hair as if he were a wee tot. "We have much to discuss, boy," Torg said, setting his hand on Terin's shoulder.

"I am pleased to see you again, grandfather," Terin almost wept with joy, never believing he would see home again after all he endured. It seemed all his dreams were coming true. He only wished his father was still here to share in this glorious moment, but Cronus said he departed just before he and Elos departed for Tro. He didn't miss the secretive undertone when Cronus spoke of his father, wondering where he journeyed, guessing he returned home to his mother as he intended.

"I see you brought more friends with you, Highness," General Bode interjected, wondering what to make of the diverse group, the most notable of which was Raven, whom he recognized from their time together before the Battle of Tuft's Mountain.

"General Bode, it's been a long time since Rego," Raven regarded the Torry General.

"You and your crew were most helpful, Captain Raven. I am grieved by the tidings of Kato's demise. Your friend was a brave warrior, and a better man. We owe him a debt we can never repay," Bode acknowledged.

"Don't worry, General, Kato will be avenged, I'll see to that," Raven said, his fierce tone so unlike his usual jovial banter. It was the same dark tone he used when he learned of Cronus' capture, and later when Corry told of Terin's enslavement. This was far worse, though, with Kato actually dead by Thorton's hand. There was such intensity surrounding Raven's aura, forcing the others to grant him a wide berth.

"Introductions are in order, General," Corry interjected, calling out each of her companions by name, starting with Raven, with Orlom and Ular receiving the most curious stares. Orlom couldn't help looking around with his mouth open, taken aback by the size of the throne room. Ular impressed Torg with his quiet resolve, the Enoructan Champion's reputation preceding him. Lucas quickly added his voice to Ular's accolades, briefly informing Master Vantel of Ular's exploits at Bansoch and Tro.

"It is good to have more of my charges returned to the fold considering our pressing need," Torg said, calling out Cronus and Lucas, who bowed their heads respectfully. "And Ular, you have come to aid us in the battles ahead?"

"My people will certainly declare war upon Tyro, and as Morac's hammer shall likely fall here, I felt it prudent to represent Enoructa in the coming battle," Ular said, his watery voice echoing strongly throughout the chamber.

"War?" General Bode asked, wondering what brought about Enoructa entering the conflict?

"Tyro attacked Tro Harbor, General. He damaged our ship, killed thousands of apes and Troans, and sank most of the 1st Ape Fleet. Now the sorry bastard will suffer for his stupidity," Raven said, his words causing a stir throughout the chamber. The commanders were pleased and concerned with the grim tidings, weighing the strength of their new allies with the dark possibility that they might submit to Tyro before bringing any force to bear. The guards standing post across the throne room couldn't mask their glee, overjoyed with the glad tidings. The apes, Enoructans, Troans and the Earthers were now fighting beside them.

"Ular carries a wondrous gift, Master Vantel, one given him by Brokov the Earther. It is a healing device similar to the one Kato brought with him," Corry wisely shifted the discussion. She would give the full details on the attack on Tro in the privacy of their council chambers.

"We shall make good use of it. There are still many wounded from the siege and the skirmishes since, that have not been healed," Torg said. "I shall have the steward see to our guests, while we apprise you of the state of the realm since you departed," he said to Corry.

"That would be most wise. Terin, if you and Cronus would help the steward settle in our guests, I have a council of state to attend," Corry added.

"As you wish, Highness," he bowed, knowing the time for their informal interactions was at an end for the foreseeable future. Such was life at court, both he and Corry bound by protocols they would just as soon set aside.

"I invite each of you to dine with me this night in celebration of our arrival, and I expect you to be properly attired as befits your station, Terin," she playfully reminded him.

* * *

Corry wasted little time meeting with her council, all gathering in the King's council chamber, its large oval shaped table dominating its center. The statues of the kings of old circled the room as if presiding over every assemblage that ever gathered therein. If only the statues could talk, Corry would be glad of their counsel. General Bode, Commander of the 3rd Torry Army, and General El Tuvo, commander of the 1st Jenaii battlegroup were joined by General Dar Valen, commander of all Torry magantor forces, and Nevias, the garrison commander of Corell. Chief Minister Eli Monsh accompanied Ministers of agriculture and alchemy, Torlan Thunn and Vergus Kalvar, along with the chief minister's apprentice Aldo, who attended him. Torg stood at the head of the table beside Corry. Much had changed since her departure, and he was eager for her to learn of it all, the good and the bad.

"I know you must be weary from your travels, Highness," General Bode acknowledged, recognizing the exhausted look she was desperate to conceal. Traveling over many days upon a magantor extracted a toll on the body.

"True rest evades us all, General, until we end this war. Let us begin," she said, detailing her journey from her arrival at Gregok, and then Torn, where she and Lucas joined the Earthers in rescuing Terin. She described the sinking of the Macon 4th Fleet by the Earthers before relaying the events as they unfolded at Bansoch. Terin's cruel treatment caused more than one angry snort from the ministers and commanders, not the least of which was Torg. She held back much of Terin's suffering, lest the craggy commander of the Elite further lose his temper. Her description of Raven and Lorken sinking two of Tyro's ships at Mordicay brightened the collective mood of the congregants, and an uncharacteristic chuckle from General Bode. She then explained President Matuzak asking her to oversee the treaty of Tro, which resulted in her leaving their magantor escort at Torn Harbor, while she again went by ship as the guest of the Earthers. She then described the attack upon Tro in detail, sparing no sentiments in the devastation wrought. She finished with her objective assessment of Tro's defenses.

"If the Gargoyle 12th Legion conducted the attack, that would be one more legion Tyro has committed to the south," General Bode scratched his chin, studying the eastern half of the map of Arax unfurled across the table.

"Yes, the Troan scouts spotted large elements of the 12th Legion moving upon Gotto. Elos and Lorken also spotted a large Benotrist fleet advancing south along the coast. The fleet should be in range of Tro as we speak," Corry said.

"Will the harbor fall?" Commander Nevias asked, knowing it would strengthen Morac's lines of logistics.

"If they only have to contend with the 12th Legion, I believe they shall hold, but Morac could just as easily commit more troops to finishing them. Morac's problem is the Earthers. Should they fully repair their vessel, I see no way for the harbor to fall," Corry said with a healthy respect of the Earthers' power.

"And yet their captain has joined us here," Bode wondered at that.

"Do not celebrate that fact any time soon, General. He has come to kill Thorton, and shall not engage in our battle until that is done," Corry tempered their optimism as far as Raven was concerned.

"Aye, a wise move," General Valen agreed. "I have heard the reports of Kato and Thorton's exchanges at Mosar. The key in their engagements is finding your target and shooting first. It would be a great boon if Raven can kill Thorton."

"I assume that goes for his ape friend as well, Orlom is his name?" Bode asked.

"Yes, Orlom. He will have to remain out of sight of the enemy as well, lest his weapon draw Thorton's attention," Corry sighed.

"So, once Thorton is dealt with we shall have the equivalent of two Earthers aiding us in battle. That is one better than last time, and we have our Champion returned to us," Nevias happily summarized.

"Terin's power may be compromised," Corry reminded them.

"Compromised? How so?" Torg asked.

Corry went on to elaborate on what befell Terin at Bansoch, having only touched upon it during her first telling. She described the loss of his power and the events that followed, explaining how he was almost invisible to the enemy at Tro, but couldn't drive them off in great numbers as he had before. She hated describing his plight as a punishment from his God, but that was how he described it, and she simply relayed that to the council.

"So, you see, Commander, Terin might not be able to repeat his success from the first siege. We must temper our expectations," Corry cautioned.

"I am not one to understand this God that Terin and our Prince follow, but I trust them to sort it all out. In the short term, we are much better positioned than the last time Morac besieged our walls. We have restored much of our garrison strength, fletched 200,000 arrows and are reinforced with Bode's 3rd Army and the ten telnics of General El Tuvo's Battlegroup. When Morac comes, we shall be ready for him," Torg boldly stated.

"These factors weigh to our advantage, as well as the tidings from the south," Chief Minister Monsh smiled happily.

"What news from the south, Chief Minister?" Corry asked, her gaze shifting suddenly to Eli Monsh.

"General Valen would best speak of it, Highness," Eli directed her question to the magantor General who just returned from the Macon Campaign.

"General Valen?" Corry looked to him, raising an expectant brow.

"Prince Lorn invaded the Macon Empire to relieve the siege of Sawyer. He achieved victory at Cesa and the Horns of Borin, catching the Macons by surprise. He then advanced several forces to the

Macon Capital, forcing King Mortus to negotiate a peace, resulting in the unification of our realms," General Valen stated.

"The unification of our realms?" Corry asked, taken aback.

"Yes. He wed the Macon Crown Princess Deliea, and once she bears an heir, the child shall inherit both thrones. He has further unified our two realms by wedding maidens and soldiers from both lands, as well as officials, commanders and citizens of all stations," General Valen said.

"He what?" Corry wondered if Lorn had lost his mind.

"It is an outlandish move, I confess, Highness, but when we consider the alternatives, one can see the wisdom in it," Chief Minister Monsh conceded.

"The wisdom in it?" She lifted a brow at that.

"Had Prince Lorn been forced to storm the walls of Fleace, much of the 1st Torry Army would have been slain, and the state of the war in the south would be in doubt. The south is now secure, freeing both the Macon and Torry armies there for redeployment elsewhere," General Valen added.

Elsewhere was a coy way of saying Torry North. Corry couldn't really be angry with her brother's decision. Considering the dire situation of the realms, he didn't really have much choice. In truth, they needed the Macon armies and the Torry southern armies if they held any hope of breaking a second siege. As much as they bled Tyro at Corell, the enemy still had many more legions to call upon, where their own list of allies near enough to help was rather limited.

"Very well, what is done is done. I assume my brother is preparing to relieve us," she said, looking to the brighter side of the situation.

"He is, Highness, but requires time to reconstitute his own forces, as well as those of Macon before they can begin their march," Dar Valen explained, before detailing the merging of the armies and the logistical challenges Lorn was dealing with.

"It seems your recruiting of the Earthers in rescuing Terin inadvertently caused them to intercede at Cesa at the approximate time of battle. You can be credited for helping turn the battle, and campaign to Prince Lorn's favor, Highness. It was most fortuitous," Eli Monsh opined, running his slender fingers across his chin.

A chorus of agreements followed that observation, a fact they had previously overlooked. So many coincidences lent credence to Yah's existence and intervention.

"Yes, very fortunate," Corry sighed, recalling the battle at Cesa, which she observed through the *Stenox*'s live feed. "My brother should be made aware of events at Tro and our rescuing of Terin, or that Terin is in fact alive if he is unaware."

"He is aware, Highness. The prince received two visitors just before the treaty of Fleace, two comrades of Terin who revealed that he survived Carapis and was taken to Bansoch, detailing much of his captivity," Dar Valen added.

"Two comrades?" She asked.

"Yes, one a Torry sailor named…"

"Criose?" She hurriedly asked, his nod confirming her guess.

"Yes, and the other was Guilen Estaran, son of…" Dar tried to add.

"Son of Darna, traitor to the Sisterhood," Corry nearly spat.

"Yes, as your testimony has revealed," Dar conceded.

"And both men remain with my brother?"

"They do, Highness," Dar said.

"Very well, Terin must be told. He shall be relieved his friends escaped. Now, what is the state of the palace's provisioning?" She asked. And, so it went, with the council relaying the state of the palace, including food stores, arrows fletched, conscripts recruited and the numbers of wounded still requiring attention. She inquired of their recent scouting forays, trying to build an accurate picture of the enemy's movement.

"I have ordered General Fonis to consolidate his Army at Central City, and be prepared to march in any direction needed, along with the contingent of Notsuan soldiers previously garrisoned at Besos," Torg said. The soldiers of Notsu numbered less than two thousand, and were repositioned to Central City to join the refugees from their fallen city. "As for the wounded, most are gathered here or at Besos. Ular should be put to work healing those here before moving on to Besos."

"I agree, but he needs to return to Corell before Morac's vanguard arrives," Corry cautioned.

"Aye, such a device will prove quite an advantage in battle," Torg said.

"If that is all, gentlemen, I shall take my leave. Each of you is invited to dine with me this night along with my many guests," Corry began to excuse herself.

"Corry, one moment," Torg said, allowing the others to step without before continuing to speak.

"Torg?" She asked, wary of the tone of his voice.

"You should know there is still one ill tiding I must share," he sighed tiredly, feeling his years.

"What is it?" She asked.

"Jonas received a missive the very day Cronus arrived here before traveling on to Tro. I ordered a copy transcribed," Torg said, retrieving the copy, handing it to her.

Corry read the awful words, her heart breaking for Terin. After all he went through to return home only to be greeted with this.

"Where is Jonas now?" She asked, fearing the answer.

* * *

Corry's plans for a quiet dinner with her guests were quickly waylaid by the growing list of friends she could not leave out, forcing a change of venue to the grand hall, where hundreds now gathered. The chamber was nearly square, with white stone pillars running the length of its east and west walls, supporting the base of a series of arches that bowed toward the ceiling. Large lanterns descended from the apex of the ceiling, spinning slowly, casting their flickering light along the uppermost parts of the ceiling. The guests included all in her arrival party and war council along with Galen, Leanna and countless warriors, commanders and palace officials. She presided over the grand feast, sitting at the high table with Torg on one side and Eli Monsh the other, the remaining guests seated at the long tables spread across the chamber, with servants shuttling platters of food from the kitchens. Though rations were a concern for the expected siege, she thought their arrival warranted a celebration, but limited the excess to three courses, which was more than enough to satisfy the stomachs of all her guests, except Raven and Orlom, who would likely help themselves to extra portions. She couldn't miss the two of them sitting at the long table to her immediate left front, each speaking loud enough to wake the dead. Orlom was just in the middle of an ape drinking song, ale spilling out of his tankard as he swayed dramatically back and forth, grinning like an idiot. If she was honest, she was happy he was here. There was such a raw innocence in Orlom and Grigg, that it reminded her so much of her childhood. They looked upon the world with their unassuming nature that made it difficult to be angry with them for long, despite their mischief. With Grigg gone, she wondered how Orlom would endure? She hoped he didn't lose his childlike charm. There were enough of them who were always serious, that he could afford to remain as he was. Of course, he chose that moment to release a thunderous belch, causing the more serious minded guests to turn up their noses, while many others laughed. Raven took that moment to gain his feet, lifting his tankard high into the air while addressing the assemblage.

"I don't know most of you. For those who haven't guessed, I'm Raven. I'd like to raise my cup to a few of my friends here. The first is Cronus Kenti," Raven pointed him out at his place at the end of the table, siting beside his beloved Leanna. "Cronus saved my life the first day we met, spared me getting stabbed in the back, which I thought was right neighborly of him. We have been joined at the hip more times than not ever since. I am lucky to call him my friend, but not nearly as lucky as he is for wedding the Lady Leanna!" Raven downed a sip, the crowd cheering in agreement as he continued. Raven went on to laud Elos, speaking of his impressive display at Tro, which the Jenaii warrior didn't react one way or the other, sitting among his fellow Jenaii with stoic indifference while Raven moved on to Orlom.

"Next is my good friend here, the mighty Orlom, Hero of Bansoch!" Raven slapped the young gorilla on the back, Orlom grinning at the gesture. "Orlom fought as fierce as a hundred warriors during the battle at the Queen's palace. You will all be glad he has joined us for the battle ahead. He is looking forward to a little payback to those foul, nasty, good for nothing gargoyles!"

A round of cheers followed that declaration.

"Me and Boss are gonna kill bunches of 'em!" Orlom added for good measure, receiving a chorus of laughter.

"Over there we have Ular, and Lucas!" He lifted his tankard toward their place at the next table, where they sat surrounded by members of the Torry Elite. "They seem to spend every waking moment sparring. Good luck to the lot of you training with them in the yard."

Lucas sheepishly shook his head, not comfortable being the center of attention, when Corry spoke, acknowledging his brave and loyal service.

"Lucas is to be commended for his adherence to duty. He was my brave companion throughout my quest to rescue our Champion. He is loyal and steadfast, and an asset to the King's Elite," Corry proclaimed, causing a chorus of hearty cheers. She then complimented Ular with equal praise, expounding his fell deeds at Bansoch and Tro.

"Your Princess and I haven't always been friendly. As those who know me can attest, I don't care much for most Araxan leaders, especially royals," Raven said, his harsh words drawing a pall over the crowd. "But I can raise my cup to a brave woman who journeyed all the way to Torn Harbor, with a wild story about visions and Terin being held captive, asking for our help. She proved something to me that day, that she was willing to risk her own life to save our mutual friend. Hell, she even led the mission to rescue him, cutting several throats in the process as my crewmates tell it. I almost feel sorry for Morac when he returns here with her in charge. She'll likely have his balls in a vice, and she's the type to twist them all the way off and smile while she's doing it. To you Princess!" Raven raised his tankard, before taking a generous gulp.

The room went deafly silent, few knowing how to take his lewd manner of speech, until Corry rescued him.

"For those who don't know our dear Captain Raven. His words were most complimentary, especially when you consider the crude appellation he gave to Tyro in his very throne room," Corry smiled knowingly.

146

Raven gave her a look, wondering which crude comment she was referring.

"What did he say to the emperor, Highness?" Lucas asked the question so many others wanted the answer to.

"He referred to Tyro as… an ASS," she smirked, shaking her head, the hall bursting in laughter.

"I wasn't lying," Raven shrugged, knowing she must have heard that tale from either Lorken or Terin. Of course, he said so many derogatory things at Fera he forgot most of them. "Now, my last compliment goes to the man many here owe their lives to, and a good friend of Cronus and myself… Terin!" Raven lifted his tankard toward Terin, who sat between Cronus and Aldo, at the end of his table, now attired as a Torry Elite. Gone were the Earther garb of black trousers, shirt and jacket, replaced with bright silver mail and sea blue tunic. If Raven was to guess, he thought Terin would rather have kept his Earth garb.

"I first met Terin just before the war started at Rego. All I knew then was that he was a friend of Cronus, which was good enough for me since Cronus is a good judge of character, which is why he befriended me in the first place," Raven said, drawing a few eye rolls from some, and chuckles from others. Many in the assemblage that knew Kato were taken aback by his blunt speech and immense size, wondering if there were any two men more different than the two Earthers?

"It wasn't until Cronus was captured and Terin volunteered to join in his rescue that we all knew he was a good kid. It didn't take long for him to start showing what he was capable with that sword of his, especially during our escape from Fera. Unfortunately, that was the last I saw of him until Corry showed up in Torn, saying he was captured. After hearing about all the gargoyles he killed here at Corell, and at Mosar, I can't say I'm surprised. Terin!" He proclaimed, raising his tankard high before downing a gulp.

"Caleph!" One solider shouted, coming to his feet, joining Raven's toast.

"Caleph! Caleph!" nearly the entire assemblage stood, heralding his name, save for the Jenaii and those seated at the high table. Terin cringed with the adulation, wanting to crawl under the table and hide.

Corry shared a sympathetic look with him, their eyes meeting briefly, before gifting him a small smile. She knew he felt much shame for all he endured, and the terrible secret so few of them were privy, a secret she knew held no mark against him, though he wouldn't listen. Should he truly feel guilt for being Tyro's blood when he also shared blood with Torg, and King Kal? It was silly, but then again, there would always be someone to begrudge him his Benotrist kin, and if there were, they would be certain to receive a thorough tongue lashing from her. Torg had yet to tell Terin of Jonas, as she asked him to hold off until after the celebration. She felt he deserved at least some moments of peace, wishing she could protect him from all the grief and sorrow that was constantly thrown at him.

The festivity continued with many others standing forth, heralding one comrade or another who distinguished themselves during the siege and the countless skirmishes since. Many of the tales she had heard before, but some she hadn't. She listened as one after another provided harrowing tales of courage, brotherhood and sacrifice. Commander of the west wall, Cors Balka, raised his tankard, recalling the painful loss of his fellow wall commanders during the siege, Sergon Vas and Gais Luven, who died defending the north and east walls. His tribute followed several more with equal emotion. Nearly seven in ten defenders died in the siege, a terrible cost that would have meant certain defeat if not for the timely intervention of the relieving armies. This was followed by the men and commanders of General Bode's 3rd Army, who suffered many losses at Costelin, Rego and Corell. Each telnic commander rattled off countless names, leaving so many more unspoken, for it would take days to fully list the fallen. It was Commander Mastorn who drew Corry's attention most, the man was once Cronus' telnic commander before his capture at Tuft's Mountain.

"Among all the brave men who have fallen in this cursed war, I dare not overlook the valiant one hundred of the 5th Unit of my 9th Telnic, the men that King's Elite Cronus Kenti led heroically into battle. There stands the only survivor of the brave one hundred.

Most died in battle, while a few unfortunates suffered terribly in the foul dungeons of Fera. I knew many of those men, all friends and brothers to their commander, a man I respect more than any other. Cronus Kenti, I salute you and all those fought beside you in the 5th Unit!" Commander Mastorn declared, looking at Cronus while thrusting his fist to his chest.

Cronus gained his feet, returning the salute. Leanna looked up from her seat, noticing the watery depths of her husband's eyes, that heart felt reminder of all that he suffered and lost. She thought he might not be able to speak without crying, but he swallowed the tears, and spoke aloud. "I only stand here free and alive because my friends risked all to set me free, two of which are in this very chamber. I wish I could fully honor the memory of my men with great deeds worthy of a song, but such is vanity. I can only truly honor them by seeing this war to its end and the preservation of our land and people. Once Raven, Lorken and Terin rescued me from that fell place, only Arsenc and I remained from the 5th Unit. But he has since fallen at Kregmarin. I dare not overlook those brave men who bled the enemy to their last. I could continue on with those we lost in Yatin and Maconia, so many Torry sons that shall never return home. Commander Mastorn has spoken kindly of my honor, and I am touched by his words, but am equally humbled by all of you, and all those I have fought beside in this awful war. I know well the dangers each of you has faced, standing to post in the face of impossible odds. You, my brave fellows of Corell are the truest heroes, my brothers of blood and steel. I salute you!"

With that, nearly every man stood, saluting in kind, a serene quiet settling over the crowd. It was then Corry called Galen forth to perform, stepping into the open space between the rows of tables in the center of the chamber. Raven mentally shook his head as Galen stood with mandolin in hand, attired in long green tunic with billowy sleeves and wearing long pointy shoes. Raven thought he looked like an idiot, which matched his dull wit and gangly face. Of course, the minstrel being the minstrel, he sucked up to all his friends, making them think he was decent.

If they only knew you as I know you, he growled to himself, still recalling all those miles he walked after Galen stole his ocran, and the mob that beat him up after Galen stole his pistol. *I wonder if anyone will notice if I toss him over the castle wall later tonight?* He mused happily at the thought as Galen began.

> *"Kal, Kal, oh ancient king*
> *That bards write and poets sing…"*

Galen sang the ancient ballad once again, just as he sang it on the eve of the final assault upon Corell. He strode back and forth between the rows of tables, plucking the strings of his mandolin, his gaze sweeping the sea of faces staring back, seeing the effect the melody played on their emotions. What greater thrill was there for a bard or minstrel than to move their audience's emotions with a powerful ballad? He smiled inwardly finding Leanna and Cronus looking back, pleased to again seeing them reunited. Of all the men of Corell, it was Cronus he counted among his closest friends, having journeyed so far together. He was pleased to see Terin returned from the dead, taking his rightful place among these brave warriors. He regarded Raven briefly, refusing to acknowledge the oversized buffoon, rightly guessing the Earther was thinking of how to kill him. He recalled one of his many conversations with Prince Lorn, when his future king advised him to pen ballads celebrating the common folks and soldiers whose deeds were small but vital to their cause. He penned many since that day, but thought this night belonged to all the people, and what could unite all than an ode to the ancient king?

This was the first time Terin heard the ballad since he learned of his kinship to the ancient king. Kal, the name was but a word, a casual utterance that held no more meaning to him than that. How wrong he was. Kal was his ancient kin, his father many times removed, and the source of all his power. He couldn't help but think he had failed his ancestor, his full power now blocked by Yah, replaced with what it was now. So much rested on his shoulders now, so much hung in the balance. He could see it in the eyes of the men, each expecting him to do what he did before, driving the enemy off time and again. *What will they do when they learn that he can no longer do that?*

THE CHRONICLES OF ARAX

Would they give up, or curse him? What will happen when they learn all his secrets? Will they believe his kinship to Tyro has cursed him in the eyes of Yah? He thought of the first siege, and how simple it all was then. All he had to do was fight as he felt himself led. Now, his mind was torn in so many directions. He was the blood of Kal, the blood of Torg, and the blood of Tyro. He wished his father was here, wondering where he had gone off to, though where else would he go but to see his mother? Torg told him they had much to speak of after the festivities, and did so with his serious tone. Of course, Torg always used a serious tone. The man couldn't say good morn or good evening without doing so with terrible authority. Kal… he heard that name again fall from Galen's lips, another reminder of all that weighed upon him. It was all too much. He wasn't Kal or Tyro, or even Torg. He was the son of Jonas and Valera, and they were only simple, honest people at heart. That was who he was, no matter how others saw him.

The festivities continued late into the night, with bawdy drinking songs sung by soldiers deep into their cups. Cronus and Leanna retired early, sharing their first night together since his last visit. Galen and several other minstrels played lighthearted tunes, fueling the merry atmosphere. Raven and Orlom attracted a small army of soldiers listening as Raven regaled them with his adventures. Most wanted to hear the tale of his escape from Fera and his journey to Tro. Most everyone in the garrison heard the tale, but only few knew any details. They listened with rapt attention as he told of his battle in the arena, his wedding and bedding Tosha and his escape from that foul place. The gragglogg attack and their trek across the wilds of the north were equally exciting, not to mention Axenville and Tro. Few knew any of these details, and none heard of his adventures after Tro. Speaking of the Ape Republic and the attack on Tro, drew several more questions.

"Will the apes come?" One soldier asked after Raven finished describing the battle at Tro, his eyes pregnant with hope.

By now, Raven was sitting on the table, with his feet resting on the bench, with the crowd gathered in a large circle around him and Orlom.

"Of course, they'll come. Most of you never saw an ape before tonight," he said, slapping Orlom on the shoulder, the young gorilla looking back at him with his toothy grin. "And those that did, haven't seen a pissed off ape. Well, our boy Tyro isn't going to be happy when an ape army comes barreling out of the Ape Hills crushing everything in its path."

"We just have to live long enough to see it," one soldier said glumly, knowing they might all be dead before that happened.

"Listen fellas, Morac ain't taking this castle. I don't care how many idiots he brings with him. You got something you didn't have last time," Raven said.

"What is that?" more than one of them asked at the same time.

"Me," Raven jerked a thumb at his chest.

* * *

Torg retired early from the festivities, waiting for Terin upon Zar Crest, the command platform perched high above the inner keep. He ordered the guards away, leaving the platform for himself. He rested his forearms upon the parapet, gazing off toward the north, the horizon disappearing into the starry night. It was times like these he dearly missed his late wife, his dearest Veanna. Torg was never one to yield to emotions, but even his iron heart could bleed from time to time, especially when he thought of her. What would she think of the heartless façade he displayed with practiced regularity? She would either laugh at his stupidity for thinking anyone would believe it, or scold him for scaring the children.

"Bah, she'd laugh at me, and say I couldn't scare anyone," Torg shook his head. It wasn't true though, for Torg scared everyone, save for his wife. She would simply laugh at him before planting a sweet kiss on his cheek. Oh, how he wished she was here for another reason, filling a role poor Torg felt wholly unsuited for, comforting their grandson. And with that thought, said grandson appeared behind him.

"Grandfather?" Terin called out from the edge of the platform, before Torg waved him forth to join him, the boy resting his elbows upon the parapet in similar fashion.

"It's a lovely night," Terin added, feeling the need to say something considering Torg was in no hurry to do so.

"Aye, a lovely night. I spent a good many nights since you left, standing here and looking at this sky, wondering if you would ever make it back to us. Thankfully your father's visions gave us the direction to find you," Torg said, keeping his eyes to the horizon, in no hurry to look at him, lest he break.

"You said we would speak of my father and where he went. I thought he would return for my mother. Is he with her or did he go somewhere else?" Terin asked, sensing something amiss.

"He went to find her," Torg sighed.

"Good."

"But she wasn't at their home," Torg's words were like ice down his back.

"…" Terin was a loss for words.

"He received a missive from one of your grandfather's elite, claiming to have taken her to Fera, inviting Jonas to answer his father's summons," Torg said, looking over at Terin's ashen face.

"How did he find her? Was it the necklace?" Terin's voice nearly broke.

"Necklace?" Torg wondered at that, but Terin didn't hear him. The boy sunk to the floor, resting his back to the parapet, too weak to move.

"I've failed them too," he moaned.

"Get up, Terin!" Torg growled, reaching down, grabbing him by the collar of his mail, dragging him to his feet. "There's no place for self pity in the heart of our Champion. It is a luxury for others, not for you."

"I am no champion, not anymore," he shook his head.

SLAP!

"Enough!" Torg growled. He wasn't good at these sorts of things. Mothers and grandmothers were made to comfort children, not cranky old men. "It was only a matter of time before Tyro figured it all out. You couldn't hide what you are forever. Your mother is probably safe as far as we know. Tyro will use her to draw your father to him, and what I wouldn't give to be able to overhear the conversation between them. Your father didn't want you to know any of this until you returned to Corell. It is here where you must stay to fulfill your duty."

"Grandfather, my power is gone. I can't do what I did before," he sighed.

"You still have great power, only different. Your God is tempering you like fine steel, shaping you into the weapon that serves his purpose," Torg felt strange speaking of Terin and Lorn's God, but the boy needed to hear it.

"There is a difference between shaping a weapon, and trading a sword for a knife. That's all I am now, a blunted knife," he felt ashamed for his self-pity, but was weary from putting on a good front for others, despite his promise to Yah to follow him faithfully.

"Then be the best blasted blunted knife there is, and stick it in Morac's eye. Now listen good, Terin. Tyro isn't your only grandfather. As you well know, I'm more frightening than he is. Get some rest lad, for tomorrow you're mine. The training arena awaits you. You won't suffer alone, as Cronus and Lucas have been absent for a long time as well," Torg said, stepping briefly away before stopping in the middle of the platform.

"Oh, I almost forgot to give you this," Torg said, walking back, drawing his sword from its scabbard, handing it to Tern.

Terin received the weapon, able to see starlight reflecting off its inky black blade, with flashes of milky white shimmering along its surface as it moved. It was sharpened to a fine edge, and felt light in his hand, with finely woven steel bands around its hilt, and crafted cross guard. It was a beautiful weapon, a sword bult for a king.

"Is this…" he was at a loss.

"This is yours. I meant to have completed it when you were marked at your initiation, but I was distracted with the siege. I began working on it the day you left. It's not a blade I expect you to wield in battle considering the Sword of Light you again carry, but I forge such a blade for all the King's Elite, and you deserve one for that alone, let alone being my grandson. I'm proud of you boy. Don't ever forget that," with that Torg stepped away, leaving Terin there clutching the blade to his chest as if it were his most prized possession.

* * *

She watched the two of them from the shadows below, waiting for Torg to leave before joining him upon the platform. Corry found him holding the blade in his arms, looking down at it, his watery eyes visible in the starlight. She didn't want to startle him, but couldn't slow her pace, wanting to comfort him after Torg delivered the ill tidings. He looked up just as she neared, his beautiful face framed against the starlit sky. She couldn't look at him without her heart beating beneath her breast.

"Corry," he gave her that easy smile that set everything to right.

"He gave you your sword, I see," she regarded the impressive weapon with a discerning eye.

"Yes. He must have labored on this for many days. It is the finest gift I have ever had, except maybe my father's sword. This one required a great effort to forge it, so its meaning is greater, at least to me," he sighed.

"It is a wondrous blade, Terin. Might I hold it?"

"Of course," he handed it to her gently.

She held it aloft, starlight playing off its inky black steel. She found it surprisingly light, and not overly long, almost as if Torg intended it as a second blade, which made sense. Could Terin learn to wield two blades at once? Considering his ability to learn, she had little doubt, and handed it back to him.

"A blade worthy of you. I can tell the pride Master Torg put into forging it, forging it especially for you. He loves you," she said, cupping his chin in her hands, keeping his eyes to hers.

"And I, him. At least his blood is something to be proud of," he sighed.

"All your blood makes you who you are, and what you are is the man I love, Terin Caleph."

"Despite my father's father? How can you love me knowing who sired my father?"

"And who are you to question your Princess? You swore an oath to the throne, to my royal kin, and to me. You are worthy of my love,

Terin. Tyro's sins are not yours to bear, nor are they your father's. We all stand upon our own actions and choices."

"I said something similar to my father, and where is he now? He seeks out my mother, turning himself over to Tyro when the realm needs him most. As much as it pains me to think of my mother alone in Tyro's keeping, my father's blood is needed here, especially with my power impaired."

"Your father knows what he is doing, Terin. All I have to do is look in his eyes to know it true. He sent you off long ago to Rego with only your sword in hand, trusting your path to his God. He knew it was perilous, but did it all the same. He trusted me with his vision, and it led me back to your arms. Trust him in this, just as he trusts you to carry us through the battles ahead."

"But why put all that on me when he could turn the battle by himself?" he hated the way he was whining, but needed to vent his true feelings.

"Perhaps because your mother is alone and with child, while you have many here who love you," she reasoned.

"With child?"

"Yes, did Torg not tell you?"

"It didn't come up."

"Well, place that among Jonas' reasons for going. He is going to make certain the woman he loves is safe and alive. I can sympathize," she smiled knowingly.

"I… I can sympathize also. If anything happened to you, there is no where I would not go, anything I would not do," he set the blade down, taking her into his arms. He ran his fingers gently along her cheek, losing himself in her beautiful eyes.

"When this battle is ended, you and I shall wed. Is that understood, Terin Caleph?" she lifted her chin, holding his gaze.

"As you command, Princess," he smiled, pressing his lips to hers.

CHAPTER 10

The following days found Terin, Cronus and Lucas suffering Torg's full attention. The craggy Master of Arms drilled his charges to exhaustion dawn to dusk, extracting every breath from their labored lungs. They practiced with blunted training swords, pairing up or taking on multiple opponents simultaneously. Corry no longer watched from the shadows, but joined in the training, donning thick leather mail and high boots as she shuffled amidst the sand of the arena. Torg would not pair her with Terin, for the boy could not or would not fully engage her. He recalled what Jonas said of their Kalinian blood, that they could not harm those they loved, or were fond of. It explained much in why Terin never performed as well in their training environment as he did in combat. His mind was always holding him back, crippling him in their mock engagements. He did notice that the more Terin trained with his comrades, the more power and skill he was able to exert, as if his mind was teaching his body that he would not harm his friends. Torg smiled inwardly as Terin managed to defeat Lucas on several occasions in hand to hand bouts, a rarity for any of the royal elite to pull off.

Elos led many of the Jenaii in the training sessions, each displaying their unique advantages in individual combat. They were able to lift into the air, slashing with their taloned toes at exposed flesh, or driving an opponent backward, thrusting their swords and spears at their enemies' legs with devastating efficiency.

After several days, Ular joined in the training, having passed on his healing device to the matron Dresila, who was accustomed to the device Kato lent them the use of after the siege. Ular instructed Matron Dresila on the differences with the newer regenerator, which held a charge longer, and was far easier to use. They worked tirelessly in the wards, healing as many wounded men as possible, prioritizing the most crippling wounds first. Soldiers with eye injuries were the quickest to heal, and displayed the most impressive transformation from liability to asset. Men who were crippled with broken spines were prioritized second, removing the intense car they required tending them day and night. Most of these types of injuries were taken care of when they still had use of Kato's regenerator, but the wounded continued to filter in long after Kato departed. Now they were free to heal all sorts of injuries, clearing the wards and restoring many soldiers to full duty. Once Corell's wounded were healed, Ular and the Matrons would move on to Besos, healing the wounded gathered there, under the strict guideline that the device must return before Morac's army appeared.

With Ular joining their training bouts, the Torry Elite were treated with his and Lucas' relentless battles, a contest of Lucas' physical strength and Ular's elusiveness. The Enoructan Champion darted to and fro, flipping backwards with unnatural speed and flexibility. Torg painted brown circles above and alongside Lucas' helm, designating them as eyes for Ular to target with his daggers. The Enoructan landed blow after blow, the blunted knives leaving indentations where they often struck true. Ular quickly became a favorite of the men, sharing with them many of his techniques, which they impressively began to copy, though few if any could match his natural gifts.

It was Terin, however, that drew the most interest. His unusual gifts in battle were rarely seen in the training arena, but Torg and the others quickly came to realize that his new gifts were far easier to discern, if not understand. He moved with almost a fluid motion that matched the air itself, making him difficult to see unless one concentrated on him, excluding all other stimulation, which was nigh impossible in the arena, let alone combat. Torg heard the men complain that fighting Terin was like fighting blind, or striking at the wind.

It was Terin's bouts with Ular that were the most inspiring and frustrating for poor Torg. They were inspiring by the impressive skill and fluidity of battle they each displayed, but even Ular couldn't keep pace with the Torry Champion, finding Terin's blade touching his neck at the end of each session. Ular saluted Terin with his sword held across his face, nodding his head respectfully, honored to hone his skill against the fabled heir of Kal. Their bouts were frustrating for Torg as they drew crowds, his men stopping their own training to observe the dazzling display before Torg growled for them to return to their drills.

Surprisingly, it was Cronus that gave Terin the most difficulty, the hero of Tuft's Mountain gaining the upper hand in several of their bouts. Torg scolded Terin for holding back, but the boy pleaded that he hadn't. The men would gather around Cronus, trying to glean whatever they could learn from him, thinking he must have the answer in combating Terin. Torg eventually realized the answer, so simple that it should have been obvious. Cronus was Terin's closest friend, almost a brother to him, and his mind couldn't allow any harm to come to him, even in mock battle. Eventually his mind would overcome that as it had with the others, but Cronus was the last holdout, with Terin gaining the upper hand in more and more bouts as they practiced. Torg couldn't imagine Terin battling Corry. She would probably win every time as much as the boy was smitten with her.

Eventually Raven and Orlom made their way to their training sessions, the large Earther taking Orlom aside to hone their shooting. Torg arranged several targets set up according to Raven's recommendations. He personally found Raven to be nothing as he expected. His reputation for brutality seemed rooted in his massive size and irreverent demeanor, but he sensed the friendliness in the man that others often couldn't or wouldn't see. He was quick with a joke or jovial banter, and didn't seem to take anything too seriously, even the prospect of facing hundreds of thousands of enemy soldiers. His optimism could be infectious, as many of the men gravitated toward him, hoping victory would be as easy as Raven claimed. Unfortunately, Torg knew better, but wouldn't douse a flame of optimism that the men so desperately needed. Hope was that one thing that could drive men onward despite the darkness rising to swallow them. One thing he would say in favor of Raven.... he was loyal to his friends, and proved that with both Cronus and Terin.

Torg decided to let the men gather about and observe Raven and Orlom's first practice, knowing it was best to sate their curiosity before sending them back to their drills. They looked on with wonder as Raven drew from his holster with blinding speed, his laser striking the wooden targets Torg erected, with a series of painted circles one within the other. He struck the centermost circle with uncanny regularity. Orlom was another matter, but the young gorilla showed steady improvement with every day. Raven had Orlom advance his skills with movement drills.

"In battle the enemy is constantly moving, and so are we. We'll start with our movement and advance with both us and the target moving," Raven said, before walking slowly back and forth in front of the target, firing as he went. Orlom copied his movement, before they increased speed. Eventually Raven engineered a pulley system, drawing the target back and forth on a rope, while Orlom fired at it.

Torg often stood off to the side, tossing sticks at Orlom's head, simulating arrows and spears being tossed about to simulate combat conditions they would likely face atop the palace. Torg reminded Raven of Coach O'Brien back in the academy who would throw foam tubes at Lorken during practice, simulating pass rushers in his face. He could imagine Torg and O'Brien getting along like pigs in slop. He once referred to Torg as COACH, in passing, which Orlom immediately picked up, using the moniker whenever speaking with the Master of Arms, especially when he started practicing bladed weapons with the others.

"Watch your feet!" Torg would caution Orlom, who struggled mightily in that regard.

"How is this, Coach?" Orlom would offer back, bouncing back and forth on the balls of his feet, balancing his shield and sword as he moved across the sand.

Terin nearly facepalmed overhearing their exchanges, but Torg took it all in good humor, focusing more on Orlom understanding

THE CHRONICLES OF ARAX

what he was teaching. Raven would stand off to the side, watching the two of them, shaking his head.

"Something humors you, I see," Corry said, approaching him while removing her helm, shaking her hair free while taking a break from her sparring.

"Just watching Torg and Orlom. I think Orlom is rubbing off on him," Raven lifted his chin in their general direction just as Orlom hooted excitedly upon executing a simple task Torg had asked of him, as if he managed some grand achievement.

"Rubbing off on him?" She wondered if she truly wanted to know what that meant.

"It means wearing him out until he starts thinking just like Orlom," Raven said.

"Oh," she shrugged, looking over at the two of them for a time. "Perhaps he is," she couldn't think of two people more different than Orlom and Torg. Perhaps Elos, but the list was very small.

"Nice place you have here," Raven said, looking at the high domed ceiling with its stone arches arcing toward its center, and the seating set high upon the walls that circled the chamber, where spectators could observe the activity below in safety and leisure. It was almost like a sporting arena back on Earth, albeit a small one.

"The training arena is vitally important for honing the skills of our warriors. It can also be quite humbling, as I can well attest," she gave him a knowing look.

"You're no pampered Princess, I'll give you that."

"Captain Raven, was that a compliment directed at me? I am flattered," she smiled, touching a hand mockingly to her breast.

"Any woman that goes through what you did to rescue my nephew over there, is alright in my book," he smiled, jerking a thumb over his left shoulder in Terin's general direction.

She stifled a laugh. Every time he referred to Terin as his nephew made her realize why Terin and Cronus were so taken with the big oaf. He always made light of EVERYTHING, as if all the problems they faced were no bother at all. She had to admit she was wrong about Raven, especially after her first encounter after Molten Isle. Perhaps all they needed was a second chance, proving their first im-

161

pressions wrong. It was then she recalled Raven's dislike of Galen, and the events surrounding their first encounter.

"You are much different than I expected, Raven," she smiled.

"Is that good or bad?"

"Good. Very good. Perhaps all we needed was a second chance, with the life of someone we each care about in the balance. I am very glad Terin was your friend, and not just for your help in rescuing him. He is so very fond of you, as well as all your crew. He seems much happier with you around, as well as Cronus and the others. It brightens my heart to see it after he suffered so."

"Sometimes all someone needs to know is that someone has their back, that they're not alone," he sighed, recalling a memory, and not a happy one at that.

"You weren't here during the siege. If ever ten thousand souls felt alone, it was all of us trapped here, surrounded by Morac's host," she said with a faraway look, recalling the awful visage of her father's head so cruelly displayed by Morac. It was meant to taunt her, to crumble her resolve, and frighten her in surrendering the palace. Morac learned that day that Corry was made of sterner stuff.

"From what I've been told, you are much stronger now, with Bode's army and the bird people," Raven could barely pronounce Jenaii, using the crude description instead.

"In many ways, yes. But these forces now guarding us, were counted among our relief forces last time. This time we have to rely on forces farther afield, that might not reach us before the battle is ended. It is all very fluid, and unpredictable," she coldly stated their position.

"Last time, you didn't know Kato was with your cavalry. He would have been better positioned here. He could've perched himself way up in your highest towers, and targeted the enemy for miles around, taking out all their commanders and working his way down the chain of command. Hell, he could've leveled their launch towers as soon as they appeared. I doubt the palace would've been in any danger of falling when the cavalry arrived," Raven said, though his definition of cavalry represented the entire relief force, not just the mounted units as she interpreted, though she could guess his meaning. Sometimes she had to interpret half of what he said, filtering his many expressions.

"Your presence will be most appreciated," she conceded.

"Eventually. Unfortunately, I won't be able to do all that until Thorton shows himself. I need to kill him before he realizes I'm even here. In the mean time the rest of you have to hold Morac at bay. Of course, if things are looking grim, I might have to adjust that plan. It reminds me of something Admiral Kruger used to tell me, *a good commander adjusts his plans to the situation, not the situation to his plans,*" Raven said, wondering if the Admiral actually said, or repeated it from General Patton.

"Admiral Kruger?" She made a face.

"My old boss in Space Fleet. I was very fond of that man. He was tough, grizzled commander who I would have followed anywhere. Maybe someday you'll meet him, if they ever find us that is," Raven shrugged.

"Perhaps I shall. I am pleased we have come to an accord, Raven. Perhaps you could do likewise with another that you are openly hostile to," she said.

"Who's that?"

"Galen."

"The minstrel? That two bit, lying weasel? I'd just as soon blast a hole through his skull…" he growled before she interrupted.

"He has been a loyal comrade of Terin and Cronus, as well as Leanna and myself since arriving here. Perhaps we can learn something from Terin when it comes to forgiveness," she said, reminding him of the strange occurrence in Queen Letha's throne room when Terin invoked the blinding power of the Sword of Light through his forgiveness of Deva. If Terin could forgive Deva, then Raven certainly should be able to forgive Galen, shouldn't he?

"I'll tell you what, Corry, if Galen stays away from me, I'll steer clear of him."

"Is forgiveness beyond you?" she challenged.

"He's still alive, ain't he? If that ain't forgiveness, then I don't know what is, just don't expect me to act all buddy buddy with the scoundrel."

"Fair enough," she conceded. With that she excused herself from the arena, matters of state requiring her attention.

* * *

Two days hence.

It was early morn when a cohort of Jenaii magantors appeared in the southern sky, bringing tiding from their King El Anthar, summoning Elos to their capital fortress of El Orva. Rumors spread of a Nayborian host gathering along the Jenaii border, believed to be led by Dethine himself, requiring Elos' presence to counter the Naybin Champion's Sword of Light with his own. And so, Terin met with Elos upon the southeast magantor platform jutting from the inner keep, bidding his friend farewell. Elos' warbird was stabled beside Wind Racer, its silver coat and black beak and talons a similar hue to Terin's mount. Terin visited Wind Racer each day, feeding his friend personally while stroking his beak and neck, the soothing gesture connecting him to the great avian. That was where Elos found him as he prepared to depart, looking on as Terin stood in Wind Racer's stall, comforting the beast.

"A kingly mount worthy of the blood of Kal," Elos said, causing Terin to turn about at the sound of his friend's voice.

"A wondrous gift from your King, one unworthy of this poor servant," Terin sighed, caressing Wind Racer's beak one last time before joining Elos in the center platform that connected the surrounding stalls. Elos already saddled his own warbird, drawing him from his stall onto the center platform, before leading him toward the archway upon the southeast corner of the structure, daylight spilling through the opening. Terin walked beside him as they led the strutting avian onto the outer platform where the roof gave way to open air, with the surrounding view of the southern approaches of Corell displayed in panoramic wonder. Elos' dark mane lifted in the balmy air before settling his blue helm over his head, his silver eyes staring through the narrow slits like a bird of prey.

"You are worthy, Terin. Yah still speaks to you when you deign to listen. I know you fear your weakness, but hold firm in what you have learned and trust in his divine guidance," Elos stated matter of fact.

"I will do my best, Elos. I would be lying if I said your leaving didn't bother me. I hoped to have you fighting beside me when Morac arrives," Terin confessed.

"As I would favor your company in my battles in the south. Should we win the day, I shall hasten back to join you in battle," Elos assured him, before climbing into the saddle, bidding him farewell. His magantor strutted forth, spreading its wings as it bounded from the platform, dipping below Terin's line of sight before ascending.

Terin looked on as Elos' magantor swept into the sky, joined by his escort who were already in the air, circling the castle several times awaiting him to join them. They sped off southward, disappearing over the horizon.

"Hurry back, Elos. I need you," Terin sighed, his words lost in the swirling winds of those airy heights before returning to his training.

* * *

Three days hence.

The late afternoon brought ill tidings to the garrison, the returning magantor patrols reporting of enemy movement along their eastern border. The Battle of Torry North had begun.

CHAPTER 11

Kriton's eyes blazed like embers, transfixed by the carnage wrought in the valley below. He gleefully observed the small distant forms scurrying amidst the burning huts of the small village, fleeing the Benotrist cavalry who struck them down with their long swords, like brittle grass before a scythe. The small village rested along the narrow steam that meandered the shallow valley, easy game for the Benotrist raiders. Kriton dispatched mounted units both up and down stream before the assault, trapping the populace as his larger host swept down from the east. Gargoyles swarmed amid the chaos, each ocran carrying one Benotrist rider and a gargoyle upon its back, the creatures springing from their mounts amid the fray, striking out at any targets upon uneven ground the cavalry might struggle with. It was a unique tactic that Kriton developed for this campaign, blending the speed and power of the cavalry with the flexibility and range of the gargoyles. He spent a great deal of time since the previous siege working these tactics, and conditioning their ocran to tolerate gargoyles, which they were naturally averse. With the additional cavalry Thorton redirected from Nisin, they now had plenty to secure their lines of communication, freeing him to raid deep into the enemy's territory.

Kriton's lips twisted with wicked delight, watching as one Torry peasant after another fell to his Benotrist cavalry and gargoyle auxiliaries. He spotted one Torry man evade a hasty sword strike from a charging mount, before stepping into the path of another, taking a slash across his back. He toppled in the matted grass along the stream just beyond the village, attempting to rise before another ocran trampled him underfoot. Women carrying their babies were run down, slaughtered just beyond the village outskirts along the west bank, the Benotrist cavalry easily traversing the shallow stream in pursuit. The awful scene unfolded in ghoulish horror, the Torry peasants slaughtered beneath the midday sun, smoke painting the blue sky above in mocking hues of black and gray.

"Bring me prisoners for the stakes!" Kriton ordered Borgon, 8th among Tyro's Elite. The Benotrist warrior acted as his second in their cavalry raids.

"Aye, with pleasure," Borgon grinned, kicking his heals, urging his mount down the near slope toward the village.

Kriton breathed in the cool spring air, his dark nostrils flaring, savoring the coming season and the promise of victory. This was the fourth village they sacked in as many days, sweeping deep into the Torry countryside ahead of their main host. The Torries abandoned every village and holdfast within thirty leagues of the road connecting Notsu to Corell, forcing Kriton to expand his cavalry raids beyond that range, striking hamlets and villages the local populace thought safe. He waited impatiently for his men and gargoyles to finish the pitiful rabble and drag forth the captives he requested, which amounted to a disappointing three old men and a young mother, whose child was slaughtered after being stripped from her arms. They were dragged up the shallow rise, dragged by ocran with ropes around their shoulders or midriff, holding desperately to the unforgiving twine, trying desperately to steady themselves while suffering the ground passing painfully beneath them. They were deposited before Kriton's mount in a disordered state, the young mother unconscious, the men faring little better.

Kriton signaled his men to begin, each drawing away their helpless victims, stretching them out upon the grassy hillside, tying their wrists and ankles to long stakes driven deep into the ground. They flailed helplessly, held down by four men or gargoyles apiece. Once secured, Kriton dismounted, drawing his dagger as he knelt over the

nt.

nearest one to him, a frightened older man with silvered hair and desperate gray eyes that looked upon him pleadingly for mercy that did not abide in him. Kriton carefully dug his dagger into the man's lower belly, blood oozing from the shallow cut. He deftly worked his clawed digits into the small opening, before widening the wound, his men holding the flailing man still as he slowly disemboweled him, setting the organs gently upon his upper stomach. It was done methodically, with as much care as Kriton could manage to prolong the man's suffering. He repeated the cruel act upon the others, one at a time, leaving them dying painfully upon the hillside overlooking their dead village.

Kriton wiped the blood on his hands upon the grass before mounting his ocran, ordering his men north and west, hoping to find the Torry cavalry somewhere ahead and destroy them.

* * *

Ten leagues within the Torry Eastern border.

The spring sun shone upon Morac's face as he bathed in its soothing warmth. The smell of fresh air invigorated his lungs as the open plain spread invitingly before him. He was relieved to be free of the stifling air of Notsu, the dying city torturing his senses like a rotten corpse. That was behind him now, his army again on the march, returning to the place of his only defeat, redemption resting beyond the horizon to the west, to the Torry heartland, to Corell.

He contemplated his decision releasing his cavalry at the outset of the campaign. Perhaps he should have used his mounted forces to secure his lines of communication, but that was not in his aggressive nature.

'Draw out the Torry cavalry and destroy them!' Morac commanded Kriton, releasing the large gargoyle to wreak havoc upon the Torry countryside, drawing the enemy forces to battle, where they could not harry his own supply trains. The die was cast, forcing Morac to attack now, or risk his precious cavalry to piecemeal annihilation.

The Torry cavalry would go where his cavalry went, leaving Morac free to press his attack.

Long columns of infantry marched in ordered ranks to his left and right, marching ever westward to Corell, their standard blowing strongly in the breeze, silver crossed daggers upon a field of black, the sigil of the 11th Benotrist Legion. They were uniformly dressed in their distinct bronze hued armor over gold tunics. They were his brave veterans from his previous campaign, though more than half their number missed the siege while dutifully garrisoning Notsu. This time an additional seven telnics joined them from the garrison force at Notsu, bringing their total to twenty-four telnics, making them the smallest of his legions in the coming battles. They would act as the vanguard of his vast host, most being familiar with the Torry lands east of Corell.

Trailing the 11th Benotrist Legion, marched the men of the 10th Benotrist Legion, attired in their uniform gray mail and black tunics. Their standard lifting in the breeze at the head of their columns, a black broken shield upon a field of red. The 10th Legion recently arrived from Pagan Harbor to participate in this spring campaign, joining the 14th Gargoyle Legion and the 9th Benotrist Legion supplementing Morac's winnowed forces from the previous campaign. They joined with the 5th Gargoyle Legion and the 8th Benotrist Legion, giving Morac nearly six full legions to seize Corell and bring Torry North to heel. The 5th Gargoyle Legion marched just north of the 8th Benotrist Legion, while the 14th Gargoyle Legion rested several leagues to their south, each shadowing their advance. The 8th and 9th Benotrist Legions followed far to rear, each still marshalling their telnics west of Notsu. Morac was pleased with the arrival of one hundred and twenty dracks, long range heavy ballista platforms from Laycrom, that were sorely lacking in the previous siege. Enhanced with coiled springs, they fired iron spears nearly four hundred yards, able to punch through stone, though not walls as thick as Corell's. They could cause incredible damage to the close ordered ranks serried atop the palace, or tear large gashes in the Jenaii host if they attempted to assail their grounded forces from above. The dracks were presently with the 9th Benotrist Legion, positioned safely and secretly in the rear of his advancing forces. Supporting these deadly platforms were hundreds of wagons laden with shaped munitions, long iron spears that were designed specifically for the dracks.

Dethine drew his mount up alongside him, the Nayborian Champion's golden braids draping beneath his steel helm.

"A fine day to renew our old acquaintances at Corell, Lord Morac," Dethine smirked, his cruel eyes envisioning the ruin and plunder of the Torry realm. With most of his contingent slaughtered north of Corell's fabled walls during the breaking of the siege, he marched mostly alone with only a few hundred of his brave Nayborians in his company. He spent much of the time since their defeat at Corell southward, returning to his native Naybin to present himself along their western border in full view of their Jenaii enemies. It was a clever tactic, making the Jenaii believe Dethine planned a full invasion of the Jenaii Kingdom. If his ruse was successful, it would keep large portions of the Jenaii battlegroups along the Naybin border, and away from Corell. His king approved the plan, knowing the fate of his realm depended on the battle of Torry North. Should they win here, then the Jenaii would be crushed soon after, and if they didn't, then Nayboria was doomed in turn.

"Together we shall give battle, old friend, our two swords against the enemy's two, and perhaps only one if your ruse worked as planned," Morac referenced Elos being drawn off to defend his native realm, leaving only Terin to fend off Morac and Dethine.

"Aye, and you are not hobbled as you were the last time. The Torries will be graced with your full measure," Dethine said.

"Yes, my full measure. We would be richly blessed if they think I shall sit idle whilst the battle unfolds. They will be painfully instructed on what my full health means to the fate of their doomed realm. I am eager to set them to right on that matter," Morac said with the coldest voice.

"Then onward we shall march, to Corell and to victory," Dethine said as Morac gazed skyward, observing a formation of Benotrist magantors circle overhead, their numbers swelled with nearly every avian east of Fera. 'Twas another reminder of the stakes of the campaign ahead, ultimate victory or defeat hanging in the balance.

* * *

Gotto. West of Tro.

The city of Gotto was almost two thirds empty when the standard of the 12ᵗʰ Gargoyle Legion appeared before its northern walls, crashing red fists upon a field of green. Most of the populace fled to Tro, taking whatever, they could carry, desperate to escape the expected slaughter. Those that remained withdrew to the inner city, the original walled fortress that rested at the western side of the confluence of the Veneba and Flen Rivers. The fortress part of the city consisted of a strong west wall the height of eight men, with towering battlements and large iron gates. It was the only land facing wall, with a lower curtain wall running along the opposing river banks, joining together farther east where they met, giving the fortress city an oddly shaped triangle appearance from above, with its outer suburbs spreading in all directions beyond the protection of its walls. It was wholly unsuited against gargoyles, but the men of the city garrison made their stand there all the same, with the city's standard blowing above their battlements, two rivers upon a field of gray. Those remaining outside the fortress trusted their safety and fortune to a brokered peace, should the enemy appear reasonable. A sane man would doubt the gargoyles civility, but these men could not move their fortunes, their wealth bound up in their landed assets.

The gargoyles entered Gotto unopposed, sweeping through the streets in surprisingly good order, their columns converging upon fortressed walls of the ancient part of the city. General Krakeni, commander of the 12ᵗʰ Gargoyle Legion, ordered his troops to avoid slaughtering any locals that remained in the outer sections of Gotto, his apparent mercy well received by those that remained. In truth, Krakeni did not want to further thin his legion in the slaughter of civilians who might be an asset after their full occupation of the vital city. Unlike most gargoyles, Krakeni knew that wealthy merchants and tradesmen could be very useful when subject to Benotrist-gargoyle authority. Besides, he already lost far too many of his telnics on the Tro raid, greatly reducing his strength. He would waste no more than necessary talking Gotto, especially if he had to advance upon Tro after doing so.

And so it was, that Krakeni gave the beleaguered soldiers defending the inner city his list of terms, terms he felt more than fair. They were to open their gates to his legion in return for their lives. They must surrender their arms, and every male under the age of forty would be sent north as guests of the Benotrist Empire, hostages to insure the city's loyalty, no doubt. In truth, they would be slaves, toiling where their labor was desperately needed. It was to Krakeni's disappointment when his offer was refused.

The very night of their refusal, Krakeni ordered a full assault in the dead of night, his gargoyles using the surrounding structures to gain easy lift, soaring over the battlements of the inner city, confounding the defenders. Once released, the gargoyles could not be directed, but their overwhelming numbers more than evened the odds, the battle immediately descending into complete chaos. The defenders fought as well as they could, using their shield walls to some effect wherever they could gather together, but they were simply too few to hold for long. All nine hundred men of the garrison were eventually slaughtered, along with those holed up in the inner city. Krakeni ordered them killed to a man, while sparing those that remained in the outer city, planning to use them to reorganize the city under Benotrist-Gargoyle authority.

By the following morn, Gotto was subdued, the standard of the 12th Legion gracing its bloodied battlements, costing the legion 1400 dead and wounded. General Krakeni quickly reconstituted his legion, leaving a token force to garrison Gotto, before advancing to Tro.

CHAPTER 12

Fera. The Black Castle.

A thousand emotions swirled in his brain as Jonas made his way along the dark stone corridors of Fera; angst, anger, hope and anticipation just a few of the myriad vying for their place in his mind. His arrival caused quite a stir, his sea blue tunic and silver mail and helm well marking him as a Torry elite. He was greeted with a considerable escort upon their arrival, and it continued to grow as they advanced to the throne room. He lost count at over one hundred and nineteen, but guessed the number well over two hundred by now. They marched beside, in front and behind him, though kept several paces away from him, unsure how to treat with him. They knew he was a *Special* guest of the emperor, and were instructed to treat him with the deepest respect, allowing him to retain his sword. Many thought he might be here to negotiate peace between their respective realms, while others thought he might be a spy, delivering vital information to their cause. None, other than a select few, knew his true purpose for being here, and he wondered what would happen if the truth spread throughout the palace?

Jonas shook his head, wondering what he would say to his father once they met? His father had much to answer for, and probably thought the same of him. He steeled his heart for the task ahead, wondering what sort of reception he would receive once he entered the throne room, which looked to be just ahead by the massive doors that were opening with an immense statue resting in front of them. Upon nearing the statue, he was taken aback by its impressive size and craftmanship, and equally disturbed by its grotesque nature, an amalgamation of human and gargoyle forms, melding into a single abomination. A tarp wrapped about the statue's middle likely hid the alteration Lorken made upon their escape, when he altered its genitalia, as Terin relayed to him the tale. If true, then his father was responsible for crafting this grotesquerie, justifying all his doubts and misgivings he harbored through the years concerning his sire.

They circled the face of the massive statue, before passing sharply left, entering the cavernous chamber, the court crier heralding his arrival. Most of the guards peeled away, with only his original escort preceding him into the chamber. Jonas was taken aback by the mirrored red stone floor, that appeared more akin to a lake of dark blood than the floor of a great hall. He noted the silver plated pillars that spiraled to the ceiling, knowing that behind each waited two archers clad in shimmering silver tunics, if what Terin said of this place was correct. He was equally impressed by the celestial design of the arched ceiling, with its jeweled stone embedded along its surface, alit by its swirling lanterns bringing its surface to life, like a thousand flickering stars.

The grand adornments of the vast throne room were but gaudy trappings of the emperor's power, each paling before the majesty of his massive golden throne resting at the chamber's far end, set atop a raised dais with a large wide stair before it. The throne looked large enough to sit several men, but the figure that occupied it radiated his presence from afar, causing even the mighty to quiver. Jonas felt the man's gaze upon him, golden eyes meeting vibrant purple, a match of wills, as each took the other's measure. More guards peeled away, stepping to the side and taking a knee, until only two imperial elite remained, each finally being waved off by the emperor, leaving Jonas advancing alone before stopping at the base of the dais.

There he stood, staring up to the emperor, neither man saying a word for a painfully long time. Looking into those turbulent golden irises confirmed that the emperor was in fact his father. Though he hadn't seen him since he was a child, Jonas would never forget his face. It sadly established that all his fears were confirmed, meaning Tyro and his father were one in the same. There was always that faint possibility that another took up his father's name if he died, using it to advance his dark agenda. It would have vindicated his father, laying his sins upon another, but alas, it was not so. Tyro was his father just as his mother always claimed and feared. He could see his father's eyes confirming his own identity, establishing that Jonas and Joriah were indeed the same man.

They continued to stare for what felt an eternity, neither knowing where to begin. Both had planned what they would say, but neither seemed able to utter it. They each had a thousand questions, but no voice to ask them. In truth, there was but one priority for Jonas that came so clearly into focus, freeing his tongue to speak of it.

"Where is she?"

Jonas's words rang out like thunder in the deafly quiet hall, every eye going to the emperor, awaiting his response. Men were struck dead for speaking so brazenly to the emperor, and many expected this Torry emissary to suffer in kind. What they didn't expect was Tyro's strange response.

"Come with me."

* * *

Jonas followed Tyro through the winding corridors of the upper palace, neither speaking a word, their strange silence continuing, each overwhelmed by the conversation that was to come, neither knowing where to begin. What they could agree to was Jonas' need to see to his wife. The guards held back by Tyro's order, wondered how they could protect their emperor with the armed Torry between them and their liege? Their emperor didn't see this man as a threat, and the Torry didn't seem interested in harming the emperor by his purposeful gait. The guards trailed the two men at a healthy distance, before Tyro ordered them to stay upon approaching the royal apartments where the lady Valera was housed.

Jonas followed his father within a spacious and richly decorated chamber with fanciful furnishings and large tapestries adorning its black stone walls. There, on the far side of the chamber sat his beloved Valera sitting upon a large backed chair, nursing a child, a preciously tiny infant held lovingly to her breast.

"We shall speak later," was all Tyro said, stepping outside, closing the door behind him.

"Jonas!" Valera gasped, joyous tears running the length of her lovely cheeks, her rich olive skin radiating with her recent motherhood.

He rushed to her side, kneeling beside her, pressing his hand to her flushed cheek.

"I feared for you and the baby when I learned what happened, and that you were with child," he cringed in shame for having her suffer so while he was elsewhere. "I should have been there," he lowered his head.

"No. You were required at Corell. Terin needed you, and so did the realm. My only regret is that you came here. The realm needs the blood of Kal for the battles ahead. Now you are here, and your father will never let you leave," she sighed.

"My duty is to you, not the Torry realm."

"You are their champion, their true champion," she reminded him.

"Nay. That mantle falls to Terin. It is his destiny and duty, just as you are my destiny and duty. I would never leave you here alone."

"I doubt your father would harm me," she reasoned.

"Not intentionally, but he is blind to his actions and the consequences that spring from them. I can only hope he listens to reason."

"Have you spoken with him?"

"Only a few words," he shook his head.

"Then you have much work to do, my love. There will be time for us after. I am well cared for as you can see, and so is our daughter," she smiled, drawing his gaze to the infant suckling her breast.

"A girl?" he returned her smile with his own, running a finger along the baby's wrinkled forehead, overcome with emotion.

"Yes, a lovely girl, with her father's eyes," she said, noting the peculiar hue of the baby's irises.

"Have you named her?"

"Not yet, but I have one that comes repeatedly to mind," she said knowingly.

"What name is that?"

"Cordela," she smiled, saying the name of his mother.

"Truly?" he asked, unable to hide his pleasure with that name.

"I see that it pleases you. Cordela it shall be. Now, go speak with your father," Valera ordered before directing him closer for a kiss.

* * *

Tyro was more than surprised with the brevity of Jonas's visit with his wife, quickly rejoining him in the outer corridor, before following him to his private sanctum. His guards were equally surprised when he ordered them to remain without, while he treated with Jonas all alone in his private chambers. There were so many questions Tyro wanted to first ask, needing them answered as a thirsty man needs water. Upon entering the spacious dimly lit chamber, he walked toward the small wooden table where rested a large pitcher of strong Bedoan ale, pouring two goblets and handing one to his son.

"I think a drink will serve each of us good," Tyro said.

"I don't partake fermented drink," Jonas politely refused.

"Truly?" Tyro didn't know if he should be impressed or offended.

"I never have. It clouds the mind, and I have needed my full cunning since the day uncle Aleric led his men into our vale," Jonas sadly recalled the grim event, when Tyro's half-brother vented his fury upon the Kalinian Vale, slaying everyone save Jonas and his mother.

"It is my one great regret, not slaying him before he fled my blade. I could have spared us such grief, spared you such grief, my son. Perhaps your mother might still live had I done so," Tyro reflected sadly, his sorrow fighting with his anger for dominion of his mind. Rarely did any emotion reign above his rage, save for cunning when it was required. One didn't build an empire without managing their base emotions, and Tyro was more than capable of such.

"That's why I gave you the Sword of the Sun... to protect us," Jonas's words came harsher than he intended.

"And I failed you, and ever since that fateful day when I learned of what he had done, I swore to not fail ever again!" Tyro growled bitterly, the mere mention of his brother causing his anger to build.

"Not killing uncle Aleric, but siding with gargoyles over mankind, was your true failure."

"Gargoyles were never my enemy. Gargoyles didn't enslave and brutalize MY people, the Menotrists did!" Tyro growled.

"You are Menotrist," Jonas reminded him.

The coldest look passed Tyro's face, causing Jonas to nearly back a step, but he held his ground.

"If you were not my SON, I would…" Tyro growled, stopping himself from completing the sentence.

"Kill me," Jonas shook his head.

"Do not speak of my kinship with those people. Am I understood?" Tyro asked in a deathly quiet voice.

"Denying your paternal heritage does not change it. Agar was your father, just as you are mine. I do not deny you, and you should not deny him."

Tyro's eyes blazed briefly; his rage kindled to an extreme he hadn't felt in a long time. "They are no longer my kin, not after all they have done."

"And yet, you are my father, after all that you have done," he reminded him.

"And what have I done but try to protect my family and people?"

"You are so blind," Jonas sighed, turning away, unable to bear looking at him.

"Gargoyles again, I assume? Is it such a sin to align with those we find common cause?"

"Humans can never find common cause with them. They are accursed by Yah. You know this. My mother told you this, and yet you used them to gain your revenge upon the Menotrists," Jonas said, looking again to his father.

"Do you care to know how I came to befriend them?" Tyro asked, swallowing his rage and trying to use reason and compassion to sway his son.

"You saved a gargoyle chieftain from uncle Aleric's keep when you went to kill him. The chieftain rewarded you with his friendship," Jonas heard this tale.

"That chieftain is now known as Lord Regula, my second, and my truest friend. When I came upon my brother's holdfast with the sword you had given me, I heard the ghastliest sounds issuing from the smithy, screams of unbearable anguish that rent my heart. It reminded me so much of the tortures visited upon my own people from their Menotrist masters," Tyro sighed, taking a pause before continuing.

"I came upon two of my brother's men standing outside the smithy, catching them unaware, their gaze drawn to the activities within, amused by the happenings therein. I slew them instantly, the *Sword of the Sun* dancing beautifully in my hand, its blinding radiance terrible to behold for lesser men, and from that day forth, I was no lesser man. I entered the smithy, finding Regula strapped down over a work bench, his limbs stretched taut to each corner, with his wings pinned painfully below him as he stared helplessly at his tormentor, Gul Dabrorin, my brother's master of arms and right hand. I slew him where he stood, before freeing Regula. It was only then I discovered the depths of Menotrist depravity. It was in that place I found the dismembered remains of many of my kin, Benotrist cousins, aunts and uncles. They were tortured beyond measure, suffering my half brother's cruelty. Many more adorned the walls, their heads preserved by Menotrist foul means, their once vibrant eyes replaced with unseeing stones, staring blankly, ghoulish trophies for my brother's amusement," Tyro took a generous sip from his goblet before continuing.

"The Menotrists had long visited such cruelty upon my mother's people. As for my father's holdfast, he curbed much of this abuse out of deference for my mother, but only halted the most extreme practices. His Benotrist serfs still suffered terribly at his hands, their labors extracted at the end of the overseer's lash. My father died between the years I fled with your mother and you giving me the sword. It was then my brother had a free hand in dealing with my mother's kin. And so it was, he brought them to his smithy a few at a time, torturing them unto death, as well as any gargoyles he could capture, both suffering in kind at his hands."

Tyro could have gone on to detail their suffering, but spared Jonas the full telling. It was enough that he now understood the source of his rage.

"What did you do?" Jonas asked, trying to separate rumors he heard of the early days of his father's revolution, from the facts.

"Regula and I slew nearly everyone we came upon, sweeping through my brother's holdfast like a cleansing wind, bringing justice to our peoples. Aleric tried to face me, believing he held the greater blade. It cost him several fingers before relenting and taking flight, the coward that he was, leaving his men and kin to face me. We slew them all, even his wicked mother, Dresela. I remembered looking into her hateful eyes, watching her die, confessing her crimes against my mother." A glossy look passed Tyro's eyes, as if lost in a memory.

"Her crimes?"

"She killed your grandmother, ordering her evil matron to bleed her out upon the birthing bed, taking my newborn sister with her. I long suspected it to be so and when I first presented my father with the truth of her crimes, he did nothing, denying my mother justice. So, I served justice where no one else would, as I have done every day since."

"If it is justice you sought against the Menotrists, you have succeeded. You have destroyed their people, reducing the survivors to a servile class, and yet, your vengeance is not quenched. Tell me, what crimes are my people guilty of to suffer your aggression?"

"Your people?" Tyro raised an eyebrow at that.

"The Torry realm. They are my people. My wife is Torry, as is my son. You would see all that they love brought low to sate your vengeful thirst. The same could be said of most of the lands you conquered. None of those people were allies or even friendly with the Menotrists, and you still waged war upon them," Jonas challenged his father's delusions.

"Where were the Torries when the Menotrists murdered and enslaved my people? Where were the Venotrists, Yatins or any of the realms that once dotted northern Arax? Nowhere, that is where they were. None are friends of mine, and for you to forsake me in my time of greatest need, is unforgivable!" Tyro roared, unable to curb his tongue.

"Forsake you? I gave you what you asked for when I placed the sword in your hand. And how have I been rewarded? With you choosing our age old enemy over your own wife and child!" Jonas matched his father's furor.

"I made no such choice. One does not exclude the other!"

"Yes, it does. Our Kalinian blood cannot abide the gargoyles. Should we align with them in any way, the power of our blood will reverse itself. The gargoyles would tear us apart, their maddened fear replaced with unfettered courage and rage. Mother knew this, and she told you this, but you either didn't understand her or you ignored her. After uncle Aleric and his men slew everyone in our vale, mother and I were spared because we were camped in the upper part of the valley, separating ourselves from the others over the shame of my giving you the sword. When we emerged from hiding, we discovered every one of our kin dead. We gathered whatever we could and fled, making our way south away from Menotrist controlled lands, avoiding bandits, gargoyles and slavers throughout our journey. When we heard rumors of a rebel leader wielding a golden sword who aligned with gargoyles and slew a Menotrist lord named Aleric, we knew it was you, or at least she knew," Jonas didn't reveal that his mother had visions of his father claiming the name of Tyro, knowing Taleron and Tyro were one in the same.

"She should have sought me out!" Tyro shook his head.

"She couldn't. It is as I explained, our blood cannot abide gargoyles. When we realized what I had done by giving you that blade, we fled to the only realm on the continent that could stand against you."

And there it was, the truth Tyro feared. His own wife and son deliberately worked against him all these years, secretly aiding the one realm that was a threat to his empire.

"It was you that found the sword Terin wields, wasn't it?" Tyro asked, guessing the truth.

"Yes. The sword called to me just as the Sword of the Sun called to me before I gifted it to you. I gave the Torry realm what it needed to face you, a sword of light, and a champion to wield it. Your plan to conquer the Torry realms will be destroyed by your grandson, your own blood."

"You have poisoned his mind against me!" Tyro growled.

"You've done that yourself."

"I did nothing to the boy for him to vex me so."

"Truly? What of his friend, who you tortured in your dungeon, killing most of his men in such gruesome manners?"

"Friend? Speak sense, BOY!"

"Cronus Kenti, the hero of Tuft's Mountain. You tortured and murdered his men that you had taken captive. They were innocent of any crimes against you but defending their realm, which is the duty of any soldier. They deserved better than what you did to them. Is that the justice you seek? Is that the justice the people of Arax will receive should you conquer all the land?"

Tyro glared at him, biting his tongue.

"There is a point where justice turns into revenge. Once you cross that line, you will seek vengeance on those who never wronged you, punishing them for imagined slights." Jonas's words stung with truth, truth that no one else dare utter to him.

They stood there for a painfully long time, staring at one another, bereft of words but not emotions.

"What now, father? You stole away my wife to lure me here. You know I cannot stay here, and I doubt you will kill me, but considering your position, that is a possibility."

SLAP!

Tyro couldn't help striking him, weary of his insolent tongue.

"I protect what is mine, BOY! You, your sister and your children are safe in my keeping. Never assume I would harm my children, even if they are insolent whelps like you."

"Then what are your intentions? I will not serve you, or your realm. And as I explained, I cannot stay," Jonas sighed.

"You are free to leave. I will not stop you."

"Free to leave?" Jonas couldn't make sense of it. Why lure him here just to set him free?

"Does that surprise you? I needed the truth, to know where you were all these years, and to be certain you were in fact my son. I will not keep you. You are free to go," Tyro shrugged.

"Very well. I will tell Valera to gather her things."

"Of course. You may leave together. I am certain her father is very worried for her safety."

Jonas wasn't a fool. He knew there was something his father wasn't saying.

"Speak sense, father. What are you holding back? You wouldn't just let me walk out of here so easily, especially after searching for me all these years."

"You are free to leave, Joriah. Take your wife and depart. You will be given a full escort to the border, where you can make your way home. Of course, a magantor is hardly appropriate for an infant, so my granddaughter WILL remain with me."

"My daughter is coming with me!" Jonas took a step toward Tyro.

"No. The Princess remains here. I will have one heir who isn't poisoned against me. She will learn to rule at my side, preparing to be the empress she was born to be. Should I ever retrieve Tosha's son, I shall wed her to him, so they might rule together. It is not uncommon for cousins to wed. As for Terin, I have given Morac specific orders to take him alive. He will live out his days in captivity, in a far off keep. I have many loyal vassals with daughters willing to wed him, giving me more grandchildren, whose loyalties will not be compromised by your influence. What are you waiting for, my son? Leave. Fetch your wife and depart!"

"Valera will not leave our daughter to you."

"And you will not leave Valera," Tyro was smiling now.

Jonas drew his sword, holding the point to Tyro's neck.

"You forget," Tyro kept his smile, grabbing hold of the blade's edge, twisting it from Jonas's grip. Tyro retrieved the weapon, examining it closely, admiring the sword. There was not a mark on his hand, not even an indentation from the blade.

In the heat of the moment Jonas forgot the terrible truth of his Kalinian blood, and his inability to harm those he loved. He was helpless against Tyro, and somehow Tyro knew this, likely learning it from his mother during their years together.

"This is an excellent blade," Tyro admired the craftsmanship.

"It was a gift from Princess Corry for my help lifting the siege of Corell. It was hand crafted by Valera's father," Jonas spoke to its origin, disgusted with his father.

"The legendary Torg Vantel. Even here his legend precedes him. As beautiful as this sword is, it is unworthy of you," Tyro said knowingly, returning the weapon to Jonas, who looked at him questioningly. "You might have need of it. At least until I can arrange something more worthy of my son."

Jonas wondered at that. He was torn between leaving to fulfill his duty to the Torry throne and staying to protect his daughter.

"See to your wife, Joriah. We shall talk again latter," Tyro dismissed him, a reserved smile gracing his lips. He knew his son would never leave without his wife and child, and he could hardly sneak them to the magantor platforms without alerting the whole garrison. An infant child was stronger than a thousand chains to keep him in place.

* * *

Jonas found his wife fast asleep, their daughter tucked within the crook of her arm as she lay upon her bed. He was tempted to press a kiss to her forehead, but dared not wake her, choosing to simply kiss the air above her brow. He admired the motherly glow radiating from her perfect skin, bathing her in femininity. He stared for a long moment, to see if she stirred, before stepping toward the window, where the stars shone in the clear night sky.

He stood before the window, gazing up to the heavens to beseech Yah's guidance.

"Show me your will, Oh Yah. Was I foolish for coming here? Have I betrayed my birthright? Please do not forsake me for speaking with my father. He is a deluded fool, twisted by his own imaginings and ambitions. I have followed your will since that fateful night when I placed the sword in his hands, but what child wouldn't try to please their father? I have raised Terin as you advised, as Lore advised, free of the privileges of court to ascertain his character and nurture his humility and honor. I placed him in your care when I sent him off to Rego so long ago. He is the champion anointed to fulfill Kal's purpose. My duty now lies with my wife and child, but I will forsake them if you will it. I will return to defend the Torry Realms if that is your will. Only a few times have I heard your voice so clearly in my mind, but since venturing here you have been silent, and I fear to lean on my own understanding," Jonas spoke desperately to the heavens, overcome with loneliness.

He stared for an eternal moment, waiting upon his God, doubt beginning to creep upon his heart.

REMAIN. GUARD YOUR DAUGHTER WITH YOUR LIFE.

Yah's words thundered in his brain, nearly driving him to his knees. He gathered himself, gazing gratefully to the sky, thankful for Yah's approval and guidance. Whatever may come, he was where Yah intended him to be, and with that he retired to his bed, joining his beloved.

CHAPTER 13

Corell.

Raven sat off to the side of the central courtyard upon a stone outcropping, where several adjoining tunnels met in the vast open space, with the open roof above resting atop vertical walls he guessed were well over a hundred feet high, perhaps more. Gazing skyward was akin to sitting at the bottom of giant empty well, with pristine white walls circling to the summit above. Looking up, he could make out a couple of the palace towers peaking above the lip of the opening overhead, and Jenaii flying across his line of sight.

The activity in the courtyard was more interesting, drawing him here to begin with. Most of the traffic flowed through the north bound tunnel, which led through a series of gates to the outside, most of which were in a state of repair from the previous siege, when Morac and Dethine tore them apart with their magical swords, if the rumors were to be believed. Raven thought it a little far fetched, but seeing the damage for himself, made him a believer. After meeting Master Orvon, the chief blacksmith tasked with the repairs, he offered his help, showing the man what a laser could do in melding steel. The man's eyes alit, realizing what they could do with such power. He immediately set about replacing the missing wood within the main gate, before placing sheets of iron over the sections Morac cut away. His men hammered the shards back into place, placing the raw iron overtop of it, where Raven used his laser to meld them together.

This completely changed the dynamics of the task, hastening its full repair. After the first siege, they managed to raise the broken gate enough to open the passageway, but it was still a hinderance, and they thought to remove it completely unless Master Orvon could perform a miracle. No one suspected that miracle would come in the form of a giant Earther who had all the manners of a starving gragglogg. With the difficult part in repairing the gate behind him, Master Orvon went about working on the gear mechanisms that were partially damaged when the Nayborians breached the wall.

With his part accomplished, Raven basked in the glory of the grateful garrison, visiting the courtyard every morn, looking for something to do.

He noted the cavalry coming and going throughout the morn, running messages to nearby keeps, or participating in long range patrols. Once Morac's legions drew closer, the cavalry would be sent away where they could do the most good, harrying the enemy supply chains.

The news of the Benotrist invasion swept through the palace with expected result. Preparing for a likely event and actually having it come to pass, were different things altogether. He could see the fear and worry in the Torries eyes, but also courage and determination. He had to hand it to them in the courage department. He wouldn't favor his chances if he was one of them during the last siege, holding out against several hundred thousand enemy with only ten thousand men armed with swords and spears. He was happy to have his rifle and pistol, though he couldn't use them until he accounted for Ben, wherever he was. He doubted his old friend would miss the battle this time, considering the importance of it.

With his friends busy preparing for the coming battle, he didn't see much of them in recent days. Their training was cut back severely, with most of them attending tasks at the behest of the Princess, General Bode or commander Nevias. Cronus left early this morn, joining a cohort of cavalry scouting the approaches of Corell, identifying likely enemy encampments for the coming siege, as well as watering points. He would be back before the day was out. Terin was tasked guarding the princess, with Corry refusing to let him linger too far from her side. Ular and several matrons departed a few days past with their tissue regenerator, General Valen ordering a full magantor escort to accompany them to Besos, where they would heal all the wounded gathered there. Lucas went with them, at Ular's behest, which Torg reluctantly agreed. The two friends had become nigh inseparable. Corry demanded they return well before Morac's vanguard neared the walls of Corell.

That only left Orlom from their group they traveled with from Tro, and the young gorilla was almost joined at the hip to Torg Vantel, following him around like a lost puppy. Raven laughed whenever he thought about it, with Orlom constantly referring to the craggy Master of Arms as *Coach*. Torg didn't know how to respond to the strange moniker, but Orlom spoke it with such deep respect, that Torg allowed it. Raven even overheard several of the Torry Elite referring to Torg as *Coach*, but never to his face. Any one else would be mortified having started the whole affair, but Raven smugly patted himself on the back, happy to stir up a little mischief.

Like Torg, Raven had drawn his own entourage of followers, who would gather around him whenever their duties allowed, asking him to share his adventures, which he happily obliged. This afternoon was no different, with several of his enthusiasts joining him in the courtyard, showing him the layout of the lower palace, before stopping here, where he observed the comings and goings, with servants, soldiers and riders moving from one tunnel to another. Besides the main north bound tunnel, the second largest rested off Raven's left, which led to the palace stables, the wide causeway lined with torches along its impressive length. Beside the entrance to the tunnel was a sizable corral holding a lone ocran, a sorry looking creature that caught his attention.

Raven eased off the outcropping, walking across the courtyard, before resting his elbows on the fence of the corral, getting a better look at the ornery brute. The ocran's coat was an even mix of brown and purple, blending and twisting in uneven spirals, giving it a most off putting appearance. The ocran snorted loudly, glaring at Raven with small mismatched eyes of pale green and dark purple. Whisps of hot breath issued from its broad, misshapen, runny nose. It had equally hideous crooked teeth, and its right horn was cloven in half, while the other bent unnaturally to the left. He spied a gash along its right hindquarter.

"You are one ugly animal," Raven said, thinking the beast the ugliest thing he ever saw.

SMASH!

The ornery brute ran its head into the fence, its crooked left horn just missing Raven's head as he jumped back with no time to spare.

"Why you…" Raven growled, reaching for his pistol.

"He's wild," a soldier warned, stepping near, wearing the braided cords of a unit commander of cavalry, with a mop of black hair peeking below his steel helm.

"Wild?" Raven said, holstering his pistol as the commander stepped close, with Raven's small entourage filling in around them.

"Yes. We found him northeast of here some time ago, wounded by gargoyles," the man explained.

"Guess he can't be all bad if he hates gargoyles," Raven shrugged, wondering why the commander had a strange look on his face, as if they were long lost pals.

"You are Terin's friend, are you not?" The man asked.

"Yes. The name's Raven," he said, offering his hand.

The soldier offered his, uncertain of the meaning as Raven shook his hand.

"Just a custom of my world," Raven explained the gesture.

"Very well," the man smiled, shaking Raven's hand a little harder. "I am Jacin Tomac. Any friend of Terin's is a friend of mine. He saved my life during the siege, pulling me from beneath my slain ocran before a horde of gargoyles could finish me. I bore the scars of that mishap until your friend Ular healed me upon your arrival," Jacin said, lifting the hem of his tunic, showing Raven where he was wounded, running his hand along the length of the injury.

"That's a pretty big chunk of your leg. You're lucky you didn't bleed out."

"I was most fortunate, and am able to return to full duty thanks to your incredible healing device. I missed my unit's glorious ride when our cavalry swept in from the west to break the siege. While my brave fellows led the vanguard of Corell's salvation, I lied helpless upon my bunk, nursing my mangled leg. That shall not happen this time, thanks much to your friends," Jacin said gratefully.

"Glad they could help, and if you want action, you'll have plenty coming this way real soon."

"Yes. It appears to be so," Jacin conceded sadly.

"What are you going to do with this ugly brute?" Raven asked, jerking a thumb toward the ornery ocran standing in the middle of the corral still glaring at him.

"Probably slaughter him once we are besieged. We can ill afford to feed him, but he can feed many of us," Jacin sighed, hating to see an ocran used for food, but such was war.

"Slaughter him? I thought you needed mounts?"

"We do, but as I said, he is wild," Jacin explained, wondering if Raven hadn't heard him.

"So, break him."

"You cannot tame a wild ocran. It is never done. They must be broken when they are young," he explained, rightly guessing Raven wasn't aware of this as he was a stranger to their land.

"Nonsense, I used to break wild mustangs on my grandfather's ranch all the time," Raven boasted, failing to mention that horses were smaller than ocran and were less violent. He did spend many a summer working his grandfather's ranch in Wyoming during his youth. His grandfather used much of his retirement credits from his time as an admiral in Space Fleet to purchase his ranch, enjoying life away from civilization.

"No, no. We cannot tame him," Jacin insisted, shaking his head.

"Sure, you can."

"No, it's too dangerous."

"Fetch me saddle, reins and blinds and I'll show you how it's done."

"It would be suicide to attempt this. You are Terin's friend, and I cannot let you do this," Jacin insisted.

Several other soldiers overheard their conversation, and began to encourage Raven as they gathered around.

"You can do it, Earther!" One of them shouted, causing several others to join in, including his small band of followers who crowded closer.

"Tame the beast, Earther!" Another shouted.

"Show us how it is done!"

The encouragement continued, some condescending, some genuine, but most simply curious.

"Just fetch me some gear and I'll give it a go," Raven said, causing Jacin to shake his head.

"This is folly, Raven. I owe a great debt to Terin, and could not reward him by allowing his friend to do this," Jacin implored.

"I'll fetch them for you Earther!" One fellow happily offered, racing off to retrieve them.

"Please do not do this," Jacin pleaded again as Raven lifted a rope from a nearby hitch post, tying a loop before tossing it over the beast's head, trying to pull the ocran to the side of the corral.

"I'll be alright. Why don't you fellas lend me a hand," he asked those gathered about to help reel the beast in. Several joined in drawing the beast to the side of the corral, where Raven fixed a harness around its large head, the animal spitting and snorting as Raven jammed the bit into its mouth. Araxan bits, reins and saddles were far more advanced than their ancient counterparts on Earth. Their designs were almost equal to Earth's 19th century, with stirrups wide enough to slip the front half of your foot into. The saddle and blinds followed with Raven climbing atop the fence, preparing to mount the suddenly calm beast.

"Raven, you really should reconsider," Jacin pleaded one last time.

"I can't let everyone down. Look at all these fellas watching," he swept his hand over the small crowd. "What do you think, fellas. Do you want me to stop or give this a try?"

"Do it!" More than one shouted.

"Tame the beast!"

"Ride it, Earther!"

"Don't worry, Jacin, I got this," Raven reassured the apprehensive commander. "Hold onto these for me," he said, removing his jacket, handing it to Jacin along with his holster and rifle before climbing into the saddle with reins in hand, while signaling the others to lift the blinds and cut the beast loose.

Call it courage, overconfidence, bravado or just plain stupidity, for all applied to Raven at one point or another, causing him grief whenever his stubbornness conflicted with the laws of physics. The beast released a curdling snort, kicking its hind legs and thrusting its back skyward as soon as the blinds were lifted, nearly tossing Raven from the saddle. The beast kicked again, twisting about, its head scrapping the ground before rearing high into the air, with Raven holding on for dear life. The beast did a flurry of moves before thrusting its ass high overhead, sending Raven flying. He sailed half way across the corral, landing painfully on the unforgiving ground.

He lied motionless for a painfully long moment, aching head to foot as Jacin set his things upon the ground, jumping over the fence to help him.

"Ughh!" Raven groaned, slowly coming to his senses, rolling over on his back, staring blankly to the sky above. He slowly lifted his head, rising up on his elbows, staring down the beast who stood across the corral glaring back at him, clopping his right front hoof into the ground, hot breath escaping its flaring nostrils. Fortunately, it stayed in place, simply snorting and glaring at him with its mismatched eyes.

"Come, Raven," Jacin said, tugging on his arm.

"No," Raven growled, slowly coming to his feet. He climbed over the fence, closing on the spot where he started, taking hold of the rope, tossing it around the beast's neck, drawing it back to the side of the corral.

"Are you mad, Raven?" Jacin argued, following him back over the fence.

"He's going to try again!" More than one in the crowd shouted in disbelief.

"Do it again, Earther!" another said, Raven unable to determine if he was cheering him on, or mocking his idiocy.

Many began to take bets on how many bones he was certain to break. Two broken legs or a broken neck drew the most wagers.

Ignoring their laughter, cheers and taunts, Raven climbed aboard for a second go around, quickly slipping his boots into the stirrups and grabbing the reins as they cut it loose. The ocran again bowed its massive head, thrusting its hind quarters up, Raven holding on as the animal uncoiled an empathic jolt. Raven's victory was short lived as the ocran reared high into the air before planting its head to the ground, thrusting its hind legs vertically into the air, sending Raven sailing over the fence. The crowd separated, scattering as Raven landed roughly in their midst. He lied on his back, again staring through the opening in the courtyard at the clouds drifting above, his eyes unmoving.

"Is he dead?" One soldier asked.

"That had to hurt," another exclaimed.

No one noticed Cronus ride into the courtyard just before Raven's second attempt, the strange scene drawing his attention the moment he cleared the opening of the north tunnel. For the life of him he couldn't make sense of what he just witnessed, wondering what possessed Raven to attempt such a thing.

"Make way!" Cronus bellowed, pushing his ocran through the crowd. The soldiers quickly parted upon recognizing his esteemed rank, his blue tunic and silver mail denoting him a member of the Torry Elite.

Cronus came to halt beside his friend before removing his helm, those gathered about recognizing his face, most saluting him with a fist to their chest, respectful of the hero of Tuft's Mountain. Raven lie like a stone corpse, starring blankly, his chest rising with his shallow breaths.

"What were you thinking?" Cronus sighed, looking down at him from his mount as he dismounted, tossing his reins to the soldier nearest him.

"Cronus, you're back!" Raven hoarsely whispered, his eyes shifting painfully to his friend.

"Yes, but it appears not soon enough," he shook his head.

"I tried to convince him of the folly of this, but to no avail," Jacin said, setting Raven's weapons and jacket on the ground beside him.

"You are blameless, commander. No man can talk Raven out of anything once his mind is made up. Help me get him inside," Cronus said, putting his neck under Raven's right shoulder as he helped him to his feet.

"I'm alright," Raven said hoarsely, gently pushing Cronus' arm away to stand on his own. "I can still tame the beast," he turned back toward the corral, before falling over with his first step, betrayed by his swollen right ankle.

"Sure, you can," Cronus rolled his eyes before recruiting a dozen men to help move him to the inner keep.

* * *

"What have you?" General Bode asked as Cronus joined him and Commander Nevias in the council chamber, where a map of Torry North was spread across the table. The two commanders had long planned for Morac's inevitable return, focusing on the Benotrist's most glaring weakness… logistics.

"They finished faster than yesterday. I don't see how much quicker they can be," Cronus reported on the cavalry detachment he rode with the past few days. They were assigned well poisoning duty of all lands northwest of Corell, up to seven leagues out. These practice runs near the palace would continue until the enemy drew closer, then the poisonings would be fully executed.

Other units were similarly charged with the remaining sectors circling the palace. Well poisonings were a delicate matter, requiring a deft hand. The wrong poison could taint a well for many years, while others were temporary. The preferred choice was depositing diseased animal carcasses in the wells, but they could be cleansed and restored if the invaders were knowledgeable in the matter. Such tactics would be required with larger bodies of water, such as watering holes and ponds. There were few rivers or streams near the palace, and those would be impossible to poison, with most damage happening downstream and likely beyond the enemy encampments.

"I have already given the order to cripple every well along the east road up to ten leagues out. These others can wait until the enemy draws closer, just in case they march elsewhere," General Bode explained, sweeping his hand across the eastern approaches of Corell upon the map. The wells should have been poisoned before the last siege. It was one of many oversights that Bode would correct this time.

"Tainting the water sources nearest the palace will force Morac to find ones farther afield, stretching his logistical lines in several directions," Cronus said approvingly.

"Aye. Once the cavalry poisons the surrounding well sites, they will reassemble twenty leagues either north or south of Corell, raiding the enemy lines of communications along this circumference," Bode swept his hand around the palace in a wide arc.

"Just as you did last time," Nevias nodded approvingly. Nevias and Cronus lamented their lack of knowledge of the success of the Torry cavalry during the siege, with Morac's perimeter too strong for messages to slip in or out of Corell. They were blind to nearly all happenings that transpired beyond sight of the palace walls.

"Aye, but last time we had Kato helping to neutralize any enemy riders contesting our cavalry. We don't have that advantage now unless your friend Raven would lend a hand, but we'll have more use of him here if things go poorly," Bode said.

"Even then, he shall not help us until Thorton reveals himself. He needs to kill him before Thorton returns the favor," Cronus explained.

"I'd wager that will be frustrating for your friend as well as for us," Bode reasoned.

"True. Raven is not one for patience I am afraid," Cronus sighed tiredly, thinking of his actions earlier. Raven was currently being seen to by the matrons, the injury to his ankle requiring their full attention. If the injury was serious, they could not heal it until Ular returned from Besos with the tissue regenerator.

"Aye. He is nothing like Kato. Could there be two men more different than them? Especially considering they hale from the same place," Nevias wondered.

"Earth is very large, if what I have learned about it is even partly true. Their people come from many places that are far different from each other. Even those born in proximity can vary greatly in personality and disposition. Are we any different? Look no further than Galen and Master Vantel," Cronus smiled, his comparison proving that to be true.

"Fair enough, Cronus," Bode conceded.

"How fares your Earther friend?" Nevias asked curiously, having only heard of the mishap just before their meeting.

"Hard to say, Commander. Raven tends to complain over small injuries, and make light of the serious ones."

"He's an odd one, I'll give him that," General Bode sighed, having recalled his first interaction with the big Earther at Rego.

The three men's gaze were instantly drawn to the entrance as Princess Corry entered, with Terin close behind, the rest of her guards remaining in the outer corridor.

"Highness," Bode greeted her as they bowed their heads.

"Gentlemen. General Valen and Chief Minister Monsh shall soon join us. What have you?" Corry asked as Terin took up position near the door, keeping a watchful eye through the narrow slits of his helm. Since arriving at Corell, Corry kept him close to her side, her ever vigilant guardian. He took to the role zealously, savoring every moment in her company. It was the one way they could spend such time together without raising the suspicion of the court on their true feelings. Once the coming battle was decided, Cory would formally announce their betrothal. Until then they would continue as they were, a Princess and her loyal Champion.

"We were discussing the watering sites about the palace," Bode explained, expounding on Cronus' morning ride with the detachment assigned the northwest sector.

"Expand the poisonings another three leagues," Corry ordered, examining the map with a critical eye.

"Highness, should we win the battle we also will have need of these watering points after the siege is lifted," Bode pointed out, trying to limit the damage of this bold tactic.

"We can dig new wells and repair poisoned ones. We want the siege to be as brutally painful for *LORD* Morac as we can manage. I believe this battle shall decide the fate of the war. To achieve that end, I will leave no advantage unused," she said.

"Very well. I will give Tevlin and Connly their new orders," Bode regarded the commanders of the Torry 1st and 2nd Cavalry.

"What of the sightings of enemy cavalry?" She inquired.

"Last magantor reports placed a sizable force numbering over three full units here, and another of equal size… here," Bode indicated separate points northeast and southeast of Corell.

"Commander Tevlin's 4th and 5th Units clashed with another group along this line," Nevias pointed out the eastern ridge of the Nepar Valley some forty leagues north of Corell.

"Casualties?" She asked.

"A dozen to either side. The enemy drew away. General Valen's scouts have spotted numerous enemy magantors to our direct east. Morac seems to have learned from his previous mistakes," Bode said.

"Terin, you and Cronus are excused to see Raven and ascertain his injuries. I will join you shortly," Corry dismissed them.

Cronus and Terin stepped without just as General Valen and the Chief Minister arrived. Corry received their assessment of all happenings in the northern realm. Food provisioning and the evacuation of all peoples in the enemy's likeliest path, were prioritized. The state of the main gate was thankfully resolved, as well as most of the interior gates. The matter resolved one of their unending list of priorities. She was pleased with Torg's preparations during her absence, the craggy master of arms continuing her work without respite. Of course, all she learned of statecraft came much from his tutelage. With her father's death, she came to realize how much she loved Torg. He was the surrogate grandfather she never had, and ironically, the true grandfather of the man she loved.

The commanders went to update the state of their readiness and countermeasures they prepared for the enemy. After much deliberation Corry presented General Dar Valen with a scrolled parchment, which he carefully read. It held the likeness of a most disagreeable woman with intense gray eyes and light auburn hair bound in braids. WANTED ALIVE was written atop the parchment, while at the bottom read: Veneva, Captain of the *Queen's Dagger*, 200,000 certras.

"I had the royal artists make a dozen copies of that for your messengers to deliver to every port from Faust to Tro," Corry instructed.

"Who is she, Highness?" Eli Monsh asked, examining the likeness over General Valen's shoulder.

"She is the slaver captain that sold Terin to Guardian Darna," Dar answered for her, recalling the testimony of Terin's fellow captive named Criose who relayed the details to Prince Lorn during the siege of Fleace.

"Yes. And I want her brought before me in chains to stand account for her crimes," Corry said with a cold anger.

* * *

"I'm alright," Raven complained as the matron Dresila examined his swollen ankle.

"I shall be the judge of your health, good sir," Dresila sternly rebuked her stubborn patient as she knelt before the cot where he sat, examining his large foot.

"It ain't broke, I can tell that by the way it felt when I stood on it. It's probably just a sprain, and I should know considering how many times I had a teammate roll into it over the years," Raven said, wanting nothing more than to leave the matrons' ward. Why he allowed Cronus and the others to bring him here, was beyond him. He was just about at the end of his rope, and would leave here very soon, even if he had to crawl out.

"It is difficult to guess the swelling considering the size of your foot. Is your other one this large?" she asked, thinking of removing his other boot for a comparison.

"They are both big, Matron. You know what they say about the size of a man's foot," he smiled.

"No," she said dryly, guessing his reference alluded to something unseemly. She sighed in frustration trying to determine the extent and nature of his injury. He was right in that it wasn't likely broken, but the sprain appeared high on the ankle, and those sorts of injuries required a lot of time to heal.

He wasn't surprised when a small gaggle of matrons crowded near to have a look. He was used to receiving strange looks wherever the *Stenox* ventured, but here it was manifested many times. He felt like a circus freak, drawing curious stares by the good people of the palace. He thought they should be used to Earthers by now considering the time Kato spent with them. At least the matrons were nice enough, most smiling sweetly and tending to him like mother hens. Some were downright frightened of him, trembling whenever he looked at them, which forced him to smile more than he wanted, just to set them at ease. If they were this taken aback by him, he could just imagine their reaction to Argos and Zem.

Torg and Orlom were the first to visit him during his examination, the craggy Master of Arms shaking his head at his stupidity while crossing his arms over his chest. Orlom stood beside Torg with his usual stupid grin, the two of them making the oddest pairing Raven had ever seen.

"It's bad enough my grandson is prone to acts of madness. I now know where he learned them from," Torg snorted.

"Me and coach came here as soon as we heard what happened, Boss," Orlom grinned.

"Her Highness learned of it first and sent us ahead to check on you," Torg clarified, relieved that the injury did not appear serious.

"I didn't think she cared?" Raven shrugged, trying to act surprised.

"You helped her save Terin, along with your crew. Gratitude is one of her many great attributes. Besides, she needs you to kill Thorton," Torg added in good humor.

"Is that a smile I see on your lips, Torg?" Raven couldn't help remark.

"If it is, you should have the decency not to speak of it to anyone else. You neither, Orlom," Torg gave each of them a look.

"Sure thing, Coach," Orlom gave him an Earther salute, touching the flat of his hand to the edge of his brow.

Torg released a weary sigh, wondering how he became saddled with the mischievous ape.

"Orlom, can you fetch me a thick walking stick? I might need it for a while," Raven asked.

"Sure thing, Boss. I'll be right back," he happily obeyed, taking several steps toward the exit before thinking to ask where he might find one, before Torg told him where to search.

"If anyone gives you grief, you tell them I told you to fetch it," Torg added before Orlom hurried off.

"Is he growing on you yet?" Raven grinned, enjoying the tired look on Torg's rapidly aging face.

"You know, Raven, I have heard many rumors about you since you came to our world. They said you were a ruthless, dangerous mercenary who brought destruction wherever he went. The rumors failed to mention you are a complete ass," Torg shook his head.

"Guilty," Raven confessed, his stupid grin causing Torg to chuckle, with poor Matron Dresila wondering what to make of it. There were no two men more frightening than Captain Raven and Master Vantel.

"From one complete ass to another," Torg confessed as well before Matron Dresila scolded both of them for their language, causing the other matrons to giggle.

"My apologies, Matron," Torg said before inquiring of Raven's injury.

"He should be fine with proper rest, and avoiding any further foolish antics," she scolded Raven.

"You sound worse than my wife," Raven said, imagining Tosha saying the same thing to him.

"A wise woman indeed, Captain Raven," she said, stepping away to fetch a dressing, while ordering the other matrons to return to their duties.

"She's a handful," Raven said as she stepped beyond earshot.

"She's a good lass. She was quite fond of your friend Kato. Every matron in Corell was deeply saddened with his passing," Torg explained.

"They're not alone in that regard. Kato was a good man," Raven sighed, hating to think about it, and what he had to do.

"I haven't told you this yet, but I want to thank you," Torg said in all seriousness.

"Thank me?"

"For saving my grandson. Corry could not have done it without you and your crew. I have many faults, but ingratitude isn't one of them."

"Don't mention it, Torg. Terin's our friend, and we don't leave our friends in places like that if we can do something about it. That kid journeyed to Fera with us to rescue Cronus, and fought his way through the palace right beside us. That's something I won't ever forget."

"Aye, he's a brave lad. I am pleased he has friends worthy of him," Torg briefly put a hand to Raven's thick shoulder, giving him a hardy pat as Cronus and Terin made their entrance, joining Torg at Raven's bedside.

"Shouldn't you be laying down?" Cronus playfully scolded, looking over Raven's bare right ankle and foot, where his trouser leg was rolled up to his knee.

"I can sit up just fine, and don't you start in on me," Raven growled, hating all the fuss he was getting.

"You won't do any of us any good if you don't take care of yourself, you big oaf," Cronus teased, keeping beyond Raven's reach, lest his friend strike his arm.

"I'll be alright. I just need time to heal. Besides, I don't need to do a lot of running around while waiting for Thorton. All I need is a high point to sit down and scan the battlefield through my scope, and my trigger finger works just fine. I'll gladly take a sore ankle than a gragglogg attack, I'll tell you that."

"I agree with you there," Cronus nodded.

"Gragglogg attack?" Torg asked darkly, knowing the danger the creatures posed.

"We were attacked by them after escaping Fera. That was why we had to continue our journey on ocran after the creatures slew our magantors," Cronus explained.

Torg had forgotten that detail when Cronus first spoke of his journey from Fera, or he hadn't paid attention when he did speak of it.

"I'll leave you rascals to talk amongst yourselves. When Orlom returns, tell him he'll find me in the training arena," Torg said, before making his exit.

"Sure thing, *Coach*," Raven said.

Torg just shook his head and stepped without.

"I always wondered what it would be like with you here at Corell, Rav. You certainly don't disappoint," Cronus japed.

"I actually saw Torg chuckle yesterday," Terin shook his head in disbelief, trying to recollect what exactly Orlom did or said to bring it about.

"Torg's the life of the party once you loosen him up a bit," Raven said, the others wondering what the *life of the party* meant.

"Can we bring you anything, Rav? I expect you shall be here for a few days at least, and I…" Cronus began to ask but Raven was having none of it.

"I'm not sitting here for several more minutes, let alone days. The matrons can't do anything to fix my ankle. All I need is time, and I can do that anywhere. What you two jokers can do is help me up to the roof where I can get some fresh air, and bring me my dinner while I'm up there."

Cronus just sighed, knowing that was how it was going to be, no matter how strongly Matron Dresila protested.

* * *

The early evening found Cronus and Leanna upon the ramparts of the outer wall, gazing off to the west as the sun slipped below the horizon, its orange glow painting the western sky. The cool spring air lifted his dark mane as he wrapped his arms around her from behind, drawing her back to his chest. She savored the warmth of his embrace, his strong arms holding her with such strength and gentleness. He slowly lowered his hands, running them over her belly. Her bulge was much lower now, a stark reminder that the baby would soon arrive. He tucked his head into her neck, squeezing her tightly.

His duties kept him busy since his return, joining countless patrols around the palace. His training under Torg was as intense as his first lessons when he was first named to the Elite. Torg drilled all of them to exhaustion, emphasizing hardening of the body to absorb blows, his generous lessons leaving Cronus sore from head to toe. It was painfully efficient and effective, humbling Cronus and the others, revealing how weak they truly were. Cronus was well schooled in all combat arts, but training constantly with Torg revealed how little he really knew. Torg could kill a man in seconds using nearly anything, even sticks, stones or his bare hands.

"You can collapse a man with a single blow!" Torg barked time and again, pointing out the knee joint, the eyes and the throat as the most vulnerable points on the body. He constantly reminded them that victory was oft decided not by who was strongest on a certain day, but by who was better at a particular moment. *"Victory can be snatched from defeat, and defeat from victory at any time. Battle is fluid and you must adapt."*

Cronus pondered Torg's words, realizing how very true they were. Often times it wasn't even who was stronger or more skilled, but who could exploit a fortuitous moment or just dumb luck. He need look no further than their victory at Cesa to prove that point, when the Earthers sunk the Macon Fleet in mere moments. The Torry admirals were not stronger or wiser than their foes that day, but exploited their good fortune, parlaying that victory by convincing the Macons they possessed a special weapon, tricking them into a full retreat. He wondered what turn of events would shape the battle to come?

"You are thinking too much, my love," Leanna sighed, knowing when her husband's mind drifted elsewhere by the way he held her.

"Sorry," he smiled wanly, reaffirming his embrace, scolding himself for allowing anything to distract him from their precious moments together.

She knew what distracted him, thoughts of the battles ahead robbing them of their time together. She wanted to savor every moment with him, fearing it could be their last. She thought of all the brave men that had already fallen in battle, knowing Cronus could just as easily count among their number. She then scolded herself for being distracted, recovering by touching her hands to his forearms that wrapped snugly about her. She sighed after a time, the glaze coming over her eyes a reflection of the calm that overtook her every time he held her. In his arms she felt safe, for he was her rock, her guardian, her love. As the tide of war raged about them, it seemed trivial weighed against his reassuring presence.

"I love you," she whispered, closing her eyes, resting the back of her head against his chest.

He squeezed her tightly, wishing to never let go, lest the fates draw her away as they were prone to do. Just as he fought to keep the thoughts of war from his mind, they came rushing back. His minded drifted painfully east, where Morac's legions marched unmolested toward Corell in vast numbers. They were coming and he knew not how they would be turned back a second time. Morac could fill the sky with gargoyles and magantors, while legions of Benotrists assailed the palace gates.

How long can we hold? he asked himself, his imagination unfolding the consequences of defeat, and what that held for his beloved Leanna. Such thoughts crippled him with fear, a fear he never knew until he met her on that bright sunny day so long ago in Central City. Death never bothered him in those days, as he waged his life for glory and position, reward fueling his courage. But now, he knew better. He now loved, and was loved, fearing anything that might take that from him, that would rob him of a lifetime with Leanna.

"You are my world," he whispered back, kissing the top of her head.

* * *

Raven rested on a rampart of the inner wall, observing Leanna and Cronus below from afar. He sat with his back against the thick bulwark with his rifle across his lap, and his left leg dangling over the wall. Several onlookers thought him mad for sitting so dangerously, but didn't voice their thoughts. Seeing Cronus and Leanna brought back memories of happier times, memories he suppressed. They were memories of his best friend, and the love his friend shared with the most beautiful woman to ever don the uniform of a Space Fleet pilot. He hoped that fate showed Cronus and Leanna the kindness and mercy that it failed to grant his former friend.

"I don't think it is wise to be sitting on the wall like that," Terin's voice drew him away from the scene below, standing off his right, able to clearly see his face in the wanning daylight.

"I'll be alright. It's more comfortable like this," he said with his sprained right ankle resting along the top of the wall, while his left dangled over the steep drop to the causeway below.

"If you happen to fall and break your neck, Tosha will never forgive me," Terin pointed out.

"Don't worry. She'll know it was my fault, just like everything else. Women," he shook his head.

"Only if you live. She cannot argue with a corpse, and will look to the next person to blame."

"That's where you're wrong, kid. If the corpse in question is mine, she'd stuff it, drag it back to Bansuck and spend several hours everyday yelling at it just for fun," he chuckled.

Terin smiled, shaking his head, imagining her doing that very thing.

"How fares your leg?"

"Not so bad. I just need to rest it a few days is all. The only thing that really bothers me is taking a piss or dropping a load. Takes me forever moving about on Orlom's makeshift crutch," he pointed out the long stick with the cross piece affixed to its top, resting beside the wall.

"It's strange seeing you like this," Terin said, never seeing Raven hurt before. No matter what they suffered or faced, Raven always came through as if nothing could hurt him. He was larger than life, and Terin loved him dearly.

"I've seen worse days, believe me. I once had my left leg shattered below the knee during a sky jump near Jakarta. That hurt like hell. Dislocated my left shoulder five times playing football, and broke my right collar bone twice. Had all my ribs cracked along my left side during my first deep space patrol when my fighter got hit with an energy blast. Luckily, I made it back to the fleet, but that was a painful trip," Raven went on to describe several more gruesome ailments, with poor Terin trying to understand what he was talking about.

"I wish you a fast recovery, for we need you healthy."

"Come on, kid, you don't need a broken-down gunslinger like me when you have that fancy sword of yours, and the blood of Kal to use it," Raven japed.

Terin stepped closer, placing his hand on Raven's thick shoulder, looking him in the eye. "WE NEED YOU."

Raven chuckled, touched by his young friend's sincerity. If there was one thing he always liked about this kid, it was his loyalty to his friends. Even if they didn't need him, Terin would still try to convince Raven that they did, just to make him feel accepted and wanted. Raven knew most of the Torries didn't see him that way. In truth, he was more like a terrible monster they needed to kill another monster, and once that monster was slain, they would just as soon see him leave.

"Don't worry, Terin. I'm not going anywhere until the job is done. Meanwhile I'll just enjoy the fresh air while I can, at least until Morac arrives and sends me into hiding. I hate to admit how much I'm not looking forward to being stuck inside the castle all day, at least until Ben shows his face," Raven's voice trailed mournfully off at the mention of his friend.

"I am sorry for your what you have to do, Raven," Terin lowered his head sadly.

"It's one thing to have to kill a man, but it is so much worse when you have to kill your best friend, one who is closer than any brother."

A long silenced passed between them, each at a loss for words before Terin braved the question he long wanted to ask.

"What happened between you and Thorton to bring you to this place?"

There it was, the one question so many on Arax wondered about, and only the Earthers knew. Raven regarded him for a time, pained by those awful memories before relenting.

"It was sometime ago. Several months before we were stranded on Arax…" Raven began.

"Take 'em, Rav. I got your back!" Ben Thorton barked through the comm.

Raven engaged his boosters, closing the distance between his star fighter and the Aurelian raider. Laser fire burst all around him, streaming past his canopy in hues of red and white.

"I thought you had my back?" Raven grunted, swerving to avoid another blast.

BOOM!

A pulse wave passed through his fighter, flowing aft to nose..

"I do. Stop whining and get that guy," Thorton replied, blasting the raider encroaching his captain's backside.

Raven closed rapidly on his prey, pushing within three thousand meters before opening up with all cannons. The Aurelian fighter imploded in a brief burst, with Raven's ship veering off, avoiding the pulse from the dead ship.

"Good shooting, Rav," Thorton said.

"Not bad yourself."

"Besides, I promised Jen, I'd keep you alive, and with you that's a full-time job," Ben quipped.

"That's funny, I promised her the same thing about you," Raven countered.

"Perhaps, but I'm not the one doing one reckless maneuver after another."

"That's a load of crap," Raven refuted.

"I'm not the one that purposely flew through the landing bay of an Aurelian command ship," Ben shook his head.

"That was your idea," Raven pointed out.

"I might have come up with the idea, but no one in their right mind thought you would actually do it."

"We are Space Fleet pilots. None of us are in our right minds. It's like my dad used to say, 'Everyone around here is nuts but you and me, and you're a little bit off.'"

"I knew you'd say that," Ben laughed, recalling how many times Raven and Jen's father said that over the years.

"What's our ETA to the rendezvous point?" Raven asked, unable to get a clear read on his console.

"Three minutes, twenty seconds," Ben said, with the intense brightness of the nearby star shining dully through his shielded canopy as they raced their sleek star fighters wingtip to wingtip. Space Fleet regulations

required at least one thousand meters spacing between fighters on deep space patrol, and at five meters, they were in clear violation, but neither of them was much for following protocol.

"Blue Squadron, report!" Raven commanded once they were within short distance comm range.

"Blue one," Lorken's voice answered back.

"Blue two," another said.

"Blue three."

"Blue four… Blue five…" They rattled off until all twenty reported in procession.

"Blue Bravo," Ben said, with bravo the designation of the squadron executive officer.

"Blue Alpha," Raven finished, with alpha the designation for squadron commander. "Let's return to the fleet."

* * *

The 2ⁿᵈ Earth Space Fleet consisted of fourteen star ships, including life support vessels, marine transports, a medical vessel, several space destroyers, two cruisers and the battle carriers STALINGRAD and MID-WAY. Each battle carrier stretched 6,000 meters in length with four landing bays running the length of the vessels, two along the top of the ships and two running the length along the bottom of the super structure. A series of heavy laser batteries ran along the flanks of the large vessels, complementing the fourteen squadrons of star fighters assigned to each carrier. The heavy armaments of the battle carriers were powerful enough to devastate the surface of a planet and destroy enemy vessels at great distances, making them the most powerful starships in the known universe.

The Aurelian alliance's largest warships were their command ships, each half the size of Earth's battle carriers, requiring several of the large vessels to trade blows with one Earth ship. Since their earliest encounters, the Aurelian and Earth civilizations came to blows over the terraformed colonies the Earth Space Directorate established in its neighboring star systems, their ever growing rivalry culminating in a larger conflict spanning several hundred light years across the galaxy. Eight months prior, the Aurelians slipped a raiding fleet past Earth's Space Fleet, reaching the outskirts of Solar System Prime. With a complement of three command ships and twenty squadrons, the Aurelian Fleet devastated the Earth colony of Titan, destroying most of Earth's defenses in the outer reaches of Solar System Prime before advancing to the inner planets, where only one Earth battle carrier blocked their path. With all of her sister battle carriers away in other star systems, the defense of Earth fell to the Battle Carrier STALINGRAD, responding from its Earth orbiting space dock, its crew recalled from shore leave and underway before the battle at Titan was concluded. Commanded by the mercurial Admiral Von Kruger, the STALINGRAD planned to fight a delaying action until other battle carriers could be recalled from deep space and the nearest star systems, and until Earth could fully muster all its defenses. That strategy changed once a brash young pilot with the call sign RAVEN, discovered a fatal flaw in the Aurelian Command ship design.

The Aurelian command ships' landing bays ran from the center of the bow before breaking off in a Y formation, exiting both sides of the stern, one to port, the other starboard. The bays ran through the center of the superstructure, with the ship's vital sections positioned above and below. The shielded doors closed the bays during sub-space flight, but were open during combat to launch and retrieve fighters. Evading a fighter phalanx and the warship's batteries, Raven passed though the landing bay of the lead Aurelian vessel. His ship slipped through the opening on the bow, passing through the superstructure of the vessel, depositing his torpedo payload before exiting portside stern, the Aurelian warship erupting in his wake.

Once Raven destroyed the lead Aurelian command ship, the STALINGRAD closed in to exchange blows with the survivors. The Aurelians immediately withdrew before other Earth pilots repeated Raven's maneuver with their remaining two command ships. For his actions, Raven was promoted to Captain of Blue Squadron. During formal inquiry of his actions, Raven acknowledged the audacious maneuver was the brain child of his friend and fellow pilot Ben Thorton, who covered his attack by single handedly engaging and distracting many of the Aurelian fighters guarding the lead command ship. For his brave contributions to the *success of Raven's attack, Thorton was formally acknowledged by Earth's Space Directorate and promoted to Executive Officer of Blue Squadron.*

Seeing the STALINGRAD as he drew near, never failed to impress Raven, the massive ship growing larger in his viewport upon their approach. The superstructure of the vessel was made of pure Trundusium, the powerful hybrid material essential for the skin of any vessel attempting hyper space travel. The ship's exterior was a collage of rounded bulwarks with powerful laser batteries centered upon them, and a cone shaped nose forming the bow of the warship. The skin of the battle carrier was tinted in shifting hues of silver and black, each melding into one another like a reflective pool. The lights of the open landing bays stood out along the dark surface of the vessels, like luminous eyes of a giant beast drawing them in. Surrounding the vessel were the smaller ships of the fleet, with the MIDWAY and its support vessels farther in the distance.

"Blue squadron, you are cleared for landing!" A woman's voice echoed through the comm.

"Landing code submitted. Blue squadron approach in sequence!" Raven ordered.

"Blue one coming in!" Lorken replied, slowing his fighter as he approached Delta landing bay, landing astern above the glow of the carrier's after burners. He entered the magnetic code into his console, guiding his fighter to its landing pad.

"Blue two coming in!"

The squadron sounded off as each landed, with Thorton and Raven setting down last.

* * *

Raven opened his canopy, climbing out of his fighter, onto its landing pad as automated units attended his vessel. No sooner had he removed his helmet then he was greeted by an attractive Chinese woman wearing the standard silver uniform of a ship's operations officer, bearing the fleet rank of a full lieutenant with two silver bars. She was equal to his space marine rank of captain. All Battle Carrier pilots held marine ranks, while ship operations held traditional naval ranks.

"Your presence is required in the admiral's briefing room, Raven," the

young officer greeted him warmly, rolling her eyes as Lorken approached, joining them on the fighter pad.

"Right now, Bao?" Raven asked, wondering what the urgency was.

"Right now! Ben as well," Bao stated firmly, trying not react to Lorken's insistent flirting, as he stood beside her with that stupid look on his face. Bao Chang was the niece of their flight operations commander, Colonel Chang. She and Lorken had an on and off again relationship through the previous year, with him dating numerous others during their off again phases, much to her annoyance.

"What about our post mission debrief?" Raven asked.

"I'll handle the debrief, Rav," Lorken said.

"I'm sure Major Hadi will love hearing about the two raiders you bagged out there," Raven shook his head, regarding the Aurelian fighters he saw Lorken destroy before he and Ben chased down the last fleeing enemy raiders.

"Three actually. You didn't see the third I got when you and Ben were chasing the stragglers," Lorken said, trying to impress Bao with his exploits.

"Two and a half, Lorken. Lieutenant Leal already crippled the third ship before you finished it, according to the flight data," Bao corrected him.

"A kill is a kill. How about you join me for dinner in the pilots' lounge after the debrief, Bao?" Lorken asked.

"I am on duty for the next six hours, LORENCE," she shook her head, knowing he hated her using his given name. "Save your smooth talk for another girl who is easily charmed." She turned and walked away.

"Her loss," Lorken shrugged.

"I'm sure she'll be heartbroken, Blue One. Just don't screw up the debrief by talking about your kills and not anyone else's," Raven slapped Lorken on the shoulder, before heading across the hanger toward the central lift, where Ben was already waiting for him.

* * *

Admiral Helmut Von Kruger stood at the viewport of the command briefing room, staring at the surrounding stars and the endless expanse of eternal space. His thoughts drifted beyond what his mortal eyes could see. Despite exploration that took them across many light years of the galaxy, they only touched an infinite sliver of the greater Milky Way. What dangers awaited the men and women they intended to send into the unknown? The name Von Kruger was gaining notoriety through the colonies and inner circles of Earth's Space Directorate. He commanded the STALINGRAD battle fleet for three years, but with the fleet's performance defending Solar System Prime from the Aurelian incursion, the command of the battle carrier MIDWAY was added to his fleet, along with its supporting vessels. A lesser man might boast the great power entrusted to him, but Admiral Kruger was neither boastful or humble, but a stern and capable commander guided by logic with enough charisma to inspire his men to greatness.

"Admiral?" Colonel Chang, the commander of flight operations of the STALINGRAD, asked. He sat at the briefing table in the center of the room where the committee of exploration and settlement was assembled. The committee just arrived, and were immediately ushered to the briefing room where they awaited Admiral Kruger and Colonel Chang, who were overseeing the skirmishes between their squadrons and the Aurelian raiders that plagued this sector.

"You may continue, Colonel," the admiral said, before turning around to take his seat at the head of the large oval table, its murky black surface contrasting with the silver walls and ceiling of the prestigious room. Admiral Helmut Von Kruger cut an imposing figure with sharp facial features and a thick, muscular build, each matching his warrior's face he used to great effect in projecting his authority.

Colonel Chang sat to the admiral's right, the seasoned veteran commander striking an equally imposing figure, having served with the admiral during his entire time as head of flight operations aboard the STALINGRAD. "Gentlemen, and ladies, our orders from Space Directorate are as follows. Once our campaign with the Aurelians is concluded, the fleet is to proceed to the edge of the Varan System, where I am to co-lead an explorative expedition beyond our known frontier. Since our current conflict with the Aurelians is over the control of recently terraformed planets, the directorate plans to continue terraforming operations in systems far beyond the Aurelian threat. Finding suitable planets and systems that meet our requirements shall be this expedition's primary mission. Admiral Kruger has assigned myself to co-lead this joint military and civilian expedition, granting me overall command in matters pertaining to security, navigation and any formal interaction with alien contacts should they arise. Mr. Flores shall share command, heading the civilian team from the Department of Exploration and Settlement. Mr. Flores, if you would like to speak and present your team," Colonel Chang *deferred to his Peruvian counterpart.*

"I was deeply honored when director Hadad selected me to co-lead this mission, and to share command with a man of Colonel Chang's reputation. It is little secret to those of us seated around this table that the future of mankind depends upon our expansion beyond our current sphere of influence. Over the last three centuries, we have vastly improved our techniques in terraforming planets to suit human life, from cooling hot worlds to warming cold ones, as well as removing poisonous atmospheres as we first did with Venus. The diversity of Solar System Prime allowed us to experiment and perfect these techniques, which we repeated with the systems most similar to our own. Our techniques have improved greatly to allow us to successfully terraform worlds that do not reside in the most favorable locations, as our first colonists on Varan 3 can attest. Though nominally successful, we still would not consider operations far afield under such conditions. For deep space colonization to be successful, we must seek out the most optimal systems for consideration, which is where the team I have assembled shall fully assess. The members of my team are equally diverse in their knowledge base, and highly accomplished. I ask each of them to introduce themselves, but to forgo their past achievements, as we lack the time to fully name them, so great they are. Ms. York, if you would begin," Mr. Flores *introduced the woman sitting to his right, a green-eyed woman with dark hair tied in a high bun upon her head, wearing the tight fitting green uniform of her department, and appearing in her mid thirties.*

"I am Dr. Rebeca York, civilian rank C-16 in the Department of Agriculture and Science. I am native to Manchester England. My expertise is in the field of botany and alien soils," she said, *looking to the man to her right to continue.*

"I am Dr. Ahmet Bahadir, civilian rank C-16, Department of Medicine and Science. I am native to Ankara, Turkey. I am a surgeon

and expert in the fields of alien science and gravitational impacts on organic development. I shall act as the lead medical officer for this mission," Ahmet explained.

"I am Dr. Jillian Davenport, team geologist, civilian rank C15, Department of science. Native to Edmonton." Dr. Davenport was a tall, blond haired woman, 32 years of age. As the team's leading geologist, she would have final word on each planet's suitability.

"I am Pierre Clemence, native to Lyon, France, civilian rank C-18. I am the ranking engineer in the Department of Planetary Engineering," the suave Frenchman said. Like Dr. Davenport, his approval was required for all planets considered for terraforming.

And, so it continued with the rest of the civilian team's introductions, eleven in all, each a foremost authority in their fields of expertise, concluding with Dr. Leon Peterson of Liverpool, astrophysicist.

Colonel Chang then introduced the military personnel chosen for the mission, the first two of which stood along the wall behind him.

"The first members of my team are fleet officers. Lieutenant Junior Grade Grigory Borovkov is the 2nd Fleet's science officer, and Ensign Kaito Nakamura scores highest among the fleet's navigators," Colonel Chang called each of them forth where they exchanged pleasantries with their civilian counterparts.

No sooner had he done so, then Raven and Ben entered the room, saluting the admiral before he directed them to their place beside Brokov and Kato.

"Mr. Flores, I present your escort pilots, Captain Mekiana and 1st Lieutenant Thorton," Admiral Kruger introduced them, further explaining their marine rank designations, the meaning of a flight captain equal to that of a fleet full lieutenant.

Mr. Flores' eyes alit with recognition with their faces and names.

"Captain Mekiana and Lieutenant Thorton, your names circle in the citadels of Brussels with awe and admiration. Admiral Kruger has chosen well selecting you for this mission. We asked for the very best, and he has obliged. Welcome to our team," Mr. Flores greeted them.

"Team?" Ben asked, sharing a look with Raven before Colonel Chang explained the mission and their place in it.

"As ranking member of the military portion of our joint contingent,

outside myself, you shall act as my Executive officer," Colonel Chang said to Raven.

"And as such, I am allowing you to choose the third pilot assigned to this mission," Admiral Kruger added.

This was all bit much in so short a time, but Raven and Ben took it all in stride. The look the admiral gave them showed his displeasure for losing them for any period of time. It was little secret that Raven and Thorton were Admiral Kruger's favorites, but the importance of this mission required of him to offer up his best pilots, and that was obviously the two of them. Raven quietly discussed the candidates for the third pilot with Ben before offering up Lorken's name.

"Lorken?" Mr. Flores asked curiously.

"Lieutenant Lorence Umaru. He is currently Blue One in their squadron," Colonel Chang explained.

"If he comes highly recommended by the two of you, then he has my utmost confidence," Mr. Flores said.

"Tell me, Captain Mekiana, do you prefer your surname, or your more famed moniker… the RAVEN?" Dr. York asked whimsically with her English accent.

"Raven. Mekiana is a mouth full. I like to keep things simple, miss," Raven shrugged with his characteristic half grin.

"She is Dr. York, Raven," Colonel Chang reminded him.

"Dr." Raven corrected, which drew a smile from the attractive woman.

"We are each going to be spending a great deal of time together over the coming months. It will be quite tedious to be calling each other sir, ma'am, Dr., Colonel, Captain and so forth. I am Rebeca, Raven," she said before offering the same curtesy to Kato, Ben and Brokov. Most of the other civilians chorused her sentiment. Admiral Kruger interceded before Colonel Chang could voice his disagreement.

"Perhaps a loosening of protocol is not such a bad thing for this mission, Colonel, considering its stressful nature and the professionalism of every member of this team, both civilian and military," the admiral said. He would be certain to remind Ben and Lorken not to engage in their usual antics, recalling the incident with a certain Major Prescott a while back, which still made him laugh when no one was looking.

"*As you advise, Admiral,*" *Colonel Chang agreed.* "*Since we shall not embark on this mission until our upcoming operation is concluded, I invite your people to accept the hospitality of the STALINGRAD, Mr. Flores.*"

"*Thank you, Colonel. I am certain they are equally tired as I am from our journey here. If you would excuse us, we shall settle in to the gracious accommodations Admiral Kruger has provided,*" *Mr. Flores dismissed his team, with Colonel Chang, Brokov and Kato following them out the door.*

"*A moment, you two,*" *the admiral ordered Raven and Thorton to remain, waiting for the door to close before speaking freely.*

"*Admiral,*" *Raven greeted him as they stepped near.*

"*First thing's first. Is there anything in the post mission brief that I should know about?*" *the Admiral asked.*

"*Nothing unusual, admiral. Seven raiders destroyed. No casualties for our squadron,*" *Ben said.*

"*What of Red and Green squadrons?*" *the Admiral asked.*

"*We don't know off hand. They were scheduled to land just after us, and we were called up here,*" *Raven said.*

"*Very well. I shall check with their squadron commanders. I have other news the two of you should know. The first is that I am sending another asset along with you on your mission, an asset that shall be assigned to Blue Squadron for the upcoming campaign so that we can fully assess his capabilities in combat.*"

"*HIS?*" *Raven made a face, wondering what or who the admiral was talking about.*

"*An old friend of yours, Zem,*" *the admiral said with a rare grin, knowing Raven's annoyance whenever his brother's pet project was brought up.*

"*Zem,*" *Raven shook his head.*

"*He will be a fine addition to our squadron,*" *Ben laughed, slapping Raven on the back.*

"*When will he arrive?*" *Raven asked, hoping it wasn't any time soon.*

"*He is already here. He arrived with the civilian delegation you just met. Which brings up my other news, which is more for you than Raven,*" *he said to Ben.*

"Is it good or bad?" Ben asked, not able to say by the impartial look the admiral liked to assume.

"That is for you to decide. Your wife, his sister, is here," the admiral said, pointing first to Ben and then Raven.

"Jennifer?" Thorton growled, wondering why his wife was with the fleet when she should be safely assigned at Solar System Prime with their infant son.

"What's she doing here? She is supposed to be assigned to an Earth based defense squadron," Raven asked.

"When they announced for pilot volunteers for the upcoming campaign, she applied for one of the vacancies aboard the MIDWAY," the admiral explained.

"And Fleet HQ let her? They know Ben's already deployed. Why didn't they deny her application?" Raven asked.

"She went around HQ and applied directly to the selection committee. No one there knew her true situation, so she applied, manipulating the bureaucracy. She was qualified and they sent her here," the admiral added, equally frustrated with the situation.

"What about the Sullivan doctrine? No two family members are supposed to serve together," Raven pointed out.

"That would be true if she were assigned to the STALINGRAD, but she is assigned to the MIDWAY," the admiral said.

"But it's the same fleet. Shouldn't that count for something?" Raven argued.

"Apparently not. I'll have a word with the captain of the MIDWAY, and assign her flight control duties for the next six months. That will keep her out of the cockpit long enough for us to send her home," the admiral assured Ben.

"Thanks, admiral," Ben said gratefully.

"Where is she now?" Raven asked.

"I would guess the pilot's lounge waiting for you, along with Zem. You have 24 hours together before her shuttle takes her to the MIDWAY. Use the time wisely, Lieutenant," the admiral said, dismissing them.

"Thanks, admiral," Raven said before turning to catch up with his irate XO.

* * *

Pilots' lounge. Battle Carrier STALINGRAD.

"Another song, Jenny," Lorken urged, standing in a gaggle of pilots with a drink in hand.

Jennifer Thorton sat atop the music amplifier in the center of the pilots' lounge, with the members of Blue Squadron gathered round. Many of them knew her as Raven's kid sister, and Ben's wife, and a few were in her academy class the year prior. She was well known for her angelic voice, and striking beauty. Her lovely black hair was disappointingly cut in a short pilot's bob, with soft bangs framing her large brown eyes. Her skin was soft and lighter than her brother's. Her generous curves filled out her black pilot's uniform, from her thick black jacket and form fitted trousers, to the pistol tied down to her right hip. Though tall for a woman, she was still a full head shorter than her brother Raven. Despite their few similarities, it was their many differences that made everyone that knew them wonder how she and Raven sprang from the same parents.

"Do any of you have a certain request?" She asked, looking out at the small crowd of faces, with a dozen hands going into the air. She smiled inwardly at Zem, who stood off to one corner with his massive arms over his chest, making it known what song he preferred, humming ANCHORS AWEIGH loud enough for her to get the message.

"Sing the LESSER LOVE," one pilot pleaded.

"No! Sing the MOONS OF TORBIN," another shouted.

She ran her finger over her lacquered lips, pondering her choices when her eyes found Ben Thorton passing through the entrance on the far side of the lounge. She couldn't bite off her smile as she met his gaze across the room. How she sorely missed him after all these months apart, wondering if her plans to reunite with him would bear fruit. She knew that look in his eyes, the one that was equally angry, but yet drawn to her, like a hungry tiger. All she needed was a few moments alone with him to douse his ire, moments that she would have once she finished her next song, and she knew which song it would be, entering the code into the amplifier.

"This is an ancient ballad, and my husband's second favorite," she said before beginning, her eyes fixed across the room where her brother now joined her husband, both staring at her with most disapproving looks.

"From this valley they say you are leaving
I shall miss your bright eyes, and sweet smile
For they say you are taking the sunshine
That has brightened my pathway awhile
Come and sit by my side if you love me
Do not hasten to bid me adieu
But remember the Red River Valley
And the girl who loves you so true…"
The Red River Valley

Jennifer continued with all the lyrics, keeping her eyes upon Ben's, a mischievous smile touching her lips as she finished, before easing off the amplifier. She ambled across the room, the other pilots looking on as she closed upon her husband, wrapping her arms around him as she reached up, pressing her lips to his. The lounge erupted in applause and hearty cheers. It took Ben Thorton a while to disentangle her enough to pull her briefly away, while still keeping her in his firm grasp.

"What are you doing here?" He growled.

"Don't be angry, Texas. I just had to see you," she cooed sweetly, breaking down his scowl with her feminine charm.

"This is no place for the mother of my child. You were safe on Earth, and you volunteer for THIS!"

The other pilots nearby drifted to different corners of the lounge, pretending not to hear. Only Raven remained close, standing beside Ben with his arms crossed, nodding in agreement with everything his friend said.

"I had to see you, Texas. I miss you. Don't worry, for my tour is short term. I'll be back on Earth once this campaign ends," she batted her lashes shamelessly, disarming his anger with her devious antics.

"No! You will be on the next transport back to Earth. I'll have the Admiral request it personally to high command. They'll back me in this if they have any sense. Our actions during the invasion of Solar System Prime bought Raven and I a few favors to call in," he said.

"I volunteered for this campaign, this ENTIRE campaign. I am a fully trained combat pilot, and I will not be sent home by an overbearing, short tempered ogre!" She jabbed her finger into his thick chest to make her point.

"Who's watching Mike?" Ben asked quietly through his flaring nostrils.

"Mom and dad have him," she crossed her arms, returning his heated stare.

"An infant needs its mother."

"And a wife needs her husband."

He shook his head, frustrated by her stubbornness.

"Come, Texas. Let us just enjoy this moment?" She softened her tone, running her fingers across his chest.

"Alright," he conceded for the moment. There was little point in arguing about it now. What was done was done until he could fix it. In the mean time he might as well enjoy her company.

"Don't be gloomy, Texas. I know just the song to cheer you up," she returned to the amplifier and entered the sequence for his favorite refrain.

Thorton remained at the door with Raven at his side, staring at his beautiful wife with the view of space behind her where the large viewport dominated the far wall. She looked like an angel silhouetted by the starry sky, save for the heads of the surrounding pilots ruining the picture.

"There's a yellow rose of Texas
He's going back to see
No other cowboy knows her
No body only he
She cried so when he left her
It like to broke her heart
And should they ever meet again
They never more shall part…"
The Yellow Rose of Texas.

"You have your hands full with that one, Ben. Don't say I didn't warn before you tied the knot," Raven said.

"No, you didn't," Ben said dryly, watching his wife step off the ampli-

fier, making her way back to them, with the other pilots clamoring for another song.

"Don't go easy on her, and for crying out loud, don't let her use that look on you that she is wearing now. You best let her know who's the boss," Raven warned.

Ben looked over at him with a raised eyebrow. "You are the last man in the galaxy I'd take advice from when it comes to women, Rav. You've never had a girlfriend more than a week, and all of them ended with you being slapped, having something poured on you, or your credits stolen."

"All those girls were just practice. My luck is bound to change. Somewhere out there, there is a beautiful angel waiting for me, a kind, loving woman made just for me," Raven waved his left hand toward the far wall, where the starlit sky shone through the viewport.

"You'll get the woman you deserve, and if that doesn't concern you, it should," Ben shook his head.

Before Raven could refute that notion, Jennifer rushed back to Ben's arms, planting a kiss on his lips.

"Did that brighten your sour mood, Texas?" She asked, brazenly batting her lashes, tearing down his resolve with those beautiful brown eyes of hers.

"Of course, it did, you little vixen," Raven answered for him, knowing the spell she put him under with her feminine wiles.

"I've missed you too, big brother," she gave Raven an equally warm smile before sticking her tongue out at him.

"Look, you only have twenty-four hours, so don't waste it here with us," Raven said, pushing them toward the door, seeing little point in arguing with her now anyway.

Jennifer disentangled herself from her husband long enough to give Raven a hug.

"Thank you for keeping him safe," she whispered in his ear, recalling the promise he made to her every time they parted to protect Ben.

"I keep my promises, sis, especially to you," he whispered back before letting her go.

"Actually, I'm the one keeping him alive," Ben nudged Raven, having overheard what they said.

"Zem is waiting for you, big brother," Jennifer pointed him out

across the lounge with his massive arms crossed over his chest, looking in their direction, before taking her husband in tow for the exit.

* * *

    Every eye in the pilots' lounge followed Zem as he strode across the floor toward Raven, his blackish silver exterior mostly concealed by his pilot's uniform, stretched by his massive frame. His luminous blue eyes unnerved everyone with their superior intensity, save for Raven, who was quite familiar with the hulking brute with the brain of an insufferable intellectual, Zem's two dominant traits. The fact Zem was created by Raven's brother Matt, who instilled in him the familial bonds they both shared made him more like an annoying brother than a creature conjured up in the lab.

    In truth, Zem was the product of years of programming, research, and revolutionary advancements in created intelligence, a unique development in andro-robotics, ANDROs as they would be called. Much of the breakthrough work was completed by Raven's brother, who received much of the credit for Zem's completion. Though Matt was of similar size and stature with Raven, they were both dwarfed by their other three brother. Their similarities diverged after that, with Matt being an intellectual genius, where as Raven was… well, he was Raven. Where Raven entered the Space Fleet Academy, Matt flourished at the Wellington Academy of Science, where he began his work with Zem. Upon his graduation at the age of seventeen, Matt assumed his post at the Earth Department of Artificial Intelligence in Melbourne, where he continued his work on Zem, finishing just a few months before.

    By the end of the 21st century, almost all of Earth's defense forces were dominated by artificial intelligence. Even in the present 25th century, all aircraft that operated within the lower atmosphere were manned by some level of automated technology. The problems arose in deep space combat, where Aurelians, pirates or other nefarious groups could manipulate artificial intelligence, and commandeer Earth's defense forces. This necessitated human-piloted starships, with manual override capabilities. The deficiencies in human pilots instigated the research that led to Zem's development. Zem would be the first artificially intelligent pilot in

THE CHRONICLES OF ARAX

Space Fleet. The defense directorate planned to fully integrate androids into the human ranks of all frontline defense forces, even command. No andro would be commissioned unless it achieved nearly human levels of independent thought and individuality, which Zem excelled in both areas.

"I guess I should welcome you to Blue Squadron, big fella," Raven greeted him by shaking Zem's massive hand as he drew close.

"Yes, your squadron's reputation is exceedingly high, a suitable place for my first combat assignment," Zem stated with his deep metallic voice.

"Weren't you just recently commissioned?" Raven noticed the single silver bar on the corner of Zem's thick bomber jacket, denoting his rank as a space pilot 1st Lieutenant.

"Recently is a subjective determination of time. Such a question should be framed specifically within objective standards of measurement," Zem said as if Raven was the stupidest human he had ever known.

"Alright, Einstein, so just when were you commissioned?"

"I assume the mention of that 20th century scientist is meant to be a derogatory comparison between his impressive intellect and my own, it is truly a false comparison. The human you know as Einstein could hardly match my unequalled level of intelligence. It is my esteemed opinion that humans of his mental acuity should represent the bare minimum standard for entrance into any levels of higher learning, let alone positions of power."

'Did he just call Einstein STUPID?' Raven shook his head.

"As for the specific date of my commission, I received a direct commission on April 4th of this year after completing the curriculum at Annapolis," Zem added.

"How long were you at the Naval Academy?" Raven didn't recall Matt mentioning anything about that.

"Two weeks standard Earth time."

"Two weeks? You graduated in two weeks? How'd you manage that?" The average cadet required two years of full academic immersion to graduate from Annapolis.

"I received a waiver for all unnecessary instruction from the defense directorate. They wisely understood it would be a waste of my valuable time to spend two years at such an institution when I could simply demonstrate my mastery of all academic and physical requirements in an abbreviated curriculum. I must say that I thoroughly enjoyed my time there, and consider the esteemed institution my Alma Mater. It is a shame Space Fleet doesn't adopt ANCHORS AWEIGH as its official song, but I shall submit my esteemed opinion on that through the proper channels," Zem stated dryly.

"Wait a minute, if you graduated the Naval Academy, why aren't you an Ensign? In fact, you should be wearing a gold bar for that instead of silver," Raven pointed out the inconsistency.

"I was commissioned an ensign upon graduation, and assigned to Space Fleet operations in Beijing, where I was summarily promoted to Lieutenant Junior Grade upon completing my initial assessments. At the conclusion of those six weeks, I was reassigned to the Earth orbital Space Fleet docking station. It was then Admiral Okello advised me to transfer to the Space Marine fighter Division, as all battle carrier squadrons fall under, with my official rank changing from Fleet officer Lieutenant Junior Grade to Marine Pilot rank of 1st Lieutenant. This assignment shall fulfill my desired combat experience to justify my next promotion," Zem explained.

"Wait a second, Zem, back up a step. How were promoted to 1st Lieutenant in six weeks?" Raven asked, knowing the promotion period for O-1 to O-2 required at least two solar years.

"I know it was a lengthy waiting period for a sentient of my esteemed standing, but fleet HQ thought it best if I wasn't promoted to grade O-2 until completing that initial assessment. Unfortunately, my next promotion to Captain, O-3, requires 120 days of flight operations or the completion of a combat campaign. Admiral Kruger has informed me that I shall receive that promotion at the conclusion of this campaign and the expeditionary mission that we shall both partake after."

"Wait a minute, are you telling me you're going to be promoted to captain in less than six months?" Raven asked, more than a little annoyed considering he waited more than three years to get promoted to that rank, and even then, needed to destroy an Aurelian command ship to get it.

"I concede it is a lengthy process, but I have been assured that if my flight skills equal my previous performances, and if our exploratory mission is successful, I shall make colonel in eighteen months," Zem added, as if his rapid advancement was too slow yet richly deserved.

"Colonel! Colonel! They said you'd make colonel in eighteen months?" Raven shook his head, realizing in a few months he'd be taking orders from Zem. He could just imagine his brother Matt getting a good laugh about now.

"Of course, though I might transfer my commission back to fleet operations, and assume the comparable rank of Space Fleet captain, in which I should easily excel, clearing my promotion to admiral," Zem said with confidence, much to Raven's annoyance. A casual observer might conclude that Zem's boasting was simply done in jest, as he was more than capable of employing due to his unique individuality that set him apart from previous attempts of artificial intelligence, but Zem truly believed in his own superiority. This narcissistic trait was further fueled by Raven's father and grandfather, who each lauded his accomplishments, his father going as far as telling Zem that he was his favorite son.

'Why me?' Raven sadly shook his head.

"You look a little down. Come. I'll buy you a drink," Zem slapped him on the back, before heading to the bar.

* * *

"Can you forgive me now?" Jennifer Thorton asked raising an expectant brow, standing naked in her husband's cabin, starlight shining through the viewport behind her.

He sighed, locking the door before pressing the viewport shield closed on the console at the side of the room, not wishing any passing ship to get an eyeful.

"I forgive you, but you're still a brat," he drew her into his arms, crushing his lips to hers before she could refute it. She certainly wasn't playing fair, knowing the effect she had on him. He wanted nothing more than to remain in her arms, the war, the fleet, and the fate of mankind be damned. She was his everything, his very purpose for living. She was life itself, and the last place he wanted her to be was anywhere near the battle zone they were currently in. Since there was no fixing that at this moment, he would certainly enjoy their time together.

He scooped her into his arms, setting her down upon his narrow bunk, wishing they had a bigger bed to share.

"Aren't you forgetting something?" She reminded him as their lips drew briefly apart.

"Not really," he shrugged.

"Your clothes, you big oaf."

"Fair enough," he smiled, stripping off his black pilot's uniform and holster, letting them drop where he stood before climbing back atop of her.

"I've missed this," she cooed, running her hands along his back as he kissed her neck, his lips moving slowly across her breasts, taking his time. This was why she came, needing to be near her husband, her beloved, her very life. She closed her eyes, arcing her back as he continued, savoring his sensuous ministrations.

There among the stars and far from home, they made love.

* * *

"What are you thinking, Ben?" She asked, resting her head upon his chest as he stared at the ceiling. It was the middle of the night, Earth Standard Time, and they finished making love for what seemed the hundredth time. He lost count at seven, and she never counted such things. Either way, it was heaven, two people joined so intimately as if they were one.

He looked down as she looked at him, her ear pressed to his chest with her gaze fixed to his. She was like an angel, a soothing balm to his iron heart. Ben Thorton had many attributes that drew the praise from his fellow pilots and every commander in his chain of command. He was a hero every much as Raven, and opportunities abounded with whatever he wished to do after his tour of service came to an end. He cared nothing for any of it, his only thoughts centering on his wife. He planned for each of them to conclude their promised service in the next two years, and take up civilian posts in some obscure isolated place anywhere on Earth or on one of her growing number of colonies, someplace quiet and peaceful. The admiral would be disappointed, hoping to convince him to stay with promises of rapid promotion and a squadron of his own very soon. Colonel Chang was equally convincing, already planning his advancement to become his air operations X/O aboard the STALINGRAD. Raven was even worse, hoping Ben would remain his wingman until they were old and gray. He smiled at that, knowing Raven would always be a child at heart, an obnoxious, overgrown child at that. He was deeply fond of them all, but none held a candle to his wife, his beautiful Jen, who was as madly in love with him as he was with her. The fact she used his given name just now, rather than her playful nickname of TEXAS, meant her question was serious.

"Just thinking of our future," he smiled back at her. Oh, how she loved his deep voice, especially late at night when it became soft as a whisper.

"The future is the future, Ben. Try enjoying the moment. Years from now you shall look back at this time, wishing to relive it all over again. Don't waste it by thinking of something else. You can think of the future when you are strapped in your fighter on a long patrol," she said, running her hand over his muscled chest.

"I can hardly talk with you when I'm in my fighter. And since you are the one that I'm sharing my future with, who better can I speak about it with?"

"Fair enough, Texas, talk away."

"I want you to promise me that you will return to Earth as soon as the admiral can arrange it. We owe it to our son to have at least one parent out of the war zone," he began.

"You could just as easily fill that role as I?"

"You are his mother. A child needs his mother more than anything else."

"And you are his father. Every child needs his father more than…" she tried to counter, but he was having none of it.

"Fathers play a large role later on, but not in infancy."

"That sounds like a convenient excuse to send me away."

"It is a good excuse to protect my WIFE."

"What about my HUSBAND?"

"Jen, you must understand that I cannot do this with you here," he tried to calm his racing heart.

"Do what?"

"Fight this war. My thoughts should be on the enemy, but now all I can think of is you, and the danger you are in."

"What of the danger you are in? Don't you think that is constantly on my mind? If not, I can assure you that it is."

"You don't understand. I cannot live without you. I won't live without you," he looked at her desperately, trying to get her to see reason.

"And I cannot live without you. Do you think I would leave Mike with my parents to race across the galaxy to be near you without a good reason?"

"There is no good reason. Before, all I had to worry about is bringing myself and your brother home safely. Now I have you to worry about, and you are assigned to the MIDWAY, where I can't help you."

"I had a good reason, Ben," she said, pushing herself into a siting position.

"What was it?" He didn't believe her.

"I dreamed of you dying far from home, and I couldn't say good bye, or how much I love you. I needed to see you. I needed you to know how much I love you, and can't live without you. If you thought I would die, and that I was far away, wouldn't you do whatever you could to see me? To hold me one last time in the event your dreams were right?" She was crying now, not wishing to share such fears with him.

"Jen," he sighed, taking her into his arms, holding her tight. They remained in each other's embrace for an eternal moment, oblivious to the passing time.

"Damn this war," he whispered, pained by the choices that brought them here.

"On that, we can agree," she smiled wanly, wiping her eyes as they drew briefly away.

"Listen, Jen," he said, gently lifting her chin with his meaty hand, "I promised to return safely to you, and to keep Raven safe as well. I have kept that promise so far, haven't I?"

"Yes," she conceded.

"Then trust me to do so for just a few more months. And in turn, you must finish this assignment as quietly and peacefully as you can, and GO HOME. I will soon join you, and we will never go anywhere near a war zone for the rest of our lives. We will find someplace quiet and peaceful to live, someplace with few people around, and live there the rest of our days."

"You would be happy in such a place?" She asked skeptically.

"As long as I'm with you, yes. I have traveled the stars and countless worlds, and done things I could only have imagined not so long ago, but there is nothing that compares to spending your life with the one you love. Life is fleeting, Jen, and passes so quickly that it will end before you are ready. In the 17th century and before, people usually died by age thirty. In the twentieth and twenty-first century they lived to be about eighty, and even then, their last few years were wretched. Now we live to one hundred and fifty, and live well, but that is still woefully short. We are young now, so another thirteen decades might seem an eternity, but it is not. I don't want to look back and regret not savoring these years with you."

Oh, how she loved him, losing herself in his deep blue eyes that stared so intently into her soul. Ben Thorton was a hero of Earth, his name whispered upon every lip for what he and Raven did. He could do anything he desired, but all he wanted was to be with her.

"Could you be happy living in obscurity? Would you regret passing on all the opportunities that lay before your feet, just to spend them with me?"

"I don't care for fame or fortune, or the accolades of lickspittles. As I said, I have traveled the stars, and anything anyone offers me means nothing. All I want is to spend my life with you and raise our family. If our children want to explore the universe, they can have at it. But as far as I'm concerned, I've had my fill. Besides, I can do many things remotely, even teach history at the Space Fleet Academy."

"A quiet life with Ben Thorton and his growing brood," she tapped her lips with a finger, considering what that would entail, and smiling. "Very well, Texas. After this campaign is over, we shall do just that," she grinned deviously, climbing atop of him, crushing her lips to his.

* * *

The following weeks continued with the 2nd Fleet clearing the approaching sectors of the Aurelian home star system, where they were joined by the Earth 3rd and 7th Fleets. The 3rd Fleet was commanded by Rear Admiral Yamaguchi, native of Tokyo, Japan, with a complement of eighteen support vessels and the battle carriers AGINCOURT and AUSTERLITZ. The 7th Fleet was commanded by Rear Admiral Ahmadi, native to Saveh, Iran, and boasted 23 support vessels, including seven marine transports and the battle carrier BADR. The vast armada was led by Full Admiral Ernesto Garcia, a cool headed commander native to Tampico, Mexico, who was charged by the Earth Defense Directorate to penetrate the Aurelian home star system, and establish a permanent base there, bringing their enemy to heel.

Much to Admiral Kruger's annoyance, and Ben Thorton's ire, Jennifer filed a formal grievance when she was assigned to flight operations duty, which violated her formal agreement when she volunteered for the campaign. She joined the 2nd Fleet under assurances of being assigned squadron flight duty. The bureaucratic Corp, which was notoriously slow to respond in all other matters, ironically responded swiftly to her complaint, ordering Admiral Kruger to return her immediately to flight status in Orange Squadron.

Ben took out much of his frustration with the situation during small arms practice in the STALINGRAD's pistol range, where Raven often joined him. The two friends would spend countless hours drawing from the holster, with unnatural speed and accuracy, their competition drawing most of their squadron members to watch, with Zem and Lorken their most vocal critics, mocking any shot that went awry. Brokov and Kato would continuously join them whenever their duties allowed, building camaraderie with their future crewmates for their upcoming exploratory mission.

It was two days before the fleet entered the Aurelian Home System when Admiral Kruger met Thorton in the flight hanger after a brief training exercise, greeting the pilot as he climbed out of the cockpit, standing off to the side of his circular landing pad. The small landing pads would extend out into the larger hanger, before receiving their assigned fighter craft, and retracting into the walls, where their automated crew would oversee maintenance and refurbishment of each craft. Ben stepped off the platform as it retracted, rendering the admiral a salute.

"Another fine practice run, if our readouts are accurate," Admiral Kruger said, returning the salute, before drawing Ben aside.

"We'll find out soon enough if they are, admiral," Ben said, tucking his helmet under his arm while looking beyond the admiral's shoulder where Raven just landed several pad lengths away toward the bow.

The admiral followed his gaze, watching as Raven's canopy opened. "I'll speak with him in a moment. I meant to have a word with you in private without raising too many questions. This ship has more ears than a corn field."

"If you came all the way down here to speak with me, there could only be one reason," Ben guessed it had something to do with Jen.

"Aye, clever man. I can't pull her from flight duty, Ben, but I wanted you to know that neither your squadron or hers will be assigned to the phalanx. Once we jump into their star system things will be happening fairly quick. Our cruisers will bombard the outer planets before we commit our fighters. Most of our fleet will advance to engage the enemy fleet, wherever they are positioned. I don't like flying blind into battle, but there is no other way. Every pilot will see action, but the phalanx will likely see the most."

The phalanx was the preferred method of attacking an enemy fleet, with multiple fighter squadrons preceding the larger warships in battle. The enemy was likely to counter with a phalanx of their own, the sides often devolving into a thousand dogfights before the big ships closed in.

"We win this battle, and then we send her home, and you with her," Admiral Kruger placed a hand to his shoulder.

"You're forgetting our exploration mission after this."

"I can pull you from that if you'd like. This rank should be good for something."

"And leave Raven to fend for himself? No, I promised my wife to bring her brother home alive. Once that is done, I can rest in peace, or at least I hope so unless Raven drags me off on some other fool errand."

"I cannot imagine him doing such a thing," the admiral tried to say in all seriousness, causing Ben to smile at the absurdity of it. Raven was always dragging him into one mess or another.

"Perhaps if you complete the exploration mission, I can arrange an Earth based assignment for Raven as well, one that will keep him safe long enough for that wife of yours to rest easy. He will hate it, but that's the least he can do for his best friend and brother-in-law."

"Thank you, admiral. You are a good man, and I couldn't have asked for a better commander," Ben's easy smile reflected his affection for the man.

"I repay loyalty with loyalty, Ben. I will never forget what you and that rascal over there did in destroying that command ship. I was prepared to lose this old girl (the STALINGRAD) holding off that fleet, but out of the blue, or the black of space if you were, came two brash pilots to save the day," he said, jerking a thumb in Raven's direction.

"Brash is a nice way of saying stupid. But in all fairness, we were risking more not doing it, so what did we really have to lose?" Ben reasoned, for had they not destroyed the Aurelian command ship, Earth might have been devastated, and them with it.

"Bravery and stupidity are forever joined, depending on one's point of view. Since it's my view I care about, I call it bravery."

"Bravery it is then. Who am I to argue with an admiral," Ben shrugged.

"Good man. I plan to conduct my command briefing today aboard the MIDWAY, and require two escort fighters to accompany my shuttle. Since Blue Squadron is scheduled for a twelve-hour standdown, its Alpha and Bravo are free for other duties. I expect you and Raven to be ready to depart on the hour," the admiral slapped him on the shoulder.

"Thank you, admiral." That would give Ben time to see Jen one last time before battle.

* * *

Two hours later.

Jen Thorton waited at attention with the receiving party in the hanger of the battle carrier MIDWAY as Admiral Kruger exited the ramp of his shuttle craft. Captain Johnson, skipper of the MIDWAY, greeted the admiral at the base of the ramp, leading him to the command briefing room, with their escort following close behind, all except Jen. She was the assigned liaison with the escort pilots during their brief stay. She was *pleasantly surprised to find her husband and brother as the pilots she was charged with, along with Zem, who had accompanied her to the fleet when they first arrived. The three of them joined her from their respective landing pads, approaching from three directions with their helmets in hand, all of them handsomely filling out their form fitting black pilot uniforms. Of course, the only body she lusted for was her husband's, though he was slightly smaller than her brother, and both were smaller than Zem.*

"Gentlemen, welcome aboard the MIDWAY," she greeted formally despite the smile on her face.

"Little sister," Raven drew her into a crushing hug, forgoing all formalities with the junior officer, lifting her off the flight deck.

"Nanouk," she whispered his given name, returning his embrace.

"You got one hour, maybe more to spend with lover boy over here. Make good use of it," Raven said, setting her down, jerking a thumb toward Ben.

"I am charged with escorting all of you," she explained, not wishing to violate her orders.

"Me and Zem can…"

"Zem and I," she corrected his terrible grammar.

"Me and Zem can handle ourselves, Jen. Take your husband some-place quiet and do something indecent. Just don't give me any of the gross details," Raven said, refusing to correct his lousy grammar.

"Nanouk!" She blushed, scolding his blunt speech.

"Don't bother correcting him, Jen. It's a waste of time, and I should know," Ben shook his head, preparing to drag her off before she insisted to say one last thing, leading Raven away from the others a short distance.

"Thank the admiral for allowing this. I would thank him myself, but he hasn't the time to speak with a lowly 2nd Lt., and you have his ear if what half the things everyone in the fleet says is true," she said.

"I'll tell him, but don't believe everything you hear, kid."

"I don't, but when it comes to you, Ben and the admiral, I know you are all as thick as thieves."

He just shrugged, not denying it.

"Just promise me you will keep Ben safe. Don't do anything foolish

during the battle. Bring him safely home to me," she said, staring at him intensely.

"I promise. He will come home safely," Raven smiled, ruffling her hair like she was a child to her annoyance.

"And bring yourself home, too, you stupid oaf," she reminded him. "I'll manage."

"You better!" She shook a fist at him before stepping back to the others, giving Zem a hug as well, the large andro returning the gesture.

"You take care of yourself as well, Zem. Remember we all love you," she said as they drew apart.

"The sentiment is returned," was all he could think to say, his enormous mind strangely at a loss for words.

"And bring my husband back alive," she smiled.

"I will see it done, unless my squadron leader orders me elsewhere," Zem looked over at Raven. Of course, he didn't say that Raven wouldn't be his commander for long. He would have a squadron of his own in a few months, and his own fleet in a few short years. He couldn't wait to implement his many ideas for improving fleet operations.

"Go on you two. Me and Zem will see ourselves to the pilot's lounge," Raven pushed Jen toward Ben, before he and Zem headed in the opposite direction.

And so, Ben Thorton enjoyed his last visit with his wife, sharing that brief respite before the battle to come.

* * *

During the early years of interstellar travel, the first explorers discovered the budding civilization of Aurelia, a planet populated with a humanoid species that were slightly built with gray skin and large blue eyes, who appeared to be in the late stages of their first industrial revolution, entering their information age and early space travel. Contact with the advanced Earth explorers fueled the Aurelians technological advancements, quickly bringing them to a level of parity within two centuries. This cordial friendship quickly descended into distrust and rivalry as Earth began to terraform and colonize nearby star systems, a process the Aurelians still had not perfected. The following conflagration shaped the histories of both planets for many years, culminating with the invasion of their home star system.

The decisive battle would be fought at the outer reaches of the Aurelian Home star system, where rested the lifeless planets of Mutor and Cragnellon. The Aurelians could not tolerate Earth controlled star bases on their outer planets, which would represent a constant sword to their throat, and an Earth defeat there would prolong the war for many years, perhaps for decades or centuries.

The planet Mutor was the eighth planet in the Aurelian star system, a rocky, lifeless world beyond the habitable zone, making it unsuitable for terraforming. It was home to a sizable Aurelian contingent, based on its surface, with countless squadrons and laser batteries to defend it. The 3rd Earth Fleet under Admiral Yamaguchi was tasked with leveling its defenses, paving the way for the 7th Fleet and its space marine landing force. The 3rd Fleet took the planet by surprise, its warships pounding the surface batteries and command sites before the first enemy fighters were launched. The battle went quickly to ground, with the 3rd Fleet gaining air supremacy, the squadrons from the AGINCOURT and AUSTERLITZ sweeping the skies, and targeting Aurelian troop concentrations.

As the battle of Mutor was well underway, the Earth 2nd Fleet jumped into space above Cragnellon, the 7th planet in the Aurelian Star System, a cold icy planet whose surface was a mix of milky white with slate gray rock peaking above its icy layer. The fleets heavy cruisers quickly targeted its known laser batteries and missile sites before devastating its spaceports and orbital defense systems. With much of Cragnellon's defenses in ruin, the fleet was alerted of the approaching Aurelian Home Fleet, consisting of seven command ships and thirty supporting vessels. The 3rd Fleet quickly dispatched the Battle Carrier AGINCOURT to support the 2nd Fleet, the large warship bringing its complement of support vessels from Mutor. Admiral Garcia, the overall commander of the Earth fleets, dispatched the Battle Carrier BADR fro the 7th Fleet, which was currently landing its first marine forces upon the surface of Mutor, while the other troop transport vessels approached Cragnellon. Admiral Garcia oversaw the battle form the bridge of the BADR, following the bulk of the 2nd Fleet toward the approaching Aurelian armada.

Admiral Kruger dispatched four squadrons to support the marine *landings upon Cragnellon, before meeting the Aurelian fleet half the distance to the next planet in the system, the gas giant Bular with its numerous moons. It was there in the dark of space between the 6th and 7th planets of the Aurelian Star System that the decisive engagement would be fought.*

* * *

Raven looked out of his fighter's viewport to the dull daylight reflecting off the milky white and gray surface of Cragnellon, his readouts picking up the debris fields of the destroyed Aurelian orbital defenses littering the surrounding space. With nearly the entirety of the 2nd Fleet moving on to face the Aurelian armada, only the cruiser *SAO PAOLO* remained to provide support, while awaiting the arrival of the transports of the 7th Fleet and the invasion forces that they would be landing upon the surface. Their four squadrons should more than cover the areas assigned them. Blue and Green squadrons from the Battle Carrier *STALINGRAD* would probe the near face of Cragnellon, while Orange and Red Squadron from the *MIDWAY* probed the far side of the planet. Raven doublechecked his squadron indicators, displaying his two air wings on his readouts. He would command Blue 1 through 10, while Ben took 11 through 20. Zem was assigned designation Bravo 21, and operated as Raven's wing man. Raven planned to keep him close to observe his reactions in his first combat mission.

"We got the northern hemisphere of that rock ahead," Raven said, reminding his squadron of their assigned area, with Cragnellon growing larger in their viewports.

"It looks dead. Seems our big ships did most of the work for us," Lorken remarked, finding little sign of activity on his readouts.

"Looks can be deceiving, Blue 1," Ben cautioned, before checking the status of the other squadrons, his eye focused on Orange 17, Jennifer's fighter.

"No worries, Blue Bravo, we are going to kick some Aurelian ass," 2nd Lt. Abel Sanchez said, the boast pleasing several of the squadron.

"Just try not strafing your wingman this time, Blue 12," Ben reminded him, recalling the unfortunate incident at Ruelon 4, where

236

Sanchez grazed the tail of Lt. Epson's fighter. A chorus of chuckles and good natured ribbing followed Ben's comment, the light humor settling the squadron as they made their final approach.

"Aye, Blue Bravo," Lt. Sanchez sheepishly agreed.

"This is where we part, Blue Alpha, good hunting," Ben said, leading his half of the squadron toward the polar regions of Cragnellon.

"Good luck Blue Bravo," Raven replied, angling for the equatorial region of the planet with the other half of the squadron.

* * *

Ben Thorton warily eyed the lifeless planet. His sensors indicated no activity on the dull gray and white surface below, but something felt amiss. The Aurelian sun shone dully through his portside canopy, its distant light barely illuminating the cold surface of Cragnellon. He tried to focus on the task at hand, but thoughts of Jennifer consumed him, knowing she was in Orange Squadron, and approaching the far side of the planet at this very moment. This battle would be far easier if he wasn't burdened thinking of her safety. He cursed the bureaucrat responsible for her being here, likely some bean counter with a stick up their rectum, with an insatiable urge to enforce obscure regulations. He was sorely tempted to take Admiral Kruger and Colonel Chang up on their offers for a rapid promotion, eventually working his way to place of real authority. Once there, he would destroy the bureaucratic Corp, even if it cost him his life. The only thing holding him back was his wife. All he truly wanted was to leave the service and take up residence in some quiet corner of the world, and savor every moment with her. Despite being here, he was thankful that Admiral Kruger assigned her this mission, or else she would be going into battle against the Aurelian fleet, taking a dangerous position in the fighter phalanx that would meet the enemy head on. No, this mission on Cragnellon was much safer, but if so, why did something feel amiss?

"I have contact!" Lt. Banisay's(Blue 18) voice echoed through the comm.

"What is it, Blue 18?" Thorton asked, switching his sensors in the direction of Blue 18.

"It is some sort of orb like ship," Banisay explained, transmitting the *image to Ben's readout. The young Filipino's eyes drew wide with alarm as the object started to glow, causing him to open fire.*

"Blue 18, disengage!" Ben warned once the image popped up on his screen. He immediately transmitted the image to Raven before ordering his wing to withdraw before everything went dead.

The orb exploded, stunning every fighter over several hundred miles away, sending Thorton's entire wing adrift in low orbit. Ben recognized the orb as a new version of a paralysis mine, designed to disable small fighter craft. He encountered a cruder version on Denton II, but the fleet's battle cruisers swept them away before they could detonate. Somehow this new orb evaded the cruisers detection.

"Blue squadron, break off!" Raven commanded his wing just before the orb set off a chain reaction with hundreds of paralysis mines exploding around the planet. Raven's fighter sped away, rising high above the surface of Cragnellon, evading the paralysis wave.

* * *

Ben Thorton drifted helplessly, trying to restart his fighter. His life support backup system came immediately on as he switched to his secondary comms.

"Blue Alpha!" He haled Raven.

"Here, Ben. What's your status?" Raven asked, his own readouts beginning to report the sorry state of his squadron.

"I'm adrift. Total shutdown."

"How long to reboot?"

"Thirty minutes, give or take," Ben replied, quickly going through his diagnostics, beginning the restart sequence. He hoped he was in high enough orbit to give him thirty minutes before he crashed into the surface.

Raven's sensors spotted six others of his squadron helplessly adrift, all in Ben's vicinity. Just as he was working out a recovery plan, the intersquad distress call sounded from Orange and Red Squadrons from the far side of Cragnellon.

"TO ALL FLEET WARSHIPS. ORANGE AND RED SQUADRONS HAVE BEEEN COMPLETELY NUETRALIZED BY PARALYSIS MINES. NO SHIPS FUNCTIONING. REQUESTING

ASSISTANCE. MOST URGENT!" Orange Alpha's voice echoed ominously over the comm.

Ben Thorton's mind shifted to Jennifer, knowing she was adrift on the far side of Cragnellon... helpless, and there was nothing he could about it.

"Enemy fighters coming from the surface," Lorken(Blue 1) observed, his sensors wild with activity. Aurelian fighters meant the danger of the mines was past, but the danger to their friends was just beginning.

"Blue squadron. ENGAGE!" Raven barked into the comm as he spied Aurelian raiders closing on Blue 18 and 19. He sped back toward Cragnellon, the white and gray of its frozen surface looming ominously in his viewport, hoping to reach his crippled comrades before it was too late, the enemy drawing dangerously close.

Blue 19 disappeared.

Blue 18 disappeared.

Raven raced toward Thorton's ship, firing on an Aurelian raider fixing Blue Bravo in its sights. Laser fire rained past Ben's canopy, striking the enemy raider, the ship imploding, releasing a pulse wave that passed through his stricken ship. Raven circled in front of Ben's fighter, scanning afield for the next approaching raiders.

"Raven!" Thorton shouted. "DISENGAGE. Take the squadron to the far side of the planet. Protect Jen."

Raven knew he had to do something but couldn't leave his own ships helpless while saving his sister, his eyes fixed on the next approaching raiders.

"Lorken, take Blue 2 through 12 and protect Orange Squadron," he ordered.

"Aye, Captain," Lorken answered. "You heard him boys, follow me and keep tight."

Green Squadron followed Raven's lead and sped off to protect Red Squadron on the far side of the planet's southern hemisphere.

Raven moved forward, engaging two Aurelian raiders before they could target Thorton.

ZIP!

Raven's blast tore through one raider's canopy, the vacuum of space freezing its controls, sending the fighter awry.

ZIP!

A second laser pierced the center of the next raider's fuselage, the ship imploding as it turned hard right, tumbling harmlessly away.

"Raven! Disengage! GO save Jen!" Thorton growled, desperately trying to start his useless fighter.

Raven ignored his friend's plea, knocking out another approaching raider as four more closed in. He took evasive action with laser fire erupting all around him. Fixing another in his sights, he fired, imploding the Aurelian ship as he passed. The maneuver was costly, allowing the other three to triangulate his position. A phalanx of laser fire swept toward him, the Aurelians gloating their triumph as Blue Alpha's ship neared their deadly volley. They failed to notice Blue 21(Zem) approaching their backside.

ZIP! ZIP! ZIP!

Laser fire tore into the Aurelian ships, imploding them in quick order, their pulse waves passing harmlessly through Zem's fighter as he closed on his commander.

"Good shooting, Zem," Raven said, speeding back to Thorton's position.

"It was simply done, a mere sampling of my superior skills over these primitive organics," Zem dryly boasted.

"Raven, help Jennifer!" Thorton growled pleadingly, tormented by his inability to do anything while his wife was in desperate need.

"I've already sent most of the squadron, Ben. If you look at your sensors, you can see a dozen more raiders closing fast on YOUR position," Raven pointed out.

"I don't care. Go save Jen. Leave me. The others are not good enough. She needs you."

"I'm not leaving you to die," Raven growled back.

There was a brief silence between them before the reports started coming in. Orange 7 disappeared. Then Orange 5. Orange 13. Orange 15. The pleas of helpless pilots haunted the comm with their brief dying cries. Lorken's sensor info was transmitted to all of Blue Squadron, so Raven and the others on the planet's near side could see the battle unfold. Thorton trained his eyes on Orange 17, watching desperately as Jenifer drifted aimlessly amidst her helpless squadron, with Aurelian raiders fast approaching.

Orange 6 disappeared, their signal dying with their imploding ship.

Orange 10.

Orange 4.

Lorken's wing pulled into range, pouring their deadly fire into the approaching raiders, striking several on their first pass, the two groups of fighters intermingling in a hailstorm of dogfights and death.

"Raven, GO help them! They're outnumbered two to one," Thorton implored him.

"And we're outnumbered three to one," Raven grunted with a dozen raiders coming into range.

Blue 13, 14 and 15 joined their captain and Zem as Blue 16, 17, 20 and Thorton drifted helpless behind them.

Raven pushed his thrusters, bursting forward, catching the Aurelians off guard by his suicidal act, taking out two in quick succession. Zem followed, shooting one raider while disabling a second. The other eight raiders pushed on toward Thorton, their laser fire ripping into Blue 15's canopy, blasting his lifeless corpse into space. Blue 13 struck the offending Aurelian ship, but another struck his starboard thruster, disabling his fighter. Raven swept in, striking another ship as Blue 17 imploded. The other six raiders broke off to reform, providing the survivors a brief respite.

Lorken's situation was equally desperate. Four of his fighters had been struck, three dead and one disabled. Three more of Orange Squadron succumbed to Aurelian fire, including Orange Alpha, 3 and 19. Lorken's wing knocked out seven raiders but were still heavily outnumbered. The SAO PAULO pulled within range of the southern hemisphere, its lighter batteries aiding Green Squadron to great effect.

Jennifer had taken several close shots but still survived, but for how long?

"Raven!" Thorton growled.

Raven knew it was going to be a close affair. There were six Aurelian raiders facing him, Zem and Blue 14. He had only one trick left up his sleeve.

"Zem!"

"Yes, captain," the deep metallic voice answered.

"Go help Lorken. Go as fast as you can."

"Aye." Zem responded and sped away.

"He's not good enough, Raven. You go. Zem can protect us," Ben pleaded.

"He's as good as I am, Ben. 14, follow me and stay close to my ass!" Raven barked, speeding off to engage the Aurelians, leaving Ben to pound his console in disgust.

* * *

Lorken shifted, shaking his pursuer, laser fire grazing his portside thruster. He circled about, the Aurelian imploding before he could fix it in his sites.

"Good shooting, Blue 6," Lorken thanked his comrade, bringing his fighter about to seek his next prey, eyeing Orange 18 disappear, followed by Orange Bravo. He knew he couldn't hold out indefinitely, the task nearly impossible with them being outnumbered and tasked with defending Orange Squadron, or what was left of them. He picked out the nearest raider and closed to target as Zem called into range.

"Blue 21 reporting," Zem's beautiful metallic voice echoed through the comm.

"Pick a target and go to work, big fella," Lorken happily welcomed, striking another raider before it could kill Orange 12.

* * *

"You know what to do?" Raven asked Blue 14, eyeing the approaching Aurelian phalanx, with five ships forming a line and a sixth in the center rear.

"Yes," Blue 14 responded. If the kid was nervous, he didn't sound it.

"Tighten it up and bank when I tell you!"

14 took a deep breath, inching his fighter closer to Blue Alpha. 'So much for fleet regulations,' he thought as they closed within three meters, his fighter's nose just off Raven's portside wing.

"NOW!" Raven barked into the comm as the Aurelians came swiftly upon them, banking hard right as 14 turned left.

As Raven expected, the five lead fighters turned on 14 as the following raider chased after him. Raven reduced his thrusters, looping *vertically, angling in the opposite direction, coming in behind the five raiders pursuing Blue 14, spreading a quick volley across their line, striking three with the other two breaking off. Blue 14 turned quickly for Raven's maneuver exposed him to the sixth raider that was now on his aft. Raven shifted down, giving 14 a clear shot on his pursuer, imploding the Aurelian fighter.*

"Good shot, 14."

"Aye, Captain," the young Lt answered, breathing a sigh of relief.

The other two raiders sped off as Raven rushed back to Thorton's position just as the arriving 7ᵗʰ Fleet fleet hailed them. Two fresh squadrons assigned to the landing force rushed to reinforce them, along with the Battle Cruisers TANARIVE and ANKARA.

"14, stay with Blue Bravo. I'm going to help Lorken," Raven said, preparing to race off to the far side of Cragnellon when Thorton's voice came across the comm with a tone as cold as the depths of space.

"You're too late, Rav. She's gone."

Those words ran through Raven's mind, chilling his blood. He could almost feel her absence, tuning his sensors to Lorken's feed, eyeing where Jennifer's imploded ship drifted dead in space.

Fresh squadrons flooded his screen, overwhelming the Aurelians. The cruisers ANKARA and TANARIVE blasted the planet's ground-based defenses from where the raiders sprang, while sweeping the remaining mines still operational in lower orbit. Victory was assured, but to Raven and Thorton, it was the end of so many things. Blue Squadron was decimated, and the love that bound them was severed.

Thorton eyed his console as all systems came back on line. He pulled away from Cragnellon, looking down to his console as the words bitterly appeared across his comm… MESSAGE RECEIVED.

"Report message," Ben Thorton commanded, his voice tight with emotion.

"I love you, Texas," Jennifer's voice echoed faintly. It was sent manually just before her ship was struck.

Ben Thorton fought back the pain, denying the tears pressing boldly upon his eyes. Raven pulled up alongside him, neither speaking a word as Ben Thorton's heart waxed cold.

* * *

"So that was it. What a waste," Terin said sadly.

"I know," Raven sighed. "Thorton was as good a friend as anyone could have. He was honest and true. He'd give you the shirt off his back if you needed it. When I took out the Aurelian Command ship, he wasn't jealous of the glory heaped on me, even though it was his plan. I made sure he got the recognition he deserved, though I doubt he really cared. All he cared about was Jen. She was what motivated him, and what distracted him. If not for her, he could have had a stellar career in the fleet, he was that good. He could fly, shoot, fight and think on his feet better than anyone I knew. Was a pretty good fullback at the Academy too. He was a strong character that everyone loved."

"Much like you," Terin smiled.

"Of course, who do you think taught him everything he knew?" Raven boasted.

"Lorken," Terin laughed, using the banter the Earthers always used against him.

Raven gave him a playful nudge that nearly knocked him over. After his laughter subsided, Terin's mood grew somber with the next question he needed to ask.

"Even though he lost her, how can Thorton hate you?"

"He blames me for not rescuing her," Raven sighed.

"But he would've died if you tried, and you sent the others to aid her."

"I sent everyone I could spare, but they were not as skilled as I, not even Zem at his level of experience. In truth, even I might not have been able to save her. I couldn't leave my command and we both knew if I didn't, she would likely die. If I left, then Thorton would have died. I couldn't risk losing them both and leave my nephew an orphan, so I made the decision that was most logical. I dispatched as many fighters as I could spare to help Jen's squadron, while staying to protect my crippled force. I saved who I could. Thorton lived and Jen died, and he will never forgive me for that."

"But if you did as he demanded, he would be dead," Terin couldn't make sense of it.

"His heart died with her, so what difference did it make?"

"It just seems so unfair," Terin shook his head sadly.

"That's war, Terin, it never is. You make decisions on who lives and who dies and you live with the consequences. I was dealt a losing hand and now I have to kill my best friend."

With those words they both stood there for a time, with Terin reflecting on that sad tale, as Raven looked below where Cronus still held Leanna in his arms, her head resting back against his chest. Terin leaned over the rampart, curious to see what Raven was looking at, before finding it. It struck him then how eerily similar Cronus' friendship with Raven was to Thorton's. He felt Raven's gaze shift to him, looking at him with his dark piercing eyes as if he knew what Terin was thinking.

"What would you do Terin, if you had to make a choice between them? You could probably save Cronus, or maybe save Leanna, but not both. Who would you choose?"

Raven's question tore at him. How could one answer? Logic said that if saving Cronus was likelier, then that should be his choice, but if all things were equal, he would choose Leanna, as men always protected their women over themselves, and Cronus would expect it of him. Only then could he fully understand what tortured Raven so.

"It is a no-win scenario," Terin sighed, looking down at their friends before looking back at Raven.

"Add to it the fact they share a child. Right now, I would choose Leanna, as she represents two lives. But once she gives birth, choosing her might condemn their child to be an orphan. And there lies the miserable truth. If the same scenario played out again with Cronus and Leanna, I would save her, for I know what she means to him," Raven confessed, knowing if history repeated itself, he would lose his friend anyway.

"No," Terin shook his head. "You spare their child that awful fate. You would save Cronus."

"Are you sure?"

"Cronus is not Ben, Raven. He knows the choices we must make every time we go into battle, choices that decide who lives and dies based on logic and probability. I know Cronus would forgive you, because like me, he loves you as a brother," Terin placed a hand to Raven's shoulder. "If Corry and I have children one day, I would rather live in pain without her, than condemn our child an orphan. She would expect that of me, and I of her. Ben is a fool for not seeing it."

Raven thought on that, recalling Admiral Kruger's offer to send Thorton home after Jen's death, but Ben insisted on going on with their exploratory mission, for some reason, though he would barely talk to Raven, let alone look at him. Why did he not rush home to see his son? All Raven sacrificed that awful day was for nothing. His sister died, his friend hated him, and for all intents and purposes, his nephew was an orphan. And here he was on some far-off world waiting for that friend to show himself so he could kill him.

"Isn't one foolish stunt enough for one day?" Corry said, regarding Raven's choice of sitting positions as she stepped from the shadows, her guards holding back as she drew nigh.

"Good evening, Corry," Raven greeted her with that infuriating grin he so easily wore.

"Raven," she answered dryly, not impressed with the dangerous position he occupied.

"You don't like me very much, do you?" He said, keeping that stupid grin.

"No, I don't. I do love you like I love Cronus and the others, you insufferable oaf, but I certainly don't like you."

"Well, at least you're honest."

"Just what were you thinking trying to break a wild ocran?" She crossed her arms, waiting for an answer.

"I figured your people needed all the mounts they can get. I almost broke the ugly brute, and will give it another go once my ankle is heeled."

"No, you will not."

"I won't huh?" Raven almost laughed, wondering what she could do to stop him.

"Listen, you insufferable pirate. As much as I don't like you, I still care about you, as does the man I love," she gave Terin a knowing look. "If our feelings count for so little in that small brain of yours, remember why you are here. You came to kill Thorton, and if you get your fool self killed before then, we are all doomed. Not to mention how Tosha will receive the news if you die so stupidly. Now, get to bed, both of you. And get off that wall before you break your neck," she scolded, turning to leave before he could say anything back.

"She has a point," Terin shrugged, not able to hide his smile, rarely seeing Raven take such abuse, though it didn't seem to phase him in the least.

"You got your hands full with that one, Terin. She used to be so polite and proper. I guess I'm wearing off on her."

CHAPTER 14

"What have you?" Commander Nevias asked the lookout upon clearing the last step of the Tower of Celenia, hurrying up the endless stair from his post upon Zar Crest to see for himself.

"Benotrist cavalry, Commander," the lookout reported, pointing to the southeast, where the open grassland kissed the horizon, just beyond the blackened fields of the previous siege lines.

Commander Nevias' aging eyes narrowed against the morning sun now high upon the horizon, counting dozens of riders clustered at the edge of his vision in the distance. Though they couldn't make out their insignia from this far away, Nevias was certain that they were Benotrist based upon the most recent sightings of their magantor scouts. General Bode released their Torry cavalry two days prior, having them poison the last wells to the west of Corell before reconfiguring at their designated rally points north and south of the palace. That left the garrison with less than thirty mounts, should they have need of them. Their magantor patrols skirmished with enemy warbirds for the past six days, with nearly a dozen avian succumbing on each side. They were still uncertain of Morac's full strength, but were certain of at least one new legion, the 10th Benotrist Legion, last reported at Pagan Harbor. Elos reported numerous forces reinforcing Morac throughout the winter months, filling out the decimated ranks of his surviving legions from the first siege of Corell. Stripping many of the garrisons throughout the empire to bolster Morac, made the

Benotrist Empire even more vulnerable to the slave revolts sweeping throughout its eastern regions. It seemed Tyro was throwing caution to the wind, committing every available resource to finish Torry North once and for all.

"More over there, Commander!" Another lookout pointed to the northeast, where stood a sizable group of riders just now emerging along the horizon.

"Good eye, men," Nevias complimented them, before scanning in all directions, spotting another group to the southwest, and a fourth directly north. He found the first reports of Benotrist cavalry troubling when they first learned that Morac had recruited a large mounted force, but wasn't certain of their strength until seeing them here with his own eyes. To parade brazenly before their walls indicated there was strength in their numbers, enough to contest the Torry cavalry, which would make it difficult for Tevlin and Connly to raid the enemy supply trains. The Benotrist cavalry wouldn't bother appearing here if their infantry weren't far behind. They were either advance scouting for Morac's legions, or were establishing a perimeter. Either way, the second siege of Corell had begun.

* * *

News of the enemy riders beyond the walls spread like wildfire through the palace. Unlike the previous siege, the defenders were better prepared and held Corell with much greater numbers, fueling their resolve. Barely one in three of the original garrison survived the siege, numbering shy of three thousand men, but their ranks were bolstered with conscripts and garrison troops reassigned from Besos and Cropus. With freshly raised archer levies and the full complement of Dar Valen's magantors, Commander Nevias was confident in his position. Impressive as his position was, his forces were the lesser partner to General Bode's 3rd Army, numbering between 12 and 14 telnics, and General El Tuvo's 1st Jenaii Battle Group, numbering nine to ten telnics. Princess Corry already called a war council, waiting for the latest scouting reports from General Valen's outriders before commencing. Meanwhile, the garrison went about their duties, knowing the true battles were still many days off, perhaps longer. With nearly 25 to thirty telnics defending Corell, Morac had little hope of taking the palace quickly.

Fortunately, Ular and Lucas returned the day before from Besos, having healed nearly every wounded soldier and civilian in the holdfast before they were summoned back to Corell. Upon arriving, Ular went about charging the Tissue regenerator before immediately clearing the remaining wounded. The most recent injuries were the gravest, many of which were cavalrymen wounded in skirmishes with the Benotrist cavalry. The gravest injuries now received the highest priority, save for highly essential personnel, whose health and mobility were vital to Corell's defense.

With the first sighting of enemy riders, Raven reluctantly withdrew to the inner keep, remaining out of sight should Thorton be among the Benotrist cavalry. He was none to pleased when Cronus led Ular and Lucas into the great hall where he was sat, ordering him to remove his right boot.

"What are you doing here with that thing? Save it for the seriously wounded," Raven protested, but Ular was having none of it, setting the device on his bad ankle.

"You've been hobbling on that foot for seven days now, Rav. It's more serious than you're letting on. Besides, this is the Princess' orders," Cronus said as the readout revealed the extent of the sprain, so grave as to require surgery if he was back on earth and the regenerator was not an option.

"I'm all right. You're making more of it than it is," Raven waved off his concern.

Before Cronus could answer that idiotic assessment, Ular was finished, packing up the device and heading back to the infirmary.

"Good luck, Rav," Lucas grinned, slapping Raven on the back before following Ular toward the exit.

"Well, can't look a gift horse in the mouth," he shrugged, stretching his foot before putting his boot back on.

"You and your expressions," Cronus shook his head, learning what a gift horse was by the number of times his friend spoke of it during their endless trek from Fera to Tro.

"You like my stupid phrases, Cronus. Otherwise, you wouldn't repeat them as many times as you do," Raven finished putting on his boot, before testing his ankle, walking around the chamber in a small circle.

"After hearing them so many times, they've become part of my language. Come, we are expected at the war council," Cronus said.

"Why us? Are we something special? I'm not much use until I kill Ben. Until then I'll just be hiding out and eating your rations," Raven said, putting his full weight on the restored ankle, confident in its recovery.

"The Princess favors your insight. We might already be late, so *let's get a move on*," Cronus smiled using that phrase Raven used repeatedly.

"Are you doing that on purpose?" Raven gave him a look.

"Absolutely. We don't want to be late, but if we are, it's *better late than never*," Cronus couldn't help himself.

"Alright, you made your point."

"*Easier said then done.*"

"Very funny."

"*Even a blind squirrel finds a nut every now and then.*"

"I don't remember using that one."

"Oh, you used it every time we sent Alen fishing for our supper," Cronus reminded him as they made their way to the outer corridor.

"I wasn't wrong."

"*You're special alright, just like all the other girls in the galaxy*," Cronus recalled what he said to Tosha more than once.

"Yeah, that really pissed her off," Raven smiled.

"*You shake any family tree and a few nuts will fall out*," Cronus recalled what Raven said to her referencing her father.

"Yeah, she didn't like that one either," Raven chuckled as numerous soldiers hurried past them in each direction, rushing off to different parts of the castle.

"Was it like this during the last siege?" Raven asked as they traversed the wide corridor, with torches bracketed high upon its white walls, the castle buzzing with activity.

Cronus recalled that first day of the previous siege, when Torg tasked Terin and he to walk the battlements countless times. He now wondered if it was just busy work to keep them focused on something simple, or if it truly served a purpose in teaching them the layout of the castle? Looking back on it, it was all surreal. The men were inexperienced, few if any having faced battle before then. They were fearful but ignorant of the true horrors of war. Now they knew better. They were practiced in concealing their fears, but those fears were far greater than before. One thing that was true then as it was now... war is madness.

"Yes. It's like your father used to say, Rav. *Everyone around here is nuts except you and me, and you're a little bit off?*"

"I created a monster," Raven mumbled.

* * *

"Maybe we're not so special anyway," Raven mumbled upon entering the council chamber. There, gathered around the large map table in the center of the room, was a small multitude. General Bode stood off to the left, with several of his telnic commanders present, Commander Mastorn among them. Raven recalled he was Cronus' telnic commander before he was captured. The man and Cronus regarded each other briefly upon their entering the chamber.

General El Tuvo, commander of the 1st Jenaii Battle Group, stood opposite Bode, with several of his telnic commanders. The Jenaii General's silver eyes studied the map unfurled across the table intently. With Elos away south, the defense of Corell rested much upon El Tuvo and his brave warriors, numbering nearly ten thousand. Their presence went far in reassuring the defenders. Any gargoyle assault upon Corell would fair poorly with the Jenaii well positioned upon its battlements.

Along the near side of the table stood Commander Nevias with his back to them, along with his commanders of the east, north, west and south walls, two of which replaced their predecessors who fell during the last siege.

On the opposite side of the table stood Princess Corry, Torg Vantel, and Chief Minister Eli Monsh, as well as ministers Thunn and Kalvar. Surrounding the chamber stood nearly twelve of the Torry Elite, including Lucas and Terin, who stood statue still behind the Princess, ever vigilant. Ular and Orlom stood off to the side of the chamber, the former's bulbous eyes blinking repeatedly, while Orlom simply looked around, staring curiously at the impressive surroundings. Raven thought Orlom might strike up a tune and start whistling by his relaxed posture. He wished he would. It would take some of the edge off the dour faces standing around the table. Raven thought they should all lighten up and not take all this business so seriously, since all they had to do is kill a few hundred thousand Benotrists and gargoyles.

"Come on, Buddy, let's get this over with," Raven dragged Cronus to the edge of the table, standing between the Jenaii and Commander Nevias' group. Cronus thought to take his proper place along the wall with his fellow elite, but Raven asked him to stay put. He wasn't going to stand there by himself like an idiot, and phrased it just that way. One look from Corry reassured Cronus to acquiesce to Raven's not so diplomatic request.

The last to enter the chamber was General Dar Valen along with several of his recently arrived scouts. They took up position beside General Bode's contingent.

"General Valen. We shall hear your report!" Corry ordered, beginning the war council. She presided over the impressive assemblage dressed in regal raiment rather than her warrior garb, wearing a shimmering, azure gown that reflected her royal authority. Raven had to admit she looked far different from the girl who stormed ashore at Bansoch wielding her sword like a madwoman. Now she looked like a terrifying queen, with all the warmth of a glacier. He had to hand it to her, she knew when to put on her *bitch face* when it was needed, reminding each of the men here that their regent was no frail flower.

"Highness, Benotrist cavalry are currently positioned here, here and here," General Valen indicated different points on the map, covering the eastern, southern and northern approaches of Corell.

"Which we can see with our eyes," Cors Balka, the ornery commander of the west wall growled. Cronus noticed the aging craggy warrior looked even skinnier than he was during the last siege.

The man was too stubborn to die, having cheated death several times in that engagement.

"Cors," Commander Nevias reproached him for interrupting, allowing Dar Valen to continue.

Commander Connly's 2nd Cavalry is currently twenty leagues to our direct north, while Tevlin's 1st Cavalry is positioned an equal distance to our south. They have completed their poisoning of all the wells in their assigned zones, and will commence engagement with the Benotrist cavalry before raiding the enemy's supply trains," Dar explained.

"Do you have an accurate count on the number of Benotrist cavalry?" Torg asked.

"At least a thousand riders, perhaps more. Those are the numbers we can confirm are currently operating within our borders," Dar answered.

"And their legions? How far off are they?" General Bode asked, their last sighting putting them five days to their east.

"I would expect their first foot soldiers to arrive by midday on the morrow. The 5th Gargoyle Legion should be the first to parade before our walls, unless it breaks off to attend other tasks," Dar said.

"How much is left of them? They lost much of their strength during the first siege," Nevias asked.

"According to Magistrate Adine, his spies in Notsu reported that all the surviving gargoyle legions from the first siege have been reconstituted under the 5th Legion. He places their strength between 35 and fifty telnics," Corry revealed, relaying what Klen shared with her before they departed Tro Harbor.

"Aye, that would explain their numbers we have observed," Dar said before continuing. "Trailing the 5th Legion, are the 14th Gargoyle Legion, the 10th Benotrist Legion, the 8th Benotrist Legion and the 11th Benotrist Legion. The 8th and 11th are less than whole, though only slightly so. All of these legions should arrive within seven to ten days."

"Five legions, two of which are gargoyle. Almost the same size force as the previous siege," Chief Minister Monsh said, rubbing his chin in thought.

"Equal in size, but not ability. Last time Morac brought four gargoyle legions to bear, now he has two. The Benotrist legions are more formidable upon open ground, but count for little against our walls," Nevias pointed out.

"Two FULL gargoyle legions. By the time Morac brought his legions to bear during the last siege, all four of his gargoyle legions were greatly reduced. These legions present nearly an equal danger, but are supported by three human legions," General Bode cautioned.

"True, but humans are harder to provision, and that portends poorly for their chances," Nevias countered.

"Not if they savage our lands to feed themselves. They could surround us with four of their legions, freeing the fifth to raid our heartland between Central City and Corell," Torg said, for that was what he would do.

"If that is their plan, what do you suggest we do?" Nevias looked to Bode and then Torg for an answer.

"Then I shall move to blunt their advance," General El Tuvo said.

His bold declaration caused an eerie silence to fall upon the chamber. They well knew what his suggestion entailed, stripping away a third of Corell's defenders, and exposing them to Morac's launch towers, should he repeat that tactic.

"All of our people are aware of our perilous position. We have ordered every citizen to prepare to take up arms should Corell succumb. If Morac decides to extend his reach beyond this siege, then we must suffer the consequence. We cannot defend every part of our realm in the face of such numbers. If Morac is willing to sacrifice his troops to raid our heartland, then so be it," Torg spoke the awful truth.

Corry wasn't so certain of this tactic, but understood that any measure to counter such a move by Morac, weakened their position at Corell. It was at Corell where the war would be decided, and nothing should distract them from that.

"Let us consider that option should the need arise, General El Tuvo," Corry diplomatically stated, before Raven opened his mouth, turning the whole debate upon its head.

"Once Thorton is accounted for, Morac's troops won't come close to your walls. That should free up General Tuvo to do what he pleases," the big Earther jerked a thumb toward the Jenaii commander.

"Your confidence is admirable, Captain Raven, but even with your weapons, you cannot stave off Morac's vast host," Corry regarded him evenly from across the table, the others looking on as if caught between a cyclone and a tempest.

"The rumors say your weapons cannot overcome Morac's blade," Chief Minister Monsh added, tempering Raven's overconfidence.

"I don't have to kill the weasel. That's Terin's job. He kills Moron, and I'll kill the rest, once Ben is taken care of, that is."

"It is not as simple as you state, Captain Raven. The enemy host vastly outnumbers us. It would take…" General Valen tried to explain, before Raven cut him off.

"You just use your scouts and find out where Ben is, and I'll take care of the rest. That's why I'm here," Raven said, with the others looking at him as if he grew a second head, all except his friends. Cronus, Terin, Ular and Lucas were well aware of what he was capable of, if not in total agreement of his boasting. Orlom, however, nodded in approval, adding his voice to cheer him on.

"Boss will slaughter them. He's the best," Orlom grinned stupidly, almost causing Corry to face palm.

"That may be true or not, Raven, but we must plan in the event that Thorton doesn't present himself any time soon. In that, we must prepare to resist Morac without your impressive aid," Torg said, redirecting the conversation to the task at hand.

And so it went, with them discussing the state of their provisions, their troop strength and placement, and likeliest route of any relief forces. The last point centered upon both the 2nd Jenaii Battlegroup that was currently engaged with Nayborian forces along their border, and Prince Lorn, who currently sat at Fleace.

"I have sent out messengers to his highness since the first movement upon our border was spotted. I have continuously sent messengers apprising him of the enemy movements since then," General Valen informed them.

"And how long shall it take him to reach us?" Commander Nevias inquired.

"He must either move north to the Nila, and advance to Central City, before marching northeast to reach Corell, or advance to Sawyer and travel across Lake Monata, approaching Corell from the south. Either path will take time. Thirty days would be the bare minimum, but I would guess forty to fifty, considering the size of the forces involved, and the provisioning they require," Dar Valen soberly stated.

Corry's eyes narrowed at the map, assessing the distance separating them from her brother. He might not reach them before the battle was decided. He needed time, time they might not have. Everyone else could see what she was looking at, sharing her pessimism in the task before them, everyone except Raven and Orlom. Those two idiots didn't look concerned at all. She would laugh at their antics if there wasn't so much currently weighing her shoulders. She needed to stiffen this council's resolve, giving them something to focus their efforts.

"Despite Prince Lorn's accomplishments in the south, and his resolve to come to our aid, he lacks one vital resource that only we can give him," she said, pausing for effect as her eyes swept the faces gathered around the table, waiting upon her to continue.

"Time. He needs time to reach us, time to move his armies before the battle is decided. We can give him that time. We can give him that time by denying Morac Corell, no matter the cost. We shall bleed him upon these walls just as we did before. We shall deny him at the battlements, at the towers, at every chamber of the palace. We shall bathe in their blood as they choke on ours. We shall give Prince Lorn the time he needs to reach us. And if not, he can bury our bones," Corry finished, her words causing more than one to smile in approval.

* * *

One day hence.

By midday the 14th Gargoyle Legion paraded before the east wall, holding at a distance where they raised their standard, a red headless corpse upon a field of black. Lookouts atop the golden tower observed their movements as the creatures began to fortify their positions, the sound of spades striking soil echoing through the spring air. Gargoyles didn't usually carry such tools, indicting the legion was laden with excess baggage, which explained their slower advance.

By late evening, the banners of the 5th Gargoyle Legion appeared along the southern horizon, a black mailed fist upon a field of white, the gargoyles' winged forms silhouetted along the horizon in the wanning daylight.

The early evening found Cronus and Terin standing upon the outer battlements of the south wall, staring off into the distance, where the sound of spades echoed hauntingly in the dark. It was a rare occurrence when Terin was not at Corry's side. The Princess excused him of his duties for the night, while she entertained the few ladies of the court that still resided at Corell, as well as Leanna. It was Cronus that took him in tow, dragging him to the palace walls to enjoy the fresh air, their mood tempered by the eerie sounds of the gargoyles working in the dark.

"I look to the day when that awful sound no longer sings," Cronus sighed. With twilight giving way to night, he could no longer make out the gargoyles' shapes in the distance. Memories of the last siege still lingered prominently in their minds. In some ways it felt ages ago, and in others, it felt just like yesterday.

This time they did not feel as alone and forlorn, confident in their friends and their greater strength, though this time their relief was farther afield. The one thing that tormented Terin, was his own weakness. Whenever he called upon his power during the last siege, it helped him overcome every task. That power was now gone, replaced with whatever it was now. Would it be enough? That question gnawed at him, plaguing his sleep. He prayed to Yah for guidance and reassurance, giving himself over to that unseen power that seemed to direct every step of his life. If Yah answered, he could not hear it, forcing him to blindly trust the path he was taking.

"*Lean not on our own strength, but upon the will of Yah,*" Lorn once told him.

Terin wished he knew what Yah's will was, but sadly didn't know. He recalled his time enslaved by Darna, his anger and pride clouding his vision, until Yah stripped both away. His anger and pride felt but a whisper, but his vision was still clouded.

"What is on your mind, Terin? I know when you are tormented by something, you grow quiet like you are now," Cronus looked over to his young friend.

"I… I don't know if I will be good enough this time. I am not what I was. I can no longer turn back the enemy, Cronus, and if I cannot, what hope have we against their numbers?"

"You accounted well of yourself at Tro. Your power is still great, just different. You might not frighten our enemies away, but they now seem blind to your presence. Learn to use that to your advantage."

"Even if that is so, how many might I slay in battle? One hundred. Two hundred. Perhaps a thousand. Those numbers count for naught weighed against their multitudes. Should I even kill ten thousand, it will not matter if the rest swarm our walls and kill everyone else."

"Perhaps last time that would have ended us, but we are collectively stronger now. We have three times the defenders as last time. And don't forget our large Earth friend," Cronus patted him on the back, his rare optimism taking Terin by surprise.

Terin smiled at that. Raven always had a way of making the direst situations seem as nothing. Who else would have thought to enter Fera and steal Cronus from under Tyro's nose, fighting his way from one end of that fortress to the other, leaving a thousand corpses in his wake?

"Where is Raven?" Terin asked.

"Sulking in the feasting hall, nursing a tankard of ale when I last saw him. He isn't happy having to hide out of sight for the foreseeable future. Orlom is with him." Cronus didn't have to explain why the young gorilla had to be hidden as well. Should Orlom use his weapons, it would alert the enemy that an Earther was present. They needed Thorton to believe no such threat existed if he was to draw near enough for Raven to kill. Only then could they count upon the full weight of Raven and Orlom's weapons to strike at the enemy.

"He is going to hate waiting," Terin smiled at that.

"Yes. Patience is not one of his virtues," Cronus chuckled.

"Neither is Orlom's," Terin said.

"Let us hope Thorton soon reveals himself."

Terin grew quiet again, Cronus' words reminding him of the story Raven had told him.

"Again, you are troubled," Cronus sighed, noting his dour mood.

"What if Raven can't kill him? What if he pauses, torn by such an awful choice?"

"Raven will do what he must," Cronus tried to reassure him.

"I am not so certain, Cronus. It is strikingly similar to my father and grandfather. I know in my heart that my father cannot kill Tyro, no matter the blood my grandfather has on his hands." Terin thought on his father's whereabouts, wondering if he still lived, or if he was captive at Fera.

"Your father is bound by the magic of his blood from harming Tyro. Raven suffers no such impediment."

"I hope you are right, Cronus. Raven is a good friend, and I feel sad for the choice he must make. I owe him a great debt for what he did for me. I owe all of them for what they did, especially Corry," his voice trailed, ever grateful for his friends rescuing him.

"Just as I owe you, Lorken and Raven for rescuing me. As we spoke before, only you can truly understand what I suffered," Cronus struggled speaking of what he endured in the dungeons of Fera. He couldn't speak of it with anyone, not even his dearest Leanna, only Terin. Only with each other could they speak so freely of their captivity, each overcome by shame, horror and helplessness. These were not things to be shared with anyone who had not endured them.

"We are blessed with many friends. Many GOOD friends," Terin sighed.

"Yes. We are," Cronus smiled, patting his young friend on the shoulder, the sound of gargoyle spades no longer weighing their spirits.

* * *

Corry sat in a high backed chair, placing the final stiches in the tiny gown she was sewing. She gathered the current ladies of the court in her private sanctum, each sitting in high backed chairs, forming a half circle about the glowing hearth upon the far wall. Using the wood was a rare treat, considering the state of their supply, but Corry insisted upon it for this night. Despite the beginning of the siege, she felt a celebration was in order. Master Orvon, the chief of the black smith guild of Central City, had finished fully repairing all the gates of the north tunnel, including the gear mechanisms of the main gate. The main gate would have been impossible to repair so quickly without Raven's help, which the master smith repeatedly informed her. Needless to say, she was overjoyed, and honored the smith by inviting his young daughter to join her small circle, the girl sitting beside her, dressed in a flowing emerald gown that Corry gifted her. The girl accompanied her father on this journey, eager to see the great fortress of Corell.

They were joined by the daughter of Governor Taulus, Carisa Luron, wife of Jors Luron. The young woman was sheltered at Corell in the event her father and husband's lands were overrun by Morac's invasion. The Laris Region barely escaped the carnage during the previous campaign. The young woman was finely dressed in a burgundy gown, with gold stitching along its collar and billowy sleeves. Beside her sat her sister by marriage twice over, Venna Taulus, formerly Luron, who wed her brother, Vade Taulus. It was Corry that ordered their marriages upon hearing their fathers' grievances against one another, thus binding their houses through marriage. She was thankful both ladies seemed pleased with their new husbands, knowing such things did not always work as planned.

Two other ladies of the court joined them, daughters of regional governors from the southeast, their fathers sheltering them at Corell with the fate of their own lands in peril. The last to join their small circle was Leanna, whose belly was now full with child, a feminine warmth radiating from her face, indicating her expectant labor. Corry gathered them together to sew clothing and blankets for

Leanna's child, and enjoy a feminine respite from the dangers that
lurked beyond the palace walls. After spending her day with the grim
matters of the realm, Corry needed a distraction from their troubles,
and by looking at the faces of the ladies before her, so did they.

"Does this meet your fancy, Lady Leanna?" Corry asked, raising
the tiny gown for all to see.

"It is exceptional, Highness," Leanna smiled, humbled by the
attention. Here she sat among these high born ladies, being the
daughter of a merchant. She was also the wife of the legendary Cronus
Kenti, whose name fell from every lip in the realm, she reminded
herself. But in truth, she was here because the Princess befriended
her, and she was ever grateful.

"How are you coming along, Zora?" Corry asked of Master
Orvon's daughter.

Zora blushed, holding up the half finished blanket that would
reach the width of her shoulders when finished.

"A lovely pattern," Venna Taulus smiled approvingly, noting the
red and green checkered design.

"I fear my efforts are lacking, Highness," Carisa Luron impishly
said, lifting a beautifully woven burgundy cloak, with silver stitching
along its edge. It was of a size for a small child, perhaps when the
babe was older.

"My Lady Luron, it is magnificent," Leanna smiled approvingly.

"I am glad you are pleased, Leanna. It is the least I could do for
the child of Cronus Kenti, the hero of Tuft's Mountain."

Leanna graciously bowed her head with the genuine praise, as
the others chorused her sentiments. Leanna politely inquired of Lady
Lorun's new husband, and if she found him favorable.

"I am very pleased with Jors. He has the most fetching eyes, and
handsome face," Carisa answered, thanking Corry for suggesting the
match to her father.

"And you, Lady Taulus?" Corry inquired of the Lady Venna,
Carisa's sister by marriage twice over, having wed the heir of House
Taulus.

"Vade is equally as charming as my dear brother Jors, perhaps
even more so. He also has a lovely voice," Venna cooed.

"Voice? Does he sing?" Corry perked.

"Only when we are alone. He sings verses and poems he has penned, but has sworn me to secrecy not to speak of it to his father," Venna smiled.

"Are you the source of his inspiration, Lady Taulus?" Corry asked.

"Of his most recent works, yes, Your Highness," she blushed.

Corry noticed Leanna trying to hide a smile, before calling her on it.

"Does King's Elite Kenti share Jors' talent, Leanna?" Corry asked.

"Cronus has a lovely voice when he deigns to use it, but it is I that sings for him when asks nicely," Leanna regretted her confession once they asked her to sing for them.

"Oh, you must Lady Leanna," Zora the smith's daughter asked prettily, her voice rising with excitement.

"Do not be shy, Leanna. Your speaking voice is beautiful enough, that I can imagine the greater loveliness if you sing," Venna said.

"Very well, though forgive me should I falter," Leanna said before singing the love ballad that Cronus loved so dear.

> *"He blew me a kiss across the still water*
> *He took my hand as we walked along*
> *He vowed to return from war should it take him*
> *He vowed to return and hear my fair song*
>
> *He came to me across the still water*
> *He returned to me from journey so long*
> *He took my hand in his as he kissed me*
> *He promised his love as I sang him this song."*

The ladies were quiet for a time, thinking on the gentle melody. The story touched their hearts, with each understanding the woman's pain in the melody, knowing the agony of war separating lovers, hoping their true love would safely return to their arms. It was Corry that truly understood Leanna's pain when Cronus was taken captive, having suffered Terin's absence, not knowing if he lived or died. How blessed they were to have them both back, though there were no guarantees with the war again at their doorstep. She couldn't help but notice the Lady Conela, daughter of the Governor of Dalen Province, southeast of the realm. The young woman looked about to burst into tears or laughter, or perhaps both at once.

"Lady Conela, are you well?" Corry inquired.

"My apologies, Highness. I feel like such a silly girl," she reproached herself.

"How so?" Lady Taulus asked.

"Lady Leanna's song was so lovely, and reflects the hopes and wishes of every lady that sends her beloved to war, and yet I cannot help silly thoughts from creeping upon my mind," Conela sighed.

"What silly thoughts are those, Lady Conela?" Corry asked.

"Well, I…. I cannot stop thinking of how the castle needs a good cleaning. The battlements and walls still bare the scars of the last siege. My thoughts should be on the lives of our brave soldiers holding these walls, but all I can think of is cleaning the walls, such the silly fool I am," she sighed.

Corry burst into laughter, the others quickly joining in her merriment, leaving poor Conela with an askance look upon her face.

"If only you knew how I often think the same, dear Conela. I am forced to set that desire on the bottom of our list of priorities, but oh, how it pains me so," Corry smiled. She was ever the dutiful regent, using logic and reason in her decisions, but couldn't help the inner desire to correct such an eyesore.

"I as well, Lady Conela," Leanna laughed. "I have told Cronus that very thing, and he laughs at me."

And so, they all shared their many thoughts on how the palace should look should they win the day. A thorough cleaning was needed. Something also needed to be done with the smell that was only growing worse by the day, with so many soldiers garrisoned at Corell. Dealing with the waste alone was an incredible feat of coordination and hard work. Just feeding so many required an army of kitchen servants, who cooked without rest from dawn to dusk, their chimneys jutting from several points from the palace roof.

They shared stories and spoke of their husbands and the men they found most fetching among the palace guards and royal elite.

They laughed and talked for much of the night, until thoughts of war and battle were furthest from their minds. Throughout their conversation, Corry would look over to Leanna from time to time, happy for her friend, and thinking of what it would be like to carry Terin's child.

Someday, Corry smiled at the thought.

* * *

One day hence.
Twenty leagues Northwest of Corell.

Commander Connly, commander of the 2nd Torry Cavalry, raised his lance high into the air, signaling the charge. His mounted force lumbered forth, two thousand hooves clopping the grassy soil, driving forth across the open fields with the northern edge of the Zaronan Forest sweeping behind them. Across the open fields an equal number of Benotrist mounts rushed to meet them, their human riders leveling their spears, each with a gargoyle sharing their saddle, their ocran strangely abiding the foul creatures' presence. Connly narrowed his eyes before the morning sun, tightening the grip on his lance with his right hand, and his shield and reins with his left. His steel helm drew close over his face, his eyes starring out through its narrow slits.

The 2nd Torry Cavalry skirmished with their Benotrist counterparts throughout the campaign, bleeding each other with every engagement. Of Connly's 700 mounts to start the campaign, he was down to 612, with 500 here with him, and the rest patrolling north and east. He was wary of the enemy tactic of charging into battle, with the gargoyles springing from their mounts, attacking them from the ground and air simultaneously. It was a clever tactic, if one was dumb enough to remain engaged.

To counter the Benotrist tactic, Connly outfitted his mounts with lances over their preferred spears, their long shafts lowered in unison, leveled upon their foes as the two columns drew nigh. The gargoyles sprang from their saddles as the gap narrowed, outstretching their wings with the mounts speeding from underneath them, before the two forces crashed into each other. Torry lances struck dozens of their foes before the Benotrists could reach them with their shorter spears, most striking the ocrans' breasts. Some dipped head first in the matted grass, sending their riders overhead. Others avoided the worst, Torry lances grazing their flanks, some slashing exposed legs or missing altogether. The surviving Benotrists responded with their spears, many finding purchase in Torry mounts and riders, some knocking others from their saddles. Gargoyles dropped from above, brandishing their scimitars at passing foes, but struggling to redirect as the Torry riders sped away, outpacing their pursuit.

Connly's lance found its mark upon the neck of an ocran, before sliding along its flank, taking chunks of flesh with it until he released his grip. His lance fell away, the enemy mount tossing its rider as it turned sharply left, blood issuing from its wound. Connly drew his sword, racing beyond the enemy column, ducking to avoid a slashing scimitar, the creature's blade glancing off his upraised shield.

The Torry cavalry passed through the Benotrist ranks, not stopping to engage, racing apace beyond the speed of the gargoyles. The Benotrist cavalry struggled to turn about and give chase, half pursuing, the others remaining to collect their gargoyle companions who couldn't keep pace. Connly's cavalry thundered across the open fields east of the Zaronan Forest, reforming once beyond the gargoyles flying in pursuit. Connly circled about raising his sword in the air, rallying his units to him, stretching the blade back toward whence they came, where half the Benotrist cavalry drew ominously close, with the rest lingering far behind.

"Forward!" He gave command, the Torry cavalry following him back into battle.

The two forces collided in a clash of swords, scores of Benotrists and dozens of Torries succumbing. The two sides bloodied each other to great effect, before Connly led his men from the battle, escaping before the other half of the Benotrist cavalry could engage, leaving 190 Benotrist casualties to his own 110. The Benotrists were too disordered to give chase.

Kriton looked on at the retreating Torries, his crimson eyes aflame, his mount shifting beneath him. His sword was stained with

Torry blood, having slain two himself. His mount snorted, as the other cavalry drew up alongside him, and his gargoyle companion caught up to him, standing beside his mount catching his breath.

"Finish the wounded and prepare to ride!" Kriton ordered his nearest commander of unit.

And, so it went, with the Torry and Benotrist cavalry bloodying themselves in every engagement. The Torries kept Kriton from raiding their distant holdfasts, and he kept them from raiding Morac's supply trains. The Torry riders were more skilled, but the Benotrists brought greater numbers to battle. Kriton ordered Borgon of the imperial elite, to lead the gargoyles without riders and ocran to make their way south to Corell to join the siege there. He couldn't use them with his other cavalry, for it took great training to make the beasts tolerant of the gargoyles, something he spent much of the winter doing. It was this very tactic that equalized their lacking experience against the battle hardened Torries. Each of his losses today was irreplaceable, and the Torry scum knew that.

Regardless, it would be a long and bloody campaign.

* * *

Two days hence.
Corell.

The defenders were greeted with the arrival of the 11th Benotrist Legion, and its partial complement of twenty four telnics, its remaining fifteen garrisoned at Notsu. The legion posted north of the main gate, holding at a distance before beginning their siege works. By late day the 10th Benotrist Legion arrived from the east, circling the north side of the palace before positioning to the west, where their standard was posted, a broken black shield upon a field of red. Their legion had their full complement of 50 telnics, having marched from their home base of Pagan Harbor. By nightfall their spades sounded in the dark as they began their siege works.

One day hence.

The early morning heralded the arrival of the 8th Benotrist Legion, following their standard of a gray hammer upon a field of red, their thirty-seven telnics aligning beside the 11th Legion north of Corell. By midday, Benotrist magantors filled the eastern sky, demonstrating in force, testing the Torries resolve. General Valen held his forces back, ascertaining the Benotrist strength before committing his precious warbirds. It was late in the day when lookouts upon the Tower of Cot spotted a small magantor force approaching from the south, twelve warbirds soaring apace through the sky.

"The south wall! Magantors approaching!" The cries went out, calling the garrison to arms.

Soldiers spilled out of their barracks onto the battlements, taking up positions. Trebuchets and scorpion crews prepared their ballistae, while hundreds of Jenaii warriors and Torry magantors prepared to spiring into the air if the approaching warbirds continued their course. Princess Corry stood beside General Bode upon Zar Crest, staring out across the open ground separating the south wall from the gargoyle 5th Legion in the distance.

Terin stood beside her, feeling no pull from his father's sword, his actions now guided by his own instinct, and nothing else. Terin looked on, taken aback by the gargoyles that took to the air once the approaching magantors passed over their position as if attempting to reach the airy heights the magantors were flying. It was a useless effort, and Terin wondered their motive.

"Southeast! Another Magantor group!" The cries went out from the lookouts atop the Tower of Celenia, drawing attention to the eastern sky, where two score of Benotrist warbirds filled the air.

"Most peculiar," General Bode wondered aloud. The angle taken by the eastern group indicated they were heading to intercept the first group, approaching from the south.

It then dawned on Terin, as well as many others, that the approaching warbirds from the south were friendly.

"Highness, if I might have your leave?" Terin asked of Corry, who fully understood what he was implying.

Corry was torn between her desire to keep him safe, and the need to trust his instincts. Despite her fears and desires, she knew he needed to be given that freedom if he was ever to regain what he lost to Darna.

"Go!" She relented.

He gave her a smile, but before he could take his first step, General Bode interceded.

"I don't believe young Caleph's intervention is necessary, Highness," Bode said as General Valen released a score of their own magantors, and General El Tuvo filled the sky with hundreds of his Jenaii. By the time Terin reached Wind Racer upon his platform, the battle would be decided.

They watched in wonder as the Benotrist magantors drawing from the east, broke off, returning whence they came. The Torry magantors and their Jenaii allies circled the twelve magantors drawing from the south, escorting them to Corell. Terin's eyes narrowed severely, trying to make out the riders from afar, recognizing their magantors as Torry war birds, each bearing two riders. The first riders of each avian were Torry by the look of their uniforms, and the shape of their spears, but it was the nature of their saddle companions that caused his eyes to widen in surprise and disbelief. They were APES.

CHAPTER 15

Terin and Corry made their way to the south facing magantor plat-forms as the warbirds drew nigh, before setting down one by one, the trailing avian circling to land on other platforms. Corry was elated to recognize the first Torry rider to set down before her, Datis Rols, who awaited her return at Torn Harbor. They were supposed to escort her back to Corell, but the attack on Tro changed her plans. She was equally surprised to see a fearsome ape warrior sitting behind him with two crossed axes strapped to his back and wearing a heavily built iron helm and boiled leather breastplate over thick shirt and trousers.

Several Torry Elite stood post around Corry, shadowing her every step throughout the palace at Torg's insistence and her annoyance. She felt Terin's presence was more than enough to safeguard her person, but Torg reminded her that Terin might be needed elsewhere at any time should the need arise. The Torry Elite warily regarded the ape warrior as he was first to dismount, jumping from the saddle onto the stone lip of the platform, his heavy boots sounding audibly as they hit the white stone floor. The warrior gave Corry and Terin a toothy grin. She returned his mirth, recognizing him from Matuzak's court, but not recalling his name, an oversight Datis Rols would correct.

"Highness," Datis greeted upon dismounting, before passing off the reins of his great warbird to the attendants rushing forth from the stables to retrieve them.

"Datis, I apologize for leaving all of you at Torn, but need required me to come straight here from Tro," she apologized.

"We understood your reasoning, Highness, and are most pleased to see you arrived safely here," he bowed.

"Pleased, but not surprised," she reasoned they learned of her whereabouts from the magantor scouts Magistrate Adine sent to Torn to inform them of the attack.

"We received the grim tidings from Tro, and immediately prepared to return to Corell upon learning you already had done so, Highness, but President Matuzak asked that we wait," Datis said, looking to his traveling companion, who came to stand beside him.

"Your friend's name escapes me," Corry said, regarding the gorilla warrior respectfully.

"I am Gorzak, of the President's personal guard!" The warrior boasted proudly, pounding his fists to his chest, the strange gesture the typical greeting of apes from tribe Traxar.

"We are pleased to welcome you to Corell, Mighty Gorzak," Corry greeted him, before again addressing Datis. "Gather the others, and bring them to the throne room, where I shall formally receive them."

"As you command, Highness," Datis bowed, just as another warbird set down beside them.

* * *

Corry sat her father's throne as her former escort riders entered the throne room, along with ten ape warriors, dressed in their austere boiled leather armor, with either battle axes or swords strapped across their backs. Among the Torries were the twelve magantor riders and two Torry Elite, the full complement of the men she set out to rescue Terin with, save for Lucas, who was standing along the wall to her left beside Ular. Terin, Torg, Generals Valen, Bode and El Tuvo, along with Commander Nevias, joined her upon the dais, standing to either side of the throne. Upon hearing of his fellow apes' arrival, Orlom hurried to greet them, standing along the wall to her right, joined by Raven and Cronus. Numerous other commanders, ministers and court officials gathered along periphery, curious to hear tidings from afar.

Datis Rols led the small procession into the chamber, stopping at the foot of the dais, he and his fellow Torries taking a knee as their ape guests looked on, standing behind them.

"Rise, all of you," Corry ordered, eager to hear their tidings.

"Highness, we immediately returned upon hearing that you had departed Tro for Corell," Datis again stated for the benefit of the others gathered therein.

"Very good, Datis. I informed Magistrate Adine to do so, knowing you were waiting for my return. General Valen is most pleased for the return of your magantors," she said, regarding the General briefly, who nodded happily in agreement. Twelve magantors were a significant addition to their defenses.

"I am pleased to inform the General that all of our warbirds and riders are healthy and fit for battle, Highness," Datis proudly declared.

"And I am pleased that you were of great service to the Ape Republic during your time there," she said, referring to their constant patrolling of the sea approaches to Torn. "You bring tidings from President Matuzak, I presume?"

"Yes, Your Highness. When news of the attack on Tro and the destruction upon the ape fleet reached General Matuzak, he was… most displeased," Datis said.

"Understandably so. You mentioned he asked you to wait before returning to Corell?" She asked.

"Yes, Highness. We remained at Torn whilst he journeyed to Gregok, calling a joint session of the Quam and Onom, informing them of the attack and calling upon them for a formal declaration of war," Datis answered loudly, every ear in the chamber attuned to his next utterance.

"Well, spit it out!" Torg gruffly ordered, not one for dramatics.

Datis stepped aside, waving Gorzak to step nearer to address the assemblage. The fearsome ape warrior removed his thick helm, revealing a square built head, and intense brown eyes that bespoke his incredible power, impressing the court with his strong carriage.

"WAR!" Gorzak roared, his booming voice sounding off the

throne room walls. His ape companions chorused the declaration, raising their furry arms into the air, shaking them violently. Those gathered in the throne room almost winced with the loud proclamation echoing in their ears, but the pain was overtaken by a thrilling joy. The Torry soldiers and commanders gathered in the chamber cheered, pimples raising across their flesh. After suffering one siege and caught amid a second, and suffering so much loss, the defenders of Corell were no longer alone. The Jenaii, Prince Lorn and their southern armies, the Macon Empire and now the apes were aligned with them against the common foe.

Corry's heart sang with joy looking out at the cheering faces gathered throughout the chamber. A single tear escaped her eye, slowly running its course down her left cheek. She tried to steel her emotions, denying such weakness before the men, but she was only human, subject to all that that entailed. She recalled the eve of the final assault during the last siege, when all hope seemed lost, recalling what she asked of Terin, ordering him to forsake the castle once the enemy breached the palace. She remembered him denying her order, proclaiming his love for her, and taking her in his arms. She was prepared to die fighting beside the man she loved, but holding no hope for victory. Then at the pinnacle moment, when they were about to be overwhelmed, their countrymen and allies arrived, sweeping the enemy away like a strong wind. She remembered standing upon Zar Crest watching the incredible victory unfold, recalling the emotion that filled her heart at that joyous moment, the very same emotion she was feeling now... HOPE.

At that moment, Gorzak removed a rolled parchment from his satchel, unfurling it as the chamber grew quiet to hear him speak.

"I bring these words from President Matuzak, addressed to Princess Corry, and the brave men and women of Corell," Gorzak began to read the declaration.

"To Princess Corry and the people of Corell.
The Ape Republic has suffered a grievous attack.
The 1st Ape Fleet is reduced to a handful of vessels.
Thousands of our sailors are dead.

Every tribal leader and member of our legislative body,
Has demanded total war upon the perpetrators of this vile crime.
As President of our young republic, it falls upon me to lead us into battle.
Though we are strong in numbers, we are also far from the current battlefield.
Mustering our great strength is already underway,
But projecting it is an obstacle we must overcome.
To you, falls the greater task, as the enemy shall soon be at your walls.
We cannot greatly, nor quickly, aid you in this task,
But have sent ten of our bravest warriors to join you in battle.
Be it known, that every ape warrior
asked to be among the precious few that we have sent,
But we could send only ten upon your magantors.
We chose ten that demonstrated their martial prowess during our revolution.
These warriors each hail from a different tribe,
And look to deliver a heavy blow to Morac's legions.
Should any question the might the Ape Republic will bring to bear
Look no further than the prowess of these ten.
Every one of us wishes we could join you upon your walls
To strike a blow and smash gargoyle skulls.
To those that ask, tell them SOON.
Soon we shall bestir from our sacred hills
And bring destruction upon our common foe.
To Corell
To Princess Corry
To Prince Lorn
Victory!"

Gorzak lowered the parchment upon finishing, receiving thunderous cheers from the assemblage. He looked to Raven and Orlom standing alongside the near wall, giving them an Earther salute with a toothy grin, which Raven casually returned, shaking his head. Corry let the noise subside before speaking.

"We are overjoyed that you shall fight beside us, Mighty Gorzak. Would you care to introduce your comrades?" Corry asked.

"Princess," Gorzak regarded her with a broad smile, drawing his nearest comrade to his side, a lanky, gorilla warrior with twin swords crossed over his back. Removing his helm revealed a shaggy head of black fur and a long face.

"I am Huto, son of Hutoq, of tribe Hutor. I have come to kill gargoyles!" The young gorilla roared, as the next warrior stepped forth.

"I am Carbanc, son of Hukok, of tribe Narsos. I have come to smash gargoyle skulls!" Carbanc roared, with a battle ax and hammer strapped across his broad back. He was shorter than Huto, with a thick head, and wide, flaring nostrils.

"I am Krink, son of Jurtok, of tribe Manglar. I have come to… cut off the heads of gargoyles!" He paused trying to think of what exactly to say.

And so it went, with the others introducing themselves, ten warriors in all, prepared to fight beside the Torries, brothers in arms.

* * *

The following days found the new arrivals in the training arena, demonstrating their prowess while Torg evaluated where they would be best placed. Gorzak was the most impressive of the warriors, able to swing both battle axes simultaneously with impressive strength and skill. The one called Carbanc, displayed an uncanny ability to use both axe and hammer in unison, often caving a shield with his hammer, while driving his axe into his opponent's head. Both apes' power was quite impressive. The ape called Huto, was more fluid in his movements, using two slender blades with a very slight curve to them, aiding in their drawing ability and speed. Huto demonstrated a dizzying array of spins and strikes, which would prove deadly amidst many foes. Torg took wicked pleasure watching his bouts with Ular, both moving fluidly, sparks flying off their blades in a whirlwind of strikes.

It was not surprising for Orlom to plant himself beside Torg, as if he were in the chain of command, parroting Torg's every instruction.

"Let's pair Ular with Huto, against Gorzak and Carbanc," Torg was curious to see the contrast in styles, the former's grace against the latter's power.

"Pair up with Ular, Huto! Just like coach said!" Orlom shouted, causing Huto to snort dismissively, not acknowledging Orlom's self-appointed authority.

"Come with me, sport. Need to work on your gun handling skills." Raven, who was looking on from the side of the arena, snatched Orlom by the collar of his earther jacket. Torg gave Raven an appreciate nod as he dragged Orlom away, much to the others delight.

Raven took him aside, going over his fundamentals, and reminding him that they had to remain within the palace until Thorton was spotted, where Orlom would continue to remain out of sight until Thorton was dead. Only then, was Orlom free to shoot away to his little heart's content. Orlom would look at the others from time to time, especially Krink, who played opposite him in the football championship they played at Gregok, where Orlom played receiver, with Krink playing corner. He was still bitter over losing, only to remind himself that the teams were unfair since Raven and Argos were on Krink's team, while he only had Lorken, voicing his complaint with Raven.

"Cheer up, kid. How do you think I felt all those years at the academy when Lorken was my Quarterback? We actually cheered whenever he got sacked, knowing he wouldn't throw an interception on that play," Raven chuckled, slapping the young gorilla on the back.

* * *

One day hence.

Morac rode at the head of the 9th Benotrist Legion, its long columns stretching to the horizon in an endless train. Once the towers of Corell broke the western sky, he rode on ahead, his personal guard filling in around him. He drew his gruesome helm over his head, his dark brown eyes staring through the empty sockets of the ape skull affixed to its front. He rode a midnight black ocran, with silver horns spiraling from its wide set skull, with his blood red cape trailing him like a flame. Sunlight reflected off his golden cuirass, shining brightly beneath his standard born by the rider beside him. He galloped forth, passing through the rear pickets of the 14th Gargoyle Legion that guarded the eastern approaches of Corell. Gargoyles hailed their commander as he passed, their guttural hisses echoing through the crisp spring air. He eased his lathered mount to a halt upon the very same rise that he stopped upon during the last siege, when he first set eyes upon Corell.

His gaze went to the airy heights of the palace, where its mighty towers rose imperiously into the heavens, with scores of Jenaii warriors circling its citadels, their winged forms soaring gracefully above the storied ramparts. Corell's white walls were still soiled from the previous battle, blood and smoke marring their ancient beauty. He eyed the standard of the house of lore waving above the tower of Celenia, a golden crown upon a field of white, lifting in the breeze. Even from afar its massive size could be seen, taunting him, a bold reminder of his failure. He would see that misfortune corrected, envisioning his own sigil gracing those ramparts, a glowing golden sword upon a field of black, the very sigil that blew above his head, held aloft by his standard bearer who rode beside him, heralding his approach like an omen bringing judgment to the Torry realm.

His attention was quickly drawn to several riders approaching, an odd mix of gargoyles and Benotrists. One of the men was Borgon of the imperial elite, riding a brown ocran whose animated disposition matched his own. Beside Borgon rode the commander of the 14th Gargoyle Legion, Trimopolak, an unusually tall gargoyle with prominent fangs curving over his blood red lips.

"Hail, Lord Morac!" Borgon greeted, bringing his mount to stop atop the small rise, the others filling in around them.

"How fares our cavalry?" Morac inquired, having last seen Borgon in Kriton's company, raiding the Torry countryside.

"We have had several significant engagements with the enemy cavalry since crossing into Torry North, the most recent just north of here a few days ago. We suffered many casualties, as did our foes," Borgon stated, before further explaining his returning with the survivors who lost their mounts.

"Very well. Where is Vetino?" Morac inquired of the imperial elite tasked with organizing his pavilion, and coordinating their supply caravans.

"He awaits you at your pavilion, north of the palace," Borgon stated.

"General, how fares your legion?" Morac then addressed General Trimopolak.

"Forward trenches complete. They are building a second line to the rear, Lord Morac," the general pointed a clawed digit south of their position, where several thousand gargoyles were digging a series of trenches and palisades. Another few days and the line would reach this position, before continuing north, where it would eventually link with the that of the 8th Benotrist Legion.

"Have the other legions begun similar fortifications?" Morac looked off to the southwest where the 5th Gargoyle Legion awaited in the distance.

"Yes, but none have advanced as far as mine," Trimopolak hissed, his split tongue running along his lower lip, struggling to keep it moist in the crisp spring air.

"I shall see for myself. Summon all legion commanders to my pavilion, posthaste, where I shall treat with them shortly," Morac ordered, before riding southward, with his guards and standard bearer following. He would circumnavigate the palace, inspecting each legion in detail.

* * *

Corry stood upon Zar Crest, observing the 9th Legion approaching from the east, their long columns angling north, taking up temporary position behind the 8th and 11th Legions. She released a weary sigh, regarding the incredible forces that now surrounded them, wondering if even more were approaching somewhere beyond the horizon. A full listing of Tyro's legions was in order, to properly ascertain just what he could bring to bear. She couldn't help but voice those concerns to General Bode, who stood beside her, observing the enemy movements with his discerning eye.

"If our reports are correct, the only legion unaccounted for is the 13th Benotrist Legion. The rest of Tyro's forces are garrison troops, and if Elos' reports were accurate, he stripped the garrisons of Nisin and Pagan to fill out the losses suffered to the 8th and 11th Legions," Bode surmised.

"Tyro had eighteen legions. Surely, he has more available than what we see here?" Corry wondered. Though the army that surrounded them was overwhelmingly large, she believed Tyro must have great power in reserve.

"The 1st, 2nd and 3rd Legions constituted Yonig's invasion force of Yatin. According to General Valen, those forces now number around twenty to thirty telnics garrisoning Telfer and Tenin. The 4th, 5th, 6th and 7th Legions have been reduced to the 5th Legion, which rests to our south, if our spies are correct. The 8th, 9th, 10th, 11th, and 14th are presently outside our walls. The 12th is much reduced after the attack on Tro, and is moving against the harbor with the telnics it has left. The 15th, 16th, 17th, and 18th Legions were all but destroyed at Tuft's Mountain. The fifteen telnics positioned along the Cot River are all that remain of their once impressive strength," Bode explained, rattling off each of Tyro's Legions in order.

"Is Tyro so blinded by hate that he would risk his empire by sending all that he has against us?" Corry asked, looking at the vast army that surrounded them. Even if Lorn arrived with a vast host from the south, with the Jenaii with him, they would still be outnumbered by Morac's legions.

"Though hate defines the man, I believe he knows, as we do, that Corell is the key to the war. Should he take it, he can garrison it with a strong enough force to never be dislodged. From here he can ravage our crop lands and strike out at our remaining holdfasts, destroying them at his leisure. It might take many years for us to recover, if we are not destroyed outright, and by then the gargoyles will spawn a new generation to replenish their lost legions. No, we must win here, or the war is lost. As far as emptying his empire, Tyro still has powerful garrison forces holding every major city and fortress in his realm."

"But he would be vulnerable to revolt," she reasoned.

"Yes, just as Elos and Alen have helped ignite, but even if successful, it will likely not factor in the battle before us. It is Corell that shall determine the fate of the war, and the fate of the Torry Realms."

"Then we must win," she determined.

"We hold these walls with nearly thirty telnics. They shall not overtake us without bleeding themselves dry, even if they have the Golden Sword," Bode said, shifting his gaze southward, where Morac's standard bearer proceeded his lord through the encampments of the 5th Legion. Even from this great distance, he could make out the faint sigil of a golden sword upon a field of black.

Corry's gaze followed where he was looking, a visible scowl torturing her lips upon seeing it. How she was tempted to ask Raven to shoot the foul wretch and be done with him, but that would defeat his need to remain hidden. Besides, he might not be able to harm Morac, as the swords of light had an unusual power to protect those who wielded them. If there was one enemy she desired dead, it was him, but justice would only be served if Morac's death was painfully slow and agonizing. If she had her way, it would be so, but there was no justice in war, and rarely in life. Darna deserved a most fitting death, and that did not happen. If she had her way, Darna would have been flayed or burned in a slow turning spit, and Deva with her. Alas, she was denied her vengeance, with Deva mercifully slaying her mother, and Terin forgiving Deva, granting her reprieve. They deserved far worse than what they received, but as angry as she was, it was Terin who was most aggrieved. She spared a glance behind her, where the boy in question stood guard, his eyes turning sharply to hers, attuned to her every action. She spared him the slightest smile, before he returned his gaze to the surrounding sky, ever vigilant in his duty to protect her, his blue eyes staring intently through the slits in his silver helm. She admonished her girlish weakness, her every thought leading back to him in some way.

"It appears Morac is inspecting his siege lines," Bode's observation drew her from her amorous leanings, returning her gaze to Morac, who now proceeded toward the west, where the 10th Benotrist Legion was fortifying their position in the distance.

"Does that mean he intends to commence his attack?" She wondered aloud.

"They appear in no hurry to do so, but things could rapidly change. We must be ready, regardless."

"We must know what awaits in the east. Inform General Valen that a reconnaissance in force might be required to ascertain if Morac has more forces enroute. We must keep an equal vigilant eye to our west, should Morac threaten lands beyond Corell," she ordered.

"I am afraid you are correct. I hate risking our precious warbirds, but we must know what we are facing," Bode agreed.

* * *

It was late afternoon when Morac reached his pavilion, easing his mount to a halt as a score of servants hurried forth to prostrate themselves before him, before seeing to his ocran. He swiftly dismounted, testing his healed leg as his sandaled boot struck the ground, reassured of its firmness. A number of imperial elite were posted around the makeshift structure, thrusting their fists to their chests as he stepped nigh. The standards of each legion stood prominently before the entrance, where his own was soon to be planted, standing taller than the others. Borgon and Dethine greeted him at the entrance, waving him through the open flaps of the pavilion.

Stepping within, he was greeted by a line of his collared slave girls, kneeling with their heads respectfully bowed. Behind them was a map table already arranged with his legion commanders and General Polis, commander of his magantor forces, along with select members of the imperial elite, gathered around it. A clap of the hands sent his slaves about their tasks, several hurrying to serve drinks to his guests, while others attended him personally, taking his helm and offering him a bowl of water to wash his hands. Another offered a cloth to dry them as he stepped toward the table.

"Status of your legion, General Felinaius?" Morac asked the commander of the 11th Benotrist Legion.

"I hold position north and west of the main gate of Corell with twenty-four telnics. We have completed the forward siege works, aligning with the 8th Legion to our east, and the 10th Legion to our southwest, running in a curved arc from here... to here," the general stated, running a pointer in a sweeping motion around the portion of Corell upon the map.

"And your reverse trenches?" Morac asked.

"Under construction, Lord Morac. We hope to have them completed in the coming days," Felinaius said.

"General Vlesnivolk?" He looked next to the commander of the 8th Benotrist Legion, whose thirty-seven telnics were aligned east of the 11th Legion, their siege works running from their forward position north of Corell's main gate, angling east and south, where they joined the siege works of the 14th Gargoyle Legion. Like the 11th Legion, the 8th completed their forward siege works, and were working on their rear trenches.

"...Foraging parties have swept the lands as far north as here, and as far west as... here," Vlesnivolk swept his hand over a large portion of the approaches of Corell, ten to fifteen leagues from their current position.

"We have also resecured the rock quarry to our north that we used during the last siege to forge munitions," Borgon, of the Imperial Elite stated, tapping the point on the map where the quarry was located.

"That shall not be necessary. The catapults I have ordered hither shall be used for an entirely defensive purpose," Morac smiled knowingly, keeping his mirth in check.

"Defensive, Lord Morac?" General Polis asked curiously. The entire point of the invasion was to seize Corell before it could be further reinforced.

"Defensive," Morac stated firmly, leaving it at that. He then asked the status of the other commanders of legion, continuing with General Trimopolak, commander of the 14th Gargoyle Legion. The 14th was firmly entrenched along the eastern side of Corell, their siege works the most complete of all the legions. General Concaka's 5th Gargoyle Legion covered the southern portion of the siege, his forty-four telnics cobbled together from the remnants of the 4th, 5th, and 7th Legions. General Gavis' 10th Benotrist Legion was well positioned along the western approaches of Corell, the grizzled commander's fifty telnics positioned to counter any relief force the Torries might send. General Marcinia was the last to report, his 9th Benotrist Legion having just arrived, and currently positioning itself to the rear of the 11th and 8th Legions, north of Corell.

"And you, General Polis?" Morac inquired of his magantor forces.

"We currently have one hundred and forty warbirds patrolling our supply routes from Nisin to Notsu, and Notsu to here. We have done as you ordered, limiting our presence to the eastern approaches of Corell and all points between here and Notsu," General Polis stated, the others curious of the limits placed on their patrolling.

"Increase your strength along the eastbound roads in the coming days. I do not wish our Torry friends to chance upon what we are bringing to bear," Morac stated, eyeing the map keenly.

"Lord Morac?" General Felinaius asked, wondering of what he had planned.

"Trailing Marcinia's legion are one hundred and twenty dracks, with many wagons bearing proper munitions," Morac said. This news brought a chorus of relived sighs around the table. The powerful weapons could hurl iron spears a great distance, punching through wood or stone with ease, let alone the flesh of a magantor.

"Shall we forward position them?" General Gavis asked, the light of the basin torch nearby illuminating his scarred face.

"Not yet. I want them positioned here... beside Marcinia's legion," Morac tapped the position on the map north of Corell.

"Why there, Lord Morac?" General Polis inquired.

"To safeguard Marcinia's men while they work," Morac said, his cryptic answer drawing their attention, before addressing General Felinaius directly. "You are to hand over your place in the siege lines to the 8th Legion, who shall extend their lines to cover the entire northern face of the encirclement."

"Where am I to reposition?" Felinaius asked.

The others followed Morac's eyes to Dethine, where the Nayborian Champion stood to his right.

"Your legion shall follow me to… here," Dethine said, pointing out the position on the map.

* * *

The following morn.

The rising sun drew back the curtain of darkness, revealing the grim landscape surrounding Corell. General Bode and Commander Nevias stood upon Zar Crest, looking beyond the north wall, where the 9th Benotrist Legion busied themselves along the horizon, the sound of twenty thousand spades echoing in the distance like a buzzing hive.

"What are they doing?" Nevias wondered, his aged eyes squinting to discern their activity.

"Time will reveal, but whatever its purpose, I doubt we shall find favor with it," Bode said, before catching sight of the returning magantor patrol approaching from the west. He hoped they could speak of the whereabouts of the 11th Legion, which they observed forming up and marching west, before disappearing in the Zaronan Forest last eve.

* * *

Corry again presided over a council of war, with Bode, Nevias, Dar Valen, and Torg, along with General El Tuvo gathered about the table with the map of Torry North unfurled across it. Only these select few were present, indicating the delicate nature of the decision before them.

"What have you, General?" She asked of Dar Valen.

"Our patrols spotted elements of the 11th Legion emerging from the western side of the Zaronan Forest, about... here," Dar pointed out the location on the map.

Even a novice tactician could see their purpose, marching toward the holdfast of Besos, several days march along the east-west road. The small garrison was stripped of much of its strength to reinforce the garrison of Corell, its combined force numbering less than three telnics. Corry looked to Bode for his assessment.

"With only human infantry, it would take time to prepare a proper siege to breech the walls of Besos. Have your scouts spotted any siege engines accompanying them?" Bode asked of Dar.

"None as yet, but much of their strength is still emerging from the forest. The walls of Besos exceed eighty feet, with powerful turrets and a wide moat. If they intend to storm the fortress, they would be better served with gargoyles, rather than infantry which shall further strain their supply trains," Dar said.

"Perhaps, or it might portend something worse," Bode sighed, rubbing a digit over his chin, mentally placing himself in Morac's position to gauge his purpose.

"Do you believe Morac will simply trap us here with part of his forces, while moving west through our heartland?" Corry asked, fearing it might be so.

"His current siege works seem aimed at doing that very thing, and should Besos fall, the way is open to Central City. He could quickly shift his gargoyles west, destroying everything between here and Central City. Even if we evacuated all of our people from his path, they shall not return before planting season has passed. It would mean certain starvation next winter," Bode reasoned.

"If he weakens his position here, we might strike out at him," she pointed out.

"Even weakened, he would still greatly outnumber us. And he would gladly exchange soldier for soldier on even ground rather than ten for one upon our high walls," Bode said grimly.

"Then he intends to trap us, while moving much of his forces west?" She asked.

"That would be my guess, but there is still the strange activity of the 9th Benotrist Legion north of the palace," Bode said.

"What purpose do siege trenches serve so far from the palace?" El Tuvo asked.

"They don't appear to be digging trenches. From what I have seen they are moving a great deal of soil from farther north to that location," Bode said.

"They could be building a structure to store their provisions. Considering the problematic nature of their logistics, that would be a reasonable choice," Nevias said.

"Perhaps, but it bears watching over the coming days. Meanwhile, we must decide whether to reinforce Besos, or leave them to their devices," Corry said.

"We cannot reinforce them with General Bode's army, or the garrison. Only magantors and my battlegroup can reach Besos with enough strength to secure it," El Tuvo stated with his serenely calm voice.

"We cannot risk your warriors when they are needed here, General. Only you and General Valen's warbirds can counter Morac repeating his use of his launch towers," Corry reminded him.

"Does it require all ten thousand of my warriors to counter such a threat, Princess?" The Jenaii General asked.

Corry considered his question, before Nevias interjected.

"A telnic of Jenaii would greatly reinforce Besos, leaving nine here to counter whatever devilry Morac conjures, Highness."

"Perhaps, if all they face at Besos is Benotrist infantry, but they would fare poorly should Morac slip a host of gargoyles there, before we could counter. It would be folly to sacrifice a thousand precious Jenaii when they might count for so little. If we decide to reinforce Besos, it should be with enough force to deny Morac an easy conquest, and disavow any thoughts of invading the lands to our west," she reasoned.

"A force that strong would weaken us here," Torg pointed out.

She considered that, but the choice was not easily made.

"Bode, you are a brilliant strategist. I would hear your counsel," she ordered.

"Considering the options available to Morac, it would be unwise to allow him to trap most of our strength here. I see the wisdom of sending a strong enough force to make a difference, but not too strong to weaken us here. I suggest three telnics of Jenaii reposition to Besos. There they can hold and wait," Bode advised.

"Wait?" Nevias asked, making a curious face.

"Wait upon the enemy. Should Morac simply besiege Besos, and advance no further, those three telnics will occupy the 11th Legion. Should Morac bring a greater force to bear to assail the fortress, those three telnics can reposition farther west, where they can harry the enemy's advance, just as our cavalry are doing," Bode explained.

"You would send them there only to abandon the fortress to the enemy?" Dar asked, thinking it harsh to consign the garrison to certain death.

"Yes. Their purpose is to check a smaller force, or slow a larger one's advance. Those are our choices, our only logical ones as I see it," Bode said.

"What say you, General El Tuvo?" Corry asked.

"It seems wise. I shall appoint Commander Ev Yaro of the 4th telnic to lead the force," the Jenaii general said.

"Good. Then we can wait and see what Morac is planning," Corry said, concluding the council.

* * *

The following morn saw the great host of Jenaii take to the heavens, angling southwest, intending to approach Besos from the south after moving several days away from the Benotrist and Gargoyles forces surrounding Corell. The gargoyles of the 5th Legion, and Benotrists of the 10th Legion could do naught as the winged warriors passed high overhead. Though the Jenaii were also limited in flight, they had the benefit of lift from the high walls of Corell, and could attain heights much greater than the gargoyles, and possessed much greater endurance.

Morac considered contesting the Jenaii's flight, but thought better of risking his precious magantors. He could guess their intentions, and if the absence of his 11th Legion removed three telnics of Jenaii from Corell, then so be it. His spirits were bolstered as the first of the dracks finally arrived by mid-morning. They were quickly positioned around the structure the 9th Benotrist Legion was constructing, twenty-three in all, with the remaining ninety-seven arriving over the coming days, followed by an endless train of munitions. They would guard his construction site, until needed for the assault upon Corell, when he would move them forward. He waited until nightfall before ordering ten telnics of the 5th Gargoyle Legion west toward Besos under the cover of night.

* * *

The following morn.

Commander Nevias joined General Bode upon Zar Crest, gazing north at the massive structure rising behind the enemy siege works to their direct north. They spied the newly arrived siege weapons positioned around its base, recognizing them as large ballista of some sort, but could not ascertain from this distance. The structure in question appeared to be a growing mound of soil, with thousands of soldiers adding to its height, bucket by bucket, like an endless stream of bugs working in a hive.

"I should have known," Bode sighed disgustedly with his failure to not have anticipated this.

"Known what?" Nevias asked, his expression mirroring Bode's alarm.

"They are building a launch ramp. One that we cannot burn."

* * *

One day hence.

The morning sun broke upon Corell, illuminating the clear sky where forty Torry warbirds and a thousand Jenaii warriors soared northward over the battlements. Half bore munitions, flames flickering above their sealed pouches dangling safely beneath them, the rest flying guard, protecting their brethren. Horns sounded through the Benotrist encampments, echoing the alarm as the enemy drew nigh, men scrambling toward their trenches, seeking cover as the great host filled the heavens. Benotrist magantors scrambled to react, the half dozen already airborne performing their morning patrols, the only ones positioned to respond.

Morac stirred from his slumber, disentangling his slave girl, pushing her aside while springing from his bed, his others girls lying about his pavilion, slowly stirring. Donning his tunic and boots, he grabbed his sword, stepping through the entrance flaps, bright sunlight torturing his eyes.

"What is the cause of this?" He barked to his guards, who stared off to the south with spears leveled.

"Enemy magantors, Lord Morac!" They shouted; his eyes immediately drawn to where they were looking.

He quickly went about donning his armor.

* * *

General Valen's warbirds came swiftly upon the forward trenches, manned by the 8th Benotrist Legion, passing safely above, the Benotrist arrows falling hopelessly short. Up ahead was the partially completed ramp, where the men of the 9th Benotrist Legion were serried along its reverse slope, struggling to flee, with thousands breaking in different directions once they reached its base.

"Packaww!" The sound of enemy warbirds sounded over the din, drawing his gaze to the northeast, where a handful sped to meet them.

Dar raised his spear, directing half his column toward the enemy warbirds, the resting continuing on toward the ramp. A unit of Jenaii broke off to join him, their blue helms and breast plates resplendent in the morning sky. Each Torry and Benotrist warbird had two riders, one driver and one archer. Dar drove for the lead Benotrist magantor, his archer rising up behind him, arrow notched as he dipped below the opposing warbird. His archer loosed his arrow into the beast's underbelly, the creature's talons nearly taking him from the saddle. Dar veered sharply left, avoiding another avian following close behind the first. A terrible screech from the stricken beast proved the arrow struck true, but Magantors required many such blows to bring down.

Dar circled about as the two forces collided in a terrible flurry, arrows spewing back and forth, spears thrusting true, or snapping uselessly in half. Several riders to each side were plucked from their saddles, flailing their limbs through their descent as they were tossed aside. He spied a Benotrist warbird dropping suddenly, a spear protruding from its eye, tossing its riders in its death spiral. A Torry warbird suffered a wounded left wing, its right wing flapping uselessly to compensate. Dar watched helplessly as it glided to the ground, its riders beset by a mob of Benotrist warriors. Despite the carnage, the enemy magantors were swiftly dispatched, four slain and two speeding away. Dar quickly took stock of his surroundings before redirecting his force back to the others.

The greater host of Torry warbirds closed upon the ramp, ready to deliver their munitions, the lead avian drawing dangerously ahead, angling for the mob of soldiers crowded atop the makeshift structure, struggling to break through the crowd.

WHOOSH!

The magantor shifted violently, a large metal spear barely missing its left wing. The warbird swerved right, readjusting its course before a second shaft struck its breast. A quiet scream escaped its dying throat, its wings collapsing before falling freely away, its riders tumbling from the saddle, their limbs flailing with their rapid drop.

The following magantors looked on in horror as another warbird was struck, a metal spear piercing its right wing, its riders holding helplessly to its back through its shallow descent. Other spears followed, spewed from the terrible siege engines positioned below. A Jenaii commander of flax shifted, avoiding a spear as the warrior beside him took a bolt through his middle, passing through his back. Those bearing munitions began to deposit their loads, the gelatinous material splashing below, erupting in flames. Some fell short, splashing upon empty ground. One found purchase upon a drack, caking its crew in flames as they readied a second shot. Others held their munitions a little farther, dropping their loads amidst the serried Benotrist ranks crowding at the north base of the dirt ramp. Flames erupted amid the crowd, fire consuming those closest to where they struck, others farther field suffering severe burns, with particles of the hellish material clinging to exposed flesh.

Some Jenaii angled lower, risking archer fire to improve the accuracy of their strikes. Several were struck by arrows, two suffering mortal blows, the rest enduring, with feathered shafts embedding limbs or wings. Their risk was rewarded with numerous hits in the serried mob below, flames splashing impressively in their midst.

General Valen skirted the left flank of the attacking columns, keeping a vigilant eye upon the surrounding skies, before spotting more Benotrist magantors drawing from the north. He directed his warbirds to engage, purchasing time for the others to drop their munitions. His warbirds soared headlong toward the enemy, the wind pressing their faces as they drove forth. He counted more than twenty magantors, each with two riders, marking them warbirds rather than scouts. He fixed his gaze to the nearest foe, speeding apace to engage. Head on clashes between contesting magantors forced one to angle above your opponent and pluck the enemy from the saddle, or dive below either wing, inflicting whatever damage one could with spear or arrow. Dar chose the former, angling above his foe, his magantor's talons just missing the Benotrist driver, while taking an enemy arrow to its own wing. The embedded shaft caused his warbird to shift suddenly from the sting, but did little damage.

A Torry rider off his right was plucked from the saddle, magantor talons piercing his chest before releasing him above open air, the rider's screams growing faint through his descent. Another Torry warbird off his left suffered a spear thrust under its left wing, faltering slightly, its driver steadying its course, before disengaging. Dar had a standing order that should a warbird suffer any injury, you must return immediately to Corell. The only exception was himself, as he needed to direct the battle as best as he could. The skirmish continued in a flurry of dizzying clashes, several magantors falling to each side before the host of Jenaii caught up to their weary comrades, joining the battle.

A Jenaii warrior swept alongside his magantor, brandishing a short sword in his right hand, and a small circular shield in his left.

The winged warrior regarded him briefly before dropping suddenly from sight. Dar stole a glance below, where the warrior fell upon an enemy warbird, the weight of his descent snapping the archer's neck, before tumbling off the warbird himself, his spreading wings breaking his fall as he neared the ground, gliding briefly before gaining lift, avoiding a mob of Benotrist warriors standing below, shaking their spears futilely at him.

And, so it went, with several more warbirds falling out of the battle, some dying, but most returning to their base to recover. Several Jenaii succumbed, overtaken by the swifter magantors plucking them from the sky with pitiful ease. Dar watched in satisfaction as the last of the enemy warbirds succumbed, or withdrew, surrendering the skies to them. He circled back to the greater portion of their attack force, who finished delivering their munitions. The grounds surrounding the great ramp were awash in flames. He spied men running to and fro, with flames pouring off their backs, trailing them like fiery sails full with the wind. Smoke drifted above the hellish landscape, briefly masking the ghastly scene below. Hundreds lay dead or dying, the bodies of burning men flopping about the ground like fish thrown upon the shore. The pitiful cries of burning men echoed hauntingly over the din.

Dar sighed with grim satisfaction, the small battle achieving its aims. He prepared to give the order to withdraw when another force of magantors came from the east, smashing into the flank of the greater host. The sounds of battle again rang out, with magantors and Jenaii circling about the heavens, spears and arrows flying back and forth. Talons snatched men from saddles or Jenaii from the air, blood staining their sharpened digits. Dar led his weary cohort back into the fray, falling upon a Benotrist magantor from behind, plucking driver and archer from the saddle in one grab, his warbird releasing them briefly after, over open air. He ignored their distant screams while pressing on. He caught sight of a flash of brilliant light ahead, luminous like a crimson flame dancing through the air with terrible power. His heart went to his throat, recognizing the *Sword of the Sun* in Morac's fell hand. The Benotrist Lord sat behind the driver of a Benotrist warbird, slaying Torry warbirds in detail. He swerved beneath the wing of another avian, slicing it in half as he passed. The Torry warbird dipped severely, nearly tossing its riders, its other wing working feverishly to compensate, to little avail. The beast glided to the surface, dooming its crew to slaughter.

Far off in the distance, thousands of gargoyles of the 14th Legion took to the air, filling the sky. They were too far afield and could not hope to reach these airy heights, but his Jenaii allies could not fly much longer without exhausting themselves. He could not risk them by remaining.

WHOOSH! WHOOSH!

Giant spears spewed from below, where drack crews moved their ballistae in position, the first shafts just missing a Torry magantor.

WHOOSH!

The third spear struck true, drilling another warbird through the breast, lifting it suddenly into the air before dropping altogether. Dar ordered retreat, watching grimly as Morac struck down another magantor, slicing its wing in half before flying off, seeking other prey. Jenaii warriors swarmed some Benotrist warbirds, slaying their crews before driving their swords into the beasts' backs before jumping clear. Most of the Jenaii were quickly growing weary, easy prey for Benotrist warbirds plucking them from the sky. Dar was half tempted to order all his forces to converge upon Morac, ending his threat for good, but thought better of it. Torg warned all of them the danger the swords of light presented, sparing those who wielded them against impossible odds. Attacking him would cost many warbirds and Jenaii that they could ill afford. No, he would leave Morac to Terin.

The Jenaii host raced back to the safety of Corell, with the Torry magantors guarding their slower Jenaii allies, holding back to engage pursuing Benotrist warbirds. Dar circled about, engaging a Benotrist magantor closing upon the trailing Jenaii, his archer striking the underbelly of the beast before breaking off. He caught sight of another Torry magantor falling to Morac's blade, its severed wing dooming avian and riders to grisly deaths.

Dar met Morac's gaze across that deadly space, the Benotrist Lord directing his driver toward him, separated by a mere hundred yards, with the walls of Corell painfully afield. Other Benotrist warbirds swept between them, snatching Jenaii from the air, crushing their wings in their powerful talons. Dar steeled himself for battle, the other Benotrists leaving him to Morac as they battled elsewhere.

"So be it," Dar relented, driving headlong toward Morac, certain to deny his warbird access to his magantor's underbelly or wing. Keeping out of range of Morac's sword was essential, but that was what Morac's other victims thought as well.

WHOOSH!

A sudden white blur passed between them, driving toward Morac with terrible speed. Dar looked on as Wind Racer drove toward Morac, his massive wings pounding the air like claps of distant thunder. Terin held his sword with his right hand, and the reins in his left, keeping his eye upon Morac's warbird, keenly following its movement. Morac smiled wickedly, savoring the chance to again cross swords with the boy.

"Dive below his left wing!" Morac barked into his driver's ear, the space between them rapidly closing.

His driver heeded his council, angling downward just as Wind Racer drew nigh. Terin squeezed his legs tightly to the saddle, his ankles and feet bound in place with heavy rope. Morac's glee turned to ash as Wind Racer spun upside down just as he dipped below him. Terin held tight, swinging his sword as he passed overhead of Morac's warbird, his blade striking true, passing though steel and bone as he twisted upside down. Wind Racer fully spun upon passing Morac's mount, leveling off before circling about. Terin released a baited breath, his heart rising in his throat, wondering how he held on, thankful for the ropes holding him in place. Turning about, he stole a glance toward Morac, seeing the result of his grizzly strike. Morac returned his gaze, staring at him with dark blazing eyes, malice and hatred pouring off the man in unending torrents. Morac's driver sat lifeless before him, his head cloven skull to neck, each half drooping left or right.

Morac pushed his rider aside, grabbing hold of the reins, the dead driver's corpse sliding off the side of the warbird to the distant ground below. He regarded Terin briefly for an eternal moment, neither moving upon the other as their mounts circled lazily in the air. He found Terin's dull blade eerily disturbing, its once vibrant energy replaced with an unsettling coldness. This was a different foe than when they last met upon the ramparts of Fera. Even from afar he projected a deadly aura, a surreal calm that made his blood run cold. The only man who ever projected such terrible power with only his gaze was Tyro.

Another day, perhaps, Morac wisely mused, withdrawing from battle.

* * *

Corry watched the battle from the heights of Zar Crest, cringing as Terin joined the fray, following his every move with baited breath. Once he saw the struggling nature of the melee, he took to the sky, soaring into battle. He met the returning host beyond the walls of Corell, dispatching two Benotrist magantors in quick order before pressing farther north. It was then Corry's heart went to her throat, watching his clash with Morac, the evil Lord's glowing blade shining brightly from afar. Her heart nearly failed her watching Wind Racer spin upside down upon meeting Morac midair, with Terin still clinging to his back upon completing the deadly spiral. She placed her hand upon the parapet, steadying herself as the two champions circled each other in the air, before withdrawing.

"Blasted fool!" Torg growled beside her, watching his grandson return from battle, Wind Racer soaring alongside General Valen, with the greater part of the Jenaii force preceding them to Corell. Of the forty magantors Dar Valen led into battle, only twenty-five returned. The Benotrists lost an equal number, and the Jenaii lost nearly ninety brave warriors. The damage wrought upon the Benotrist 9th Legion was exceedingly high, with hundreds, if not a thousand dead, and many more wounded. The work on the ramp would stop for a day, perhaps two, but continue it would. Corry would not risk such losses again, and once the ramp was high enough, the gargoyles would use it to assail the castle.

CHAPTER 16

THE SIEGE OF BESOS.

The fortress of Besos rested sixty leagues west of Corell, positioned along the east west road connecting Central City and Corell. The fortress itself rested atop an imposing hillside overlooking the Besos divide that ran northeast to southwest, with the Desos River running along its north face. The Desos was one of the headwaters of the Stlen, a shallow headwater at that, that was easily forded at nearly every point. The fortress itself possessed high curtain walls running the circumference of the base of the hill, with an impressive moat circling it, with a north facing drawbridge, and a series of strongly built turrets liberally spaced along the walls. A tall inner keep rested atop the hill, overlooking the outer walls, with a series of redoubts circling it, connected by an inner curtain wall.

The commander of the garrison was one Lord Darus, who wisely evacuated most of the inhabitants of Besos when word reached him of the encroaching army. With much of his strength sent to Corell, the garrison numbered a paltry fifteen hundred men, with only fifty archers. They were reinforced by the three Jenaii telnics led by Ev Yaro. The Jenaii commander joined Lord Darus upon the upper ramparts of the inner keep, looking out over the north wall of the fortress at the great Benotrist host encamped along the banks of the Desos. He could spy the large banners of the 11th Benotrist Legion flying above the center of their encampment, two silver crossed daggers upon a field of black.

Lord Darus was a slender, silver haired commander, approaching his sixth decade. He was clad in austere gray armor over a matching tunic. He served the realm faithfully all his days, reigning as Lord of Besos for nearly thirty years. He served with King Iore during the Sadden War, fighting gargoyles along the Plate, and gaining renown as an able leader of men, and a brave warrior. Upon his father's passing, he assumed Lordship of Besos, overseeing the fortress guarding the realm from gargoyle incursions that managed to bypass Corell and Cropus. His loyalty and duty brought him to this pinnacle moment, standing to post upon these walls against overwhelming odds. They counted over twenty telnics in the Benotrist legion, perhaps more.

"The enemy seems ill prepared for a counter attack," Lord Darus said, regarding the lack of palisades along their siege lines, and an obvious lackadaisical air about their encampment.

"Most peculiar," Commander Ev Yaro said, his silver eyes narrowed against the midday sun.

"No general worth a spit would expose his legion's neck like that unless it was a trap. He taunts us, begging us to attack and leave the safety of our walls," Lord Darus surmised, knowing one defender upon the wall was worth ten outside it.

"They don't appear to be moving upon us, and yet, they cannot safely advance into the interior of Torry North while we occupy this position," Ev Yaro pointed out.

"Then we hold, and see what they have planned," Darus said. His Jenaii ally would remain as long as his presence could preserve the Torry hold on Besos, but he would have to withdraw if the enemy breached the walls. Should Besos fall, Ev Yaro's three Jenaii telnics were all that stood in the Benotrists path toward Central City. Three telnics of Jenaii warriors could not stop an army as large as the 11th Legion, but could greatly slow their advance. With the aid of the Torry cavalry, they would be most effective in weakening the 11th legion, stringing it out before General Fonis could move his 2nd Torry Army from Central City and destroy them. The problem with

297

that strategy would be the destruction the 11th Legion could wrought to the Torry heartland. For now, that problem could wait, for the enemy was not strong enough to storm the gates of Besos without significant reinforcements, or a complement of gargoyles that could fly over the fortress walls.

* * *

Two days hence.

The grim news was relayed to Lord Darus that a second large host was advancing upon Besos from their southeast, ten telnics of gargoyles detached from the 5th Gargoyle Legion, more than enough to breech the walls. Commander Ev Yaro was now forced to withdraw his three telnics to the west, as they were needed to harry the enemy's advance from Besos. Under the cover of night, the Jenaii withdrew, leaving the garrison to its fate.

* * *

Two days hence.

Dethine stood before the walls of Besos amidst his Benotrist allies, surveying the tall battlements of the ancient holdfast, beckoning him like a wanton mistress. Glory awaited the Nayborian Champion, eager to test his sword of light against the gates of the fortress. He stood resplendent in the morning air, sunlight playing off his golden cuirass and helm, matching the coat of his ocran that stood dutifully beside him. His overtures to the garrison to surrender were rudely rebuffed, filling him with a determined resolve to finish this siege in quick order. He had great plans for its stubborn commander, thoughts of how the man would suffer playing evilly in his mind.

"Give the order, General," Dethine said, his eyes still trained upon the battlements above the main gate, resting inconveniently beyond the wide moat circling the fortress.

General Felinaius gave the signal, horns sounding the commencement of the attack. The sky quickly filled with gargoyles, a thousand flying overhead from the north, and the other nine thousand assailing the walls from the south. The Benotrist infantry waited beyond the moat, waiting for the gargoyles to clear the battlements above. Arrows and spears greeted the gargoyles as they drew nigh, dozens dropping short of the fortress walls. Burning ballistae arced overhead, falling short of the Benotrist soldiers aligned in front of Dethine. Others splashed along the approaches of the main gate, setting the ground ablaze, slowing any ground advance while the defenders fought off the gargoyles.

Dethine smiled with grim satisfaction as the gargoyles began to set down upon the north wall, making steady progress, though suffering great loss to do so. From his vantage point, he could not see the overwhelming attack upon the south wall, where thousands of gargoyles swarmed over the battlements. Torry soldiers fought desperately, contesting every foot of the wall, slaughtering gargoyles to great effect. Men kept tight to their formations, thrusting spears or swords between their interlocked shields. Eventually the gargoyles breeched several places along the battlements, forcing the defenders into separate pockets of resistance. The gargoyles swarmed over these positions one by one, overwhelming them with greater numbers. Upon the north wall, the gargoyle attack was concentrated above the main gate. The creatures swarmed over the battlements, or set down behind the main gate from above, before being set upon by the defenders guarding it. Torry soldiers cut down the first to land in their midst in quick order, the gargoyles lack of armor making them easy kills for trained swords. Eventually more set down, their bodies piling up all around the causeway, hindering the defenders' movements before more descended. Eventually, the defenders were overcome, one by one, until none remained to prevent the gargoyles form opening the gate.

Dethine followed the Benotrist infantry across the lowered drawbridge as the gate was opened from within. The area between the outer and inner curtain walls was now flooded with Benotrists and gargoyles, with the Torries upon the inner curtain wall lobbing fire ballistae into the deadly confined space. Torry archers fired rapidly into the Benotrist infantry crowded below to great effect, unable to miss. Dethine weaved his way through the masses, moving aside whenever a fire ballista dropped in his midst, escaping the flames consuming the men and gargoyles around him. Gargoyles flew overhead, assailing the inner battlements. Dethine made his way toward the main gate of the inner walls, where Benotrist infantry crowded before it, suffering flame and arrows from the Torries manning the battlements above.

"Make way!" Dethine bellowed, working his way to the front, his blade igniting a fiery gold, imbuing him with its terrible power.

The Benotrist infantry looked on as Dethine cut into the gate, each strike tearing off pieces of the iron door. Within moments large shards were torn off, daylight peeking through the growing gaps he wrought. Torry spears thrust through the now gapping holes, met by Benotrist shafts and swords jabbing back. Dethine continued his assault upon the gate, moving left as he rent it asunder, until it gave way completely. A great cheer went up from the Benotrist host, men pouring through the fissure, swarming the inner castle as gargoyles pressed the attack from above.

Passing through the now ruined gate, men broke off in every direction, some fighting their way up the stairwells to the inner curtain wall above, while others advanced to the inner keep. Dethine struggled working his way through the river of humanity sweeping before him, stealing a glance to the towering inner keep before them, its uppermost battlements now swarming with gargoyles.

* * *

Lord Darus stood among his men upon the battlements of the inner keep, gargoyle blood dripping from his sword. The Torries stood shoulder to shoulder, jabbing their swords between their shields without respite, with gargoyles pressing upon them. So few remained to hold the walls edge, forcing them back as the gargoyles took hold, more setting down upon the lip of the battlements, fueling the inevitable. Darus thrust his blade around his shield, feeling it slide into flesh of some sort, the guttural sound of a gargoyle screaming proving he struck true. He jabbed repeatedly, making sure of his kill. The soldier beside him found similar success, killing another to their front, before jabbing overhead at another creature clambering overtop of their shields. Darus shifted toward the new threat, thrusting his blade into the gargoyle's side as it slid off their shields, dropping dead at their feet. He pressed forward, jabbing again as another creature slammed into his shield, clawed digits reaching over the top of it, trying to tear it from his arms. He angled his thrusts around his shield, blindly trying to find purchase in the creature's flesh, before a terrible pain shot up his arm, his sword falling from his hand. He retracted his arm, a large dent imprinting his steel vambrace, his hand numb as he tried to shake it off to little effect. His shield gave way, a creature ripping it from his left arm. The soldier to his left thrust his blade into the creature's middle, the gargoyle screaming madly, its jowls snapping as the soldier kicked it off his blade, just as another slammed into his back, driving the soldier to the floor.

Darus looked on in horror as gargoyles swarmed over the soldier, hacking his limbs and devouring his flesh, his desperate screams drowned in the din. Darus clambered for the man's sword, grabbing with his left hand, lifting it just as a scimitar came down upon his head, blocking the blow. He let the curved blade slide off his sword, shifting to his right to counterstrike when his eyes went suddenly blank.

A gargoyle stood behind him, Darus' blood staining his blade, the Torry Lord's head dangling from his neck before the creature lopped it off with his second blow. Darus' dying eyes looked up as gargoyles swarmed the battlements, smoke billowing from the place darkening the sky above like an evil shroud. Besos had fallen.

* * *

Dethine stood upon the battlements of Besos as the sun settled in the western sky. The fortress was now theirs, its garrison put to the sword, the head of its commander resting atop a pike above the main gate, his plan to torture Lord Darus ruined by his death in battle. He only regretted not slaying more of the enemy, but his allies gave him little chance to, sweeping before him like a terrible wind. He looked out to the west, knowing that the way to Central City lay open before them. General Felinaius would garrison Besos while raiding the Torry heartland. The fortress was now a bulwark against any foray of the 2nd Torry Army positioned at Central City in this direction. He would now return to Corell to aid Morac in the upcoming assault. The Benotrist 11th Legion would remain here, while the gargoyles returned with him to Corell, though with fewer than they arrived with, having lost two thousand in the assault.

"First Besos, and then Corell," he whispered, visons of final victory dancing enticingly before him.

CHAPTER 17

Fera.

Jonas pivoted in the loose sand, mirroring his opponent, bringing his shield to meet the explosive thrust. He shifted his shield, glancing the follow thrust before delivering his counter strike, tapping his blunted training sword to Davor's knee, the Benotrist warrior grunting in frustration as the training master called out the strike. Despite their many bouts, Davor had yet to defeat Jonas. He was not alone in that regard, with every member of the Imperial Elite falling to the stranger who was of special interest to the emperor.

Jonas trained with the men every morning in the very pit where Raven battled during his visit, with the large block resting in its center. More often than not, his father sat in the viewing stands above, watching him dismantle his best warriors with pitiful ease. To Jonas' credit, he never boasted his victories, acknowledging each defeated foe with utmost respect, often helping them to their feet. He wished Valera could oversee his bouts, but his father refused to allow her outside the royal apartments. Whether it was to constrict her movements or for her protection, Jonas could only guess. More likely he wanted the child kept from curious eyes, at least until she was old enough to formally present as his heir, as he repeatedly claimed he would, much to Jonas' protest. The situation was surreal, and Jonas couldn't see a way out of it. When his father invited him to train with his men, he thought to refuse, but Valera reminded him that sharpening his martial skills might be useful at some point. He smiled at that, proud of her sound advice. She was ever his sage councilor, tempering his anger and helping him to focus his thoughts. His father found her quite impressive, which he found equally proud and disturbing. If one found favor and praise with Tyro, Emperor of the Benotrist Empire, and sworn enemy of all you held dear, one could hardly not be disturbed. It was madness.

"Again!" The training master ordered Davor to step back into his starting position.

Jonas regarded his foe studiously, noticing his sound stance but disordered bearing. The man was out of sorts facing Jonas, which affected his timing and perception, two principles his father emphasized during his first lessons in sword handling when he was a boy. Without proper timing, one would miss one's target and find a sword pressed to one's throat. If this were true combat, Jonas would rush forth, taking Davor by surprise and finish him quickly, but the benefit of the training arena was he could take the measure of each of his opponents at his own leisurely pace. He simply stood back and received Davor's attack, parrying his vigorous thrusts before disarming him with a decisive riposte.

"Agghh!" Davor growled his displeasure, watching his sword fly from his grip.

Jonas lowered his sword, rather than claim his victory with its blade pointing to Davor's throat. He found such displays unnecessary. He won, and Davor knew it. With that, Davor retired to the opposite wall where Jonas' other vanquished foes gathered, watching as his next victim paraded forth, with no better success.

"Enough!" Tyro ordered as the training master called out another to face his son.

"Emperor!" The training master bowed, before looking up to the emperor's box above, waiting upon his decree, and fearing the failure of his charges, each trained religiously by his own hand with such poor showing.

"Be still, Master Hochan, you have not failed. There is only one man who can face Joriah," Tyro said, ordering them to remain in place as he stepped away, though they could barely see him in the shadows of the stands with the arena's high walls and lighting directed below. Anyone siting behind the torches appeared as little more than shadows to those training below.

They were not surprised to see Tyro emerge through the entrance to the arena, dressed in training leathers and wielding twin blunted swords, with a stout steel helm covering much of his face. Unbeknownst to Jonas, his father trained constantly with his chosen elite, both gargoyle and human, defeating them all just as Jonas had, save for Thorton whose weapon of choice made such bouts pointless. The men looking on failed to notice that no gargoyles were present in any of their bouts with Jonas, as Tyro feared their obvious reaction to his Kalinian blood.

"Two swords?" Jonas regarded his father's unusual choice. No true blade master would use two blades over one. Any second blade was a poor stand in for a shield, and to master the use of twin blades required years of training and ambidextrous leanings, which his father had both, as he was soon to discover.

"You are free to match me!" Tyro said coldly, looking to Master Hochan, who stepped forth, presenting Jonas a second blade, which he reluctantly took, tossing his shield aside.

With that, they began, Tyro advancing upon him in a flurry of moves, his blades working in unison, taking Jonas aback. Tyro slightly smiled, noting Jonas' footwork, his feet moving with precision in small semi circles, or economical pivots, keeping easy balance as he fended off his assault. Joriah was quick to master his feet when Tyro first trained him, and he would praise him, but there was no time for such banter in the heat of battle. Jonas parried Tyro's left blade, before delivering his dangerous riposte, but Tyro was ready, as they drew briefly apart.

"Distance," Tyro said, reminding him of the first lesson he gave Joriah on the principles of swordsmanship, on the necessity of using the space separating you from your foe to determine which strike and technique to use.

Jonas demonstrated the mastery of that lesson, driving his father back with a flurry of strikes, able to wield two blades as well as Tyro. The others looked on with jaws agape, barely able to follow the action with the four blunted blades swirling like a winter gale, before part-ing, circling each other at a measured pace. Jonas thought to ask his father why he trained with two swords, the tactic inferior to one in his opinion, but couldn't think on that now, with Tyro upon him in an instant.

They continued apace, their blades matching each other blow for blow, before Tyro disarmed Jonas' left hand, before catching the other in a bind, his blade moving in a rapid semicircle, pinning Jonas' remaining blade away as his second blade touched his son's chest.

Jonas simply shrugged, acknowledging defeat, inclining his head toward his father, respecting his victory. Tyro regarded him for a long moment, as the men cheered their emperor. Tyro saluted his men with a fist to his heart, releasing them from their duties for the remainder of the day. Once the men filtered out of the arena, Tyro removed his helm, waiting for Hochan to depart, following the others out, leaving only the guards on duty standing at the entrance, out of ear shot if they spoke lowly.

"You are a poor liar, Joriah," Tyro glared at him, knowing he held back.

"I gave you my full effort," Joriah stated.

"Indeed." He didn't believe it.

"If falsehoods displease you, then tell me true. Why do you train with two blades?"

"Need you ask?" Tyro thought the question foolish.

"A shield is useless against a *Sword of Light*, but you had the *Sword of the Sun,* which you gifted to Morac. Why then would you fret over facing it?"

"It was not the *Sword of the Sun* that concerned me."

"The *Sword of the Moon* then, but you were not aware of its exist-ence until Terin arrived at your keep, revealing it so," Jonas reasoned.

"There was always the possibility one could emerge, and that has proven prescient. I always plan for the worst, and that has contributed greatly to my conquests."

"But you don't have a *Sword of Light* to use. Morac does. And the only foe you would need it against is Terin, and a second sword is as useless as a shield against his blade," Jonas pointed out.

"There are others besides my troublesome grandson that have such swords, and mastering two blades gives me a great advantage, a lesson you seem to have mastered as well. Tell me, Joriah, when did you have time to train considering you have been a farmer for the last twenty years?"

"There is always time to practice, if you make time. And I had no better partner to train with than Terin."

"Aye, and I could have helped you with that if you and your mother hadn't run away," Tyro tried to keep his tone even, though the bitterness bled through.

"I already explained why, and as I see you have kept any gargoyles of your elite from my training sessions, you now understand our reasons for leaving."

"Do not mistake my precautions with agreeing with you, they are merely that… precautions. Back to my first point, why did you hold back in our spar?"

"You know why."

"Aye, you cannot harm me, but training is different, and you held back all the same, and I can well guess."

Jonas simply shrugged, allowing him to continue.

"You plan the long course, holding back to assess your opponent's strengths and failings, to use them at a future time, when real consequences rest in the balance."

Jonas just shook his head, for his father was so wrong.

"Then speak it true, Joriah!" Tyro growled.

"I have no cause to harm you, or see you defeated before your men, as my very life, and my wife and daughter's depend upon you remaining strong in your keep."

"You would question my strength here? Are you truly so foolish, boy?"

"I wouldn't cast aspersions that can be thrown back."

"You dare call me a fool?" Tyro growled, taking a step closer.

"You bring my pregnant wife here, luring me as well, where we are trapped, surrounded by creatures that despise me and my daughter for the blood in our veins, and the only thing holding them at bay is YOU. Tell me, father, what should become of us if you die? It needn't be an assassin or battle death, but simply age. What would happen then? Have you thought this through? My sword arm can only carry us so far. Terin navigated these corridors to the palace roof, but he had mighty friends and was not saddled with a wife and infant, and he had my sword to protect him. What do I have but my blood and skill? So, you see, I have every reason to see you live." Jonas held his gaze for enough time to drive his point before stepping away, leaving his father there to his tumultuous thoughts.

* * *

Tyro stood in his chambers staring out its high window to the lands beyond, his mind a torrent of anguish and rage, focusing on the horizon until his emotion cooled. The tidings from Tro concerned him greatly. Somehow their plans to attack the ruling forum and discredit the Ape alliance was changed to an attack on the ape fleet itself as well as the *Stenox*, a change that didn't come from himself or Thorton. The report of the *Stenox's* destruction was ambiguous at best, and what if his grandsons were aboard? Madness. He would find the fool responsible for attacking the *Stenox* and the ape fleet and have them dealt with. Such was the confusion in war, where plans were waylaid and communication broke down over long distances, which brought him back to his son.

He hated that Joriah was right. He couldn't let him go, not after spending so many years searching for him, but he wasn't fully safe here. Despite his faults, Tyro was loyal to his blood, and to his friends and people. Joriah was his blood, and he would do what he must to keep him safe, just as Regula was his friend and he would do what he must to protect him and his kind, just as he vowed to do for his Benotrist peoples. He stood there for a time, searching for an answer, for some solution to balance the scales, until his eye was drawn to the fitted stone on the floor off his right and the treasure hidden below it. He worked his fingers around the stone, lifting it free, before drawing out the three Swords of Light he long ago retrieved, one from his brother's dead hand, and the others in the Kalinian Vale when he scoured it looking for Cordela and Joriah. He kept them secret through the years, for what use had a man for more than one, or two if he was able to duel wield?

He set them upon the floor, drawing two from their nondescript scabbards, holding one in each hand, spinning the blades slowly, before picking up speed, moving them with graceful ease. What use was wielding two swords, Joriah had asked him. There was plenty reason to do so if one held two *Swords of Light*, one to block another in a duel, while the second gutted your opponent. Even the greater blades could not prevent him from defeating them. But he had no need for a third, considering that at length, before returning the swords to their proper place.

* * *

Valera sat upon their bed nursing Cordela, while Jonas stood at the window, staring in the distance, not saying a word as her maid servants attended her. Whatever transpired between him and his father had bothered him intensely. He had not changed out of his sparring leather mail and tunic, removing only his helm, which he set on the floor with little regard. She did her best to not call out to him with the servants about. Young Aina had just finished setting her hair for the day, fussing with it for far too long, in Valera's opinion, but the emperor insisted on such pampering. Dola and Mayla were equally occupied with her feet, brushing a scarlet coloring upon her toenails, and rubbing oil on her feet, over her protest. She constantly rewarded each of the maids with extra food, ordering far more than she personally needed in order to give the excess to them. They refused at first, but Valera was insistent. If she could do nothing else while here, she would do what she could to protect them and see to their needs. Jonas tried the same, asking his father to give Cronus' surviving men over to him, to serve as his attendants, but Tyro refused, which was another point of contention between them. Valera found herself becoming the peacemaker between them, a role she never thought would fall to her.

She was prepared to dismiss her servants when the emperor entered their chamber, sending them out with a wave of his hand, his guards holding at the door, before he ordered them to wait in the corridor. Valera looked to her left where Tyro stood, and then to her right, where Jonas waited at the window, turning back to look at his father, each ignoring her as she sat on the bed between them.

Tyro stepped toward the window holding a sword still sheathed in its scabbard, its finely crafted hilt contrasting sharply to its simple sheath. She thought he might draw it and slay Jonas right there, but he simply held it out for him to take.

"This belonged to your uncle Terik before my brother murdered him, and claimed it for his own. It is yours, and guard it well," Tyro said, turning to step away.

"You had this all along," Jonas said, though his tone made her believe he already knew this.

Tyro stopped halfway across the chamber, keeping his back to him. "You have the foresight to find the blades if you choose, son. You know what I have and where."

"Thank you, father," Jonas said, ignoring the insinuation in his father's statement.

"Use this to keep them safe should I succumb," Tyro regarded her and Cordela, which caused her to wonder what was the reason of their discourse.

"I shall," Jonas said, drawing the sword from its scabbard, the blade alit in otherworldly light, its golden glow igniting tenfold in Jonas' hand, sending beams of faux starlight to every corner of the chamber. Tyro looked on, as if torn by a memory, before turning away, as Valera sat in awe, her eyes wide with wonder.

Tyro stood there with his back to Jonas for the longest time, as if conflicted. "I shall find the men you asked about, and give them to you. Do with them as you will." With that, he passed through the door.

CHAPTER 18

Corell.

Corry stood upon the outcropping of the inner keep where she and Terin shared their first kiss. She stared longingly in the distance, ignoring the great host surrounding the palace, her thoughts on happier times, and the future she could only dream would come. She leaned back into Terin's arms, savoring his comforting embrace as he wrapped his arms around her, drawing her even closer to his chest. The wanning sunlight cast its weakening rays upon the surrounding lands, with the enemy host growing fainter by the moment, before their thousands of cookfires alit, marking their place in the darkness. It was a stark contrast, darkness and light, the darkness of the enemy and the light of hope for a better future. Each rested before her, vying for dominion for her destiny. What would it be? Death or victory?

Victory! She thought determinedly. They had come too far to lose, suffered too much to fail, and most of all they loved each other too much to not grow old in each other's arms.

"You are thinking so loud I can hear you," Terin whispered in her ear, holding her tight within the shadows of the outcropping, lest anyone see them share their embrace. She was still a Princess of the realm, and he but her loyal warrior in the eyes of her people.

"If so, then what am I thinking?" She challenged, her hooded eyes gazing dreamingly now, the horrors of what waited beyond far from her thoughts.

"The future, together, you and I," he smiled, closing his eyes, pressing his head to hers, savoring the smell of her hair as it tickled his nose.

"Impressive," she sighed happily. It was as if they were mentally linked, joined by invisible bonds connecting them so deeply, that it sent tendrils of excitement and happiness throughout her being.

"I could tell by how relaxed you are. Thinking of what waits beyond our walls would make anyone tense. Only happy thoughts could take that away. I know, for I feel the same whenever you are in my arms."

"Oh, Terin," she smiled, turning in his arms. She pulled slightly away so as to look at him, his blue eyes sparkling with life. She caressed his cheek, losing herself in his beautiful gaze. Oh, how she loved him, wishing for nothing more than for an end to this madness.

They both knew that time was growing short, the enemy's preparations for battle nearing completion. The great ramp north of the castle was approaching the height of ten men, and was protected by many more dracks than before, preventing them from assailing it a second time. The gargoyle telnics that assailed Besos had returned the day before. They received the grim tidings of the fall of that vital fortress the day prior to that. Morac was tightening the noose about their throat, his legions coiled to attack. Unlike last time, he wouldn't fritter his forces with a series of weak assaults, wearing down the defenders. No, he would strike with his full strength at one time, and that time was drawing ominously nigh. They knew the battle would be soon, perhaps on the morrow, or the next. This could very well be their last moment together.

"If tomorrow is the day, promise me you will remain safely guarded should I get drawn elsewhere. I cannot go on without you. I WON'T go on without you," he said with the saddest voice that nearly broke her heart.

"You cannot think like that, Terin. When the battle comes, we all must do our part. I was wrong trying to shield you from such danger before. We might all die tomorrow, or not. What matters is that we have each other now. If you desire to grow old with me, there is only one thing that can bring that to pass."

"What is that?" He asked.

"Win," she cupped his cheeks, kissing him.

* * *

"I've brought your supper," Galen said upon entering Leanna's chamber, bearing a bowl of porridge and bread upon a small platter. He found her resting upon her bed with cushions behind her back and between her legs, trying to get comfortable and failing miserably.

"Galen, how very kind of you," she smiled, wiping the sleep from her eyes, working her way into a sitting position as he stepped near, placing the platter upon the small table beside the bed.

"You shouldn't have gone through such a fuss considering your many duties as late," she smiled, touching a hand to his shoulder. Galen had assumed many duties, especially helping the ministers' scribes, his ability to read and write proving quite beneficial.

"No fuss, my dear lady Leanna. Besides, the Princess insists we take care of you considering your condition," he regarded her swollen belly.

"You are all so very kind," she sighed appreciatively, taking the bowl in hand, spooning a portion into her mouth. Between Galen, Raven, Orlom and Aldo, she was not lacking in attention. They each visited her throughout the day, helping with whatever she required. It was strange to see Raven removing her waste bucket without a complaint. She was most embarrassed to have him do such a menial task for her, but he insisted, claiming *Anything for Cronus' wife*. She knew it was very difficult for him to remain so long inside the castle, not able to show himself, lest the enemy know he is here. It had been a very long time now, and still no sign of Thorton. Orlom was equally helpful, fetching water and keeping her company with his ridiculous stories, which she found strangely endearing. Aldo was the most attentive, though spoke the least of all of them, which was odd considering he was a minister's scribe. He would often watch over her while she slept, ever vigilant for any sign of labor. He would take whatever time his duties allowed to attend her. She knew they all loved Cronus so very much, and her as well, helping her in any way they could. Corry would visit when her duties allowed, though her visits were rare as late, with the weight of the throne bearing so heavily upon her at this time.

"It is my pleasure to be of service, my dearest lady," he bowed, before drawing a chair to the side of the bed, taking a seat.

"What tidings have you?" She asked. Being confined as she was, she hungered for any news of the siege, or idle gossip that Galen was wont to offer.

"I have heard the men speak that the attack shall be soon, perhaps tomorrow or the day after. Besos has fallen," he whispered that last bit, having read the missive while helping the scribes transcribing parchment earlier in the day.

"Besos? What of the men garrisoned there?" She asked worriedly, her spoon stopping halfway to her mouth.

"Put to the sword, if the reports are accurate." He left unsaid what that portended for the realm. There was little to prevent Morac from raiding the Torry heartland now, unless General Fonis moved from Central City to contest him.

"Those poor men," she mourned.

Galen was quiet for a moment, wishing he hadn't shared that, considering how sad it made her, but he couldn't shield her from such important tidings. They were at war with the enemy at their gates, and such things were their reality. Besides, Cronus would certainly speak of it if he did not.

"My apologies for causing such grief. Perhaps I might brighten your mood with a ballad I have penned?" Galen offered.

"Is it a new work?" she wondered.

"Indeed. No one has heard it, and I would have you be the first."

"I would be honored, Galen. What is it called?"

"Tessa the seamstress," he smiled mischievously.

"A seamstress?" She wondered at that. It certainly didn't sound entertaining, and was probably a pun of sorts.

"Oh yes, a most diligent and brave woman whom I have had the pleasure of meeting. She labors in the palace fletching arrows and mending garments for our soldiers. She labors dawn to dusk without respite, refusing to relent. Her dedication to our cause is most inspiring, and I thought her tale worthy of song."

"Oh, Galen, do sing it for me," his explanation intrigued her.

Come rest from your labors dear Tessa
Come rest from your labors this night
The sun has set on our troubles
So, we might rest for the night

The sun does not rest on our troubles
Tessa refuted this claim
My husband and sons have I given
I labor to honor their names

I shall labor yet longer
For the enemy still lingers nigh
I shall labor yet longer
Until gargoyles abandon our sky

Tessa was a wife and a mother
A seamstress who three sons she bore
Her husband and three sons have left her
Left her to fight in the war

One son she lost at Costelin
A gargoyle blade struck him down
One son she lost at Kregmarin
Where arrows fell all around

Her husband fell at Danartha
Their village where he made his last stand
Defending his home and his people
His blood he did spill for their land

Her last son fell with our cavalry

315

In Connly's troop he did ride
His last fight fought in the fields
North of Corell where he died

Now at Corell does she labor
Mending clothes for our men
Fletching arrows for our archers
Working without cease once again

Though Kings and heroes are lauded
Where poets sing of their fame
Let Tessa's deeds be remembered
Let ages remember her name

She wiped a tear from her eye as he finished, touched by the sad and inspiring tale.

"Does it find your favor?" He asked with a hopeful voice.

"Very much so. You often sing of kings and heroes of great renown. What caused you to think of her?" She asked.

"Prince Lorn suggested it. He said kings and heroes are always remembered and honored in our legends and songs, but the common men and women are not, even though their contribution to our victory is of greater worth. It is the quiet work that no one thinks of that is essential to any victory. Our brave matrons, our foot soldiers, tanners, and magantor handlers all contribute, and yet no one sings their praises," he sighed, ashamed for having never thought of them before now.

"They will be remembered now, thanks to you, Galen."

"I do hope so. Perhaps it can be my small contribution. This war will be remembered for all time, the greatest conflagration our world has ever known, and we must all share in the glory, every one of us, including the brave wives of our royal elite, especially the one who traveled half the world to help rescue her beloved," he smiled, causing her to blush. She meant to refute that, but was bereft of words. Before she could think of something, Cronus finally made his appearance, his tall frame passing through the door.

"Cronus," she beamed, her face radiant in the candle light. How she loved this moment every night when he finished with his duties, and returned to her arms.

"How fares my wife?" He asked of Galen, stepping nigh, and taking a knee at her bedside.

"She is as brave as any warrior of the realm, my friend. As you have finally relieved me of my post, I shall take my leave. Until tomorrow, my fair Leanna," Galen bowed and stepped without.

"Please sit. The stone floor is hard on your poor knees, my love," she insisted, running her free hand over his check, while he kissed the other, pressing his lips tenderly to it.

He obeyed her gentle request, inching the chair closer to her bedside. They just stared at one another for the longest time, their eyes sharing more than words could say. They never knew if each night was their last, savoring the precious time given them. He repeatedly said he wished she was safely elsewhere, just as he said during the last siege, but she reminded him that there was nowhere safe. If there was nowhere safe, then she preferred to spend every last moment with him. She could read that unspoken fear in his loving eyes.

"We are promised nothing in life but death, my love. We have been blessed with wonderful lives, despite our suffering and trials. Even they are blessings in a way, for how can one appreciate the wonders of life without such troubles to weigh in compare," she smiled wanly, trying to set his mind at ease. For all his attributes, her Cronus was a worrier, often letting gloom take hold of his heart.

"I know," he meant to say something more, but knew she was weary of hearing his misgivings. He wanted her away from here, somewhere safe, but she was right in that. There was nowhere safe.

"Do not be morose, my love. You are to be a father soon," she smiled, moving his large hand to her belly, where she felt the baby bulge along her side. No sooner had his hand rested upon her, he felt the baby kick.

"It moved," he smiled, looking up at her.

"He has been doing that all day," she smiled back.

"He?"

"Your son. We are having a boy. A boy just like his father," she couldn't help smiling.

"No, a daughter. One as lovely as her mother," he countered.

"A son," she insisted. "But if it comforts you to believe so, you are not alone in that belief. Raven says it shall be a girl, though Galen says a boy."

"Is everyone making their opinion known?"

"Of course. The princess says it is a girl, and Terin a boy. Torg says boy, while Lucas and Ular say girl."

"What of Orlom? He is never one to not offer an opinion," he chuckled.

"He couldn't bring himself to disagree with Raven or Torg, so he claims we are having twins, one of each," she laughed.

"I shouldn't be surprised. I am pleased we have provided our friends such entertainment."

"Some are more easily entertained than others, but yes, it is a nice respite."

"Easily entertained describes Orlom perfectly," he smiled.

"How ever did you guess," she laughed.

"My powers of observation have rarely failed me."

She laughed at that as well. Oh, how she loved his laugh, and his smile. She would not be disappointed with a daughter, but she really wanted a son as handsome as him. They talked a little while longer before he climbed into bed. He lay beside her, playing with her hair as she rested her head upon his chest, before falling asleep in each other's arms.

* * *

The following morn.

"TO ARMS!" Men shouted, rousing the garrison as the morning sun broke the horizon.

Men flooded the battlements from their barracks resting just within and below the inner walls, racing through the wide, lit stairwells that opened behind the inner battlements. Once in the free air, some raced up the stairs to their post along the inner walls, while others rushed through the raised portcullis' leading to the outer battlements. Once they took up position along the walls, their gaze drew northward, where a great host filled the heavens. Thousands upon thousands of gargoyles approached the north wall, their winged forms shading the sky like a dark storm fast approaching the shore.

General Bode joined Commander Nevias upon Zar Crest, the raised, open platform affording them a clear view to direct the battle, overlooking the inner and outer walls. Horns sounded the alarm, alerting the entire palace that battle was upon them. Gazing east and south, they beheld thousands of winged forms filling the sky, nearly level to the outer walls, indicating the gargoyles from those directions came from the ground level. Those approaching from the north were much higher, soaring higher than the inner walls, nearly level with the inner keep, taking them easily above the outer walls, where they could land atop the defenders fresh for battle.

"That damnable ramp!" Nevias cursed, guessing the number approaching from the north at ten thousand, perhaps more.

Bode couldn't disagree. They moved all of their long range ballista to the north wall in recent days, the crews releasing their first volleys, spewing long spears into the approaching mass. He spied several winged forms dropping away, like dark raindrops from a pregnant cloud. More shafts followed, to great effect, but could not slow the advancing tide.

"Kai-Shorum!"

Gargoyle war cries echoed through the morning air, chilling the bones of the hardiest of men as they stared into the black abyss, thousands of fangs and demon eyes staring back at them.

Jenaii horns sounded above the inner keep, where Jenaii warriors sprang into the air to meet the enemy host. The defenders manning the outer northern wall cheered heartily as the Jenaii passed overhead. Torry ballista crews held fire as the two masses clashed just beyond the walls. The forward ranks collided midair, Jenaii short swords clashing with arcing scimitars. The Jenaii were better protected with thin, light weight blue armor and helms outclassing the gargoyles simple gray round helms and small circled shields. The forward most ranks were nearly two hundred abreast, spaced barely enough apart for their wings to work freely.

Gargoyle war cries met the stoic Jenaii, the two groups clashing in a storm of swords, and breaking bones. Dozens fell from either side, swords slicing wings as they passed, or vital points on the body. A Jenaii warrior glided above a gargoyle foe, his swift strike taking a chunk from the creature's left wing, the gargoyle dipping severely, before dropping out of the battle altogether, gliding to the surface below. The Jenaii dodged another circling about, before catching sight of a Jenaii lopping the head of a creature off his right, before colliding head on with a gargoyle from the second rank. The Jenaii's neck snapped, his eyes drawing vacant as he fell suddenly away, impacting the ground below.

* * *

"Shift all archers from the west wall to the south!" Nevias sent his messenger to relay the order. He eyed the approaching gargoyle columns drawing ever nearer the east and south walls, row upon row of winged creatures strung out as far as the eye could see. He deployed nearly a thousand of his garrison troops along each of the outer walls, with another thousand manning the trebuchets and ballistae along the adjoining turrets. Another thousand manned the inner walls, overlooking the outer battlements, with Bode's men reinforcing his men with an additional two thousand men to each outer wall, and two thousand upon the inner battlements. The remainder of Bode's army guarded the tunnel behind the main gate, as well as all the gates leading to the inner courtyard, as well as every stairwell and passageway throughout the palace. The remaining men of Nevias' garrison manned the inner keep and the towers jutting proudly above the palace. General El Tuvo's telnics defended the inner keep when not guarding the surrounding skies, though nearly every one of them was engaged north of the castle.

"They appear ready for battle," Bode shook his head, looking down the ramp of their platform where Gorzak and his fellow apes guarded the base of Zar Crest, the ape warrior spinning his twin axes, impatiently waiting for battle.

"They shall have their fill by day's end," Nevias sighed.

"As will our other recent addition," Bode looked below to the uppermost battlements of the inner keep where Ular stood guard beside Princess Corry and Torg Vantel. They could not see Terin standing farther back, but knew he was never far from Corry's side. Bode knew the boy was looking afield for any sign of Morac, prepared to counter his threat before committing elsewhere.

* * *

"Men of the east wall, stand your posts!" Guln Turlon, the new commander of the east wall shouted, his order relayed along the battlements as the enemy host drew nigh, their approach masked by the blinding sunrise. They came in the thousands, their ranks in lines that stretched to the horizon. The morning sun casting their fell shadows upon the east wall like specters summoned from the grave. Torry and Jenaii archers narrowed their eyes before the blinding glare of the morning sun, struggling to keep their targets in view, catching sight of them just short of the wall. Torrents of shafts soared over the battlements, peppering the gargoyle ranks, dozens falling away, wounded or dying, their guttural cries echoing through their descent. The rest of the first wave arrived at the outer wall, greeted by Torry spears, slaughtering them in great numbers.

Few of the first wave survived before the second wave arrived, their own ranks further thinned by Torry and Jenaii archers standing upon the inner walls above and behind the outer battlements. Dozens fell before reaching the wall, the rest succumbing after, driven back by walls of shields, swords and spears. Few lingered, clutching hold of the outer part of jutting ramparts, desperate to catch their breath before the next wave arrived, to rejoin the fight. The Torries cleared away whatever stragglers they could reach before the next wave arrived, with arrows passing overhead.

"Kai-Shorum!" The gargoyle battle cry echoed through the crisp air, a harbinger of death and ruin as they threw themselves upon the east wall.

* * *

The battle along the south wall fared equally well, the first gargoyle waves faring poorly, slaughtered at the wall with their survivors descending to the surface before making their way back to their encampments on foot, trying to avoid their dying comrades from crushing them as they fell. Steady archer fire thinned each arriving wave to great effect, the sixth wave faltering with the seventh following on their heels.

Corry observed the carnage from high atop the inner keep, guardedly optimistic with their performance, cautiously reassured with their stalwart position. The ramp to Zar Crest rested off her right. She couldn't help but notice the ape warriors standing at the base of the causeway, eager for battle. She could ill imagine an entire army of such warriors giving battle. Unfortunately, they only had the ten who currently fought beside them. She took solace in the fact that unlike the previous siege, the garrison had nearly three times the number as before, with a third of them Jenaii warriors, and a full complement of magantors. Terin was not as before, but was still a force to behold, and if all else failed, Raven and Orlom were hidden below. Once Thorton was spotted and dealt with, their considerable power would be brought to bear, but for now, that was not happening, much to her frustration. She felt Terin stir behind her, the situation to their north the source of his concern.

She watched with knowing dread as the Jenaii and gargoyle host battled short of the north wall, their gallant friends giving better than they received, but suffering great loss all the same. The Jenaii telnics swept through the forward ranks of the gargoyle host, before splitting off, half going east, and half west, leaving five hundred of their comrades dead or wounded in their wake, inflicting three times that number upon the gargoyles. She watched as the Jenaii circled around the northern corners of the palace to regroup, while the enemy host continued for the north wall. Torry ballistae crews resumed their volleys, spewing their deadly fire into the gargoyle cluttered sky. Scores tumbled from their dark mass, some dropping like heavy stones, others working their wings in distress, wounded from the heavy blows. The constant barrage could not stay their terrible advance, their endless thousands passing over the outer battlements of the north wall.

"Shields!" Bors Datev, the newly named commander of the north wall shouted, his order relayed along the battlements before the enemy host coursed overhead. The men lifted their shields overhead, crouching low with spears ready to thrust between their seems. Archers atop the inner walls fired without respite into the encroaching mass, dropping many short of the wall. Others were struck passing high above the wall, the bodies falling upon the Torries crowding the battlements below, caving holes in their formations.

The gargoyles passed over the outer walls, continuing on for the less guarded inner walls. Torry archers fired rapidly into the encroaching mass, unable to miss. Some withdrew, racing down adjoining stairways, seeking safer positions to continue their volleys, their attendants following on their heels, bearing bundles of arrows. Others held their ground within walls of infantry, firing desperately as the creatures swept down upon the crowded walkways.

"Kai-Shorum!" Gargoyles chanted, slamming into the men upon the inner walls, slaying a hundred upon impact, driving into their faltering ranks. An equal number of gargoyles were slaughtered at the outset, the causeway littered with dead and dying men and gargoyles, countless more wounded lay strewn about, bodies flailing upon mounds of corpses and wounded. Men struggled finding footing to give battle, forsaking spears for their short swords in the close confines of the wall. Some were pushed off the walkway, falling painfully upon the causeway below, suffering broken bones upon impact. The Torries tried to collect themselves, forming lines and counterattacking, but the following waves were too much, diving upon them.

The Telnic commanders of the 3rd Army assigned to reinforce the outer battlements of the north wall, sent hundreds of their men through the raised porticus' passing under the inner walls to aid their beleaguered comrades. Other reinforcements shifted from the quiet west wall, with thousands of gargoyles now setting down within the inner walls. The battle just within the north inner wall degenerated into a thousand melees, men grouping themselves wherever possible, with reinforcements pouring through the gates from the outer battlements, while others fed into the fray from points west and the inner keep. Thousands more gargoyles swarmed above, setting down wherever they could, weathering archer fire from the adjoining walls and the inner keep. Some managed to soar higher, circling the citadels rising above the inner palace.

Torry magantors swept in from the upper palace, plucking gargoyles from the air. General Valen led the first sortie, soaring above the inner east wall before turning sharply toward the north wall, his warbird snatching a creature in its left talon, while his archer raised up in the saddle, drilling another gargoyle passing below them between the shoulder blades, his feathered shaft striking true. Dar's magantor sped higher, avoiding a cohort of gargoyles joining the fray from the north, soaring beyond their feeble reach. Dar circled high above the outer battlements, looking down at the endless waves of gargoyles passing below, their damnable ramp enabling them to soar above the outer walls. His fellow magantors followed in his wake, sweeping the periphery of the encroaching mass, plucking creatures at random from the sky, their archers rising in their saddles, firing rapidly into the dark mass below.

* * *

Corry felt a hand touch her shoulder, pushing her aside. She stumbled briefly, turning as Terin stood between her and a gargoyle climbing over the parapet lining the edge of the roof of the inner keep, the creature somehow managing to claw its way from below. It slithered over the battlement like a serpent from beneath a rock, struggling to gain its feet, its scimitar still grasped in its right hand. The creature's glowing red eyes gazed obsessively into hers, as if possessed by an unholy power.

SPLIT!

Terin lopped its head without hesitation, its severed crown tumbling into the air, while its carcass slid from the parapet, striking the causeway below. Terin shifted, scanning afield for any other immediate perils. The skies around the inner keep and upper palace were clear of threats, most of the gargoyles swarming the inner walls below. The open expanse between the inner palace and the northern inner wall was a collage of men and gargoyles giving battle, the creatures dropping at nearly every point onto the defenders below. He caught sight of several exchanging blows at the edge of the open courtyard, wincing as a soldier was driven over the lip, hearing his screams as he fell, growing fainter through his vertical drop.

Archers along the east and west walls directed all their fire into the gargoyles pouring over the north wall, while the longer ranged ballista continued to pour their deadly volleys into the approaching masses before they reached the palace. Looking farther north, one could see the mass of creatures formed up behind the great ramp, waiting their turn to race up its slope and spring into the air. Torry magantors soared even higher, keeping above the fray, while swooping down upon the enemy where they were most vulnerable, alone or exhausted.

Corry stepped closer, looking at the carnage below with growing dread. The defenders were holding their own, but suffering incredible losses all the same.

"Perhaps it is time for you to join the fray," she relented, hating having to send him into that mess.

Terin quickly looked east and south, where the gargoyles attacking both walls were still held at the battlements, a few pockets forming at places along the entire front, but not enough to force a breakthrough. The east wall's archers were now directed to the north wall, sparing the gargoyles there their withering fire.

"Ular, Lucas, please guard the Princess in my absence," he said to their friends, who stood beside Torg. Ular's bulbous eyes blinked hypnotically, observing the battle around them.

"On my life. By my oath," Ular vowed with his watery voice.

"I so avow," Lucas smiled, slapping Terin's shoulder.

With that, Terin raced off to the magantor stables below, where Wind Racer was saddled and waiting.

Corry watched as he departed, her heart torn with uncertainty, but such was war and the battle before them. She drew her sword, preparing herself for what lay ahead, her gaze drawn to what the others were now looking at, looking north where The Jenaii host swept back over the northeast and northwest corners of the palace, assailing the gargoyle stream from both sides.

HAROOM!

Horns sounded to the north.

* * *

HAROOM!

Benotrist horns sounded again, heralding the advance of the 8th Benotrist Legion, who bestirred from their siege lines, forming up north of Corell's main gate. Twenty of their thirty-seven telnics aligned forward of their siege works, each equipped with heavy rectangular shields, best suited for interlocking above and beside their formations as they advanced under a barrage of arrows and ballistae. A third blast of their horns signaled them forth, with their standard bearers preceding them, lifting their banners high into the air, a gray hammer upon a field of red, sigil of the 8th Benotrist Legion.

The defenders along the north wall looked on with knowing dread as the ground attack commenced. Few had yet noticed, occupied with the gargoyles passing overhead in great numbers, their own ballista tearing gaping holes in their winged formations. The threat of dying gargoyles dropping in their midst was a constant danger. Commander Datev ordered his men to hold position, while the telnic commanders of the 3rd Army reinforcing him, continued to feed reinforcements through the gates to the inner walls behind them, where the gargoyles were assailing. Commander Datev didn't see any siege engines or a giant ram among the advancing infantry, wondering how they would assail the gate without them? Fueling his angst was the sight of the Benotrist drack crews trailing the ground assault, moving well south of their siege lines. He counted at least thirty of the wickedly dangerous weapons being moved into position, with more joining them, along with their munition wagons. The question of how they planned to breach the castle gate without a ram was soon answered by the arrogant warrior riding up alongside the Benotrist center column, wearing his distinct golden armor, and brandishing a glowing bronze sword emitting a bright yellow glow… Dethine.

* * *

Dethine, son of Dethar, rode forth upon his golden ocran, his braided locks trailing below his golden helm. The Nayborian Champion gazed upon Corell with contempt, recalling their bitter defeat here the previous fall, despite their rending of the main gate, which looked fully repaired, much to his annoyance. How the Torries managed to repair it was beyond him, but he would gladly see to its ruin a second time, though he would be doing so without Morac, whose presence was required elsewhere. He pointed his sword toward the gate, directing the legions to their objective, before circling about, signaling the drack crews to commence.

THOOSH! THOOSH! THOOSH!

Drack hurled spears sped overhead, striking the bulwarks along the north wall, their long iron shafts spraying rock fragments wherever they struck, leaving sizable indentations. The crews adjusted aim; their following shots spread from just below the battlements overlooking the main gate to points higher. One managed to strike the inner wall of Corell, where gargoyle and Torry infantry battled without respite. Another impaled a soldier atop the outer walls, just east of the gate, the shaft punching through his chest, before embedding into the causeway behind him. He lay there, his eyes staring briefly before going slack, the metal shaft pinning him to the walkway. Another man cried out to his west, a shaft piercing his upraised shield, tearing his shoulder form its socket.

Torry ballistae answered in kind, sending fire munitions into the advancing infantry below. Gargoyles flying overhead, redirected their assault upon the Torry ballista crews upon the turrets of the north wall, with Jenaii giving chase, contesting their assault.

* * *

The east wall.

The gargoyles gained footholds along several points of the east wall, pressing the defenders back as successive waves fed their advance. Fissures began to spread along two of the points, with the defenders trying to drive them off the battlements with their walls of shields and spears, while gargoyle reinforcements clambered over the ramparts, springing upon the Torry ranks from above. With their archers redirected to the inner wall, the east wall defenders faced each successive wave at full strength. The battle degenerated into a tough slog, with the gargoyles making steady, but costly, gains.

The south wall.

Torry archers and ballista greatly reduced the gargoyle waves before they set down. The gargoyles held several weak points along the battlements, paying dearly for every step gained. With nearly half of the Gargoyle 5th Legion committed to the assault, the defenders were hopelessly outnumbered, but were slaying twenty for every one they lost, an exchange that the Gargoyles could not long maintain.

* * *

North wall. Before the main gate.

Dethine followed the Benotrist cohorts within the shadows of the north wall, the main gate resting a hundred paces before them. After fending off their gargoyle attackers, Torry ballista spewed fire munitions from the adjoining turrets, their deadly flames erupting throughout the Benotrist formations. The smell of burning flesh tortured his nostrils, coupled with the sounds of wounded and dying men, each fueling his resolve to end this battle, putting the garrison to the sword. He felt the pull of his sword holding him back, staying the urge to rend the gate and open the way into the castle.

Gargoyles recommitted their attack upon the north wall, swarming the outer battlements above, greatly reducing the withering arrow fire that plagued them for the past several hundred paces. The sound of clashing steel echoed hauntingly upon the ramparts above. From his vantage point, he could not see much of the battle. A fair mix of bodies were thrown over the walls, both men and gargoyles, but not enough of either to determine who was winning. He was determined to press toward the gate, needing to open the path for the ground assault, but the sword warned against it.

SPLASH!

Another Torry munition struck off his right, caking a dozen men in flames, with several others killed where it struck.

THOOSH! THOOSH!

Dracks returned fire, their iron shafts spraying the turrets along the north wall, one finding purchase through the workings of a fire ballista, snapping it off as it was being loaded, spilling flames across the stone floor of the circled platform. Dethine watched gleefully as Torry ballista crews thrashed about along the turret above, engulfed in flames, several throwing themselves over the side of the palace walls, striking the ground nearby, ending their suffering. The other Torry ballista continued to rain upon their serried ranks, ignoring the drack crews who were too far afield. It was almost too much to bear, the men of the 8th Legion wavering as they held short of the gate. They looked to Dethine to make his move, dependent upon him to break the gate.

His patience was soon rewarded as the gate suddenly lifted, much to his confusion. A great cheer sounded through the ranks as the men rushed toward the opening of the tunnel. Dethine wondered why the Torries did this, guessing they did not wish their gate ruined by his sword, but to allow them free passage was madness.

"Very well," he shrugged, trying to take a step, but again the sword held him back.

The Benotrists poured through the gate, chasing after the retreating Torries as they raced along the tunnel, with each interior gate opening as they ran.

* * *

The inner keep.

Cronus ventured from the inner keep, leading a flax of palace guards into battle, each adorned in their uniform silver armor over golden tunics, with silver wings adorning their helms. The guards carried large rectangular shields with a slight inverted curve at their top, and medium length swords, designed for more forceful swings than the standard short swords of the regular soldiers. Passing under the raised porticus of the inner palace, he was greeted with a hellish visage, with thousands of men and gargoyles spread out across the open area of the inner palace. The massive opening to the courtyard rested some fifty paces from the gates to the inner keep, where a number of Torry soldiers were backed to its stone lip, pressed by a larger number of gargoyles, trying to push them off, sending them to a quick death to the courtyard below.

Cronus rushed forth, the palace guards following at his heels, striking the gargoyles from behind. He took the first by surprise, hacking its right wing. The creature released a curdling scream, turning upon him, its wing dangling from its back, blood spilling from its wound. The bloody wing grazed Cronus' shield as the creature turned, nudging him briefly before he drove the point of his blade into the gargoyle's stomach.

"Kai-Sho…!" The creature's battle cry died in its throat as Cronus twisted the blade inside its innards, before kicking it free.

The guard beside him cut into another gargoyle's shoulder, driving his blade almost to its spine. The creature thrashed violently, nearly tearing his grip from the hilt. With his blade stuck in the creature's back, the man dragged him backwards from the fray, while another drove his sword into the creature's stomach with several quick jabs before moving on to other foes, leaving his comrade to work his sword free. Cronus and the others cut into the remaining gargoyles, like peeling the layers of an onion, hacking them down where they stood, until the rest fled or were struck down from the soldiers to their front, or Cronus' men from behind. One creature managed to break free, launching itself into a soldier standing upon the lip of the courtyard opening. The man lifted his shield to receive the blow, but the weight of the gargoyle forced him back a step, a step he could not afford.

"Agghh!" The poor wretch screamed, falling 160 feet to his death below, his body striking the edge of the courtyard. The gargoyle managed to spread its wings following the man over the side, struggling to gain lift. A Torry archer standing across the opening opposite Cronus, took aim, firing two feathered shafts into the creature, forcing it to descend to the courtyard below where Torry soldiers there cut it to pieces.

Cronus looked over the precipice, watching as the men below finished their kill, the soldiers looking back up at him, trying to make out the happenings upon the palace roof, while they waited upon the Benotrists racing south through the main tunnel.

The men Cronus saved thanked him and the palace guards before moving on to their next target, a mass of gargoyles setting down nearby. Cronus and the others joined them in battle, cutting down the new arrivals to great effect, their unarmored flesh easy game against their heavy shields and thick helms and mail. Cronus cut down the last of them, pausing to catch his breath, taking stock of his surroundings. The sky was filled with gargoyles and Jenaii battling in all directions, all sense of order cast aside. More gargoyles were afoot, fighting with the men of Corell upon the length of the north inner wall, scimitars and short swords clashing in an unending sea. The dead were piled in each direction, their growing heaps a hinderance to their every movement. Scores of men lay writhing along the base of the inner walls, many with broken backs having fallen off the causeways above. Arrows and ballista flew overhead, striking targets beyond his line of sight.

The base of the Tower of Cot rested off his left, spiraling high into the firmament, with archers perched upon its jutting platforms, taking aim at gargoyles passing before it. It stood opposite the Tower of Celenia, which rested off his right, its highest peak rising above the citadels that protruded from the roof of the inner keep, rising higher than even the Golden Tower, which jutted prominently from the roof of the inner keep. Between the basses of these towering structures, and the inner walls of the palace, men formed shield walls, driving north toward the base of the north wall, sweeping the gargoyles before them. They were shadowed by smaller formations atop the inner east and west walls, driving north along the causeways toward the adjoining turrets connecting each with the north wall.

Above this, the sky was filled with gargoyles, Jenaii and Torry magantors, battling for dominion. Cronus caught sight of a magantor crossing over the inner wall, its lifeless corpse crashing somewhere along the eastern outer battlements, probably killing a dozen men upon impact. Torry archers took careful aim, trying to pick out targets without Jenaii or magantors nearby, trying their utmost to avoid striking a friend.

"Kai-Shorum!"

Cronus' blood ran cold, looking up just as a cohort of gargoyles descended upon them. He immediately crouched, lifting his shield to brace for impact, his sword coiled to counter strike. His fellow warriors took similar precautions, each schooled in the proper tactic to receive a descending attacker.

THUMP!

Cronus shifted, avoiding much of the blow, the creature sliding along his shield, its scimitar glancing off his helm. The blow rattling his brain, intense ringing filling his ears. He immediately jabbed his sword around his shield, seeking out the gargoyle's flesh, but finding empty air, the creature sliding to his left, as he barely kept his feet. He began to follow the creature, shuffling his feet to shadow its movement, when another creature appeared in his periphery, having already slain the man to his right. Cronus swung his blade to his right, slicing the creature's left wrist, a terrible scream issuing from its bright red throat, though Cronus could hear little of it. He immediately followed with another strike to its middle, spilling its innards as he withdrew his blade.

THUMP! THUMP!

Cronus crumbled under the weight of two more gargoyles dropping from above, their clawed feet striking his helm and shoulder, driving him to the floor of the causeway. He gasped, trying to catch his breath, trapped under their combined weight. He was on his back, face to face with one of the creatures, its foul breath blasting his senses, its jaws snapping, trying to bite into his cheek. He managed to get his right hand to the gargoyle's forehead, trying to force it back, his sword lost somewhere underneath him.

"AGGHH!" Gargoyle screams sounded nearby, though rang dully with his injured ears. He felt the ground vibrate nearby, the creature atop him pulling briefly away in alarm, before lifting fully from his face. Cronus noticed a large furry hand grip the creature about the collar of its tunic, tossing him off him. Cronus looked on in disbelief as an ape warrior stood over him, driving an ax into the creature's skull. The gorilla warrior swung again, striking another creature coming at them from somewhere off Cronus' right, but he couldn't see from this angle.

"You still live. Good!" The ape warrior grinned, looking down at Cronus, before helping him to his feet, though Cronus could barely hear him, his ears slowly clearing.

"Gorzak," Cronus recognized the large ape warrior from tribe Traxar, the leader of their small contingent.

"Aye! Quit lying about. We have gargoyles to kill!" The warrior grinned, slapping poor Cronus on the back, before moving on. The gorillas had followed Cronus from the inner keep, barely catching up with him as he was beset by the last group of gargoyles, arriving just in time by the look of things.

Cronus gathered up his surviving guards, deciding to follow Gorzak and his fellow apes into battle. The apes were already engaged up ahead, cutting down several screaming gargoyles, the wretched creatures struggling to escape the simian onslaught. Cronus almost winced catching sight of Carbanc bludgeoning a gargoyle's skull with his hammer, while Krink stood over another, trying to twist its head off, wearing a stupid grin on his face. The apes seemed to be enjoying this a little too much. Two others ganged up on another gargoyle, chopping away at its head and legs simultaneously, chucks of leathery flesh flying off their axes. Another gorilla met an on-rushing gargoyle by extending two fingers, poking the creature in the eyes. The gargoyle staggered, wincing in pain as the gorilla grabbed hold of his head, snapping his neck.

* * *

The main tunnel.

The Benotrist warriors rushed along the wide lit tunnel, finding every gate raised as they passed, the fleeing Torry soldiers keeping just ahead of them. They could see daylight up ahead, where the main tunnel met the open courtyard of the palace. From there they could branch out to every part of the palace. None stopped to consider why the defenders allowed them free passage. It had to be more than just Dethine able to cut away the gates. Why give up so easily? Such thoughts escaped men in the heat of battle. Like water flowing downstream, they followed the only path open to them, racing through this deadly passageway seeking the enemy in the only way they could reach them. Their poor decision was all too apparent as the fleeing Torries passed into the courtyard ahead, the last gate's porticus lowering between them, right at the end of the tunnel. It lowered just as the Torries touched a torch to the floor.

WHOOSH!

Flames ignited along the tunnel, shooting northward, where oil coated the entire floor of the passageway. Men screamed in agony, flames erupting all around them, engulfing their oil soaked sandals and feet. They tried to turn about, to return whence they came, but were caught up in a crowd disaster, men trampling those before them underfoot, before falling down altogether into the gathering flames. Those nearest the entrance backed away as some escaped the tunnel into the open, flames pouring off their feet and garments, throwing themselves on the ground, desperate to douse the flames.

Dethine stood north of the gate, where his sword kept him in place, watching the smoke issue from the tunnel. They would have to wait for the flames to die out before advancing. He ordered the Benotrists to withdraw at a safer distance to wait out the flames.

* * *

Terin held tight to Wind Racer as the great avian sprang from its platform, soaring over the battlements of the south wall. His gaze swept the outer battlements below where the gargoyles began to take hold, several pockets bulging, each gargoyle wave feeding their expanse. Thousands of the creatures now lay dead along the wall, most resting at its base, thrown off the ramparts by Torry spears, or dropped short of the palace by archers. The approaching waves couldn't climb much higher than level with the outer battlements, their labored wings working desperately to gain even that level of lift. He was tempted to set down among their pockets, expelling each in quick order, but his sword no longer invoked such power. He could do little more than slaughter a few hundred, but the rest would press on. No, the south wall was strongly held, and the defenders would have to do without him, as he was needed elsewhere.

Circling east around the castle, he found the east wall in slightly worse shape, the pockets of gargoyles pressing strongly into the wide causeway separating the inner and outer battlements. The Jenaii pressed upon the gargoyle flanks as they neared the north wall, greatly thinning their ranks before they assailed the castle. The tactic provided the added benefit of falling bodies striking the Benotrists gathered before the main gate, rather than falling upon the defenders of Corell. Even from afar, Terin could see General El Tuvo lead his warriors into the gargoyle host, striking from the east time and again, reforming and striking with grace and precision. The surviving gargoyles swarmed over the northern inner battlements, their numbers bleeding into the adjoining causeways connected to the east wall. It was here he could make a difference, before pressing elsewhere.

Wind Racer angled low over one of the adjoining turrets connecting the north and east walls, his sharp talons snatching several gargoyles from the battlements, while knocking others off the side. He circled about, dropping his crippled foes upon part of the causeway serried with gargoyles, before briefly setting down. Terin sprang from his back as Wind Racer again took the skies, staying above the waves of approaching gargoyles.

Terin scanned his surroundings, spotting Torry soldiers making their way north toward him along the inner walls, with gargoyles crowding the walls to his north and west, where they battled the defenders along the inner battlements from every point along the north wall. Thousands more battled below in the open space between the inner walls and the inner keep. He caught sight of the ape warriors battling alongside palace guards below, with gargoyles flying overhead in every direction. The sky itself was a maelstrom of gargoyles and Jenaii battling for the firmament, sunlight playing off their swords like ten thousand flickering stars.

Watching Wind Racer soar above the gargoyle host, Terin went to work.

"Yah, guide my hand," he whispered, making his way along the short causeway connecting the northeast turrets. The inner walls mirrored the outer walls, with twelve smaller turrets connecting the inner battlements, with two turrets at each corner of the four inner walls, and another connecting each wall at an inverted angle. It was at the inverted angle turret connecting the east and north walls that he began. He need only take three steps before falling upon two creatures pressing a Torry defender against the parapet, their scimitars pounding upon his shield, his back leaning dangerously over the rampart. Any further and he was sure to drop upon the outer battlements below, a quick drop and sudden death.

Terin swept behind the creatures, chopping their backs clean through, splitting wings and spines in one fluid movement. He moved on, ignoring their dying screams in his wake, not stopping to see the Torry soldier recover and finish them. He took another gargoyle across the face, the creature turning just as he approached, its red eyes staring vacantly beyond him.

SLASH!

His cut was swift and short, the top of the gargoyle's skull flying off his blade, its body dropping where it stood. He severed the right wing off another, pushing its flailing body over the edge of the causeway, where it dropped thirty feet to its death, nearly striking another creature standing below.

And, so he went, moving along the north inner wall, clearing it east to west, the creatures oblivious to his presence, freeing Torry soldiers from their foes as he passed. It wasn't as before, where his mere presence sent thousands of gargoyles to flight, but different. They were blind to his presence now, allowing him to cut them down in detail, though he was limited by his own mortal exhaustion. He could move only so fast, fatigue limiting his impact. Though he couldn't instill great fear in the gargoyles, he DID instill great courage in his friends. The Torries cheered his arrival, renewing their spirits, and granting them greater strength and resolve.

The gargoyles knew something was amiss, feeding off the Torries strength, though in reverse, their collective will beginning to falter. Terin spared a glance to the north, where the gargoyles continued to spring into the air from their massive ramp, approaching Corell in an endless dark stream.

"PACKAWW!"

The terrible sound drew Terin's eye to the encroaching columns of gargoyle just beyond the palace walls, trying to make out even larger winged forms flying above the hundreds of gargoyles blocking them from view. His face paled recognizing the brown and black feathers of northern magantors, marking the advent of the Benotrist warbirds, and the bright glow of a single outstretched blade among them… Morac.

* * *

General Dar Valen circled above the upper reaches of the Golden Tower, preparing to again drive into the gargoyle host streaming over the castle from the north when his eyes fell upon the greater threat flying above them. A flax of Torry magantors followed his lead as he broke toward the Benotrist warbirds drawing near the north wall. He outstretched his spear, directing his men forth, coursing above the carnage below. Another flax of Tory magantors approached from the east, and another from the west, converging on the enemy warbirds.

"PACKAWW!"

Dozens of magantors sounded, their screams rending the air like sword tips twisting in ears for miles around. They met in the crowded heavens in a massive collision, talons tearing gashes in passing warbirds, or snatching riders from their saddles. A few archers managed to fire off their arrows as they passed, most of their shafts fluttering uselessly awry. Dar dove underneath an onrushing magantor, driving his spear into its wing as he passed, the shaft snapping off its rough, feathered hide. He released the broken weapon before drawing his sword, coursing higher, barely avoiding the next warbird. He swooped down upon another just beyond, his magantor's talons snatching driver and archer from their saddle, depositing them soon after. He circled about, not able to see the Benotrists flailing limbs through their quick descent, striking the ramparts along the outer battlements of the west wall.

Dar swept underneath another warbird, his archer firing twice into its exposed underbelly, the shafts embedding into its breast. He didn't have time to see if they had any effect with another warbird sweeping down upon him. Dar crouched low, clinging desperately to his magantor's neck, feeling a blast of air upon his back from the other warbird's draft.

"Agghh!" He heard his archer scream. He looked over his shoulder, looking on in horror at his archer's terror filled eyes drawing swiftly away, his chest pinched between the Benotrist magantor's talons.

He circled above to gain his bearing, quickly scanning afield. Thankfully the greater host of gargoyles was still being thinned by the Jenaii, just short of the north wall, but too many were still bleeding through. Nearly a dozen magantors were dead or riderless to each side, their empty mounts flying off in several directions, while the dead dropped painfully upon the roof of the palace below, killing many where they struck. One crashed among the crowded outer battlements along the north wall, killing a dozen upon impact, its beak coming to rest against a rampart above the main gate. He caught sight of Morac's blade flashing amidst the fray, running his fell blade along a magantor's wing, severing it with ease. He winced as the stricken avian dipped severely, descending rapidly, its remaining wing working desperately to slow it descent, crashing upon a turret along the west wall, before continuing over its edge, disappearing beyond the palace wall.

Dar drilled his men constantly in the event Morac should appear upon a magantor. They were to avoid him altogether, while engaging his comrades. They appeared to be doing this as well as they could, but not everyone could escape his fell blade. It went against their nature to avoid fighting, but Morac's blade could not be availed. Only Terin could face him. But it still fell to Dar to slay every other Benotrist magantor. Resolving himself to that task, he found an inviting target passing across the face of the northern inner battlements. He swept down from above, snatching its driver from the saddle, before passing to the east, depositing his flailing body beyond the castle walls.

* * *

Morac grinned demonically, his magantor driver closing upon a Torry warbird trying to flee his reach, catching it as it circled the Tower of Cot. He reached out as they drew alongside of it, rising up in the saddle, slicing the tip of its right wing. The Torry warbird screamed, the painful wound causing it to turn sharply left, its left wing smashing into the face of the tower. Morac looked back, pleased to see the stricken beast throw its riders, before correcting itself, flying awkwardly southward, disappearing beyond the palace walls. He circled back, passing between the fabled Tower of Cot and the Tower of Celenia, driving north to reengage, coming upon another Torry warbird heading straight for him. The Torry magantor dove below him, just missing his warbird's outstretched talons. He continued on, passing back over the north wall where the Jenaii were assailing the gargoyles below, thinning their ranks before they passed over the palace.

Morac ordered his driver through the Jenaii host assailing the gargoyles' eastern flank, the avian diving into their midst, snatching one out of midair in its talons, scattering a dozen more. Morac reached out, lopping a Jenaii's leg as they passed, before taking another across the belly, nearly splitting the winged warrior in half. One Jenaii managed to climb upon his bird's tail, driving his sword into its hindquarter. Morac drew a dagger form his belt, throwing it at the warrior, the Jenaii springing away to avoid the blow. Morac's magantor shifted suddenly, pain shooting though its back, before leveling off, proving the wound superficial.

His fellow Benotrist magantors followed his lead, circling back from the castle to engage the Jenaii, aiding their gargoyle allies streaming toward the north wall. Borgon sat upon another magantor, ordering his driver forth, his eye drawn to Jenaii warrior leading a cohort of warriors into the gargoyle flank, wearing four braided cords upon the shoulders of his blue mail, the rank denoting a commander of army or battlegroup as the Jenaii were organized under. He drove onward, dropping into the Jenaii midst, his magantor's talons snatching the fellow from his formation, crushing his wings in its closing talons, before speeding northward, with several Jenaii giving chase. He would deposit his prisoner at their encampment before returning to battle.

The tactic briefly hindered the Jenaii attack, allowing a greater number of gargoyles to assail the palace. Morac circled about, watching as the gargoyle assault upon the north wall intensified. He ordered his magantors back into the fray above the castle, reengaging the Torry magantors. He needed to take full advantage of the moment. He only had two gargoyle legions available, which he fully committed to this assault. The east and south walls were chewing up many of his winged warriors, their sacrifice keeping the defenders upon those walls from reinforcing the north wall, where the gargoyles using the launch ramp were assailing to great effect. If he was to take Corell without starving it out, it needed to be now. Looking below, he spotted the mass of Benotrist infantry before the main gate of the palace waiting to enter. He wondered their delay, before spotting trails of smoke issuing from the open gate of the palace, with numerous men flailing about before the entrance, suffering severe burns, by the look of things. Dethine stood off to the side, waiting for the tunnel to clear of smoke and fire before continuing the ground assault.

Morac's gaze swept the palace roof, looking for any sign of Caleph, but finding nothing, before his eyes fell upon the raised command platform jutting above the inner keep, where the Torry commanders were perched.

"So be it," he said, his eyes alit, a terrible thought coming to mind.

* * *

SLICE!

Terin's blow split the gargoyle, shoulder to opposite hip, its upper half sliding off his blade. He moved along the inner wall, slaying another with its back to him, lopping its head while it was engaged with a Torry soldier to its front. He caught several more unawares, chopping them down with effortless grace, before racing down the nearest stair to the inner palace below, having cleared much of the northern inner wall. The defenders upon the wall reestablished their defensive positions, interlocking shields to receive the oncoming gargoyles, while the battle within the inner palace continued with walls of Torry infantry squeezing the gargoyles between them, while fending off those setting down from above. Terin cut into the gargoyle ranks, their startled looks seeking for the source of their affliction, slaying a dozen in as many moments. He was no longer guided by the sword's unseen power, but his own inclination, slaying every gargoyle he came upon. His blade turned murky, and eventually dark, a reflection of his somber spirit as he went about killing. Gone was the vibrant luster emanating from his blade, sending the enemy to flight. In its place was this darkened blade, a reflection of the shadow that his presence took in the enemies' eyes. He cut one creature down from skull to chest, kicking its carcass off his blade, before locking eyes with a familiar face… Cronus.

His friend smiled briefly, having gutted a foul creature, twisting his blade free, while a gorilla guarding his flank buried an axe in the skull of another. His heart sang, happy to find his friend amid the chaos. Cronus had led a small band of gorillas and palace guards into the enemy host, forward of the walls of Torry infantry pressing from the west and south, pushing the gargoyles toward the base of the inner northern wall, when Terin emerged behind their foe.

They cut down the few creatures separating them, with Cronus finishing the last with a thrust to the belly after Terin lopped its right wing while Gorzak rent the left with his axe. Cronus caught his breath, meaning to say something to greet his friend when a strange look passed Terin's face.

No longer guided by his father's sword, Terin learned to lean fully upon Yah's voice, if the deity deigned to give it. That required a quiet place and his full attention, which neither were possible at this place and time, or so he thought. He felt a sudden chill course his flesh, with a simple word whispering loudly through his brain... GO.

Cronus could do naught but follow Terin through the crowd of gargoyles and then men, making haste for the inner keep, with his motley band on their heels.

* * *

The main gate.

Dethine stood before the north wall of the palace, keenly watching the skies above where the gargoyles and Jenaii battled, thousands perishing short of the palace walls, the stricken dropping upon the Benotrists' serried ranks below. He kept a constant vigil, trying to avoid a falling corpse, lest it crush him underneath. Their dracks kept a heavy barrage upon the ramparts above the main gate, their steel shafts punching through parts of the battlements, and multiple bodies in their path. Several Torry magantors attempted to quiet the long-range ballista, dropping several fire munitions into their midst before being chased off by Benotrist warbirds. Morac's magantor assault seemed to drive off the Torry warbirds, at least for now. Dethine needed to renew the assault upon the tunnel, waiting for the smoke to clear and fires to die down. At last, it appeared time, the smoke issuing from the main gate reduced to a narrow stream hugging its roof.

"FORWARD!" He ordered, the Benotrist 8th Legion relaying the command as they poured into the open passageway.

* * *

General Bode stood upon Zar Crest beside Nevias, watching the battle unfold with his steely nerve. The south and east walls appeared sound, the gargoyles making slow, but unsustainable progress, their tenuous holds along several points costing them thousands of casualties. His main concern was the north, where the damnable ramp allowed unnumerable gargoyles to pass freely above the outer battlements, assailing the inner walls, setting down into their midst in great numbers. The state of the main gate was also in question. He ordered it raised should Morac or Dethine appear before it, and so it was, allowing a great host of Benotrists to enter, before they were driven off by fire. That tactic would only keep them at bay for a time, and for all he knew that times was at hand. The first report he received was that Dethine waited outside their north wall at the head of the Benotrist 8th Legion. That left Morac, who he now observed wreaking havoc among their Jenaii and magantor ranks. He followed him with his eyes as he soared about the castle, slaying many of Valen's warbirds in detail, before assailing the Jenaii north of the palace, and returning to Corell to continue his foul work. As to where he would strike next, the answer became clear.

Morac sped through the crisp air, soaring above the battle filled skies below, and the palace rooftop lower still, his keen eye fixed to Zar Crest through the ape skull affixed to his dark helm. He ordered his driver forth, cutting a path through any Torry magantors and Jenaii in his way. His magantor soared higher, his golden cuirass and greaves reflecting the morning sun, his cape trailing him like a crimson flame, fluttering in the wind.

The lookouts atop the Tower of Celenia gazed with knowing dread as the Benotrist Lord circled the white citadel like a carka bird seeking carrion, staring back at them at eye level upon their airy heights. He gave them a wicked smile that was veiled by his macabre mask, before dropping suddenly from sight.

"Kai-Shorum!" Morac shouted, his magantor sweeping down upon Zar Crest, several Benotrist magantors following in his wake.

General Bode drew his sword upon turning about, looking skyward as the fell beast drew ominously nigh. The air was filled with arrows and ballista, all trained upon Morac, and all going awry or missing altogether. Bode's aides scattered and Nevias drew briefly away as time slowed in the General's eyes. Morac looked over his driver's shoulder, his eyes fixed upon the Torry General below, guessing his identity by the four braided cords adorning either shoulder and the proud carriage he carried himself. This was the man who spoiled his previous campaign, sending him east in disgrace. Bode was now his, and he would take him. The Sword of the Sun alit like a blazing fire in his outstretched arm. Bode stood defiant, lifting his shield and holding his sword at the ready to receive him. He was a Torry Commander of Army, the ranking general of the Torry Kingdoms, and the greatest tactician the realm had known in centuries. He was brave, cunning and true, and he yielded to no enemy of his people.

The magantor landed abruptly upon Zar Crest, its large golden beak striking Bode's shield emphatically, driving him to the stone floor. Bode winced, feeling his ribs break as he landed. Morac sprang from his mount as two soldiers rushed forth, placing themselves between the Benotrist lord and their General as the magantor's large head swung around, blasting hot air into their faces, lifting their hair behind their helms. Morac changed direction, leaving Bode where he lay, while cutting the soldiers down in detail, his blade cutting a swath across their shields and swords, splitting their tempered steel like parchment, with pieces of bone and flesh flying off his sword. Quick follow thrusts finished the two as he turned back to Bode, who managed to gain his knees, trying to stand fully erect when Morac closed upon him.

Bode threw his shield at Morac's head, buying time to gain his feet as the Benotrist Elite knocked it away with his blade, cutting a large chunk from it as he sent it flying. Bode could barely breath through the pain running along his ribcage, knowing his time was short. No common blade could prevent Morac from gutting him, so he needed to make his last breath count, moving around Morac's magantor, placing it between them. The beast shifted, its driver scanning afield before noticing the Torry General skirting the right side of his mount. He shifted the beast sharply, its wing thrusting out, striking Bode flat in the chest, knocking him back as Morac circled the beast, his eyes fixed on him, his sword ready to strike. Bode recovered, ignoring the pain in his ribs, driving his sword into the magantor's flank.

"PACKAWW!"

The warbird screamed, shifting violently as Bode twisted the blade in its side as Morac closed upon him, driving his blade down upon his helm, splitting his head in half from skull to chest, before yanking it free. Morac kicked Bode's still corpse from his blade, blood and gore dripping from its glowing tip. He retreated to the edge of the parapet as the magantor thrashed about, briefly springing into the air before settling back down, blood issuing from its wound. Morac skirted the dying avian as his driver dismounted, drawing his sword to fight beside his Lord.

Morac raced across Zar Crest, slaying the last remaining warriors who remained, both wounded from the magantor landing in their midst. He made sure of them with hurried blows to their remaining good legs, while his magantor driver finished them, before making his way toward the ramp leading to the roof of the inner keep below. He came upon Commander Nevias fleeing down the ramp, flanked by several guards. Nevias ducked briefly as another Benotrist magantor passed dangerously low, its terrible scream paining his ears, only to be set upon by Morac from behind.

Morac took the rear most guard across the back, his follow strike lopping the head off the second before he was upon Nevias. The aged garrison commander turned back briefly as Morac's fell blade met his chest, lifting the top of his body from his sword.

Morac paused, staring down to the serried palace rooftop below, where a hundred pairs of eyes stared back at him. His own gaze swept the gathered host, finding the one of interest standing along the near wall… Corry.

"Kai-Shorum!" The battle cry went out as dozens of gargoyles poured over the ramparts behind him, following Morac onto the palace roof, with several Benotrist magantors sweeping down from above. The gargoyles managed to attain the airy heights after again swarming the inner walls that Terin earlier cleared, though most were slain along those serried causeways below.

"Kai-Shorum!" Morac parroted their war cry, racing down the ramp from Zar Crest, cutting down the first palace guards he came upon, their winged helms clanging off the stone floor as they fell.

* * *

Torg drew Corry behind him, his sword taking a gargoyle across the breast, its scimitar grazing his upraised shield. Corry stepped around him, driving her blade into the creature's gut, as he slipped around her, taking another across its right wing. The roof of the palace was madness, gargoyles springing from the ramparts, throwing themselves upon them as Morac raced down the ramp, cutting down their men with pitiful ease, his golden sword alit in a fiery glow, as if the very sun itself was at his command. Lucas guarded Corry's right, his blade soaked with gargoyle blood, parrying another blow, his counter strike gutting the creature hip to hip. Ular guarded her left, shifting quicker than water, cutting down foes with practiced ease.

"Go below!" Torg growled, blocking another scimitar with his shied.

"Not without you!" She grunted, fighting desperately beside them.

"Go! If Morac follows he shall find more than he cares to," Torg advised. Raven and Orlom waited within the halls just below the rooftop, keeping out of sight, lest Thorton learn of their presence, but once within the corridors below, the enemy could be slain without prying eyes knowing how.

"Raven's weapon is of no use against his sword," she pointed out.

"Agghh!" A Torry commander of flax shouted off their far left, caught in the talons of a Benotrist magantor. The avian swept over the east wall below the base of the Golden Tower, depositing the poor wretch to his death, before a Torry magantor swept in above it, taking its riders from their saddle. More Torry magantors appeared, contesting the skies above the inner keep, while archers positioned along the platforms of the Golden Tower and the citadels of Tarelia and Vantor fired into the enemy host below. The three prominent towers protruded from the roof of the inner keep, towering over everything save the Tower of Celenia, which rose imperiously from the inner palace below.

* * *

Morac lopped a Torry head from its neck, stepping aside as the dead guard fell forward, dodging an arrow fired from an archer posted above on a platform of the tower of Tarelia. He shifted as another struck the stone floor beside him, where he just stood. He raced to the base of the tower, venting his fury on the base of the massive structure, his sword tearing a sizable chunk from its wall. If he had time he would rend the structure from its foundation, but was pressed by the battle at hand.

"Packaww!" A Torry magantor screamed overhead, sweeping down upon him, met by his upraised blade, cutting the right talons from the warbird's outstretched leg. He moved on, ignoring its screams as it flew off. He strode forth, catching another Torry trying to back away, splitting his spear and gutting him before he drew his blade. Gargoyles sprang past him, assailing the line of Torry warriors formed to receive him across the middle of the palace roof. The Torries cut several down, backing away with leveled spears and swords, while more gargoyles filled in around him, along with his magantor driver. Dozens of Jenaii swept over the battlements, setting down beside the Torries as Benotrist and Torry magantors battled above.

Morac paused briefly, scanning the foes arrayed before him, and finding them lacking.

"Kai-Shorum!" He shouted, racing into their midst, slashing through the spears blocking his chosen path, gargoyles swarming his flanks. He worked his way into the Torry line, cutting men down in a flurry of swings and thrusts, constantly shifting, catching them unawares. The Torries drew back, like summer grass bending before the wind, yielding to his fell blade. He found Corry's eyes staring back at him, standing behind several choice warriors to his right, including an aged man who was stoutly built and an Enoructan brandishing a pair of blades, gutting any gargoyle to come near him. Morac moved to engage them, determined to kill her protectors. He still wasn't certain what he would do to her, but something would come to mind.

WHOOSH!

Morac ducked, a blur of white passing overhead. He barely kept his feet as Wind Racer set down before him, crushing a gargoyle underfoot, squeezing its guts beneath its talons.

"Packaww!"

Wind Racer bellowed, his hot breath twisting his helm agar, contorting Morac's face like a strong northern gale, lifting his dark hair behind him. He struggled fixing his helm before the warbird was upon him, driving him to his back. He managed to raise his sword, but the avian shifted away, dodging his errant thrust. He gained his feet, keeping low as its black beak snapped where his head was but a moment before. He shifted left, running his blade under Wind Racer's left wing, nearly severing it in half before stepping behind it as it stumbled, screaming in torment. He raised his sword to strike it fully from behind when his sword cautioned him to turn about, meeting a hurried strike from Lucas.

Morac left Wind Racer in his wake, driving Lucas to his back, splitting his sword, before cutting his shield in half, taking his arm with it. Before he could finfish him, Torg was upon him, throwing his shield toward his face. Morac blocked the object with his sword, recovering only to find Torg lunge a strike to his right leg from the side.

Morac winced, feeling the blow to his knee, his reinforced greaves preventing serious damage. He was thankful for that costly lesson from Kregmarin, giving his joints extra protection. Torg withdrew before he could finish him, the aged warrior a craftly and nimble fighter. Taking a step toward the Master of Arms, his sword cautioned him again, turning to meet Ular who came upon him in a flash, his swords striking at his in a dizzyingly array. He managed to meet one of the blows, splitting one of his blades, and then the other as more gargoyles swarmed over the surrounding battlements, setting upon the surrounding Torries.

Morac drove Ular back, the slippery Enoructan dodging every blow as he pushed him to the edge of the parapet. Ular nearly stumbled, his bulbous eyes blinking repeatedly, following the path of the Sword of the Sun, knowing its danger. Morac paused before finishing him, sensing peril behind him. He turned swinging his sword in a forceful arc, expecting to kill the fool attacking him, when his blade stopped.

* * *

Morac's gaze stopped with his sword, meeting Terin's steely countenance staring back, his once silver sword now black as a moonless night, casting his visage in a deathly shadow. He meant to say it had been a long time since Fera on that dark night when they last crossed swords, but words escaped him at this time. There was no place or time for boastful threats and idle chatter in battle. There was no time for anything but the fighting at hand. More gargoyles set down in their midst, battling the Torries and their allies while he and Terin battled.

Morac and Terin backed a step, tossing their shields aside, each useless against their blades. Terin struck first with a hurried thrust, Morac jumping back, avoiding the strike while bringing his sword down upon Terin's blade. Terin's sword vibrated in his hand as he nearly lost his grip upon it. He recovered, just as Morac swung, meeting his stroke, a strange ethereal light emitting wherever their blades touched. Terin nearly disarmed him with a devastating riposte, Morac recovering in time to parry his follow thrust.

Corry held back, waiting for a moment to strike Morac from behind, but the two of them circled and shifted faster than she could follow with her eyes. It was both frightening and wonderful to behold, a fluid dance of life and death that poets would sing of long after they were gone, but all she could think of was the danger to Terin's life. The others were equally engaged, with Torg pinning a gargoyle to the floor, repeatedly jabbing his sword into the creature's stomach. Ular moved to defend Lucas, who nursed his missing left arm, the Enoructan managing to retrieve another sword, parrying a strike from Morac's Benotrist driver. Cronus followed Terin onto the roof with a considerable party of palace guards and apes. The apes accounted well of themselves with Carbanc braining several gargoyles with his hammer, and Gorzak cutting down an equal number with his twin axes. Cronus tried to aid Terin, only to be beset by a gargoyle rushing to engage him. Terin managed to back Morac toward the parapet, nearly forcing his back to the stone battlement, catching the Benotrist Elite by surprise. Morac growled his displeasure, unaccustomed to such parity in battle. Corry watched in horror as a gargoyle set down several paces behind Terin, its feral red eyes trying to make out his presence as it moved to strike him, Terin's visage partially revealed by his proximity to Morac's blade.

"Agghh!" The creature hissed in agony as Corry drove her sword into its back, twisting her blade free before stabbing him again. She immediately backed a step, preparing to strike it again when Torg stepped beside her, chopping its right wing and leg in quick order as it flopped to the floor, writhing in agony.

Morac watched in horror as his gargoyles were cut down in detail, their ranks growing desperately thin. He backed Terin a few steps with a dizzying array of strikes, before retreating along the wall toward the ramp leading to Zar Crest where Borgon's magantor set down, his fellow elite beckoning him to retreat. He paused his retreat, again driving into Terin with a flurry of strikes to keep him back, his sword glowing brighter as Terin's darkened, the two blades feeding off the other's power, sending off tendrils of multiple hued light in all directions whenever they clashed. He could barely see Terin without focusing fully on him, his form growing blurry whenever he stepped away.

"Packaww!" A Benotrist magantor swept overhead, passing dangerously between them, its rider barely able to see Terin fighting his Lord.

Terin backed away from Morac, slashing the avian along its underbelly, stepping further away as its innards spilled on the palace roof. The creature released a curdling scream, dropping suddenly upon its side, flopping painfully about before Terin hacked its wing and then its neck for good measure. Torg and Cronus rushed forth, killing its riders as soon as they spilled from the saddle.

Terin spun about to reengage Morac, only to find him climbing aboard Borgon's magantor and springing into the air. He stood there frozen in time as the son of Morca drew away, the two warriors looking upon each other as the remaining gargoyles withdrew from the palace like the tide retreating from the shore.

CHAPTER 19

Terin lost track of time as he watched Morac retreat, flying off to his encampment, leading his surviving magantors and gargoyles from the battlements of Corell. He felt Corry's hand upon his shoulder, and turned to look into her moistened eyes. They stared for a brief and eternal moment into each other's eyes, saying so much without speaking a word, before drawn by the pitiful cries around them. He rushed to Lucas' side, his friend pressing a torn rag to the severed stump on his left arm. Ular and Cronus stood at his other side, tying a tourniquet around his bicep, but failing to stay the blood loss completely.

"Take him below! The matrons must heal him immediately!" Corry ordered, Ular and Cronus tucking him over their shoulders, carrying him off, much to his protest.

All across the roof of the inner keep men, gargoyles and magantors lay dead or wounded, blood and gore caking the white stone battlements or smeared across the floor. The midday sun was suddenly shrouded, clouds casting an eerie pal over the palace, matching the dour mood gripping their hearts. There, amidst the fallen, Terin's eyes found Wind Racer, the majestic warbird resting on his side, exposing his crippled wing, bent at an unnatural angle. The great avian returned his stare, his silver eyes finding Terin across the palace roof, dozens of wounded and dead laying between them.

Corry hurried after Terin as he fell to his knees beside his friend,

THE CHRONICLES OF ARAX

wrapping his arms around Wind Racer's neck, hugging him tightly, tears pouring from his cheeks. She felt her heart break as Terin wept, begging Wind Racer not to die. The only time she saw him cry was when she rescued him, but those were tears of joy. This was different, as if all he suffered to this point finally broke him, his tears pouring out in an unending flood. She wanted nothing more than to take him in her arms and hug the pain away, but she had her duty to attend, forcing her to be the voice of strength and reason.

"I think he shall live, Terin. His wounds look to be along the wing. We shall bind it for now until we can use the Earther's regenerator to heal it," she said encouragingly, touching a hand to his shoulder before calling upon Krink and two other apes to help him.

Corry left Terin with Wind Racer before joining Torg, the two of them stepping to the battlements to see the carnage wrought below. The entire northern inner wall was a collage of corpses and wounded piled high upon the battlements above and along the open causeway of the inner palace below it. Bodies were strewn across the inner palace from the north wall to the gates of the inner keep below, and around the opening of the courtyard. She wondered how many men lost their lives falling over its edge to the courtyard below? The outer battlements of the north wall suffered as well, with hundreds of men dead or wounded along its length. She caught sight of enemy munitions still peppering the battlements above the main gate, their long metal shafts powerful enough to punch through the edges of the stone bulwarks lining the parapet. Their own ballista returned fire, but their aim seemed to be set directly below the north wall, where the Benotrist 8th Legion was again retreating from the tunnel, abandoning their attack. She could only imagine how many died along the main tunnel connecting the main gate to the courtyard. Their Jenaii allies began to return to the palace, passing over the north wall. There were far fewer of them than before from what she could see. Even from these airy heights she could make out the numerous Jenaii fallen strewn across the fields north of the palace. She looked for General El Tuvo amidst the returning warriors, but there was no sign of him. Her fears would be confirmed later when he was reported taken captive. It was easy to lose track of things during the heat of battle, which led her to look suddenly to Zar Crest. She did not see what befell Bode and Nevias, her view of the elevated platform obscured from where she had stood. The events that followed Morac's attack happened so quickly she didn't have time to consider all that transpired, the battle at hand requiring her full attention.

She followed Torg across the palace roof and up the ramp, coming upon Nevias' dismembered body beside his loyal guards.

"You should remain below. This is not for your eyes, Corry," Torg advised, not wishing her to see this.

"We are beyond such courtesies, Torg. This is war, and I am acting Regent. I ceased being affected by its brutality when Morac presented my father's head during our parlay," she steeled her heart for the task at hand, though he didn't believe her. No one truly became used to such ghastly sights.

"Very well," he sighed, looking down at his old friend, Nevias' dead eyes staring skyward at nothing, the top half of his body separated from the rest.

They continued on to the platform, finding several more bodies including Morac's slain magantor, and Bode's body beside it, nearly spilt down the middle, the two halves of his head drooping to either side like a peeled fruit. Corry clenched her lips lest she weep, and she would not give Morac the satisfaction. Torg knelt beside the slain general, touching a hand gently to his right shoulder.

"Rest well, my friend," he whispered, honoring his great deeds and sacrifice.

"He didn't die alone," Corry managed to say without crying, pointing out Bode's sword driven into the magantor's side.

"No, he did not," Torg agreed, admiring what Bode apparently did. Knowing his blade was useless against Morac, he struck a blow to something he could kill.

"Come. We have much to do," she said.

* * *

Raven and Orlom had waited in the great hall throughout the battle, watching as the matrons used it as a ward, healing the wounded as they trickled in. The trickle became a flood as the battle progressed, with men and Jenaii lying across the large open floor. The cries of the wounded echoed off the stone walls in deafening levels. The floor was soaked in blood and waste, the foul stench torturing the nostrils of everyone in the upper palace, filtering its noxious fumes through every corridor and passageway. To the matrons' credit, they managed as well as could be expected, arranging the wounded in an orderly triage, keeping them alive long enough to be healed with the regenerator. Most the injuries required their age-old treatments as the regenerator could only work so fast, and its power was quickly waning. Now that the battle was ended, it would need to be taken to the roof to be recharged, though the cloudy sky would hinder that. Despite their best efforts, many of the wounded succumbed, either before they were seen or during treatment, usually from the loss of blood.

Minor injuries were set aside until they could be treated. Matron Dresila put Raven to good use in this regard. Early in the battle, a soldier appeared in great pain suffering a separation of the shoulder. Fortunately for the soldier, Dresila had time at the moment to reset it, popping it back into place. Raven, having observed the action, told her of having done that for his teammates on occasion during his playing days. Dresila recruited Raven to handle all such injuries as they arrived, taking advantage of his unnatural strength.

"Are you sure about this?" He had asked at the time, wondering if it was a good idea.

"What is one of those ridiculous sayings of yours? Oh yes, WHAT DO WE HAVE TO LOSE," she said, directing him to the corner of the hall where they eventually sent nearly twenty such injuries throughout the battle. The men looked none too pleased to see who was going to heal them, writhing in pain as Raven handled them roughly, popping their shoulders back into place. Most responded fairly well, though a few didn't go so right, and would require the regenerator to fix, but that would take days as they would be low on the priority list. Orlom acted as his assistant throughout the battle, helping hold men in place as he worked on them. He would

periodically send Orlom to check on the status of the battle up top, making sure Thorton hadn't appeared.

With all such injuries now attended to, Raven and Orlom merely stood off to the side watching the chaos around them. Raven had watched holo videos back on earth of military hospitals throughout the ages, and they were eerily similar to this. It was a depressing sight. He and Orlom began to make their way through the rows of wounded, before coming upon one poor fellow with a vicious cut along his lower left calf, where a scimitar struck the exposed part behind his greaves, with only a thin, blood-soaked rag staying the blood loss. Raven tore off a large strip from the man's tunic and removed a knife from the soldier's belt. Within seconds he wrapped the cloth around his thigh, using the handle of the knife to twist it tightly before tying it off.

"Whatever you do, kid, keep that on until they treat you with the healing thingy," Raven patted the young man's head before moving on.

"Boss, look," Orlom nudged him, pointing toward the doorway where Cronus and Ular carried Lucas.

"He doesn't look so good," Raven said as they made their way to them.

Cronus and Ular paused upon entering the vast chamber, looking for direction until seeing Raven approach, much to their relief.

"What happened?" Raven asked, looking Lucas over until seeing the stump on his left arm with blood oozing heavily from its makeshift bandage.

"Morac," Cronus said, shaking his head in disgust.

"That looks pretty bad," Orlom said, noticing the grievous injury and pale look on Lucas' face, the Torry elite's eyes going in and out.

"Looks like he could use a hand," Raven couldn't help to say, the others not getting his stupid joke or finding it in bad taste. Raven directed them to the priority area where the most time sensitive cases went. Even with Ular's torniquet, the wound would continue bleeding profusely. They had seen enough men die today by loss of blood. The area was near the front of the hall at the base of the dais.

Nearly all the matrons were busy moving men up and down the lines where they lay, working feverishly to keep them alive.

Much to their disappointment, there were too many ahead of Lucas to heal him right away.

"Hold him down," Cronus said, going to retrieve a poker from the hearth along the near wall. By then Lucas was already unconscious, as Raven grabbed hold of the bicep of his arm, holding him down as Ular and Orlom held his legs and free arm, putting their weight on him. Cronus tore away the bandages, taking a deep breath before pressing the hot metal to the wound. Lucas awoke with a painful cry, his eyes half wild half and half delirious. He eventually calmed, as they eased their hold. Raven checked his pulse, which was faint but holding, and carried him to his place in line. Ular remained with him as the others stepped outside in the outer corridor where Cronus told Raven of all that transpired, to the extent that he fully knew. Though Cronus wanted nothing more than to check on Leanna, duty required him elsewhere, and Galen was to see to her throughout the day. He had to trust his friend in that regard, and decided to return to the palace roof, where Torg could direct him where he was needed.

"I'm coming with you," Raven said, weary of being cooped up all these days.

"Wouldn't that reveal your presence to the enemy?" Cronus asked, knowing that was the primary reason he didn't help them in the battle.

"Just hand me a giant cloak or something to cover me. That should work for a short while."

"I don't think we have a cloak big enough to conceal you, not even a tent," Cronus shook his head.

"I'll see what I can find," Cronus conceded.

"What about me, Boss?" Orlom asked excitedly, eager to go as well.

"Either change out of those clothes or we'll have to cover you up as well. And both of you should leave your rifles below," Cronus said regarding Orlom's earth garb before leading them to the roof.

* * *

Cronus couldn't find a cloak large enough for his friend, but used a ragged tarp which seemed to do the job. Raven looked more like a ghostly specter haunting the battlements than a warrior in hiding, or more like a walking blanket. They noticed Wind Racer sitting off to the side, nursing his wounded wing, which was heavily bandaged. Several apes stood watch over the great warbird, pounding their fists to their chests as they passed. Terin was not present, attending other matters while leaving his beloved friend in their care. They certainly received a few strange looks as they crossed over the roof of the inner keep before entering the Golden Tower, Raven's strange appearance taking many aback. They ascended several levels before keeping within the shadows of a north facing outcropping, affording them a generous view of the primary field of battle.

Raven was taken aback by the carnage, guessing the casualties in the thousands. Perhaps tens of thousands if he was being honest. At the base of the inner battlements, just within the walls, there were mounds of bodies twenty feet high in places. Most of the slain appeared to be gargoyles, but it was difficult to tell what was within the piles. He saw enough human limbs sticking from the ghastly mounds to know both sides suffered greatly. The outer battlements were only slightly better, though most of those slain there were tossed over the walls upon the Benotrists below as they tried to enter the main tunnel. From here they could see the carnage upon Zar Crest, where Morac's slain magantor was difficult to miss. By now they were informed of Bode's and Nevias' deaths. The east and south walls were battered, but held firm, losing far less than the north wall.

"Something has to be done with all the bodies before disease starts to spread," Raven said, knowing it wouldn't take long for that to happen.

"We have large furnaces in the bowels of the palace for that," Cronus said, pointing out several shoots were the men were already tossing corpses into. They would slide to the bottom of the palace and be thrown into the great furnaces there, which could be heated hot enough to dispose of the bodies. It was grim but necessary work.

"I guess whoever built this castle thought of everything," Raven said, impressed by the engineering of Corell. He spotted the familiar spires of smoke issuing from the chimneys across the palace, wondering which ones were from the furnace, planning to avoid them if he could. The smell of burning bodies was not one to savor.

"Not everything," Cronus pointed out the launch ramp Morac constructed that allowed the gargoyles to easily assail the north wall. Nothing prevented them from building more along the other walls. Thankfully only two of his legions were gargoyle, and many of them perished this day.

"Yeah, that's kind of dumb. Why didn't they think of that before putting all that time in building this place?" Raven wondered.

"Gargoyles never constructed anything before Tyro. Having human allies has changed that," Cronus sighed.

Raven took that moment to draw his pistol with as much stealth as he could manage, using its scope to scan the enemy siege lines. If Thorton was anywhere, it would most likely be near Morac's pavilion.

"What do you see?" Cronus asked.

"The men along your northern perimeter seem to be refortifying their trenches. I see a lot of them digging, but nothing extraordinary. They have a number of wounded they are gathering behind their siege works," Raven spotted numerous pavilions with Benotrist matrons attending the injured men and gargoyles, dressed in the same red gowns the Torry matrons wore. Many of the Benotrist wounded were left behind in the fields north of the main gate. A quick scan revealed many were still alive. He could see many of the fallen moving slightly about, trying to crawl away on useless legs, or shift painfully with their guts ripped open, waiting to die. He shifted his scan to Morac's pavilion, watching as Morac was speaking to a few of his lackeys before entering the structure, catching sight of a scantily clad slave girl meeting him at the open flaps of the entrance.

"He's got good taste at least," Raven added, regarding the comely wench attending him.

"Who, Boss?" Orlom asked.

"Never mind," Raven lowered his pistol, not feeling like explaining it.

"Come. We are expected at the commanders call," Cronus said as a soldier ascended the tower to inform him.

* * *

Raven followed Cronus into the somber chamber where gathered many commanders, royal elite and ministers of the realm, joining Torg and the Princess. Terin stood quietly along the far wall behind Corry, his eyes weary from battle, but they brightened upon seeing his friends enter. Orlom followed after, taking up position beside Torg with his arms crossed as if he was his bodyguard. Cronus thought he overheard him refer to the commander of the elite as *Coach*, but was not certain. He would laugh if things were not so dire. He recognized several commanders of telnic from the 3rd Army gathered around the map table, including his old commander of the 9th Telnic, Mastorn, along with three of the garrison commanders of the east, west and south walls, and General Valen. The absence of the north wall commander was later explained by his death. Bors Datev perished defending the inner battlements of the north wall at some point during the battle. Two Jenaii commanders of telnic also joined them, standing to Corry's immediate left, their stoic indifference making it difficult to determine if they had seen battle at all, though they certainly had. Cronus couldn't help but admire the Jenaii for their unflinching loyalty and professionalism. They were steadfast and unyielding, and never prone to the emotional outbursts that plagued mankind.

"Gentlemen, I wish not to keep you from your duties. I shall be as brief as is practical considering our position," Corry began. "As most of you are aware, we have lost many of our bravest men today, including Commander Nevias, General El Tuvo, and General Bode. General El Tuvo was taken captive, while Bode and Nevias perished at Morac's hand. Upon conferring with my counsel, I have decided upon Commander Cors Balka, commander of the west wall, to assume command of the palace garrison. Commander," Corry called out the stick thin, grizzled warrior standing to her right along the adjoining side of the table.

"I will do so as you command, Highness," Cors bowed respectfully. This was a position and honor Cors Balka never expected considering his cantankerous manner and blunt speech. Cronus approved of this appointment, and considering how few commanders of rank within the garrison remained, it was not unexpected.

"I shall leave it to you to name your replacement for the west wall, as well as filling the vacancy upon the north wall," she reminded him.

"Aye, Your Highness. I'll find the right sort to fill them," he said gruffly.

"As for command of the 3rd Army, I have decided upon Commander Mastorn of the 9th telnic. Commander," Corry called him out from his place along the table to her left.

"I am humbled and honored, Your Highness," a surprised Mastorn bowed deeply, noticing Cronus nodding in approval, which Corry noticed as well.

"King's Elite Kenti speaks well of you, General, and though I hold his opinion in very high regard, it is your reputation and performance that weighed most heavily in my decision," Corry affirmed.

"Again, Your Highness, I am most humbled," Mastorn said.

"Now on to pressing matters. What is the state of your forces, gentlemen? General Valen, shall you start?" She looked to her magantor commander, who stood across the table.

"At least thirty warbirds dead or wounded. Many more suffering minor injuries or missing crewmembers. Enemy magantor losses match our own, perhaps a few more. It was a costly exchange, Your Highness," Dar reported.

"How many magantors have you left?" she asked.

"Forty-one, and many of those require new riders or archers. Some of the wounded magantors might bolster that number if we can have use of the Earthers' regenerator," he added.

"That will not be for some time, General. Wounded men take priority," Torg reminded him.

"Of course, Master Vantel," the General agreed.

"As we are discussing our air assets, I would look to you next,

Commander Ev Avoran," she asked the ranking commander of telnic, who assumed command of the Jenaii battlegroup.

"Our tallies are incomplete as of this time. A simple estimate would conclude three thousand dead, wounded or missing. This does not include minor injuries. Once reorganized, we can field four full telnics," the acting General said with characteristic Jenaii indifference. The others contemplated the severe reduction of the 1st Battlegroup to its current size. Four thousand Jenaii still were more than adequate to blunt a concentrated gargoyle assault of half a legion. Unfortunately, Morac had more than a legion of gargoyles to throw at them.

"And our garrison forces?" Corry looked to Commander Balka and his subordinates.

They reported losses along the south wall of two hundred dead and wounded, inflicting four thousand casualties upon the Gargoyle 5th Legion. The east wall suffered more than double that number, with four hundred and sixty dead or severely wounded, having inflicted three thousand four hundred casualties upon the Gargoyle 14th Legion. The north wall suffered the greatest losses, numbering over nine hundred and seventy dead or wounded. Gargoyle casualties upon the north wall were estimated from ten to fifteen thousand, from what they assumed was the 14th Gargoyle Legion. Most of the casualties along the north wall were suffered by the garrison troops assigned the inner battlements.

General Mastorn followed with the losses suffered by 3rd Army, including eight hundred dead and many more wounded, with most of their losses concentrated at the inner palace. It was a costly battle, one they could not afford to repeat.

"Commander Balka, you will need to rebalance your forces," Torg reminded Cors, who nodded in agreement. Thankfully, the west wall incurred no losses in the battle, and could reassign many of their men to the north wall. Thankfully, the 3rd Army's men were also distributed along each wall, backing the defenders who manned the battlements.

"The question remains, when will Morac renew his assault?"

General Valen asked, looking forlornly at the map spread out before them, detailing Corell and its surrounding regions.

"It could be tonight if he can reorganize his gargoyles," Torg snorted, shaking his head with disgust.

"The ramp they constructed changes everything we know of their capabilities," Chief Minister Monsh opined, having remained silent until now.

"Yes, very industrious of them," Cors Balka snarled with derision. If there was one thing he hated most in the world, it was gargoyles.

"The ramp was constructed by human hand and ingenuity. I doubt they could have thought of it on their own, or executed its construction by their own effort," Corry added.

They went on to discuss the status of the wounded and the main gate, which was raised before Dethine could rend it, much to their relief. They finished with the latest scouting reports to their southwest, one of the few directions open to their reconnaissance, though there was yet little to report. Dar was loathe to send any patrols out without significant reinforcements, as Morac's warbirds would attack them in force. His patrols were growing more infrequent as the siege progressed, requiring him to husband his strength for an attack upon Corell. With that, they were dismissed to attend their duties, leaving Torg, Corry, Raven, Cronus and Orlom alone in the chamber.

Corry ordered Terin to accompany his grandfather, who followed the others out of the chamber, heading for the great hall, leaving Cronus, Raven and Orlom.

"See to your wife, Cronus, for I fear the enemy may renew their attack by nightfall," she advised, her fears founded in what she would do in Morac's place. He knew they were weak, and would strike now, when victory was never as likely.

Cronus bowed, regarding Raven one last time before stepping without. That left Corry with Raven and Orlom, the Princess looking into his dark eyes for the longest time before saying a word.

"You came here for a purpose, Raven, to kill Thorton and then help us defend Corell," she stated.

"Yep," was all he could say to that.

She wanted to scream at him, to vent her frustration for his blindness. What good did waiting for Thorton to show himself do, if they were all dead? She wanted to say that and so much more, but wouldn't. Part of her knew the wisdom of his waiting, but hated what it cost them in blood. She looked into his dark eyes that stared back with cold indifference, as if he were separate from them in this conflict. He was the most mysterious person she ever knew. He would risk his life for a dear friend, but do nothing to save ten thousand. He was here though, that fact she repeated to remind herself that he did care for the ten thousand. She wanted him to do something, but knew he couldn't, not yet anyway. She was torn between her desires and cold logic. She desired him to stand to post and cut down Morac's legions with impunity. Logic demanded he wait for Thorton to appear, and surprise him with a laser blast to his brain. Once that transpired, he could move on to Morac's minions. Even cold logic wasn't without emotion in this regard. To prove that, all she had to do is think of poor Kato, and what Thorton did to him. No, Raven had to remain hidden, as much as it pained her to admit. What could she say to him now? He looked at her awaiting a response, and all she could do is look back.

"We shall do our best to fend off the enemy, and buy you the time to wait for Thorton," she placed her hand upon his chest. The gesture calmed her rage for some reason she couldn't fathom. With that she left him standing there as she turned and departed.

* * *

Terin followed Torg, his grandfather strangely quiet as he marched through the corridors of the palace, trying to keep pace with Torg's forceful gait. For a man of his years, Torg was still as spry as a young man. As Terin felt spent from battle, his grandfather seemed tireless. He thought of all his time training under him, never recalling him weary. Torg was never one to instruct his pupils without exerting himself with equal measure. Long after Terin retired each day, Torg remained, drilling others until dusk, as tireless as a mountain enduring the seasons without complaint.

"Grandfather, I should…"

"I'll tell you what you should do," Torg curtly cut him off, passing through the open doors to the great hall, the sound of injured men echoing off the stone walls. Torg led him directly to the front of the vast chamber between the rows of wounded men. It was a ghastly sight with so many men suffering in terrible pain. It was a sight he would never grow accustom, no matter how many battles he fought. Torg led him directly to Matron Dresila. Who appeared to be expecting him by the look on her weary face. Terin doubted the poor woman would sleep anytime soon, and already was weary enough to fall dead.

"Master Vantel," Dresila bobbed a curtesy, greeting him with such grace despite the conditions that surrounded her.

"None of that, My Lady. Spare no effort in addressing me. Now where do we stand?" He asked, his voice softening while addressing the woman. Terin could hear the respect Torg had for the matron in his tone.

"We are almost drained. I shall treat three more and follow you to our last patient before we must recharge the device," she said, looking to the endless line of men that would not be healed for some time. Many would not survive the day, but such was the state of things.

As she healed the next three men in line, Terin found Lucas in the crowd, which was made easy as Ular stood over him like a guardian spirit. He spoke with them briefly, as poor Lucas did his best to convince them he was not in pain. It was a pitiful lie with the agony written on his face, as well as the blood leaking through his bandaged stump. Their brief exchange was cut short by Torg's growl, ordering Terin to follow him and Dresila.

He walked quietly behind them, following them up the adjoining stairwells before stepping onto the roof of the inner keep, where he left their ape friends watching over Wind Racer. He was surprised when Dresila set the regenerator upon Wind Racer's damaged wing, the great avian turning his massive head in her direction with an eerie calm, as if privy to her intention. The warbird turned to Terin with a soulful look, before looking back to his benefactor as Dresila initiated the device. Wind Racer bathed in the warmth radiating from the restored flesh, pressing his black beak into Dresila, rubbing it along her chest and face. She was taken aback, returning his affection by running her hands along his feathered neck.

"Thank you, Matron," Terin said gratefully.

"I believe your friend has already thanked me sufficiently, but you are welcome, all the same, Champion Caleph," she smiled warmly while retrieving the device, taking it to the middle of the roof to place it for its recharge. With the sun moving in and out of the clouds it might take longer than she hoped.

"Your bird is safe!" Carbanc, son of Hukok, declared, slapping Terin on the back, he and his fellow apes stepping away, leaving him alone with Torg.

"I don't know how to thank you," Terin sighed, overcome with gratitude.

"Corry ordered it done, and I agreed, though it was not to save your friend. The princess may hold you in high regard, Terin, but she ordered Dresila to use the last of the regenerator's energy to save Wind Racer for the greater good. We could have healed three more men for the energy we just spent on your mount. At least one of those men we left below untreated, will likely perish before Dresila can restore its power. When you speak of gratitude, know that healing his wing will cost a man his life," Torg said grimly.

"Why? Why do that then?" Terin was horrified. He had been too tired to think of the ramifications, and now was pained with guilt.

"Why? Why do you think, Terin? It doesn't require deep reasoning to decipher. It certainly wasn't done to keep you safe, which is her true desire. No, Wind Racer was restored because he is your trusted mount, and gives you the mobility to counter Morac should he return this night. Look beyond our walls and you can see the enemy is not broken. If I were Morac, I would return before we can reorganize our defenses. He knows he cannot defeat you, at least not easily, just as you cannot defeat him. We were mistaken to let you roam freely throughout the battle, especially afoot, freeing Morac to strike where you were not," Torg explained.

"Here," Terin sighed, looking at the carnage around them.

"Yes, here. With you fighting below, he was able to slay Bode, Nevias and countless others, as well as wound Lucas and Wind Racer. Had you not arrived when you did, he would have killed Ular and me as well. Only you can stop him, and you must remain mobile to do so. For that, we had to sacrifice healing three men in order to heal Wind Racer. It is a heavy burden to bear, knowing what we sacrificed, but such is war, and the decisions it forces upon you."

"No matter the reason, it still weighs upon me," Terin shook his head, thinking of the families of the men who might die because of it.

"You haven't the luxury of being weighed by it. You must make their sacrifice worth it by preparing to meet Morac, your blade against his own. Now, you need to eat and rest, and be ready for battle at any moment," Torg sent him off, watching as he disappeared through the adjoining stairwell.

* * *

Morac's pavilion.

Morac stood before the table with a map of Corell unfurled across it, richly detailing its outer and inner walls, with each turret, along with the inner castle and its myriad of towers and platforms. He stripped his armor upon entering his sanctuary, as he came to view his pavilion, with its many comforts and delights. He lifted his goblet, draining its wine with his eyes fixed upon the outline of the castle, working out the plans running through his mind. He placed the empty vessel forcefully upon the table as his slave girl Velesa hurried forth to fill it, her head bowed respectfully, before returning to her place along the near wall, kneeling beside her sister captives. He brought only nine of his fifteen girls for this campaign, leaving the rest at Notsu. He brought four golden collars, planning to use them to celebrate his victories, along with his two favorite silvers, Velesa and Corry, the later sharing the hair and name of his nemesis. Oh, how he would savor exchanging the false Corry for the true one, returning her discourtesies a thousand-fold.

367

His Generals began to filter in one at a time, heeding his summons for a war council. The first to arrive were Generals Marcinia and Gavis, commanders of the 9th and 10th Legions, their role in the attack little more than holding in reserve along the western and southern siege works. The insufferable Gavis looked upon Morac with obvious contempt, thinking poorly of his plan of attack. Morac thought to remove his head where he stood, but killing Generals needed to be done judiciously. The ornery Gavis could be displeased all he wanted, but as long as he kept his tongue, Morac would let him keep his head. Their legions were nearly at full strength, fielding fifty telnics each. General Vlesnivolk entered next, his battered mail and blood stained tunic reflecting his arduous day. He spent much of the battle dodging ballista spewing from Corell's battlements or dropped into their midst from the enemy magantors. He nearly entered the tunnel, stopped only by the crowding that slowed their advance to a crawl before their path was alit with fire. Their second entrance into that deadly passageway faired little better, forced to withdraw once the attack upon the upper palace was turned back. He left five thousand dead and wounded within the tunnel and the approaches of the main gate. Even now many of their wounded could be seen strewn across the battlefield between their forward trenches and the main gate of Corell. He could barely field thirty telnics, his legion suffering casualties throughout the construction of the ramp combined with what he lost today.

General Polis followed next, his magantor forces greatly reduced, losing thirty warbirds, though incurring an equal or greater loss upon the Torries. He was followed by General Trimopolak, commander of the 14th Gargoyle Legion, whose forces attacked Corell from both the east and the north, via the ramp, thus suffering the highest casualties of all the legions. The gargoyle general looked none too pleased with the result, his losses not yet tallied, but could be guessed over twenty telnics, perhaps more. He barely escaped the battle unscathed, Torry archers just missing his wings by the barest of margins, and another grazing his helm. Of his telnic commanders, more than twenty-four were unaccounted for, forcing him to designate unit commanders to organize their cohorts. Another similar attack would finish his legion.

The next to enter was General Concaka, commander of the 5th Gargoyle Legion. His attack upon the south wall was strongly met, accomplishing little more than keeping the Torries positioned there in place and unable to reinforce the north wall and inner palace. He was still awaiting the final tallies, guessing his losses to be four thousand. Coupled with his losses at Besos, his legion was now reduced to thirty-eight telnics.

The last to enter were Dethine and Borgon. Dethine's golden mail appeared as resplendent as a new day sun, as if he hadn't seen battle at all. Though he spent the entire fray dodging Torry munitions and falling corpses, he looked no worse for the wear. Borgon was equally vigorous, celebrating his capture of the Jenaii General El Tuvo, his magantor having snatched him from the air, returning him to their camp. The Jenaii waited outside the pavilion chained hand and foot, his broken wing preventing him from flight.

"What have you?" Morac asked Borgon, any information he might have gleaned from his interrogation taking precedence.

"He is most stubborn. All that I learned is that he commands the 1st Jenaii Battlegroup, and that he is named El Tuvo. And this was learned from Torry prisoners that we managed to take, as he refuses to answer," Borgon said, the Benotrist elite impressed with El Tuvo's resistance to torture.

"The Jenaii will tell you nothing. You should kill him and be done with it," Dethine stated flatly, his people knowing the Jenaii character better than any other, having battled them for centuries.

"I shall consider it," Morac said, deciding when and where to do so to their full advantage. He then asked them to list their losses, and the status of their reconstitution of forces, which they detailed. The 14th Legion was the most problematic, and would struggle to reposition before nightfall. Morac ordered Trimopolak to move his entire legion to the north side of the perimeter, behind the ramp. The 5th Gargoyle Legion would shift east, and the 9th Benotrist Legion would reposition to the south, and he wanted it done before dusk.

"Impossible!" General Gavis sneered. "They can't reposition their legions so quickly, especially after the battle they just fought. We only have part of the day left to do so."

"It will be done as I have ordered," Morac glared at the obstinate General Gavis.

"Why such urgency? Better to do it come sunrise, giving us a full day to complete it, and more time to tally the dead," Gavis pushed.

"Tomorrow will be too late. We attack tonight," Morac stated firmly, slapping the table where the center of Corell was displayed upon the map.

"Tonight? That is madness. How can we plan to do so in the dark? The gargoyles might surprise them, but they will suffer in kind, unable to coordinate their…" Gavis pointed out, but Morac was having none of it.

"At dusk the 14th Legion will again use the ramp and assail the palace, but this time they are to Passover the inner walls and concentrate… HERE!" Morac tapped the opening to the courtyard which rested on the roof of the inner palace between the northern inner walls and the inner keep.

"The courtyard?" General Vlesnivolk mused, running a finger under his chin, examining the outline of the palace curiously, while Trimopolak looked unimpressed, his legion in no condition to attack again. It would take all they could muster to reform, let alone soar high enough to pass over the inner battlements. Even then, they would have to navigate the opening of the courtyard, before dropping back to the ground level, some one hundred and sixty feet below the opening.

"The courtyard!" Morac affirmed. "The 14th Legion will take the courtyard and clear the tunnel to the north gate from within, while the 8th Benotrist Legion attacks from without. General Trimopolak, your gargoyles must clear the levels above and the chambers beside the tunnel, where the defenders have use of their deadly openings," Morac referenced the small holes lining the length of the tunnel, where defenders on the level above could fire arrows or jab spears through their openings into the men crowded below in the tunnel. He recalled how many of their men they lost during the attack during the last siege. This attack could eliminate that threat, clearing those areas before the Benotrists entered the tunnel from the north.

"And once the castle is breeched?" General Marcinia asked, his eyes alit with the realization of what the plan would mean if successful.

"Then, we feed the rest of our legions through the tunnel, secure the base of the palace, and work our way to the roof. It means, General, the conquest of Corell," Morac smiled.

"And what of their Champion? Will he not waylay these lofty plans?" Gavis asked.

"Once he shows himself, Dethine and I shall finish him. His sword might protect him from my blade, just as mine protects me from his, but it will not protect him from two *Swords of Light* striking at the same time," Morac explained. He planned for Dethine to join him with the following waves of gargoyles, who would assail the inner palace itself, occupying the defenders upon the roof, while the first waves continued to the courtyard below.

With that, Morac dismissed his generals, as each needed the remaining daylight to complete his orders if the attack was to commence as planned. Dethine and Borgon remained, the former regarding the line of kneeling slave girls appreciatively, while Borgon removed his dagger, twirling it in his fingers while surveying the layout of the palace.

"There are many lovely beauties awaiting your collar within Corell," Morac reminded the Nayborian champion.

"I doubt there are few as lovely as the fair Belicia," he said, naming the golden collared girl Morac gifted him at Notsu, who now wore his silver.

"She eagerly awaits you in your pavilion," Morac remarked, drawing Dethine's mirth from the crude comment.

"Indeed, and I look to add several more Torry lovelies to my collection," Dethine smirked.

"Have your fill with the high-born females. I'll take my fill with the country girls. They are far more pliable and have seen less suitors. Once Corell falls, the Torry heartland awaits," Borgon smirked.

"I anticipate its bountiful yield," Morac said.

"Then let us make it so. What shall you have us do before the attack?" Borgon asked. As eighth among Tyro's elite, he was a Benotrist warrior of great renown. He was rumored to have slain over sixty

371

men in combat through the years, using his cunning master sword handling.

"Our dracks have kept the north wall of Corell under barrage since we withdrew. Let us give them respite until the battle commences. But we would be remiss not keeping our Torry hosts entertained once our dracks grow quiet," Morac said.

"Aye," Borgon smiled, knowing just what entertainment Morac intended.

* * *

The defenders worked feverishly after the battle clearing the dead from the battlements, sending many to the furnaces in the bowels of the palace, while others were piled into mounds and set ablaze, or tossed from the walls, to clear the walkways for the next assault. The men along the north wall struggled tossing bodies over the parapets while under duress, with Benotrist dracks still within range of the battlements. Jars Volen was the newly named commander of the wall, his predecessor having fallen during the fray. He overlooked the activities from the inner battlements, directing his diminished ranks to his utmost. Cors Balka, the newly named commander of garrison, reassigned three units from the west wall to bolster his position. He immediately put two of them to work clearing the inner battlements and the area behind them, while the third he ordered to the outer battlements. There was still time left in this day to clear many of the dead, and he would see that it was done. Fortunately, the bodies thrown over the walls were near the main gate, where they could be more easily gathered and burned, once there was a lull in the battle.

THOOSH!

A drack spear drilled a soldier through the chest, striking another behind him at the shoulder along the outer battlements, just above the main gate. Another shattered the edge of a rampart further east, a large chunk of the ancient stone dropping upon the causeway behind it, the spear continuing on, striking just below the inner wall beyond it.

Jars Volen looked on miserably, cursing the foul devices striking at them with impunity with no means of returning the favor. They lost two dozen men to the deadly fire since the assault ended. The enemy seemed to possess an inexhaustible supply of the strongly built munitions. After one managed to kill a soldier, the others would huddle beneath the parapets, fearing to show themselves. After a while, they would bestir from hiding, and continue with the clearing of the dead until another spear struck true. He hated admiring the enemy, but their drack crews were well trained, pausing fire, and waiting for his men to show themselves. Eventually his men emerged, getting back to work, awaiting the next spear to strike, but nothing happened. After a long period of quiet, it was obvious the dracks stopped firing, and he wondered why?

"Commander, look!" His aide pointed out beside him, the young soldier directing him beyond the palace walls where Dethine rode forward of the line of dracks.

* * *

Dethine paraded before the walls of Corell, just beyond range of their ballista, astride his golden ocran. He drew his sword, his mount cantering before their line of dracks, the ancient blade alit with a golden glow, drawing the eyes of the defenders with men and Jenaii gathering along the palace walls.

"Men of Corell!" Dethine taunted, his voice booming over the battlefield with terrible authority. "I present our trophy, taken so courageously from your trembling ranks. BEHOLD!" He outstretched his sword behind him, where Borgon and a flax of gargoyles marched forth, dragging General El Tuvo to the fore in full view of the defenders, his arms and legs bound, and his broken wing sagging unnaturally at his side. The defiant Jenaii General stood unmoved, his silver eyes staring stoically and unyielding in defiance of his captors. A thousand gasps and moans echoed from the palace walls, bemoaning the General's sorry state.

Corry and Torg made their way to Zar Crest, drawn by the commotion running through the palace. She felt the overbearing presence of the Jenaii gathering along the battlements of the inner

373

keep, their quiet rage held in check by their trained indifference. She quickly recognized the source of their silent ire, seeing their commander captive before the palace walls, helpless to intervene.

Corry sensed Terin standing behind her, feeling the torrents of anguish pouring off him, urging him to act, but held in check by reason and discipline. It was times such as this that she understood his sword's yearnings, wanting nothing more than to charge forth and save their comrade. It would be satisfying but foolish, and here they stood, helpless observers in Dethine's cruel game.

The onlookers grew silent as Dethine circled behind the captive general, bringing his sword down as he shifted in the saddle, lopping El Tuvo's good wing, before striking the other. The Jenaii released an uncharacteristic scream, blood issuing from his severed appendages. The Jenaii host gathered atop the upper battlements, stared intently at the ghastly sight. Corry felt their festering rage at this insult, Dethine's cruel act an abomination, the violation of a sacred taboo.

The desecration continued as Borgon ordered the gargoyles to force El Tuvo to his back, freeing his limbs briefly before stretching them to their utmost, tying them to stakes driven in the ground. Once fastened, Borgon knelt beside him, drawing his dagger, and cutting away the Jenaii's tunic, exposing his torso before sliding the blade carefully into his abdomen, fueling his screams as he dug his fingers into the wound.

"Shalls we mufflesss himss?" One gargoyle asked, El Tuvo's anguished cries carrying over the battlefield.

"No! Let his friends hear his song," Borgon commanded, working his fingers deeper into the cut, before drawing his innards out through the hole, laying strings of them upon his belly.

The Torries, Jenaii and their ape allies looked on with gloom, El Tuvo's agony tearing at their hearts as darkening clouds gathered above, casting the land in despair and shadow. The cries of the wounded still echoed through the halls of the palace, filtering to the roof top of Corell. The smell of burning flesh drifted freely, twisting amid the swirling winds, torturing the defenders with their noxious fumes. Behind the Benotrist siege lines Morac's legions began to chant their dispiriting death songs, their merriment contrasting the defenders' dread while Borgon made sport of the dying Jenaii general. Just as all seemed hopeless for Corell's brave defenders…

ZIP!

A flash of blue streamed from the Tower of Celenia.

Borgon's lifeless corpse crumpled to the ground, his brains spilling from his punctured skull.

"Payback's a bitch," Raven shrugged, shifting to his next target.

CHAPTER 20

Raven's second shot streamed toward Dethine astride his tall golden mount, the Nayborian managing to bring the flat of his blade to deflect the blast, sending it harmlessly into the eastern sky. Raven cursed under his breath, recalling Darna doing the same at Bansoch. He sent a volley at Dethine, the Nayborian again deflecting all three, convincing Raven to shift aim, sending the next blast through his ocran's hindquarters. The beast thrashed violently, throwing Dethine to the ground, before Raven brained the animal, dropping it dead at its master's feet.

Raven shifted aim to the gargoyles surrounding El Tuvo, dropping them in quick succession, catching most in the back as they retreated to their siege trenches. His next blast pierced the skull of a Benotrist unit commander, sending his still corpse tumbling into the siege trench, just north of Corell's main gate. Two telnic commanders fell next, followed by the 8th Legion's standard bearer.

Panic ran through the enemy ranks, with gargoyles and men pouring into their siege trenches, dodging Raven's fire, with those farther afield fleeing away from the palace toward the outer encampments. The defenders of Corell shouted in triumph, cheering the turn of events, many more rushing to the battlements to witness the glorious slaughter.

Corry gazed to the Tower of Celenia, where perched Raven upon its highest platform, firing at will upon the enemy. She recalled that glorious day when she found him at Torn harbor, beseeching his aid to save Terin, when all he said was for her to step off his ship, unless she was coming along.

"Are you going to help me?" She had asked.

"If Terin's on that island, we'll find him. We lift anchor in an hour," he said as a matter of fact, as if the impossible task were but a small thing. And here he was again, throwing Morac's great host in confusion and panic with such pitiful ease.

Torg stood at her side, shaking his head in disbelief as Raven went to work strafing the Benotrist siege trench, before shifting his fire farther north and east, striking Morac's pavilion. Torg felt someone nudge his shoulder, turning to see Orlom step to his side with his rifle in hand.

"Boss said to target their spear throwing machines, Coach," Orlom grinned excitedly, taking aim over the parapet, fixing his aim on the drack furthest east, firing away. Torg looked on as his laser blast dropped the remaining crewmen that hadn't taken cover in the siege trenches behind them. He watched as Orlom dropped two, sending the rest running away, before targeting the weapon itself. A few more blasts tore apart the coiled spring, and the support beams, toppling the powerful weapon over. Orlom couldn't resist blasting one of the crewmen in the rear, sending him sprawling in the dirt.

"HOO! HOO!" Orlom grinned excitedly, before shifting aim to the next drack.

"He is having too much fun," Torg shook his head, causing Corry to smile, finding the entire scene surreal.

* * *

Morac's pavilion.

Morac just downed a goblet of wine, wearing only a half tunic, having just enjoyed the use of the fair Velesa, partaking her delights before the night's battle. The girl climbed out of his furs, collecting herself as the other slaves prepared his meal. He smiled inwardly at the sight of their frightened obedience, feeding off their fear, their fear of him. Such power was intoxicating. The more control he exerted, the stronger he felt. He wanted nothing more than to rule, to have others prostrate themselves before him. What is greater than to have a slave girl call you master when you bed her? Nothing was better, he reminded himself, a cruel smile twisting his lips.

ZIP!

Morac jumped back as the laser blast tore through his pavilion, grazing the thigh of the slave girl Denesha, causing her to drop a pitcher of water.

"Who?" Morac uttered, reaching for his sword which rested beside his furs, as another blast struck his map table, smashing it to pieces.

"Lord Morac!" Emperor's Elite Vetino, his aide de camp, shouted, rushing through the flaps of his pavilion.

"Speak! What devilry is this?" Morac growled.

"It is coming from the castle. An Earther must be up there," Vetino declared, just before a laser blast pierced his back, dropping him at Morac's feet.

Wearing naught but a half tunic, Morac strode from his pavilion bare chested with his sword at the ready, deflecting the next blast Raven sent his way. He was greeted by a horrific scene, several members of the imperial elite lying dead before his pavilion, and his great army in chaos. Men clambered from their shelters, rushing toward the siege trenches.

"Packaww!" Magantors screeched from their holding pens to his north, laser blasts ripping into the tethered avian. Another warbird took flight, fleeing north to escape the carnage, before a blast gutted it rear to throat. Morac scowled watching it drop from sight. He immediately called the nearest surviving elite to his side, issuing orders to be relayed. The man took two steps before laser tore through his chest. Morac found another aide, giving him the same order, and again he was struck once stepping away. He cursed the heavens as every soldier within fifty paces of him was targeted, dropping one after the other like some cruel lark.

"Agghh!" Morac cursed, shaking his fist at the Tower of Celenia, wondering which of the foul Earthers had rallied to the Torries cause. He winced as more laser fire spewed from Zar Crest, targeting his dracks, breaking them apart like fragile toys. He stood defiant, waiting for the Earther to fire at him, outstretching his arms, daring him to do so. Nothing. The Earther would waste no more blasts on him, leaving him standing before his pavilion like a half-naked fool. He despaired, marching toward the siege trenches forward of his position, and jumping in. Only once within the safety of the dirt walls could he begin to issue orders, relaying them along the siege lines.

* * *

"Enjoy the dirt, dumbass," Raven smiled, watching Morac jumping into the trench. He spotted three lightly clad girls emerge from Morac's pavilion, joining countless others fleeing north toward the outer encampments in the distance. He next targeted their food distribution points that circled the palace, marked by their outer facing palisades, and newly erected hearths with smoke billowing from them, and the wagons laden with stores being unloaded at each location.

ZIP! ZIP!

He dropped two ocran hitched to a large wagon at the north center position, shifting aim to several cooks huddling amongst the stacked provisions, sending blasts through crates and barrels, slaughtering them in detail. He spread a few more blasts throughout the position, destroying casks of wine and water before shifting to the northeast, where the next one lay. The high level of the tower where he stood, afforded him a panoramic view of the entire siege, with a low parapet circling the floor, with the area above it open, with five supporting columns spaced evenly along the perimeter, supporting the weight of the level above. A stairwell led to the floors below, and a single ladder to the level above. Looking below, he spotted Orlom atop Zar Crest, doing a fine job of destroying the dracks. He just hoped he remembered not to hold the trigger in a continuous stream or he would burn out the rifle's core, but so far, he was doing as he was told… for once.

He held his fire, sensing a presence behind him, turning to see several Jenaii warriors pass through the opposite side of the platform, setting down behind him.

"You fellas need something?" He made a face, not able to read their expression, which he found unsettling. Of all the peoples of Arax, he found the Jenaii the most boring and unapproachable. He had no idea what they were thinking, each staring at him with those deep silver eyes and expressionless faces.

"Protect them," the one closest to him said, directing his attention beyond the north wall.

He looked where he was pointing, watching as a unit size element of Jenaii soared over the outer battlements, heading due north.

"Where are they going?" He asked, before realizing their intention. "Oh, crap! Listen, go tell Orlom to stop shooting!"

"As you command, Raven of Earth," the Jenaii spoke with deep reverence.

"Just Raven, pal. You can ease up on the fancy speech. Oh, and can you fetch Cronus, I need him up here," Raven slapped the warrior on the shoulder like they were long lost drinking buddies.

With that, Raven went back to work, targeting anyone fool enough to poke their heads from the siege trenches behind the line of dracks. His first targets were rather easy, catching one soldier through the nose, just peaking above the palisade. A little farther west he found another one, sending his corpse back into the trench. He caught sight of Dethine retreating back to Morac's wrecked pavilion, not wasting any shots on the likes of him.

Raven lifted his aim as the Jenaii element approached General El Tuvo, whose broken body lay unmoving, still tied to the stakes.

"Good thing I didn't put him out of his misery," Raven mumbled, having considered that at the outset, but didn't when all the other juicy targets presented themselves. He didn't know if the poor bastard was still alive until he zoomed in with his scope, seeing the anguished look on the general's face.

ZIP! ZIP! ZIP!

Raven swept the siege trench just north of there as the Jenaii host set down, cutting the general's bonds and lifting him into the air. Raven wondered how they would carry him without entangling their wings, considering he was too heavy for only one to lift. One scooped their hands under his arms, while the other held his feet, carrying him vertically, one above the other, taking to the air while the others guarded their return. El Tuvo returned to the palace face first, his eyes going in and out of consciousness with blood draining from his wound, and his intestines dangling freely. Raven watched as they bore him through the air, passing safely over the battlements, setting down upon the inner keep where Matron Dresila was waiting.

* * *

Dresila stopped the regenerator in the middle of its charge at forty three percent in order to treat the dying Jenaii general. No sooner did they set him down beside her, she placed the device upon his belly where his entrails were spilling out. She quickly pressed the initiate switch once it gave her a positive read. Within moments the wound was sealed, though El Tuvo was asleep, likely from the loss of blood.

"Will he live, my lady?" One of the Jenaii warriors asked, his even voice betraying little emotion.

"He is still very weak, commander, and I dare not restore his wings as it will drain the regenerator. Once he awakens, reassure him that his wings will be restored once the severely injured soldiers have been saved," she said, noting the rank adorning the warrior's shoulders, before removing the device, restarting the charging process. She frowned looking at the darkening sky, the cloud cover greatly reducing its ability to recharge.

"We shall see to his comforts, my lady," the Jenaii bowed reverently, calling upon his fellows to bear their general to his quarters.

Dresila bowed in kind, her respect for these brave warriors matching theirs for her. The Torry realm had no greater friend than the Jenaii, and she was proud to have helped them in this way.

ZIP! ZIP! ZIP!

She winced as Raven and Orlom continued to fire over the palace walls, reminding herself that every blast took a life. It was odd that the device she now used and treasured, healed the gravest of injuries, and saved countless lives, was a gift from the Earthers, whose weapons took life so easily. They were both instruments from the same people, great tools of life and death. Then she thought of the many Torry lives that were saved by the death Raven and Orlom were visiting upon the enemy, and she was thankful for it.

* * *

ZIP!

Raven targeted a magantor taking flight from its pen far north of the palace. He slew over twenty by his last count, with the rest fleeing beyond the horizon. Tens of thousands of Benotrists and gargoyles huddled in their trenches, with the rest of their army scrambling away from the palace. Once they passed beyond six thousand feet, he let them be, which kept them in sight if they were fool enough to remain, which they were. Once they realized they weren't being targeted at that range, they became confident, and began reestablishing their perimeter around their outer encampments. There were still thousands fleeing between their siege trenches and the new perimeter, giving him plenty to freely shoot at. Raven shifted aim back to the food distribution points, wreaking havoc along the western perimeter where the 10th Benotrist Legion was mostly untouched to this point. He saw no reason to leave them out of the suffering. He continued to the southwest, where the bulk of the 9th Benotrist Legion was caught repositioning to the south by the look of things. He got bored breaking up their logistical positions, and went back to targeting their commanders.

ZIP!

He brained a commander of unit or telnic, not certain which it was. The poor fellow flopped to the ground, sending the men around him in panic. He dropped two more soldiers at random before shifting back to the east, where the gargoyles were. He wasn't clear which gargoyle legion was which, but didn't really care, blasting away into their midst. By this point, Orlom had already finished off the dracks, and was having a good old time shooting at will.

"You called for me, oh great and magnificent Raven?" Cronus

gave him a mock bow upon clearing the stairwell, causing Raven to turn, shaking his head.

"Real funny, which of the idiots did you learn that phrase from?"

"Brokov. He and Lorken shared many such idioms over the years," Cronus laughed, stepping to his side, looking over the parapet at Raven's handiwork.

"That figures. Well, now that you're here, I need a few favors," Raven said, returning his attention to the east, looking through his rifle's scope, firing off another blast, this one burning a hole through a gargoyle's back, dropping the creature some three hundred feet beyond the siege trench.

"I think that can be arranged. What did you have in mind?" Cronus asked, watching as he dropped another gargoyle trying to take flight, the creature barely in the air before face planting in the ground.

"I didn't really think this out when I came up here, and I'm getting a little hungry. Can you have some food sent up. Something to drink would be nice too. Maybe a bucket for me to piss in wouldn't be a bad idea. I'm going to be working late tonight, and won't have time to go all the way back down to do those things."

"Did you call me all the way up here because you're hungry?" Cronus couldn't believe it. Here they were in the middle of battle, with the whole world in flames, and Raven wanted dinner.

"A man's got to eat, Cronus. When you're done with that, I'll need you to come back and stay with me. Terin too," he said, blasting another gargoyle in the back of the head, the creature dropping to the ground far to their east.

"Stay with you? You need some friendly company?" He asked, wondering if Raven was getting bored.

"Company is good, but that's not it. In the event Thorton is close by, and kills me, you are one of the few men who can use my weapons. I suggest you pick them up, but don't use them, or he'll shoot you pretty quick. Save them for their big attack, and catch him by surprise. Hopefully it won't come to that if Terin comes up here, and stands beside me with that fancy sword of his. Maybe he can deflect Ben's shots, like Morac and that other idiot did with mine. Two can play at that game."

"Two can play? That's a new one," Cronus chuckled.

"That phrase is older than Lorken's pick up lines. It means if a tactic works for one side, it will work for another."

"Pick up lines?" Cronus made a face.

"It's what you say to a woman to get her to date you, or to initiate courtship in your case," Raven said, blasting another gargoyle through the back, shifting aim as it dropped.

Cronus just shook his head, trying not to burst in laughter at the absurdity of it all.

"Something funny?" Raven gave him a look, taking a pause between shots.

"Looking back before I met you, I now realize my life was rather dull."

"Of course it was, now how about getting me that food."

"Alright, I guess you earned it. I'll fetch Terin also, but Torg wanted him near Wind Racer so he can quickly respond to wherever Morac or Dethine might attack."

"I wouldn't worry about Moronic or Death boy. If they attack it is going to be on the ground, so Terin will have plenty of time seeing them coming. Right now, both of those idiots are stuck in their trench with the nearest available magantor miles away. The only hope they have is if Ben shows up and spoils my party, but I don't see any sign of him. Kinda strange that he's not here, considering how important this battle is," Raven reasoned.

"Where else could he be?"

"If not here, the only other place would be Tro," he shrugged, hoping that wasn't the case. Even so, even Ben couldn't beat the others by himself. There was also the chance that Ben was dead. That would explain a lot. Sometimes he couldn't bring himself to believe Ben would attack them like that. Then again, he didn't think he would kill Kato either.

"Wherever he is, I am certain he shall quickly learn that you are here."

"Yep, so let's hope wherever he is, it's far away. That should buy me time to thin out the herd."

"I know I have spent too much time in your company when I know what that means. I best fetch your food. I wouldn't want our beloved hero to starve," Cronus smiled, slapping him on the back.

"Oh, and ask if the kitchen staff have that special bread with the sprinkle stuff on top of it," Raven said, causing Cronus to smile and shake his head.

* * *

"Switch to pistol, charge rifle," Orlom said to himself all too loudly, recalling Raven's instructions before he sent him up here. With the sun now breaking the clouds, dipping dangerously toward the western horizon, now was the time to recharge the rifle before sundown. He said to only drain the pistol to seventy percent, and to stop shooting come nightfall.

"Did you say something?" Torg asked him, still standing at his side upon Zar Crest.

"Just Boss's instructions, Coach," Orlom said, setting the rifle's solar conductor toward the sun while drawing his pistol, raising the scope from its internal workings, taking aim before firing away.

"Good work, lad," Torg affectionately ruffled his head as if he were his son, which Orlom gave him a toothy grin between shots.

Corry smiled at the gesture, wondering how the two of them became such fast friends. Of course, Orlom didn't really give Torg a choice in the matter, latching on to the master of arms upon his arrival. With Terin having joined Raven atop the tower, she took this moment to step away, deciding to check in on the wounded as Dresila completed the recharging of the regenerator some time ago. She hoped the matron could heal most of the mortal wounds before sunrise, the fate of many resting on just how much power that wonderful device could muster.

Corry took one last look beyond the palace walls, where lie strewn thousands of enemy dead and dying, their mournful cries building into a ghastly chorus, carrying upon the wind. She steeled her heart to their suffering, knowing the invaders deserved far worse. Despite their losses, they still outnumbered her brave defenders many times over, but for now, she felt confident in their position.

* * *

Corry was greeted with the anguished groans of wounded men crowding the corridors outside the great hall, a few sitting along the walls, and others laying down. Most were glassy eyed, staring vacantly at nothing, each moment passing painfully slow as they awaited treatment. The matrons would move along the crowded corridors, picking out which ones required immediate treatment, moving them into the great hall to the front of the line. They patched up countless others, buying them time to treat later. A few noticed her approach, trying to stand or kneel respectfully before she ordered them to remain as they were, her guards relaying the order as she made her way along the corridor. She stopped upon seeing an upraised face staring at her as she passed, before turning to look down at the soldier. Corry knelt in front of him, noting his bloodstained face and mail, nursing a broken leg, his left knee bent at an unnatural angle, the joint swollen and the skin discolored along the length of the limb.

"Princess," he said weakly, pain coursing his body without respite, though he was growing accustomed to it after suffering for so long.

"Your leg looks very painful," she kindly said, touching a hand to his armored shoulder. She noticed the greave and sandaled boot missing on the injured leg, likely the work of his friends that brought him here.

"Others are far worse, Your Highness. I…" he winced, his slight movement sending tendrils of pain shooting up his leg.

"Though I yearn to show you politeness and inquire of how you came to be in this state, your speaking shall cause you undo pain. Rest easy, my brave warrior. The matrons will treat you as soon as they are able," she gave him a comforting smile before kissing his forehead and standing up, finding the others sitting nearby looking at her with love and admiration. Every soldier at Corell proudly served her, honored to fight for and beside her. She had proven herself a warrior by her fell deeds and determined leadership. Word spread throughout the realm of her defiance of Morac during their parlay, and her harsh rebuke to the upstart Lord. They also knew how she journeyed to find Terin, rescuing their champion. Here she was, visiting the wounded, her own armor and tunic stained with gore, with her sword tainted with the blood of the gargoyles she slew.

She gave the men a few words of encouragement before moving on to the great hall, where the scene was even more horrifying. Men and Jenaii lay strewn across the chamber, with blood, gore and excrement spilt upon the floor. One could hardly take a step without soling their sandals. Despite the apparent chaos, the wounded were arranged in some order by the coldly efficient matrons. Dresila managed to heal thirty men after recharging the regenerator, working on number thirty one when Corry approached.

"Keep working, Matron Dresila. Never mind my presence," Corry said, stepping to her side as the Matron looked up.

"You are always welcome in our presence, Your Highness," she said, kneeling beside her patient with the regenerator resting upon his chest, a severe puncture driven through his right breast. He would have been treated much earlier, but was not brought to them until the device was drained during their first period of treatment. So it was with many of the wounded. Many of the injured were difficult to move, or expired while doing so. Others were injured at the base of the palace or along the outermost battlements, taking much longer to gather and move. Nor did they have the luxury of moving the device to the wounded, as many others would perish while they were moving about.

Corry watched as the soldier was healed, the man's color slightly returning to his face, though he would need a few days to recover his blood loss. He thanked Dresila profusely, and Corry as well before rising to his feet and being led away by another matron. Corry remained for a short while as Dresila continued with number thirty two, visiting with the men waiting their turn. She made certain to pay them her respects, especially Lucas, who was far down the list, with nearly twenty men in front of him. He was easy to spot in the crowd with his distinct blue tunic and Ular as his companion.

"How fares my brave friend?" Corry greeted, looking down as he sat on the floor, nursing his cauterized stump of a left arm, with Ular standing beside him.

"As a royal elite sworn to your service, Your Highness, it is but a minor inconvenience. As an honest man, it hurts like the blazes," Lucas managed to say in good humor.

"It was very brave what you did, Lucas. I shall be forever grateful. Not only for that, but for everything you have done. My journey to Bansoch would have been unbearable without your good company," she said with deep admiration.

"It was my honor, Highness," he smiled at that. He would follow her to the ends of the world if she asked. She was a good ruler, fair and brave, and as worthy as any regent to ever sit the Torry throne.

"Thank you for watching over him, Ular. You were very brave up there as well. You a worthy champion of your people, and I am deeply honored that you are fighting beside us," she touched a hand to his shoulder.

"It is I who is honored to be fighting beside you, Princess Corry. We have shed blood together at Bansoch, Tro, Flen, and now here. My people consider those who shed enemy blood together as brothers and sisters. In this, you have been my sister since Bansoch, and even more so now," he said with his watery voice. She knew these bonds extended to the others in their company as well, especially Lucas.

"How fares things out there? We have heard rumors about Raven. Are they true?" Lucas dared ask.

"If the rumors are of Raven killing the enemy in great numbers, and causing panic in their legions, then yes, they are true," she said loud enough to cause a chorus of cheers among the many men in the hall listening in on their conversation.

"It is true, then?" Another soldier asked, overcome with joy despite his mangled right arm, wrapped with blood-stained rags, and dangling uselessly at his side.

"Very much so," Corry affirmed. There she stood, in the middle of the great hall, surrounded by the bravest men in the world. She thought of her father at that moment, recalling how he loved to march beside his men, enjoying their company. She loved her men very much, and couldn't be prouder of them.

Hearty cheers rang through the hall, filling her with hope, pride, but most especially... love.

* * *

"Can I ask why we are still up here?" Cronus asked. It was well past sundown, with the star lit sky peaking through the overcast in uneven patches. Raven's gun fell silent for some time now, and yet he insisted on remaining here at his self-assigned post.

"You have someplace else to be?" Raven quipped, staring through the scope of his pistol, scanning 360 degrees as if waiting for something.

"Other than seeing my very expectant wife, no, I have nowhere else to be. What are you waiting for, anyway?"

"Just waiting for all the rats to climb out of their holes," Raven said, watching as the enemy began to emerge from their trenches, making a hasty retreat to their new perimeter where the others already began constructing siege trenches. Raven wondered where they got the spades to do the shoveling, since most of their equipment rested near or within the first siege trench.

"Rats?" Terin made a face, standing at his other shoulder, keeping a constant watch for any sign of Thorton.

"Invasive rodents about this big, spread disease and reproduce in great numbers," Cronus explained, having asked the same question during their trek across northern Arax.

"Good answer," Raven said, rather impressed with his memory.

"These rats you are referring are those still in the trenches," Terin correctly guessed.

"Yep. I'm just waiting for them to fully empty out of them, which looks about now," Raven holstered his pistol, picking up his mostly charged rifle.

ZIP!

His first blast brained a Benotrist commander of some rank north of the palace. He dropped amid scores of his fellows, the blast send-

389

ing them in panic. That's all it took for thousands of Benotrists and gargoyles to break into a full run away from the palace toward the new siege line in the distance. The crescent moon poorly illuminated the battlefield, causing many to trip in the dark, or crash into each other. Some stopped at the food provisioning sites, grabbing whatever they could before continuing on.

ZIP! ZIP! ZIP!

His next blasts found Benotrist wagon drivers drawing from the east, hoping the dark would mask their approach. They made use of the main thoroughfare connecting Corell to Notsu, most them held up beyond the horizon by Raven's laser fire until braving the road at night. Raven dropped them in quick order, despoiling any notion of resupply by that route, though this violated his six-thousand-foot rule. He just hoped they wouldn't figure that out. He went back to strafing the retreating enemy, taking guilty pleasure in dropping the men running alongside Morac and Dethine, trying to pick out elite warriors to target.

ZIP!

Raven's next blast found a Benotrist Elite through the back, identifying him by the sigil emblazoned upon his cape, a sword and whip dividing the sun and moon. If Morac had any friends in his army, it would be among the elite, and the way Raven figured it, Morac shouldn't have any friends. By now, Orlom had started firing, targeting the gargoyles along the eastern perimeter, thinning their ranks as they withdrew.

"I don't think Ben will show up before tomorrow, so if you want to see your wife, this would be a good time, Cronus," Raven said between blasts.

"What about you?" Cronus asked.

"I'm working late tonight, as you can see."

"I shall stay with him," Terin said, drawing his sword to have it ready if needed, the weak moonlight shrouding its now murky blade in otherworldly light.

"Go on, Cronus, me and the boy hero here can handle this. Give that wife of yours a kiss for all of us, you lucky dog," Raven waved him on.

"Dog?" Terin made a face.

"Small animal, about this big, barks a lot," Cronus said, holding his hands shoulders' width apart.

"Barks?" Terin asked.

"Never mind," Cronus used the Earthers' famous line, before stepping away, disappearing down the stairwell.

Raven continued his deadly fire, moving apace through the enemy ranks, unable to miss in the retreating crowds. Terin looked on, trying to follow what was happening in the dark, but noticing that he stopped shooting at a specific distance.

"I know you can shoot farther," he inquired.

"Yeah, but apparently they don't realize that."

"But why not continue shooting at them?"

"Because if they stop there, they are too far away to attack the castle, but close enough to keep an eye on," Raven explained, dropping several gargoyles to the south, spreading his deadly volleys all around the perimeter. He fired into the 10th Legion, retreating to the west, before targeting the north again, finding Morac standing mid distance between the forward trenches and the new perimeter, looking in his direction with his sword at the ready, as if to challenge him, while his men ran past him.

"What a jerk," Raven shook his head, targeting those beyond him.

∗ ∗ ∗

Morac stood unmoved, staring back at Corell with sword drawn, in defiance of what stood against him. He was not one to cower before such ruin. He swore to all that was true, he would see the Earthers dead. He cursed them, hoping to draw their fire so his men might witness his power in deflecting their weapon, giving them courage to soldier on. His army was on the precipice, and might break apart if pressed. With half of his soldiers huddled in their trenches for half the day without food or water was bad enough. Suffering more losses on their withdrawal was even worse. And so, he stood, drawing no interest from the Earthers. They ignored him, leaving him standing alone like a fool. He cursed and ranted, shouting to the heavens the injustice of it all, venting his fury before succumbing to what he must do.

He spotted the outline of his pavilion, finding his way to it in the dim light. He was surprised to find two of his girls still huddling within, his Corry and one of his golden collars. He grabbed as much of his things as he could manage, filling their arms as well, ordering them to follow him. He would later discover that three had fled to the new perimeter, and three others were missing. The last thing he grabbed on his way out the entrance was his helm with the ape skull affixed to it.

Stepping without, the girls cringed as laser fire alit the sky, streaming in all directions from atop the palace. Morac hurried them north across the open fields to where the army was waiting, though he could see little of them in the dark. Flashes of laser swept overhead, and to their east and west, striking down his soldiers one at a time, their mournful cries haunting the battlefield.

* * *

Cronus entered his bedchamber bloodied and bruised, his tunic soaked in grime and blood. His dented mail, and greaves weighed upon him like stones fixed to a swimmer's limbs. He stripped his armor, setting it quietly to the floor before staggering to their bed, where Leanna was fast asleep. He sat upon the bed, gently touching a hand to her shoulder, causing her to stir. She wiped the sleep from her eyes as they adjusted to the dim candlelight.

"Oh, Cronus. You look so very tired," she greeted him, pressing her warm palm to his cheek.

He had checked on her earlier, to reassure her that he had survived the battle, which Galen had already told her, for which he was grateful. Now, he could retire for the night, and share these precious moments with his love. He ran his hand over her swollen belly, knowing it would be soon. Most women did not suffer as she did at this stage, but she could barely take a step without labored breath. She felt helpless, and hated herself for it, voicing that with him.

"If that is the sacrifice you must take for our child, then I do not begrudge you for it. I am thankful that you are here and not seeing what has happened out there," he smiled, gently moving the hair from her face, smoothing it behind her ear. He was so very grateful for the love they shared, which contrasted with the horrors he witnessed this day. He thought of the thousands of dead and dying upon the battlements above, many of them young boys who would never sire children of their own, or partake in all the blessings that life offered. He spotted hundreds that fit that description all along the castle walls, their bodies shredded and broken by enemy swords and spears. The corpses of older men were just as common and tragic, each a father, brother or husband who would never hold their children, or kiss their wives upon their return. Their story ended upon the battlements of Corell, and it fell to their kin to honor their memory and sacrifice.

With that in mind, he lay down beside her, exhausted and spent, holding tightly to her as they fell asleep in each other's arms.

* * *

Terin stood vigilantly beside him as Raven struck down the enemy in every direction. To the west he dropped two Benotrist soldiers making their way across the open fields separating the forward trenches and the new perimeter. To the southeast he blasted three gargoyles rummaging through an overturned supply cart. To the east he brained a gargoyle unit commander just short of the outer perimeter. Of course, the enemy didn't know where the outer perimeter began or ended. They were merely herded there by Raven's laser, with him shooting at them up to six thousand feet. It was at points beyond that, that they began to reorganize themselves conveniently where many of their outer encampments lay. Everything short of that was his self-ascribed kill zone. He had one rule, if it moves within that zone, it dies. And, so it went... ALL NIGHT LONG.

* * *

Sunrise.

As morning broke upon the east face of Corell, Raven lowered his rifle, its power nearly drained. The morning sun shone upon the battlefield like a curtain drawing back the night, revealing more than three thousand gargoyles and Benotrists littering the grounds surrounding the palace. Their deaths joined with those Raven and Orlom slaughtered the previous day, sending panic through Morac's disordered ranks. Raven began recharging his rifle, while looking through the scope of his pistol, scanning Morac's new perimeter. He shook his head with their stupidity of setting their new siege line well within his sites, but that was the point of not shooting beyond the imaginary line he placed around the castle. The hardest part was instructing Orlom to respect these self-imposed restrictions, and to his surprise, the young gorilla did as he was asked.

Thank goodness for small miracles, he thought as Orlom's gun went silent as soon as his did, the ape following his key.

Terin stood quietly beside him, having stood watch all night. He hadn't said much in the last hour or so, looking about to fall over from exhaustion. Raven was thankful for his help, the two of them making an unbeatable pair under these conditions. From this vantage point, Raven could target any enemy forces for miles around, and they couldn't touch him. The only threat was Ben, and Terin negated that if his old friend decided to show up unexpectedly. The only hope Morac had for victory was to order an all out assault, but his gargoyles ranks were growing thin, and their ramp rested well within the KILL ZONE. Without it, they would have to assail the walls the old fashion way, exhausting themselves just to reach the outermost battlements. With how few were left, he doubted they would make much progress before they were all slain or driven off. Any magantors left to them would also be easy kills for his laser. That left their last option, which was sending the Benotrists across the open fields to assail the palace afoot, breach the main gate, and fight their way through the lone tunnel to reach the palace interior. Not to mention they would be under constant fire from Orlom and Raven throughout the entire trek. And even if they breached the tunnel,

Terin could blunt their advance in those narrow confines. Their only advantage was that they had two swords of light to Terin's one, but by the time they fought to get in that position, half their army would be dead or dying. He just hoped they were smart enough to realize that, because he didn't want to chance Terin's life with that remote possibility. Either way, it was time to get some rest, but he had to wait for his rifle to charge.

"Alright, junior, time for you to get some shut eye. I'll be right behind you once I charge this," Raven nudged Terin to the stairwell.

"What of Thorton?" Terin asked tiredly. He hadn't felt this exhausted since he was slaving away in Darna's keep.

"If he was close by, he'd have already showed himself by now. That means he is far away and won't arrive today or tomorrow, or maybe longer. Either way, we need to get some sleep. All you have to do is walk down those stairs without falling asleep and breaking your neck. Your girlfriend would never forgive me if you did."

Girlfriend? Terin was too tired to smile at his crude reference of his and Corry's relationship.

"Very well, uncle," Terin managed to say, causing Raven to laugh before stepping away.

* * *

Torg stood upon Zar Crest with General Mastorn, the commander of 3rd Army, and Cors Balka, the newly named commander of the Corell garrison, along with Ev Yaro, the acting General of the 1st Jenaii Battlegroup. General El Tuvo was still recovering from his wounds, his severed wings still not healed, forcing him to recuperate in his quarters. Matron Dresila assured Torg that the ailing General would be healed before the day was out, after all those with mortal wounds were healed.

The commanders examined their surroundings, fully assessing their situation. With the enemy now encamped far afield, Commander Balka began sending men outside the walls to gather the dead and set them ablaze, or bury them in their trenches. Others went to search the abandoned encampments, killing stragglers, or taking prisoners for questioning, as well as equipment they could make use off. Several dracks were recovered, along with their munitions, particularly those in the best condition for repair. If they could be repaired, they would be placed upon the outer battlements. They discovered many of the enemy wounded left behind just beyond the forward trenches. Torg ordered several taken prisoner for questioning, with the rest put out of their misery. They discovered a Benotrist magantor rider among the wounded, pinned beneath his dead mount with a broken left leg, clad in his distinct steel armor and gold tunic. General Valen would be certain to oversee his interrogation. Commander Balka sent men to scour Morac's pavilion, retrieving everything he left behind. Most interesting was the discovery of three scantily clad slave girls found hiding in an over turned wagon just east of the pavilion. They were brought before Princess Corry for questioning.

The men sent to clear the dead remained outside the palace walls for much of the day, under the watchful gaze of Morac's legions, who remained in place, fearful of Raven's rifle. Both sides took advantage of the respite, reorganizing themselves for the next stage of the siege. Morac's task was made much harder due to the lengthening of his siege lines, with the enlargement of Corell's encirclement. He struggled mightily reestablishing communication with his legion commanders spread out as they were. His legions also suffered from the decimation of their command structures, with so many telnic and unit commanders slain by Raven and Orlom. Fortunately, all of his legion generals survived, and were accounting well of themselves reordering their ranks. It would take several days to adequately establish his new perimeter and reassess his strategic position.

Torg's task was made far easier than Morac's, with his interior lines of communication compact and easily reordered as needed. Despite their losses along the north wall, and with the Jenaii, the defenders were well entrenched at Corell, and would not be easily dislodged. At no point during the first siege was Corell so strongly held.

* * *

Corry received the freed slave girls in a secluded chamber, not wishing to subject them to the audience of the throne room. The girls were thoroughly searched before being presented to her, and she was well guarded by several members of the royal elite, including Lucas, whose left arm was finally restored. She was joined by Aldo, the chief scribe and apprentice of the Chief Minister, who was also tasked with reviewing the many parchments recovered from Morac's pavilion. The slave girls were surprisingly calm considering what they had endured. She sympathetically regarded the three of them, understanding much of what they endured by the testimony of the previous three who stood before her. Did Morac's slaves always escape in threes, she wondered?

"Welcome, ladies. I am Princess Corry, acting regent of Torry North. I am told you were captive to Morac, and have since escaped. Might I have your names, and who speaks for you?" She began, her gaze fixed to the one wearing the silver collar, understanding its significance.

"I am Velesa, formally of house Betaras, youngest daughter to Havin Betaras of Bacel, Your Highness," the dark-haired beauty bowed deeply, her eyes trained to the floor.

"I know that name," Corry said, ordering Velesa to lift her chin.

"You have heard the name Betaras? Do any of my kin live?" Velesa asked, daring to hope.

"Perhaps," Corry said, snapping her fingers as Aldo produced a scrolled parchment, bearing hundreds of names of refugees given sanctuary in Torry North, each subdivided by place of origin. The list for Bacel was unsurprising brief compared to Notsu and points nearer Corell.

"Do you know Luven Betaras, My Lady?" Aldo asked, finding the only surname to match her own.

"He lives?" Velesa's voice broke with emotion.

"He is kin of yours, My Lady?" Aldo asked.

"Yes, my brother," she nodded, affirming it so.

"He arrived at Torry north before Kregmarin, accompanying a large caravan of your father's estate. He was given sanctuary at Besos, and later moved to Central City. If he is who you claim he is, he should be there waiting for you," Aldo explained. Most of the refugees from Notsu and Bacel were moved to Central City, along with the contingent of Notsuan soldiers loyal to Torry North.

Velesa nearly wept for joy. After all she endured, she could never have dreamed anyone she loved still lived.

"Did you know Geneve Jordana of Bacel?" Corry asked, naming one of the previous slave girls that escaped Morac.

"Yes. I knew her in passing, but came to know her very well. She was a fellow… slave in Morac's tent. He claimed she died during our retreat to Notsu," Velesa sighed sadly.

"That was a lie. She lives, and escaped him along with two other of your fellow captives," Corry countered, pleased the girl didn't speak falsely. If she didn't know Geneve was captured, then Velesa was not who she claimed to be.

"She lives?" Velesa asked happily, overcome with such good tidings.

"She does, along with Keya and Mia," Corry said kindly, setting them all at ease.

The other girls then introduced themselves as Helana Fabis of Gotto and Daynaria Lutis of Cestarina, a small city may leagues south of Notsu. Corry asked how they came into Morac's keeping, and how many others were still captive. They went on to explain all that transpired since Notsu, and the many men of renown that treated with their former master throughout the winter at the beleaguered city, including Thorton. This revelation caused the obvious reaction from Corry, Lucas and the others.

"When was this?" Corry asked harsher than she intended, nearly causing the frightened girls to jump.

"It was long before we departed Notsu, Your Highness. We do not know how many days for certain, or in which direction the Earther fled," Velesa quickly said.

"Did you hear Morac or any of his supplicants speak of the Earther and his whereabouts?" Corry pushed.

"I believe he is at Nisin, or someplace near there, Your Highness. We have heard them speak of it in passing at times, sending and receiving missives on his activities there," Helana further explained.

"Lucas, bring Raven here. He should hear of this," Corry ordered.

Lucas was out the door immediately. Though Raven was fast asleep, he needed to hear of this.

"You shall tell us everything you know about the Earther Thorton," Corry said.

* * *

"What do you think?" Torg asked of Raven as they overlooked the full map of Arax unfurled across the table, joined by Commander Balka, Corry, generals Mastorn and Valen along with Ev Yaro. They just finished questioning Morac's escaped slave girls at length, placing Thorton as far away as Nisin. They gathered in the council chamber immediately after, trying to determine how many days they had before Thorton COULD arrive. Chief Minister Monsh and his scribes were currently reviewing the many parchments they retrieved from Morac's pavilion, the potential information taking priority over attending this council of war. He was to apprise Corry of anything of interest.

"Your guess is as good as mine. It should take anywhere from five to seven days to reach Nisin by magantor, perhaps longer. If Morac sent one as early as yesterday, that would be ten days minimum for a roundtrip. That assumes Thorton is there and not in the field chasing rebels," Raven surmised.

"Five days would be a very generous estimate. I would estimate nine to ten days," General Valen said.

"That is better still. That would guarantee that Thorton shall not arrive for twenty days at the earliest," General Mastorn reasoned.

"That's only if the girls are telling the truth. How can we be sure of anything they said? I doubt Tyro assigned Ben cleanup duty in his eastern empire while the fate of the war is happening here," Raven snorted, not liking this at all.

"From what I heard, the ladies said Morac was displeased with the attack on the *Stenox*, claiming Hossen Grell did so of his own volition. The true target of the broken rifle was the council forum of Tro. That means it is very likely Thorton did not know they used his gift to attack the *Stenox*," Corry said, her analysis giving Raven pause.

She was not one to dismiss Ben's actions, but needed to base their decisions on what logic determined to be true. If Ben intended to attack the *Stenox*, he would not be away in the north attending other objectives. He would be close by to make certain they were finished. This was coupled with the tidings of Kato's demise, where Ben returned his body to Lorn, and was reported to have regretted what transpired between them. If he was truly regretful, then she doubted he would attack the *Stenox* so brazenly. Logic therefore determined that he was ignorant of Hossen Grell's intentions, and that would explain why he is elsewhere. She could see Raven coming to that same conclusion, though his stubborn nature was slow in doing so.

"If Ben is that far off, which I'm not yet convinced of, then we have a decision to make," Raven scrubbed his chin with his left hand, looking intensely at the map.

"And that is?" Commander Balka asked.

"I've held my fire at six thousand feet, letting those idiots out there think that's the limit of my Rifle's range. This keeps them camped far enough away to not be an immediate threat to the palace, but close enough to keep an eye on. If Ben isn't here, then this advantage will only hold until he does show up. That means we can keep things as they are for the next few days, waiting to see what Morac does. If he does nothing, then we can guess he is waiting for Ben to even the odds. If he pulls away his army, then he has other plans, either withdrawing to Notsu or advancing deeper into your territory. I can light him up where he sits right now at any time. If I do that, I can kill another four to six thousand soldiers before he withdraws beyond my range and your line of sight. When that happens, you won't know what he's up to. The only question is, is it worth doing? Four thousand dead soldiers in exchange for losing sight of the enemy. If it was me, I'd take the four thousand and let Morac decide what to do from there. But that's just me, I like eliminating problems, that's why I was always a fan of dodge ball when I was a kid."

"Dodge ball?" Ev Yaro asked, raising a sharp eye brow over his silver eye.

"It's a game where you divide up in teams and throw rubber

balls at each other. If you get hit by one, you're eliminated and your team goes on without you."

Raven's explanation was met by silence, the others looking at him with blank looks painting their faces.

"What is a ball?" Commander Balka asked the question they were all thinking.

"What's rubber?" General Mastorn added.

"Never mind," Raven snorted.

"Considering the question presented, I would choose to keep the enemy where we can see them. We hold a strong position, and only have to wait for Prince Lorn to lift the siege, where we can join our strength to his before attacking," General Mastorn reasoned, eying the southeastern approaches of Corell upon the map, mentally charting the likeliest route Lorn would take to relieve them.

"Lorn could bring all the strength of Torry South and Maconia and still be outnumbered by Morac's host. I say we take the four thousand heads Captain Raven can give us. Every one of the bastards we can kill the better," Commander Balka growled.

"Highness?" Torg looked to her, impressing upon the others that she was regent, and that the final decision was hers.

"I would hear from General Valen. What news have we of Prince Lorn?" She looked to Dar.

"No messengers have arrived for six days. That portends many possibilities, Highness," he answered. There could be weather issues, or Morac might have placed a large portion of his magantors to their southwest, intercepting their warbirds. He also had yet to thoroughly interrogate the Benotrist magantor rider they had taken captive. Whatever information he might divulge might alter their plans.

"What was Lorn's last position?" Raven asked, forgoing the prince's title, an oversight the others allowed as it was Raven doing so.

"His Highness was last reported at the port of Sawyer, though elements of his army have been spotted at all points along Lake Monata. Other elements have even followed the land route toward Central City. And most interesting of all, numerous units of the 2nd Macon Army have disembarked at the port of Tarelis, if the reports are to be believed," General Valen stated. The Port of Tarelis was the largest harbor in Torry North bordering Lake Monata, resting forty leagues east of the Arian Hills.

"Tarelis would be the likeliest route of travel. The port is large enough to offload many ships simultaneously," Torg stated.

"Aye, but that is still a long march to Corell, Master Vantel," General Mastorn countered.

"How old are the reports placing the Macon's at Tarelis?" Raven asked.

"Ten days. All the reports after were from Central City," Dar Valen answered.

"And what condition are the roads connecting Tarelis and Corell?" Raven asked.

"They are wide, well maintained and solidly constructed," Corry said. The great advantage for a kingdom as old as Torry North, was the many years afforded it to construct numerous roads connecting all points of the realm. The regions along the northeast shore of Lake Monata possessed abundant vineyards and fruit trees, which the improved roads hastened the delivery of their goods to various markets. These same roads allowed armies to move quickly within the realm.

"Should Lorn choose that direction, it would be the quickest route to reach us, but perhaps not the wisest," Ev Yaro stated flatly.

"How so, commander?" Corry asked.

"We are well fortified in our position, and shall not be easily dislodged. Should Prince Lorn approach with a great host, it would allow Morac to lift the siege and meet him south of here, where the ground is level. He could easily overwhelm his Highness, and then turn back to reestablish the siege. The logical path would be the longer, overland march to Central City, securing the capital and blunting any invasion through the Torry heartland. From there he could join his strength to General Fonis' 2nd Torry Army and march east for Besos. Once that was secure, he could advance in strength upon Morac, using the Zaronan Forest to shield his movements. By that point, Morac's supply trains would be running thin without the bountiful yields of the Torry Heartland available to plunder," the Jenaii commander explained with so little passion that Raven thought him dead. The Jenaii were so coldly logical that he was certain Zem would fit right in with them.

'What a lively bunch that would be,' Raven shook his head at that thought.

"Prince Lorn does not know the state of our defenses to risk that we might so long endure," General Mastorn pointed out.

"Perhaps, or perhaps not. It is Prince Lorn's duty to defeat the enemy and preserve his army in order to win the war. Our lives here are secondary to that duty. We must prepare accordingly. This siege may last a very long time, and our food stores will run thin by mid-summer, perhaps earlier," Torg said.

Such was the risk with a spring siege, with winter draining food stores, leaving any garrison vulnerable, no matter how prepared they were. Corry had done well coordinating the delivery of large amounts of food throughout the winter, acquiring bountiful yields from places as far away as Teso and Zulon, but even these measures would be taxed by the size of the force defending Corell. She doubted they could last to the beginning of summer before they began to starve, and revealed this to the council.

"If food is an issue, why not eat the gargoyles? You got plenty laying all over the palace. I don't know how long they have to be dressed before the meat is tainted, but its worth a try," Raven said, the others looking at him as if he grew a second head.

"I bet they taste like chicken," he added, with no one even thinking to ask what a chicken was.

Corry mentally shook her head, dismissing that awful idea before deciding to maintain the status quo for the next five days before reassessing their position.

* * *

The day continued with the defenders clearing the dead and treating the wounded. Raven and Orlom slept the better part of the day before resuming their watch on the enemy, taking up position in the Golden Tower, this time together. They would find a few targets within six thousand feet, usually gargoyles loitering forward of their new siege lines foraging for food from the dead. It was an obvious reminder for them to keep their distance. Raven had Orlom join him upon the tower's uppermost platform to keep a watchful eye on his young friend, knowing he was likely to become bored with so few targets throughout their shift. The last thing they needed was a bored Orlom, which always led to something bad. Raven constantly reminded Orlom to never hold the trigger for a continuous stream, or it would burn out the rifle's core, making it useless.

It was early evening when Raven was visited by General El Tuvo, his wings fully restored. The Jenaii General thanked Raven for saving his life, and for the Earthers' regenerator for restoring his life and wings. He spoke briefly and direct before stepping away, wasting few words as was the Jenaii nature. With Thorton not likely nearby, Raven had no need for Terin to stand watch over him for the next few days, though his young friend would visit with him several times each day, along with Cronus, Ular and the other gorillas. The following days continued with the clearing of the dead, and sporadic laser fire to any gargoyles straying within Raven's imaginary perimeter.

Corry busied herself with the logistical situation of the palace, keeping a vigilant eye upon every provision stored within Corell. She spent much effort in preparing Corell for a second siege as soon as the first one was lifted. Every commander and soldier in the castle were well aware of this grand accomplishment, which further elevated her in their eyes. Torg marveled at her transformation from a dutiful princess to a warrior regent, leading the realm through its most perilous time. Corry ordered rations reduced to seventy percent, extending their projections of viability deeper into summer. She was disappointed that her time with Terin was limited, with his presence required elsewhere in the coming days, especially guarding Raven and Orlom. Such was their current situation, with the danger of Thorton's arrival ever looming.

Corry was kept apprised of all discoveries concerning the parchments from Morac's pavilion that Chief Minister Monsh and his scribes were reviewing. The Benotrist Lord was careless in the securing of vital missives sent to and from Benotrist holdfasts throughout the eastern empire, as well as correspondence from the emperor. Of most significance was a detailed listing of key provisioning and transport sights from Nisin Castle to Notsu, and from Notsu to Corell. She ordered the documents to be given to General Valen, where he could determine if a raid upon any of the sites was feasible. Also of interest was the concentration of Benotrist magantors southwest of Corell, which explained the lack of returning scouts and messengers from that direction.

Corry also learned of Morac's obsession with her, with Velesa revealing that he had taken a golden-haired slave girl that shared her name. The very thought of it sickened her, yet drove her determination to see him brought low. He would be surprised that she could be equally inventive in planning his humiliation and ruin. A late evening three days after the battle brought her to the battlements of the inner palace, staring to the north, where the enemy cookfires dotted the horizon. Morac had reestablished his siege lines, though they were markedly thinner due to his casualties and the larger encirclement pushing them farther afield.

"I wonder what they will do?" Terin asked, stepping to her side, his voice drawing her attention from the enemy encampments in the distance.

"Nothing good, but I am happy to let them sit in place and rot. You should be abed," she lightly admonished.

"Duty calls upon me to stand watch over Raven and my princess. Since Raven appears to be secure up there, my priority falls solely with you," Terin smiled, pointing to the Tower of Cot where Raven and Orlom were perched this night. Raven changed his location every day, affording himself a variety of views and to keep the enemy guessing where he was perched. Of the citadels of Corell, only the Towers of Celenia and Cot rested outside the inner keep, each spiraling impressively above the others between the inner palace and the northern inner battlements, with the opening to the courtyard set between them.

"I see, and how fares our insufferable Captain Raven? I have seen so little of him as late."

"Other than his usual complaints concerning the toiletries, food and sleeping arrangements, he seems content with his current situation," Terin said, leaving out Raven's many invectives, foul language and crude jokes.

"It is a cruel twist of fate that we are so indebted to a man like him. The spirits of all the kings to have ruled the Torry Realms would be aghast with our situation," she shook her head.

"I do not think they would find him in disfavor. They would be glad for his help, as we are."

"Of course they would find him favorable, but they would still be aghast. I have little doubt that Raven would endear himself to every one of them with his blunt speech and ridiculous antics. Even I have come to love the big oaf, though he tests me to no end."

"He is far worse with Tosha, I assure you," Terin laughed.

"Indeed. I will be certain to not repeat my cousin's mistake when choosing my mate," she playfully poked him in the arm.

"In all honesty, Tosha has earned his treatment."

"Perhaps, and what of your intended, what treatment has she earned from you, Terin Caleph?" She asked bemusedly.

"That is where Raven and I are different. I am deeply indebted to my intended, for she sailed around the world to rescue me from torment and slavery. I am hopelessly hers in all things," he smiled, leaning closer, staring intently into her blue eyes.

"Good, I would have it no other way," she nudged him playfully.

* * *

The following morn.

A lone Benotrist warrior emerged from the siege lines north of Corell, riding a gray ocran and bearing a blue flag lifting in the morning breeze. Raven watched his approach through the scope of his rifle, holding fire upon recognizing the truce symbol. The defenders crowding the battlements relayed the discovery to the rest of the garrison as the rider neared the palace, the gates drawing open upon his approach. A party of defenders emerged to receive him, blindfolding the emissary, and leading him into the castle.

* * *

Corry received Morac's emissary in the throne room, sitting her father's throne, the fellow wincing under her intense gaze as his blindfold was lifted. He was clad in the vestment of a Benotrist elite, wearing dark mail over a black tunic, with the infamous sigil emblazoned upon his chest, a sword and whip dividing the sun and moon. He was solidly built with a mop of dark hair framing his square jaw. He was escorted to the base of the dais where he took a knee with Lucas and several other Torry elite surrounding him.

"Speak!" Corry ordered, the members of the court flinching before her harsh tone.

"Your Highness, Lord Morac requests an audience before the walls of Corell, mid distance between our lines, with two as escort as tradition holds," the Messenger stated, his voice higher than intended, unnerved before Corry's intense gaze.

"For what purpose? What leverage does your master hold to draw me hither? I stand unmoved, behind thick walls, fully stocked stores and a strong garrison. What does he boast other than numbers, numbers blunted by disorder, starvation and huddled in miserable trenches for fear of being struck down by our Earth friend's laser? And why ask to meet? Does he have another trophy he wishes to present to me? Is it another severed head of someone I love, my brother perhaps, or cousin? I think not. Inform LORD Morac that he holds no leverage to call me from my keep," she coolly stated.

"Lord Morac in his infinite wisdom respects your stalwart position, Your Highness, and desires only to present terms favorable to both your mighty realms. As a token of good faith, he offers the release of several captives you might find of interest, including a young lord whose kin sits among your ladies of court," the messenger offered, pausing long enough to leave the obvious question in the air.

"Spare me your theatrics and petty games, knave, and speak of whom you are referring!" She demanded.

"Of course, Your Highness. No offense was intended. I am…"

"Speak of it!" She cut off his drivel.

"One Jors Luron, once heir and now head of House Luron, as

his father Gais succumbed to wounds while engaged with our brave cavalry," the emissary said, his tight lips unable to conceal the smile in his eyes.

Corry refused to yield any emotion, internally venting her disappointment with this tiding. She recalled her dealing with the dispute between Gais Luron and Governor Taulus in this very chamber, negotiating the joining of their two houses with the marriage of their heirs and daughters. Both daughters were currently among her ladies of court, Carisa Luron, and Venna Taulus. She would spare them further suffering if she was able, and that required treating with the contemptable Morac.

"How many captives in total? Be specific!" She sternly ordered.

"Lord Morac offers seven. Three are nobles in high standing, the rest lesser gentry that may draw your interest."

"They will be released PRIOR to our meeting. Return to your master and inform him we shall meet." She dismissed him, her guards escorting him out as Torg stepped to her side from the shadows of the dais.

"What think you?" She asked, her eyes following the retch's exit before shifting to his.

"He obviously has something to say. If he plans to negotiate a peace, he stands in a poor position to do so."

"That is my sentiment as well," she sighed.

"Who shall you take with you?" Torg asked.

"Last time I chose Terin and Cronus."

"Fine choices, but I sense you are leaning differently."

"Terin is needed should things go poorly, but Cronus shall remain here, considering Leanna's position," she said.

"Lucas then?" He asked, knowing her affinity for the Torry warrior.

"He would be my favored choice, but not the right one," she sighed, hating to admit who she was considering.

"The spirits have mercy," Torg laughed, rightly guessing her choice.

* * *

Corry sat astride her snowy white mount forward the main gate, waiting as the freed captives made their way south, where they were handed over to her soldiers some three hundred paces to her north. She watched as they made their slow trek toward the palace dressed in brown woolen tunics, their bare feet suffering the open ground. She did not know Jors Luron by face, calling upon his sister, the lady Venna Taulus, to stand beside her to confirm that he was among them, confirming it so as they drew nigh. The captives were all men ranging from eighteen years to sixty, with their hair disheveled and soil caking their exposed limbs as if they were toiling under duress, which their sunken eyes and the indentations of shackles upon their ankles and wrists strongly indicated.

"Oh, Jors!" Lady Venna shouted, rushing to his side as they stopped before the princess.

Corry looked on as the siblings embraced, satisfied that Morac upheld his price for their meet before riding forth to treat with him. She rode forth, head strong and proud, her steely gaze fixed north, where Morac awaited beneath a large blue flag lifting in the breeze, flanked by his two companions. As during their first meet, she was clad in silver mail, greaves and vambraces over a white tunic, her golden tresses trailing her silver helm as she rode forth, her own companions following in her wake.

"She doesn't look happy," Raven said, riding at Terin's side, trying to catch up with her as she rode apace.

"For good cause," Terin said, recalling her previous meeting with the Benotrist Lord at nearly the same place. He spoke of that meeting in detail with Raven, before they mounted their ocran, reminding him of Morac's cruel display of her father's head.

What did she expect from a jerk named Morac? Raven thought to himself. He didn't see Kriton joining the parlay this time either, noticing that both of Morac's companions were human as they drew close.

Morac awaited them before the abandoned siege works of his former forward trenches, a sorry reminder of his hasty retreat before the Earther's fell weapon, the identity of said Earther revealed as Raven's large form rode forth from Corell. Morac sat astride a pale ocran, adorned in polished black armor over gray tunic, his blood red cape draping his shoulders, with his helm lowered, his fiery gaze staring intently through the empty sockets of the ape skull affixed to it. If his grim façade intimidated the Princess, she showed it not, returning his intense stare with her own steely gaze, her intense blue eyes peering through the narrow slits of her helm. His mount stirred as she approached, shifting uneasily, unaccustomed to its new master. He lost count of the ocran he lost in his campaigns, his latest a victim to Raven's deadly fire as they were driven from their siege works. He spent the previous days reordering his legions, made difficult by his expanded lines of communication, and his tenuous supply trains. Many of his men went days without eating as they struggled reestablishing food distribution points. Morac spared a glance to his previous command pavilion, which was now toppled in a heap somewhere over his left shoulder, its contents pilfered by the thieving Torries. 'Twas another offense he would see them punished for, unless their princess saw reason, said princess drawing to a halt before him, flanked by the contemptible Earther and Torry Champion.

"Princess," Morac received her, lifting his helm, baring his face and faux smile.

"Morac," she curtly replied, giving him no more acknowledgement than that.

"Lord Morac, keeper of the golden sword, first among the emperor's elite…" Dethine began to rattle off his many appellations.

"Spare us your mindless drivel, Dethine. You needn't list his useless titles, each cheaply won or given. You are a pitiful sight, the champion of Nayboria reduced to Morac's lickspittle!" Corry cut him off, her eyes never leaving Morac's.

"Rudeness is unbecoming a girl of your high station, princess. Did your late mother never teach you manners?" Dethine asked smugly.

"Patience, my friend. Our dear princess is a spirited woman, a rare flower among the thorns," Morac interjected before she cut the poor Nayborian apart with her next barb. "When last we met, Princess, you were joined by the boy and Cronus Kenti, and I with Dethine and the mighty Kriton. Unfortunately, Kriton is presently occupied with other *DUTIES*. In his place I present General Vlesnivolk, commander of 8th Legion. As for your NEW companion, I have had the displeasure of his company before," Morac regarded Raven with a most sour look.

"Do not waste words with flippant introductions, Morac, Lord of bones and ash. Speak to your purpose for drawing me from my keep!" Corry snapped.

"Patience, Princess. I was merely acknowledging the presence of your newest acolyte, though in all my imaginings I would never have ascribed the brutish Captain Raven among your devoted followers. I wondered the past few days which of the Earthers flocked to your hopeless cause, though I should have known," Morac said, now regarding Raven with a false grin.

"Not hopeless anymore, sunshine. How do like sleeping in your trench? Not as comfortable as that big tent you were used to," Raven shot back, resting his hands on the pommel of his saddle, his ocran cooperating with its unfamiliar master.

"I sleep well, Earther. I plan many contingencies for each campaign, affording me other pavilions to draw upon should the need arise. Your interference is but a minor thing, a mere inconvenience that weighs little in the grander scale. Soon Corell shall fall, and you with it."

"If you're going to storm the castle, you have a funny way of showing it. When I look around, all I see are your dead soldiers," Raven spared a glance past Morac's shoulders to the corpses still littering the battlefield.

"There are other ways to take a castle beside bleeding my legions, which is why I called for this parlay," Morac smiled, returning his gaze to Corry, his hand resting upon the hilt of his sheathed blade, causing Terin to reach for his. Terin's ocran shifted forward, shielding Corry should things go awry.

"Guard yourself, boy, for we are under a flag of truce!" General Vlesnivolk warned.

"He is eager to renew our battle. 'Tis a pity your pet magantor will no longer meddle in my affairs. I am sure his carcass will help feed your garrison in the coming days," Morac taunted, believing his crippling blow to Wind Racer doomed the avian.

"When next our swords cross, you shall draw your last breath," Terin answered.

"Bold words for a boy whose sword has dimmed. Even in its full glory it could not attain mine, lest now, its luster dimmed and power broken. I look forward to adding it to my belt, twin blades for my fell hands," Morac smirked, drawing Corry's ire.

"Speak to your purpose or this parlay ends!"

"Patience, Princess. If you recall our last meet, I promised to consummate my victory upon your dead mother's bed with your father's head overlooking the affair. Since I no longer possess his severed crown, perhaps I shall pluck your virtue with your companions' heads overseeing our union," Morac smirked.

"Yeah? How 'bout I celebrate our victory by bending you over and shoving Terin's sword up your ass!" Raven growled.

"Mind your tongue, Earther!" Morac snarled.

"You mind yours!" Corry countered. "My patience has run thin with this farce. Speak to your purpose or we are done here."

"I offer a proposal, princess, one that is reasoned and fair, and can end your people's suffering," Morac gestured, his tone changing as quick as a shifting wind.

"A proposal?" She asked skeptically.

"Yes, a very generous offer from where I stand. It seems we find ourselves in an apparent stalemate, but it only APPEARS so. Despite the Earther's theatrics, your garrison is doomed. Yet, grinding your bones to dust, as I am wont to do, would bleed my legions heavily. I see no reason to do so, when other options lay before me."

"There is nothing we can agree to, this I assure you," she shook her head.

"Considering your position, you might wish to reconsider," he pushed.

"Our position is strong," she refuted.

"Is it? You may believe so if the only choice left to me was storming your walls, but I have many options before me, none of them leaning to your favor. You are strongly entrenched behind your thick walls and high towers, but Corell is as much a prison as it is a fortress, a prison that keeps you here while my legions can move elsewhere.

Should you prove unreasonable, I can leave a small portion of my vast host to keep you in place, freeing the larger share of my army to raze the Torry heartland. Envision it if you will, all the lands between Corell and Central City laid bare, your people slaughtered or enslaved, their farms and villages easy plunder for my rampaging legions. I can sweep across the land like a great wave cresting the shore, pressing to the very walls of your capital, and what are such shallow walls before gargoyle legions? Central City will fall, and Fonis' army with it. Perhaps it shall take time to accomplish this, or perhaps not. One can never gauge how motivated one's army might be plundering freely as they march. Of course, I shall allow you to receive the count-less messages sent by your people beseeching your help. In fact, I have many now," Morac nodded to General Vlesnivolk, who drew a bundle of parchments from his satchel, presenting them to Corry.

Corry scowled as the Benotrist General handed said parchments to Terin, who passed them on to her. She opened the first one, reading the desperate missive penned by a magistrate from the Torry village Canistar, pleading to her for aid. She opened a second, penned by the elder of Julota, calling upon General Fonis to protect their village. There were countless missives from Kadesha, Luturon, Delino, and Gulana, all villages bordering the approaches of Besos and parts west. Should she believe they were authentic? With Besos fallen, she had little reason to doubt their sincerity. The simple fact was that Torry North was open to invasion, their collective throats ripe for ripping. She stopped at the fourth parchment, tucking the rest away, not allowing her face to fall. She removed her helm, showing the strength of her countenance, lest Morac think he had riled her. She sat upon her mount, her golden tresses lifting in the midday breeze, meeting his sneer with a steely resolve.

"As you read, your people beg for your aid, aid you cannot give. Imagine if you will, my legions holding you here in place through spring and summer, while their comrades strip the land bare. Perhaps I lift the siege come autumn, and withdraw to Notsu. If you have not starved by then, you will surely not survive another winter with no crops to harvest. Fields cannot be planted when farmers are driven from their homes, or slain outright. I need only wait for the following spring, where I can simply walk across these same fields and enter Corell unopposed, with only starving corpses to oppose me. Of course, there is an alternative, if you are wise, and not swelled with pride. Are you wise, Corry?" Morac asked smugly, leaning forward in the saddle.

"Bold words for deeds you have not yet achieved," she challenged.

"Deeds that are as predictable as rain flowing down hill, Princess. The fate of your realm is sealed, unless…"

"Unless what?" She grew tired of his ramblings.

"You can choose peace, Princess. Peace between our great realms."

"Speak sense, fool. What peace can there ever be between us?"

"I can ensure the sovereignty and security of the Torry Kingdoms, and with this promise, I shall swear my sword arm to the protection of your realm," he declared sincerely.

"And what would we pay for such *Generosity?*" She shook her head dismissively.

"Torry North need only cede Corell and the lands east of here to a neutral kingdom, a buffer state, if you will, one between our two realms."

"What neutral kingdom would that be?" She asked, humoring his madness.

"A new kingdom which shall include Corell, Notsu, Tro and all lands between them. It shall stretch from the southern shores of Lake Veneba to the northern face of the Lone Hills. I shall be its king, and you, my dear Corry, shall be my queen. Corell shall be garrisoned by a joint Benotrist/Torry contingent. With our union, we can bring this war to its end. The emperor has several minor conditions, pertaining mostly with the surrender of your *Champion.* His presence is requested at Fera, where he shall swear oaths of loyalty to Emperor Tyro, and surrender his sword to his hand. The emperor also requires the surrender of his grandsons born of Princess Tosha, which the Earthers wrongfully absconded. As for the Jenaii, they are to withdraw to their ancestral lands, swearing to never return north of Lake Monata ever again. The Earthers shall restrict their presence to the Ape Empire, remaining there in perpetuity. These conditions are not negotiable, but they are fair. What say you, Highness? Shall you choose peace?" Morac offered.

"Your offer is bold, but hollow. Your words of peace are deceitful drivel, expecting me to give you freely what you cannot achieve by force of arms. If you want to plunder the Torry heartland, then do so. Do so, and bleed your legions. You shall lose a hundred men or gargoyles for every league between Besos and Central City, arriving before its ancient walls with half the strength you have left, and be well met by General Fonis and the might of the 2nd Torry Army. You would hardly be in a position of strength, your forces spread across the breadth Torry North. Go, march upon Central City, and we shall pluck your feathers until your wings are bare," she countered.

"You shun my offer of mercy?" He growled.

"I spit upon it! Hear my offer. Withdraw from this land with Raven cutting down your soldiers throughout your retreat, or stay and DIE. Those are the choices before you. But know this, Morac, son of Morca, Keeper of the golden blade, first among Tyro's elite, Lord of Notsu, Bane of Bacel, and slayer of King Lore..." she rattled of his many appellations, mocking his prideful boasts..."guard your loins well, for I shall have your manhood before this war is ended. They shall be bronzed and hung above the hearth in my bedchamber, where I shall look upon them every night until the end of my days and laugh!" She declared.

Morac's hand went to his hilt, his face contorted in rage.

"Don't try it!" Raven warned.

Morac turned his mount around and departed, his comrades following in his wake as Corry gave Raven a knowing look before turning about, kicking her heels, her mount galloping back to the castle gate.

Terin regarded Raven briefly as the Earther waited for Corry to pass beyond earshot.

"Sometimes she can be a complete bitch, but your girl's got balls," Raven smiled, shaking his head before following her back to the castle.

CHAPTER 21

Morac wasted little time revealing his intentions. By the next morn, the 10th Benotrist Legion withdrew from the siege, marching west before disappearing into the Zaronan forest, apparently marching for Besos. Torry captives were paraded before the Benotrist outer siege works, forced to labor in full view of the palace. Most were of peasant stock, taken in raids from the Torry countryside, suffering the lash and the inventive cruelties of their captors.

Corry learned from the captives Morac released before their parlay, that they were previously held at points north and east of Corell, laboring in the loading and unloading of wagons at different supply depots Morac established along his lines of communication. They told of the horrors they witnessed, including the slaying of the weakest of the captive males, as they had more prisoners than they could feed or had use for at the time. Some were put to work in quarries, shaping stone munitions for Benotrist trebuchets. They described the ill treatment of Torry women at the hands of the enemy, further fueling Corry's rage and determination to fight to her dying breath.

Morac gathered his remaining commanders in his new pavilion, internally scowling with its more austere furnishings and smaller size. Even his contingent of slave girls was reduced by three, with no sign of the missing girls' whereabouts. They were either slain during the chaos or escaped to Corell. If the later was true, he looked forward to recovering them, and punishing the Torry Princess for harboring them. As for the Earther, he already sent out messages calling upon Thorton to balance the scales, but that would take time, time he might not have, considering the state of things. His eyes fixed to the map of the realm unfurled across his table, taking keen interest to the lands south and west of Corell, where he ordered General Polis to concentrate his magantor forces, intercepting any warbirds trying to reach Corell.

"What is the latest?" Morac asked of said General, tapping his fore finger upon the map where his magantors were now positioned, guarding the southeast approaches of Corell.

"We have downed four magantors trying to approach Corell from points south, two here, one here, and the last... here," General Polis pointed out each location on the map, the last fifteen leagues southeast of the palace just a day before.

"What of your own patrols?" Morac asked.

"Our supply lines between here and Notsu appear sound. My scouts report no raids upon any of our caravans along that route in the past twelve days. Our cavalry have clashed with Torry cavalry at all points between here and Besos, though less so in previous days. I expect that to continue as our army advances from Besos into the Torry interior," Polis said in regards to the Benotrist 11th Legion advancing west from Besos as the 10th Legion arrives to relieve them, the captured Torry holdfast now operating as a major resupply point for all Benotrist and gargoyle forces in Torry North.

"What of Lake Monata?" General Vlesnivolk, commander of the 8th Benotrist Legion, asked, recalling the Jenaii approaching from that direction in breaking the last siege.

"We have encountered Jenaii magantors along this line," Polis ran his fingers in an arc between the headwaters of the Pelen and the Lone Hills.

"What of Tarelis?" Dethine asked, knowing the port the likeliest avenue of approach across the lake, with its impressive port and docking facilities.

"Our scouts have met heavy resistance far north of there, preventing us from seeing any activity within two hundred leagues of

Lake Monata," Polis said, that last information casting a pall over the tent.

"We are blind to what is transpiring there?" Vlesnivolk growled, his outburst uncharacteristic for the usually stoic commander.

"Calm yourself, general. They could muster the collective strength of southern Arax and we would still outnumber them. It bears watching, but that is all. This campaign will be decided to our west, from here to there!" Morac swept his hand across the map from Besos to Central City. "It is there where the Torries shall meet their end, if not in battle, then next winter, starving in their hovels. Let the battle of Torry North begin."

Such was Morac's plan until a late arriving magantor scout brought tidings that altered his strategy.

* * *

Forty leagues southwest of Besos.

Benotrist cavalry swept through the small village, slaying everyone in sight. A few held their ground, brandishing pikes or whatever they could grab a hold of, the attack taking them by surprise. Some attempted to escape, fleeing afoot toward a forest skirting a ridgeline to their south, but were easily overtaken in the open fields surrounding the settlement. Benotrist riders broke between the wooden homes, chasing down the fleeing Torries, their gargoyle companions springing from their saddles, dropping upon those evading their mounts.

Kriton rode through the center of the village, skewering a villager brandishing an axe, releasing his spear, driving the man to his back. He drew his sword, riding apace through the narrow dirt trail separating the wooden structures to either side, taking another across the back as he turned to flee. He rode to the far end of the village into the clear, leading a flax of riders, before circling about. He watched the last stragglers overtaken at the forest edge, cut down in quick order before his men returned to the village, their gargoyle companions dismounting to search the buildings, slaying everyone found hiding therein.

Kriton ordered the village burnt, leaving the bodies where they fell. He favored placing the heads of his victims on spikes as a warning to others, but time was of an essence. He kept a wary eye to the heavens, watchful for Jenaii raiders to fall upon them. Thousands of the winged warriors had escaped the siege of Besos, plaguing their advance into the Torry heartland, slaying their cavalry, foragers and supply trains to great effect. They slew many Jenaii in turn, both sides bloodying each other. They finished their grizzly work and continued on, razing every farm and village in their path.

* * *

Corell.

Four days hence.

Cronus found his way to their bedchamber at the end of another long day, finding his beloved abed, sleeping quietly with Galen sitting upon a chair, watching over her. The minstrel placed a finger to his lips, warning Cronus to silence as he entered, having watched over her throughout much of the day. Galen gained his feet, patting his friend gently on the shoulder before stepping without. Cronus eased off his helm, setting it quietly aside, before stripping off his vambraces, greaves and mail, the last making enough noise to stir Leanna from her slumber. He winced as her right eye slightly opened.

"Cronus," her face blossomed fully, both eyes opening wide to receive him.

"Sorry," he shrugged, stripping his mail fully, setting it aside before kneeling at her bedside.

"Never apologize for coming to my arms, my love. I am always happy to see you. These days are terribly lonesome without you," she ran her hand through his hair, smoothing it behind his ear. She never grew weary of looking at him, his handsome face setting her astir. She looked forward to this every day, waiting for him to join her after attending his duties. She knew how fortunate they were, with nearly everyone else in the palace separated from those they loved.

"My days are equally lonesome. I spend every day surrounded by multitudes, and feel nothing but loneliness thinking about you," he closed his eyes, tilting his head, gently squeezing her fingers between his cheek and neck, savoring her warmth.

"You are never alone, not truly. Even when we were separated, first when you marched off to war and capture, and then when you were sent to Sawyer, and then Tro, you were always with me… in here," she said, touching a hand to her heart.

He could not argue that, with thoughts of her giving him solace and hope, even in the darkest pit of misery in the dungeons of Fera.

"Beyond all hope and reason, we have been reunited time and again, as if divine providence watched over us, over you," she added.

"Divine? Have you been speaking with Lorn?" He smiled, noting the Prince's zealous leanings when word of Yah was ever raised. If she had spoken with him, it would be truly a feat considering they had never met, and Lorn was far away.

"He is not the only adherent of Yah's providence, my love. Terin and Corry both follow him, especially Corry. After what happened at Bansoch, one could understand why. And yet, you have doubts," she smiled wanly, both admiring and annoyed by his stubbornness.

"I have always believed in the things I can see and hold. Yah seems more a grand idea, than truth, but I concede he might have merit, considering the things I have witnessed," he sighed, thinking of Terin and Lorn's many incredible feats in the face of all sense and rationality.

"And yet you doubt?"

"I do, but never mind me. You know I am insufferably stubborn and obtuse," he shrugged with good humor.

"You are not dull of wit, my love. You are clever and brave, and stubborn only in the defense of those you love," she said, caressing his cheek.

"Terin and Corry have won you over to Yah's cause, I see," he smiled. If he was resistant to her proselytizing, he showed it not. He might lack such leanings, but would listen to whatever was on her heart, for he loved her so.

"No. Corry and Terin speak freely of it, but have not moved me in this."

"Oh? So, you remain a skeptic as I am."

"No. It was Jonas that convinced me."

"Jonas?"

She nodded, affirming it so.

"When you departed for Sawyer, I feared for you, and rightly so considering what transpired there. I remember one night when I stood upon the battlements, gazing longingly to the west, wondering if you were safe in that far off land, that Jonas was standing near, gazing to the west as well. He was thinking of Terin, tortured by visions he would not speak of, which became prescient. It was then I confided my fears and worries, for which he listened. He said Yah would return you to me, keeping you safe on your journey. I thought he said this to waylay the fears of a silly girl, but he said it was not so, speaking aloud my thoughts, and assuring me it was no idle promise. He said you would travel to Sawyer, Yatin, Cagan and Fleace before returning to my arms. He said you would leave again for Tro, but would return with mighty friends," she sighed, recalling that strange, yet comforting conversation they shared that night.

"He said all that?" Cronus found it unsettling the power of foresight Jonas possessed.

"Yes, and strangely, I believed him. And after it came to pass, I knew all his words were true. It was then I recalled what he spoke of Yah, knowing it must be true as well."

"And what did he say of Yah?"

"That he was God, the only God, and we must dwell in his grace, and follow his will, and that if we did so, as a people, he would deliver upon his promise to King Kal, the promise to vanquish the gargoyles for all time, and receive his blessings for our place in this world."

"And, now you are his," Cronus sighed, gently caressing her cheek, reassuring her that he was not dismissive or threatened by her new found devotion.

"I am, but what of you, Cronus? Shall you follow him? Shall you acknowledge him?"

"Perhaps one day," he kissed her forehead, his words causing her eyes to moisten, but she girded herself, guarding her fears for the coming days. She wanted to be strong for him, but her body betrayed her. It took all her strength just to rise from her bed. She feared he might perish without falling under Yah's grace. Jonas did not speak of the afterlife with her, or Yah's promise in that regard, but her heart told her otherwise, knowing Yah's adherents would walk a different path in the hereafter than others, and she needed Cronus to share that walk with her. She feared what the morrow might bring, and desperately wanted to be close to him. He closed his eyes, pressing her hand to his cheek, kissing it gently.

They sat there for a time, savoring each other's presence, the simple intimacy of their slightest touch filling their hearts with overwhelming love.

"I would know my husband," she whispered, causing his eyes to slightly open.

"I… what of… the child…" Cronus stumbled over his words, causing her to smile.

"Our child is fine, Cronus. It has been too long, my love, and I fear much longer once the child is born. I think of you constantly, and want you within me."

Cronus paused, torn between desire and concern before she spoke again, melting his resistance.

"We do not know what tomorrow shall bring. We are at war, Cronus. Nothing is assured, only this moment," she said soothingly, drawing his lips to hers.

* * *

For many days he scanned Morac's perimeter, eying the Benotrist/Gargoyle forces through the scope of his rifle while perched atop the towers of Corell, this day finding him upon the Golden Tower. Raven could further devastate Morac's ranks, with his army well within his range. With the 10th Legion now removed to Besos, the likelihood of an attack upon Corell was greatly reduced. He debated throwing caution to the wind, and start firing away, guessing he and Orlom could slay four thousand before Morac's troops withdrew fully from view. Since the only reason not to was for them to keep an eye on Morac's host, it now seemed pointless. He discussed this with Torg, and they agreed that since only one legion was withdrawn to invade the Torry heartland, they should hold off any sudden actions. If another was removed, then they would give Raven a free hand. The fear that ran forward and backward through his mind with the status quo, was Thorton popping up anywhere along Morac's siege line and fixing Raven firmly in his sights.

As the morning progressed, Raven shifted his attention to the southwest. A shifting of several units cascaded into movements of telnic sized elements.

"Hungry?" A familiar voice echoed behind him.

"Shouldn't you be with Leanna?" Raven said, keeping the scope to his eye.

"She is resting for now," Cronus said.

"Hasn't she been resting all night?" Raven asked, catching sight of another unit of the 9th Legion shifting southward. The 9th Legion recently took the place of the 10th Legion along the western perimeter, making these moves very curious.

"A woman with child requires rest even after a night of rest," Cronus said, hoping Raven wouldn't probe further, drawing from him the true reason she was kept up late. He decided to change the subject before Raven asked another question.

"Here, I brought you something to eat." He handed him some fresh bread and dried moglo meat.

"Thanks," Raven handed his rifle to Cronus while taking the food. "Take a look and tell me what you think." Raven said, tearing off a large bite of bread.

"Which direction am I to look?"

Raven pointed south and west while chewing.

"Thisss tasthes prethy good."

"It's fresh, compliments of Princess Corry, though I'm not to tell you that. And don't talk with your mouth full."

"That was nice of her," he said before biting into the dried meat, then stuffing another piece of bread in his mouth.

Cronus lifted the scope to his eye, scanning the enemy perimeter. "They seem to be shifting forces south and west."

"Yeah, all morning long. It started as a trickle. A flax here, a unit there, but now you see them shifting telnic size elements south and west," Raven said.

"You think they're massing for an attack?"

"I don't know. It wouldn't make sense from that direction or that far away. By pulling back his forces from Corell, Morac has pretty much written off a frontal assault."

"Then what is he up to?" Cronus wondered, still eyeing the Benotrist/Gargoyle line.

"Maybe Torg should send out some scouts and take a look."

"Not likely," Cronus said. "We have few magantors left, with so many raiding Morac's supply points north of here. General Valen reports great success in the supply raids, while our southern and western scouts have not returned in recent days. Whatever Morac is hiding in that direction, he is committing much of his resources keeping us from knowing. The Jenaii dare not risk anymore of their scouts unless they send a sizable contingent, which they cannot spare. Right now, we need every sword to hold Corell in the event Morac changes his mind on assaulting us."

"Just remind Dar to keep one bird alive so I have a way back to my ship. As much as I like you all, I don't plan on staying here after we're done killing these bastards."

"Rav, if we somehow destroy Morac's legions, we will find a magantor to return you to the *Stenox*," he shook his head at his friend's overconfidence.

"I'll take your word for it."

"Rav, how far does this scope see?" Cronus asked, something catching his eye to their south, a blurry image whose shape contrasted with the burnt plain around it.

Raven pressed the magnification switch on the weapon's stock. "As long as an object is in line of sight, you can make it as large as you want. Heck, you could read a book, miles away even at night," Raven answered as the image in the scope grew ever larger in Cronus' eye... Ocran.

"Riders due south," he whispered aloud. *But whose?* he pondered as the image grew. Scores of riders came into view, far beyond the 5th Gargoyle Legion that was positioned along their southern perimeter. Were they Connly's? Tevlin's? Meborn's? Or Morac's?

"Riders?" Raven asked before stuffing more food in his mouth.

"Blue tunics," Cronus' eyes drew wide. Then amidst the congregant a banner lifted magnificently in the morning breeze, the sun shining with glory upon its crest: A golden crown on a field of white. "HE'S COME!"

"Who has come?" Raven asked.

Cronus lowered the rifle, placing a hand to Raven's shoulder, squeezing tightly while locking his eyes to Raven's. "Prince Lorn."

* * *

Torg Vantel and Commander Balka were the first to join them atop of the Golden Tower, soon followed by Generals Mastorn, El Tuvo and Valen and Princess Corry and Terin. There they congregated with little room to spare, each taking their turn to scan the horizon with Raven's rifle scope. By now large elements were emerging in the distance, impressive hosts filling in along the horizon. Lorn had come, and he did not come alone.

"How is that possible?" Corry asked.

Had he come with the entire south? Did he bring enough men to break Morac's line? These questions were the first of many she sought answer to, as General Valen reported more movement to their east.

"Much of the 14th Gargoyle Legion is moving now, at least ten telnics. Perhaps more," Dar observed through Raven's scope. The 14th was greatly diminished in the assault upon Corell, fielding only thirty telnics, much of their strength left dying upon the north wall of Corell. He again looked south, spotting numerous magantors skirmishing along the horizon, counting at least twenty warbirds to each side. He followed the action keenly, watching a gold Torry warbird drop from the sky, followed by a Brown Benotrist avian, its riders thrown from their saddle, arms flailing through their severe descent.

"Valen?" Torg asked, looking at how tightly the general griped the rifle.

"Your Highness, permission to lead my warbirds to battle?" He asked, handing the rifle to Torg.

Corry hesitated, wary of releasing their magantors, pondering if this was all a ruse to lure them away, but it seemed too grand a deception for one of Morac's cunning.

"Go," she conceded.

"Wait, Dar!" Raven cautioned, the Torry Magantor General holding at the stair well, looking back to him.

"Why?" Dar asked.

"Don't attack until Cronus signals you to do so."

"Raven?" Corry questioned, noticing the strange look passing his face.

"I have an idea."

"A good idea, or a bad idea?" Cronus asked, knowing that look could go either way.

"We'll find out soon enough," Raven shrugged, with Dar descending the stairwell with all haste.

"It seems this did not take Morac by surprise," Torg said, scanning west, where another host emerged from the Zaronan forest, marshaling into formation, bearing the standard of the 10th Legion, a black cloven shield upon a field of red. Torg revealed the discovery to the others as Raven took the rifle from his hands.

"Cronus, fetch Orlom and send him up here, we have work to do," Raven said.

* * *

Lorn paraded before his men astride a light gray ocran, his silver breastplate and helm resplendent in the morning air. His armor, usually dull from use, shone brilliant, showing Morac who stood before him. His standard bearer rode beside him, hoisting his sigil for all to see, a golden crown upon a field of white, its banner lifting in the breeze. He gazed north, where the towers of Corell broke the horizon, jutting into the firmament in all their glory, rising like points upon a massive white crown. Behind him gathered many riders, nearly eight hundred in all, drawn from Avliam, Meborn and Tevlin's commands, with only Connly's cavalry absent, checking Kriton's riders west of Besos.

"Corell," Lorn whispered, his words lost in the wind, staring long-ingly to his ancestral home.

The tall white walls were far away, her towers barely breaking the northern horizon as he stared north over the burnt plain. He had come far in so short a time, marching to Sawyer, then taking ship to Tarelis, before marching in haste, skirting the headwaters of the Pelen along roads less traveled. He had set off from Fleace long before Morac's siege had begun with Yah bending his ear, whispering commands, and revealing this vision to him. Here it was where his dream took shape at this very place and time. He had followed Yah's guidance through the Yatin and Macon Campaigns, surrendering his will to the path laid before him. His victories to this point were mere proving grounds for what awaited him here upon the fields of Corell. Destiny swept him here like a fallen leaf carried upon the river to the sea. Here he would claim his Kingdom or perish in the attempt. The men that accompanied him would follow him to the gates of damnation should he have need of it. They loved him as a brother and honored him as a King, though he was only a Prince. He was Lorn II, son of Lore and his union with destiny had come.

Before him gathered a great host, Benotrists and gargoyles marshal-ing forth to give battle, their standards raised proudly in the lifting breeze, standing between them and Corell. To his northeast stood the 5th Gargoyle Legion, rallying to their standard of a black mailed fist upon a field of white, their numbers in the many thousands, thirty-eight telnics arrayed for battle, their death chants echoing over the fields like ghostly sirens. To their east came the 14th Gargoyle Legion, nearly twenty telnics bearing the standard of a red headless corpse upon a field of black, the ghoulish sigil reflective of their soulless ranks. To the west of the 5th Legion, and his direct north, stood the 9th Benotrist Legion, forty-nine human telnics, their helms and spears glittering in the sun. They dressed their lines while gathering into formation, awaiting the 10th Legion drawing from the west, adding its fifty telnics to their great multitude. Lorn gazed skyward where their magantors gave battle, waring with Morac's fell host.

Torry, Macon, Jenaii and Benotrist magantors battled in the skies above, several warbirds downed in their melees before each side briefly withdrew, circling above their respective hosts. They would certainly reengage once the battle was joined.

Jentra drew alongside his left flank and Squid Antillius his right, the later dressed for battle, exchanging his minister's robes for helm and mail, riding to war as he did with King Lore in the days of old.

"Your Palace awaits," Squid proclaimed.

"Nay. Morac awaits. Let us pray Corell still bears the Torry standard," Lorn said, but by the look of things, that still held true.

"Your orders, my Prince?" Jentra asked.

"It is time, my friend."

"Commander Avliam!" Jentra's coarse voice boomed harshly, like sand over rough stone.

The Torry Cavalry Commander galloped nigh, saluting with an open hand.

"Your orders?" Avliam asked.

"Cover the right flank with Meborn. Commander Tevlin to the left," Jentra commanded.

Those atop the Golden Tower observed the divergence of the Torry Cavalry. They broke east and west, kicking up a cloud of dust before taking up position to the army's extremes. The settling dust revealed the vast infantry drawing forth to give battle between the cavalry elements. Not since the zenith of the Middle Kingdom had a Torry Monarch assembled a host so vast as the Armies Lorn brought to Corell. The Armies broke from their column formations into a line of battle. To the far west marched the 2nd Teso and 2nd Zulon Armies, their combined strength numbering five telnics. Aligned to their east was the standard of the 1st Torry Army, a blue hammer and ax upon a field of white, commanded by General Lewins, fielding nineteen telnics of both Macon and Torry soldiers.

To the east of the 1st Torry Army marched the 2nd Macon Army, commanded by General Bram Vecious, his thirteen telnics arrayed in distinct gray mail over purple tunics, following their standard of a red sword upon a field of gold.

Aligned to Vecious' east was the joint Macon-Torry army, commanded by Dadeus Ciyon, wearing his distinct golden armor, tunic and cape, his dark hair trailing his bright helm. Guilen Estaran rode beside him, arrayed in silver armor and tunic, in contrast to his commander, the son of Darna still new to the saddle and warfare, but following Dadeus into battle none the less.

King Mortus' gray mount galloped forward of his army, bearing the Macon Monarch into battle with sunlight reflecting off his golden breastplate, greaves, and helm. He wore a scarlet tunic and a black cape that rippled in the wind. Beside him rode his standard bearer, raising his sigil of a golden crown upon a field of black. He looked to his west, where rode Prince Lorn, his gray mount riding apace to meet him. His retinue trailed him, their mounts cantering apace, the Torry standard bearer centered among them.

"Hail, King Mortus!" Lorn greeted, drawing nigh, Jentra and Antillius flanking their prince.

"Hail, Prince Lorn, though I should say King Lorn after this day!" Mortus declared, sparing a glance north, where the Torry throne awaited its rightful claimant.

"If the day is ours," Lorn cautioned, tempering his optimism with the great task before them.

"This day is ours for the taking. We did not march untold leagues to fail below the walls of your ancestral home," Mortus said with a booming voice, turning about to look east, where the Jenaii 2nd Battlegroup guarded their right flank, twenty telnics to oppose the gargoyles opposite them, and Avliam's cavalry further east, guarding their extreme flank.

Lorn followed his line of sight, where stood their winged allies aligned in loose ranks stretched endlessly east and south, liberally spaced for each to spread their wings and take flight. Circling over the Torry right, the great magantor *Sky Lord* bore King El Anthar into battle, his gray-white wings casting long shadows upon his soldiers below. *Sky Lord*, Father of *Wind Racer*, was the mightiest magantor of the Jenaii Kingdom. His silver talons hung menacingly below him, able to halve an ocran with a single slice. King El Anthar rode upon the great avian, clad in the distinct Jenaii armor of blue mail and helm over black tunic. A small shield was affixed to his left arm, freeing his hand to hold the reins. His right hand held his sword, sunlight playing off its murky steel. Two other great magantors flanked him, one bearing General Ev Evorn, commander of the Jenaii 2nd Battlegroup, and the other bearing Elos, the Jenaii Champion.

El Anthar masked much of Lorn's movements from Morac's magantors, with the Benotrist Lord believing any relief force would come via Central City along the large east-west road. Lorn sent Ciyon's army, along with those of Teso and Zulon and Avliam's cavalry to Central City, and from there along the southeast road, skirting south of the Pelen River. The greater portion of the army traveled from Sawyer across Lake Monata, disembarking at Tarelis, then marching north to join with Ciyon at the headwaters of the Pelen, taking Morac by surprise, while General Fonis led the 2nd Torry Army and the Notsuan contingent from Central City east toward Besos to keep Morac's eye trained there. Along the route, the allied forces were joined with the Torry cavalry already battling in Torry North, with Meborn's 3rd and Tevlin's 1st Cavalry joining with Avliam's 4th on the march to Corell, while Connly's 2nd battled Kriton's Benotrist cavalry west of Besos. Once King EL Anthar learned of the march from Fleace, he sent a small portion of the 2nd Battlegroup across the Monata, along with thirty magantors to shield their advance, while Elos led the greater portion of his strength against the Nayborian armies gathering to invade their kingdom across the Elaris. King Anthar feared Dethine had returned to lead the Nayborian host, but the Naybin Champion remained with Morac, leaving the Naybin armies without a sword to counter Elos. The 4th Nayborian Army was shattered, and the 3rd suffering greatly before withdrawing to Non, the golden castle, and seat of King Lichu, regent of Nayboria. The 3rd Jenaii Battlegroup remained along the Elaris River, keeping any remaining Naybin forces in check, freeing Elos and the 2nd

Battlegroup to join with Prince Lorn and King Mortus in Torry North.

Two leagues to the rear of the allied host, 2,000 soldiers of Sawyer guarded the baggage, supplies and support elements, including a small army of tanners, cooks, fletchers, and smiths. Among this vast entourage was the Princess Deliea, daughter of Mortus, wife of Lorn II and future Queen of the Torry Realm, guarded by numerous Torry and Macon elite. The young Dougar, the orphan taken in by Prince Lorn as his squire, attended the Princess as her sworn guardian for the coming battle. The City of Sawyer used all their resources to reinforce the Macon-Torry expedition. Their small merchant fleet ferried supplies across Lake Monata, while their cavalry guarded the long supply chain that ran from Fleace to Sawyer to Tarelis and across the regions south of Corell. General Gaive Dolom, oversaw the Sawyeran Expeditionary Forces.

Lorn outstretched his sword toward the enemy host, with King Mortus doing likewise, igniting a thunderous cheer through their gathered ranks, signaling the advance, eighty thousand men and Jenaii following them into battle.

* * *

Morac mostly abandoned his outer siege works throughout the morn, shifting his legions south while skirting Corell at a safe distance, while keeping a greater part of the 8th Benotrist Legion north of Corell, and ten telnics of the 14th Gargoyle Legion guarding the eastern approaches. The remainder of his forces he shifted south to oppose the relieving forces marching upon Corell. He spent the following days recalling the 10th Legion from their intended reposition of Besos, keeping them within the Zaronan Forest, until this day, where he called upon them to redeploy south. By late morning the 9th and 10th Benotrist Legions were formed into telnic sized combat rectangles, 2 telnics deep and fifty abreast, opposite Lorn's vast Army. Each rectangle was one hundred men across and twenty deep. Facing south, the 10th Benotrist Legion, led by General Gavis, aligned to the west, while General Marcinia's 9th Benotrist Legion aligned to his east. Both legions were relatively unscathed, neither suffering the heavy losses incurred by the other legions during the first siege, or from the most recent attack upon Corell. Each suffered less than a thousand casualties to Raven's deadly fire, but not enough to impair their combat effectiveness. To the east of the 9th Legion, stood the 5th Gargoyle Legion, commanded by General Concaka, the gargoyle commander a veteran of the first siege, and battle hardened. His legion included the remnants of the 4th, 6th, and 7th Gargoyle Legions, who were shattered in the first siege, their combined strength reduced to thirty eight telnics. To the east of Concaka, stood twenty telnics of the 14th Gargoyle Legion, commanded by General Trimopolak, his legion suffering heavily during the recent assault upon Corell's east and north walls, losing nearly half his strength.

Morac led ten telnics of the 8th Benotrist Legion southward, holding them in reserve behind the forces arrayed there, while riding to the fore. Dethine gathered whatever cavalry they had, both Naybin and Benotrist, nearly two hundred mounts in total, and guarded Morac's extreme right flank, checking General Tevlin's 1st Torry Cavalry.

"Kai-Shorum!" his soldiers shouted as Morac rode before his Legions upon his pale ocran, his blood red cape twisting in the wind. He gazed south where stood the great host of Torries, Macons and Jenaii, arrayed for battle, their thunderous cheers contesting his own army's chants. His dark eyes swept the grand assemblage brought against him, gazing intently through the empty sockets of the Ape Skull affixed to his helm, fixed on the Torry rider opposite him. An eerie sensation coursed his blood, passing to his extremities with festering rage and trepidation. At this fair distance, the warrior before him seemed oddly familiar. Could the azure tunic and silver breastplate be an apparition? A tortured spirit sent to haunt him? Nay, King Lore was dead, felled by his swift hand. *Then who?* Morac thought, his mind a violent tempest seeking an answer.

"Lorn," he whispered, suddenly cognizant of the man before

him. His unease only worsened, with the growing feeling that he was placed here before the walls of Corell against his will, as if all that transpired was preordained. Shouldn't he be confident? Here he stood, the mightiest warrior in all the world. He wielded the *Sword of the Sun*. The might of the Torry Kingdoms, their Macon and Jenaii allies and the Armies of the south congregated before him, and yet his Legions still greatly outnumbered them. If he destroyed these Armies, the war would be ended. He no longer needed to storm Corell or waste time with a siege. He need only to cross this field of battle and strike down the son as he did the father and Lorn's gathered host would crumble. In one fell stroke, he would give his emperor the gift of four Kingdoms. Save for the Apes and Queen Letha, all of Arax would fall under his dominion.

All of this was true, but the *Sword of the Sun,* which guided his hand in all things, held him back. For that brief moment, Morac felt what he had not felt since Emperor Tyro first placed the *Sword of the Sun* into his hands: Fear. He did not fear the Armies before him, the Castle behind him or the prince himself. He feared something else. He feared the unseen, the unknown, the spirit that he knew dwelt within the Son of Lore. His shield and mask were transparent to Lorn, as if he could see through them at this great distance into his very soul, revealing him as a weak vessel filled only with rage and hate. Looking at Lorn was as if an all-knowing being was looking back, able to see you for what you truly were. Then it seemed as if an ethereal presence passed between them, eclipsing Lorn's power for a brief moment. Morac's fear abated, fueling a resurgence coursing his blood, stirring him to act, and drawing forth his sword.

"KAI-SHORUM!" He shouted, rearing his ocran and charging to meet the Torry Prince.

Morac's Legions repeated their Lord's war cry and lumbered forth like a leviathan roused from its slumber. "KAI-SHORUM!" Echoed like a deathly groan along the Benotrist front a league in each direction as their multitude advanced. The legions sprang forth like a coiled serpent lunging to strike.

Across that deadly space, Prince Lorn leveled his sword toward Morac, pointing him out among his mighty host, as if drawing every eye upon the son of Morca riding to meet them. Despite all they endured to reach Corell for this defining moment, Lorn's vast army was still heavily outnumbered more than two to one in this very engagement, not including his own forces within Corell and Morac's forces north and east, as well as the forces engaged west of Besos. Most of his soldiers ignored the odds before them, coming to believe in Lorn, his many triumphs fueling his legend. As the armies lumbered forth, drawing upon each other across the open fields, Lorn kept his eye upon Morac and the bright glow emanating from his fell blade. Somewhere in the eastern sky, Elos circled, knowing his task was to intercede as Morac drew nigh, the *Sword of The Moon* blunting the *Sword of The Sun*.

The Benotrist front was still two hundred paces away, with Morac slightly withdrawing within the foremost ranks, twenty-five hundred Benotrist spears lowering in unison between interlocked shields, with ninety-seven thousand aligned behind them in a sea of steel, iron and flesh. To the east, the Gargoyle 5th and 14th Legions closed upon the Jenaii, their guttural tongue contrasting with the Jenaiis' stoic silence, both haunting in their own way. In the skies above, the magantor forces reengaged, Benotrist, Torry, Macon and Jenaii warbirds clashing in the heavens overhead. Most were too busy to see General Dar Valen leading his remaining warbirds from Corell to join the battle from the north, but they were still many moments away, and would not engage before the two armies collided.

One hundred paces.

The two armies were almost upon each other, when a sudden euphoria swept over Morac, with all that he fought to achieve just within his grasp. He could feel the power surging within his sword, emanating to his entire army, their spears leveled to give battle, their hearts pounding in triumph.

Fifty paces.

Morac could see Lorn's eyes through the slits in his helm, so close now he felt he need only to swing his blade to touch him. Lorn had no sword of light to contest him, no power to stay his mighty blow, and so he would end him, here before the walls of Corell. His elation faltered as a shadow passed, the wings of a Jenaii magantor sweeping dangerously above the Torry ranks, with a Jenaii warrior springing from its back, setting down beside the Torry Prince's mount, brandishing a glowing sword with a vibrant emerald hue, the warrior's silver eyes staring back at him with unnerving indifference... Elos.

Forty paces.

Thunderous cries rang out behind Morac, joined with triumphant shouts from his enemies in front of him. His Sword held him back as his ranks continued forth, cautioning him to hold in place, his mount pressed by the men crowding around it, when a burst of pure white light drew from the west, passing through the rear of his army, fueling horrendous screams of dying men, rising into a deafening crescendo. It was at that moment that all Morac's dreams turned to ash.

* * *

Moments before.

Raven watched as Morac brought most of his army south of Corell throughout the day, holding his fire until they were in position and drawing close to the allied lines facing them. Cronus stood behind him, having given signal to General Valen to launch his attack some moments before, the Torry warbirds just now nearing the skies above the enemy host. Orlom stood on the opposite side of the platform, observing the remaining Benotrist forces north of Corell, holding his fire until Raven gave him the signal to attack. The rest of the garrison was abuzz, men and Jenaii taking up position along the battlements, with Corry joining the commanders upon Zar Crest. The men were anxious to give battle, but helpless to act, watching the battle unfold far beyond the palace walls.

"Don't do what I'm about to, Orlom. When I finish shooting, hold your fire until I tell you, and then shift aim to their magantors, and whatever you do, don't shoot our guys!" Raven said, before drawing back the trigger of his rifle... and holding it down.

Thick blue laser burst from the Golden Tower in a continuous stream before blending into pure white, striking the rear ranks of the Benotrist Legions. The laser swept their lines from west to east, dropping several rows as it passed, cutting those in the rear most row in half at the upper torso, passing through their soft flesh, before striking the next row at the lower torso. The 3rd row was cut in half at the waist. The 4th row crumpled over, their bodies sliding off their severed thighs, blood gushing from their flailing nubs. The 5th row dropped, cut off at the knees. The 6th row toppled as their ankles buckled. The 7th row shifted forward, unnerved as the laser struck behind their feet, spraying soil across the back of their legs. Cries of utter torment rent the air, vying with the sounds of battle, the two merging in a ghastly chorus.

With forty men deep and 2,500 abreast, Morac's fore ranks were oblivious to the destruction wrought behind them, pressing forth, obedient to their Lord's will.

Atop the Golden Tower, Raven gripped his rifle tightly, the weapon nearly jumping from his hands, the laser continuing through the Benotrist ranks before passing into the gargoyle ranks beside them. The laser tore through the gargoyles like wet parchment, shattering their formations before passing through to the end. Raven lifted his aim, struggling to control the rifle's continuous stream while driving back in the opposite direction. Targeting the middle ranks of Morac's Legion, he swept back east to west, cutting them down like a finger of God rubbing along a terrestrial surface, laying waste to all in its wake. The defenders upon Corell's southern battlements looked on in disbelief, awestruck by what their eyes beheld.

Corry paled at the sight before her. Even at this fair distance, she could descry the Benotrist ranks crumble like sand walls before the wind. She almost felt pity for the Benotrist wretches, for who could stand against such a weapon? Though these men deserved whatever cruelties fate consigned them, she closed her eyes for she could look no more.

* * *

NO! Morac's thoughts screamed, staring helplessly as the Earther's laser swept behind them, removing all hope for victory, gutting his army with its terrible power. He watched as the laser passed west to east and back west before returning again eastward, stopping mid distance through his ranks, where it mysteriously ended. He could not withdraw his army with so many of their own dead behind them, and with his forward ranks now engaged. He shifted his gaze south, where his men drove bravely into the Torry lines, twenty-five hundred Benotrist spears leveled upon their foes. He cleared his thoughts, focusing on Elos and Lorn. He was close now... very close. He need only close the distance between them and strike them down. This one act would ensure his victory and his name would be remembered through the Ages. He threw caution to the wind, moving his mount through his ranks, before breaking through a gap, charging head long into the Torry line.

SPLIT! SPLIT!

He cut down two Torry soldiers in his path, causing those around them to falter, a score of his soldiers following in his wake.

SPLIT! SLASH!

He cut down two more, drawing closer to Elos who stood forward of Lorn, moving forth to engage him, while the Torry Prince followed the Jenaii warrior, easing his mount behind him, his men following them into the fray.

Lorn awaited him with steely nerve, his own gaze focused on the Benotrist Elite. Riding toward him was the Bane of Lore, his Father's killer and the despoiler of his Northern Realm. Revenge should be foremost in his mind, but Lorn focused on the task at hand. While his allies and men stood transfixed by the laser pouring forth from Corell, or the Benotrist ranks pressing their front, Lorn focused on Morac, but did not foolishly engage him, keeping Elos between them. Morac's eyes glowed through the eye sockets of his mask, emitting torrents of rage and malice upon his Torry foe. Lorn stood defiant, awaiting the Son of Morca, indifferent to his hate and unmoved by the *Sword of the Sun.*

"FIRE!" Lorn commanded his archers.

Heeding the Prince's command, a score of archers behind Lorn, released their volley.

Morac grinned at such futility, spinning his sword to block the harmless shafts. Alas, the shafts were not meant for him, but the beast he rode. Arrows whizzed past him, while others he knocked away, but many embedded into his mount's muscled thighs and throat. The beast slowed, stumbled and dropped. Morac jumped free before being pinned neath the dying beast. Morac embedded in the soft soil, with a taut grip on his cherished sword lest it slip from his grasp and ensure his doom. The power of his sword surged through him, hastening his recovery as he sprang to his feet, leaving his silhouetted form in the sod behind him. There he stood with his dead mount to his left and the Torry Prince a stone's throw away with Elos between them. All around them, the Torry and Benotrist front collided in a storm of clashing shields and spears.

SPLIT! THRUST!

Morac cut through the Torry soldiers pressing nigh, trying to keep Elos in view, and Lorn who was still mounted, slashing his sword left and right amid the fray. He cut down another, and another, yet Elos was slipping away, cutting down his men farther afield, drifting eastward along the line, with Lorn even farther beyond, lost amidst the shifting front. He paused, held back by his sword, warning him to withdraw.

NO! He mentally screamed, denied vengeance with victory so tantalizingly close. He barely had time to back a step when the entire allied front lumbered forth, weighing into his beleaguered ranks. He backed further, struggling amidst the crowd as everything gave way.

* * *

"%$#&&*" Raven cursed, tossing the rifle to the floor as the laser faded like a dying flame half way through his third pass, before extinguishing altogether.

"Why did you stop?" Cronus asked.

"Cause it's broke!" Raven grumbled.

"Broke?" Cronus asked.

"It can't continuously fire without burning out its core. Now it's a useless pile of junk."

"Then why did you do it?" Terin asked.

"That's why!" Raven pointed to the results while drawing his pistol, scanning the battlefield to their south, examining the devastation.

"Can I shoot now, Boss?" Orlom asked

"Yes, but remember what I said," Raven warned, looking through the scope of his pistol. Morac's legions were thrown into chaos, with many thousands dead and dying, strung out in near perfect lines east to west, and back again and a half, each pass of the laser cutting down four or five ranks. The second pass was more toward the middle of the formation, leaving tens of thousands trapped between the lines of death, surrounded by their comrades, the wounded flopping about like dying fish spit upon the shore. Raven guessed he cut down ten to sixteen thousand with each pass, gutting Morac's legions. Beyond the lines of death, the front of his legions faltered, with Lorn's armies swarming their ranks, fueled by their enemies' disarray.

ZIP! ZIP!

Orlom's laser struck a Benotrist warbird racing above the distant battlefield, the first blast missing its rider, the second taking the magantor through the breast, sending it careening northward before crashing.

"We got this, Cronus. You boys might want to check with Torg and see what he has planned for you," Raven said, targeting another Benotrist warbird, blasting it through its middle, the magantor dropping into the crowded battlefield below, probably crushing a dozen men wherever it fell, hopefully Morac's soldiers, and not Lorn's.

"What of Thorton?" Terin asked, stealing a glance northward to the Benotrists aligned before the north wall, where Thorton would most likely appear.

"If he shows up now, he's a day late and a dollar short. Morac and Dethine, on the other hand, require your special attention," Raven advised.

"Day late and dollar short?" Terin made a face.

"Never mind," Cronus shook his head, tugging on Terin's tunic sleeve as he moved toward the stair, using the Earthers' famous catch phrase whenever anyone asked what they meant.

"Looks like Morac is lost somewhere in all that mess. He looks like a blind drunk looking for the exit," Raven said, scanning the center of the battlefield where Morac was caught up in a crowd of his soldiers, half going forward, and the rest trying to flee, stumbling into one another.

Terin and Cronus hurried off with that information, leaving Raven and Orlom to their task.

* * *

"Fire!" King Mortus commanded.

A thousand archers of the Macon 2nd Army, loosed their shafts into the confused ranks of the Benotrist 9th Legion. Hundreds dropped as the volleys came in successive waves, further taxing their faltering lines.

"Onward!" Mortus shouted, waving his broad sword toward the enemy, the 2nd Macon Army advancing upon the enemy front.

* * *

King El Anthar ordered his Battle Group forth once Raven's laser faded out. His warriors slammed into the fore ranks of the Gargoyle 5th and 14th Legions, his following troops flying above the fray, setting down upon the creatures from above. Only a few gargoyles took flight to counter their charge, most thrown into confusion from the gutting of their ranks. gargoyle war cries quickly waned, giving way to frightened retreat, the creatures first withdrawing northward into the second line of the dead and dying who were struck down by Raven's laser. Behind this line and the first line of Raven's victims, were the bulk of the Legions. The gargoyles caught between the lines of death could neither retreat or advance without stepping on or over their own dead and wounded, with few having enough space to spread their wings and take flight. The forward ranks that heeded their Generals call to charge, had to choose to face the onrushing Jenaii or retreat over their wounded. Once the Jenaii host broke through the front ranks, Morac's left wing fell in full retreat.

* * *

Positioned between the Macon 2nd Army and the Jenaii Battle-group, General Dadeus Ciyon ordered his soldiers forth, crashing into the right wing of the 5th Gargoyle Legion and the left wing of the 9th Benotrist Legion. Ciyon led the combined army of Torry and Macon soldiers from Fleace to Central City, and across the southern regions of Torry North, while forging them into a single fighting element. By the time he joined with Prince Lorn and King Mortus at the headwaters of the Pelen, his newly formed army was fully integrated, though untested. Here was the crucible, the ultimate proving ground, before the walls of Corell, with the fate of mankind itself in the balance. Most of his men had never seen a gargoyle before, and were obviously unnerved by the foul creatures aligned to their front right. Even with Raven's deadly volley, enough of the creatures remained to give battle to stay their advance. With interlocked shields, his men pressed forth, driving methodically into the 9th and 5th Legions, meeting their walls of shields in turn, the two forces colliding in cacophony of clashing steel and iron. Spears and swords thrust desperately between shields with slowly measured effect. Armies could bang into each other's shield walls for an entire day without gaining much ground. Most armies practiced rotating fresh levies to the front in such battles, so as not to wear out the men fighting. Men could only swing a sword so many times before exhaustion took them, or a sword found purchase in their chest. This was Ciyon's foremost concern, watching his front carefully from atop his mount, positioned several ranks to the rear, his golden armor standing out from his men.

Dadeus reached out his circled shield, deflecting an arrow from striking Guilen, whose mount stood beside his, saving him from a blow to the chest.

"Thank you, General," Guilen gasped, his eyes drawn open in surprise. The closest the young man had ever been in battle before this day was when he escaped the Sisterhood, and even then, Terin did all the fighting. Here he found himself in the middle of one of the largest battles in Araxan history, with tens of thousands of men and gargoyles arrayed before him. Sitting atop his ocran afforded him clearer view of the enemy's strength. He and Dadeus were positioned south of where the enemy legions met, with the Benotrists to their front left and the gargoyles their front right. The men held firm in their ranks, their faces shrouded with helms and shields, but the gargoyles stood fully exposed with only small circular shields. Helms, and curved swords to protect them. He could barely look at them without fear taking his heart, their blazing red eyes staring hatefully back at him, with slather dripping from their curved fangs.

"Take heart, Guilen, and stay close to my side!" Dadeus ordered, drawing his sword, moving forward though his crowd of soldiers, ordering his commanders to press through the enemy front just as Raven's laser faded. The men on the front ranks were driven by those behind, exposing many to enemy spears, but the tactic quickly bowed the Benotrist and gargoyle lines.

"ONWAARD!" Dadeus shouted over the din, breaking forward of his men, slipping through a fissure opening in the Benotrist line. Guilen followed, with scores of infantry pouring into the breach, sending the entire 9th Legion reeling, and the 5th Gargoyle Legion giving ground before the Jenaii struck their left flank, sending them in full retreat as well.

* * *

To the far west where Lorn's extreme left met Morac's right, Commander Tevlin's 400 Torry Cavalry clashed with Dethine's 230 Naybin riders. The Torry Cavalry rushed forth, their ocran hooves kicking up soil, closing on the Naybin Cavalry, their lances lowering in unison as the Naybins drew nigh. Dethine's riders lowered their lances in kind, leveling them upon their Torry foes before the two forces collided, dozens unseated at impact, their bodies impaled on spears or lance tips. Others succumbed to ocran horns tearing into their mounts, or unnerved ocran bucking in fear. The two forces quickly intermingled in a desperate melee where spears were discarded for swords.

Amidst this chaos Dethine found Commander Tevlin, striking

his sword arm with the *Sword of the Stars*, severing the limb at the elbow, his following blow splitting his breastplate like parchment. Tevlin slipped from his mount, Dethine moving on to his next kill, his blade negating the Torries numeric advantage. His sword lighted bright yellow like a midday sun. Split. Thrust. Slash. Thrust. Split. Slash. He cut the Torries down one by one, shattering Tevlin's force, the surviving Torries fleeing west and south, conceding the extreme left as Dethine rallied his surviving mounts, reforming and turning east into the flank of the 2nd Teso Army.

The Teso and Zulon Armies blunted the right flank of the 10th Benotrist Legion, smashing their fore ranks and driving them back into the serried line of death where Raven's third laser stream had struck. The Benotrists broke under the pressure to the fore and the grizzly lines of death that gutted their ranks. The sight of men cut cleanly in half crawling briefly without legs or abdomens, drove the sturdiest minds to madness. Many of the dying cried for their mothers, while others begged their comrades to slay them and end their wretched torment. Their misery was short lived, the blood spilling quickly from their wounds.

Just as the men of Teso and Zulon pushed the Benotrists to the brink, The Naybin Cavalry slammed into their left flank.

* * *

Far to the east, General Avliam and General Meborn's Torry Cavalry rode unopposed, charging froth, sweeping around the Gargoyle 14th Legion's extreme left, striking their left flank as the Jenaii pressed their attack upon their front.

* * *

General Polis, commander of the Benotrist magantor forces at Corell, cursed his misfortune. He barely escaped Raven's first attack upon their besieging forces when he drove them from their forward trenches, slaying more than twenty of their warbirds in doing so. He was in his command pavilion when the shooting started. Had he been with his warbird in its pen, he would have fallen with the men who died there, cut down like ripened stalks. He recalled his bitter retreat across the open ground north of Corell, dodging laser fire that struck down so many commanders and elite, before diving into the outer trenches, spending a day and a half cowering in the dirt. The days since then were equally bitter, his scouts having discovered Lorn's massive army a hundred leagues southwest of Corell. They concentrated their magantors keeping this news from reaching the garrison, while constantly skirmishing with Jenaii and Torry warbirds from the relieving army. By this morn, his once robust magantor force was reduced to thirty mounts, with laser fire dropping two more in the previous moments.

Polis' warbird swept over a Torry magantor, snatching its archer from its saddle, crushing him within its talons before dropping him to the battle below. Polis swerved, dodging another Torry warbird coming straight at him, their archers exchanging shots as they passed, both fluttering awry. Bursts of laser flashed off his left, taking another of his magantors from the sky, its falling corpse dropping into a mass of Torry soldiers below. He was thankful its death served some good, taking a few of the enemy with him.

Polis contemplated withdraw, needing to preserve what remained of their magantors, but the battle was yet to be decided. Despite their cruel losses, they still outnumbered the allied army. They could hardly concede the skies when their men continuing to fight bravely.

ZIP! ZIP!

More flashes of laser dropped another of his mounts, while two more succumbed to Jenaii and Torry warbirds. *Curse the fates*, Polis thought miserably, relenting to what he had to do.

"Give the signal!" He ordered his archer sitting behind him, the fellow lowering his bow and unfurling a long, bright crimson sash, signaling the other warbirds to withdraw.

ZIP! ZIP! ZIP!

Polis slumped in the saddle, Raven's first blast taking him through the chest, the second and third piercing his magantor's neck and head, sending it tumbling from the sky, the archer's ribbon slipping from his grasp, fluttering away. Only a few had seen it before they went down, the rest hanging on only briefly.

ZIP! ZIP! ZIP! ZIP!

Raven and Orlom swept the skies, dropping magantor after magantor, with several fleeing south, east or west, desperate to escape their deadly fire. Raven shifted aim, not lacking for targets.

* * *

General Vlesnivolk observed the carnage wrought by Raven's devilry. The Earther's weapon gouged their Legions, cutting wide swaths of smoldering death through their ruined ranks. Fear swept his men as they stood in reserve behind the other legions, commanding only ten of his thirty telnics, the rest of his 8th Legion holding position north of Corell. To their detriment, his ten telnics' location upon the battlefield afforded them a clear view of Raven's deadly volley, his laser sweeping past their line of sight once, twice, and nearly a third time before mercifully ending. He struggled to assuage their fears and keep them in line. Dethine and Morac wielded the *Swords of Light,* and so armed could hold the right and middle, with Morac managing to halt the center's retreat, reforming just north of the second line of death that Raven gouged through their legions. Their left, however, was being pressed by El Anthar's Battle Group, Ciyon's Army and the Torry Cavalry. The gargoyles in the rear ranks took flight, meeting the Jenaii in the air, battling above their brethren, dark and silver wings colliding in a whirlwind of steel and blood, desperately holding back the Jenaii advance

General Vlesnivolk kept his head on a swivel, his gaze sweeping the length of the battlefield, trying to determine when and where to commit his reserves. The center looked desperate, before Lord Morac reestablished their lines. Then the right looked in trouble before Dethine swept the Torry cavalry from the field and turned into the enemy flank. The left was a maelstrom of Jenaii and gargoyles, making it difficult to determine what was truly happening. Then the center appeared to buckle, their legions being pushed back beyond their new line, catching sight of Morac's sword far south of their collapsing ranks.

Flashes of laser swept the skies above, dropping their magantors in quick detail, before they broke altogether. The General could wait no longer, raising his sword to order his telnics forth to reinforce the center, before his men broke and ran.

"Kai-Shor…" his voice died in his throat, laser taking him through his skull.

General Vlesnivolk slipped from the saddle just before Dar Valen's magantors swept overhead, followed by General El Tuvo's Jenaii, one in ten dropping fire munitions upon the Benotrist reserve, as they sallied from Corell, before joining their strength to Lorn's, assailing the 5th and 14th Gargoyle Legions from behind. Men scrambled, flames igniting in their midst. The men furthest north, broke and ran, their eyes panicked with terror watching laser fire spew from the Golden Tower in the distance, riddling their ranks as fires exploded in their midst from the Jenaii and magantors. It was too much to bear, with more and more men peeling away. Their shaken courage gave way to complete panic, with most of the 8th Legion brought south, abandoning the battlefield.

* * *

Morac managed to rally the men of the 10th Legion, halting their retreat behind the second row of death Raven cut through their ranks, trampling hundreds of wounded men laying strewn across their path before turning to make their stand. The pursuing Torries and Macons slaughtered thousands of his men gathered in the foremost ranks during their retreat, and now stopped short of his new lines, holding at the edge of the line of death, pausing briefly to dress their ranks before pressing on. Torry arrows blotted the sun, passing over Morac and shredding the Benotrists behind and beside him. The *Sword of the Sun* shielded its master from harm, but not those who followed him. The Torries and Macons knew this and focused their attack on everyone except the Son of Morca. Morac's eyes blazed, briefly finding the Torry Prince across that deadly space, before losing sight of him amidst the chaos, a Torry shield wall obscuring his view.

"Kai-Shorum!" Morac shouted, his war cry repeated by enough of his men to echo above the din. He slashed at an advancing shield, rending it in half, blood splattering from where he struck, the man's cries drowned in the chaos.

SPLIT! SLASH!

He swung desperately, cutting down the Torries all around him. The Torries advanced beyond either flank, swarming past him like water around a rock. The Torries and Macons shifted away from him as they pressed on, leaving a large space between them and him, when he caught sight of Lorn a short distance ahead, still sitting his mount, staring back at him with stoic indifference, as if he were a mere novelty. Morac paled as Lorn turned, galloping off to the east, ordering his army away from Morac as Elos stepped into view before him. The Jenaii warrior stood unmoved, staring down Morac, daring him to advance. If he backed a step, Elos advanced a step. If he advanced, Elos retreated, mirroring his every move as the battlelines moved farther and farther behind him. He stole a glance skyward, where Jenaii and Torry magantors filled the heavens, the flash of laser fire driving his own warbirds from the battle. With the castle to their rear and Lorn's army pressing his front, he could only fight and die, or flee northeast and northwest. The bitter choice was upon him, twisting his innards like painful barbs.

"AGGHH!" Morac cursed, withdrawing to rejoin his men, the advancing Torries and Macons leaving a free path to do so, as Elos followed, keeping at a safe and constant distance, never giving him a free hand to wreak havoc upon the Torries and Macons common blades.

* * *

The gates of Corell opened as Torg Vantel led Twenty-three Torry Elite into battle, using all the available mounts remaining in the palace stables. Cronus rode beside him, with Ular sharing a saddle with Lucas upon his other flank, and the ten apes led by Gorzak, doubling up on the other mounts. The apes were eager for battle, and would not be denied. They rode apace, turning sharply west, navigating the abandoned siege trenches that circled the palace before skirting the west wall, racing south to join the fray.

ZIP! ZIP!

Laser fire dropped several Benotrist stragglers that remained in their path, peaking their heads from their siege trenches along the western perimeter, Orlom's laser fire cutting down any of them fool enough to emerge. Orlom followed their advance from atop the Golden Tower with Raven standing beside him, keeping a steady fire upon the main battlefield.

Carbanc, son of Hukok, sat behind Cronus in the saddle, hooting excitedly while swinging his hammer overhead, with poor Cronus hoping he didn't hit him by mistake before they joined the battle.

* * *

General Ciyon led the joint Torry Macon Army between the left wing of the Benotrist 9th Legion and the right wing of the 5th Gargoyle Legion, driving both legions back like peeling a fruit. Thinning his own flanks, he reinforced his center and drove it forward to the Benotrist rear. Seeing his opportunity, he ordered his extreme right into the flank of the 5th Gargoyle Legion, who were currently reeling under the Jenaiis attacks, both from the King El Anthar, and those from Corell, led by El Tuvo.

General Ciyon rode among his men, slashing at the Benotrists with his long sword and advancing far past their left before ordering the greater part of his army to sweep west, rolling up the 9th Legion.

* * *

"Careful, My Prince!" Jentra scowled, swinging his sword down upon a Benotrist's arm, hewing the limb at the wrist.

Lorn followed Jentra's blow by driving his sword into the Benotrist's chest, then pressed his foot on the man's torso to pull his sword free. Lorn did not heed Jentra's admonishment as he once again pressed his mount to the fore with enemy sword tips and spears jabbing at him fiercely. Though his ocran was stabbed several times, it still bore its master with calm and courage.

Squid pressed close, guarding Lorn's right, his mount assailed by enemy shafts and blows. Was it bravery or foolhardiness that drove Lorn to such reckless abandon on the battlefield? Squid could only conjecture, but he guarded him with his life all the same.

The forward ranks of the Torry 1st Army struggled to keep pace with the prince, fighting their way to the fore. Lorn would not wait for them or allow them to separate him from the enemy. They pushed north and east, driving the Benotrists beyond both lines of death wrought by Raven's terrible weapon.

"Agghh!" Jentra heard a man cry out to his left, turning to see a Benotrist dropping short of his mount, with Criose's standing over him, removing his sword from his back.

"Blast it man, get behind our shield wall!" Jentra barked.

"Prince Lorn tasked me to guard you," Criose panted, catching his breath, doing his best to keep pace with him on foot.

"You can't guard me on foot, and I have my own fool to guard!" Jentra growled, kicking his heels, urging his mount after Lorn who again pushed to the front.

They fought on, splitting the left wing of the 10th Benotrist Legion, driving it north and east before Lorn ordered them to turn hard right, pressing the survivors into the right flank of the 9th Legion, leaving the rest of the Torry 1st Army driving the remains of the 10th Legion to the west.

"HOLD OR DIE!" General Marcinia, commander of the 9th Benotrist Legion, shouted. His troops heeded his commands, forming a sturdy line of defense with interlocked shields and jabbing spear thrusts. His archers supported them, casting their volleys over the heads of their fore ranks and into the approaching Macons and Torries. With King Mortus pressing his front, and Prince Lorn and General Ciyon pressing his flanks, he knew he couldn't hold for long. His hopes for Morac to join him were for naught as he was now withdrawing with the remains of the 10ᵗʰ Legion somewhere to his west.

"Hold!" He ordered, steeling the hearts of his brave soldiers with the enemy drawing ever closer to their front and sides. If he could stay their advance, he might counter attack. Such hopes were folly for this day belonged to Lorn as Marcinia dropped to the ground with a laser blast caving his skull.

Atop the Golden Tower Raven slowed his rate of fire, taking fewer shots lest he drain his only weapon, rendering him defenseless. He took his time, picking out high valued targets, or spreading a light volley wherever enemy resistance seemed strongest.

The Benotrist 9ᵗʰ Legion and the men of the 10th with them broke. Men could only take so much before even the sturdiest minds gave way. There was no order to withdraw or stay, because their Commanders were dead or dying. There was no trickle cascading to a full retreat. It was a complete rout as Men and Gargoyles fled north and east in the thousands. Many stripped off their armor as they ran, while others slashed those in their way to hasten their escape. Many were trampled or caught in the crowd, wedged against each other and helpless. Raven fired freely into these helpless masses, causing further panic that drove them to madness. The Torry 1ˢᵗ Army pressed upon their rear, cutting down the few who remained with stomach left to fight.

Morac cursed as the 8ᵗʰ Legion fled the battle. He nearly reached them before they broke and ran, but fortune forsook his cause and cast ruin upon his every endeavor. He no longer had the choice of flight or fight. He could only hope to escape with his life and sword as he cut his way north and east, following his minions to the safe vestiges east of Corell.

* * *

General Ciyon continued rolling the left flank of the 9ᵗʰ Legion, any enemy directly north of him taking flight, affording him a clear view of the 8ᵗʰ Legion breaking apart and fleeing to the northeast, along with elements of the 9ᵗʰ and 10ᵗʰ Legions. Morac was following those tattered remnants, leaving what remained of the 9th Legion to their fate.

"General, Morac flees. Shall we pursue?" Guilen asked of him.

"Let him flee, we have plenty of game here to hunt," Ciyon continued west to envelope the 9th Legion. He would be the hammer to Lorn's anvil, with King Mortus driving up the middle.

* * *

Sudden tremors shook her heart as if assailed by a thousand tingling nerves. She could barely catch her breath as the sensation coursed her flesh. It was the same feeling that ran up your leg when standing near a steep height. Her throat tightened, trapping her voice as it caught in those willowy narrows.

"Cronus," she said weakly as he neared.

His black mane blew free in the wind, framing his face with those dark steely eyes that undressed her from far away. He came to her, standing at the bow of the small craft as it traversed Tro's calm waters. He climbed aboard the Stenox, took her in his arms and kissed her with unbridled abandon. He ravished her like a starving beast devouring a fresh kill.

That memory of their reunion at Tro, after his escape from Fera, filled her conscious thought with the euphoria of first love. The feeling that makes you grow weak at the sight of your true love, fills an Araxan woman as she goes into labor. She did not open her eyes for she knew he was not with her. She called on Lorn's God to protect him in battle. She had surrendered her will to Yah's omnipotence, beseeching his protection for her brave Cronus.

"Please protect him!" She prayed, fearing some ill fortune would visit him this day.

"Leanna?" Galen asked, holding her hand as her labor increased.

She opened her eyes and looked kindly upon the Minstrel. Galen had tended to her selflessly these many days.

"I was praying for Cronus," she smiled as the erotic stimulation of child birth intensified, forcing Cronus' image boldly in her mind. She never imagined it could be so beautiful, so passionate, so erotic, so perfect.

"How soon?" Galen asked Jonella, the Matron who sat at the foot of the bed while examining Leanna's womb.

Galen had sent for her and she came from tending the wounded.

"It could be very soon or much later, I do not know," Jonella answered. She delivered hundreds of children in her time as a matron, knowing no two were completely alike. Jonella struggled with whether to stay or go. With battle raging outside the Castle, and thousands of wounded from the previous engagement, there was much for her to attend. Yet those from the previous battles had been given all the care she could possibly provide. The battle being fought was still far from Corell's walls and the wounded were far from her care. She would stay with Leanna until duties called her elsewhere. Besides, there were other healers working tirelessly in the wards above and below. She again pressed her fingers inside Leanna's womb to measure.

"Three finger widths," she whispered aloud. *Perhaps it shall not be so long after all,* she thought just as Leanna's water broke.

* * *

The Benotrist 9th Legion broke apart, squeezed by Ciyon to their east, Lorn to their west, and Mortus to their south. Those who could flee, did so in any direction open to them, but most found themselves trapped amidst their fellows, their pocket closing about them. Lorn broke free of his men, skirting north of their formation, into the open fields beyond where much of Morac's soldiers were fleeing. He could see them clearly now, strung out in an endless stream running north and east. Jentra and Squid followed close behind, leading several units of infantry, Jentra directing them into the north end of the shrinking pocket, cutting the 9th Legion's last avenue of escape.

Dozens of Benotrists broke free, racing north before coming upon Lorn, recognizing him as a man of importance, thoughts of killing him replacing thoughts of flight. With several archers among them, they stood their ground once in the clear, releasing a volley upon the Torry prince, whilst their comrades rushed forth to engage.

"Ride!" Jentra shouted at Lorn's side, having just eased their ocran to a trot, pausing to survey the enemy fleeing north of them.

Lorn turned as the first arrows dropped, several finding purchase in his mount's hindquarter, the beast shifting with the sting, before throwing him from the saddle. He tumbled painfully in the soil, losing his helm and sword along the way. Jentra and Squid circled about, shielding him from the onrushing Benotrist soldiers, mentally counting a fair two dozen fast approaching. Jentra cursed his stupidity, wondering how they were taken by surprise, outpacing their own lines amidst battle. A handful of Torry soldiers swift enough to keep pace afoot, filled in around them, scores of others still far afield, rushing to catch up.

Lorn staggered to his feet, still dazed from the impact. The sound of men shouting and a clashing of steel brought him to his senses, before finding his sword laying nearby in the matted grass. He found himself with a ring of Torry soldiers fighting off a larger group of Benotrists. He caught sight of Squid on foot, giving battle, the elder minister barely holding on, pressed back by the youthful vigor of his Benotrist foe. Off his left, Jentra remained mounted, moving swiftly among their foes, chopping two in quick order, swerving amid their gathering ranks. Lorn grabbed his sword, rushing to help Squid, who nearly lost his footing on the uneven ground, the deceiving landscape appearing a flat grassy sea, but was in fact a series of rolling mounds that could easily hide an approaching foe until they were fast upon you.

Lorn took Squid's opponent by surprise, smashing his left knee with the toe of his sandaled boot, crumpling him to the ground before driving the point of his blade through his thigh, twisting it free. Squid recovered, striking at the man's other leg, nearly severing his foot at the ankle. They recovered in time to meet the next foe coming at them, leaving the first crippled and screaming behind them. Lorn blocked a hurried strike with the flat of his shield, his counter strike driving the man back a step before Squid circled to his side, striking from the flank. The distraction was all Lorn needed to push forth, his reach piercing the fellow at the left knee, sending him to his back.

"Agghh!" Squid cried out, taking a blow to the back of his legs, faceplanting him in the grass before Lorn could finish their foe. He turned, finding another attacker standing behind him, preparing to finish him when a dark silver blur flashed behind him.

Lorn looked on as his rescuer crashed into the Benotrist with his shield, knocking him off balance, the man arrayed in bright silver mail, tunic and cape, his helm and armor polished to a bright sheen. The irate Benotrist quickly turned on his attacker, meeting him with a flurry of strikes, the silver clad fellow barely holding on, appearing to possess only the crudest sword handling ability. Lorn finished his first foe, before moving to help his rescuer, when the familiar visage of Dadeus Ciyon clad in his golden armor came riding up, driving the Benotrist to the ground with a slash of his sword, saving Lorn's rescuer.

"My Prince, a glorious day of battle!" Dadeus greeted, lifting his helm to greet Lorn.

There was nothing glorious concerning battle, he thought to remind his flamboyant general, but lacked the time.

"I am glad to repay my debt," Dadeus added, recalling the ma-gantor attack during the march to Fleace, when Lorn dragged him to safety, lest he be burned alive.

"There are no debts between brothers in arms, Dadeus. Nor is there time for words with enemies about," Lorn said, stealing a glance around them for the nearest foe.

"There are no enemies left standing, my Prince," Dadeus declared with his cocksure grin, waving his sword around them.

It was only then Lorn noticed the lack of clashing steel nearby, followed by dozens of Ciyon's soldiers flooding the area. The distant sounds of battle proved the fighting was now far afield. Dadeus' infectious grin widened upon seeing Lorn realizing what he already knew, their part of the battlefield was won.

"The 9th Legion is beaten, Your Highness, and what is left of them is surrendered or fled. We crushed them from the east as you did from the west. Before the final blow I shifted north of my men, where Guilen spotted this group heading in your direction, where we gave chase," Dadeus added for good measure, pointing out Guilen as Lorn's silver clad rescuer, when the young man removed his helm.

"Well met, cousin," Lorn smiled, the irony not lost on him that the man Terin helped free form the federation helped save his life this day. With that Lorn finished the last Benotrist soldier nearby that still lingered, before checking on Squid, who lay upon the ground, writhing in pain, the back of his knees bleeding severely.

"I shall endure," Squid grunted in agony as Lorn tore a strip off the nearest dead Benotrist's tunic to bandage his legs.

"Indeed, and I command it of you, old friend," Lorn said, easing Squid onto his back as Jentra came riding up.

"How bad is he?" Jentra asked, keeping his head on a swivel, as any trained warrior is wont to do.

"He needs a healer. Take him upon your saddle and take him to Ilesa," Lorn said, knowing Ilesa was waiting with the regenerator at their base camp far to the south.

"My place is to guard you, My Prince," Jentra snorted.

"I am not dying, Your Highness. There will be others whose wounds shall take precedence over my foolishness," Squid came to Jentra's defense.

"Guilen shall stay with him, Prince Lorn. You can have use of his mount, as yours appears impaired," Dadeus offered, ordering one of his men to fetch said mount, standing nearby where Guilen left it. Dadeus ordered half his men to remain to safeguard Squid and Guilen, while he, Lorn and the others continued on.

Once again in the saddle, Lorn moved farther north, stopping briefly upon a low rise, where he could better view the battlefield. Behind him was the impressive scene where the remnants of the 9th Legion surrendered, with many more dead or dying upon the battlefield, surrounded on three sides by the combined strength of Lorn, Ciyon and King Mortus, whose standard appeared above the gathered host, a golden crown upon a field of black. From this vantage point, Lorn could not see King Mortus dispatch and lead half his strength to the east, joining the attack upon the gargoyle 5th Legion, leaving his remaining men to oversee the surrender of the 9th Legion. To the west, the 10th Legion was holding upon its right flank, reinforced by Dethine wreaking havoc upon the armies of Teso and Zulon to their front. The left flank of the 10th, however, was in disarray, many thousands abandoning the battle. The greater part of them fled northwest, the rest fleeing northeast, joining many of the 8th, 9th, 14th and 5th Legions escaping the carnage, strung out in a long line, skirting the southeastern face of Corell, making their way somewhere to the northeast where they would regroup. They suffered indiscriminate laser fire from Corell throughout their flight, and fire munitions dropped into their ranks from Torry magantors that kept returning to the palace to rearm. To Lorn's southeast, the 5th and 14th Gargoyle Legions were beset by the Jenaii 2nd Battlegroup and those of the 1st led by General El Tuvo, along with half of Ciyon's Army and part of King Mortus' 2nd Macon Army, as well as the Torry cavalry of Avliam and Meborn. Torry magantors roamed freely above, snatching gargoyles midair, crushing them in their talons before flying off and returning again and again.

Even from his higher position, Lorn could see little of any of this, the battlefield too large to ascertain the full picture. He watched as laser fire continued to spew from the Golden Tower, concentrating on the remnants of the 10th Legion still fighting on to his far west, though he could barely make sense of what was transpiring there.

"What are your orders, My Prince?" Dadeus Ciyon asked of him, drawing up alongside him, with Jentra upon his other flank.

"We finish those still fighting. Once that is done, we shall see about the rest," Lorn said, deciding whether to engage the 10th Legion to the west or the gargoyle legions to their east, allowing Morac to escape to the northeast.

"And allow Morac to escape?" Jentra questioned the wisdom of that. There seemed no better time to finally finish the Benotrist warrior than now.

"Shall we proceed to engage the 10th or the 5th and 14th, Your Highness?" Dadeus asked, surmising where Lorn was looking.

Lorn struggled deciding, before catching sight of Elos' sword flashing amidst the chaos in the direction of the gargoyles, thinking their help was needed elsewhere when a familiar white Magantor passed across their line of sight to the west…. Wind Racer.

* * *

King Mortus rode apace, parading before his reformed ranks before redirecting them to the east, and into the gargoyle host fighting there. The eastern half of the battlefield was a collage of Jenaii and gargoyles fighting in midair, with thousands more engaged afoot. The right wing of Ciyon's combined Torry/Macon Army pressed into the gargoyles' western flank, their shield walls holding the gargoyles in check, but too weak to advance. Mortus caught sight of Torry, Macon and Jenaii magantors sweeping down from above, plucking gargoyles from the air, before flying off to deposit their kills. He could not see the Torry cavalry assailing the eastern flank of the gargoyle host with too much ground between them.

"Parade with me my brave warriors. For victory, glory and the fate of mankind!" Mortus shouted above the din, his men relaying his words along the lines before proceeding, their columns shifting into broad rows of shield walls advancing in force. They shifted to the left of Ciyon's troops, sweeping into the gargoyle host.

"Kai-Shorum!" The gargoyles chanted, many thousands answering the Macons' charge. A thousand creatures slammed into the forward shield wall, the sound of their scimitars scrapping off their upraised metal, sounding unnervingly above the din. Macon swords jabbed between their shields to great effect, cutting down their lightly protected foes, while other gargoyles clambered overtop, swinging their curved scimitars and clawing at the Macons eyes. Many more managed to spring into the air, setting down upon the rear ranks of the attacking soldiers.

Mortus, sitting astride his mighty ocran between the third and fourth ranks of his men, made for an inviting target, drawing the attention of several creatures. One swept low overhead, its glowing crimson eyes fixed on the Macon monarch, its wings outstretched as it glided forth like a ghastly specter conjured from his darkest nightmare. Mortus brought his shield across his chest, leveling his sword to receive the blow, twisting his shield at the last moment. The weight of the gargoyle slid off his shield, his sword tearing its left wing as it passed, sending it crashing beyond him, where his soldiers

457

finished it. He recovered in time to dodge another creature sweeping in from his right, raising his sword in time to glance a swinging scimitar, the gargoyle passing overhead, before another struck from the front, taking him from the saddle.

Mortus landed harshly, the air escaping his lungs under the force of his drop, dislodging his helm. He barely opened his eyes as another creature loomed overhead, sweeping down from above, its red eyes ablaze and fangs curved menacingly through its rapid descent.

WHOOSH!

A Torry magantor snatched the creature from the air, drawing it away, its feral eyes dulling as it died in its talons. Two soldiers helped their king to his feet, breaking formation to aid him, while others formed a protective circle, with more creatures setting down all around them. Mortus recovered his strength and wits in time to raise his sword, helping to fend off their attackers. He drove his sword into the side of one creature, while the man beside him went down, a gargoyle scimitar splitting his shoulder. Another creature dropped down upon the stricken soldier, burying its fangs into his neck before Mortus lopped its head.

And, so it went, with Mortus leading his men, slaying the creatures managing to fly over their shield wall, before advancing into them, constricting their formations, preventing them from taking flight with their wings squeezed by their ever-shrinking pocket. In all his days, King Mortus had never seen a gargoyle, consigning their horror as the thing of tales told to children to make them behave. Alas, he was wrong, the foul creatures far worse than he could have ever imagined. He vowed to battle them well into the night with the sun slipping dangerously low in the western sky.

* * *

Dethine rode through the ranks of Teso and Zulon with abandon, his sword lopping heads, and removing limbs with practiced ease, sending his foes in retreat. His men followed, charging their mounts through their foes disordered ranks, the men of Teso fleeing south before their onslaught, and the men of Zulon soon to follow.

The Benotrists of the 10th Legion were heartened by his arrival, their right flank renewing their assault all along the western front, smashing into the left flank of the Torry 1st Army, where General Lewins commanded the left wing of the Torry Army, while Prince Lorn led the right against the Benotrist 9th Legion and part of the 10th he forced eastward. With Morac abandoning the field, only Dethine remained to confound the allied army.

King Sargov and General Zubarro led the shaken ranks of Zulon, each struggling to keep their men in line with the Benotrist 10th Legion pressing their front, and Dethine tearing into their left flank, cutting men down with pitiful ease. King Sargov stole a glance west along his lines where the Nayborian champion cut down another of his men, his glowing yellow sword sweeping across the soldier's chest, nearly cutting him in half. Dethine continued apace, soldiers fleeing his blade, the entire flank giving way, with dozens of riders following in his wake.

"To me, soldiers of Zulon! To me!" King Sargov shouted, drawing his sword to meet Dethine and stiffen his men's resolve. Archers fired into the charging calvary, dropping several ocran, and striking Dethine's mount with several shafts, but the beast continued, snorting a terrible sound as it lumbered forth. More shafts followed, slowing its pace until it eased and dropped dead, with Dethine jumping from its back, landing firmly upon the ground, wasting little time to engage his foes on foot.

SPLIT! SLASH! THRUST!

He cut men down in quick order, limbs and heads flying off his blade, his golden braided locks trailing him as he moved like a yellow flame. King Sargov stepped to meet him, lest his men lose courage, knowing the futility of his task. He recalled the tale of how King Lore met his end at Kregmarin, knowing he would soon share his fate, but honor demanded no less.

It is a fine day to die, he told himself, bracing for impact as Dethine drew nigh, an evil glee filling his eyes as he strode forth. Perhaps it was a fine day to die, but not for Sargov, King of Zulon, and not today. A great shadow loomed overhead, giving Dethine pause as Wind Racer set down, where Terin sprang from his back landing between Dethine and Sargov, while his great avian took again to the air.

Dethine's glee died on his face, staring at Terin as if staring at death. He struggled keeping him in focus, as if a shrouded aura surrounded him. Terin stared blankly back, his eyes void of emotion, moving forcefully upon him with powerful strides. Dethine barely lifted his blade in time before Terin was upon him, a series of blows driving him back as he struggled to keep his feet, transfixed by the fell power Terin wielded. The men of Zulon looked on, transfixed by the clashing swords, Terin's turbid blade absorbing the glow of Dethine's lesser sword.

THRUST! SLASH! PERRY!

They moved across the mated grass in a flurry of moves, light clashing with shadow, the soldiers of the 10th Legion looming dangerously to Terin's right, with only a thin line of Zulon infantry shielding him from attacking his flank. Terin ignored that possibility, his attention focused upon Dethine, driving him back step by step, oblivious to the flashes of laser riddling the Benotrist 10th Legion, sending many to flight. Dethine's comrades attempted to circle around them, but were met by King Sargov and his guards, the Nayborian cavalry lacking enough open ground to trample them underfoot, their ocran slowed enough for the men afoot to block their advance with leveled spears and pikes.

Dethine's emotions ran the gambit of anger, hate, fear, confusion and loathing, struggling to sort them while fighting for his life. He wanted to say something, to offer a mocking sneer to rattle his foe, but was at a loss for words. Terin was unnervingly silent, moving economically, without a wasted motion, tearing apart Dethine's mechanics in a flurry of strikes, perries and thrusts. Dethine's counter strike failed miserably, nearly losing his sword to Terin's riposte.

HAROOM!

The sound of war horns echoed over the din as a band of Torry cavalry drew from the west, where Torg Vantel's small party attacked the Nayborian cavalry from behind. They drove hard from the palace, skirting the larger mass of Benotrists fleeing the battle toward the Zaronan, avoiding battle until nearing the conflagration, cutting down smaller bands of Benotrists crossing their path, before coming upon Dethine's rear. Torg gutted a Naybin rider, with Cronus passing upon his left, and Lucas his right, their saddle mates jumping from their mounts to give battle afoot. Ular sprang upon a Naybin mount, gutting its rider from behind and pushing him from the saddle. The apes were all afoot in an instant, shouting their war cries as they gave battle. They struck down Naybin cavalry with their axes, blood splattering their dark fur, the sight of battle only fueling their maddened glee. Gorzak of tribe Traxar, swung his two axes like a whirlwind, swerving among the Nayborian cavalry, chopping men from their saddles like ripened stalks. Torg struck down another Naybin while catching sight of Carbanc, son of Hukok, drag a poor wretch from the saddle, before caving his skull with his war hammer. Huto, son of Hutoq, ran forward off Torg's left, driving a poor Nayborian to the ground with his broad sword, before chopping him nearly in half, moving on, leaving the twitching wretch in his wake.

Cronus caught sight of the clashing swords ahead, one dark and the other golden, racing ahead to aid his friend. Cronus knocked several Naybins aside, drawing closer to Terin, before dismounting in a flourish, running up behind Dethine, driving his sword into his back just as Terin drove his through his front, the two blades crossing in his chest.

There, within sight of the walls of Corell, Dethine, the Nayborian champion and keeper of *a Sword of the Stars*, met his end.

Terin and Cronus retracted their swords, Dethine's dying body crumpling to the ground between them, before Terin lopped his head for good measure. Terin and Cronus shared a look, relieved and exhausted, pausing briefly amid the chaos swirling around them. Terin reached down, retrieving Dethine's sword from his dead grasp, its bright glow growing dull in his hand before handing it to Cronus.

"It is yours," Terin said, the blade igniting a fiery golden hue as Cronus took a hold of it.

"It is yours by right, Terin," Cronus said, but Terin was having none of it.

"You and I slew Dethine, and the sword passes to both of us, but as you can see, I already have a *Sword of Light*," he smiled, directing Cronus to sheath the blade given him by Torg.

No sooner did they turn to join the battle with the Benotrist 10th Legion, a great commotion arose all around them, with a mighty host of cavalry and soldiers flooding into their midst from the east, where rode Prince Lorn, Jentra and Dadeus Ciyon, along with General Avliam and his hundreds of riders, sweeping the remaining Naybins from the field. Lorn stopped short of the two of them, a knowing look passing his fair countenance.

"Well met, my friends. Well met indeed."

THUS ENDED THE 2nd SIEGE OF CORELL.

CHAPTER 22

"Well met, my friends. Well met indeed," Lorn greeted them.

"My Prince," Terin said, the two looking upon each other for the longest moment, with so much to say, and no words to do so, each traveling far since they last saw one another at Mosar.

"Only Terin Caleph could come back from the dead to save the realm," Lorn smiled, shaking his head at the wonder of it all.

"Not quite dead," Cronus corrected.

"True, not quite dead," Lorn agreed.

"Terin!" Another familiar voice cried out, coming from the man sharing Jentra's saddle, who immediately dismounted to embrace his long-lost friend.

"Criose?" Terin smiled in disbelief. General Dar Valen had informed him of Guilen and Criose's arrival at Lorn's encampment at the siege of Fleace, but never expected to see him here.

"It is good to see you well and free," Criose said, knowing there was so much for them to say and share, but this was hardly the time.

"Prince Lorn, welcome home, lad," Torg's ruff voice said as he drew alongside them, with Lucas and the others fanning out around them, along with the apes and Ular afoot.

"Master Vantel, your face is a welcome sight indeed, old friend," Lorn couldn't stop smiling, his love for his father's oldest friend and most trusted councilor evident in his countenance and voice.

"Bah, my face is only good for scaring children. There will be a time for words and sharing our mutual affections, but not now or here. We have a battle to finish, and those rascals in the tower will start to wonder why we are all standing here like fools!" Torg reminded them, jerking his thumb northward where laser fire continued to strafe wherever the enemy was concentrated.

"Rascals?" Jentra wondered at that, until realizing just whom he was referring.

"Indeed, my friends, we have a battle to finish," Lorn agreed, before giving out orders.

"Jentra!"

"Yes, Highness?" The grizzled warrior answered.

"Ride south. Tell General Dolom to set camp where he is and to fortify his position. I do not want Princess Deliea to come forward until the battlefield is secure. Have Lady Ilesa brought forth to attend the wounded. Take enough men to provide for her security. Dadeus, you will greet her upon her arrival and direct her to where the wounded are gathered. I will send reinforcements to bolster the camp in a short while. Jentra, I want you to stay with the Princess until I call her forth."

"I will guard her with my life. Come along, Criose, so you can GUARD me," Jentra snorted, causing Terin to question what he meant by that.

"I am his guard," Criose sheepishly explained before climbing back into the saddle, the two men ridding south, the others chuckling at Jentra's expense. Criose guarding Jentra was like a tersk guarding a lincor. Fortunately for Criose, Jentra grew weary of him running after him throughout the battle and ordered him to share his saddle.

"Ular has another regenerator," Torg informed the prince.

"Another one?" Lorn smiled at that. One healing device was a wonder to behold, but two would save many more lives this night.

"A generous gift from our Earther friends. Where do you have need of it?" Ular asked with his watery voice.

Torg hated to waste a great warrior with treating the wounded, but he was the ablest to use the device among them, making Torg question his own stupidity for not bringing one of the matrons along to attend that task, freeing Ular for battle.

"Dadeus, lead our Enoructan friend here to where we left Guilen and Squid. Have him start there, for I have need of Minister Antillius."

"Aye, my prince," Dadeus saluted with a fist to his heart, offering Ular a hand, drawing the reptilian warrior to his saddle, before riding off with a portion of cavalry to guard them.

"Master Vantel, it seems we have a battle to finish," Lorn smiled, receiving hearty cheers from their ape friends standing in their midst, shaking their axes, hammers and swords, eager to fight some more.

"Aye," Torg snorted in agreement.

Terin and Cronus lifted their swords, their fell power further fueling their comrades' resolve.

Lorn smiled, knowing the greater meaning of what transpired just before his arrival. Dethine was dead, and his sword was now theirs. With that, he turned, leading his men to rout what remained of the 10th Legion, the others following him into battle, including Torg, two swords of light and a band of howling apes.

* * *

The Golden Tower.

"Should I keep shooting, Boss?" Orlom asked as nightfall was fast approaching, and his rifle was nearly drained.

Raven lowered his pistol, checking the status of his own weapon, the charge showing 33 percent. With his rifle done for, they only had Orlom's pistol with a full charge, and the last thing he wanted was to be caught defenseless should Ben suddenly appear. He thought to tell Orlom to stop shooting, but even from these airy heights, the sound of the fighting still reached their ears. Every moment another Torry, Macon or Jenaii would perish, and every laser blast they sent down range could prevent that. What were the odds of Ben showing up now?

Not very high, Raven admitted to himself.

"Screw it, keep shooting until its drained, then drain your pistol. But make every shot count, Orlom, do you hear me?"

"Aye, aye, Boss," he grinned happily, getting back to work.

Let's see what Morac is up to, Raven thought, scanning his progress through the scope of his pistol, finding him directly east of the castle some 2000 meters out. He stood out among the others, fleeing afoot amid a long line of Benotrist and gargoyles. He spotted him approach another of his cavalry, trying to obtain their mount, but Raven was having none of that.

ZIP! ZIP!

Two well placed blasts dropped the ocran dead where it stood just as Morac approached, causing him to curse up a storm, kicking the animal in frustration, ignoring the poor rider who lay underneath it, struggling to pull his leg free. Morac looked back to Corell, shaking his fist at Raven, his face contorted in unbridled rage.

"Keep walking, hero," Raven chuckled, taking far too much delight in tormenting the Benotrist warrior. "Might as well check on the rest of the neighborhood," he said, shifting his attention south where the fighting continued, finding a gargoyle breaking free of the battlefield, looking to swoop down upon a Macon commander guarding prisoners of the 9th Legion.

ZIP!

He brained the creature, dropping it at the feet of its intended victim, the Macon warrior looking surprised, and then thankful, before pressing a fist to his heart in Raven's direction.

"You're welcome," Raven shrugged, scanning to find another juicy target.

* * *

"Agghh!" The creature screamed with King Mortus' blade impaling its gut, clawing at him with its dying breath, slather dripping from its fangs as its bright glowing eyes began to fade.

Mortus kicked the creature from his sword, driving it into the dirt, as his men hacked it to pieces, standing at his side. He lost count of the number he had slain this day, coming upon fewer and fewer as darkness closed about them while pursuing them north and east.

ZIP! ZIP!

Laser flashed behind them, followed by terrible screams. He turned about, finding another gargoyle writhing on the ground with smoke rising from its chest, gasping for air not ten paces from them. The king's guards were upon it instantly, chopping its limbs and wings before closing for the final thrusts to its more vital parts. Mortus wondered how the creature managed to get so close without them seeing it, but with night now nearly upon them, it was little wonder.

ZIP! ZIP! ZIP!

Laser flashed again off his right, near Cronus and Terin, who joined the Macon monarch some time ago, guarding his flank at the behest of Prince Lorn. He saw the golden hue of Cronus' blade illuminate the air around him, slashing at the foes the laser struck, finishing the creatures in quick order, while Terin scanned for other threats, the two moving in unison.

Watching the two of them was a sight to behold. They were even more impressive when Elos joined them for a time, the three of them driving the enemy before them, ending any chance of them reforming to counterstrike. Eventually Elos broke off, undertaking other duties for his king, before eventually finding Ular and guarding him as he went about rending aid to the wounded they left in their wake.

"Shall we hold for the night, My King?" General Bram Vecious, commander of the 2nd Macon Army, asked, riding up to his side, with the reigns of the king's ocran in hand.

"Nay!" Mortus growled, taking the reigns after dismounting to slay the creature, climbing into the saddle.

"Nay?" Vecious asked, uncertain he heard him correctly.

"Nay, General. We push on. The enemy is on the run and I mean to finish them!"

* * *

The cries of the wounded and dying rent the air as night closed over the battlefield, their ghastly echoes torturing the ears of the bravest of men, imprinting forever in their collective memories the horrors they had seen. Most of the cries came from Benotrists who were strewn about the plain of Corell from the southern horizon to the eastern approaches. Those who accompanied Lorn on this long trek never expected a victory so complete. Many expected this day to be their last, for Morac led a vast host that outnumbered the combined Armies of El Anthar, Mortus and Lorn. They vowed to meet the son of Morca in battle none the less, even if it cost them their lives. They knew Corell must be saved, and were willing to die to save her. But nay, such sacrifice was not needed this day for Lorn was victorious. Even the optimistic among them envisioned victory to come at a steep price. *This* victory was unlooked for. Did it come as a gift from a benevolent Creator? Or was it a fluke? Had the fates merely aligned this day, granting victory to their cause? Would such fickle winds blow against them during the next battle? Wherever Lorn passed, the men looked upon him with wonder, awed by his many deeds, so great and many they were, but none comparing to this day. He explained to them throughout their arduous trek to Corell that they were marching against a foe far greater than they, but that Yah would intervene upon their behalf, and that a sign would be given when the battle was joined. When Raven's laser tore apart the heart of Morac's legions, they took this as the sign that he spoke of.

He felt their stares as he passed, and heard the whispers extolling upon him unearned divinity. He warned his men not to raise him to such a station. There was only one God, and no mortal men should ascribe to his majesty, for to do so was blasphemy. Jentra warned him of that growing sentiment and he was quick to quash it at his every turn. He was not Yah, but merely his servant, and a very grateful one at that.

Once they crushed the 10th Legion, and his allies finished the 14th and 5th gargoyle Legions, driving their survivors to flee, Lorn quickly set about reorganizing their forces. He only released their cavalry and magantors to pursue Morac's fleeing troops, harassing them from the periphery and strafing them with fire munitions, keeping his infantry where they stood. With night now upon them, he did not wish to expose his men to a possible counter attack, as Morac would be tempted to do. A seasoned tactician would point out that

Morac was in no condition to do so, but Lorn had learned through history, to never underestimate an opponent, especially a desperate one. Unfortunately, his father by marriage thought differently, and led a great portion of his army in pursuit of the fleeing enemy. Lorn knew the dangers of battle in the gathering darkness, and the difficulty in recalling an army with its dander up, so he dispatched his greatest assets to aid him, sending both Terin and Cronus, and later Elos, after conferring with King Anthar. He would join them once he saw to another matter… Squid.

Dadeus was true to his task, leading Ular to Squid, who then healed his old friend, much to Squid's objection, rightly pointing out that others more grievously injured should take precedence, but Lorn had need of him. He and Torg came upon him at the gathering point General Ciyon established for the wounded, a makeshift, open area just south of the battlefield, where great fires were lit to illuminate the ground. There they found hundreds of men gathered, most laying upon the ground with a myriad of injuries, with Lady Ilesa moving from one to the other, providing care. Ular was nowhere in sight, with Ciyon explaining that Ilesa would treat those gathered here, while Ular moved about the battlefield, healing those that could not be moved. Lorn ordered a sizable escort to protect their Enoructan friend, and safeguard his invaluable device.

They skirted the encampment, before coming upon Squid helping with the wounded, looking much restored since he last saw him.

"Antillius!" Lorn called out, he and Torg easing their ocran to a halt, his elite guard fanning out around them, keeping a constant lookout for any threat in the darkness.

"My King," Squid bowed happily, the left side of his face lit by the nearby firelight.

"I'm not the King yet. Not until I sit upon my father's throne," Lorn corrected him.

"That is a mere formality at this juncture *King* Lorn. After this day, you are the greatest King ever to rule the Torry Realm."

"Let posterity set my place among the kings of Old, wherever that may be. I am still only a Torry Prince."

"As you wish, my Prince. Our dear Dadeus spoke that you require my services, offering that as reason for my priority in treatment," Squid said.

"He speaks true, my Friend. I need for you to go to Corell on my behalf, and treat with my sister. If she needs reinforcements then I shall oblige this evening. If not then I will keep the Army out here as we have many tasks to attend this night. Inform her of the current state of our forces, and ask that she prepare quarters for my wife and future queen, the Princess Deliea, and her father, King Mortus. And most of all, offer her my deepest affection and gratitude," Lorn said, before ordering his nearest aid to fetch Squid's mount, which was corralled nearby.

"As you command, KING LORN," Squid smiled, following the escort Lorn provided him, disappearing in the dark as Guilen appeared, Ciyon's young aide de camp looking much used after the day's events.

"Prince Lorn," Guilen bowed, hurrying to greet him after learning of his arrival.

"Cousin, how fare you this fine evening?" Lorn smiled. He oft referred to Guilen as such, acknowledging their distant kinship, which Guilen was grateful for, and made him feel welcome in the Torry camp.

"We have healed many of our men, and the Lady Ilesa hopes many more before the regenerator runs cold. General Ciyon has ordered this encampment with two rings of pickets, and guards placed every ten paces. We have brought the wagons forward, and they are constantly bringing us the wounded from across the battlefield," Guilen explained.

"Very good. And where is General Ciyon currently?" Lorn asked.

"He is with his army, overseeing the prisoners we have taken," Guilen explained.

"And how many prisoners have we taken?" Torg asked.

"I can only guess," Guilen said, wondering with whom he was speaking.

"Then guess," Torg said.

"Guilen, may I present Torg Vantel, commander of the Torry Elite and the realms' master of arms," Lorn formerly introduced them.

"You are Terin's grandfather," Guilen said, his eyes wide with wonder.

"Aye, and you befriended him when he was captive. He speaks well of you, lad," Torg acknowledged.

"Yes, I was his friend, but not as good a friend as he needed then. I was told my mother is dead, by my sister's hand, and my father dead by the hand of the Princess. I mourn my father, but he treated Terin poorly, and I can not hold any other to account for his death. My mother... well, she played a dangerous game and lost. I am glad to be free of her, and for that I owe your grandson a great debt," Guilen sighed.

"A debt you repaid with your deeds this day, Guilen," Lorn acknowledged his intervening on his behalf, sparing him a blow that might have ended him.

"What deed was that?" Torg asked.

"Guilen saved my life, tackling a man about to strike me down, just before our dear friend Dadeus arrived with a host of warriors to clear the enemy away," Lorn explained.

"Good lad," Torg grunted, causing Guilen to blush with pride, feeling he earned a place among these great men.

"My thanks, Master Torg, Your Highness," he said to both of them.

"Now back to my question, how many prisoners have we taken?" Torg asked.

"Ten thousand," Guilen shrugged, his guess wildly speculative.

"Ten thousand! How in the blazes can we keep that many contained throughout the night without them breaking free?" Torg growled.

"We will check on that matter after leaving here. General Ciyon is very capable in this regard, and if he has need of more men, we shall arrange it," Lorn said. They hurriedly met with Ilesa, watching as she worked tirelessly moving from patient to patient, her diligence impressing Torg to no end considering her condition. After this day, Lorn would have to intervene on Kato's behalf and order her to lessen her duties until her child was born, but he would give her this night. It was her own special way of honoring Kato, healing men with his wondrous gift. Lorn thought of Deliea while watching Ilesa, wondering how he would act if something befell her? With that, he smiled wanly before stepping away into the night.

Lorn sighed, lifting his eyes to the heavens above, taking in the starlit sky in all its mystery. He wondered where in the deep firmament displayed before him dwelt YAH? To which star should he direct his prayers? Or did the deity dwell in them all as well as the ground beneath his mount? He feared to close his eyes for he might fall fast asleep. His body was spent. The arduous trek to Corell and the battle that started at dawn and continued still, drained him beyond measure. The Yatin and Macon Campaigns were momentous enough, let alone the task at hand. He endured because he focused on the details, not the enormity of all that was before him. He simply obeyed Yah's will, trusting him with the larger decisions. His men came to believe that he could do anything, and trusted his judgment for he had led them from victory to victory. To them he was a God for everything he touched turned to gold.

As Lorn's eyes swept the heavens, he felt small before the majesty of creation. He was only a man, a tired, weak man. The only thing that separated him from the soldiers in his Army, or the enemy that lie in piles all around, was the gift of birth. He was fortunate to be the king's son. Was that truly Yah's will that one man should rule another based on no merit other than birth? Laser fire alit the night sky, striking someplace to his northeast, Gargoyle screams following as Raven's aim found its mark, or was it Orlom's? Lorn's men proclaimed this victory as his masterpiece, as if all transpired in accordance with his foresight. He did not wield a *Sword of Light* or Raven's terrible weapons. He merely benefited by their terrible potency.

He looked one last time to the heavens before he and Torg sought out General Ciyon.

* * *

"Confound this darkness!" King Mortus cursed. "If ever I wished a day to linger longer. Grant me only a brief time and we would finish the lot of them."

"I don't think you could bleed them any more than you have, King Mortus," General Avliam answered as he rode at his side. The Torry cavalry commander joined the Macon King after hounding Morac's retreating forces for much of the night. The Torry riders cut down the Benotrists in great numbers and guarded the Macon Monarch as his Armies swept northeast across the battlefield. Most of the enemy they came upon were the scattered remnants of the 10th Benotrist Legion, for it was the furthest west of the fleeing legions, most caught between the Torry 1st army pressing from the southwest and the Macon 2nd Army moving from the southeast to block their escape. Many were caught in the vice of the two armies, with the rest forced to shift closer to Corell before fleeing east, suffering Macon and Torries to their south and the Earther's withering fire to their north.

With Dethine's death, they were helpless to stay either. The legion was shattered. Nothing remained but scattered remnants trying to flee. Even these were being destroyed in detail. With Terin and Cronus each wielding *Swords of Light*, the enemy gave in to despair. Cronus and Terin worked in tandem through the retreat, cutting down one pocket of Benotrists after another, as well as any group of gargoyles they came upon. The only salvation afforded the wretched few survivors was night closing about them, hoping the darkness would mask their escape to the eastern approaches. Once there, however, they were on their own. No rallying points were set before the battle. Much of the Legion's leadership was slain. Each man was alone, save for the comrades in his proximity. They could not wait for others to gather as the enemy was close behind and would catch the lot. The only hope of any Benotrist survivor was to flee as fast as possible, eventually making their way east to the crossroads at Notsu. Only individuals could escape for the 10th Legion was gone.

"Let us cease this madness, Majesty!" General Bram Vecious, commander of the Macon 2nd Army, pleaded of King Mortus, while riding nigh upon his mount. "Let us halt our advance and set camp for the night. We shall lose more men in this dark than to enemy swords. I've nearly lost my ocran twice in the Benotrist siege trenches which crisscross every which way."

Mortus paused, conflicted with his heart's desire and his own good sense, before relenting. "Very well, General. Give the order to halt our advance. Set camp. Consolidate your troops. Tend the wounded!" Mortus relented. "And General!"

"Yes, Your Majesty?" Bram answered.

"Prepare your troops. Come the dawn, I intend to chase the enemy 'til their legs fall off!"

"It shall be done," Bram said before riding off to relay the command.

Mortus let out a tired breath as his General disappeared in the night. He finally could catch his breath after a long hard fought day. He too looked to the stars and felt small before the firmament above. All of his long ago dreams of conquest and Empire building seemed petty and small to him now. How could he have been so foolish? Had he been granted his heart's desire he would have defeated Torry South and handed Tyro his victory. And no victory would have been as calamitous as that. He had never seen a gargoyle before this campaign, and often thought tales of their barbarity to be children's fables. His apparent victory would have been devastating to humanity. The choice was clear to him now, the gargoyles and their allies must be destroyed.

Forgive me, Yah, I did not know, Mortus prayed to the heavens, seeking absolution for his transgressions and offering thanksgiving for redemption and the opportunity to restore honor to his name. He looked upon the sky for a time until his guards interrupted his thoughts, ushering Prince Lorn, Torg Vantel, Cronus and Terin into his presence, along with General Ciyon. Lorn and Torg collected Ciyon as they went, finding Cronus and Terin standing watch, guarding the Macon King, after leading King Mortus' vanguard in pursuit of the enemy for much of the night, cutting down men and gargoyles in great numbers. The two of them stood vigilant watch over Mortus, with his encampment nearest the enemy.

"King Mortus, how fare you this fine night?" Lorn greeted, stepping into his midst, their faces faintly alit by a torch placed some distance off. Even in the dim light Mortus could see Lorn's bloodstained armor and ill-used helm now marred and slightly dented above his left ear. He could see the way the men, both Torry and Macon, looked upon his new son by marriage. Before, he was known to many of them only through rumors of his great deeds. But this day they saw for themselves the transformation manifested in the prince. His victories in Yatin and Macon would be remembered well in those lands, but for the people of Torry North, and all those who fought here this day, he would forever be the SAVIOR OF CORELL.

"I fare well, but lament this cursed darkness. Without nightfall, we could have ended Morac's legions for good," Mortus growled.

"Despite that, we have won a great victory, and much of that is a credit to you, father. Without you and your Armies we would not have carried the day. Never again shall our peoples raise swords one against the other. Macon and Torry blood forever soak this sacred soil. From now until the breaking of the world, that shall never be undone," Lorn placed his hand affectionately upon the Macon King's shoulder, his use of the word *Father* a gesture to remind each of them of the new nature of their union.

Mortus regarded the Torry prince for a long moment, recalling his visions concerning the man before they met before the gates of Fleace during their parlay. Never in his imaginings could he have foreseen what lay before them, or that they would be riding to war together, bound by oath and blood, and yet here they were, two kindred souls bound by Yah's will, fighting for mankind.

"Aye, all have done well, Prince Lorn, but the day is yours above all others. You have won the hearts of my people, who have shed blood with you and shall ride with you to the gates of the Black Castle if need be. I too, shall ride with you to the black gates of that cursed realm, to topple Tyro's realm and vanquish the Gargoyles for all time, and by the look of things, we shall not go alone," Mortus regarded Terin and Cronus with a knowing look.

"We are with you, your majesty, to the end of the world, if need be," Cronus said, the power emanating from the sword in his hand, coursing his flesh, its vibrant glow strengthening in the starlight.

"Well said, Cronus Kenti, slayer of Dethine," Mortus regarded him.

"Such an appellation is unearned, Your Majesty, for it was Terin that struck the fatal blow," Cronus explained.

Before Terin could refute that, Torg put Cronus' humility to rest.

"Who the blazes know which of you struck the fatal blow when your swords drove him through front and back at the same time. You made that miserable wretch look like one of my late wife's needle cushions," Torg growled, causing a healthy round of laughter.

"I give you the tittle of Slayer of Dethine, for young Caleph already has a famed moniker, Champion of the *Torry Realm* and *Hero of Corell*. I can add the *Slayer of Yonig, Slayer of Mulsen* and the *Blood of Kal* to name three more that come to mind," King Mortus added for good measure, regarding the boy in question, the one whom their hopes of victory depended.

"You are too kind, Your Majesty," Terin humbly sighed, guarding his heart from prideful accolades that might undo all he had done to restore Yah's blessing, sharing a knowing look with Prince Lorn, who seemed to read his thoughts.

"I sent Minister Antillius to the palace to treat with my sister and arrange proper accommodations for both you and Deliea, father," Lorn said, looking to Mortus.

"Very kind of you, Prince Lorn. Deliea should be sent there when she can be safely moved, but as for me, I stay with the army until this battle is concluded," Mortus said, and that would certainly not be this night.

"Nor shall I, King Mortus," Lorn smiled, ordering Torg to reinforce the Macon's position with all forces they could free up to do so. With that he drew Cronus and Terin aside to join him as he continued to check in with their other allies, and inspect their encampments. They could still see flashes of laser striking out to their northeast, where most of Morac's legions fled, with an occasional blast striking to the west where a number of men from the 10th Legion fled to the Zaronan Forest, and other flashes to the north of Corell, where the greater portion of the 8th Legion still lingered.

* * *

Raven lowered his pistol. It was nearly drained and he could not recharge it 'til sunup. He was never more helpless than now, with his rifle destroyed and his pistol almost empty. Orlom fared little better, with his rifle drained and pistol at thirty five percent. This was a dangerous moment for them, but the enemy was no threat as they waited inside Corell's thick walls with Lorn's vast host surrounding it. Letting out a heavy yawn, Raven sensed the finality of that moment. If he closed his eyes he would tumble over from exhaustion. His right eye was blurred by the day's work as he picked off Morac's soldiers one at a time. The tiring part was following Lorn, Cronus, Elos, Ular, Mortus and Terin throughout the day and keeping them alive. They did not make it easy on him either, constantly throwing themselves in harm's way time and again. They were safe for now as they finally converged.

"How are you holding up?" Raven asked his young friend.

"I am good, Boss, please let me keep shooting?" Orlom asked with his stupid grin. Despite his weariness, he looked happier than a pig in slop.

"Alright, just make sure you are shooting the bad guys and not our people."

"I shoot only the bad guys, Boss," Orlom grinned.

"Good. My pistol is almost done. I'm going to step away for a few moments, and stretch my legs. Maybe I'll get some food and bring some up to you."

"Food?" Orlom's grin stretched further, if that was possible.

"Yeah, food. I'm starving and don't know where our helpers all went."

With that, Raven descended the *Golden Tower*.

* * *

She stood alone near the base of the *Golden Tower*, looking out over the battlefield from Corell's inner keep. She stared into the darkness, indifferent to the cool night air kissing her flesh. Her ears caught the cries that rent the night, expounding the pitiful sound of wounded men haunting the battlefield. This victorious day seemed surreal as if it were a passing dream. What glory was war? None at all, she reminded herself, wishing it was truly over. The only promise in war was pain, all other outcomes lingered in doubt, but pain was most assured. The cries in the dark affirmed that. Even if they won the war, her father would still be dead. The only true reward of victory was the keeping of the lives left to them, and that the toll rises no higher. Though many of her countrymen had fallen, it was those dearest to her that pained her heart. If the fates bequeathed her a choice to return to her all the lives of her fallen subjects who had thus far perished, or her father, she would choose the latter. It was selfish, she knew, but it was the nature of her human heart, duty be damned. If she could ensure Terin's survival at the cost of ten thousand Torries, she would make that bargain with any omnipotent power able to grant it. Such choices were the ramblings of a tired mind. She closed her eyes as if the burning fatigue welded them shut.

"Go to bed, kid," a familiar voice said behind her.

She turned as Raven cleared the entryway of the *Golden Tower*, stepping onto the causeway.

"Raven," she greeted him, before shifting her stare back into the pressing dark. "How can we sleep with such weight upon us," she lamented.

"You sleep 'cause you have to," he said, resting his forearms on the rampart beside her.

"You have been busy this day. You may have saved the Torry Realm with your great deeds. You watched over my brother, Cronus and Terin. I thank you for all you have done, but" .... her voice trailed off mournfully.

"But what?" He asked her in a quiet voice.

"You frighten me, Raven," she shifted her eyes to his as the pale moon light reflected eerie upon their faces.

Raven had no answer for that.

"Life should not be taken so cheaply. You killed thousands in a moment's time. How easily the Benotrists fell to your terrible weapon.

I almost pitied them. I would have if they weren't such vile people. Do you know what I thought of that troubled me most?"

"What?" he asked.

"That Thorton would do to us what you did to them. I could see him now, cutting down our soldiers in the thousands. Unlike Tyro, we have few men to spare. It would be the end of us. All of our hopes and labors painstakingly purchased with our victories would be swept away by such a small effort."

"I don't think Thorton will do what I just did. If he did, he would be without his rifle for good. He attacked the *Stenox* at Tro with Kato's rifle. He didn't try it with his own. But if he is cornered and desperate… who knows. As far as my laser goes, it is an awful weapon. But the deadlier the weapon, the quicker the war, and that is the only mercy any weapon can promise."

"Maybe so," she conceded.

"Princess Corry!" Galen's panicked voice echoed behind them.

* * *

Lorn came upon Ular kneeling beside an injured Macon commander of flax, just north of the original lines of battle, some distance south of the rest of the main army. Lucas stood over him wielding a torch in his left hand, with his shield slung over his back, holding his sword with his right, ever watchful for threats that might be hidden in the dark. Elos stood behind him, standing back-to-back, his silver eyes staring keenly into the night, a vibrant emerald hue illuminating his sword. They were joined by two flax of guards, including several members of the Torry elite, chosen to protect Ular and the regenerator. Lorn eased his mount to a halt, his men fanning out to either side as Cronus and Terin drew alongside him.

Lorn dismounted, holding back a few paces to not hinder Ular's work, as Cronus and Terin followed suite, dismounting and standing guard beside him. No one spoke as Ular knelt over the wounded man, who lay there upon the cold ground, trying desperately to hold in his innards that squeezed between his bone white fingers. The man was ripped open hip to hip, victim to an unfortunate slash of a gargoyle scimitar that managed to fall below the protection of his cuirass. The man's throat was parched from screaming, his pain giving way to delirium, his pallid lips quivering. It was clear his time was short, his only hope resting in the regenerator and whatever power it had left.

Lorn waited quietly as Ular initiated the device. A purifying glow emanated from the regenerator, sterilizing the man's intestines before the wound slowly closed, his innards withdrawing into the suture. The wound slowly closed from left to right, before stopping halfway, when the device stopped altogether. A sudden moan escaped the man's lips, cognizant of his surroundings but unable to move with the pain's return.

"Lie still, Macon friend. You are still grievously wounded," Ular spoke with his watery voice, taking the man aback at the strange sight of him, his eyes going in and out of focus, wondering if this was a nightmare or a strange dream. He clearly had never seen an Enoructan before, but had known of them, staring at Ular as he blinked his eyes, before another ripple of pain shot north of his stomach.

"What ails him?" Lorn asked, stepping closer before seeing the wound only half healed.

"The regenerator is fully drained. I must wait for sunrise to restore it. Hopefully this man can survive the night," Ular said, touching a hand to the wounded Macon's forehead.

"Will he survive the night?" Lorn asked.

"Uncertain. Much of his injury was healed, but not fully. We can only wait. I shall remain with him until sunrise," Ular said.

"Lady Ilesa's device is drained as well, Your Highness," Elos informed him, which seemed logical as she was able to move quickly among her patients as they were gathered in one place, which drained her regenerator faster than Ular's.

"There we are, then. Let us hope the severely wounded are few," Lorn sighed. The Earthers' devices were blessings indeed, but even they had limitations. Even now the cries of other wounded men haunted the battlefield, calling out from every direction. Lorn ordered men sent out to locate them, rendering whatever help they needed to stay alive until morning. Elos and Lucas vowed to remain with Ular, while Lorn and the others gained their mounts and drew away.

There was still much to do this night, and a council of war was ordered, which Lorn decided to undertake at a point between the Torry, Macon and Jenaii encampments. Cronus and Terin rode alongside Lorn, each watchful for any threats in the dark, though the wanning moonlight afforded enough visibility to guide their path. Lorn Thought of all that transpired since he last saw Terin at Mosar, before sending him off to battle at Carapis. He feared him dead, wondering how his death served the will of Yah, but his God delivered him, returning him to their cause.

"It is good to see you among the living once more," Lorn said, looking over to his young friend.

"Thank you, My King. It is good to be among the living, especially among my friends, better friends than any man has ever had," Terin said.

"As for your friends, I agree, they are loyal and honorable, but I am not king yet," Lorn smiled at that. Terin was the tenth man to call him by that appellation this day.

"The throne does not make you any less or more of a king, not after what you have achieved, *King* Lorn. You are the author of this victory, everything coming to pass as you have foreseen, or Yah has deigned to show you. Whether you sit the throne tonight, tomorrow or never, you are still the King of the Torry realm, and my king," Terin said.

"And mine as well, Highness. We will follow you wherever you lead," Cronus added firmly.

"I am humbled by your affections, my friends. Cronus, some thought me daft for allowing you to depart during the Macon Campaign. They do not think so now as your journey to Tro has borne such fruit. You not only raised Terin from the dead, but you brought Raven along as well. Your Earth friend has watched over me today like a mother Lanzar watching over her cubs."

Cronus laughed at that, never imagining Raven as a mother of anything.

"I don't recall anyone ever saying anything like that about Raven," Cronus laughed. "But he is my friend and I owe him a great deal."

"As do I," Terin added.

"And I owe all of you, and you me. Such is the nature of brothers in arms. We each owe our life to the other. I've never met Raven, but I surmise he feels the same as each of you," Lorn said just as laser cut the night sky, striking near Cronus' mount.

They were all startled, wondering if Raven had lost his mind before he fired again.

ZIP!

Laser fire streamed from Corell, searing the soil nearest Cronus and unnerving his ocran. Panic gripped Cronus' heart as fear coursed his flesh unabated. A few moments followed before Raven sent another blast, striking the ground between them, kicking up soil as they quickly dismounted. Another blast was followed by the approach of a magantor setting down in their midst, further confusing them until the rider called out for Cronus to come with him, explaining his urgency, and that Raven's blasts were a means to guide him to their location.

"With your leave, Sire," Cronus' voice came fast and desperate.

"Granted," Lorn quickly answered.

"You may have need of this," Cronus handed him Dethine's sword and climbed onto the magantor, speeding off to Corell.

* * *

Her eyelids pressed down like heavy stones as she struggled to stay awake, lifting them with what strength she had left.

"Cronus," her voice barely whispered. "Where is Cronus?"

"He is coming, Leanna," Corry's voice reassured her, holding the new born in her arms.

Matron Dresila attended Leanna, pressing wadded bandages into her womb to no avail. Blood soaked through and around without relent. Once the baby came, the blood followed without cease. Dresila locked eyes with the Princess, confirming Corry's fears. She knew the regenerator was all that could save her, but it was likely drained and was far away, unless the magantor they sent to fetch Cronus could retrieve it.

"Cronus shall come soon, my Dear Lady Leanna," Galen added, sitting by her side across from the Princess while holding her hand.

He burst into the chamber like a violent gale, his frantic eyes falling on Leanna's frail form laid out upon the low bed. Blood-soaked linens lie upon the floor and the bottom half of the bed as Dresila attended her. Her usual flush olive skin was sickly pale like stained alabaster. With his eyes fixed solely on her and nothing else, he rushed to her side as Galen backed away, joining Raven at the chamber's entrance.

"Cronus," she smiled weakly. She labored to stay conscious 'til he arrived, fighting desperately to see him one last time. "I prayed for you to return safely to me, and Yah was faithful, for you are here and well."

"My love," he said, twisting his frown into a smile. "You should rest now and save your strength."

She ignored his request while gripping his hand, her grip painfully tight as if she might drift away, desperately clinging to him.

"Once she falls asleep, she will not wake," Dresila warned in a pained whisper, urging Cronus to savor every moment left to them.

"NO!" He shook his head, his heart breaking into pieces. She can't die. Not now. Not after all they had endured. Their only hope to save her was the regenerator, and both were now drained, and she would not last to morning.

"I Love you, Cronus. I am…" She paused as her eyes fought the dark veil closing about them. "…I am sorry. Tell our daughter how much I loved her," her tears ran down her cheeks, dampening her matted hair.

He couldn't speak without crying. Lowering his lips to hers, kissing her tenderly, his tears falling into her lashes. With all the strength left to her, she returned his affection for one brief moment, savoring his embrace, before relenting, her spirit drifting away, dying in his arms.

"No! Don't go, Leanna. Please. Please don't die. I can't… I can't live without you. I won't live without you. Please don't die," he wept, holding her tightly in his embrace, begging her to live, but she was gone and she took his heart with her.

CHAPTER 23

Grief weighed upon him, contorting his spirit into a maelstrom of loneliness and rage. That which he held most dear was ripped from him. All that he had long labored for now seemed meaningless. She was gone and with her she took his joy. He would not utter her name for her memory lashed at him painfully, tearing his heart into piteous fragments. His will to live drained away as he contemplated the dagger he held in his hands. The dim light of the dying torch in his bed chamber illuminated his face in a deathly pale light.

He stood on the brink, straddling that place that many have been but few followed through, with his fingers gripping the hilt tightly, seeking the strength to drive the blade into his heart.

"Kill yourself latter. My arm needs a break and it's your turn to watch the kid," Raven said in his usual non-serious tone as he cleared the doorway with Cronus' baby in his arms.

Cronus looked up at his friend. Anyone else would have looked at him in dismay and pleaded for him to reconsider such folly, not Raven. He simply walked up to him and placed the baby in his arms while taking the dagger from his hands and setting it beside him as if nothing happened.

"The wet nurse just fed her and she's ready for her nap. The Princess was going to rock her to sleep but I figured it was your turn, Daddy'O." Raven stepped away, making for the door. He stopped and said, "You better pick out a name for her or I'll pick one myself. Three days and no name yet..." he shook his head then left.

Cronus looked down at the child, as she stared up with expressive green eyes, studying his face as if he was the most interesting thing in the world. She felt light as a feather in his arms, so delicate and beautiful. He couldn't look at her without seeing his Leanna. It should be her looking down at their daughter, not him. He could not replace her, not in the slightest, and now this small person depended on him for her survival. Cronus wondered how he could do so when his own heart was broken. How could he survive so much battle and death, and return to her unscathed, while she died birthing their child? It was madness.

As if sensing his unease, the baby began to stir, voicing her displeasure.

"No. Do not cry. Shh, please..." he pleaded to no avail before resorting to music, singing the first thing that came to mind, the very song his Leanna so often sang to him.

I blew her a kiss across the still water
I took her hand as we walked along
I vowed to return from war if it took me
I vowed to return and hear her fair song

I came to her across the still water
I returned to her arms from journey so long
I took her hand in mine as I kissed her
I promised my love as I sang her this song

By the time he finished she was quiet, staring up at him with her little mouth drawn open, forming the cutest little circle with her lips. He never felt so much love and so much pain simultaneously. It was all too much, and he wept, shifting her away from his falling tears before holding her tight to his chest, rocking her to sleep.

* * *

485

Seven days hence.

Merriment filled Corell, victory lifting the spirits of the beleaguered defenders. The siege was broken for ten days as Lorn's and EL Anthar's Armies swept east and Mortus' swept west and north, before reassembling before the walls of Corell. The garrison spent the ten days clearing the dead and tending the wounded. The enemy dead were stripped of their weapons and armor, tossed into their siege trenches or gathered in great pyres and set ablaze. The Benotrist dead were so vast, that the arduous chore taxed the garrison. They worked quickly, lest the rancid smell of rotting flesh spread disease in their wake. Benotrist prisoners were tasked with refilling the siege trenches that circled the castle every which way, before being gathered and chained, and sent south, their fate to be decided after the war.

Lorn was waiting for a full accounting of the enemy strength, with the latest reports indicating the near total destruction of the 10th Benotrist Legion, and a thirty to sixty percent reduction in the 8th and 9th Benotrist Legions, though such estimates were wildly speculative at best. The Gargoyle 5th and 14th Legions were equally decimated, with his men coming upon them in small disordered groups, slaying them piecemeal. With most of his magantor forces destroyed, as well most of his cavalry between Corell and the Torry eastern border, Morac was blind to everything but the forces around him, which resembled a large mob more than an army, making their way back to Notsu, suffering fire munitions dropped into their midst by Torry warbirds that harried their pitiful columns day after day. Thousands of his soldiers would succumb to lack of water and starvation before reaching Notsu.

To the west, much of the 11th Legion was holed up at Besos, General Felinaius deciding whether to endure a siege or withdraw. A siege would be the end of him once Lorn and his vast host descended upon him from the east, and General Fonis and the 2nd Torry Army and the Notsuan contingent drew from the west. With his tenuous supply trains from Notsu now severed, he had few options, other than to march upon Central City and escape north through Rego, or to surrender. Even if he chose the former, Lorn's forces would likely catch him from the rear before he could defeat Fonis, or evade hm.

The last force of significance that concerned Lorn was the Benotrist cavalry that was currently raiding their heartland, led by Kriton, if the rumors were to be believed. They were originally the vanguard of the 11th Legion advancing into Torry North from Besos, but those forces were recalled once the news of Morac's defeat reached them, withdrawing to Besos.

The Matrons worked feverishly in the days after the battle, using the regenerator on the mortal wounds first, struggling to keep men alive long enough to be treated. They relived Ular after the first night, freeing him to join the battles ahead, where he and Lucas joined Lorn pursuing the enemy eastward. Lorn wielded Cronus' sword throughout the pursuit, he and Terin slaying many hundreds with the powerful blades. The apes joined them in battle, sharing their mounts and wielding their axes and hammers to great effect. Some of the gorillas began to collect the heads of their kills, stringing the severed skulls on ropes they flung over their shoulders, wearing the grizzly trophies with pride.

Lorn rode through the serried ranks of his cheering men camped before the north wall of Corell, where stood many thousands of tents, shelters and pavilions. The men had dug out many new well sites, as well as using those dug out by Morac's legions, which were needed since Corry ordered all the watering points for many leagues poisoned before the siege commenced. It was a wise move at the time, but now worked against them, but they would overcome it. The greater concern was feeding their vast host, their supply caravans stretching endlessly to the south, with the west blocked by the enemy occupying Besos. That was the next priority on Lorn's mental list of tasks to be done.

"Hail King Lorn!" They shouted his name though he reminded them time and again that he was not King yet. He had not even entered Corell since vanquishing Morac's host. He spent these past days hunting the remnants of Morac's tattered Legions, ensuring Corell's safety before claiming his Kingship or title that meant little minus complete victory. Though Morac eluded him, The Benotrist

Lord had no means left to him to threaten Corell. Lorn called off his pursuit to rest his tired troops and prepare for what awaited next. Claiming his Kingship was the least of his priorities. But this day he would sit upon his Father's empty throne and become King of the Torry Realms.

Terin rode beside him, sharing the praise heaped upon them in equal adoration. The men loved them and would follow either to the world's end. Each of them knew they were raised up by providence or fate, rather than their own merits. Such knowledge kept them humble. "Yah shall crush the pride swollen heart," Lorn reminded Terin time and again. Terin returned the men's cheers with a raised hand and a hearty smile that masked his battle-scarred heart. They visited upon the enemy death in such a grand scale that his human brain could not fully comprehend. Despite all the death and wonder and battle that occupied him these past ten days, Terin couldn't help but think of Cronus and Leanna. He managed to speak with him briefly the day after she died, before rejoining prince Lorn who was many leagues east by that time. He would never forget the look on his friend's face, a pitiful shadow of the man he knew the night before. His spirit was broken, perhaps forever, lest some miracle could restore him. He said barely a word, just staring forward but seeing nothing, as if he was struck dead. It broke his heart to leave him there, but duty called him away, though Corry and Raven remained to see to him. He recalled the story Raven told of Thorton and Jennifer, and the terrible change that came over him. He could never reconcile the man Thorton was to the man he now is, but looking at Cronus that morning he realized how such a thing could be. The Cronus he saw that day was not Cronus, and he hoped his old friend would defeat whatever transformation that vied to take hold of him.

"This day is yours as much as anyone's," Lorn said to him, drawing him from his musings as the north gate came swiftly upon them.

"My thanks, Sire, but this day is yours as you claim your birthright and restore the House of Lore."

"Then let us make it so. I am certain our friend Antillius awaits us in zealous anticipation."

They were joined north of the main gate by King Mortus, sitting upon his mount in his resplendent golden armor over his scarlet tunic, his standard bearer's mount waiting behind him, hoisting the sigil of his house proudly in the wind, a golden crown upon a field of black. Waiting in his company was the lady Ilesa, who joined them in their advance after spending the first two days helping Matron Dresila heal the wounded at Corell. General Valen brought her east and then west and north, healing any of those wounded pursuing Morac's forces. Lorn couldn't look upon her without thinking of Kato as she sat there upon her mount, her face a mask of brave indifference, hiding the tumult within.

"Greetings, Prince Lorn!" King Mortus hailed as they drew nigh, Lorn's entourage coming to halt within the shadow of the north wall.

"Greetings, King Mortus!" He returned the salutation, regarding his father by marriage with a deep bow, before giving Ilesa a knowing look.

"We shall soon address you as King Lorn for your throne awaits!" Mortus said, waving an open hand toward the open gate of the palace. Lorn clasped hands with the Macon King, the two of them riding side by side through the main gate.

* * *

The two Princesses awaited their return, overlooking the procession from the ramparts of the north wall. Corry and Deliea watched intently as Lorn drew closer, joining King Mortus before the north wall. A chorus of hearty cheers rang out from the men gathered along the battlements heralding their Prince's arrival. Lorn had not stepped foot in Corell since breaking the siege, the pursuit of Morac drawing him east the days after the battle.

"Our future King arrives," Corry said, her tone one of relief rather than annoyance.

"Lorn is very proud of you, Corry. He often speaks of your strength and courage, and lauds your defense of the realm in his absence," Deliea said, her eyes fixed on Lorn and her father approaching the main gate.

"And I, him. Our father would be most pleased with his incredible acts. I regret my previous opinion of his absence, lamenting that he was in Yatin while Corell was first under siege, but I was wrong. He knew the true state of things, both there and here, though I could not foresee the forces rallying to our cause at that time, whilst Yatin desperately needed him," Corry sighed, hating how the facts refuted her excuses to be angry with her brother. In all honesty, after rescuing Terin, she no longer cared about her quarrels with Lorn. Her heart was so filled with the love she now had, that there was no room for all the things that annoyed her, though it still lingered, if ever slightly.

Deliea smiled at that, touching a hand to her shoulder. The women had not seen each other since their rescue from Molten Isle. How so much had changed since then. Once rivals, their two kingdoms now forged a potent alliance. Deliea was now with child, a child that mixed the bloodlines of Lore and Mortus.

"I never fancied that one day we would be sisters, Corry. I am most glad," Deliea said as her eyes followed Lorn fast approaching the main gate, riding beside her father. She lied, for she had fancied such thoughts long ago when her younger eyes first beheld the future Torry King. She admired Lorn then, when he was a boy and even more now that he was a man. With his victories at Borin and Cesa, he could have claimed much of her Father's Kingdom, but he returned all that he had won in exchange for her. Who would give a Kingdom for a woman? Lorn would, and she was that woman, and she loved him for it.

"Our Father would have loved you had he lived to see this day. I am honored to be your sister. I have often disagreed with my brother, but in choosing the future Torry Queen he has done well." Corry liked Deliea, but looked upon her brother with great confliction. She was torn by relief and anger, relief that the burden of the throne was now his, but anger at his long absence, though it faded as late. Corell nearly fell twice before he arrived. The tall gleaming citadels of white still bore the Torry banner when Lorn arrived because of the sacrifice of thousands, the battlements of Corell still stained with the blood of its brave defenders. *So many have perished,* she sadly reflected, Kato, Arsenc, General Morton, General Bode, Commander Nevias, Leanna... Lore... She stopped after her eyes fell on Terin riding at her brother's side, following Lorn and Mortus through the main gate below, passing from view. She had already lost Terin once, yet he returned from the dead. He was the one that she could not sacrifice even if victory and defeat were in the balance.

"Your Highnesses, Prince Lorn and King Mortus will be expecting you," Jentra said, waiting behind them with young Dougar at his side. He spent the past ten days guarding Lorn's wife and future queen, with Criose waiting farther back, guarding him in turn, much to Jentra's annoyance. The very idea of him having a guard was ridiculous. He voiced that displeasure with Master Vantel, his commander and only superior in the Torry elite.

I have my own shadow to worry about, Torg growled, jerking a thumb toward the gorilla Orlom, who was constantly at his side since the battle at Corell ended. The ape referred to him constantly with a most odd moniker of *Coach,* whatever that meant.

"Of course, Jentra, if you would kindly escort us," Deliea smiled, hooking an arm through his elbow, while Corry offered hers to young Dougar, who looked surprised.

"It is all right, Dougar. You are my brother's squire and attendant, and I can think of no better guardian to protect me," Corry smiled at the boy. When she first learned that he was an orphan boy that her brother found on the streets of Fleace the day of his wedding, and that he befriended and made him his squire, she was touched. The boy spent the past days standing watch over her and Deliea, wearing mail and greaves far too large for his small body, with the shortest sword Lorn could find riding upon his left hip.

"As you wish, Princess," Dougar bowed, offering his arm to her, leading her to the great hall.

* * *

A chorus of cheers greeted Lorn as he led their prestigious company through the courtyard, where they dismounted, handing off their mounts to attendants, before continuing into the palace proper. Soldiers standing post saluted as they passed with fists to their hearts, which Lorn and Mortus returned, before coming upon Chief Minister Monsh awaiting them before the entrance of the grand hall.

"Your highnesses, welcome to Corell," the chief minister bowed, before leading them into the vast chamber, where they were greeted by a thousand pairs of eyes, and thunderous cheers. The grand hall was impressively large, resting several levels below the throne room, with a massive dais at its far end, and white stone pillars running the length of its west and east walls, supporting the immense arches that ran the length of the chamber, and bowed toward the ceiling. It acted as the main feasting hall and the place where the wounded were treated during the battle.

The long tables were set in place with hundreds of guests standing beside their chairs as Lorn and Mortus made their way to the dais, where stood Princess Corry and Princess Deliea, each standing forward of the high table to receive them. Torg stood off to the left side of the dais, with Orlom beside him, his rifle slung over his shoulder and a stupid grin painted on his face, whispering all too loudly in Torg's ear. Lorn caught sight of Jentra, Criose and Dougar standing off to the right of the dais, opposite Torg. Between the commander of the elite and the prime, stood the other members of the royal elite along the back of the dais, standing rigidly in their bright silver mail and helms over blue tunics. Each was adorned in black capes, staring in disciplined uniformity. He spotted Lucas among them, the large built Torry standing out among his peers. Ular and Elos stood among them, the Enoructan and Jenaii Champions joining their place among the Torry Kingdoms great warriors, each a proven friend of the realm.

King El Anthar and King Sargov of Zulon stood at the base of the dais, waiting upon their fellow monarchs. Lorn and Mortus exchanged pleasantries with them, before they each ascended the dais. The apes in Lorn's company were directed to a place of honor at the table below and to the right of the dais, thankfully stowing away their grizzly trophies before entering the grand hall. Numerous Jenaii and Macon commanders and court officials sat opposite them at the table to the left. The other members of the arriving party were directed to equal places of honor, especially Ilesa, who was ordered to the high table as Lorn and Mortus' most esteemed guest. Terin did not wait to be directed, taking it upon himself to stand beside his grandfather and Orlom, the young gorilla nearly knocking him over with a strong slap on his back, greeting him with a toothy grin.

The entire assemblage grew quiet as a tomb as Lorn ascended the dais and stopped before Princess Corry, the other kings holding back as the two looked upon each other for the first time since the war began. They each endured so much grief, war and suffering, each bearing the weight of command, Corry at Corell and Lorn in the south. Though their flesh was young, their hearts and minds were aged beyond their years. They stared into each other's eyes for what felt an eternity, before Corry began to kneel, acknowledging Lorn as her king.

Lorn stepped into her bow before she could begin, taking her into his arms. There in the grand hall of Corell, Lorn and Corry embraced, holding each other, tears falling from their cheeks as the assemblage began to weep with joy and sorrow and happiness.

"HAIL PRINCE LORN! HAIL PRINCESS CORRY!" Someone in the back of the chamber began to chant, with others picking up the refrain, before the declaration reverberated off the walls of the grand chamber, echoing through the passageways beyond.

"I love you," Lorn whispered into her ear, holding tight as she cried, pent up tears releasing without cease.

"Welcome home, my king," she whispered back, holding him just as tight.

After a time, they broke their embrace, with everyone taking their seats to commence the welcoming feast. Servants brought forth steaming platters of food and wine, while bards entertained them with songs and ballads. They shared stories and merriment well into the night. Eventually the tables were moved to open the floor for dancing, after the second course was served.

Terin was never far from Corry, the two sharing knowing looks throughout the evening, and coy smiles whenever they thought no one was looking. He couldn't fully enjoy himself, noticing the absence of his two greatest friends, wondering where they were. At some point he noticed Lorn's absence as well, the monarch briefly excusing himself.

* * *

Raven sat upon a rampart of the inner keep, overlooking the north wall. Few sentries were posted this night as Corell was safely surrounded by the Armies of Lorn, Mortus and El Anthar. It was here where Raven could get away from the festive crowds. He spent his afternoon and evening avoiding his Torry hosts. He never liked formal gatherings and thought it best to leave the Torries their day of celebration. He did not know Lorn, having never met the Torry King. His taking of the throne meant little to Raven. After such a victory Raven should feel much better than he did. He hoped to find Thorton, but his net came up empty. With Leanna's passing, he could feel his friend slipping away. He wanted to leave, but he needed to know where Ben was. And how could he leave until he knew for sure that Cronus was alright? He understood the pain of being separated from those you love. Except for his sister, his family lived, but he knew he would never see them again. He was stranded on this world, a castaway far from home. Though the woman he loved was on Arax with him, she might as well be a galaxy away. He was irritable when she was not around to soothe his raging heart. All of his time with her was a maelstrom of lust and rage. He was miserable when he was with her and miserable without her. One way or another, Tosha always made him miserable. No, that wasn't entirely true. They had gotten along pretty well during his visit there, and if not for her father's interference, they could have come to a better arrangement. He could well imagine the tongue lashing she'd give him if she found out he left their sons with Matuzak while he went to Tro. But that was supposed to be a short trip. If she did find out, he would politely point out that her father attacked them there, leading to this whole mess.

Who am I kidding, she won't care for excuses, he growled to himself, trying to forget his troubles, before taking another sip from the jug of ale Torg gifted him a few days back.

He spent the past ten days watching over Cronus, hoping his friend didn't do anything stupid. He couldn't stop thinking of Ben whenever he looked into Cronus' dead eyes. History had a nasty way of repeating itself, no matter how hard you tried to change it. He wasn't in a position to question Cronus' judgement considering where he sat, resting his back against a bulwark, with his left leg dangling over the wall. He probably shouldn't be drinking when a slight shift would send him to his death on the causeway below. Oh well, he shrugged, ignoring his own warning, taking another gulp from the jug of Regoan ale. He hadn't gotten drunk in a long time and this was as good a time as any.

> *"As I walked out in the streets of... of... Laredo*
> *As I walked out in Lar... Lareeedo one day*
> *I spied a... young cowboy wrapped up in wh... whi... white*
> *   linen*
> *Wrapped up in whi... white linen as cold... as the clay"*

He mumbled the music and garbled the lyrics as he attacked the jug, taking little note of the time nor the stranger approaching in the closing dark.

"If you wish to drink yourself silly there are safer places other than a high wall of Corell," the stranger's voice called out from the shadows.

"I'm not drunk yet, pal, but I'm working on it. And no matter how drunk I get, I ain't fallin off a stupid wall," Raven answered, trying to make out the stranger's face in the dark. The man looked oddly familiar as he stood just feet away resting his hand flat upon the rampart while gazing to the north.

"I hope you are right. It would be unfortunate for you to have survived the Aurelian Campaign, crashing on this world, escaping the Black Castle and the Isle of the Sisterhood, the attack on Tro, Molten Isle and the 2nd siege of Corell only to meet your end in such a way."

Aurelian Campaign? Raven questioned how the man knew about that. He only spoke to Terin about it so the kid must have said something to the stranger.

"And I would hate to see you die before I can thank you for saving my Kingdom."

Raven thought for a moment before realizing who the man could be. "You're welcome, King Lorn. I guess I should thank you too, since Morac might've starved us out here had you not come to our rescue. That was an impressive feat, kind of like Hannibal crossing the Alps or Sherman marching through Georgia," Raven added the last for his own amusement knowing Lorn would not know the reference. His slurred speech was quickly improving.

"Or Patton's relief of Bastogne or the Athenians march at Marathon," Lorn's voice trailed off into the night. The sentries were nowhere in sight and few crowded the outer battlements below. The late spring air swept in from the north, circling about the ramparts before passing on. Lorn's eyes focused ahead, staring into the night as Raven climbed off the Rampart to stand beside him as Lorn had his full attention.

"How do you know of that? Did Kato tell you these things?"

"I am not king yet, not until tomorrow," Lorn added, shifting his gaze to Raven. They were close know, and he could see the large man's face clearly in the dim light as if it were alit by a thousand suns. Lorn was tall for an Araxan, but still looked up to Raven's imposing height. Most Araxans would fear standing this close as he looked a fearsome beast, but Lorn held no fear. He stared into Raven's intense eyes without doubt or apprehension.

"I know all about you Raven," his voice carried upon the air like a whisper, calm and assuring. "I know of your father and mother. You mourn your sister and the breaking of your friendship with Thorton. I know of your compassion for Cronus and his loss. Though you claim otherwise, I know why you came with Cronus and Terin to Corell. It was not to kill Thorton. You said it was, but deep in your heart you knew Corell would fall if you did not come. You will not admit it, but you came to save your friends. You would rather have us believe otherwise to preserve your terrible reputation. You delight in portraying a fearsome barbarian that all should fear. That is not you, Raven. You are your father's son whether you know it or not. He did not send his son to space fleet to have him sell his gun arm to the highest bidder or be driven by vendetta. Nay. You fight for those you love and those that love you."

Raven's dark eyes bore into Lorn's as if the Torry King were an otherworldly Being. "How do you know these things?"

Lorn's timeless eyes met Raven's as if they were joined by omnipotent bonds. "Some of what I tell you this night I have not told another soul, not my father, my bride or my closest friends. I was not always what my people see me as today. Not long ago I was a spoiled princeling, concerned with the pleasures that the crown afforded me. It was my birthright to rule the Torry Realms. Knees would bow to my regal station, my right as the future King. I followed my own path, my own longings. Most who knew me thought me only a normal Prince who had a lifetime of praise and adoration draped upon them for no merit other than birth. It was expected that I be confident in my ability to rule, though granting a child his every want, breeds arrogance and cruelty rather than humility and virtue. One day Squid was at Corell when I was celebrated for some small achievement made larger than it was. I was always drawn to him for some reason that only Yah can surmise. He had always treated me with undeserved kindness, and not because of my high birth. He was the only one of my father's advisors that truly was fond of me. A boy can sense such things even when words are not spoken. I remember well that day for I treated my friends poorly, made my sister cry and disappointed my father. Squid took me aside and his eyes bore into me like yours do know. I could see the hurt in his eyes at the way I treated my family and anyone else I encountered. He told me that night that I would have a dream and to take what I saw as a gift for it was a warning of what would be if my heart remained as it was."

"What was the dream?"

Lorn's eyes narrowed, his voice lowering to a ghostly whisper. "I saw my father's death in battle. I saw Tyro's Legions sweep away the Torry Realms as I failed my people. I saw Morac's Golden Blade cutting down the Torries bravest soldiers with ease. I saw my sister violated on my mother's bed as Morac celebrated his victory. My people were dragged away in bondage as Tyro claimed Corell. I was bereft of my homeland. I was naked. I was hungry. I dwelt in darkness, silence and pain. All the pleasures of this world that consumed me were taken away, leaving me an empty vessel. I dwelt in a loveless void, eternal and maddening. I awoke in a terrible state, my body trembling. As the light of day cleared the nightmare from my mind, I thought it was but a passing vision. I was wrong. The same vision visited me the next night, and the night that followed. Eventually the dreams visited me while I was awake, consuming my conscious thought until I cried out to the spirits for mercy. 'Take this vision from my sight!' I cried. 'What must I do?' Then I heard the silent voice that spoke not words but shared its will with my heart. I knew that I had to empty my heart of everything that filled it. I was shown the nature of man in his barest form and the ugliness it bore. I surrendered all that I was to the spirit, to YAH, and was filled with redemption to start my life anew. Yah revealed what I must do to save my people, but first I had to give him my heart and heed his counsel. To do this I had to acknowledge that my wicked heart was no different than those I feared. My soul had no more worth than any other. All souls are precious. Only then did Yah fill me with his love and grant mercy I did not deserve. I became his servant from that day on."

"So, Squid converted you to his religion?"

"No. I converted him."

"But he told you about the dream?" Raven was confused.

"He did. But once my heart was committed to Yah, I sought him out to share my joyous news and to thank him for his guidance. He received me as he always had, with fondness and friendship. But he did not know of what I was speaking. He did not remember telling me of the dream. He remembered nothing as if they were the memories of another."

"Interesting," Raven said, unsure if Lorn was a prophet or crazy.

"There's more."

Raven's left eyebrow rose.

"Though my heart was changed, doubt shrouded my mind as to how I was to face Tyro's Legions. Yah forgave my weak faith and told me I would not be alone. He revealed Terin in my dream and the secret he carried in his blood, and the *Sword of the Moon* he would wield. He showed me Cronus and I knew he would perform great deeds," Lorn's whispered voice lowered still as he continued. "Then I saw a star fall from the heavens and the face of the man who stands before me."

Goosebumps began to creep rapidly over Raven's flesh.

Lorn Continued.

"Yah revealed everything about you, Raven. Your coming to our world was not happenstance. It was the will of Yah."

"Now hold on!" Raven pushed back. "My actions are not subject to your God. I'm from Earth. I'm stranded here by accident, not because of the whim of an alien deity."

"Yah is not alien to anyone, Raven. His omnipotence is not limited to this world. You swore an oath to him when you were eight years old. Remember? Your Father took you by the hand once you awoke in the night from a terrible nightmare, much like my own. You feared eternal damnation and cried out for salvation. Your father converted you that night. Have you forgotten?"

Raven's heart started to race as his eyes shifted rapidly staring into Lorn's.

"It was Yah who took pity on that trembling child who is the man who stands before me. How quickly the faith of a child dulls over time as the man he becomes forgets the oaths he has taken. Yah does not forget, Raven. He does grant us free will so he may know his faithful servants from those who were never truly his. You may not know it, but he dwells in your heart. His presence drives your actions. Do you truly believe you are led by reason? Did reason guide you when you journeyed to the *Black Castle* to rescue Cronus? What was your reasoned plan to free him?"

"Tosha owed me a debt for saving her from Molten Isle. It seemed a reasonable exchange at the time," Raven's explanation sounded weak even to him.

"That is not true," Lorn corrected him. "You knew you could not trust her. She was consumed with you, but not with rewarding you. You knew you would have to rescue Cronus yourself and used her to get close to him to complete the task. You were driven by your love for your friend. You followed your heart where reason would've warned caution. You are a servant of Yah, though you follow his will unwittingly and ignorant."

Raven wasn't sure he believed any of it.

"Tell your God he is welcome, but if he wanted to thank me, he could've just told me himself."

"He can't tell you, Raven. He sent me to tell you."

"And why can't he tell me?" he smiled doubtfully at that.

"Though he occupies a small part of your heart, your pride fills the rest. Yah cannot speak to a prideful heart. Pride and arrogance are deadly twins and each are masters of your heart."

Raven did not take Lorn's assessment well.

"How do you know what's in my heart?" He growled, contesting Lorn's assessment.

"You know what's in your heart, Raven. Search yourself and tell me it is not so."

Only thunder and lightning filled his heart at that moment. "If I've done everything your God wants, then what difference does it make what's in here?" He jerked his right thumb into his chest.

"Do you believe Yah only cares to direct our actions for the collective good? No. He wants each of us to be fulfilled as individuals, letting your light shine for others to follow. Tell me Raven, what do you desire most in our world? Or whom do you desire most?" Lorn's question cut to the bone.

Raven said nothing.

"I know who owns your heart."

"Tosha made her choice, and I wasn't it," Raven twisted his frown painfully.

"Love is unconditional, Raven. If you want true happiness, it must be offered as such."

"You want me to give her what she wants? Are you crazy? Do you know what she asked of me last time?"

"If you REALLY love her, then give her what she wants. All of it. Unconditional."

"You want me to surrender!" Raven's voice rose in disbelief.

"What good am I to Yah's greater glory if I took up permanent residence on her isle? All I can tell you then is good luck fighting Thorton without me."

"If she REALLY loves you, then she will return the gesture and give herself over to you just the same."

"You don't know Tosha very well, do you?"

Raven wondered how Lorn knew so much about things he had no way of knowing. Either Lorn's God was really talking to him or Lorn was able to read minds.

"Your God is concerned with my happiness?"

"I'm concerned with your happiness," Lorn answered, gripping Raven's shoulder with his left hand while staring into his eyes. "You should not be up here alone when there is celebration below. The siege is lifted and you contributed much to our victory. In the past many have looked upon Earthers with mistrust and trepidation, but not this day. Those men celebrating our victory in all the halls of the castle speak well of your name. They are your brothers now. You are bonded for all time through the blood you shed together. I am your brother now, now and forever. You are your own man Raven and no other can command you. But as your brother, I am asking you to join us this night."

"You sound worse than my mother, putting a guilt trip on me like that. Alright, I'll go down there with you," Raven conceded.

Lorn smiled. "Very good, but first we need to check on our other lost brother, shall we."

* * *

Lorn and Raven traversed the narrow corridors of the upper keep, Lorn's guards holding at a distance, the sparse torchlight playing off the white walls illuminating their path. The area was near the royal apartments, where Cronus and Leanna were housed as special friends of the crown. Raven spent the better part of the last ten days stopping in to check on his friend, where a small army of Corry's handmaids were constantly on hand to help Cronus. They came upon Galen making his way toward them, the minstrel spending as much time with Cronus as Raven had. Raven hated to admit the minstrel wasn't as much of a weasel as he thought he was, the two coming to an accord for their mutual friend's benefit, but that didn't mean Raven liked him. Like Raven and Cronus, Galen was notably absent from the festivities below, standing vigil over Cronus.

"My King," Galen bowed at the waist, waving his hand outward as he rose, greeting Lorn.

"I am not king until tomorrow, Galen. But I am honored with your kindness. How fare you this fine evening?"

"I fare well, Highness. I was just calling upon our beloved comrade, who lies asleep in his chamber, though the little one will be sure to end his slumber as she is wont to do," Galen said, a humored smile gracing his lips.

"Your friendship with Cronus is admirable, Galen. I would ask that you partake of the festivities in the grand hall. You have earned your place among the celebrants."

"You are most kind, My Prince."

"Maybe sing a good song for once while you are there," Raven goaded, not able to help himself from ribbing the minstrel.

"My dear Captain Raven, I know of no other kind. I have penned a ballad you might find favorable, My Prince, one of a commoner as you sagely advised." Galen said.

"I would be favored to hear it, Galen," Lorn said as Galen stepped past.

With that, they approached Cronus' chamber, where Lorn asked Raven to remain in the corridor so he might speak with Cronus alone.

"Good luck," Raven said as Lorn smiled, stepping within.

* * *

He found Cronus asleep on his narrow bed, with his baby resting in the crook of his left arm between himself and the wall. The wet nurse finished feeding her a short while ago, which should only satisfy the child for a brief time, considering the infant's ravenous hunger. Cronus' eyes were welded shut from exhaustion, as a newborn took all one had to keep it alive, especially without its mother. By now,

Cronus was spent of tears, too tired to even cry. He felt his heart hollowed by his loss, missing Leanna so, but thankful for her parting gift, the child he sheltered in his arms. She was all he had of her now, and spent most days holding her close. Only his love for the child gave him a will to live.

Cronus stirred with a hand touching his shoulder, turning to find a man kneeling beside him in the shadows.

"Cronus," Lorn whispered lowly so as not to wake the child.

The voice sounded familiar, and took Cronus a moment to remember it as he was half asleep. "My King!" he started to rise, but Lorn forced him to lie still.

"Don't wake the child, I only came to check upon you."

Cronus could hardly believe his King was kneeling at his bedside for no other reason but to see that he was well.

"I am well," Cronus lied.

"Hmm," Lorn wondered at that. "I never met Leanna, Cronus. I cannot emphasize enough my sorrow for her passing. I just want you to know that you are relieved of all duties until you see fit to resume them. This is not the time for others to remind you of the blessings your precious life still holds for you, but to take solace in the gift of your daughter's life. As she breathes, so does Leanna's spirit. Through this child you and Leanna are forever joined. Rest now, my brother," Lorn said, coming to his feet before backing away as a tear rolled down Cronus' cheek.

"Thank you, My King."

"I am not king until tomorrow, but I shall be honored to be the king of men such as you, Cronus Kenti. I have something that belongs to you," Lorn said, removing Dethine's sword, placing it on the floor near the bed, the dim torchlight reflecting beautifully off its ancient blade.

"It belongs in the hand of a king, Highness," Cronus reminded him.

"It belongs in the hand of its true master, in the hand of the man who earned it in battle. I am only thankful for its use in recent days."

"Terin earned it in battle, he…" Cronus tried to explain but Lorn was having none of it.

"You and Terin claimed the kill the same moment, and he yields ownership fully to you. As he is of the blood of Kal, who are you to refuse him? By his blood is it gifted to you, and as such shall never betray you as the swords have done to their unworthy masters. You are its master, for now and for always, and when you are ready, you will carry it in battle."

"Would it not better serve our cause if our rightful king wielded a *Sword of Light*?"

"Would it not better serve our cause if our Swords of Light are wielded by our finest warriors? As king I shall lead our elite in battle, where the swords shall serve me none the less. Yah has blessed me with powerful friends, and you are among that number, as I once told you upon the shores of Carapis."

"Yes, the dream of the three that would help you in the battles to come. Terin and I, and a third you did not speak of, though you claimed he was one that I knew," Cronus recalled.

"You remember, very good."

"I do," Cronus said quietly, the child miraculously sleeping through their conversation.

"Sleep well, Cronus. I shall call on you again come the morrow," Lorn said before stepping toward the door.

"Prince Lorn," Cronus called out as he reached the door.

"Yes?" Lorn asked, turning back to look at him.

"Raven was the third, wasn't he?"

"Yes," Lorn smiled at that, before stepping without.

* * *

The Grand Hall.

Terin waited for the first chance afforded him to seek out Criose on the other side of the chamber, where he was planted beside Jentra throughout the night. The two friends embraced, overcome with emotion. Only Criose fully understood what Terin suffered, having endured the same by his side. This was the second time they had seen one another since that fateful day when Criose escaped and Terin was recaptured. The events since the breaking of the siege conspired against their sharing more than a few moments to reminisce, with the battles that followed carrying Terin to the east, while Criose remained at Corell after their brief exchange after Terin and Cronus slew Dethine. Criose spent many of the days since, being questioned by the Princess, where she gleaned every detail of Terin's captivity as she could, which only fueled her anger.

"By all the spirits, you are a sight to behold, my friend," Criose grinned.

"And you, Criose. I feared for you and Guilen when you sailed off, hoping the ship's crew would honor their word," Terin said.

"They did. We sailed directly for Cagan, where we called upon Regent Ornovis to inform him that you lived. Thankfully your Earth friends and the Princess intervened before Prince Lorn was forced to, hastening your rescue," Criose explained, though they each doubted any rescue attempt by Lorn would be successful if Darna's plans came to fruition.

"What of Guilen? I keep missing him. Wherever he goes, I am elsewhere," Terin asked.

"He serves as General Ciyon's aide de camp, and personal scribe," Criose said, causing Terin to smile. Guilen had come far since Terin's early lessons teaching him to read and write by scribbling in the sand.

"He is at Besos then," Terin sighed, knowing the danger their friend was in as General Ciyon led his army to begin the siege of the fortress city, where they would be soon joined by additional forces in the coming days, including General Fonis' 2nd Torry Army drawing from the west.

"Yes, perhaps we shall soon join him," Criose said proudly, eager to prove his worth and the faith Prince Lorn placed in him.

"Indeed," Terin smiled, placing a hand to his friend's shoulder. He noticed Jentra conversing with Torg, the two ranking members of the Torry Elite not having seen each other since the start of the war. He thought how much alike they each were, and respected them deeply. It was the first time all night Orlom wasn't by Torg's side, having drifted to where his fellow apes were. The apes were gathered in a large circle off to the side of the vast chamber, with numerous Macon and Torry soldiers, sharing stories and belching rather loudly. He could only shake his head at their antics, grateful for their friendship to the realm. They were loud and uncouth, but were fierce warriors all, each slaughtering gargoyles in great numbers. They were having a competition among themselves on their number of kills, with Gorzak claiming the most with nineteen, eight of which he retained their heads.

Terin stole a glance at Corry every now and then, catching her looking back so subtlety one would never notice unless one was looking for it. He looked for the day they were wed, and not having to practice discretion. As much as he wished Raven was here, he was thankful in one regard, for his friend would push him in Corry's direction and proclaim their love for all the realm to hear. And with that thought, the entire chamber grew quiet as a tomb as Prince Lorn and Raven passed through the entrance, followed by an entourage that grew as they made their way through the corridors of the palace.

Lorn paused upon entering the chamber, the festive crowd quieting while drawing away, giving the entire assemblage a clear view of the future king. He and Raven stood there in stark contrast, one a prince and the other a mercenary and barbarian, one the embodiment of virtue and the other the standard of individualism. But what they shared was greater than what separated them, joined by the unseen bonds in Lorn's vision. Lorn regarded Corry standing across the chamber, and his beautiful Deliea beside her. King El Anthar and King Mortus stood off to his right, each regarding him in turn. There were so many of his friends and countrymen gathered in the crowd, each contributing to their victory, whether it was Jentra, his most trusted friend and stalwart protector, or Ular, or Elos, who each performed heroic deeds that would be heralded in song long after they were gone. There was General Valen, who seemed to have fought in every major engagement, fighting without rest since the war began. There was Matron Dresila, who helped heal thousands of their soldiers, though lamented her one failure, the death of Leanna tearing her heart. She stood somberly off to the side, her morose spirit robing her of this joyful moment. Equally conflicted was dear Ilesa, who kept her thoughts upon healing others with Kato's device, keeping her mind off what she lost. She looked back to him, the pain in her eyes reminding him so much of Cronus. He gave her a gentle smile, touched by her good heart. Of course, he couldn't miss Orlom retaking his place beside Torg, with his rifle still slung over his shoulder, looking to be enjoying himself, with his infectious grin tearing through Torg's stoic veneer. He thought he saw Torg grin, if ever so slightly. It was truly a sight to behold. The other apes were impossible to miss, their large furry heads and loud voices standing out in the crowd. And then there was Terin, his brave friend who sacrificed so much in the defense of their realm. He looked different than Lorn last remembered, the toll of captivity and desperate battles aging his eyes beyond their years. He was his brother, as much as Cronus and Raven, perhaps more so in a way. They were the twin heirs of Kal, Terin the warrior and Lorn the ruler, each fulfilling his mantle as Yah ordained. With that, Lorn spoke.

"Forgive my brief absence, but I felt compelled to call upon our missing brothers, who contributed so very much to our victory. Cronus Kenti sends his regards, and is attending far more important matters than our celebration. I ask each of you to think of him fondly," Lorn began, his eyes sweeping the assemblage.

"This celebration would seem hallow without acknowledging Cronus' fell deeds, or those of Captain Raven, who I found celebrating our victory alone upon the uppermost battlements. Though content in his solitude, I was only able to lure him here through chains of guilt. It is here where he belongs, and I call upon you to great with due accolades the man who slew twenty thousand of our enemies, and tore the heart from their legions, easing our victory… Captain Raven!" Lorn proclaimed.

"RAVEN!" The room thundered in cheers, chanting his name in deafening roars.

"Here is where you belong, brother," Lorn said, placing a hand to his thick shoulder.

What could Raven say? He never liked being the center of attention. Even when he destroyed the Aurelian command ship, sparing Earth a devastating attack, he tried to weasel his way out of the formal ceremony honoring his achievement. At that time, Admiral Kruger was forced to threaten his favorite pilot with time in the brig if he refused to attend the ceremony in Brussels where he was awarded for his bravery. This felt much the same with all their eyes upon him.

As the room began to quiet, Princess Deliea stepped forth, approaching her husband and Raven with her easy grace and charm.

"With my husband's permission, I would like to offer my first dance this evening to Captain Raven," Deliea smiled knowingly at Lorn, who stepped aside, consenting with an open hand, directing her to Raven, while signaling the musicians to commence.

"The first dance!" Lorn proclaimed to another chorus of hearty cheers.

The musicians began to play a gentle melody as the future Torry queen took Raven's hand, leading him to the center of the floor. He hated dancing, and was awful at it. Like his dance with Tosha, it would have to be slow and easy, requiring little more than a shuffling of his large feet. He was clumsy at best, and dangerous at worst, which he warned her, but she didn't seem to care. Of course, he wasn't going to dance her way, with her hand pressed to his while they circled each other like flittering sprites. He simply put a hand to her waist, and held her other hand in his as they moved, with the crowd all watching.

"You know I hate dancing," he reminded her.

"I know," she smiled mischievously. "With your precious Tosha absent, it falls to someone else to torment you in her place, and I knew you would not deny a dance with the future Torry queen, especially one who asked so nicely."

He shook his head.

"Something amuses you, Raven?"

"Lorn had his hands full with you. You're devious."

"Of course, as are most women, and my beloved Lorn is slow to realize that, as are most men."

Raven spared a glance to where Lorn stood, watching them. "I don't think your husband is ignorant about anything, not even women."

"You are probably right," she laughed.

"He seems to know things he shouldn't, and I'm guessing you

noticed that too," he looked in her eyes for the truth of it, when she averted her gaze.

"He claims his God shows him visions of what is and what shall be, and in the brief time I have been his wife, I have come to know the truth of that," she sighed, returning her eyes to his, her smile returning for the benefit of those looking on.

"He seems to know a great deal of things that happened in the past as well, things no Araxan should know about Earth. I'm guessing he said something similar to your father that brought about your miraculous peace?"

"Yes, and during our march here, he encouraged the men with a promised sign upon our arrival at Corell, though in private, he confided with me the nature of this miraculous intervention," she was looking at him intensely now.

"What did he say?"

"He said YOU were that sign."

"Me?" Raven made a face, feeling goosebumps raise along his neck.

"Yes. He claimed you were sent to our world to aid him in this war, that you, Terin and Cronus were appointed by Yah to this task. And what did you do when our armies were gathered before the walls of Corell? You tore the heart from the enemy," her voice trailed at that, looking briefly away.

"I killed a lot of Morac's idiots, but most were slain or driven off by your armies," Raven reminded her.

"We could not have succeeded so easily without you doing what you did, Raven. You simply appear and do the impossible, believing it a simple thing," she said, her eyes moist now, thinking of what might have happened if he didn't. Her father and husband and so many others could have died so easily facing the great host Morac arrayed against them. She could see it now, Benotrists and gargoyles in the hundreds of thousands swarming over their soldiers, her father and Lorn fighting desperately with arrows raining upon them, and swords and spears pressing upon them from every direction. She could see it now, as if it truly happened, seeing all their brave soldiers falling in battle, their pained faces seared in her memory.

He didn't know what to say to that, allowing her to continue.

"I don't believe I ever thanked you for rescuing me from Molten Isle. So much transpired, and so quickly, that I never said thank you. I would like to do so now."

"Actually, Kato and Arg recued you, while I freed Tosha, if memory serves me right," he reminded her.

"I already spoke with Ilesa, thanking Kato through her," she explained, sparing a glance to said matron who was standing amidst the crowd, Raven following her gaze in that direction.

"Kato's wife," Raven regarded her for the longest moment. He hadn't spoken with her as yet, as she spent the days since the battle away from the palace.

"She is lovely, and my father respects her deeply for all she has done. She is but one of countless heroes contributing so much to our cause."

"I will have to speak with her, though tonight might not be the right time," he said.

"She would like that, I believe," Deliea smiled wanly, pained by Ilesa's broken heart, but such was war and all it took from them. She feared Losing Lorn as Ilesa lost Kato, or Cronus lost Leanna. She couldn't help but notice the pained look crossing Raven's face as he looked to Ilesa, wondering what he was thinking, before realizing it was empathy.

"Lorn was right about you, Raven of Earth," she smiled brightly.

"He was? Which part?"

"He said you were a good man, and I agree."

As Raven danced with Deliea, Arax became a little less alien to him, and a little more like home. As the song came to an end, King Mortus stepped forth for Deliea's second dance. Raven kissed her hand before stepping away, noticing Lorn pulling Corry to the middle of the chamber, choosing her for his first dance. Soon others joined them, the few ladies of the court forced to partake to offset the imbalance, with no shortage of dance partners.

"Tomorrow then," Corry said, dancing with her brother as the eyes of the assemblage followed them across the floor.

"Tomorrow," he sighed, referring to his sitting the throne, and being named king of the realm. When he was a boy, he harbored visions of that day, imagining the glory of the title, but such flights of fancy meant nothing to him now. He wished his father still lived rather than the crown be his. He voiced his displeasure of a formal ceremony, but Squid, Chief Minister Monsh and his sister insisted on the importance of it. Such were the necessities of regal authority, the people needing to see the importance of the event. He simply could not march into the throne room and take his seat without a formal audience and declaration, though in all practical measures, he was already king by his actions.

Looking into her blue eyes he was reminded of their mother, smiling at her familiar beauty.

"Something amuses you, brother?" she asked.

He wasn't fool enough to speak of their mother, reminding her of another loss they suffered. "You look beautiful tonight, as you do every night," he wisely said.

"Thank you," she sighed.

"It is I who thank you, for ruling so wisely in my absence. Without you, Corell would have fallen during the first siege. You would have been a great queen regent if the throne never passed to me. I am not ungrateful for all you have done, Corry. What reward would you ask of me? Name it, and I shall see it done."

"There is only one thing that I want," she lifted her chin, steeling her resolve, uncertain of his feelings on this matter. Even if he said no, she would have what she wanted, his edicts be damned.

"You need not fret over that, sister. Terin is already yours. You have earned the right to choose for yourself whom you shall wed," he smiled.

She hated how he did that, reading her so easily.

"In fact, I shall announce that this evening," he offered.

"No! I shall wed him on my own terms. I do not want a public spectacle."

"You are the princess of the realm, the heroine of Corell, and the bane of Morac, if the rumors of your tongue lashings are true. You cannot hide from the people," he smiled, the tales of her rebuking of Morac making their rounds through the camps.

"We shall see," she conceded nothing. She would have her way with this, no matter the protocols of court.

"Did you truly promise to castrate Morac?" He lifted a bemused brow at that.

"Of course, and I shall see it done before the war is finished," she said with a deadly serious tone, which caused him to laugh.

"Very well. I shall add that to your reward, of which you still haven't named, but if you would allow me, I shall find something worthy of you, Corry, for you and for Terin," he stole a glance to said young man, who stood diligently off to the side of the chamber.

"Thank you."

They danced for a time, the bitterness she harbored for him through the years melting away. Lorn was a good man, a truly worthy king and heir to their father's legacy. She thought to say that she loved him, but he could see that unspoken in her eyes.

* * *

Raven made his way to stand beside Terin, looking on as Corry next danced with King Mortus, and Deliea with Torg, the Macon Princess having to drag the crusty old warrior against his will to the floor. They noticed Lucas call upon Ilesa, offering her a dance, which she politely agreed. Another matron called upon Ular, after the gorilla Gorzak drew Matron Dresila onto the floor, making the oddest pairing. Raven didn't feel so stupid for dancing after seeing Gorzak nearly break Dresila's feet several times in their first moments.

"Should we survive this war and live to be old men, Raven, I shall never forget that I saw you dance this night," Terin looked up at him with a boyish grin.

"Oh, yeah? If you tell Lorken, Brokov or Zem about this, I'll break every bone in your body," Raven growled, giving him a gentle shove, breaking his grin into a larger smile. Raven's crew ridiculed him mercilessly after learning of his dance with Tosha at Bansoch, right before Darna launched her attack, and he didn't care to repeat their taunts.

"As you command, *Uncle Raven*," Terin couldn't help himself, Raven's humor rubbing off on him.

After a time, Galen played his ballad, *Tessa the Seamstress,* bringing a tear to the eyes of many, reminding each of them the great sacrifice so many had suffered in this war. Many felt shamed by their complaints, when their suffering paled before Tessa's tribulations.

Come rest from your labors Dear Tessa
Come rest from your labors this night
The sun has set on our troubles
So we might rest for the night…

Lorn was touched by Galen's ballad, the minstrel taking his advice to heart and exceeding anything his own mind could conjure. He immediately sent for Tessa the seamstress, who was busy elsewhere in the palace, laboring without cease until called for. She was taken aback by the summons, wondering why the prince would call upon her by name. She protested at first, claiming she was poorly dressed to treat with Lorn, but was told her presence was required as she was attired. And thus, poor Tessa entered the Grand Hall, nervously clutching her skirts, taken aback by her reception.

"Hail Tessa! Hail Tessa the brave!" The entire assemblage heralded her name as she entered, wondering the cause of their greeting, until her eyes found Prince Lorn standing in the center of the chamber, beckoning her forth.

"My Prince," she said, beginning to kneel as she approached, before he bid her to remain standing, and taking the entire assemblage by surprise by kneeling before her instead.

"My fair Lady Tessa, would you honor me with this dance?" Lorn asked, causing her to cry.

"Why, Oh Prince, would you wish to dance with me? I am old, and tattered, and beneath your eminence."

"You are beautiful, Lady Tessa. You are beneath no one, and we love you, every one of us. Now, may I have this dance?" Lorn asked again.

"Yes, My Prince," Tessa wept, overcome with emotion. So long had she labored without cease, forgetting the simplest joys in life for the cause that drove her. There in the Grand Hall of Corell, Tessa the seamstress danced with the prince, while Galen again sang her ballad, causing more tears to fall. King Mortus followed, dancing with her as the others followed in turn. She danced with kings, generals, and warriors great and small. She danced with ministers, dignitaries and men of renown. She danced with Ular, Terin, Raven and Orlom. She danced with Torg, young Dougar, Criose and Jentra, weeping tears of joy, her heart breaking after so long denying the tears yearning to break free.

* * *

The following morn found hundreds gathered in Corell's throne room and thousands more in the adjoining chambers and corridors. Most pressed to the fore hoping for a better view as Lorn strode through the vast hall, walking across the mirrored white stone floor of the massive, elongated chamber with its series of white stone arches along its length, with the azure-stained ceiling between them. Between each series of arches stood statues, twice the height of a man, cast in marble with ivory faces and sapphires set in their eyes. Each statue was crafted in the visage of the Torry Kings who once sat the throne. They stood in full armor with swords drawn and their crowns upon their aged brows, so lifelike it seemed they might come to life. The light of basin torches playing off the azure stone behind the statues looked akin to an artificial sky, further illuminating their presence.

The dais some three meters high, rested at the far end of the chamber, with the king's large black Throne centered upon it, wrought in iron with silver inlays upon its back and arms. The dais curved from one corner of the Throne room to the other in a half circle, with wide steps upon its front, rising to the throne. The lesser Throne was now placed beside the black Throne, wrought in ivory with gold inlays upon its arms. The entire royal elite stood post along the base of the dais or upon its highest point, behind the thrones, spaced between the four massive columns that rose imperiously upon the dais.

Lorn regarded the familiar faces aligned to his left and right as he passed between them. Macon and Jenaii Commanders dotted the crowd, joined by members of the Torry court and dignitaries from many lands, all gathered to honor the new Torry King. Terin and Cronus followed him, their silver helms and armor polished to a bright sheen, their armor and blue tunics matching Lorn's attire, with black capes draping their shoulders. Terin was pleased his friend bestirred himself for the ceremony, and Lorn honored him by naming him his personal guard, beside Terin.

"You wield a Sword of Light, who better could I choose as my escort?" Lorn had asked, when he called upon him early that morn.

"I am honored, My King," Cronus had said, overcome with emotion. He would find his daughter in the arms of Corry's handmaid at the front of the assemblage, a treasured guest of the House of Lore.

Lorn continued, finding the Matrons' guild standing near the front, along his left, with Dresila and Ilesa the most prominent among them. The ministers' scribes and attendants stood opposite them, with Aldo standing prominently forward among them. The apes, led by Huto, son of Hutoq, stood along the wall to his far right, at the back of the crowd, with Orlom among them, standing out in his Earther attire and his rifle slung over his shoulder. Generals Valen, Mastorn and Lewins stood along the wall to his left, nearest the edge of the dais, joined by the Macon General Bram Vecious, and the Jenaii Generals El Tuvo and Ev Evorn, commanding the 1st and 2nd Battlegroups, though the 1st was greatly diminished. Raven waited in the back corner, hidden within the recesses of the chamber, leaning against the wall with his left hand hooked in the belt of his holster, happy to be out of view.

Lorn paused coming upon the small group standing closest to the dais, within the line of Torry elite guarding the throne. The Elite parted as Lorn drew nigh, saluting with their spears slapping their shields while backing away. Among those standing below the dais were the ministers of the realm, including Chief Minister Monsh and Squid Antillius, whose silver beard glistened, matching the hue of his gray robes. He labored long for this day, proud of the boy he once knew to be crowned king. Lorn embodied all that Kings should be but rarely are, strong yet compassionate, guided by mercy, and tempered with humility. Squid held back the tears he wanted to shed for his former king and friend, Lore, knowing he would be proud of the man his son had become.

Lorn greeted each minister in kind, before stopping at Squid, placing a hand to his shoulder, as if knowing what he was thinking.

"Well done, my KING," Squid whispered, earning him a gentle squeeze to his shoulder before Lorn moved on.

Elos stood next to his king, El Anthar, each bowing their heads as Lorn received them. El Anthar's stoic face looked as if it was carved from stone. He was adorned in white raiment, contrasting his silver eyes that seemed to peer through the minds of men as if their skulls were translucent. Lorn bowed in turn, before pressing his fist to his heart, saluting his stalwart allies. They would return his smile if Jenaii were inclined to do so, but there was no greater friend to the Torry realm than their winged brothers.

Next stood Tessa the seamstress, attired in a beautiful golden gown gifted to her by Princess Corry, her hair set beautifully upon her head, her green eyes sparkling as Lorn drew her in his embrace taking her aback. She was his special guest, and stood in this place of honor at his insistence.

The next three standing before the dais were King Mortus, flanked by Corry and King Sargov of Zulon. Corry bowed her head, before Lorn lifted her chin, staring intently into her eyes, sharing so much without speaking a word. She was adorned in a white gown wrapped tightly to her torso before flowing freely from her hips to the floor, concealing her golden slippered feet. Her golden locks were styled high upon her head with her tiara nestled in her hair, with diamonds and gems embedded in its thin silver band. Lorn lifted her right hand with his left, pressing it to his lips. He lowered her hand, before greeting King Mortus, exchanging a salute with his ally and father by marriage, and likewise greeting King Sargov.

He smiled when his eyes fell upon the last person standing

below the dais, stopping at Deliea, regarding his beautiful princess, overcome with joy. A scarlet gown draped her graceful form, contrasting her deep olive skin that radiated her elegant beauty. Her black hair shone like strands of obsidian cascading to her shoulders.

"My Queen," he smiled, waving his open hand to the thrones waiting above. Her bright emerald eyes sparkled as he took her by the hand and guided her up the dais as Terin and Cronus followed, breaking left and right, posting beside the throne.

Standing between the two thrones stood Torg Vantel, the commander of the Torry elite, and Master of Arms of the realm. He presided over this grand assemblage, his gray eyes sweeping the sea of faces with austere authority. He stood in contrast to his fellow Torries, arrayed in thick gray trousers and shirt with dark, nondescript mail. His mere gaze caused the hardest of soldiers to avert their eyes. Behind Torg, stood Jentra, the Prime of the elite, and Lorn's dearest friend, striking a similar pose as Torg, his steely gaze sweeping the chamber like a warbird seeking prey as Torg addressed the assembly.

"The Torry throne stands vacant. King Lore has passed!" Torg declared as Lorn drew nigh, before stopping short of the second throne, directing his Queen to her rightful place, while Torg presented him a silver crown, its thin band embedded with diamonds and precious gems. Lorn placed it upon her head.

As Deliea sat upon the long vacant throne of the Torry Queen, those gathered in the Throne Room cheered. "HAIL QUEEN DELIEA!"

King Mortus marveled as Lorn honored his daughter by seating her first. Lorn waited before seating himself, giving the assembly ample time to honor his bride as Jentra stepped forth bearing a box, opening it in the full view of the gathered host, revealing an austere steel crown, with jagged edges along its surface, its unpleasant appearance symbolic of the burden of just rule.

Torg stepped forth, taking the crown and placing it upon Lorn's head, before turning again to address the assembly.

"Be it known to all the realms of Arax and the people of Tory North and South. Prince Lorn sits the vacant throne. Hail King Lorn!" He proclaimed.

"Hail King Lorn!" The crowd repeated several times, growing in a deafening crescendo before subsiding.

Lorn faced the quieting crowd, looking out upon that small sea of familiar faces, his black mane and deep blue eyes radiating like a King of old.

"To the Ladies gathered here and my brothers who have fought to preserve all we hold dear, I thank you. I wish my father still lived and I could merely be his son with no other obligation than that. But such is the fate of Kings and Kingdoms that I must assume his place as a poor substitute for the man that he was. I hope he looks down upon us from the House of Yah with a pride swelled heart, a pride in his people and his friends. I hope also that my mother can look down from the firmament above at the Torry Queen and approve. This War is not yet won. We have much left to do and the price shall be great. I cannot promise you victory. I only promise to follow the path Yah has placed before us and to obey his will. If any road leads to victory it shall be that. This day, however, we shall rest and make merry, leaving the future and its worries for tomorrow."

"HAIL KING LORN! HAIL KING LORN!" The great hall erupted.

Joyous tears fell like raindrops from the eyes of many, a euphoric wave passing through the crowd. Squid Antillius released a measured breath at the fulfillment of Lorn's ascendency. "Lore would be proud," Squid whispered to himself. "Hail King Lorn."

Terin and Cronus unsheathed their swords and raised them into the air. They emitted blue and gold, illuminating the air about the throne room, the light of Terin's sword fueled by his joy. There upon the dais of the throne room of Corell, Prince Lorn became King.

EPILOGUE

The festivities continued throughout the day and deep into the night, with King Lorn and Queen Deliea greeting their subjects throughout the Castle as well as the troops camped outside Corell's walls, both Torry and allied alike. They walked among the camps to the cheering throngs of soldiers. The men were given a grand feast, their first warm food in over a fortnight. Casks of ale and roasted moglo were offered in generous helpings, many taken from the enemy provisions left during their hasty retreat.

"Hail King Lorn! Hail Queen Deliea!" The men cheered.

Lorn would stop and talk to the men, hearing their complaints and listening to their stories. Deliea looked on, admiring how Lorn interacted with their men, able to see the deep affection they shared for the Torry King. They finished at the Grand Hall, greeted with the sound of music heralding their entrance. Another great feast was prepared for them as bards sang tales of ancient times and newly scribed ballads of their many battles. Galen performed many ballads of the common people and soldiers, as Lorn advised long ago, his effort well received by the court, and especially the masses, once they spread beyond the grand hall.

Lorn and Deliea again presided over the grand hall at the high table, overlooking the sea of familiar faces of apes, Jenaii, Macons and Torries. Corry, El Anthar, King Mortus and King Sargov joined them at the high table, with Terin standing post behind the Torry

Princess, her ever vigilant guardian. This would be the last of their celebrations, for the war beckoned and a large portion of the enemy still remained in Torry North, trapped within the walls of Besos, as well as their cavalry rampaging through the heartland. Despite these concerns, the battle of Torry North was over at the strategic level.

Raven stood along the side of the chamber, preparing to make his exit, mentally debating when he should return to the *Stenox*. Thorton wasn't here, that part was now obvious, making Tro the next likeliest place. He might not have killed Ben, but he achieved his second objective in defeating Morac's invasion. Lorn had called for a council of war in the morning, and invited him to attend. He would decide his next course of action after conferring with his new allies. Before he could take one step toward the exit, Chief Minister Monsh's scribe Aldo came bursting in the chamber, walking with a purposeful gait toward his master, who stood along the opposite wall sharing words with Torg. Half the people in the chamber noticed his excited disposition as he hurried across the room.

"Aldo, what news have you?" Prince Lorn called out from the high table, causing Aldo to freeze half way across the floor.

Aldo paused, looking to the Chief Minister for direction before deciding it unwise to disobey the King's request.

"Two magantors just arrived, My King, from Tro Harbor," Aldo said, waiting for direction before revealing further details.

"And what tidings do they bear, Aldo? You needn't worry about secrecy, for all shall know the truth of it at some point!" Lorn ordered.

"As you command, My King. They bear two correspondences. The first from Magistrate Adine, informing your majesty of victory at Tro!" Aldo couldn't hide his excitement, causing the entire chamber to erupt in thunderous cheers before Aldo could give details of said victory, forcing him to wait until the crowd grew quiet.

"Continue Aldo!" Lorn said as the noise subsided.

"He states the that the Gargoyle 12th Legion has been greatly reduced, and likely destroyed, and their commander slain at the hands of a General Zem," Aldo added, uncertain of whom General Zem was, or his allegiance. "The second correspondence is the first-hand account of General Zem, penned on very unique parchment."

Aldo approached the high table to present the documents to the King but was intercepted by Raven, who strode across the chamber with a swiftness none had seen from the large Earther.

"Raven?" Lorn asked as the Earther relieved Aldo of Zem's message, written clearly on paper produced on the *Stenox,* bearing his new rank at the top with the heading…

From the memoirs of General Zem.…

"You've got to be kidding?" Raven shook his head, reading Zem's first hand account of the events that transpired at Tro after they departed, with the rest of the court looking on.

Thus ends Book Five of the Chronicles of Arax:
The Battle of Torry North
The saga continues with Book Six: Fall of Empires

APPENDIX A

Armies of Arax

TORRY ARMIES

Army	Location	Commander	Size
1st	Fleace	Lewins	19 Telnics
2nd	Central City	Fonis	20 Telnics
3rd	Corell	Bode	12 Telnics
4th	Cagan	Farro	12 Telnics
5th	Destroyed at Kregmarin		

LARGE GARRISONS

	Cropus	Torgus Vantel	5 Telnics
	Corell	Nevias	3 Telnics
	Central City	Torvin	5 Telnics
	Cagan	Telanus	5 Telnics

(Currently split between Fleace and Cesa)

Torry Cavalry

	Location	Commander	Size
1st	Corell	Tevlin	300 mounts
2nd	Corell	Connly	700 mounts
3rd	Western Border	Meborn	500 mounts

Torry Cavalry (continued)

Army	Location	Commander	Size
4th	Cagan	Avliam	412 mounts

(100 reserve cavalry of the 4th attached to 1st Torry Army)

Torry Navy

Fleet	Location	Admiral	Size
1st	Faust	Kilan (Grand Admiral)	31 galleys

(Includes 3 captured Benotrist warships)

Fleet	Location	Admiral	Size
2nd	Cesa	Horikor	50 galleys
3rd	Faust	Liman	21 galleys
4th	Faust	Nylo	22 galleys
5th	Cesa	Morita	17 galleys

BENOTRIST/GARGOYLE ARMIES

Legion	Location	Commander	Size
1st (gargoyle)	Telfer	N/A	10 Telnics
	(Survivors of Mosar reassigned to 2nd Legion)		
2nd (gargoyle)	Tinsay	Torab	24 Telnics
3rd (gargoyle)	Destroyed at Mosar (survivors reassigned to 2nd Legion		
4th (gargoyle)	Surviving telnics absorbed by 5th Legion		
5th (gargoyle)	East of Corell	Concaka	44 Telnics
	(Includes all telnics of 4th and 7th Legions)		
6th (gargoyle)	Destroyed at Corell		
7th (gargoyle)	Surviving telnics absorbed by 5th Legion		
8th (Benotrist)	East of Corell	Vlesnivolk	37 Telnics
	(Augmented by 10 T from Nisin garrison and 5 T from Pagan)		
9th (Benotrist)	Notsu	Marcinia	50 Telnics
10th (Benotrist)	Notsu	Gavis	50 Telnics
11th (Benotrist)	Notsu	Felinaius	39 Telnics
12th (gargoyle)	Gotto	Krakeni	38 Telnics
	(Lost 12 T during Tro raid. Preparing to siege Gotto)		
13th (Benotrist)	Laycrom	Trinapolis	50 Telnics
14th (gargoyle)	Notsu	Trimopolak	50 Telnics
15th (gargoyle)	Tuss River	Unknown	10-15 (Est.) Telnics
16th (gargoyle)	Destroyed at Tuft's Mountain		
17th (gargoyle)	Destroyed at Tuft's Mountain		
18th (gargoyle)	Destroyed at Tuft's Mountain		

Benotrist/Gargoyle Armies (continued)

Legion	Location	Commander	Size
GARRISON FORCES			
	Fera		29 T (Benotrist)
	Nisin		10 T (Benotrist)
	Pagan		5 T (Benotrist)
	Mordicay		10 T (Benotrist)
	Tinsay		20 T (Benotrist)
	Laycrom		20 T (Benotrist)
	Border posts		10 T Benotrist), 10 T (gargoyle)

Benotrist Navy

Fleet	Location	Admiral	Size
1st	Mordicay	Plesnivolk	48 galleys
2nd	Tenin	Kruson	7 galleys
3rd	Pagan	Elto (Grand Admiral)	80 galleys
4th	Pagan	Pinota	50 galleys
5th	Tenin	Unknown	32 galleys
6th	Pagan	Silniw	50 galleys
7th	Tenin	Onab	24 galleys
8th	Tinsay	Zelitov	50 galleys

YATIN ARMIES

Army	Location	Commander	Size
1st	Mosar (Only 16 of 25 mustered at Mosar)	Yoria	8 Telnics
2nd	Faust (21 of 25 answered muster)	Yitia	20 Telnics
3rd	Destroyed at Mosar (3 surviving telnics joined with 1st Army)		
4th	Tenin	Surrendered to Torab	

GARRISON FORCES

	Location	Commander	Size
	Mosar	Yakue	3 Telnics
	Telfer	Destroyed in Siege of Telfer	
	Tenin	Surrendered to Torab	

Yatin Cavalry

Army	Location	Commander	Size
1st	Telfer	Destroyed in Battle of Salamin Valley	
2nd	Mosar	Cornyana	475 mounts

Yatin Navy

Fleet	Location	Admiral	Size
1st	Tenin	Sunk in Battle of Cull's Arc	
2nd	Tenin	Sunk in Battle of Cull's Arc	
3rd	Faust	Horician	18 galleys

Jenaii Armies

Battle Group	Location	Commander	Size
1st	Corell	El Tuvo	10-12 Telnics
2nd	El Orva	Ev Evorn	20 Telnics
	(Casualties suffered at Corell replaced with soldiers of the 1st Battle Group)		
3rd	El Tova	En Elon	20 Telnics

GARRISON FORCES

	Location	Commander	Size
	El Orva	El Orta	15 Telnics
	El Tova	En Vor	5 Telnics

Jenaii Navy

Fleet	Location	Admiral	Size
1st	El Tova	En Atar	20 galleys
2nd	El Tova	En Ovir	20 galleys
3rd	El Tova	En Toshin	20 galleys

Naybin Armies

Army	Location	Commander	Size
1st	Northern Border (7 detached to expeditionary force, destroyed at siege of Corell)	Duloc	3 Telnics
2nd	Plou	Rorin	10 Telnics
3rd	Non	Corivan	10 Telnics
4th	Western Border	Cuss	10 Telnics

GARRISON FORCES

	Plou	Cestes	5 Telnics
	Non	Rasin	7 Telnics
	Naiba	Tesra	3 Telnics
	Border Posts		5 Telnics

Naybin Navy

Fleet	Location	Admiral	Size
1st	Naiba	Gustub	10 galleys
2nd	Naiba	Galton	10 galleys

Macon Empire Armies

Army	Location	Commander	Size
1st	Fleace	Noivi	10 Telnics
	(5 telnics sent to siege of Sawyer, 5 remaining with General Noivi)		
2nd	Sawyer	Vecious	13 Telnics
3rd	Fleace	Ciyon	8 Telnics
	(reconstituting into joint Macon-Torry Army)		
4th	Null	Farin	8 Telnics

GARRISON FORCES

	Location	Commander	Size
	Fleace	Novin	5 Telnics
	Cesa	Clyvo	5 Telnics
	(Repositioning after truce of Fleace)		

Macon Navy

Fleet	Location	Admiral	Size
1st	East of Cesa	Goren	20 galleys
2nd	Null	Vulet	20 galleys
3rd	Eastern Coast	Talmet	20 galleys
4th	Destroyed at the straits of Cesa		

APE EMPIRE ARMIES

Army	Location	Commander	Size
1st	Gregok	Cragok	20 Telnics
2nd	Torn	Mocvoran	20 Telnics
3rd	Talon Pass	Vorklit	10 Telnics
4th	Northern Coast	Matuzon	10 Telnics
5th	Southern Coast	Vonzin	10 Telnics

GARRISON FORCES

	Location		Size
	Gregok		10 Telnics
	Torn		10 Telnics
	Talon Pass		10 Telnics

Ape Navy

Fleet	Location	Admiral	Size
1st	Tro	Zorgon	9 galleys
2nd	Torn	Vornam	40 galleys

Casian Federation Armies

Army	Location	Commander	Size
1st	Coven	Gidvia	12 Telnics
2nd	Milito	Motchi	12 Telnics
3rd	Teris	Elke	7 Telnics

GARRISON FORCES

	Location		Size
	Milito		3 Telnics
	Coven		4 Telnics
	Port West		3 Telnics
	Teris		3 Telnics

Casian Navy

Fleet	Location	Admiral	Size
1st	Coven	Voelin	100 galleys
2nd	Milito	Gylan	80 galleys
3rd	Port West	Gydar	60 galleys
4th	Teris	Eltar	60 galleys

Federation of the Sisterhood Armies

Army	Location	Commander	Size
1st	Bansoch	Na	20 Telnics
2nd	Fela	Vola	20 Telnics
3rd	Southern Border	Mial	20 Telnics

GARRISON FORCES

	Location		Size
	Bansoch		10 Telnics
	Fela		10 Telnics

Sisterhood Navy

Fleet	Location	Admiral	Size
1st	Bansoch	Nyla	120 galleys
2nd	Bansoch	Carel	80 galleys
3rd	Southern Coast	Daila	50 galleys

Teso Armies

	Location	Commander	Size
1st Army	Southeastern border	Hovel	4 Telnics
2nd Army	Fleace	Velen	2 Telnics

Zulon Armies

	Location	Commander	Size
1st Army	Northern Border	Zarento	2 Telnics
2nd Army	Fleace	Zubarro	3 Telnics

City State Armies

Sawyer	5 Telnics	100 Cavalry	
Rego	3 Telnics	100 Cavalry	
(Rego garrison size fluctuates with new conscription)			
Notsu	2 Telnics	200 Cavalry (Listed assets constitute free Notsuan forces located at Central City)	
Bacel	Destroyed at Kregmarin and siege of Bacel		
Barbeario	8 Telnics		
Bedo	10 Telnics	100 Cavalry	40 galleys
Tro Harbor	6 Telnics	50 Cavalry	14 galleys
Varabis	5 Telnics		30 galleys

APPENDIX B

Details of the Battle of the Elaris.

The following is the account of the battle along the upper Elaris, between the 3rd Jenaii Battlegroup and the 3rd and 4th Nayborian Armies that transpired a full fortnight before the breaking of the second siege of Corell. The Elaris river is the natural boundary separating the Jenaii and Nayborian realms, and the focal point of the many wars waged between them. Believing the Nayborian Champion Dethine had returned to his native realm to lead an invasion of the Jenaii Kingdom, Elos departed Corell to join with the 3rd Jenaii Battlegroup to counter the threat.

The battle of Elaris was centered near the ford of Elarin, the southernmost point where a human army could safely cross the river. The Zeita Forrest straddled the banks of the upper Elaris, stretching for countless leagues into each realm. The Zeita was populated with large Torbin trees, with thick trunks and needled branches that rose to impressive heights, creating a clear forest floor easing the movement of armies and negating much of the Jenaii advantage of flight.

The 3rd and 4th Nayborian Armies, led by Generals Corivan and Cuss, occupied the ford of Elarin, before crossing into the Jenaii Kingdom proper, but advancing no farther. Their objective was to present a persistent threat to the Jenaii Kingdom, without engaging them, keeping as many of their forces in the south, and away from the primary campaign in Torry North.

The Jenaii 3rd Battlegroup was reinforced with ten telnics of the El Orva garrison, bolstering their numbers before advancing upon the Nayborian positions. General En Elon, commander of the 3rd Battlegroup, demonstrated along the western flank of the Nayborian armies, while Elos led ten telnics in a flanking maneuver along the Nayborian left, cutting across the Elaris downriver, before turning back north. With the *Sword of the Moon*, Elos led his soldiers through the thin ranks guarding the Naybin flank. Without Dethine to match the Jenaii Sword of Light, the Nayborians quickly yielded, half retreating west toward the river, the rest fleeing east into Nayboria, before Elos turned sharply west, pinning a large portion of the Nayborian army against the east bank of the Elaris while the 3rd Battlegroup advanced from the west, driving those on that side of the river against the west bank. Despite their success, the Jenaii suffered thousands of casualties from a series of effective delaying actions and numerous traps set throughout the forest. Eventually the two Jenaii forces met north of the ford of Elarin, squeezing the enemy between them.

The result of the battle was a devastating victory for the Jenaii, smashing the 4th Naybin Army, capturing or killing nine of every ten, the rest unaccounted for. The 3rd Naybin Army was cut in half, with General Corivan leading the survivors to the palace of Non. The Jenaii suffered a combined six thousand casualties, including three thousand dead. The battle freed Elos in joining King El Anthar and the 2nd Battlegroup in the relief of Corell, once it was discovered Dethine was not in the south. The battle ended the Nayborian threat upon the Jenaii, forcing them into a permanent defensive position for the duration of the war.

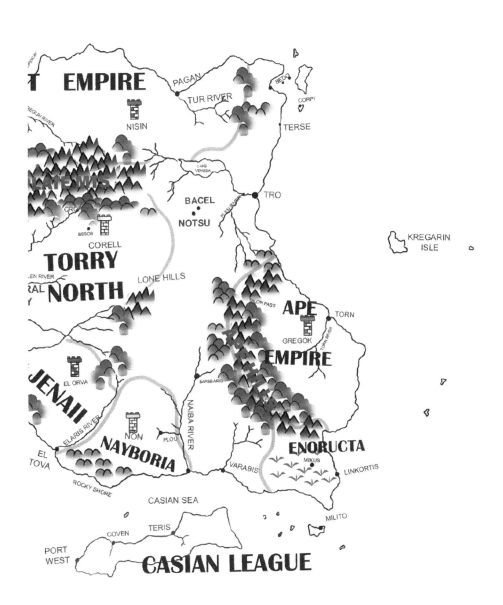

OTHER BOOKS BY AUTHOR

Free Born Saga

Book 1 Free Born

Book 2 Elysia

Book 3 Dragon Wars (coming soon)

Chronicles of Arax

Book 1 Of War and Heroes

Book 2 The Siege of Corell

Book 3 The Battle of Yatin

Book 4 The Making of a King

Book 5 The Battle of Torry North

Book 6 Fall of Empires (2024)

ABOUT THE AUTHOR

Ben Sanford grew up in Western New York. He spent almost twenty years as an air marshal, traveling across the United States and many parts of the world, meeting people from a broad range of cultures and backgrounds. It was from these thousands of interactions that he drew inspiration for the characters in his books. He currently resides in Maryland with his family.

Made in the USA
Middletown, DE
27 October 2023

41384637R00321